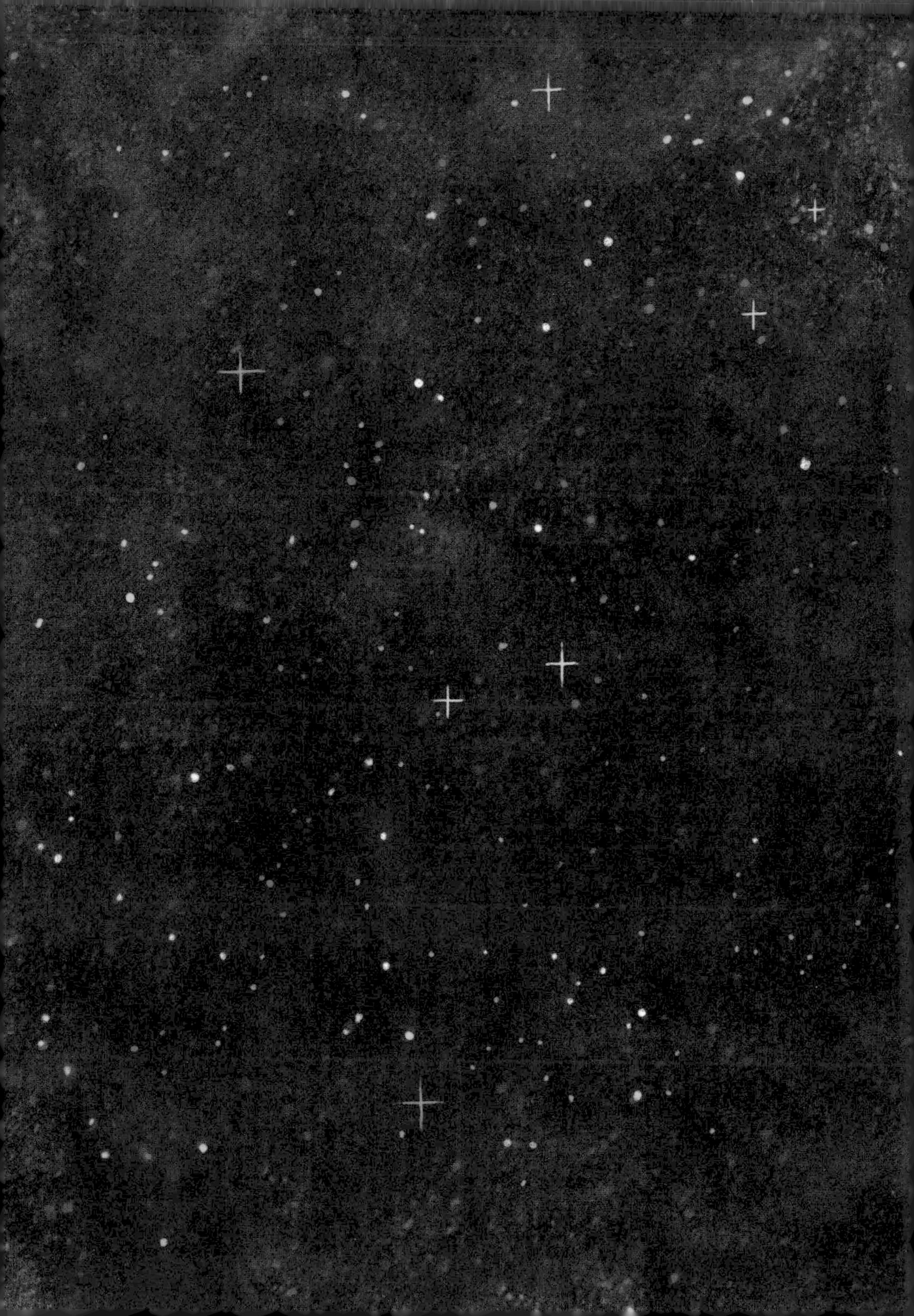

THIS WAS OUR PACT

RYAN ANDREWS

First Second
New York

For Ai

First Second

Copyright © 2019 by Ryan Andrews

Published by First Second
First Second is an imprint of Roaring Brook Press,
a division of Holtzbrinck Publishing Holdings Limited Partnership
175 Fifth Avenue, New York, NY 10010

Don't miss your next favorite book from First Second!
For the latest updates go to firstsecondnewsletter.com and sign up for our enewsletter.

Library of Congress Control Number: 2018944916

Paperback ISBN: 978-1-62672-053-4
Hardcover ISBN: 978-1-250-19695-8

Our books may be purchased in bulk for promotional, educational, or business use.
Please contact your local bookseller or the Macmillan Corporate and Premium Sales Department
at (800) 221-7945 ext. 5442 or by e-mail at MacmillanSpecialMarkets@macmillan.com.

First edition, 2019
Edited by Calista Brill, Carol Burrell, and Steve Behling
Book design by Andrew Arnold, Molly Johanson, and Chris Dickey

Drawn with Mitsubishi Uni series pencils on Arches hot pressed watercolor paper.
Colored digitally in Photoshop.

Printed in China by 1010 Printing International Limited, North Point, Hong Kong

Paperback: 10 9 8 7 6 5 4 3 2 1
Hardcover: 10 9 8 7 6 5 4 3 2 1

chapter one
THE EQUINOX FESTIVAL
1

chapter two
THE FISHERBEAR
30

chapter three
AND THEN WE WERE LOST
68

chapter four
MADAM MAJESTIC
and the AVIAN CARTOGRAPHER
114

chapter five
THE MUSTY CELLAR
160

chapter six
THE CAVE THAT
CARRIED THE COSMOS
194

chapter seven
GRAVITATIONAL WAVES
254

chapter eight
A LITTLE FARTHER
UP THE ROAD
286

CHAPTER ONE
THE EQUINOX FESTIVAL

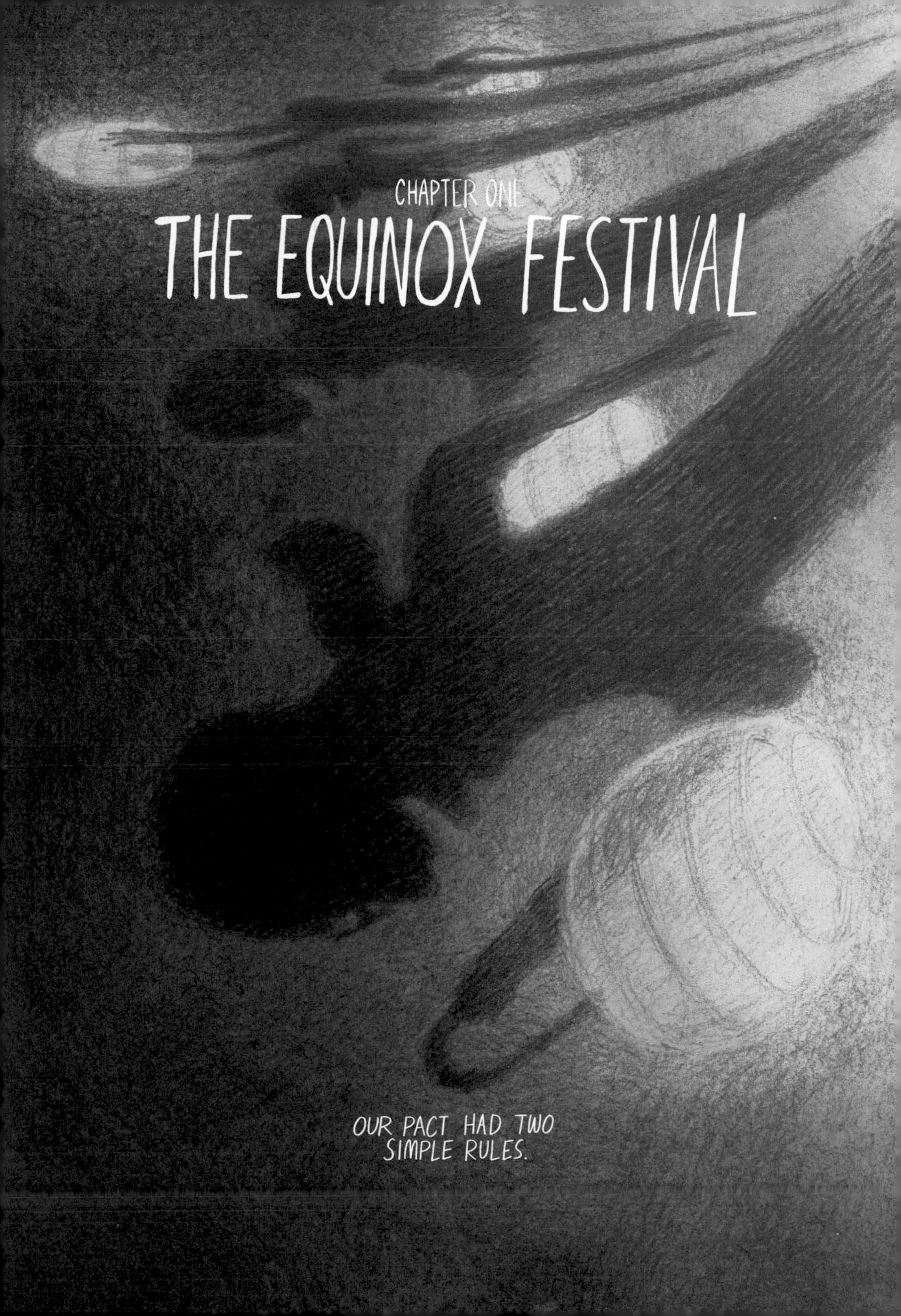
OUR PACT HAD TWO SIMPLE RULES.

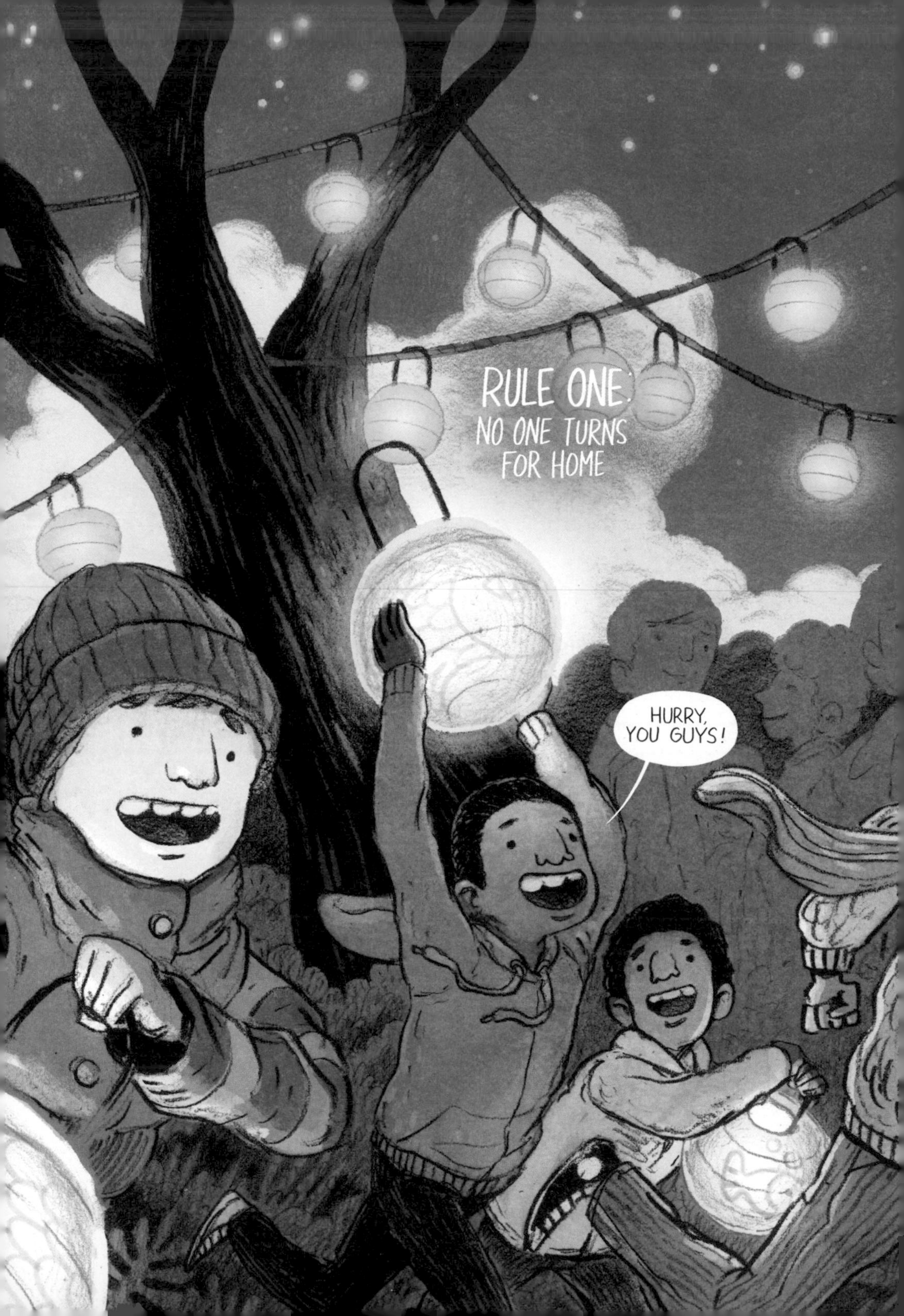
RULE ONE:
NO ONE TURNS FOR HOME
HURRY, YOU GUYS!

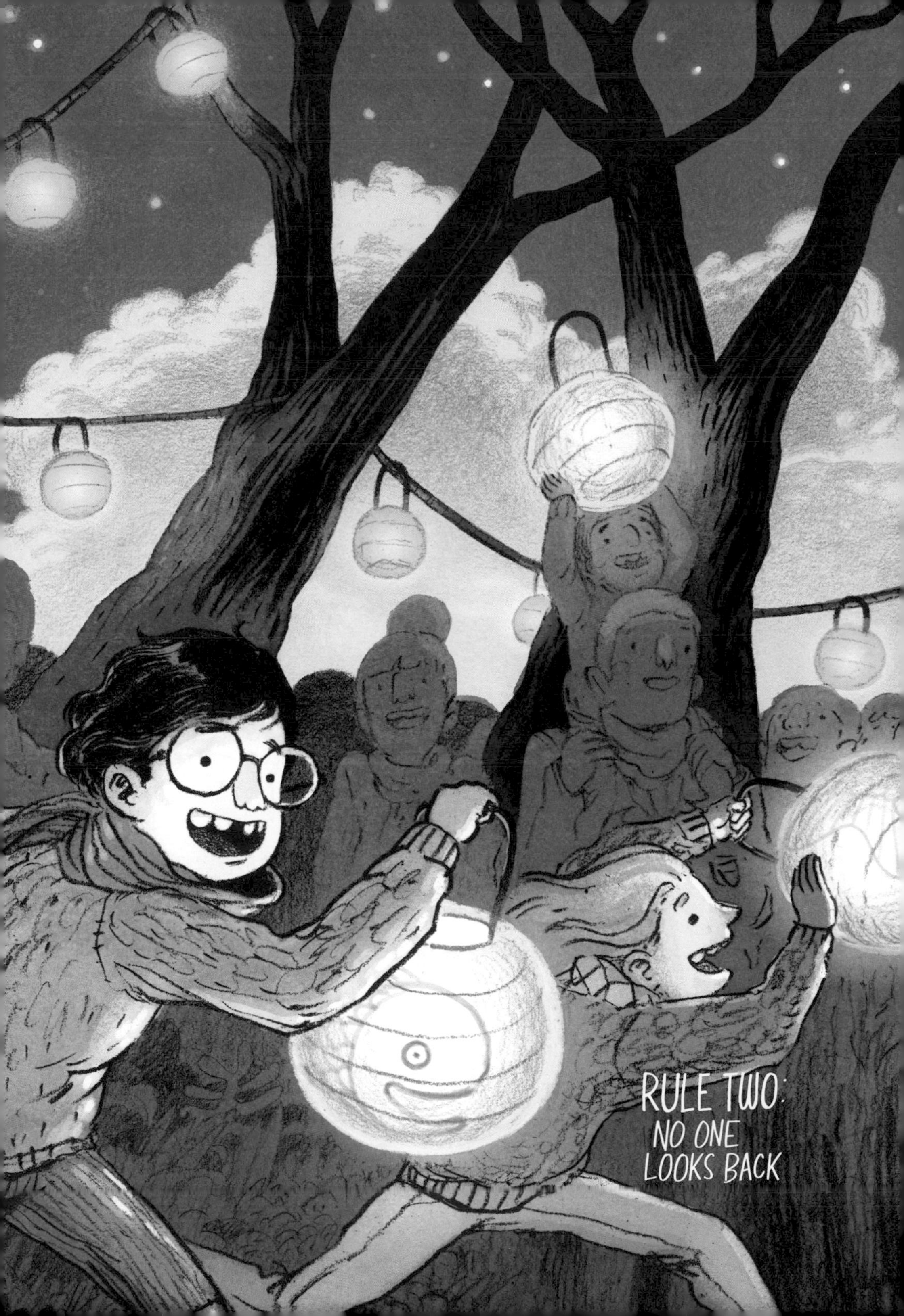
RULE TWO:
NO ONE
LOOKS BACK

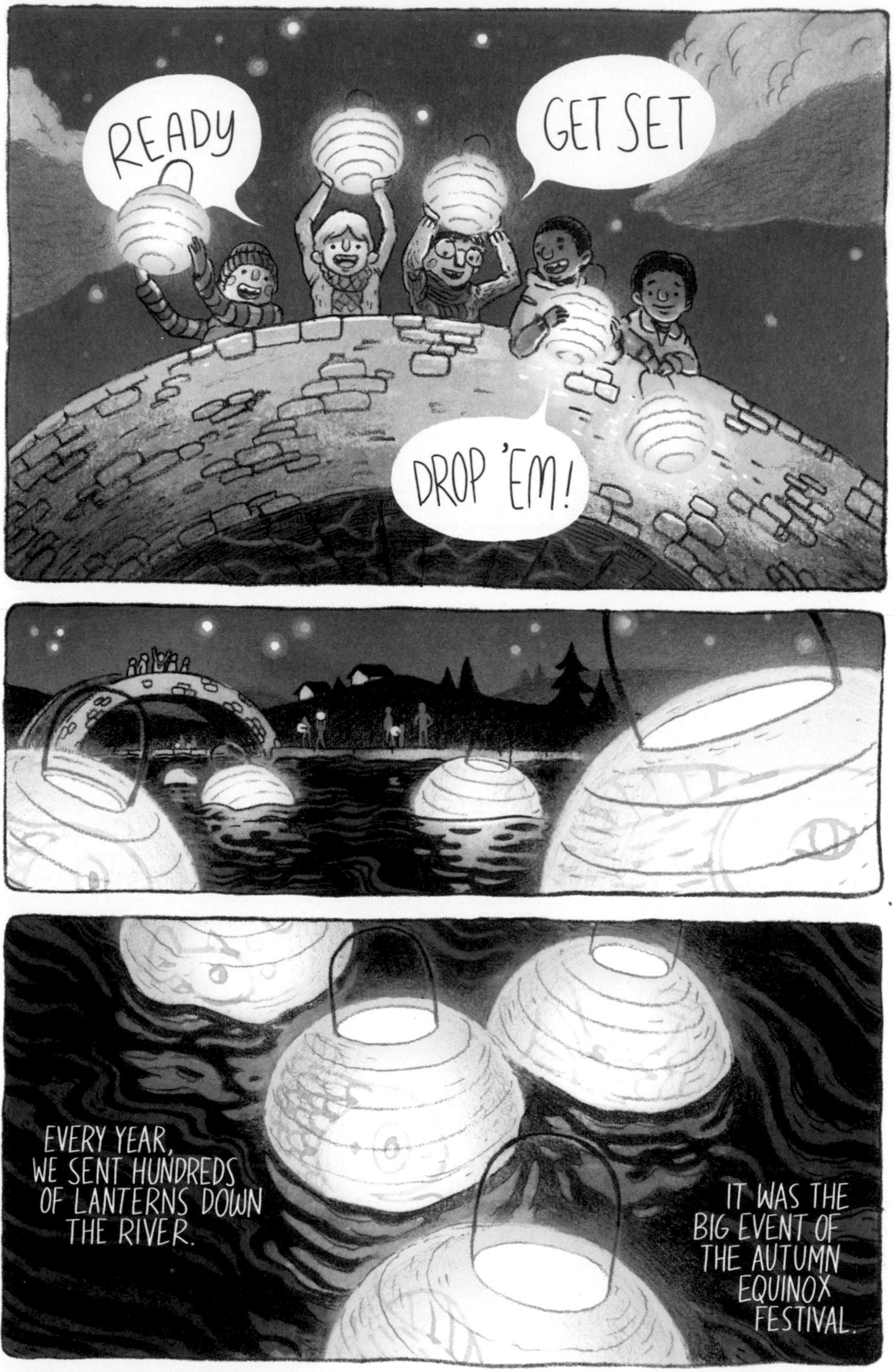
READY
GET SET
DROP 'EM!
EVERY YEAR, WE SENT HUNDREDS OF LANTERNS DOWN THE RIVER.
IT WAS THE BIG EVENT OF THE AUTUMN EQUINOX FESTIVAL.

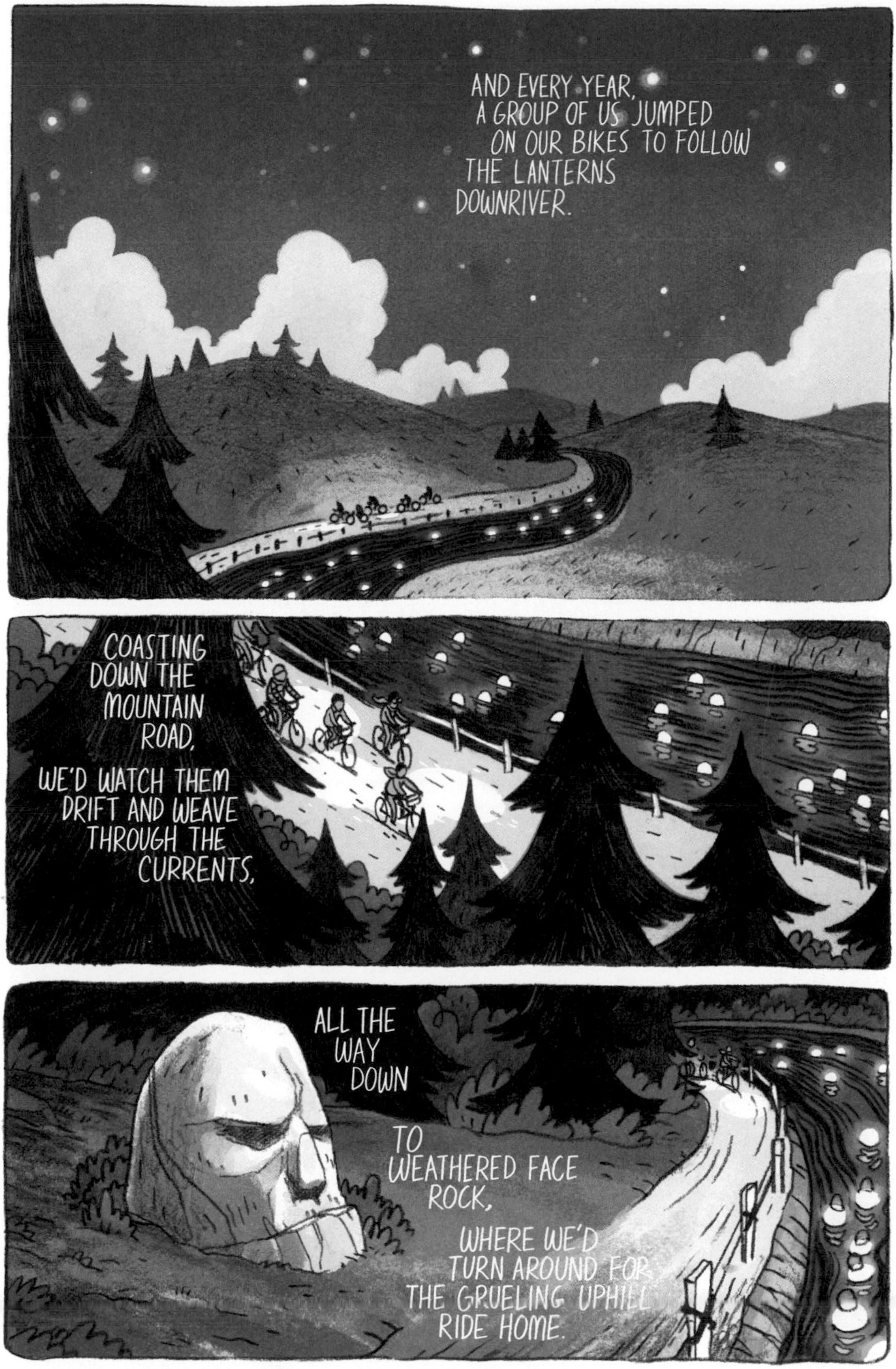
AND EVERY YEAR, A GROUP OF US JUMPED ON OUR BIKES TO FOLLOW THE LANTERNS DOWNRIVER.
COASTING DOWN THE MOUNTAIN ROAD,
WE'D WATCH THEM DRIFT AND WEAVE THROUGH THE CURRENTS,
ALL THE WAY DOWN
TO WEATHERED FACE ROCK,
WHERE WE'D TURN AROUND FOR THE GRUELING UPHILL RIDE HOME.

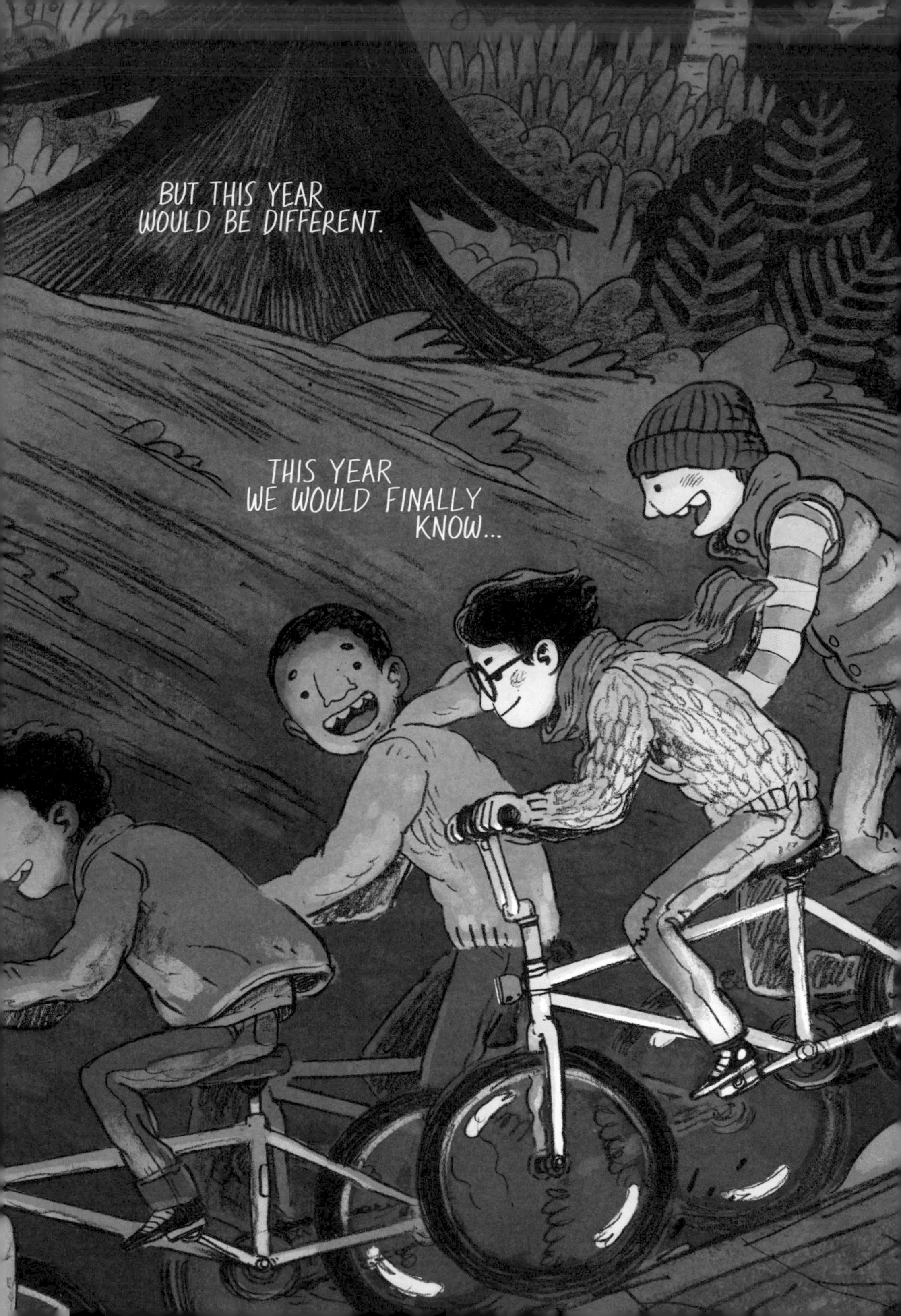
BUT THIS YEAR WOULD BE DIFFERENT.
THIS YEAR WE WOULD FINALLY KNOW...

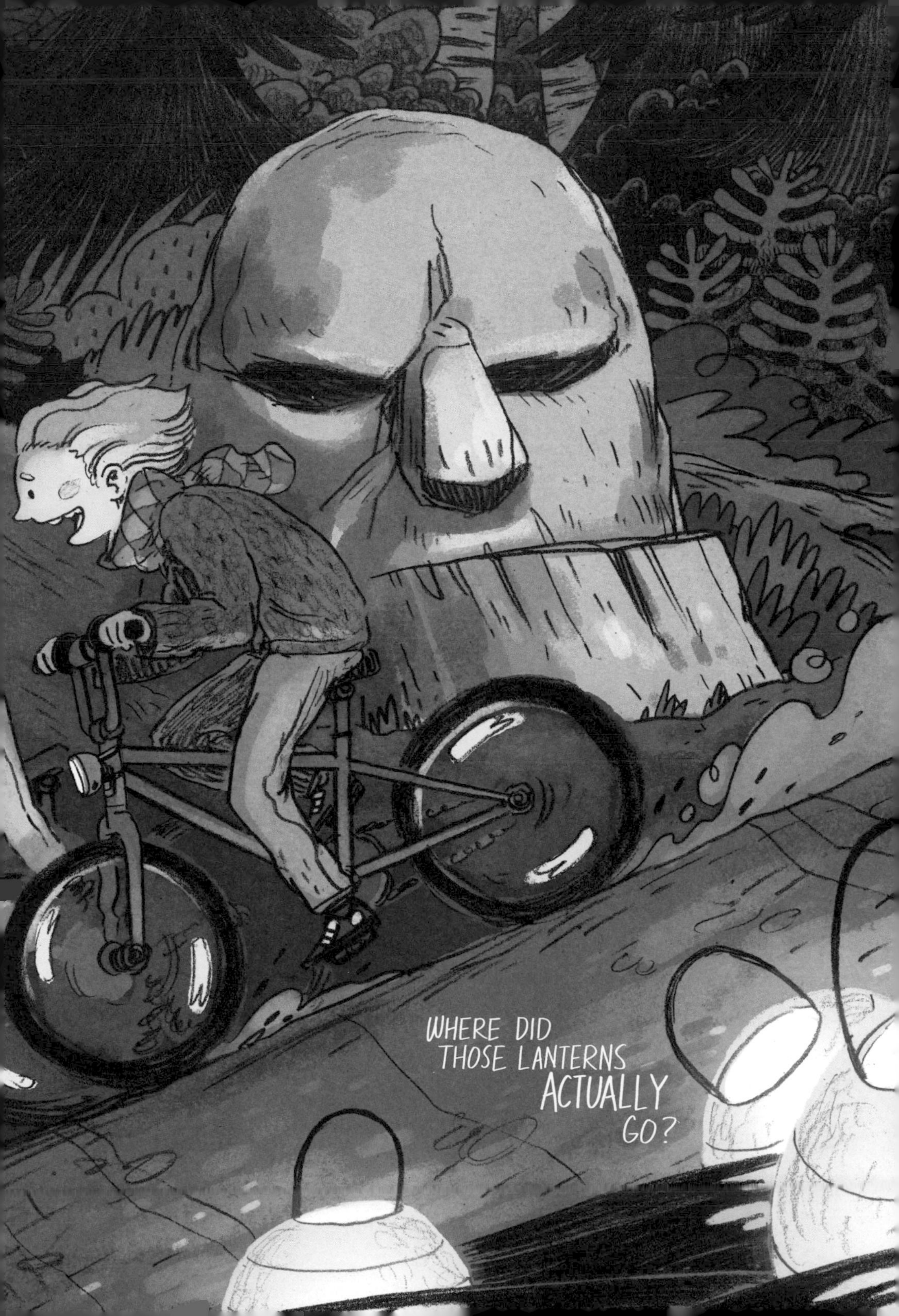
WHERE DID THOSE LANTERNS ACTUALLY GO?

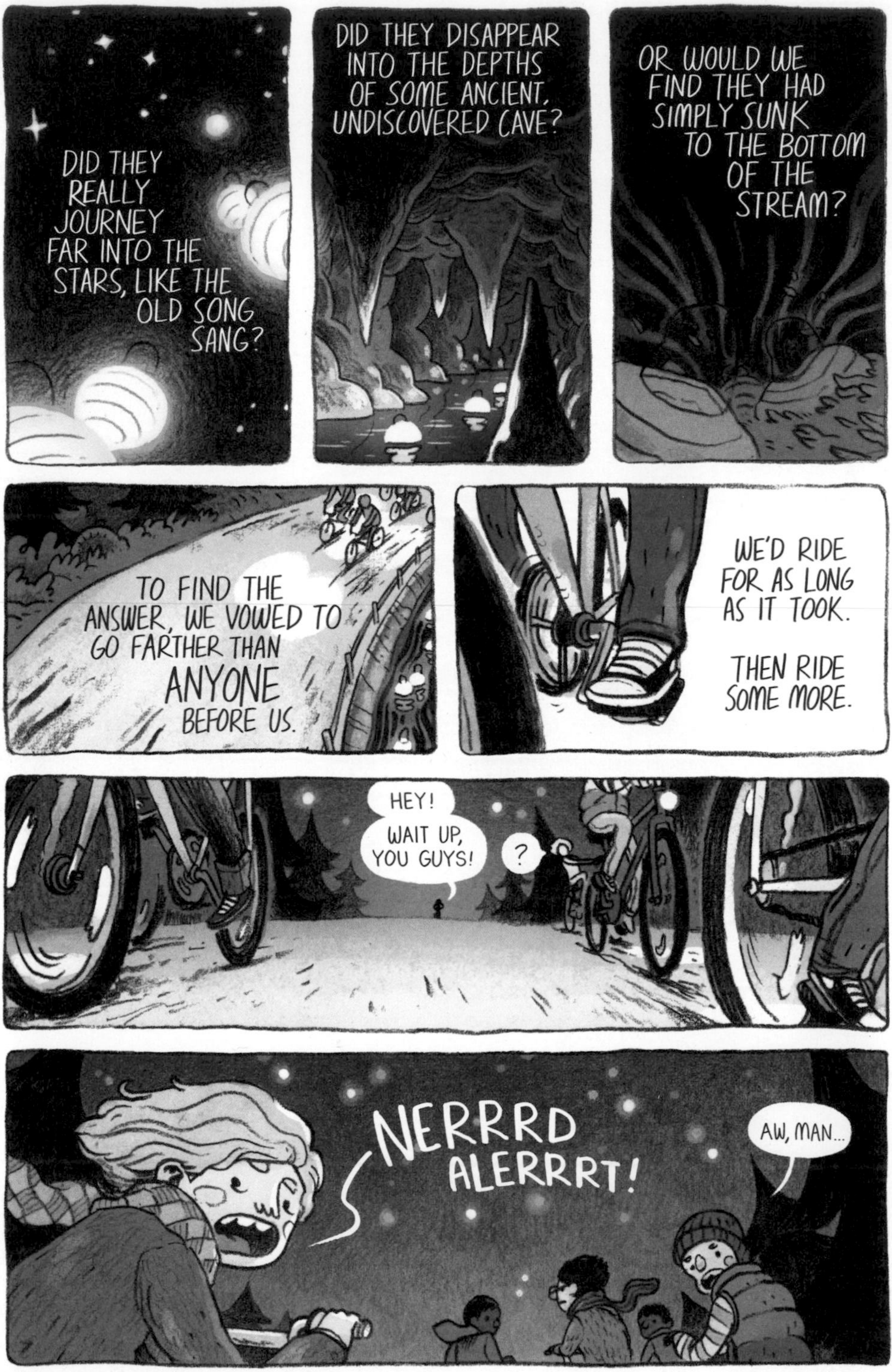
DID THEY REALLY JOURNEY FAR INTO THE STARS, LIKE THE OLD SONG SANG?
DID THEY DISAPPEAR INTO THE DEPTHS OF SOME ANCIENT, UNDISCOVERED CAVE?
OR WOULD WE FIND THEY HAD SIMPLY SUNK TO THE BOTTOM OF THE STREAM?
TO FIND THE ANSWER, WE VOWED TO GO FARTHER THAN ANYONE BEFORE US.
WE'D RIDE FOR AS LONG AS IT TOOK.
THEN RIDE SOME MORE.
HEY!
WAIT UP, YOU GUYS!
?
NERRRD ALERRRT!
AW, MAN...

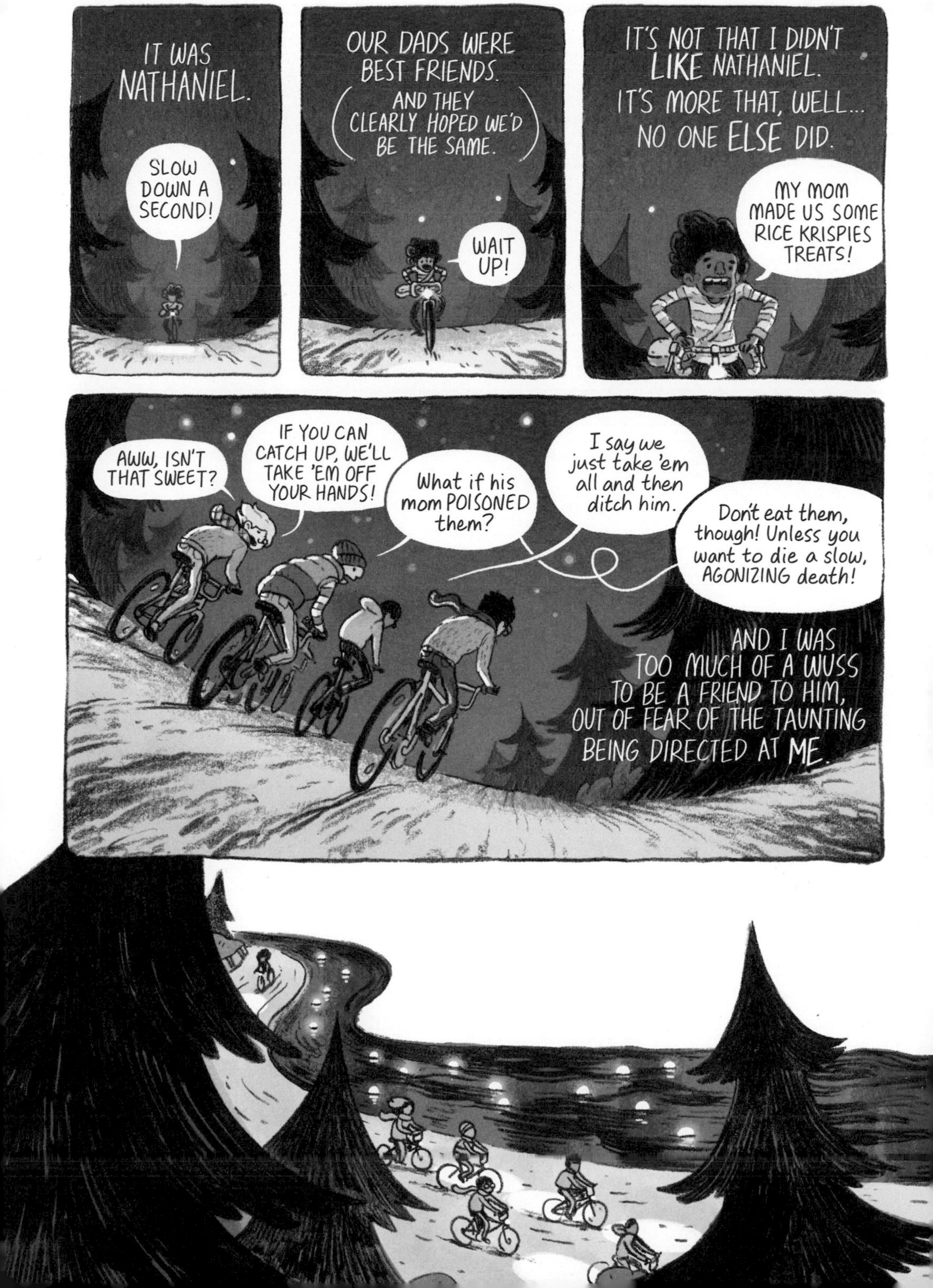
IT WAS NATHANIEL.
SLOW DOWN A SECOND!
OUR DADS WERE BEST FRIENDS.
(AND THEY CLEARLY HOPED WE'D BE THE SAME.)
WAIT UP!
IT'S NOT THAT I DIDN'T LIKE NATHANIEL. IT'S MORE THAT, WELL... NO ONE ELSE DID.
MY MOM MADE US SOME RICE KRISPIES TREATS!
AWW, ISN'T THAT SWEET?
IF YOU CAN CATCH UP, WE'LL TAKE 'EM OFF YOUR HANDS!
What if his mom POISONED them?
I say we just take 'em all and then ditch him.
Don't eat them, though! Unless you want to die a slow, AGONIZING death!
AND I WAS TOO MUCH OF A WUSS TO BE A FRIEND TO HIM, OUT OF FEAR OF THE TAUNTING BEING DIRECTED AT ME.

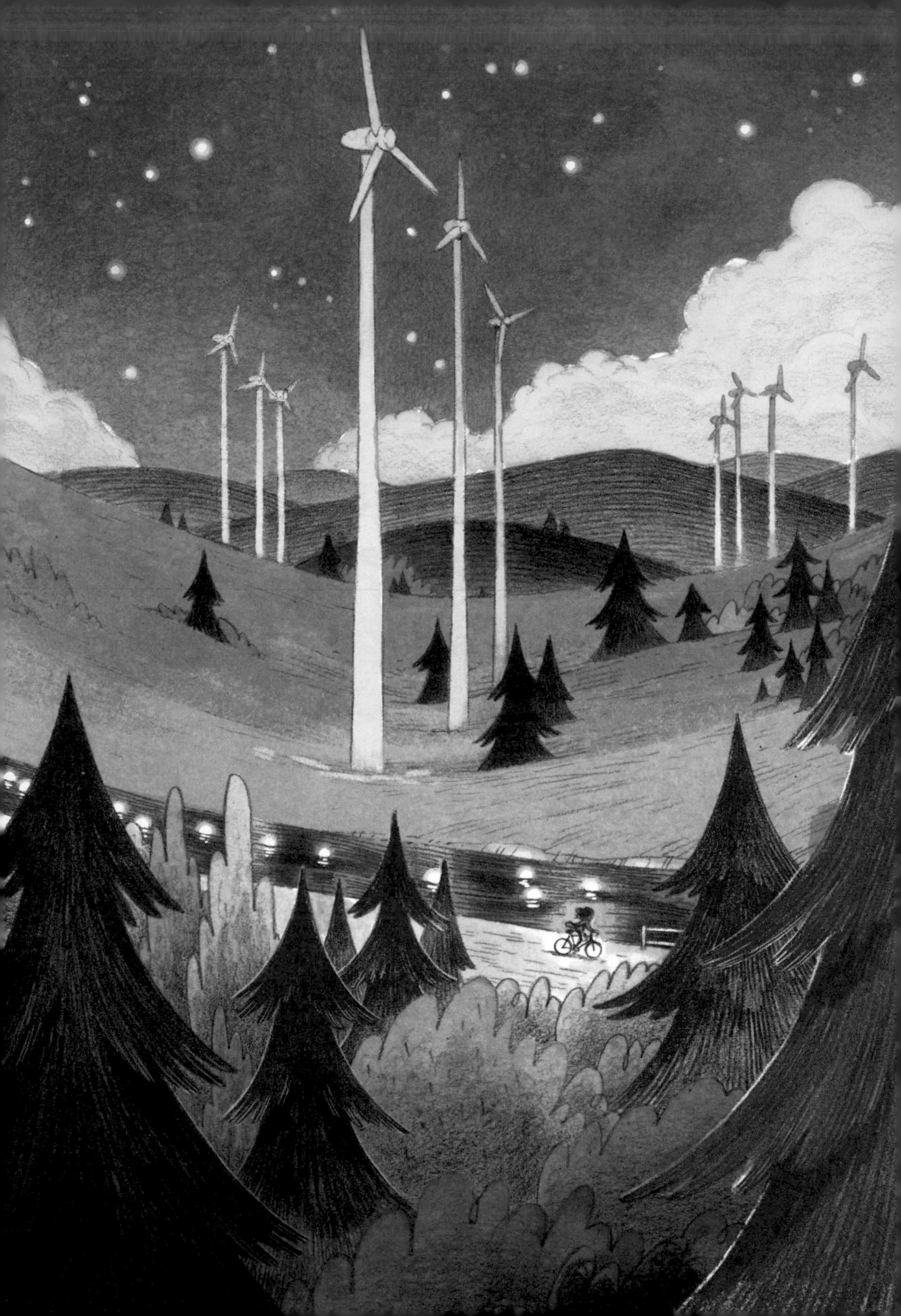

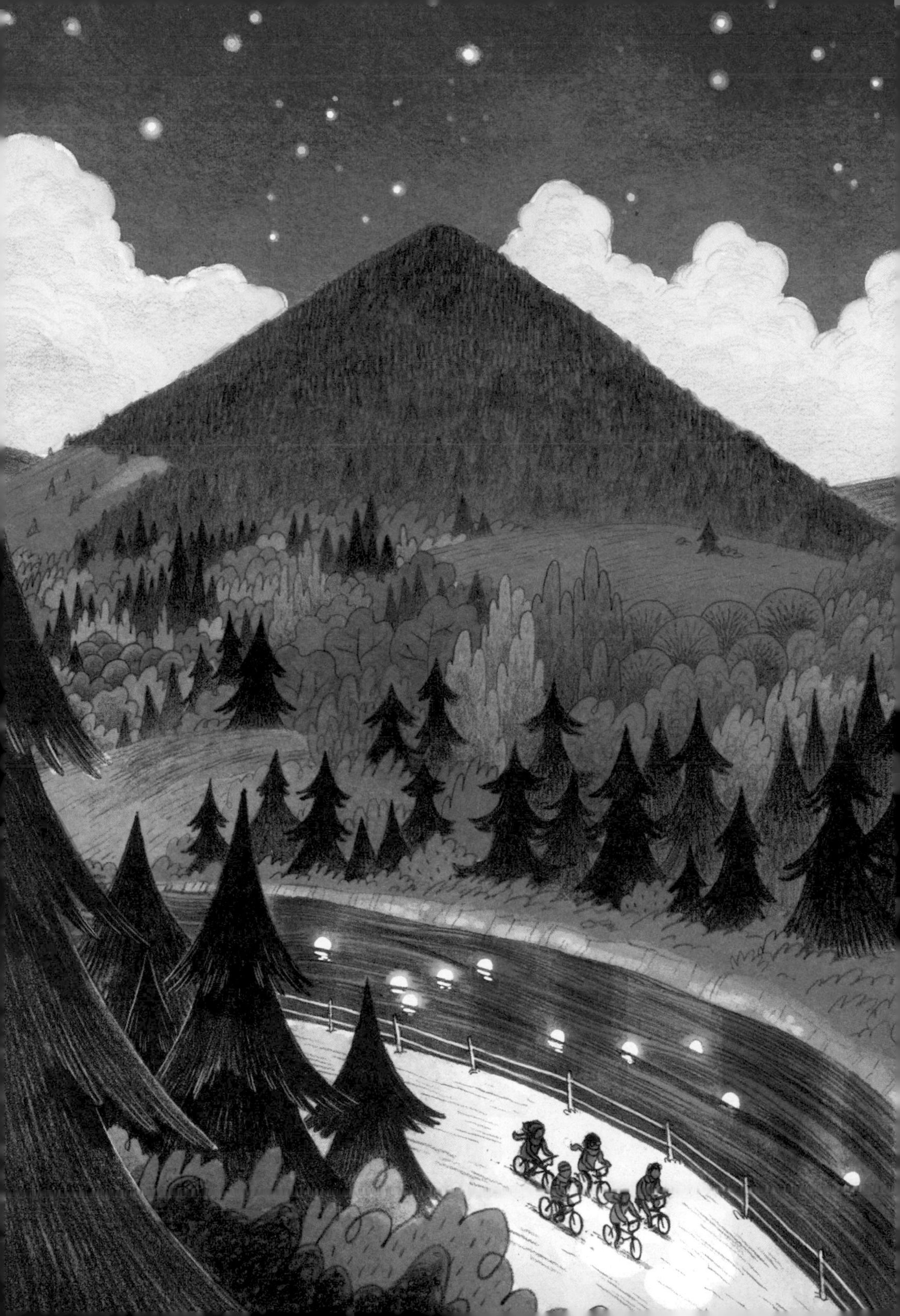

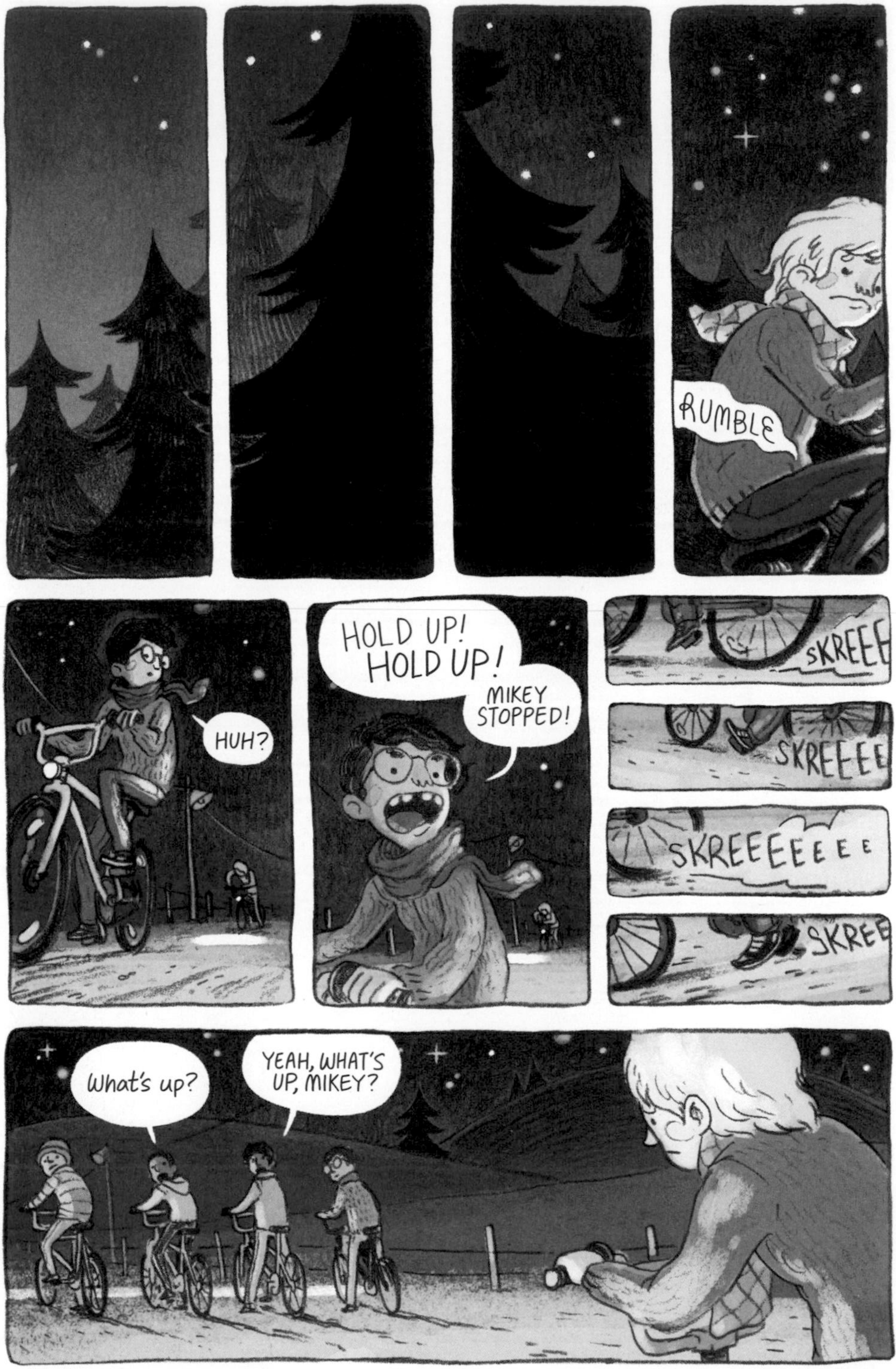
RUMBLE
HUH?
HOLD UP! HOLD UP!
MIKEY STOPPED!
SKREEE
SKREEEE
SKREEEEEEEE
SKREE
What's up?
YEAH, WHAT'S UP, MIKEY?

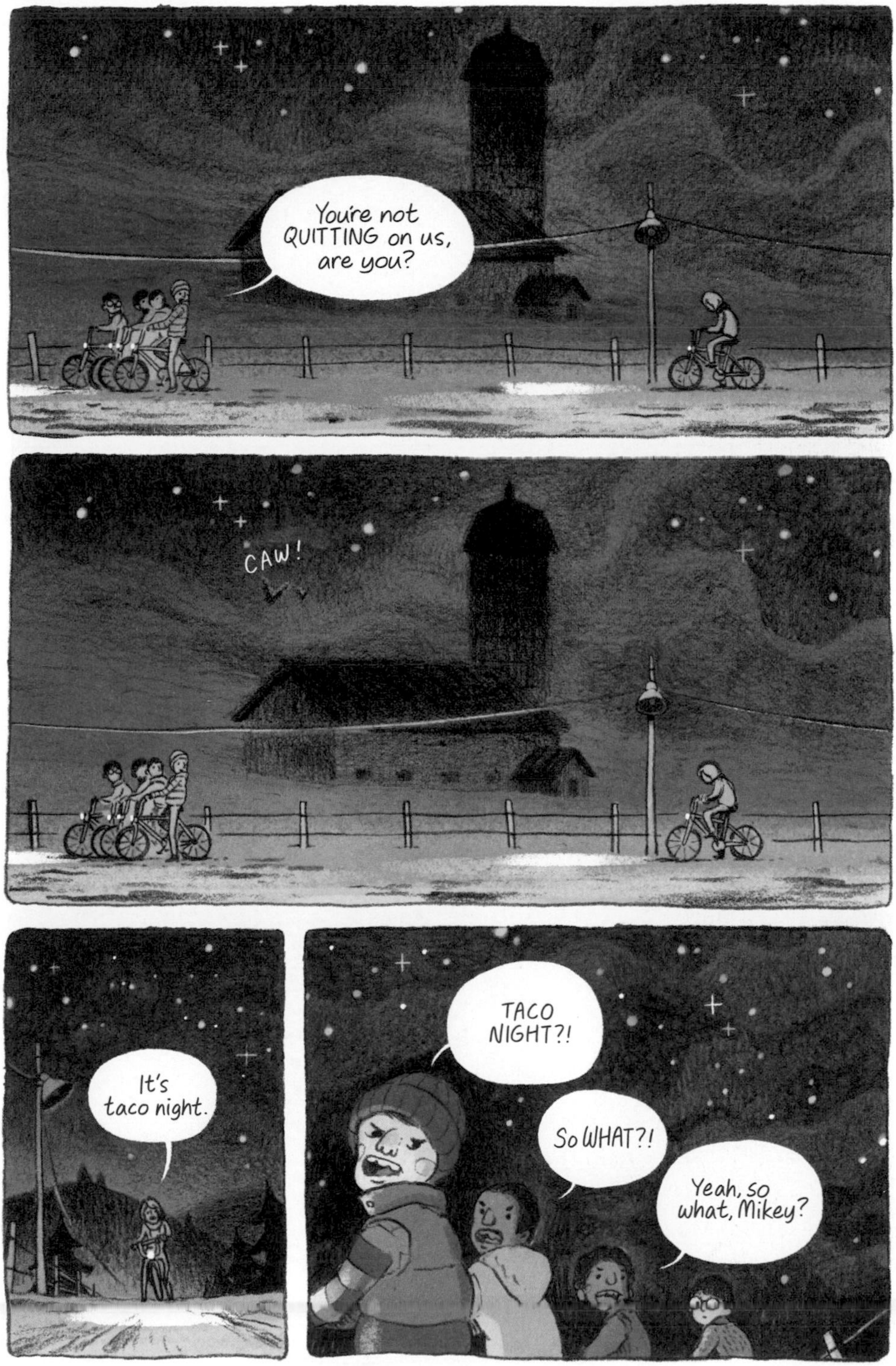
You're not QUITTING on us, are you?
CAW!
It's taco night.
TACO NIGHT?!
So WHAT?!
Yeah, so what, Mikey?

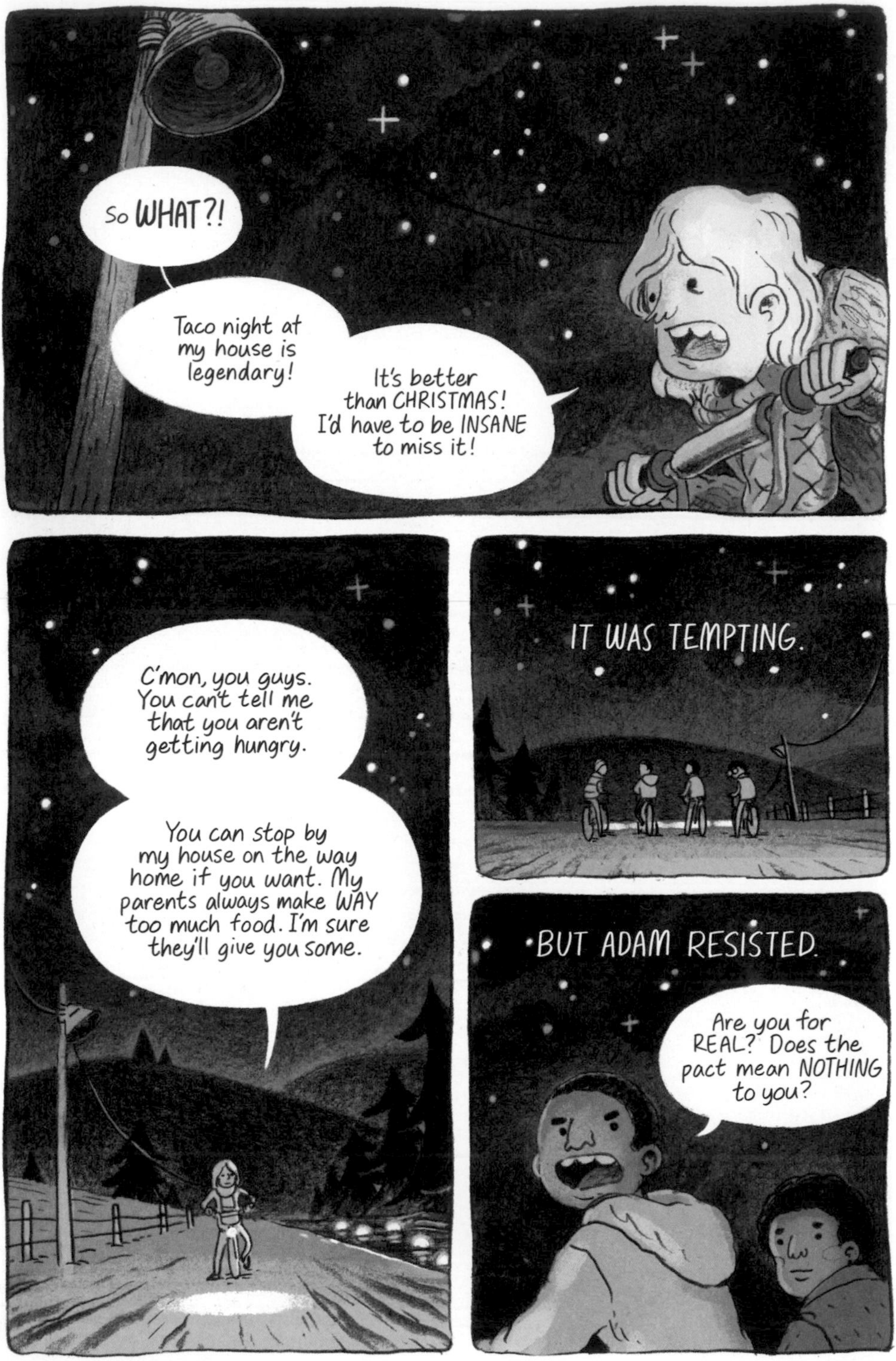
So WHAT?!
Taco night at my house is legendary!
It's better than CHRISTMAS! I'd have to be INSANE to miss it!
C'mon, you guys. You can't tell me that you aren't getting hungry.
You can stop by my house on the way home if you want. My parents always make WAY too much food. I'm sure they'll give you some.
IT WAS TEMPTING.
BUT ADAM RESISTED.
Are you for REAL? Does the pact mean NOTHING to you?

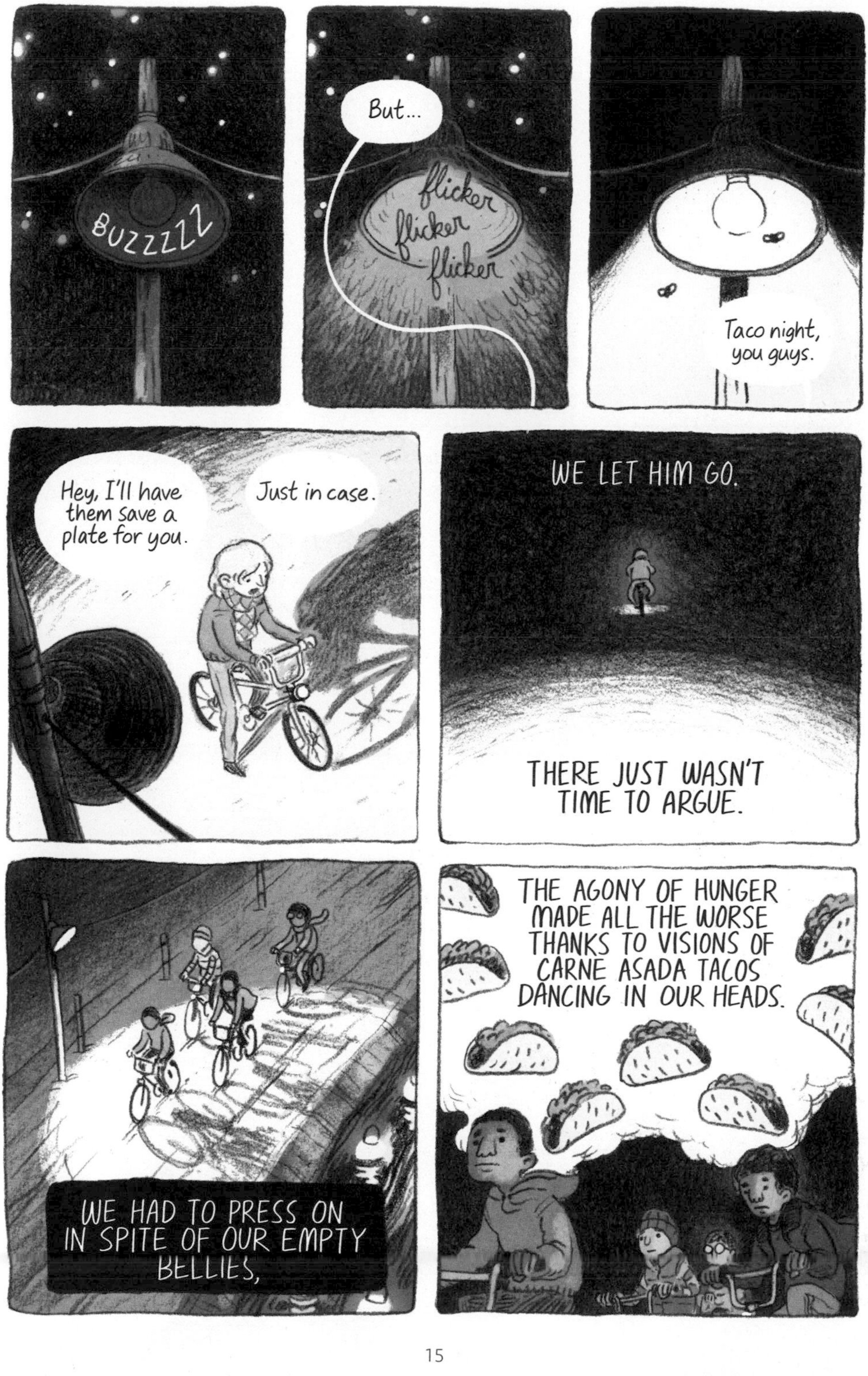
BUZZZZZ
But...
flicker flicker flicker
Taco night, you guys.
Hey, I'll have them save a plate for you.
Just in case.
WE LET HIM GO.
THERE JUST WASN'T TIME TO ARGUE.
WE HAD TO PRESS ON IN SPITE OF OUR EMPTY BELLIES,
THE AGONY OF HUNGER MADE ALL THE WORSE THANKS TO VISIONS OF CARNE ASADA TACOS DANCING IN OUR HEADS.

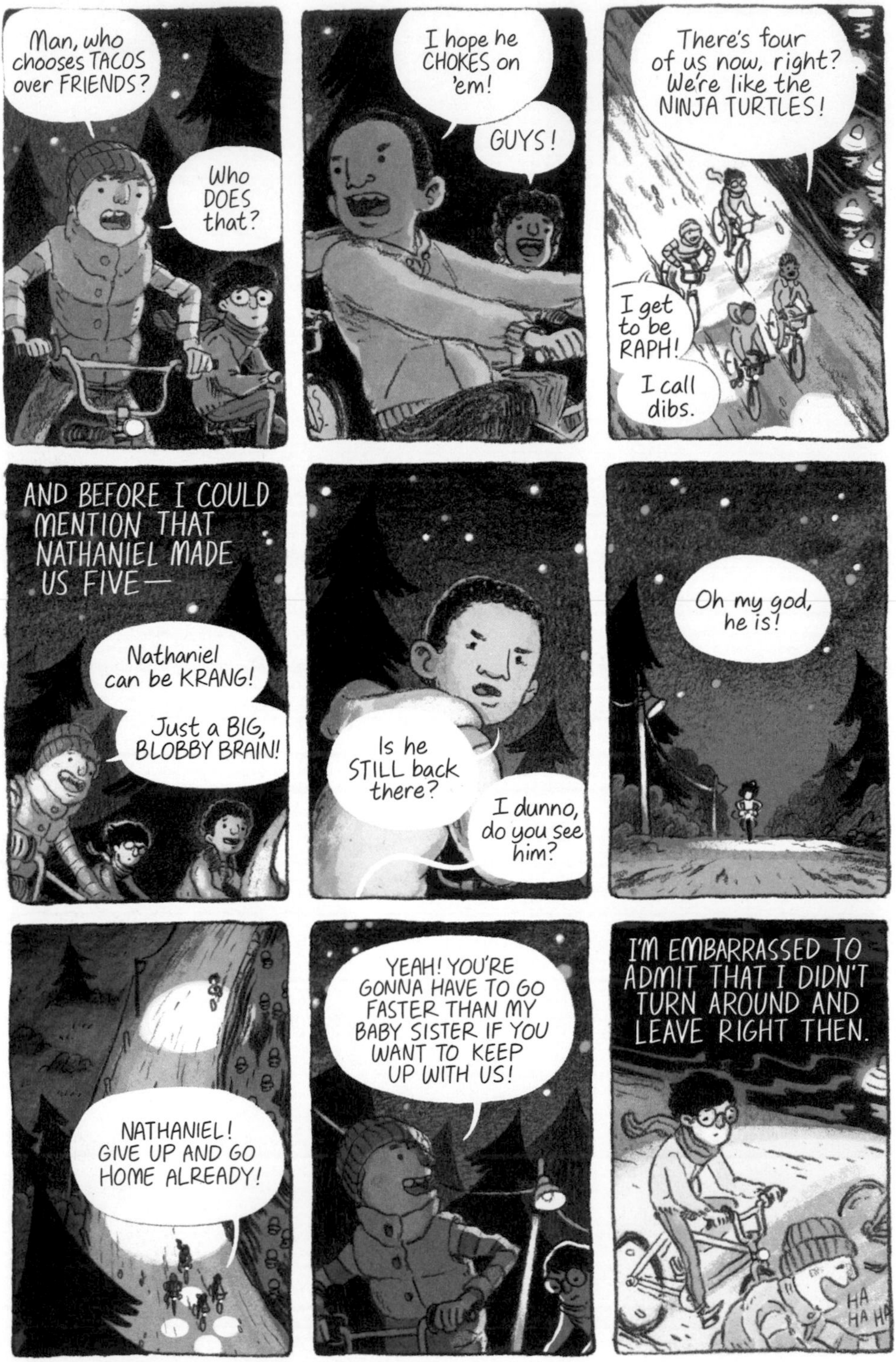
Man, who chooses TACOS over FRIENDS?
Who DOES that?
I hope he CHOKES on 'em!
GUYS!
There's four of us now, right? We're like the NINJA TURTLES!
I get to be RAPH!
I call dibs.
AND BEFORE I COULD MENTION THAT NATHANIEL MADE US FIVE—
Nathaniel can be KRANG!
Just a BIG, BLOBBY BRAIN!
Is he STILL back there?
I dunno, do you see him?
Oh my god, he is!
NATHANIEL! GIVE UP AND GO HOME ALREADY!
YEAH! YOU'RE GONNA HAVE TO GO FASTER THAN MY BABY SISTER IF YOU WANT TO KEEP UP WITH US!
I'M EMBARRASSED TO ADMIT THAT I DIDN'T TURN AROUND AND LEAVE RIGHT THEN.
HA HA HA

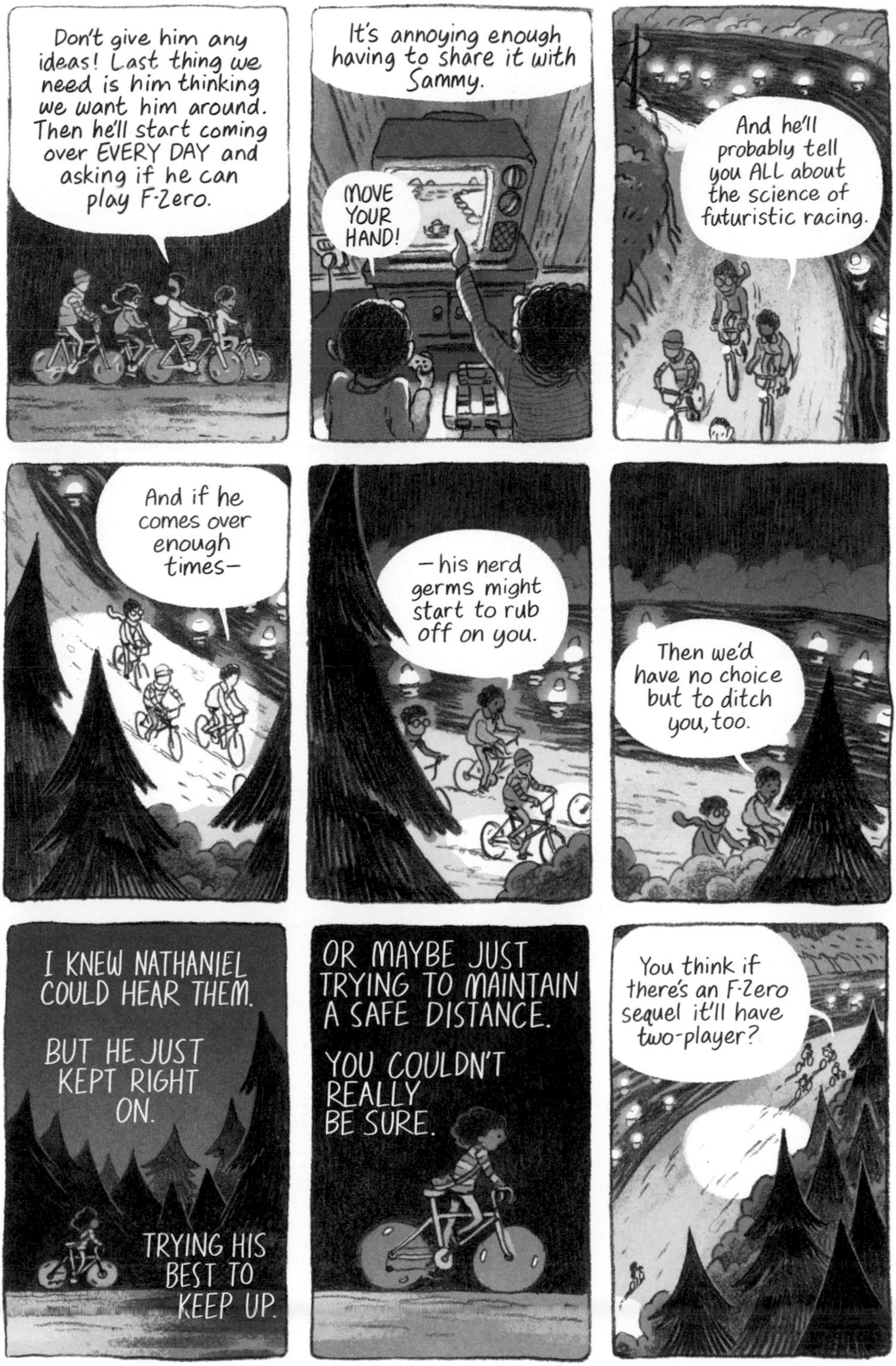
Don't give him any ideas! Last thing we need is him thinking we want him around. Then he'll start coming over EVERY DAY and asking if he can play F-Zero.
It's annoying enough having to share it with Sammy.
MOVE YOUR HAND!
And he'll probably tell you ALL about the science of futuristic racing.
And if he comes over enough times—
—his nerd germs might start to rub off on you.
Then we'd have no choice but to ditch you, too.
I KNEW NATHANIEL COULD HEAR THEM.
BUT HE JUST KEPT RIGHT ON.
TRYING HIS BEST TO KEEP UP.
OR MAYBE JUST TRYING TO MAINTAIN A SAFE DISTANCE.
YOU COULDN'T REALLY BE SURE.
You think if there's an F-Zero sequel it'll have two-player?

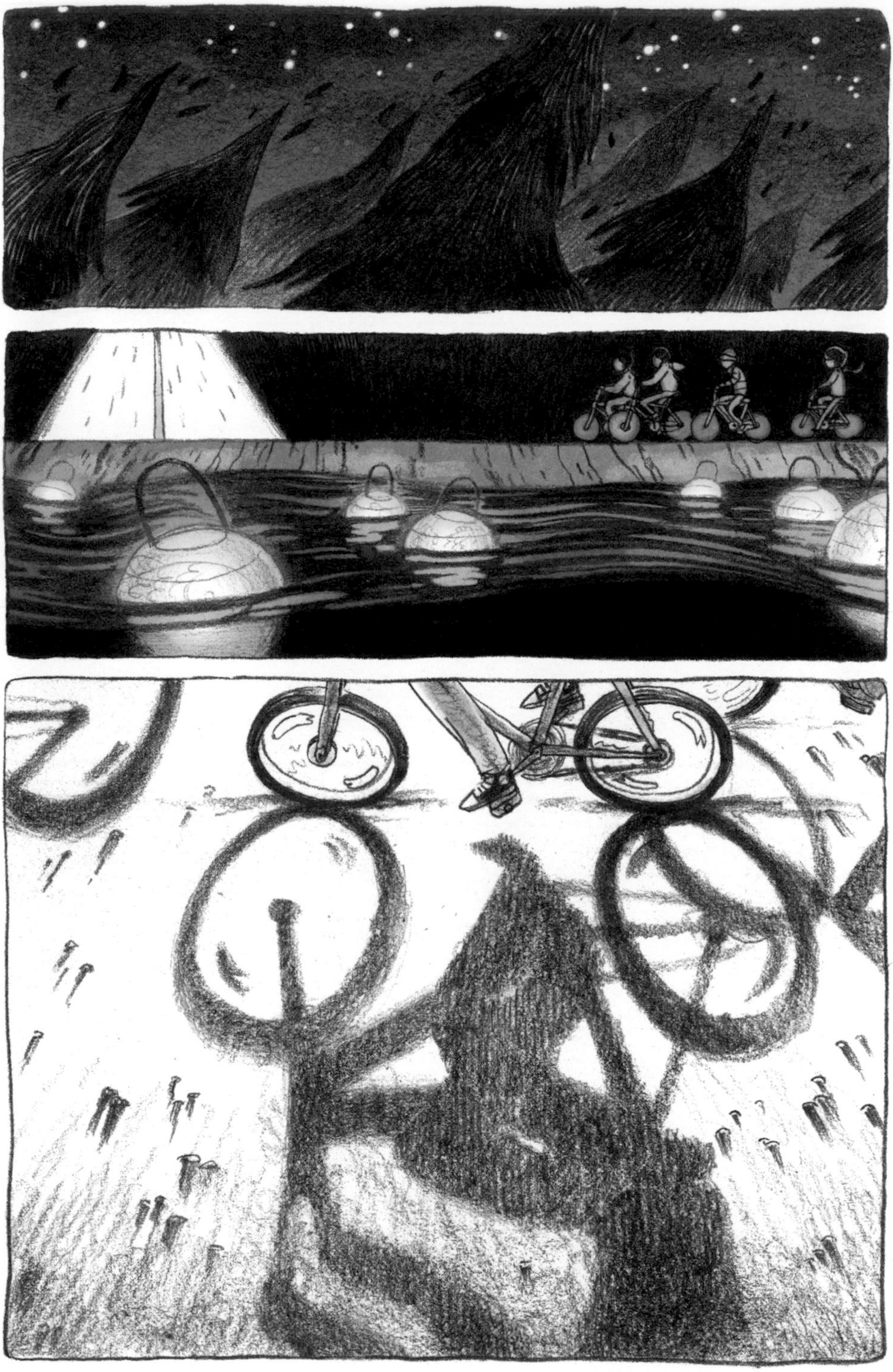

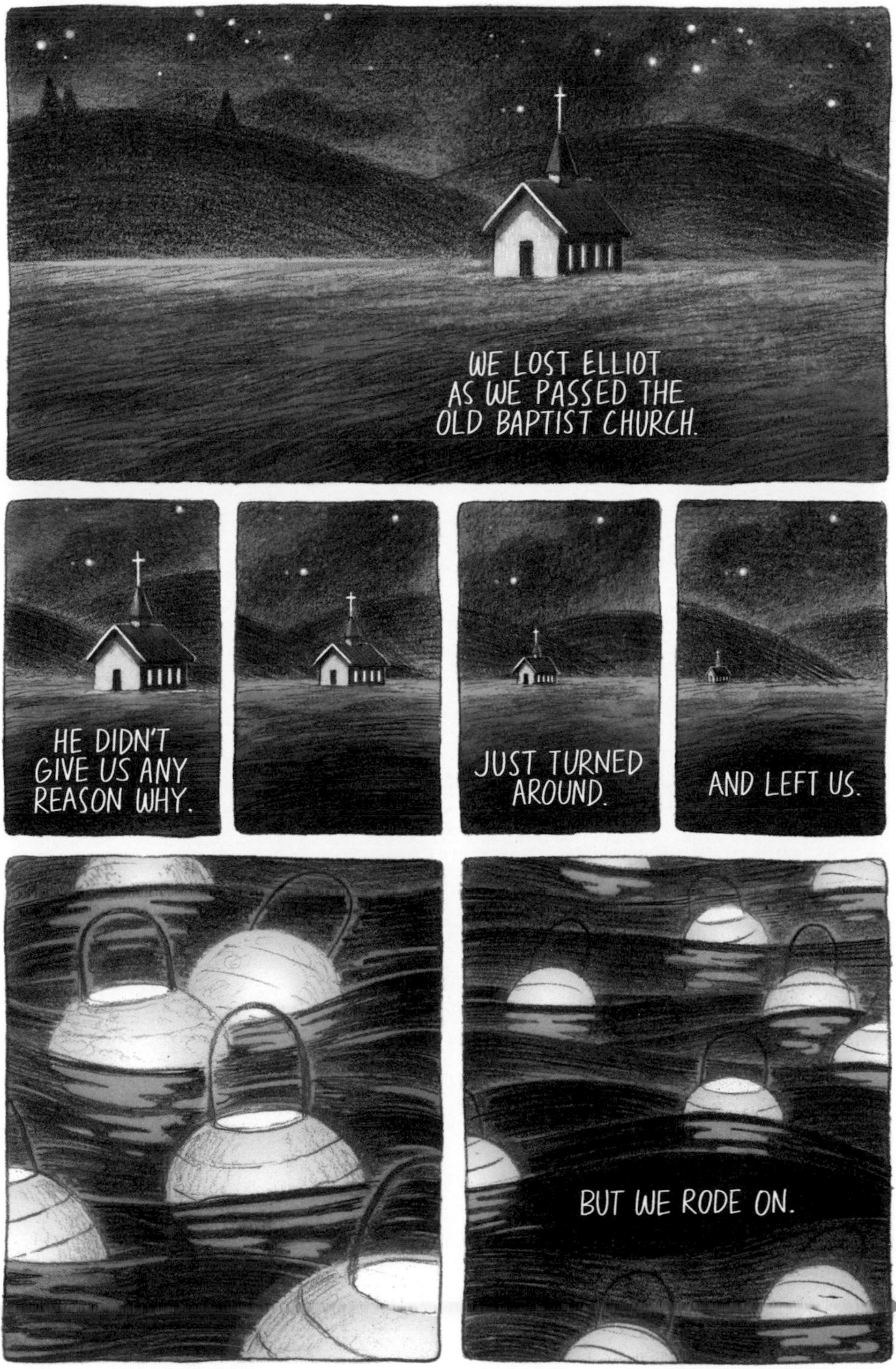
WE LOST ELLIOT AS WE PASSED THE OLD BAPTIST CHURCH.
HE DIDN'T GIVE US ANY REASON WHY.
JUST TURNED AROUND.
AND LEFT US.
BUT WE RODE ON.

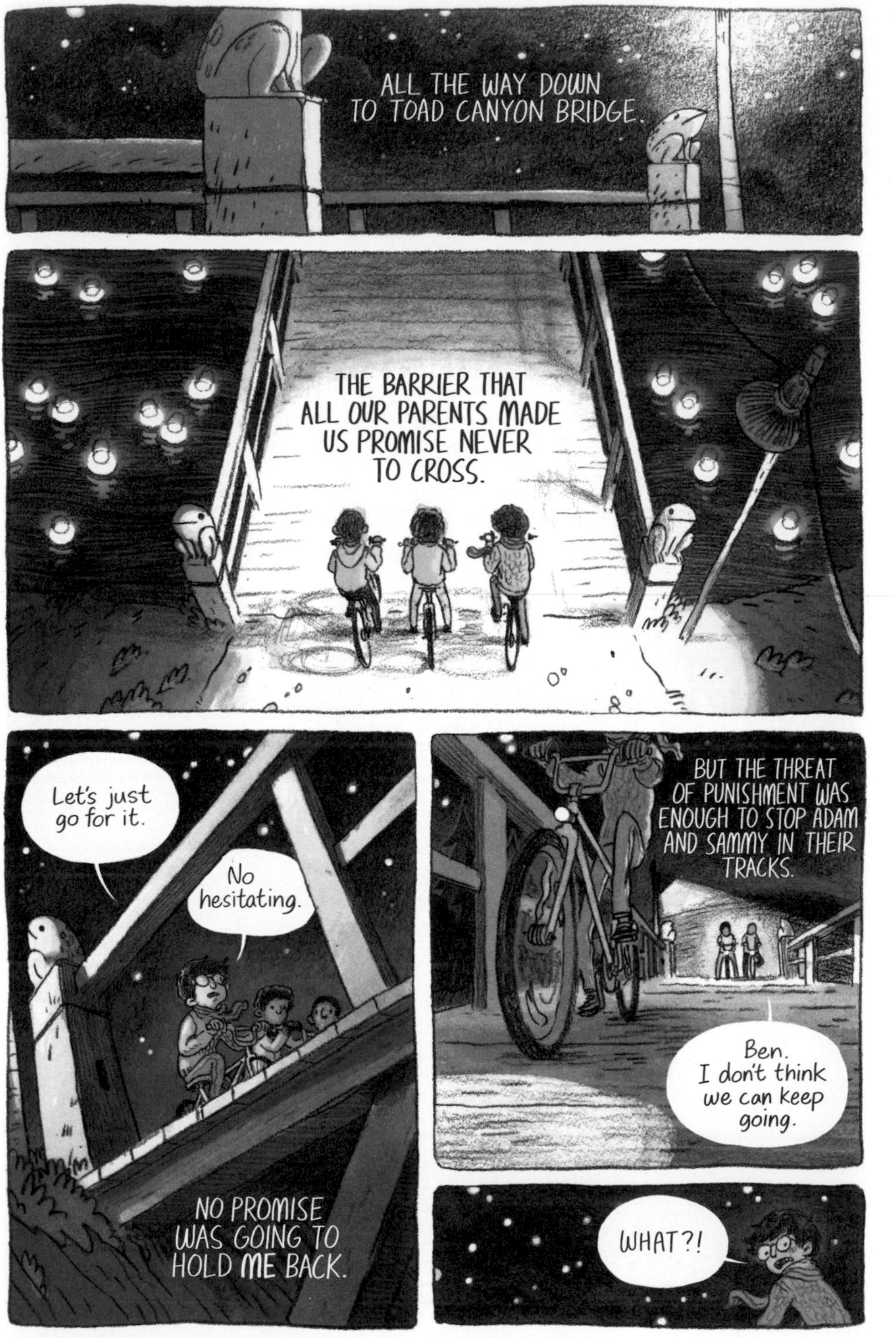
ALL THE WAY DOWN TO TOAD CANYON BRIDGE.
THE BARRIER THAT ALL OUR PARENTS MADE US PROMISE NEVER TO CROSS.
Let's just go for it.
No hesitating.
NO PROMISE WAS GOING TO HOLD ME BACK.
BUT THE THREAT OF PUNISHMENT WAS ENOUGH TO STOP ADAM AND SAMMY IN THEIR TRACKS.
Ben. I don't think we can keep going.
WHAT?!

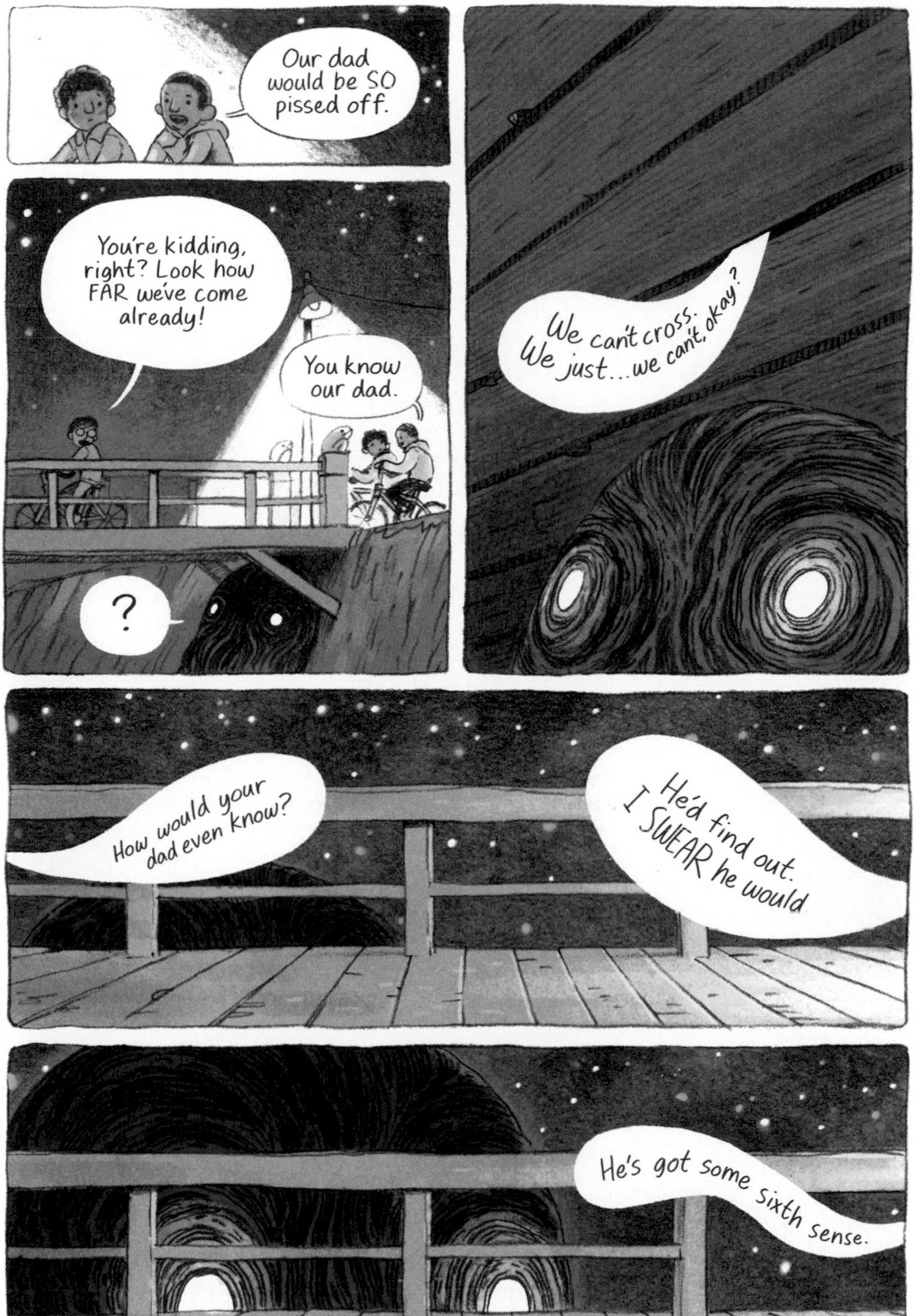
Our dad would be SO pissed off.
You're kidding, right? Look how FAR we've come already!
You know our dad.
?
We can't cross. We just... we can't, okay?
How would your dad even know?
He'd find out. I SWEAR he would.
He's got some sixth sense.

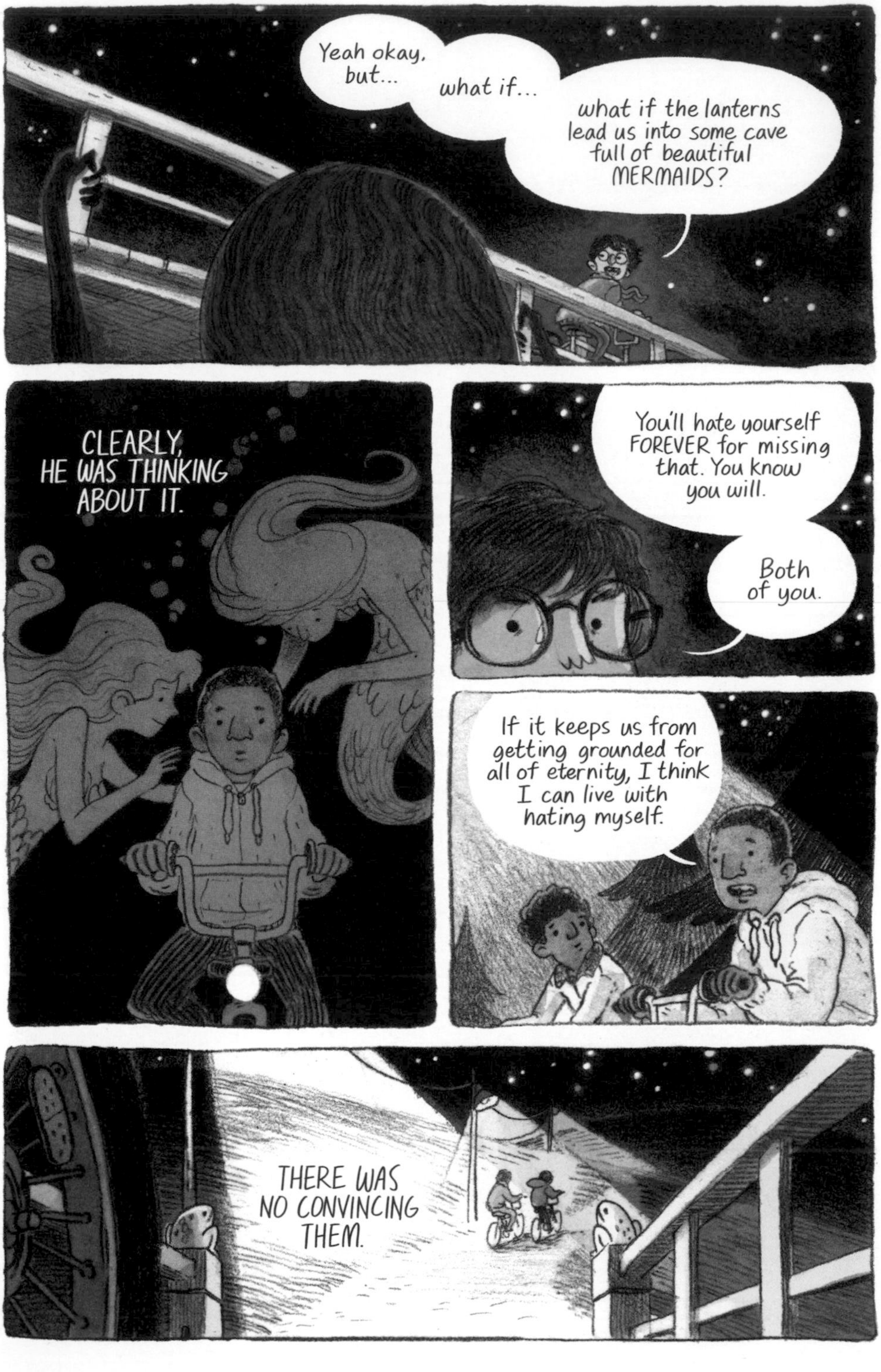
Yeah okay, but...
what if...
what if the lanterns lead us into some cave full of beautiful MERMAIDS?
CLEARLY, HE WAS THINKING ABOUT IT.
You'll hate yourself FOREVER for missing that. You know you will.
Both of you.
If it keeps us from getting grounded for all of eternity, I think I can live with hating myself.
THERE WAS NO CONVINCING THEM.

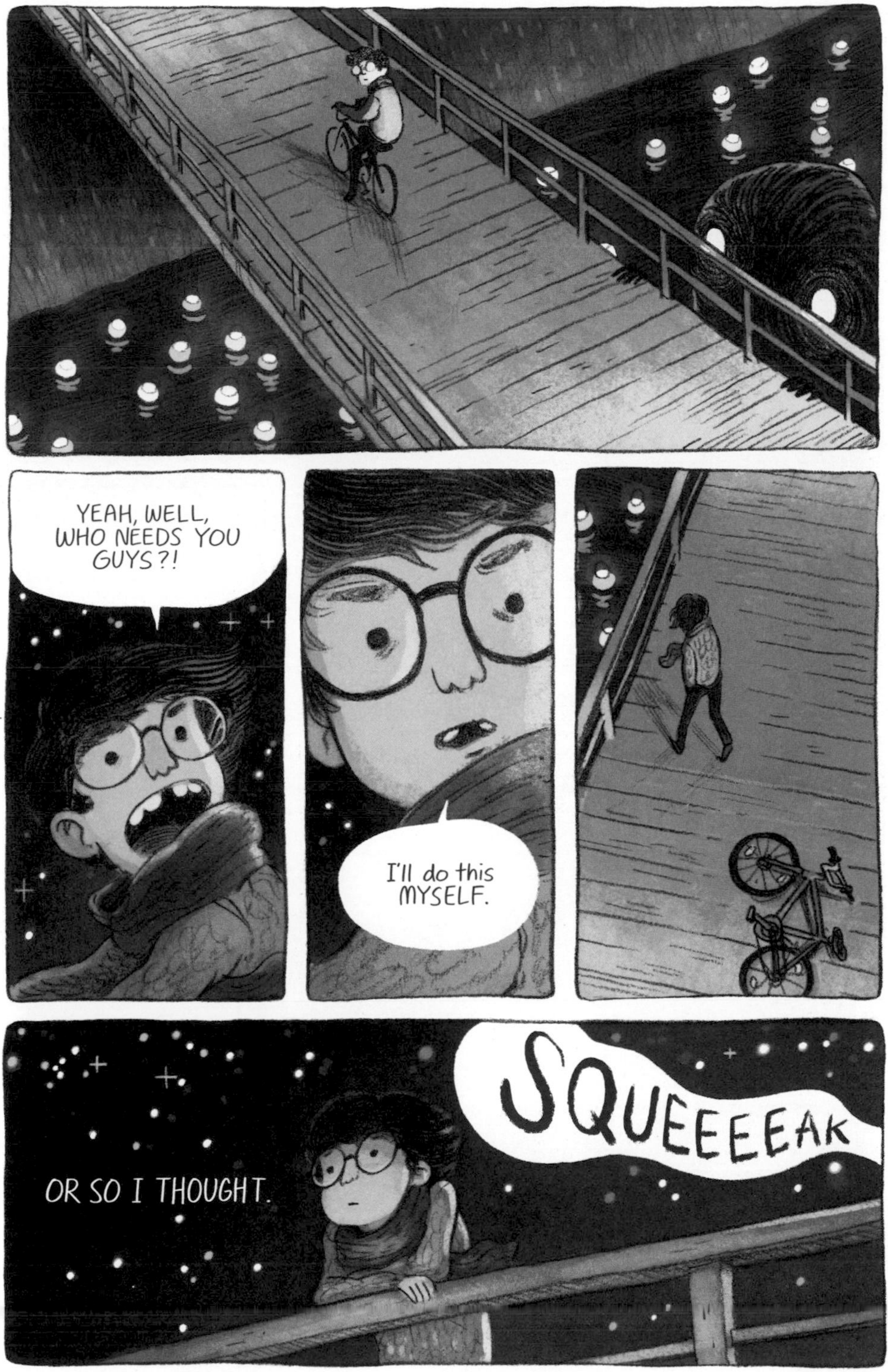
YEAH, WELL, WHO NEEDS YOU GUYS?!
I'll do this MYSELF.
OR SO I THOUGHT.
SQUEEEEEAK

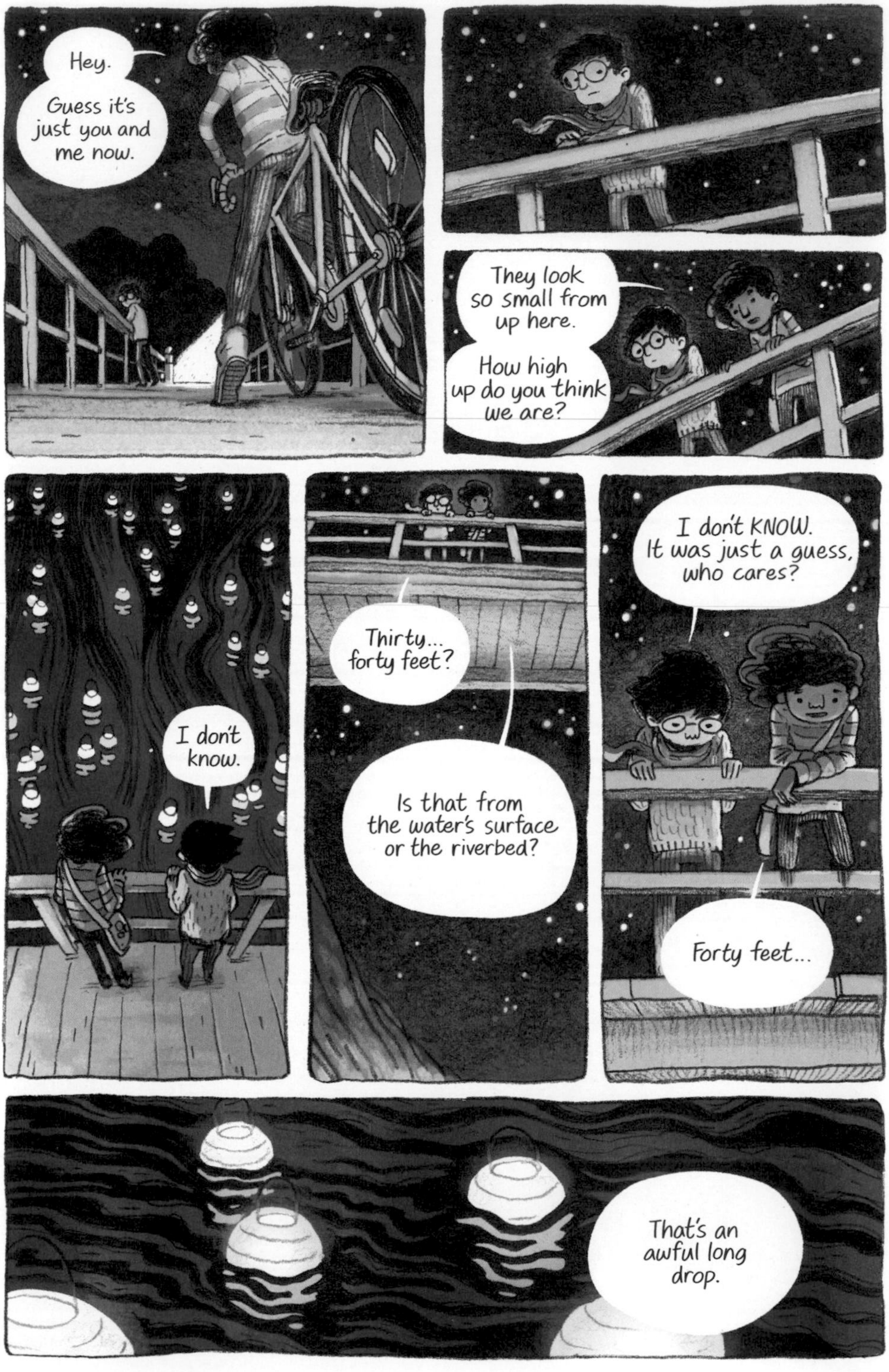
Hey.
Guess it's just you and me now.
They look so small from up here.
How high up do you think we are?
I don't know.
Thirty... forty feet?
Is that from the water's surface or the riverbed?
I don't KNOW. It was just a guess, who cares?
Forty feet...
That's an awful long drop.

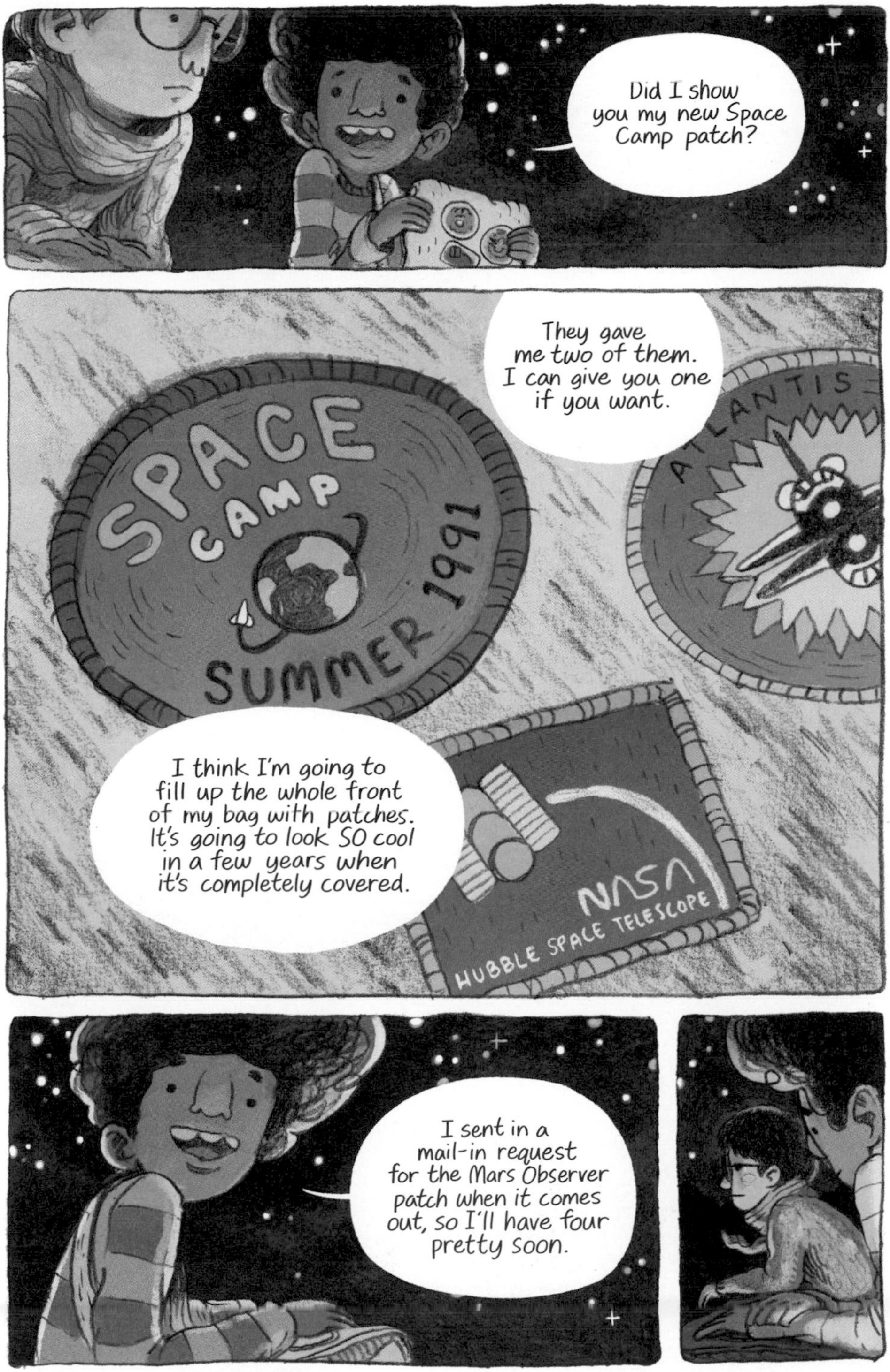
Did I show you my new Space Camp patch?
They gave me two of them. I can give you one if you want.
SPACE CAMP
SUMMER 1991
ATLANTIS
I think I'm going to fill up the whole front of my bag with patches. It's going to look SO cool in a few years when it's completely covered.
NASA
HUBBLE SPACE TELESCOPE
I sent in a mail-in request for the Mars Observer patch when it comes out, so I'll have four pretty soon.

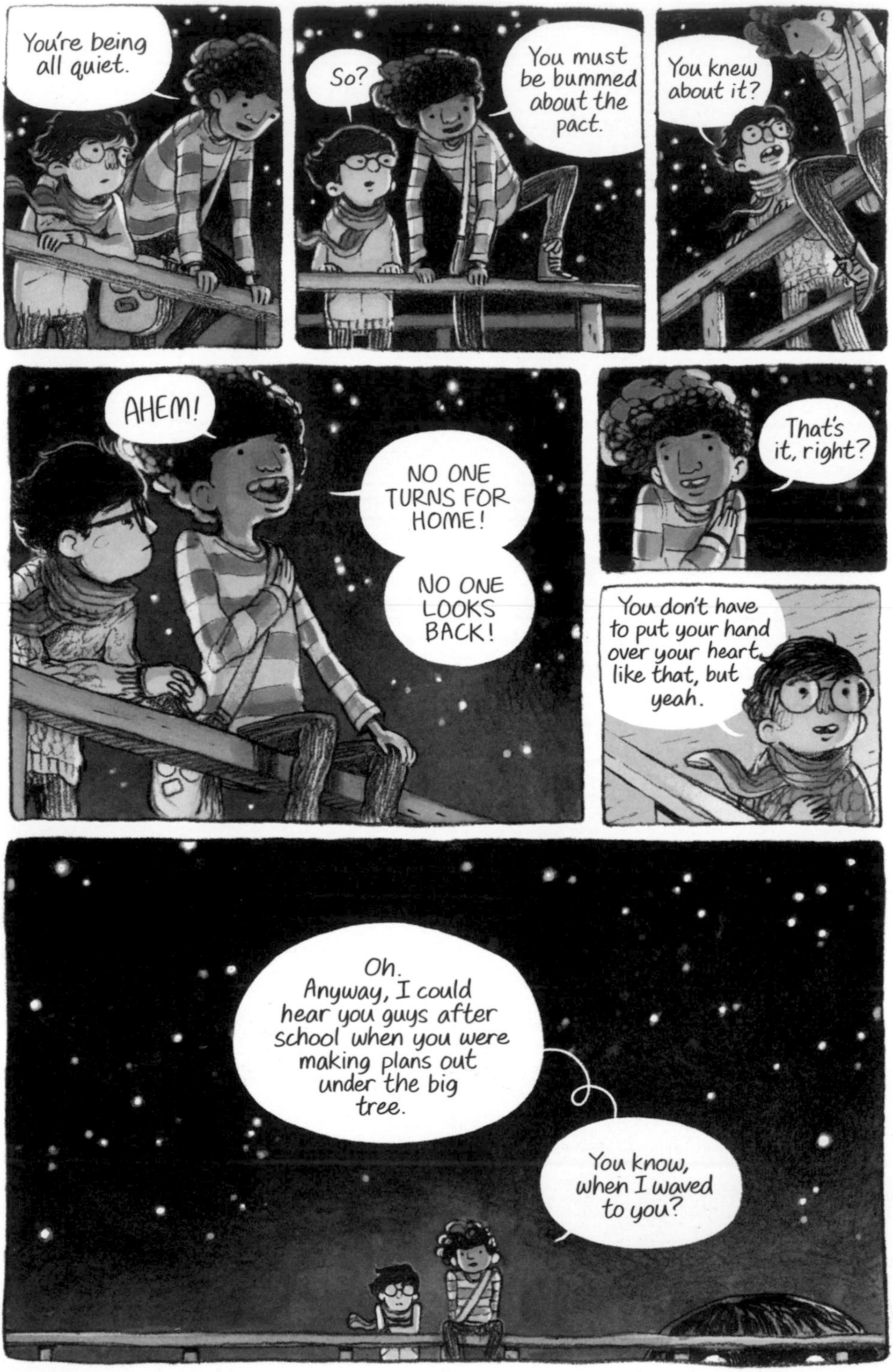

You're being all quiet.
So?
You must be bummed about the pact.
You knew about it?
AHEM!
NO ONE TURNS FOR HOME!
NO ONE LOOKS BACK!
That's it, right?
You don't have to put your hand over your heart like that, but yeah.
Oh. Anyway, I could hear you guys after school when you were making plans out under the big tree.
You know, when I waved to you?

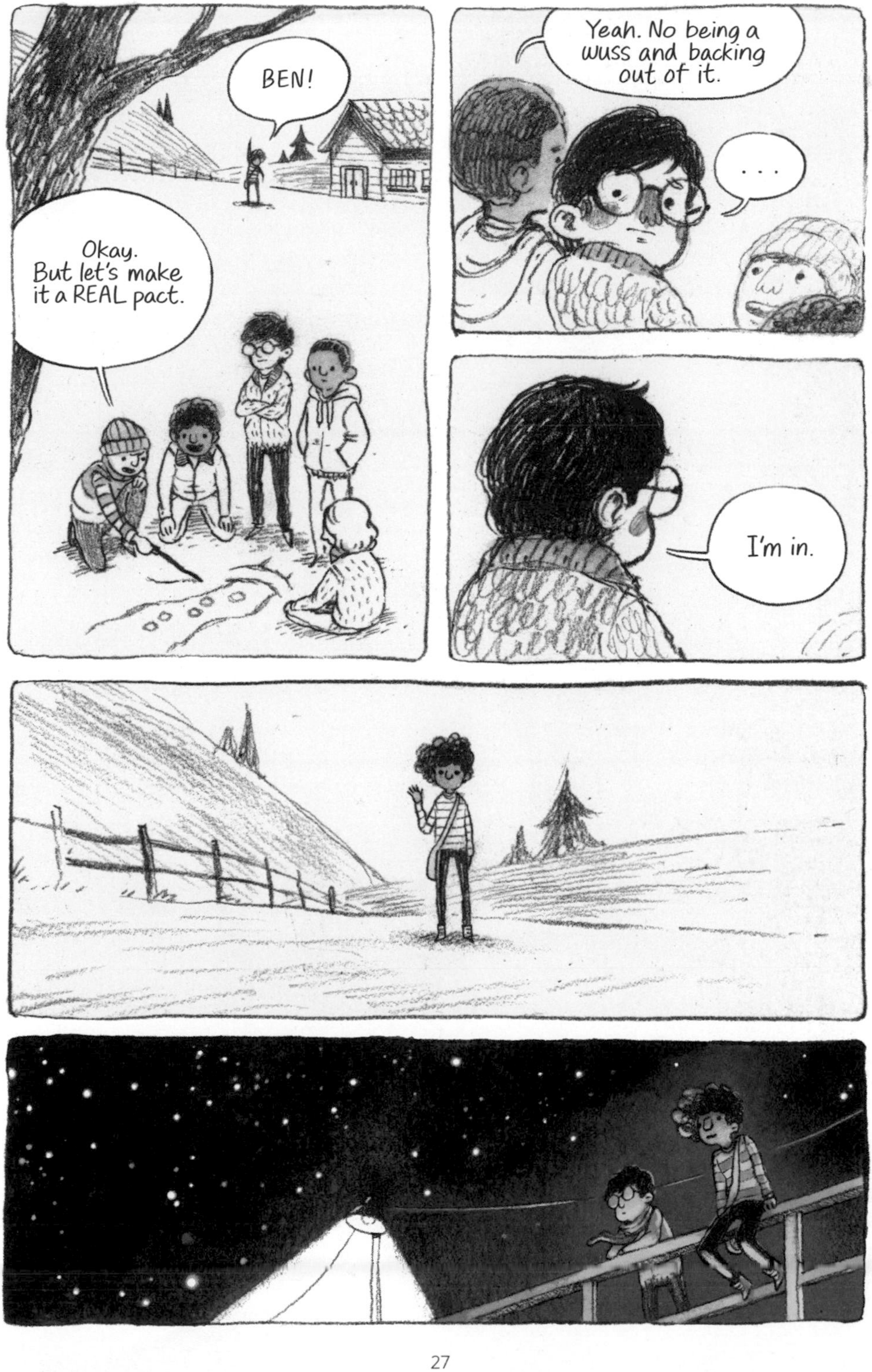
BEN!
Okay. But let's make it a REAL pact.
Yeah. No being a wuss and backing out of it.
. . .
I'm in.

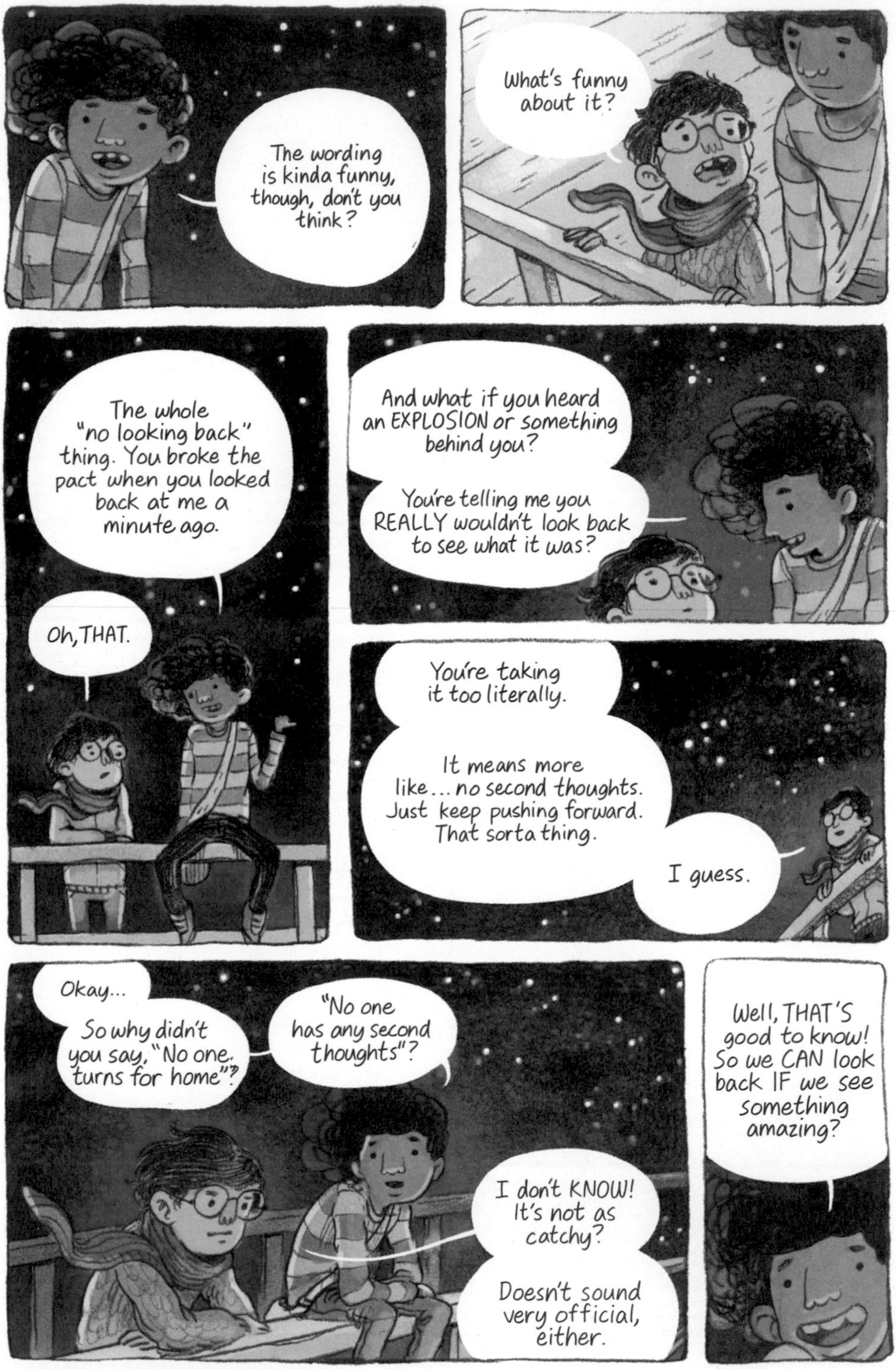
The wording is kinda funny, though, don't you think?
What's funny about it?
The whole "no looking back" thing. You broke the pact when you looked back at me a minute ago.
Oh, THAT.
And what if you heard an EXPLOSION or something behind you?
You're telling me you REALLY wouldn't look back to see what it was?
You're taking it too literally.
It means more like... no second thoughts. Just keep pushing forward. That sorta thing.
I guess.
Okay...
So why didn't you say, "No one turns for home"?
"No one has any second thoughts"?
I don't KNOW! It's not as catchy?
Doesn't sound very official, either.
Well, THAT'S good to know! So we CAN look back IF we see something amazing?

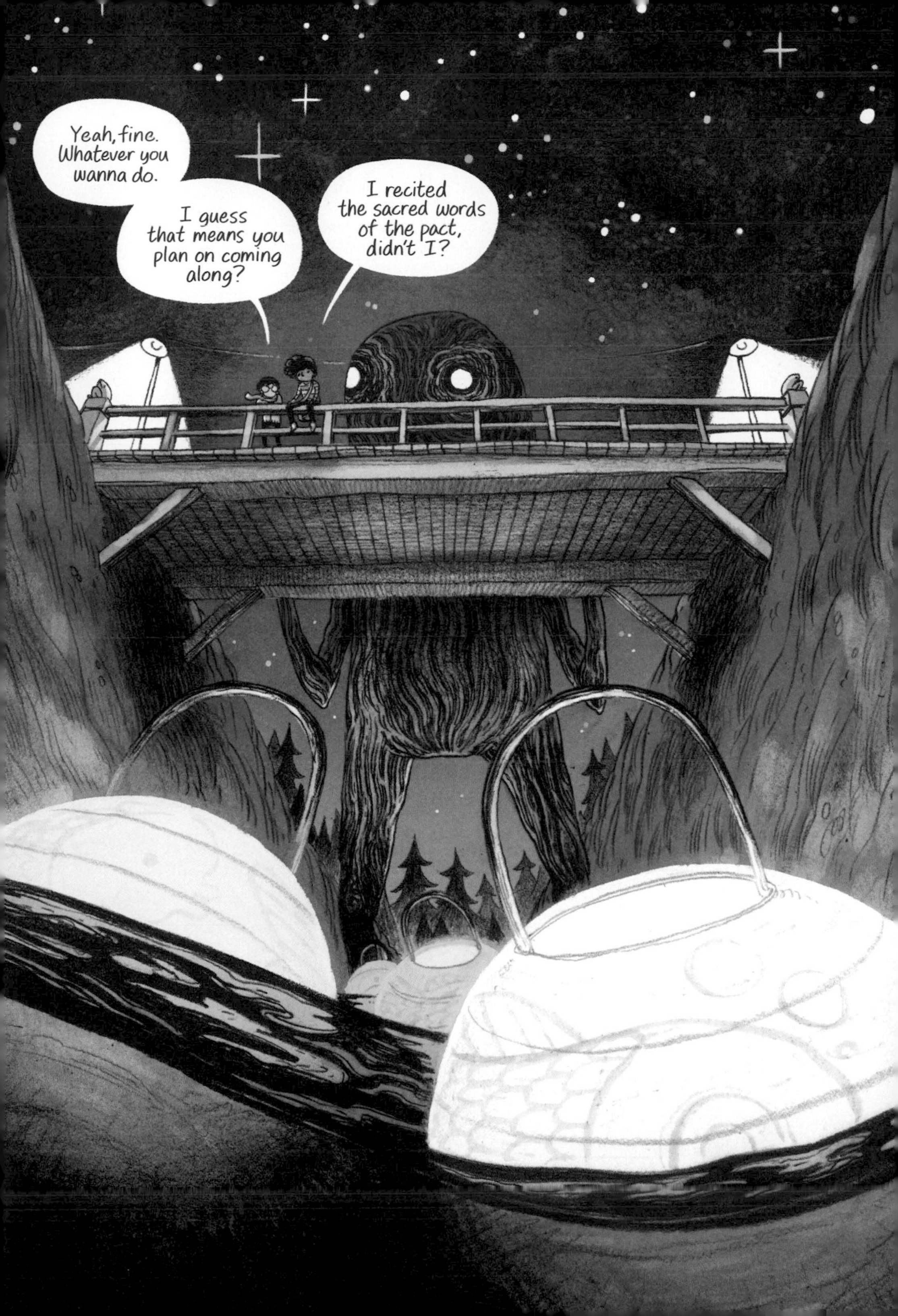
Yeah, fine. Whatever you wanna do.
I guess that means you plan on coming along?
I recited the sacred words of the pact, didn't I?

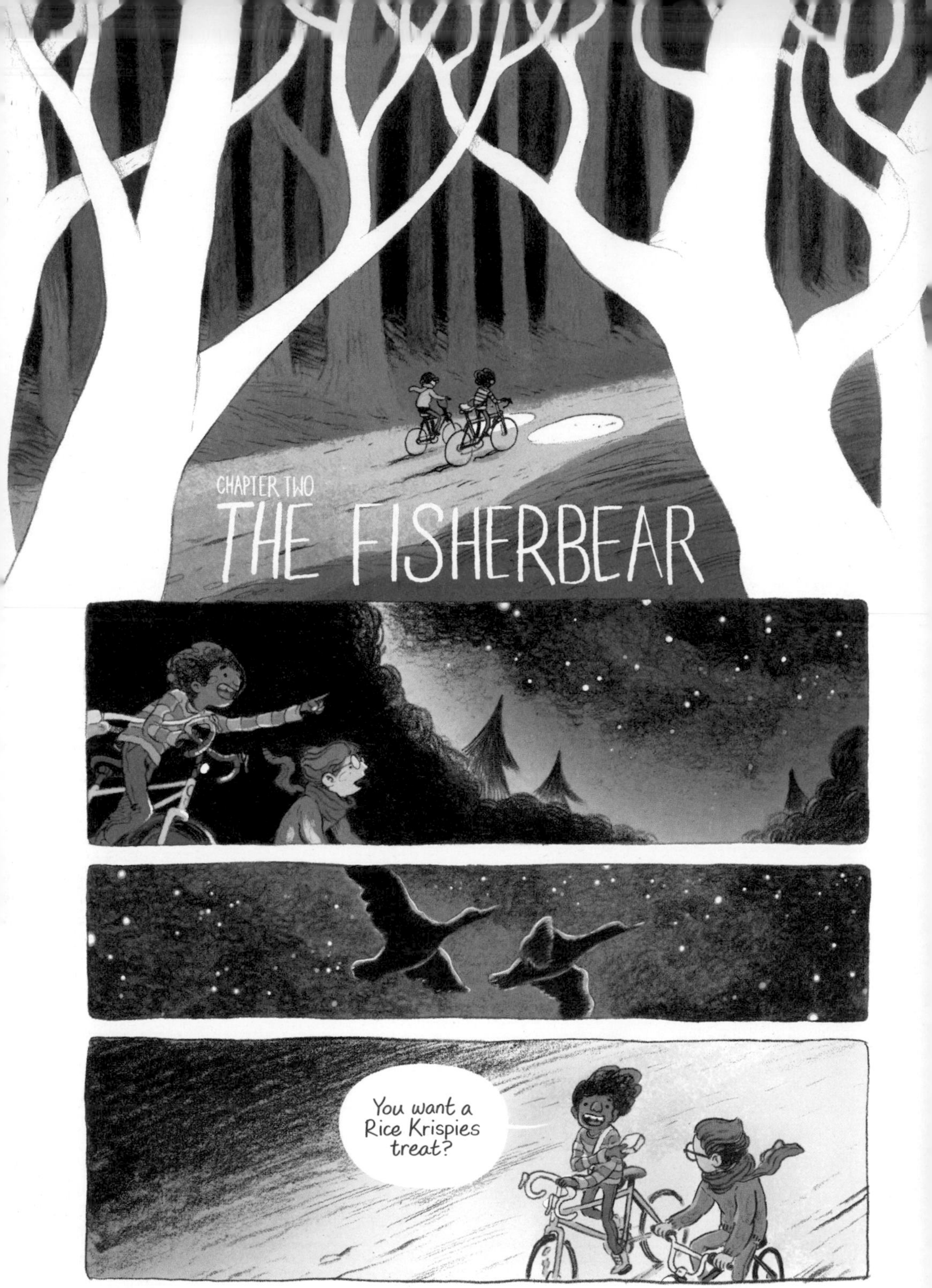
CHAPTER TWO
THE FISHERBEAR
You want a Rice Krispies treat?

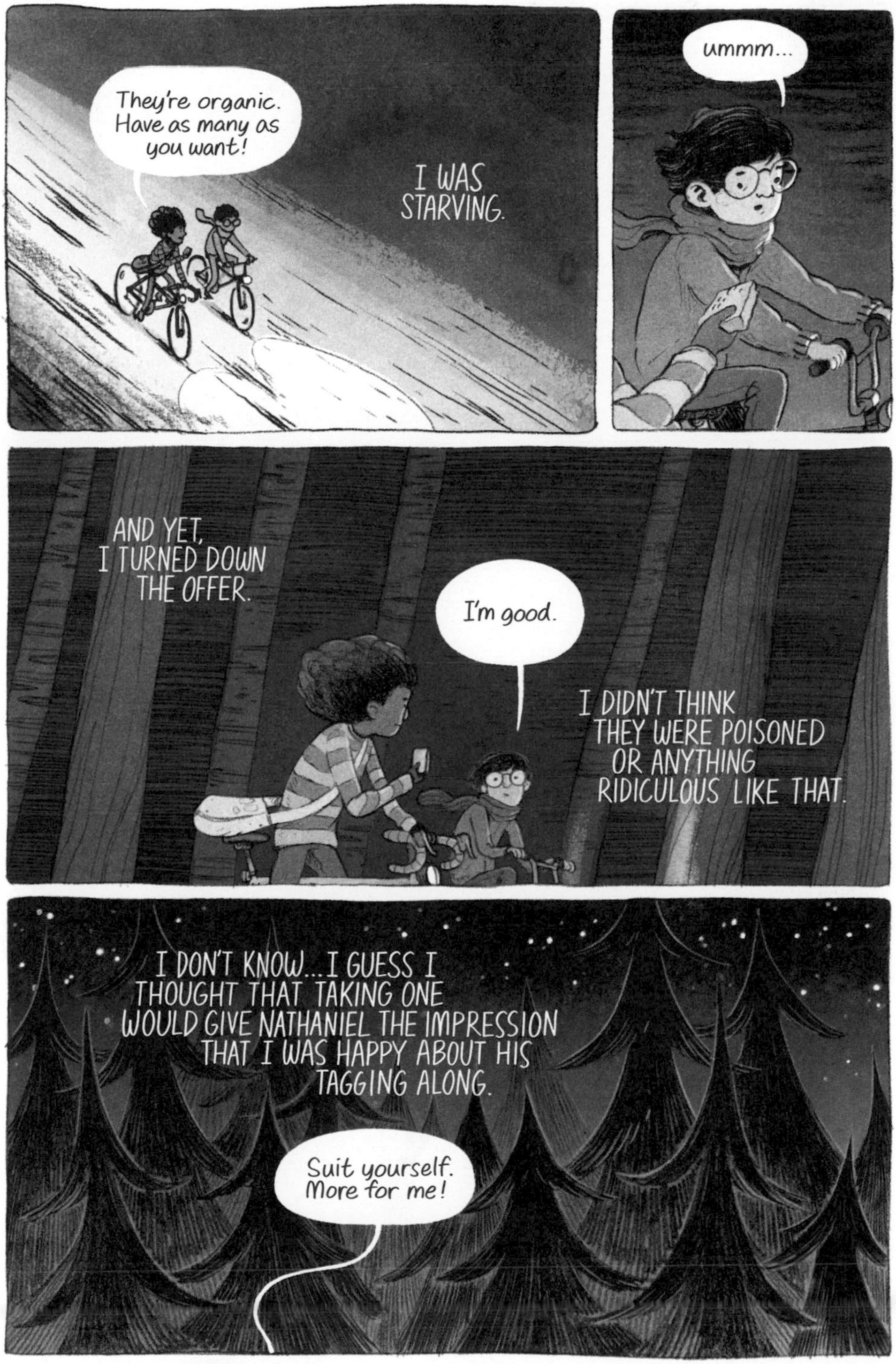
They're organic. Have as many as you want!
I WAS STARVING.
ummm...
AND YET, I TURNED DOWN THE OFFER.
I'm good.
I DIDN'T THINK THEY WERE POISONED OR ANYTHING RIDICULOUS LIKE THAT.
I DON'T KNOW...I GUESS I THOUGHT THAT TAKING ONE WOULD GIVE NATHANIEL THE IMPRESSION THAT I WAS HAPPY ABOUT HIS TAGGING ALONG.
Suit yourself. More for me!

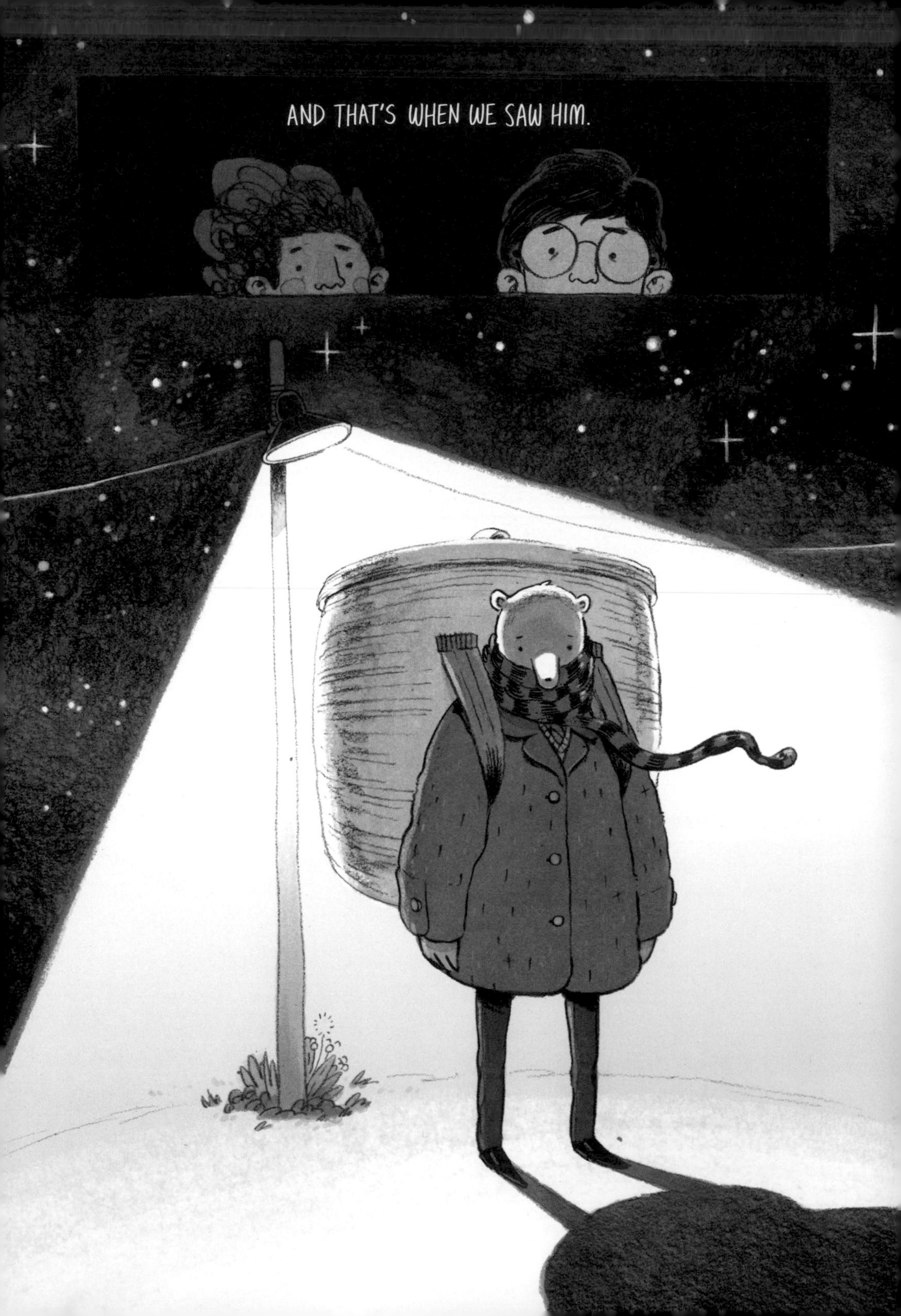
AND THAT'S WHEN WE SAW HIM.

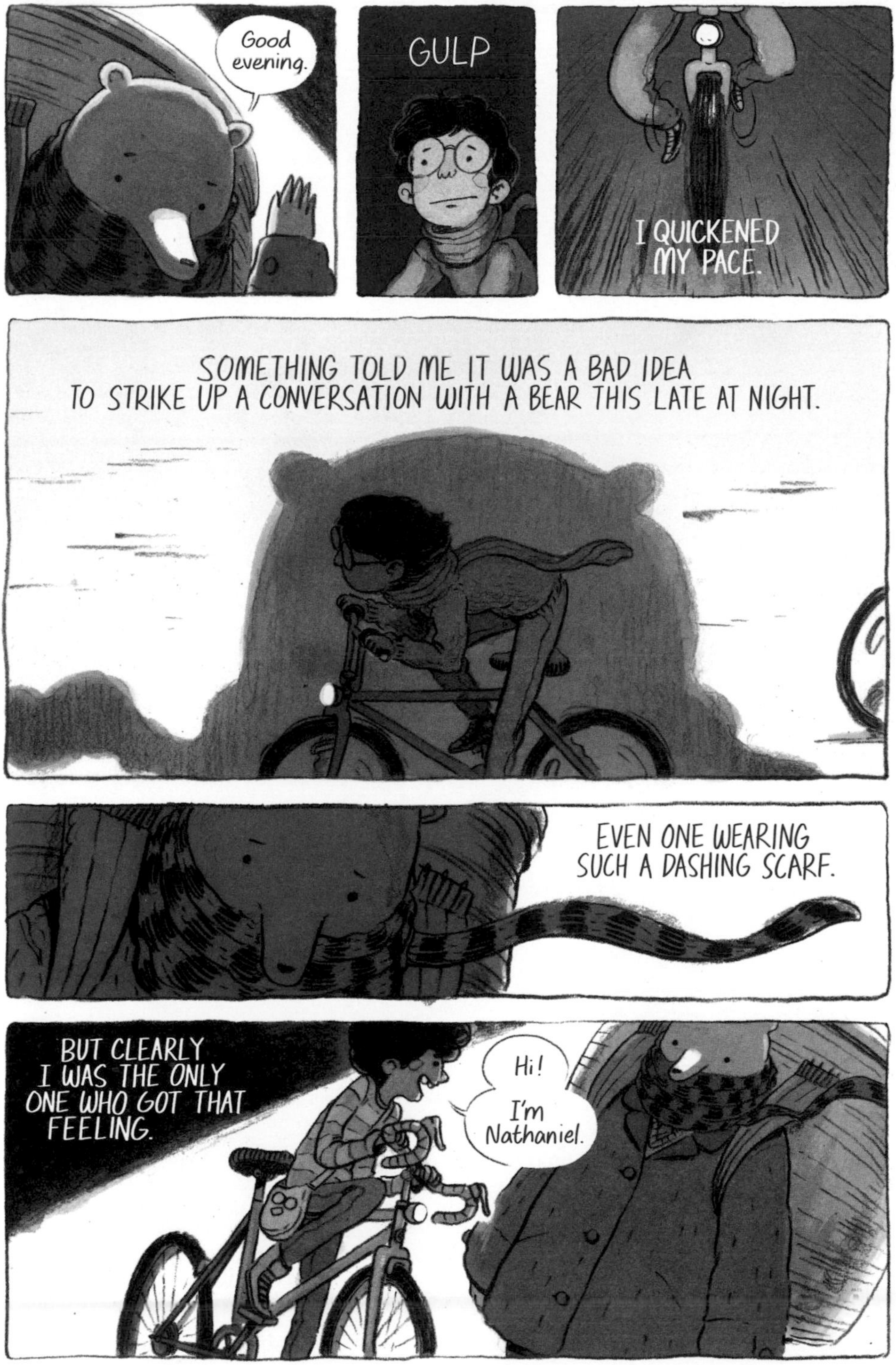

Good evening.
GULP
I QUICKENED MY PACE.
SOMETHING TOLD ME IT WAS A BAD IDEA TO STRIKE UP A CONVERSATION WITH A BEAR THIS LATE AT NIGHT.
EVEN ONE WEARING SUCH A DASHING SCARF.
BUT CLEARLY I WAS THE ONLY ONE WHO GOT THAT FEELING.
Hi!
I'm Nathaniel.

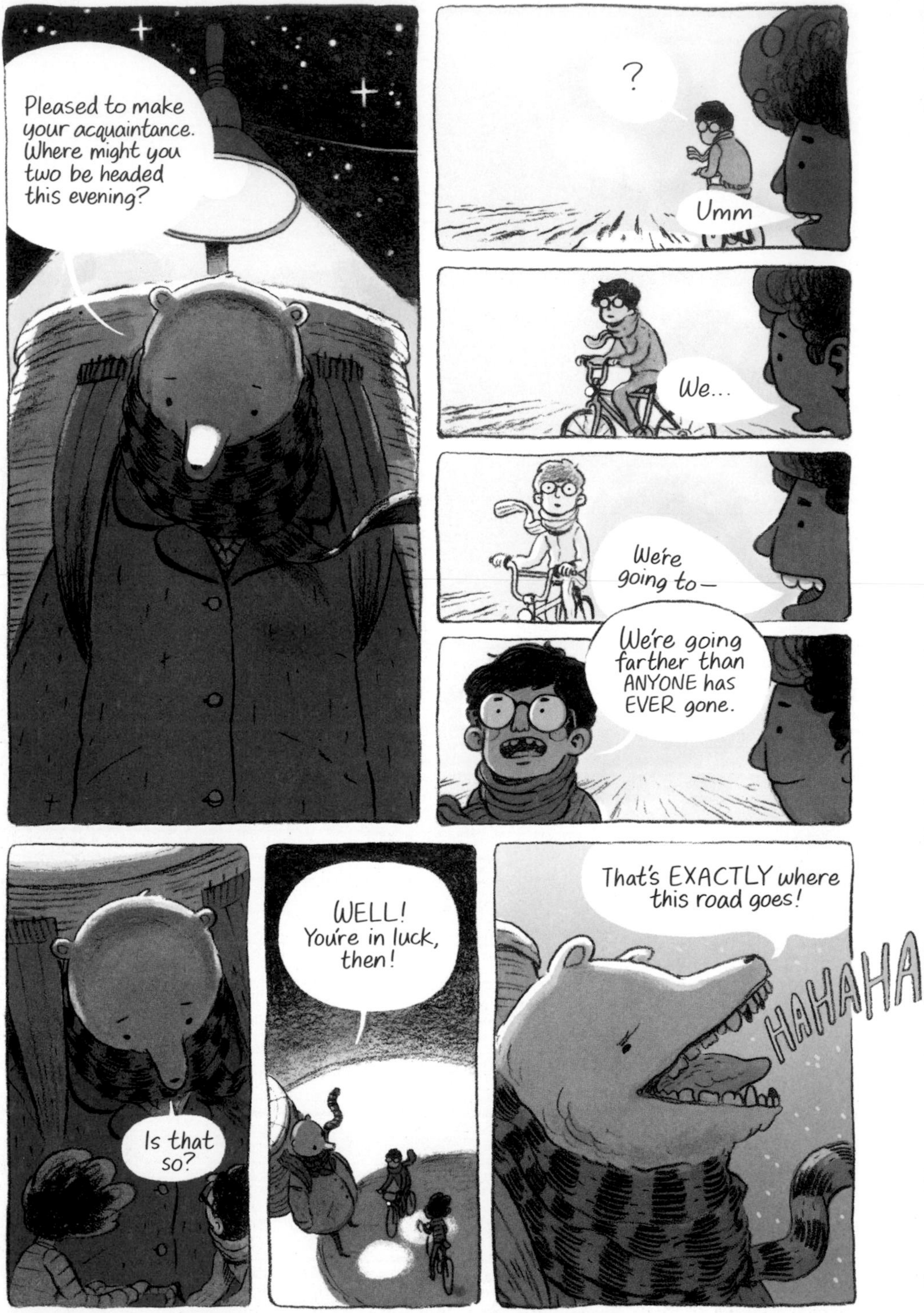
Pleased to make your acquaintance. Where might you two be headed this evening?
?
Umm
We...
We're going to—
We're going farther than ANYONE has EVER gone.
Is that so?
WELL! You're in luck, then!
That's EXACTLY where this road goes!
HAHAHA

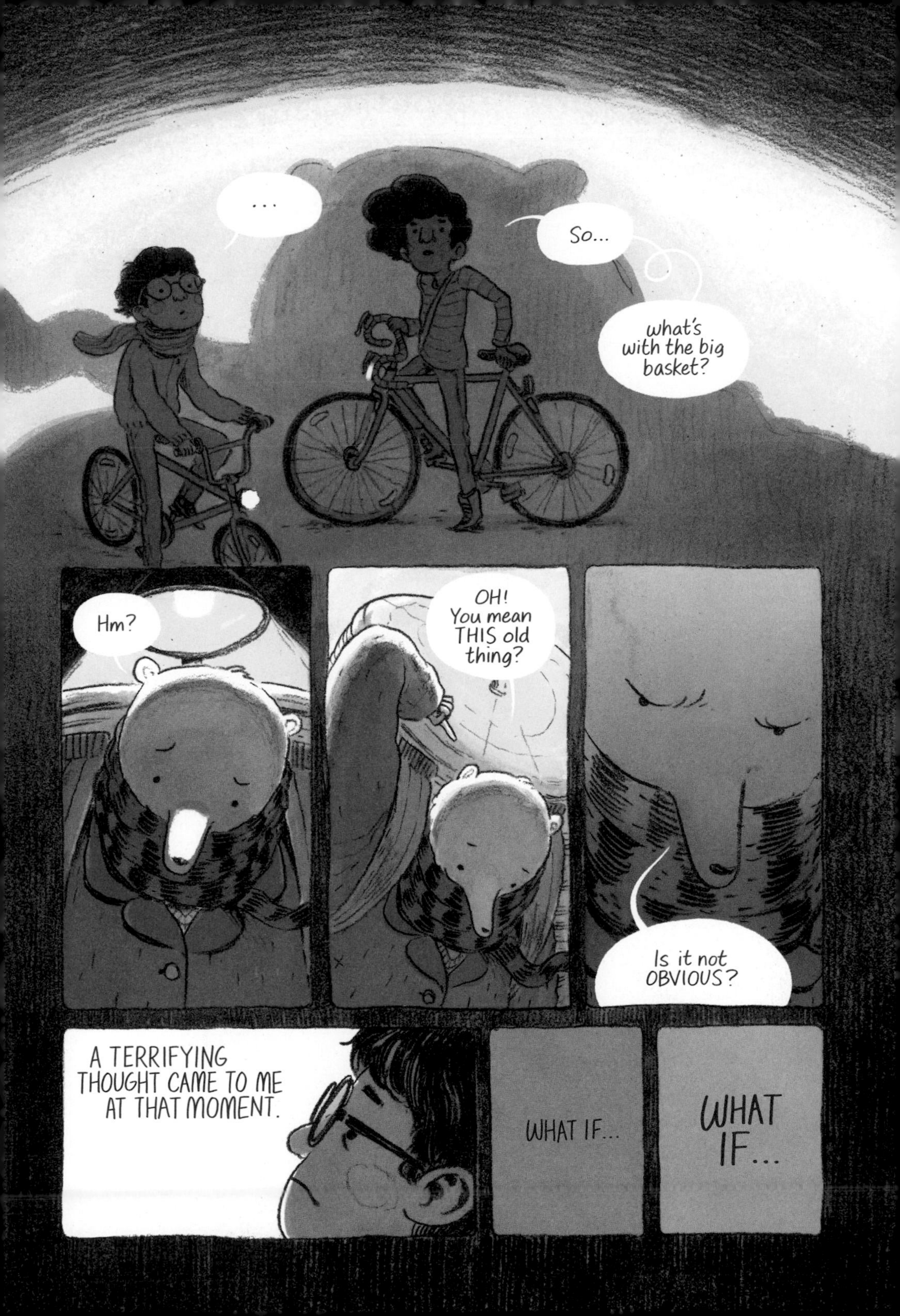
...
So...
what's with the big basket?
Hm?
OH! You mean THIS old thing?
Is it not OBVIOUS?
A TERRIFYING THOUGHT CAME TO ME AT THAT MOMENT.
WHAT IF...
WHAT IF...

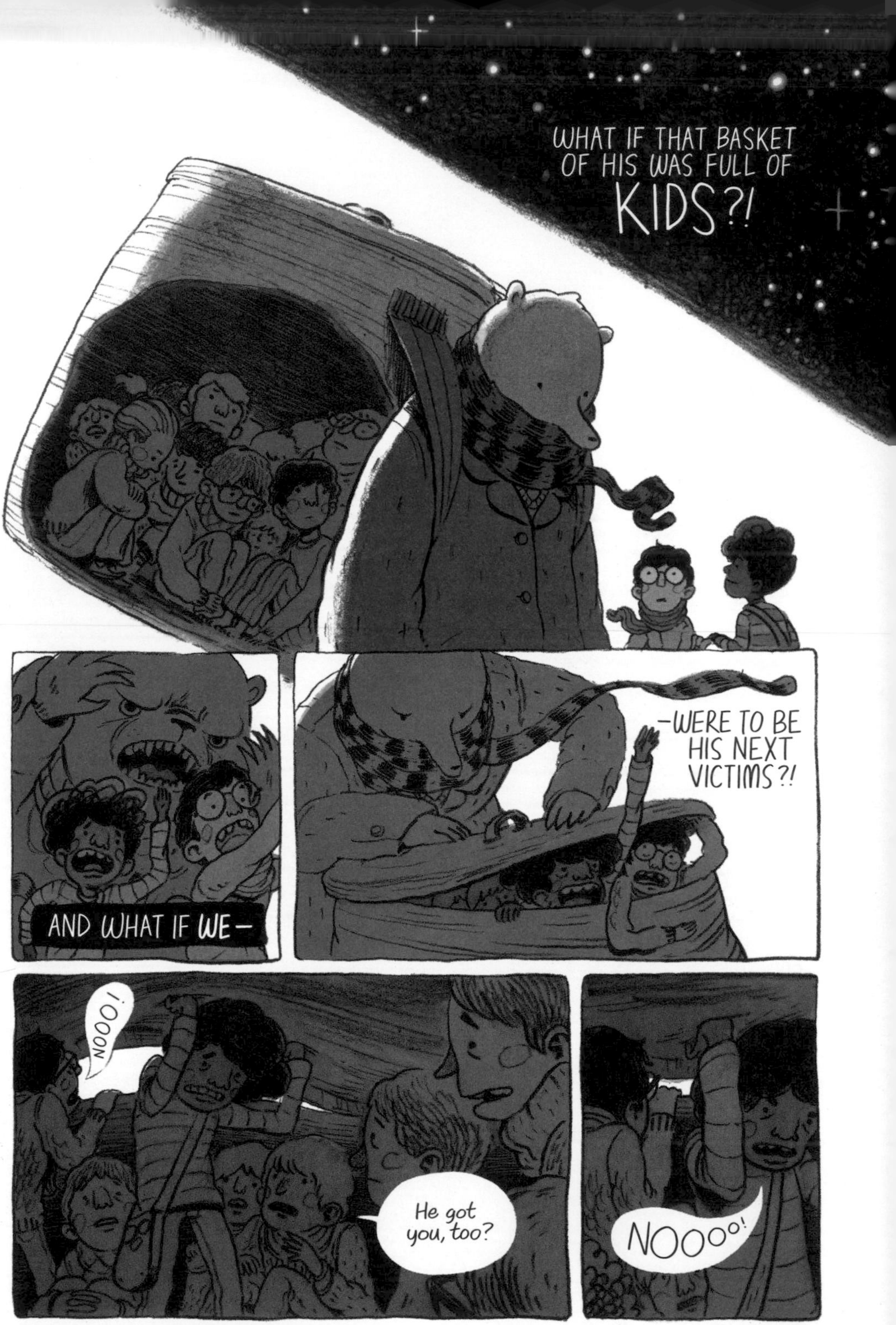
WHAT IF THAT BASKET OF HIS WAS FULL OF KIDS?!
AND WHAT IF WE–
–WERE TO BE HIS NEXT VICTIMS?!
NOOO!
He got you, too?
NOOOO!

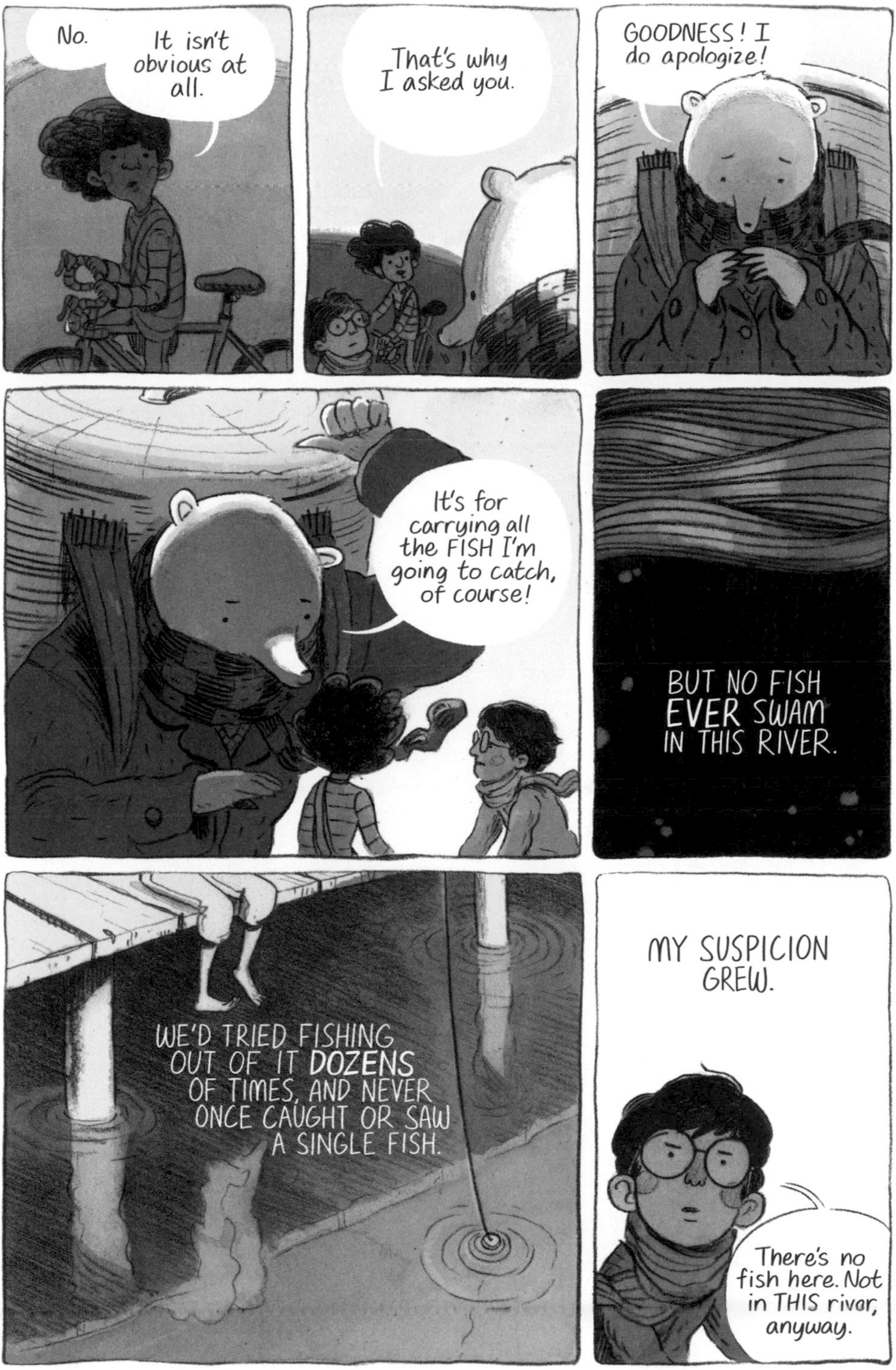
No.
It isn't obvious at all.
That's why I asked you.
GOODNESS! I do apologize!
It's for carrying all the FISH I'm going to catch, of course!
BUT NO FISH EVER SWAM IN THIS RIVER.
WE'D TRIED FISHING OUT OF IT DOZENS OF TIMES, AND NEVER ONCE CAUGHT OR SAW A SINGLE FISH.
MY SUSPICION GREW.
There's no fish here. Not in THIS river, anyway.

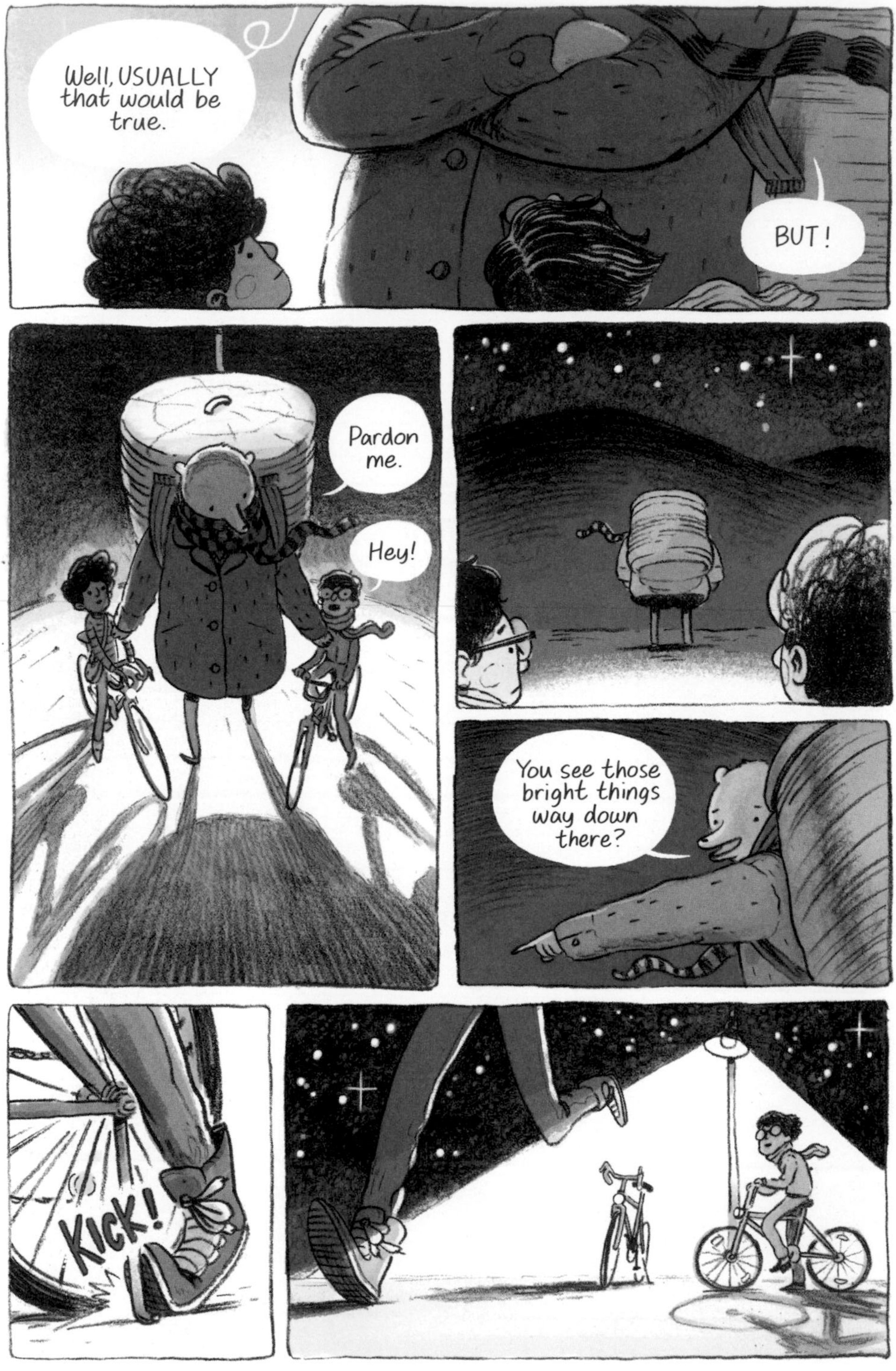
Well, USUALLY that would be true.
BUT!
Pardon me.
Hey!
You see those bright things way down there?
KICK!

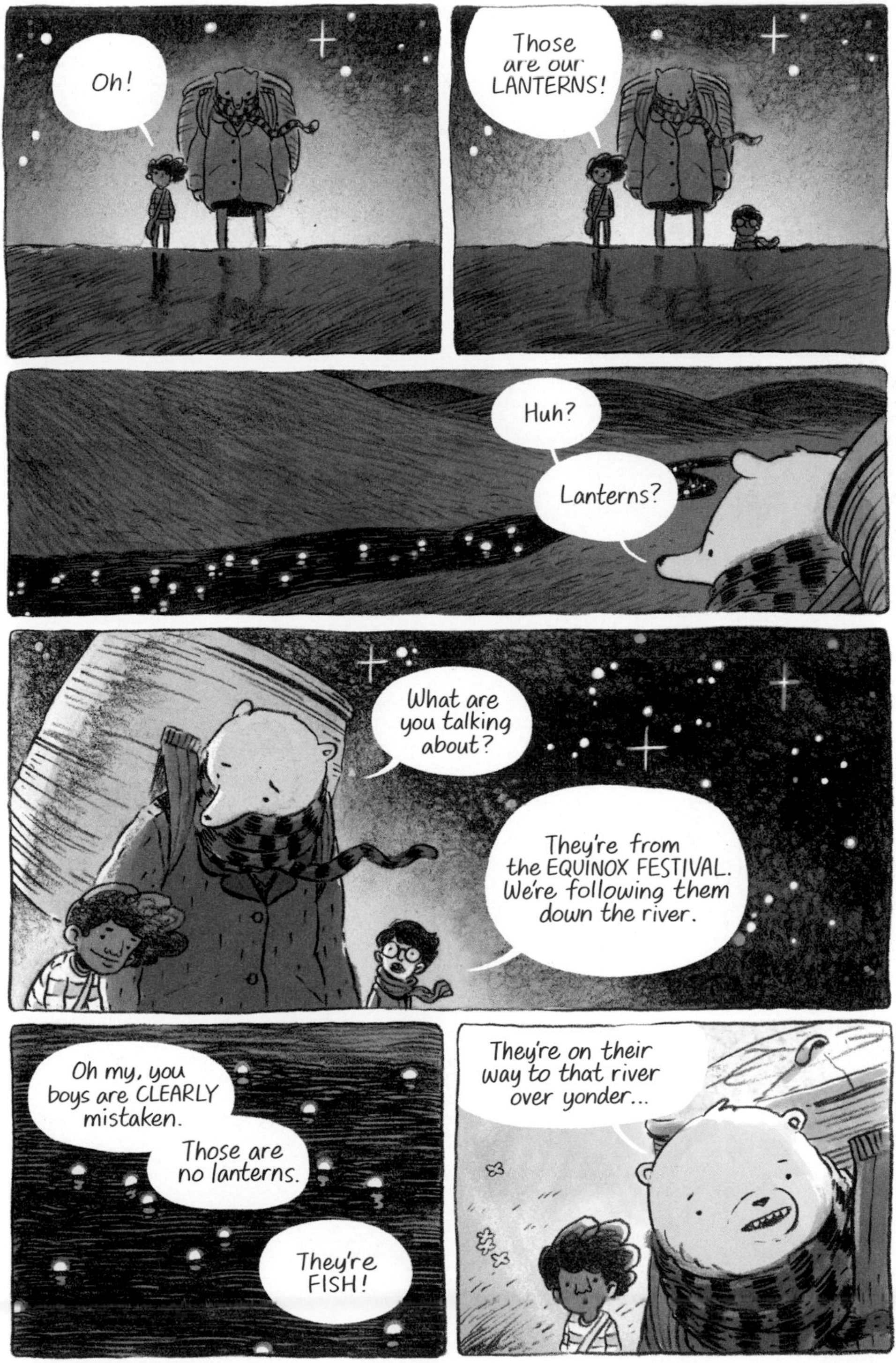
Oh!
Those are our LANTERNS!
Huh?
Lanterns?
What are you talking about?
They're from the EQUINOX FESTIVAL. We're following them down the river.
Oh my, you boys are CLEARLY mistaken.
Those are no lanterns.
They're FISH!
They're on their way to that river over yonder...

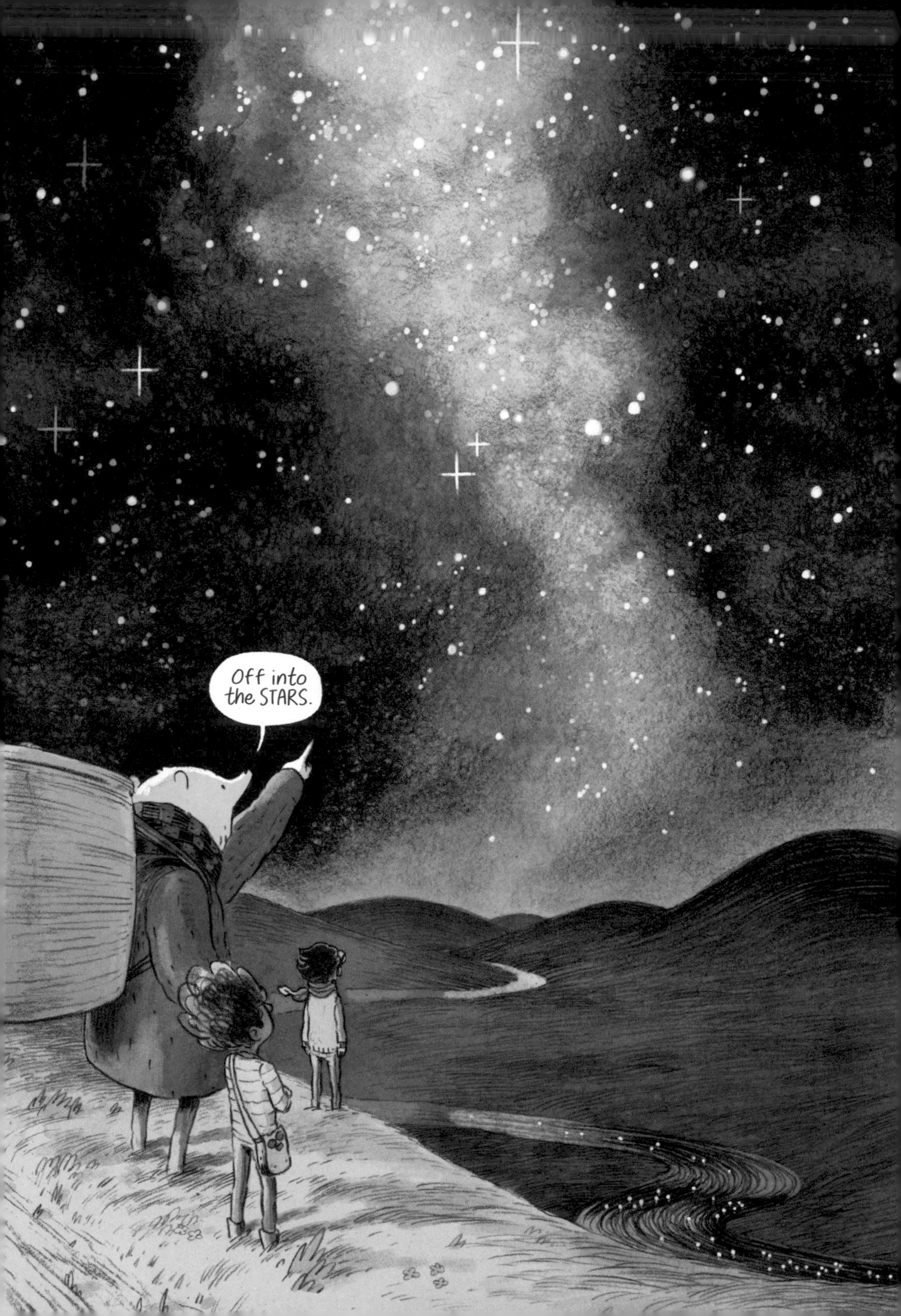
Off into the STARS.

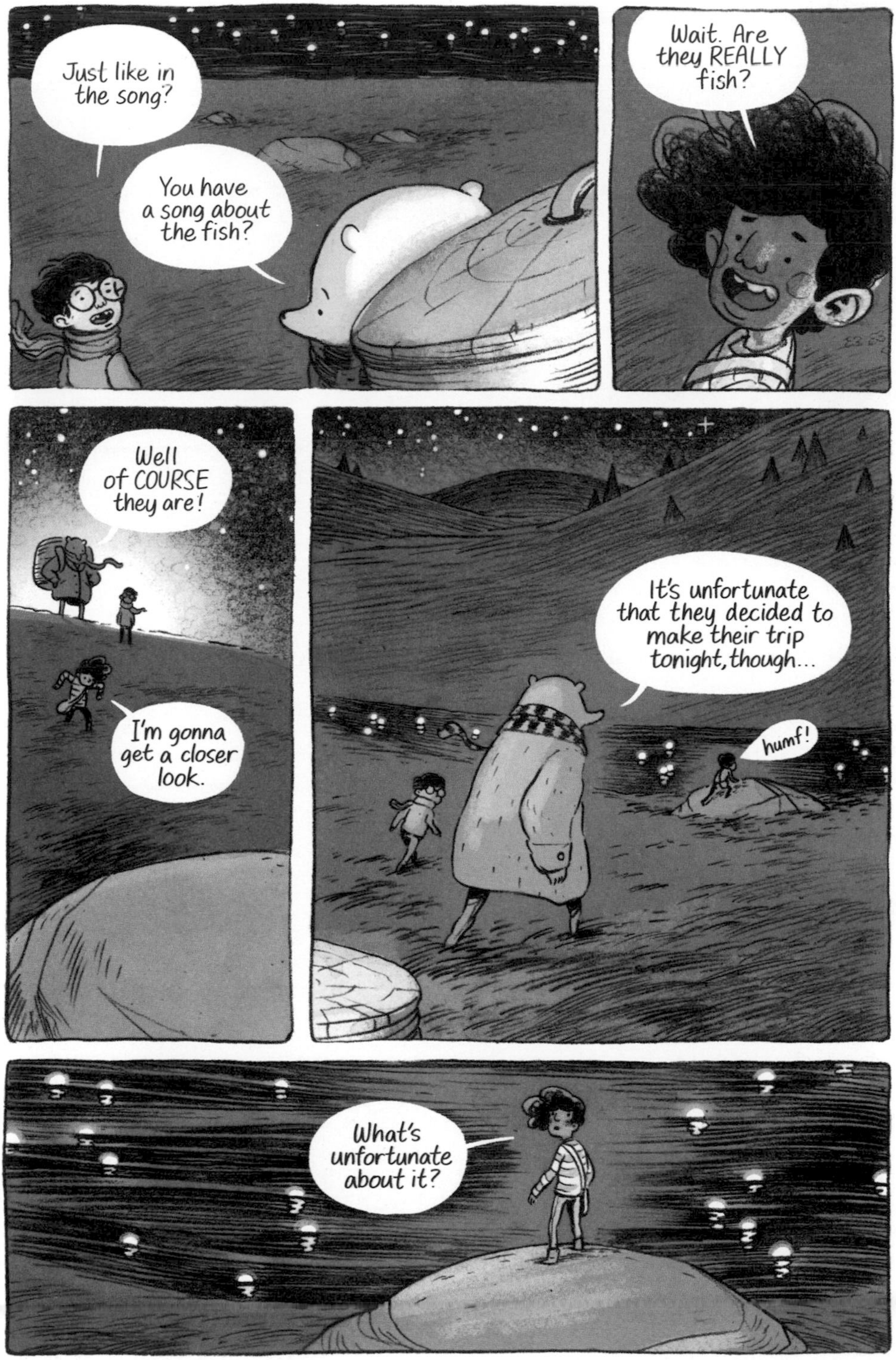
Just like in the song?
You have a song about the fish?
Wait. Are they REALLY fish?
Well of COURSE they are!
I'm gonna get a closer look.
It's unfortunate that they decided to make their trip tonight, though...
humf!
What's unfortunate about it?

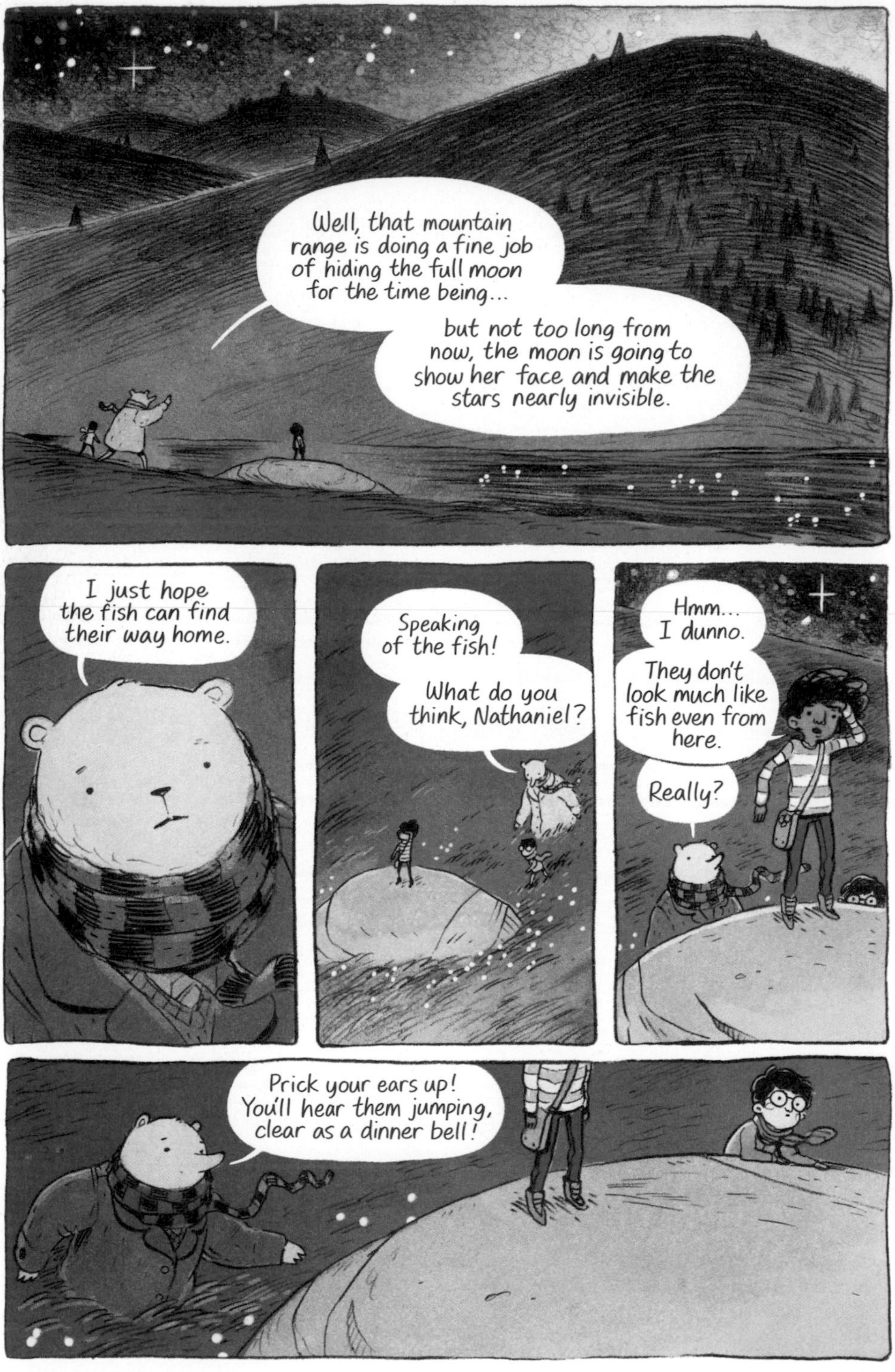
Well, that mountain range is doing a fine job of hiding the full moon for the time being...
but not too long from now, the moon is going to show her face and make the stars nearly invisible.
I just hope the fish can find their way home.
Speaking of the fish!
What do you think, Nathaniel?
Hmm... I dunno.
They don't look much like fish even from here.
Really?
Prick your ears up! You'll hear them jumping, clear as a dinner bell!

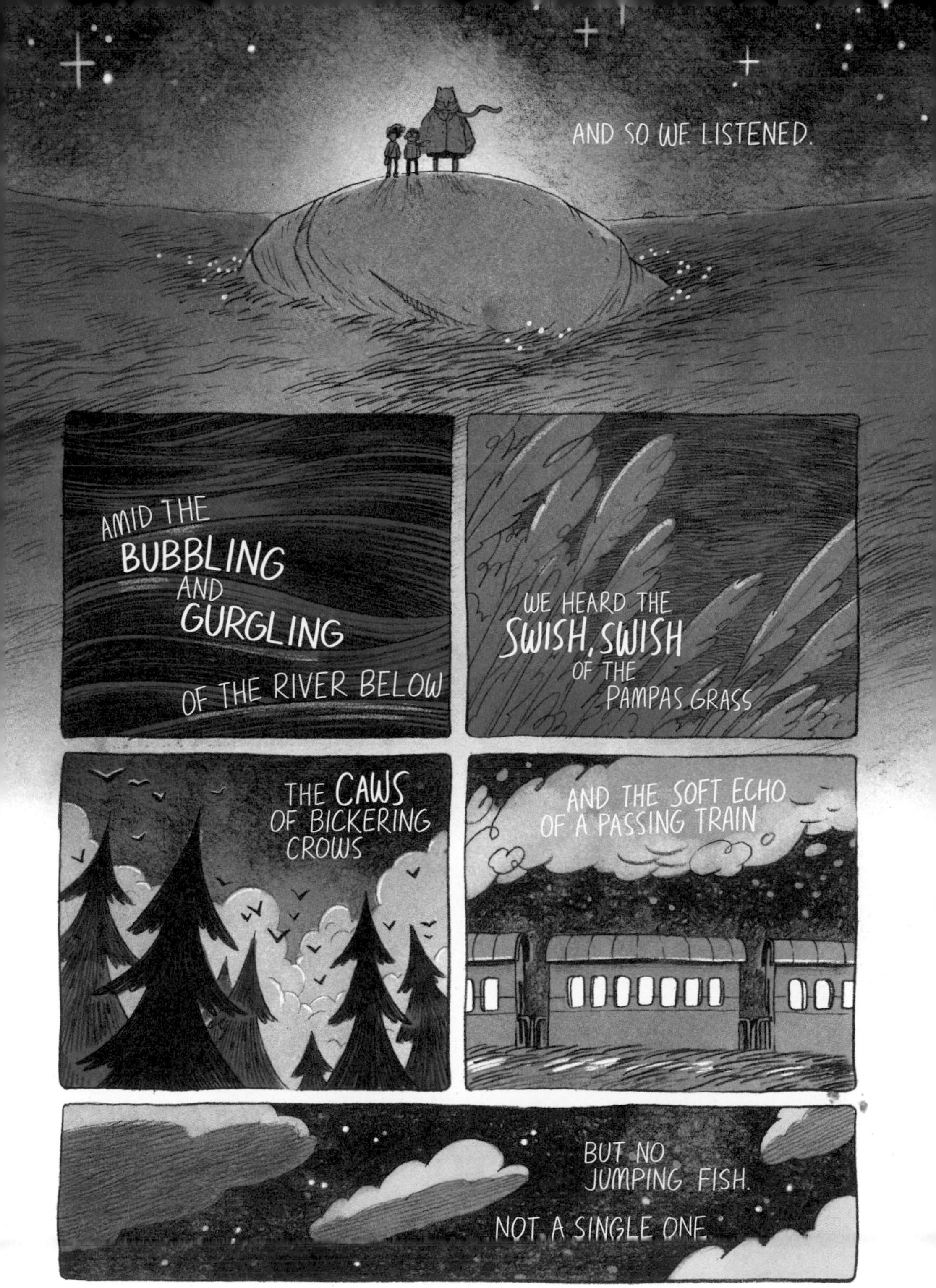
AND SO WE LISTENED.
AMID THE BUBBLING AND GURGLING OF THE RIVER BELOW
WE HEARD THE SWISH, SWISH OF THE PAMPAS GRASS
THE CAWS OF BICKERING CROWS
AND THE SOFT ECHO OF A PASSING TRAIN
BUT NO JUMPING FISH.
NOT A SINGLE ONE.

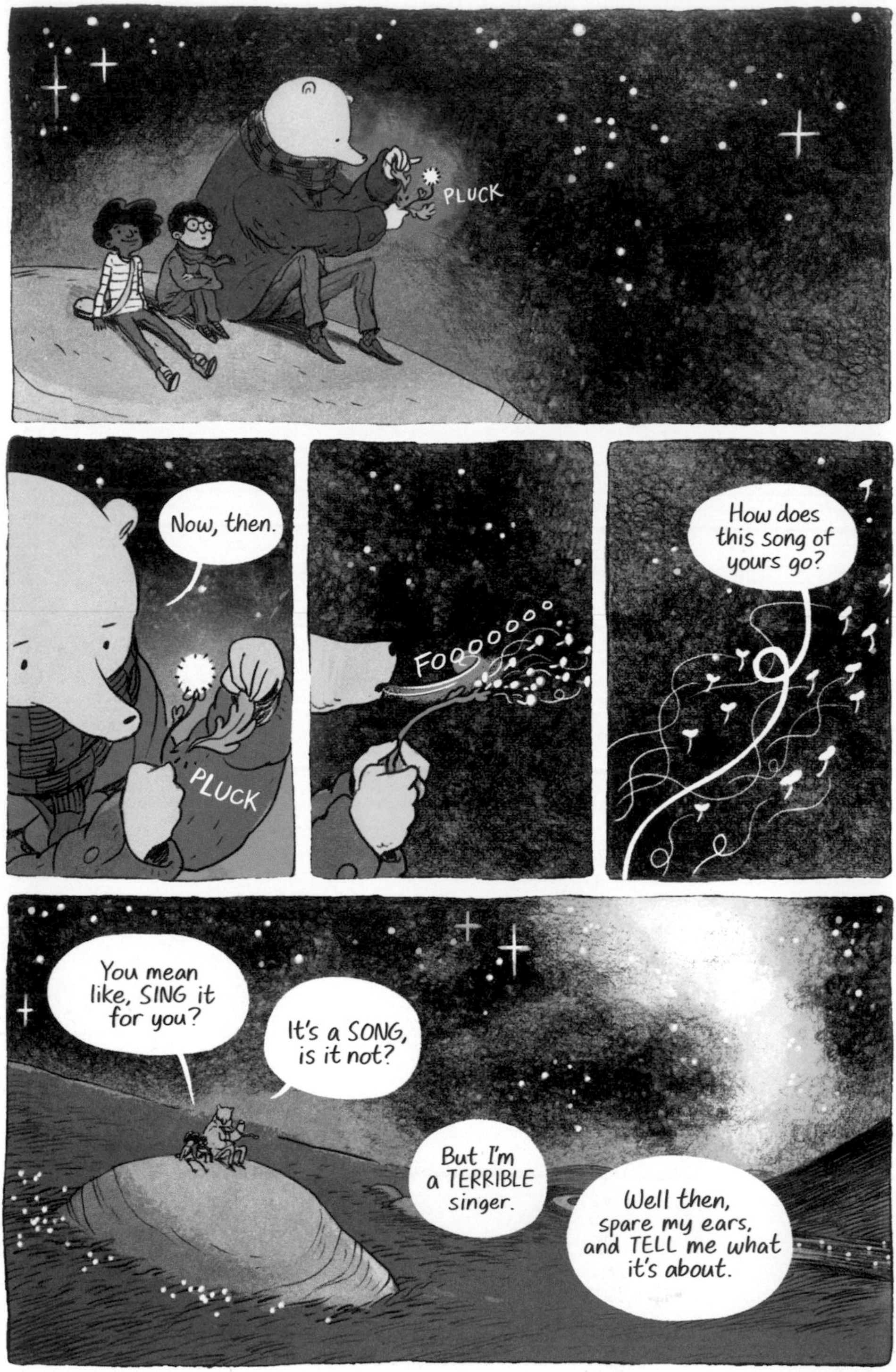

PLUCK
Now, then.
PLUCK
FOOOOOOOO
How does this song of yours go?
You mean like, SING it for you?
It's a SONG, is it not?
But I'm a TERRIBLE singer.
Well then, spare my ears, and TELL me what it's about.

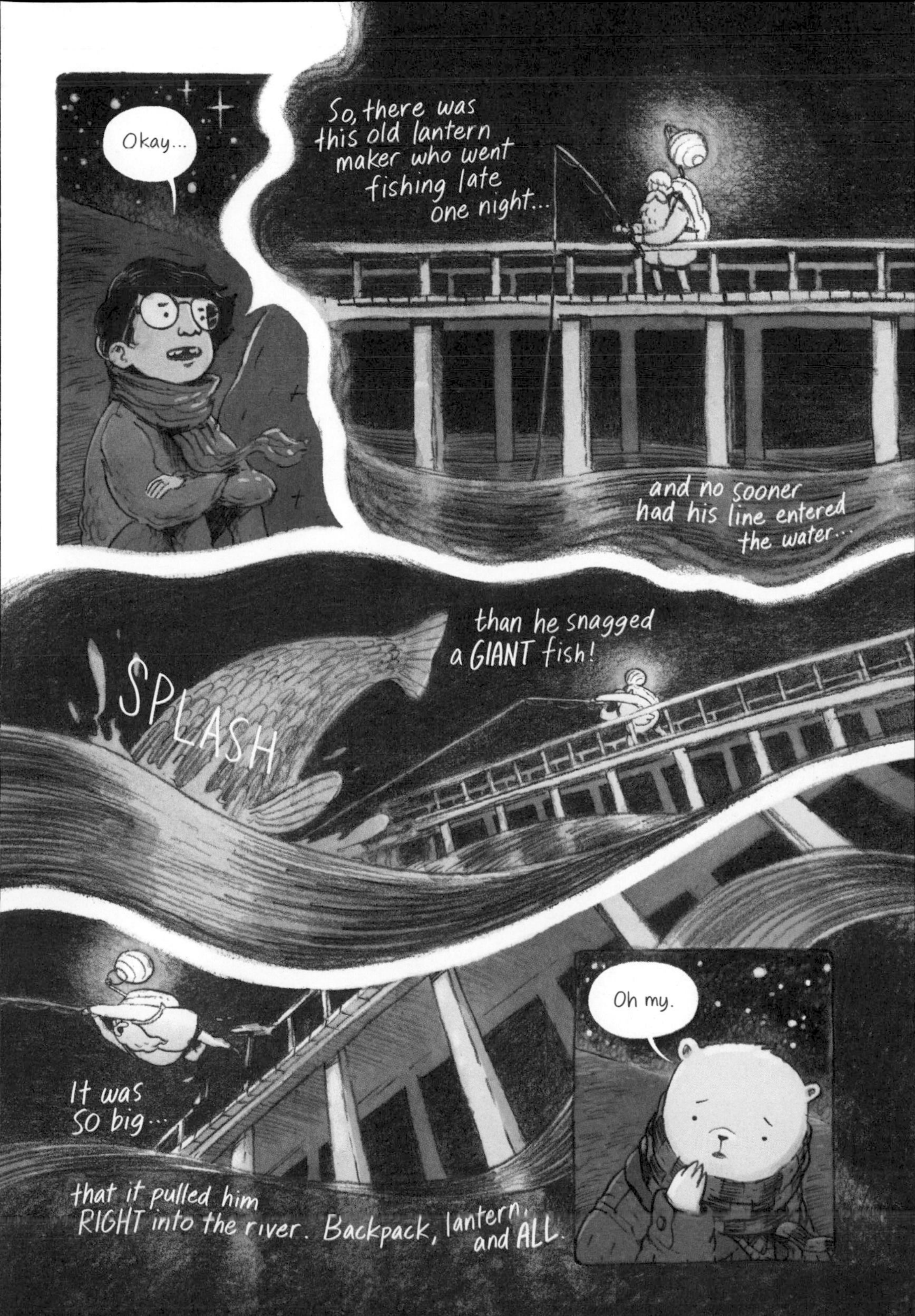
Okay...
So, there was this old lantern maker who went fishing late one night...
and no sooner had his line entered the water...
than he snagged a GIANT fish!
SPLASH
It was so big...
that it pulled him RIGHT into the river. Backpack, lantern, and ALL.
Oh my.

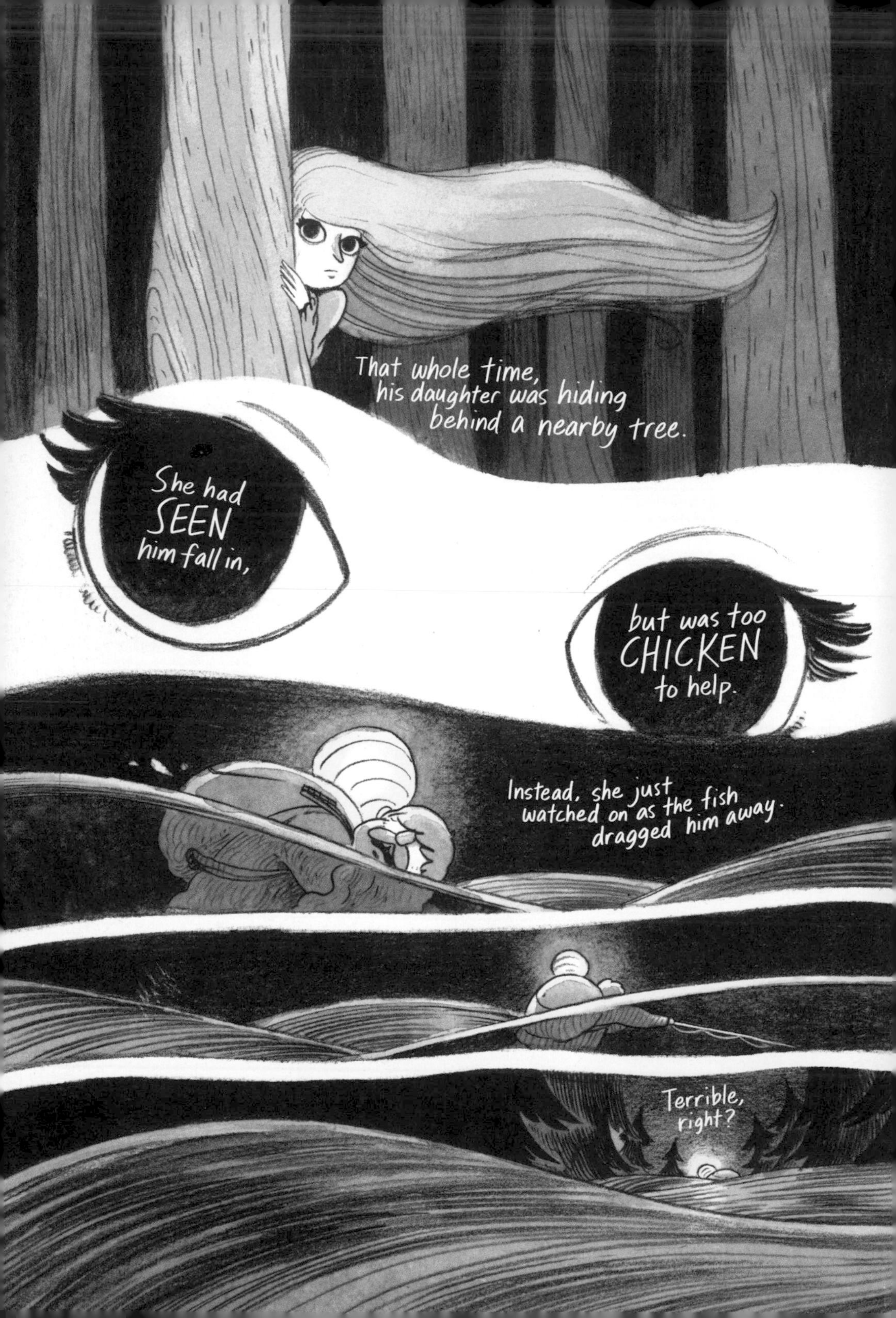
That whole time, his daughter was hiding behind a nearby tree.
She had SEEN him fall in,
but was too CHICKEN to help.
Instead, she just watched on as the fish dragged him away.
Terrible, right?

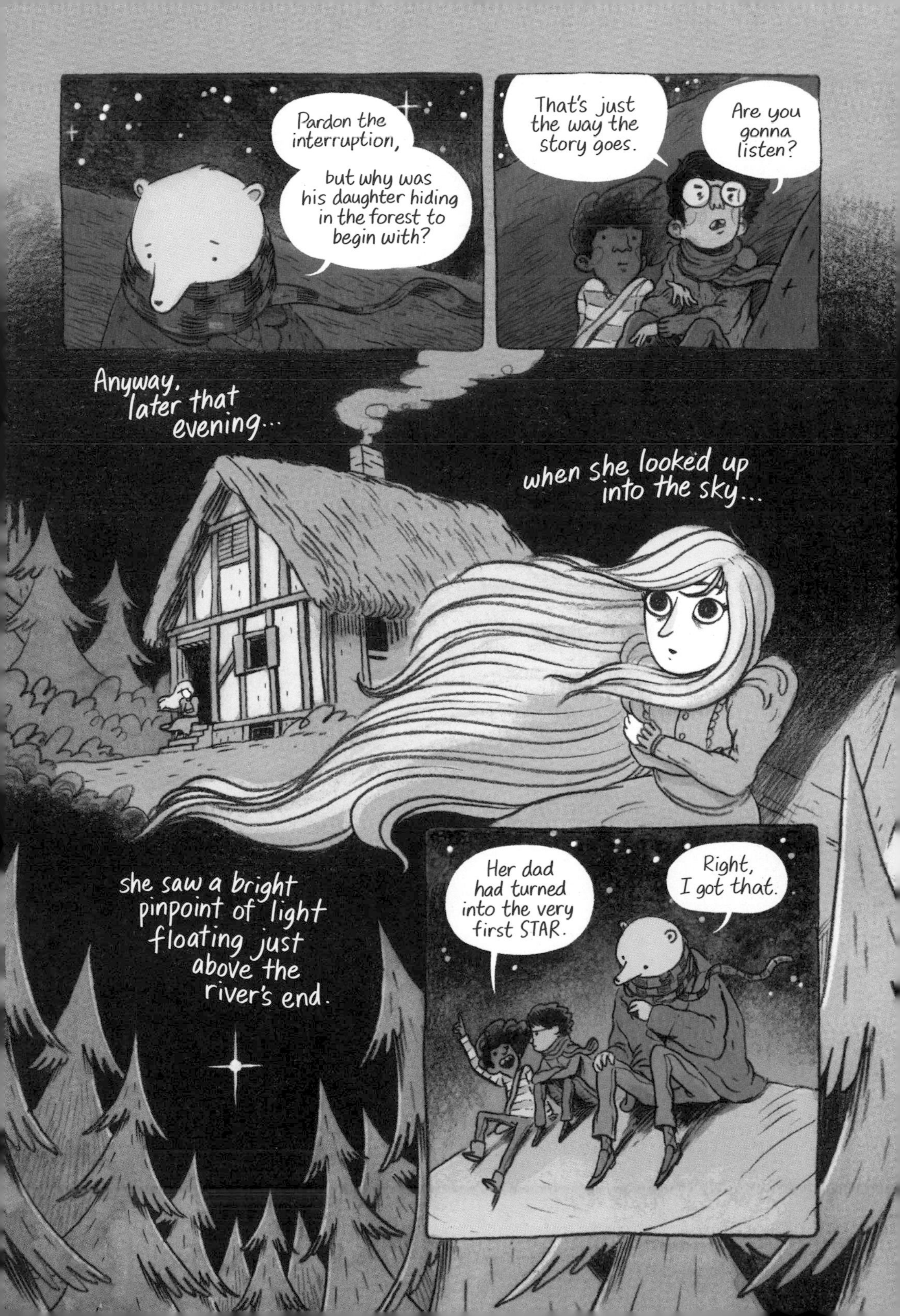

Pardon the interruption,
but why was his daughter hiding in the forest to begin with?
That's just the way the story goes.
Are you gonna listen?
Anyway, later that evening...
when she looked up into the sky...
she saw a bright pinpoint of light floating just above the river's end.
Her dad had turned into the very first STAR.
Right, I got that.

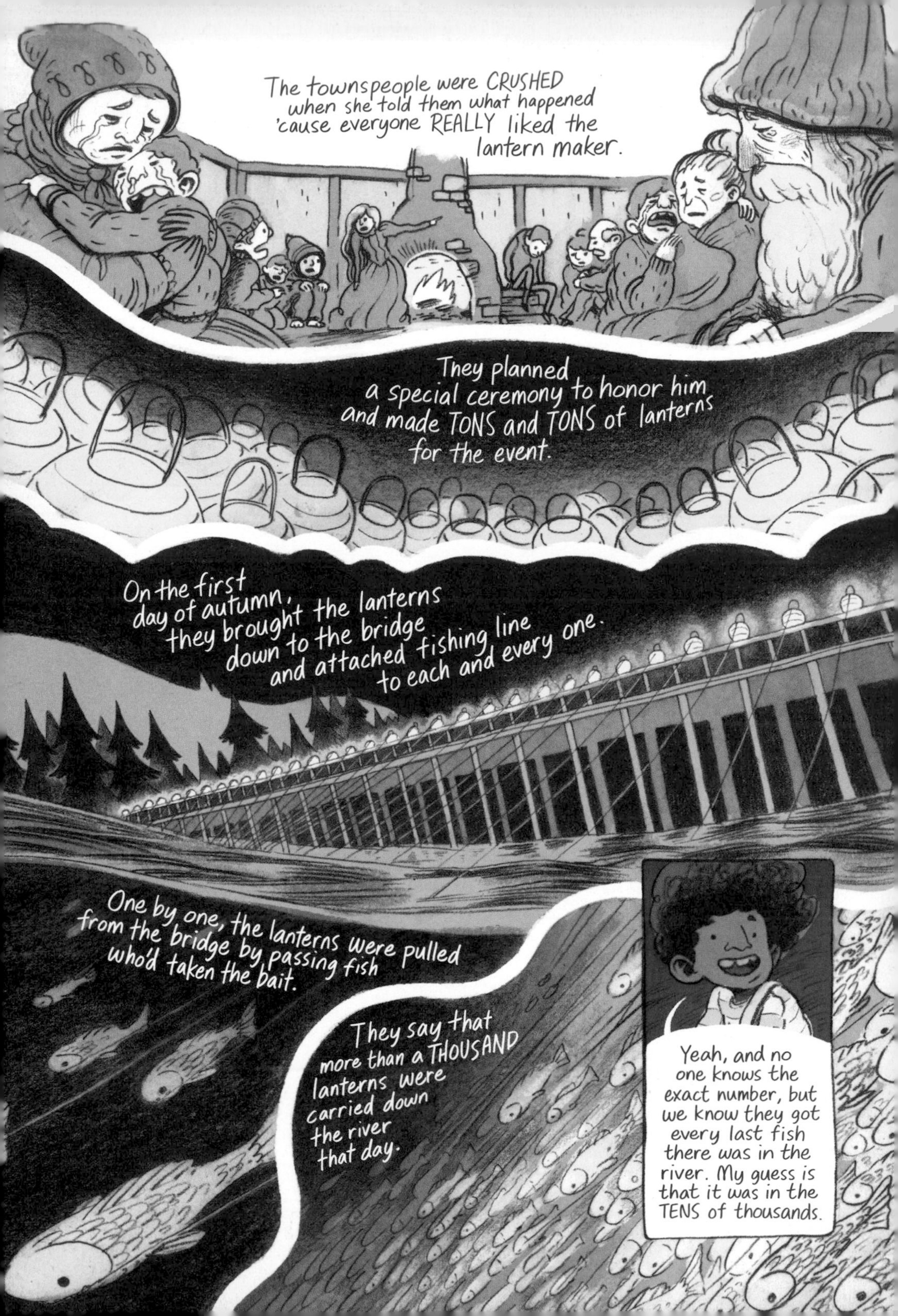
The townspeople were CRUSHED when she told them what happened 'cause everyone REALLY liked the lantern maker.
They planned a special ceremony to honor him and made TONS and TONS of lanterns for the event.
On the first day of autumn, they brought the lanterns down to the bridge and attached fishing line to each and every one.
One by one, the lanterns were pulled from the bridge by passing fish who'd taken the bait.
They say that more than a THOUSAND lanterns were carried down the river that day.
Yeah, and no one knows the exact number, but we know they got every last fish there was in the river. My guess is that it was in the TENS of thousands.

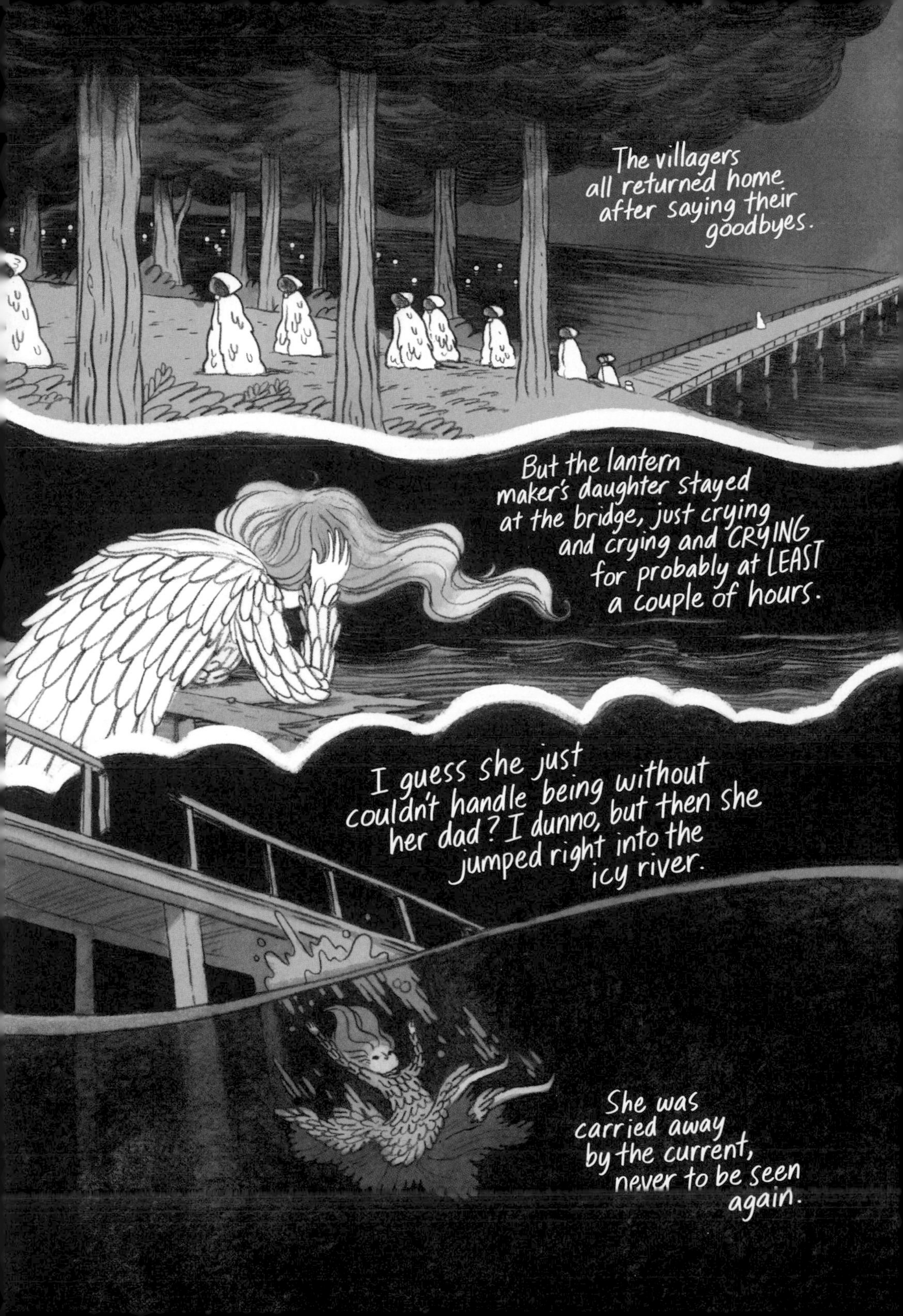
The villagers all returned home after saying their goodbyes.
But the lantern maker's daughter stayed at the bridge, just crying and crying and CRYING for probably at LEAST a couple of hours.
I guess she just couldn't handle being without her dad? I dunno, but then she jumped right into the icy river.
She was carried away by the current, never to be seen again.

Then, just as the
townspeople were getting
ready for bed, somebody
called everyone outside.

When they looked up,
they saw a shining river
of lights flowing
overhead...

and a bright white moon rising in the east.

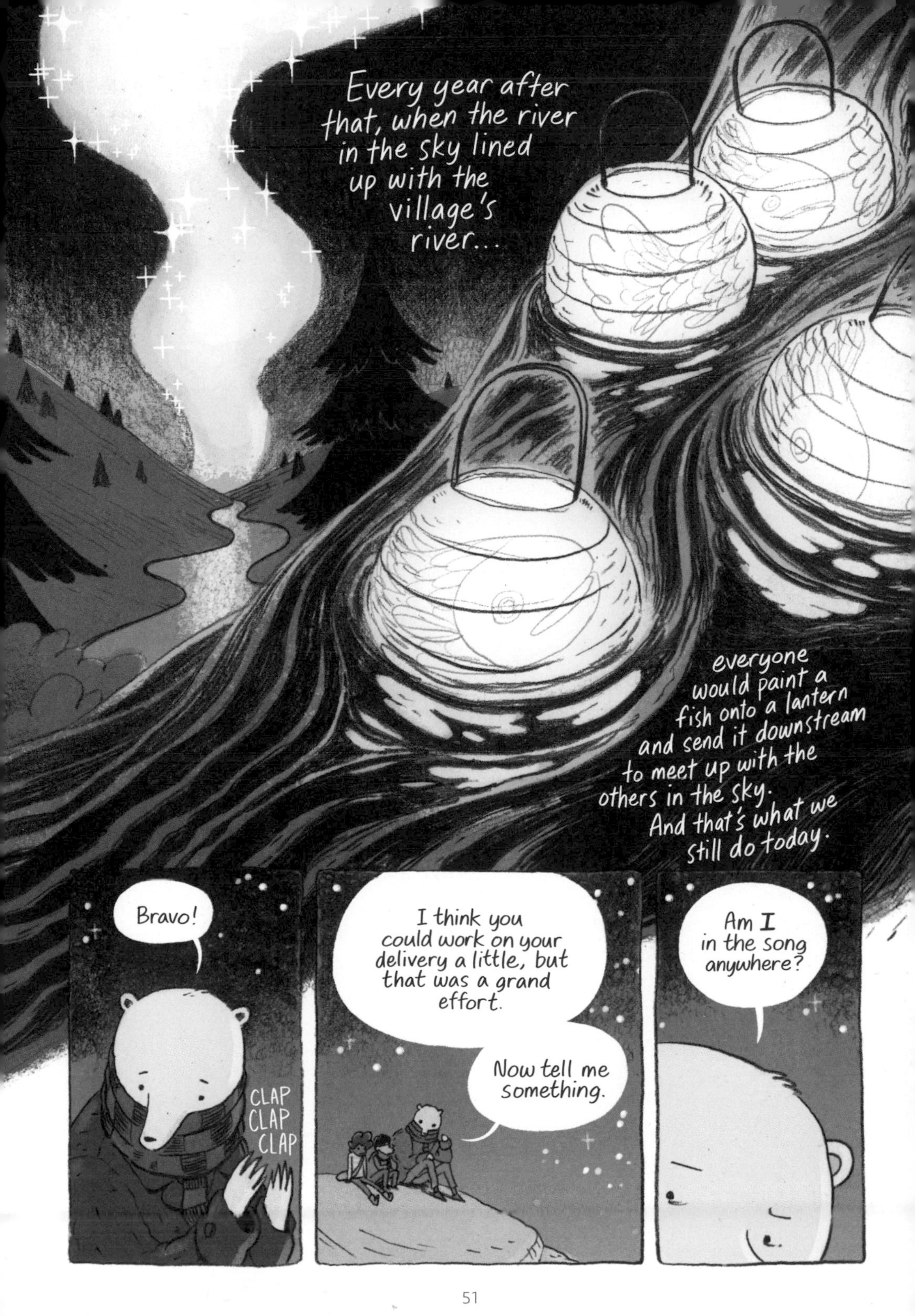
Every year after that, when the river in the sky lined up with the village's river...
everyone would paint a fish onto a lantern and send it downstream to meet up with the others in the sky. And that's what we still do today.
Bravo!
CLAP CLAP CLAP
I think you could work on your delivery a little, but that was a grand effort.
Now tell me something.
Am I in the song anywhere?

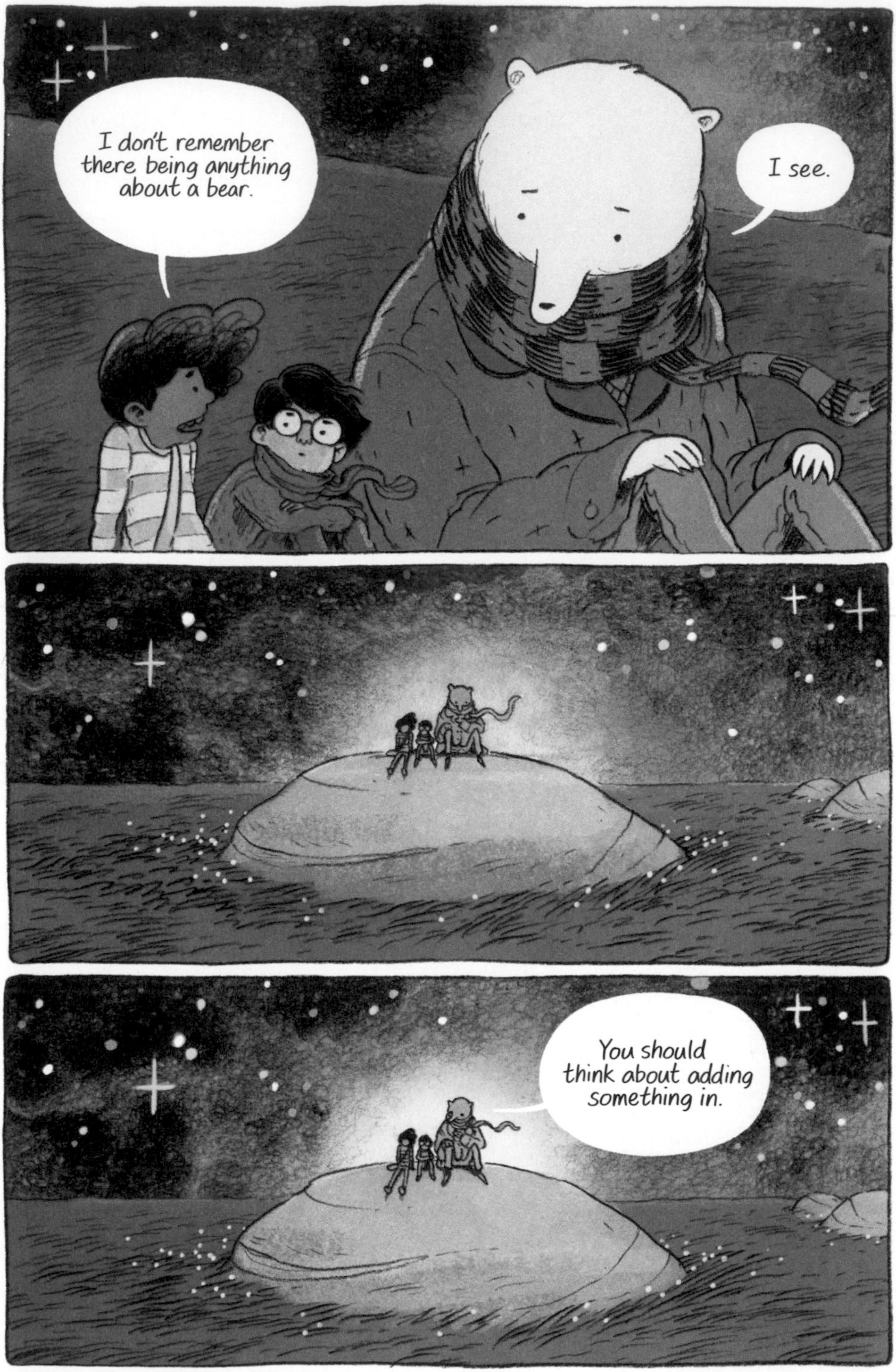
I don't remember there being anything about a bear.
I see.
You should think about adding something in.

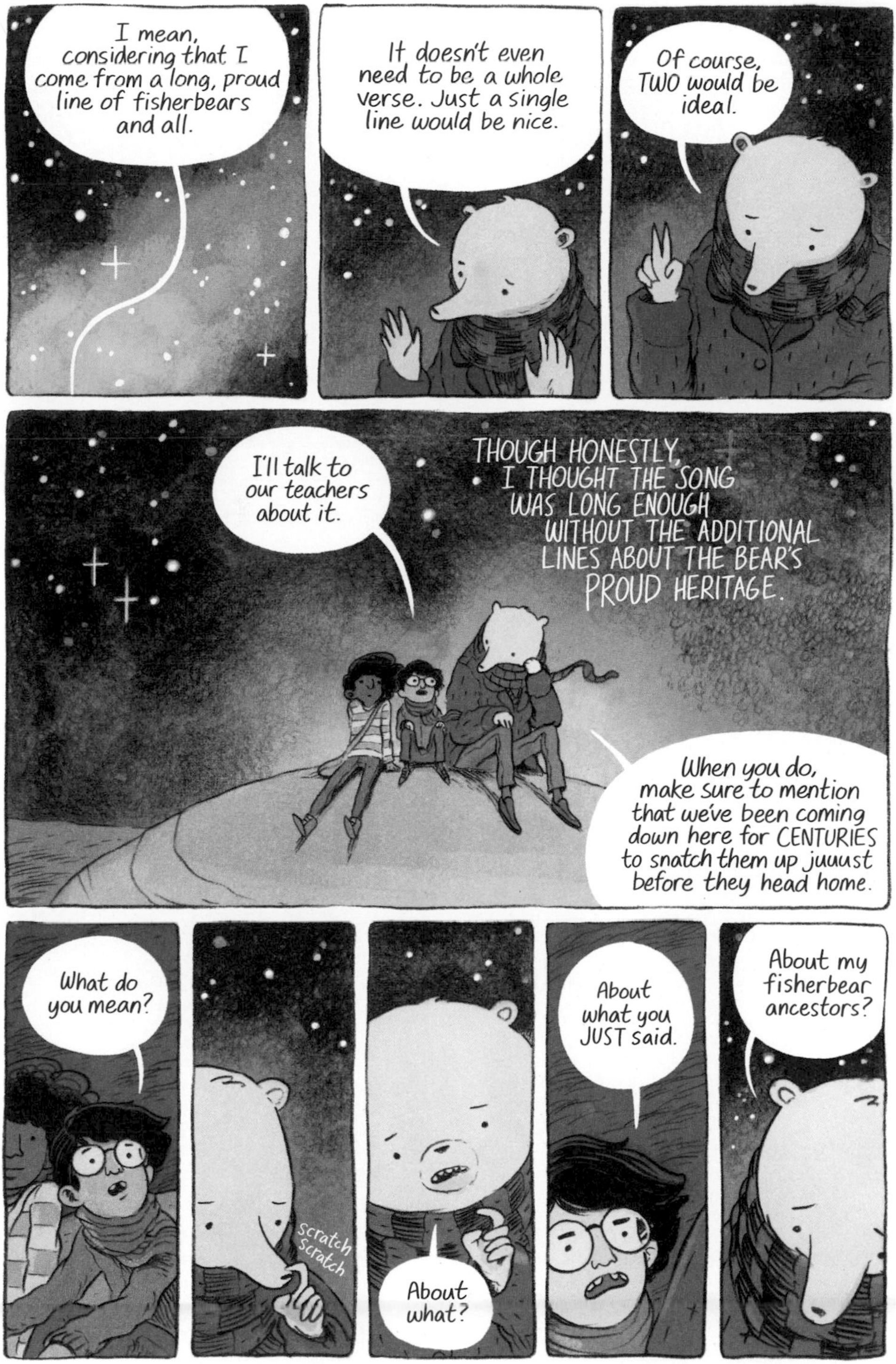
I mean, considering that I come from a long, proud line of fisherbears and all.
It doesn't even need to be a whole verse. Just a single line would be nice.
Of course, TWO would be ideal.
I'll talk to our teachers about it.
THOUGH HONESTLY, I THOUGHT THE SONG WAS LONG ENOUGH WITHOUT THE ADDITIONAL LINES ABOUT THE BEAR'S PROUD HERITAGE.
When you do, make sure to mention that we've been coming down here for CENTURIES to snatch them up juuust before they head home.
What do you mean?
scratch scratch
About what?
About what you JUST said.
About my fisherbear ancestors?

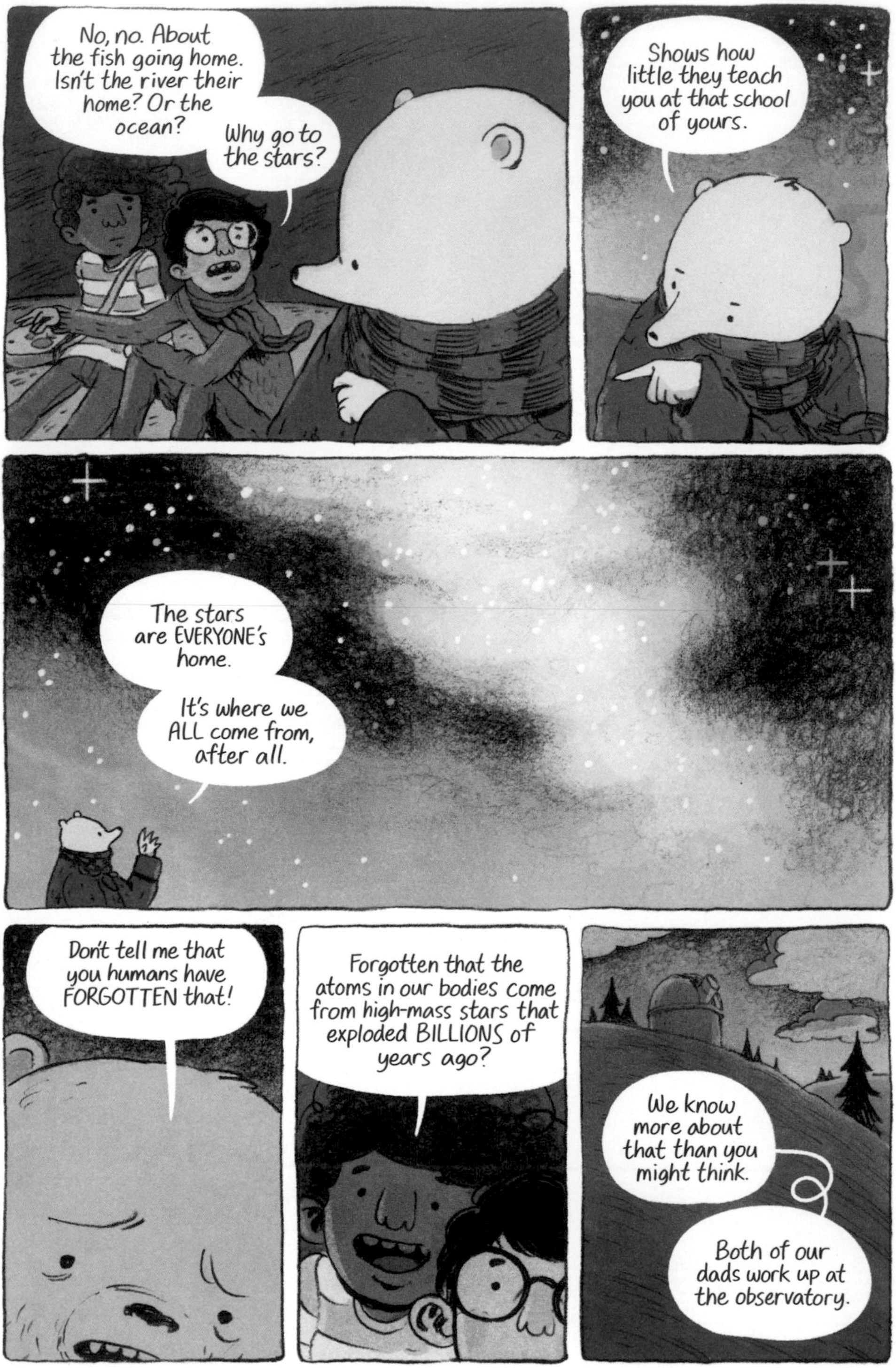

No, no. About the fish going home. Isn't the river their home? Or the ocean?
Why go to the stars?
Shows how little they teach you at that school of yours.
The stars are EVERYONE's home.
It's where we ALL come from, after all.
Don't tell me that you humans have FORGOTTEN that!
Forgotten that the atoms in our bodies come from high-mass stars that exploded BILLIONS of years ago?
We know more about that than you might think.
Both of our dads work up at the observatory.

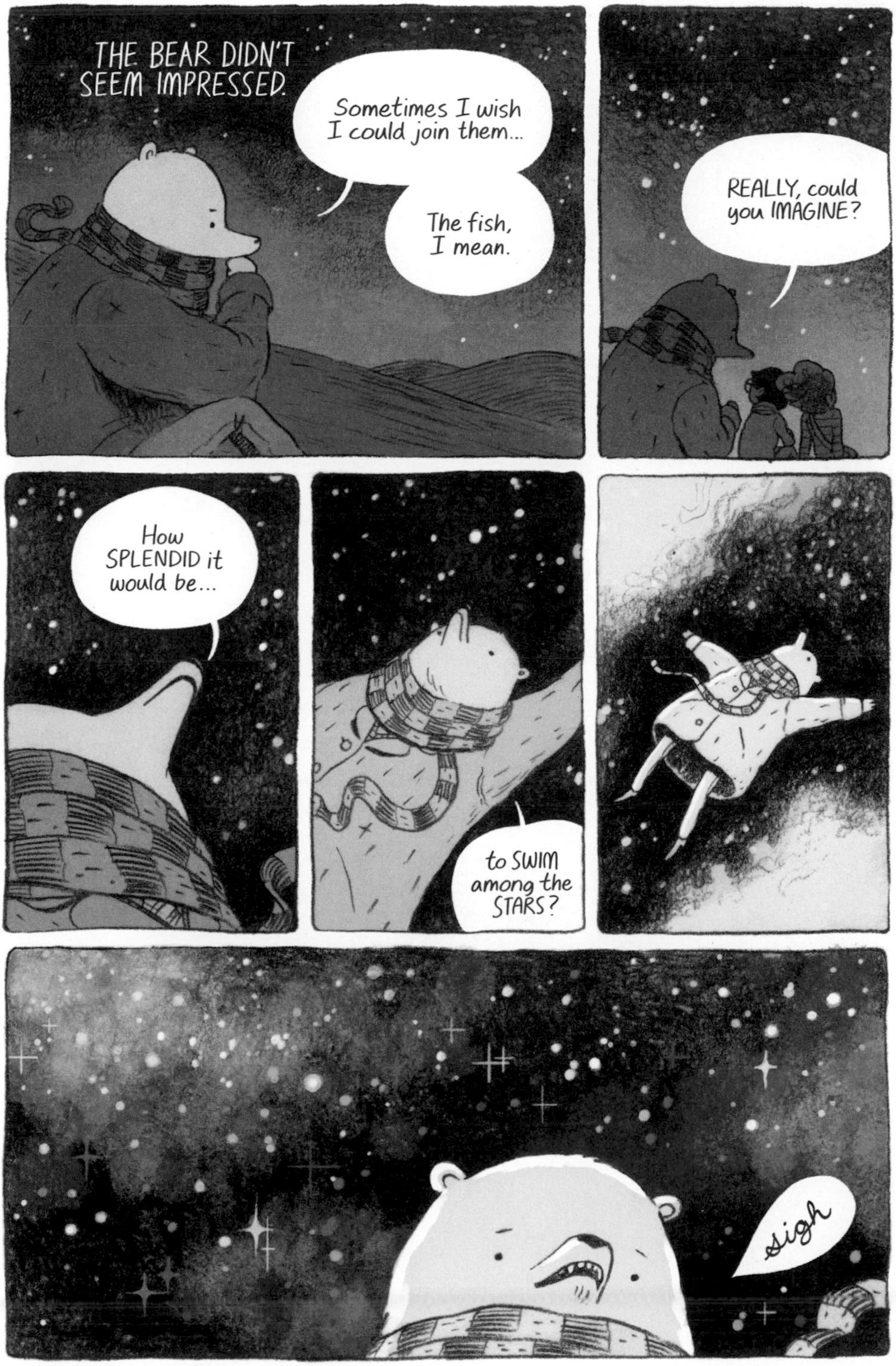
THE BEAR DIDN'T SEEM IMPRESSED.
Sometimes I wish I could join them...
The fish, I mean.
REALLY, could you IMAGINE?
How SPLENDID it would be...
to SWIM among the STARS?
Sigh

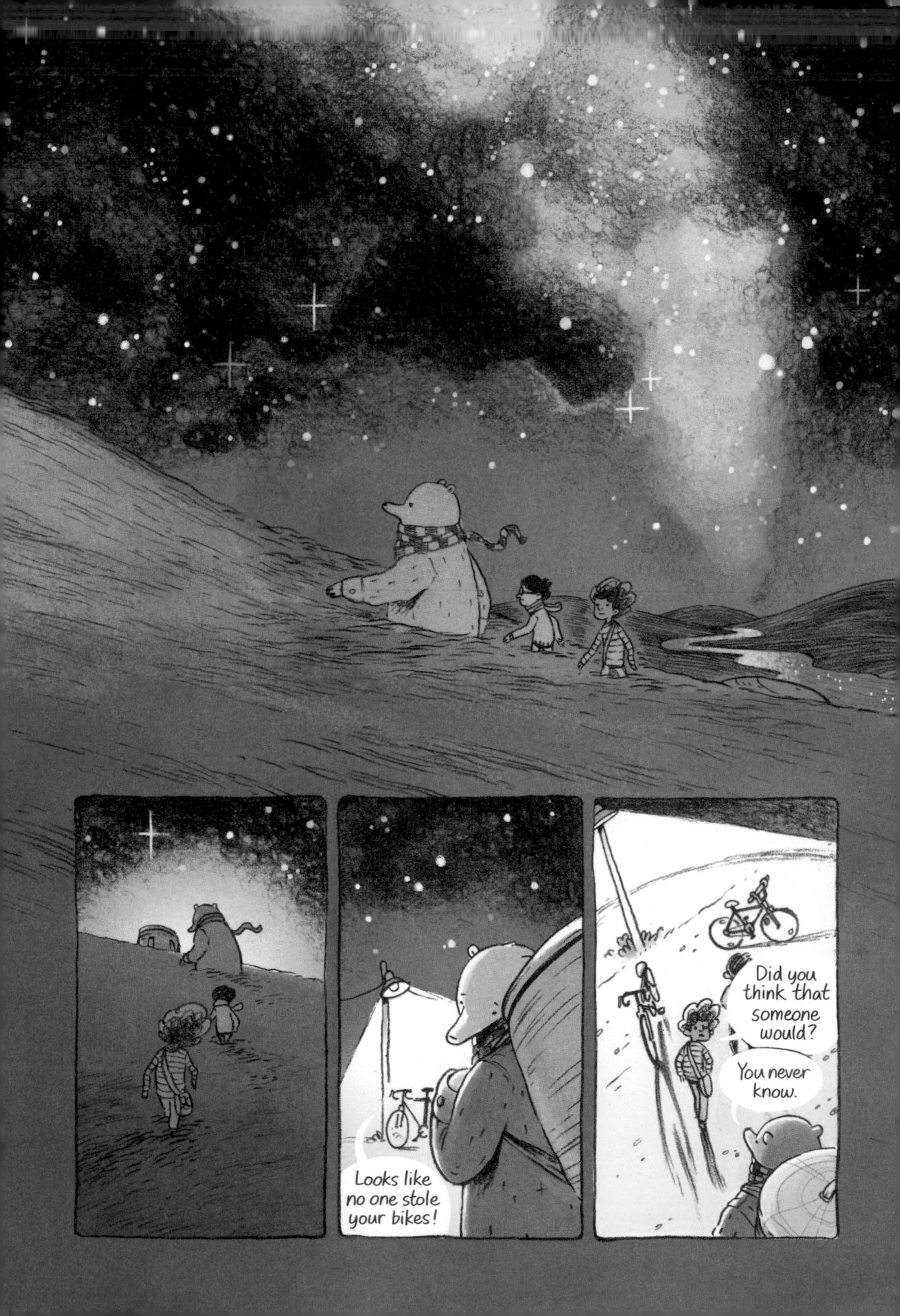
Looks like no one stole your bikes!
Did you think that someone would?
You never know.

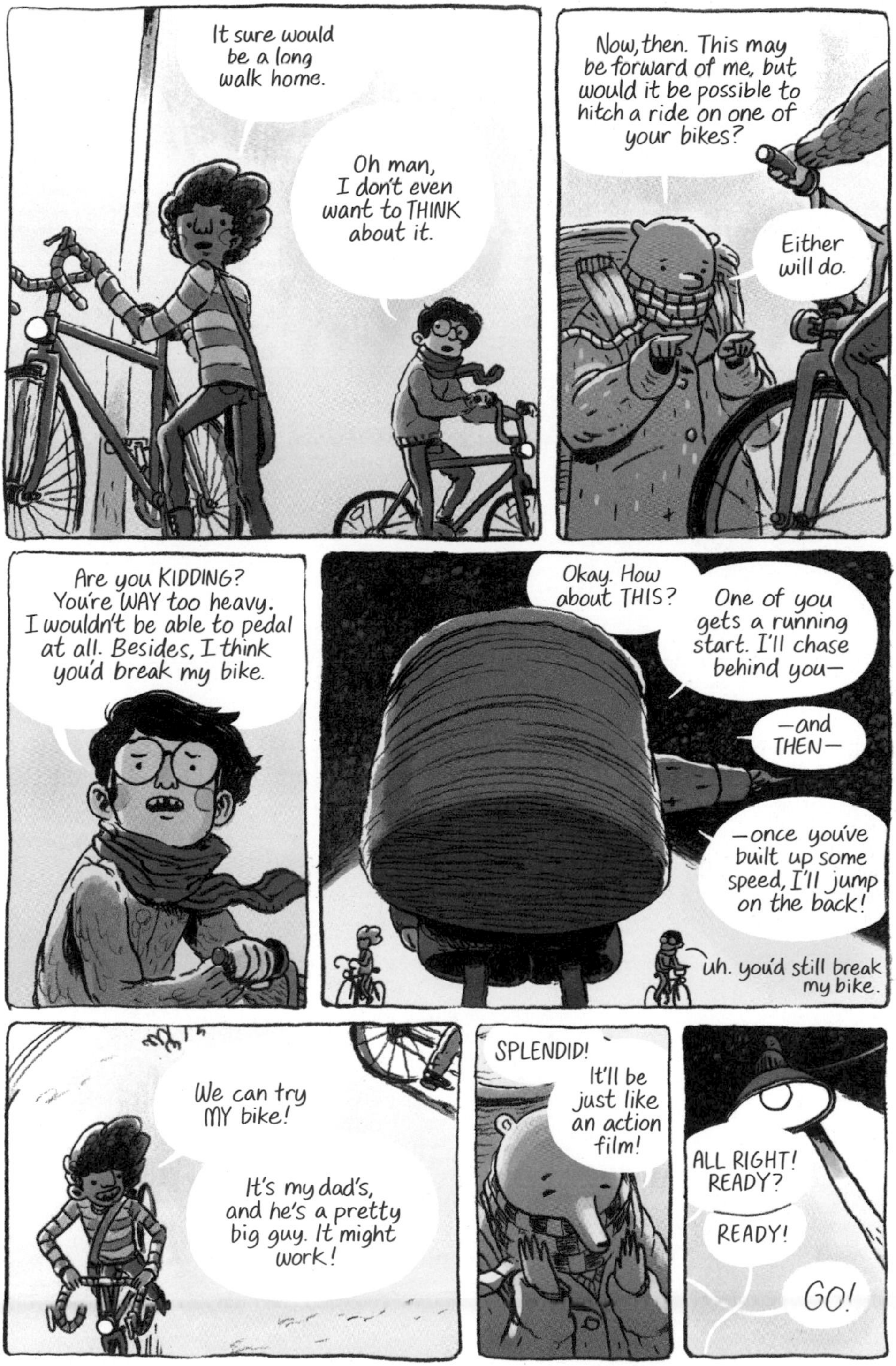
It sure would be a long walk home.
Oh man, I don't even want to THINK about it.
Now, then. This may be forward of me, but would it be possible to hitch a ride on one of your bikes?
Either will do.
Are you KIDDING? You're WAY too heavy. I wouldn't be able to pedal at all. Besides, I think you'd break my bike.
Okay. How about THIS?
One of you gets a running start. I'll chase behind you—
—and THEN—
—once you've built up some speed, I'll jump on the back!
uh. you'd still break my bike.
We can try MY bike!
It's my dad's, and he's a pretty big guy. It might work!
SPLENDID!
It'll be just like an action film!
ALL RIGHT! READY?
READY!
GO!

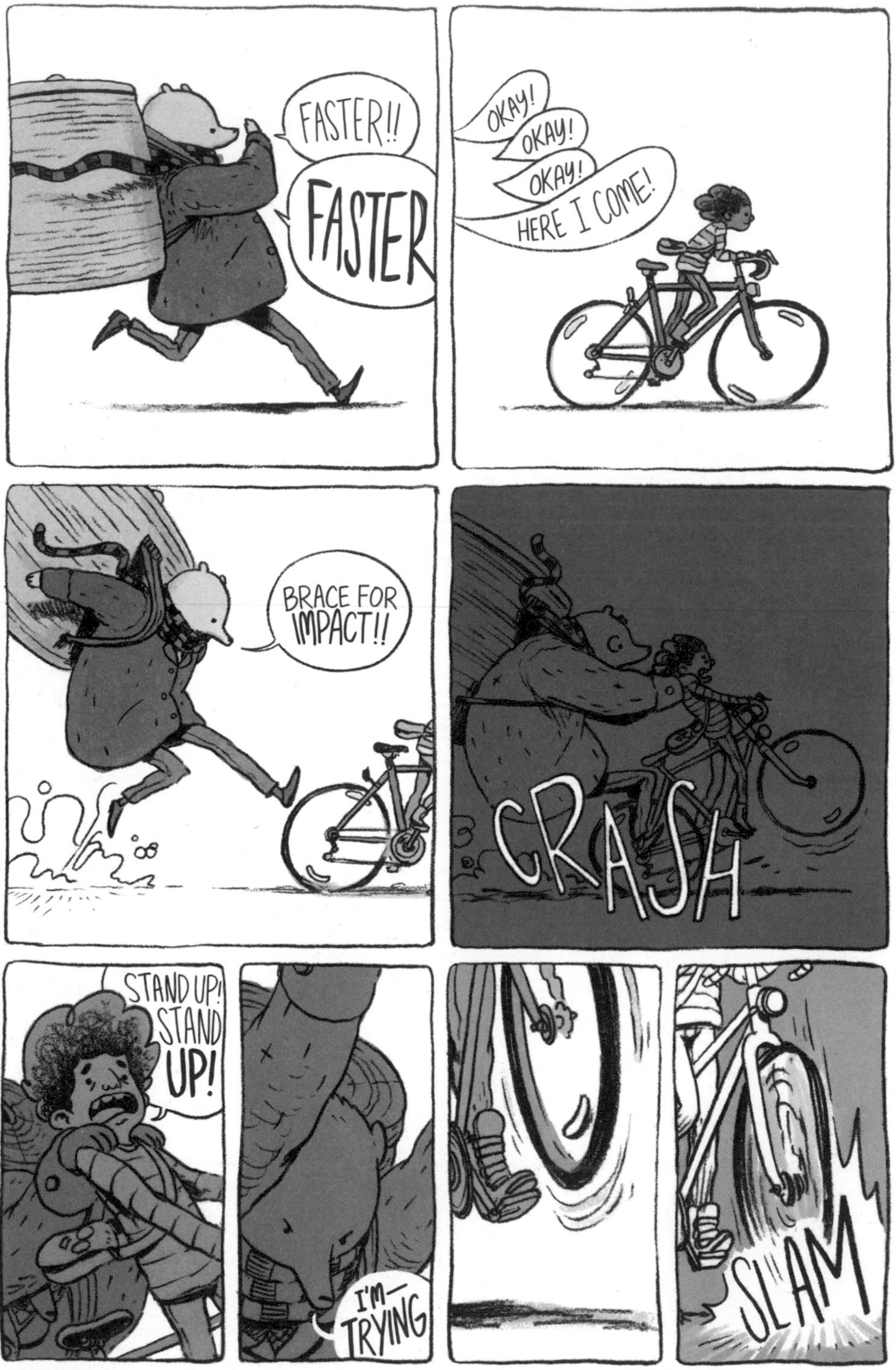
FASTER!!
FASTER
OKAY!
OKAY!
OKAY!
HERE I COME!
BRACE FOR IMPACT!!
CRASH
STAND UP! STAND UP!
I'M— TRYING
SLAM

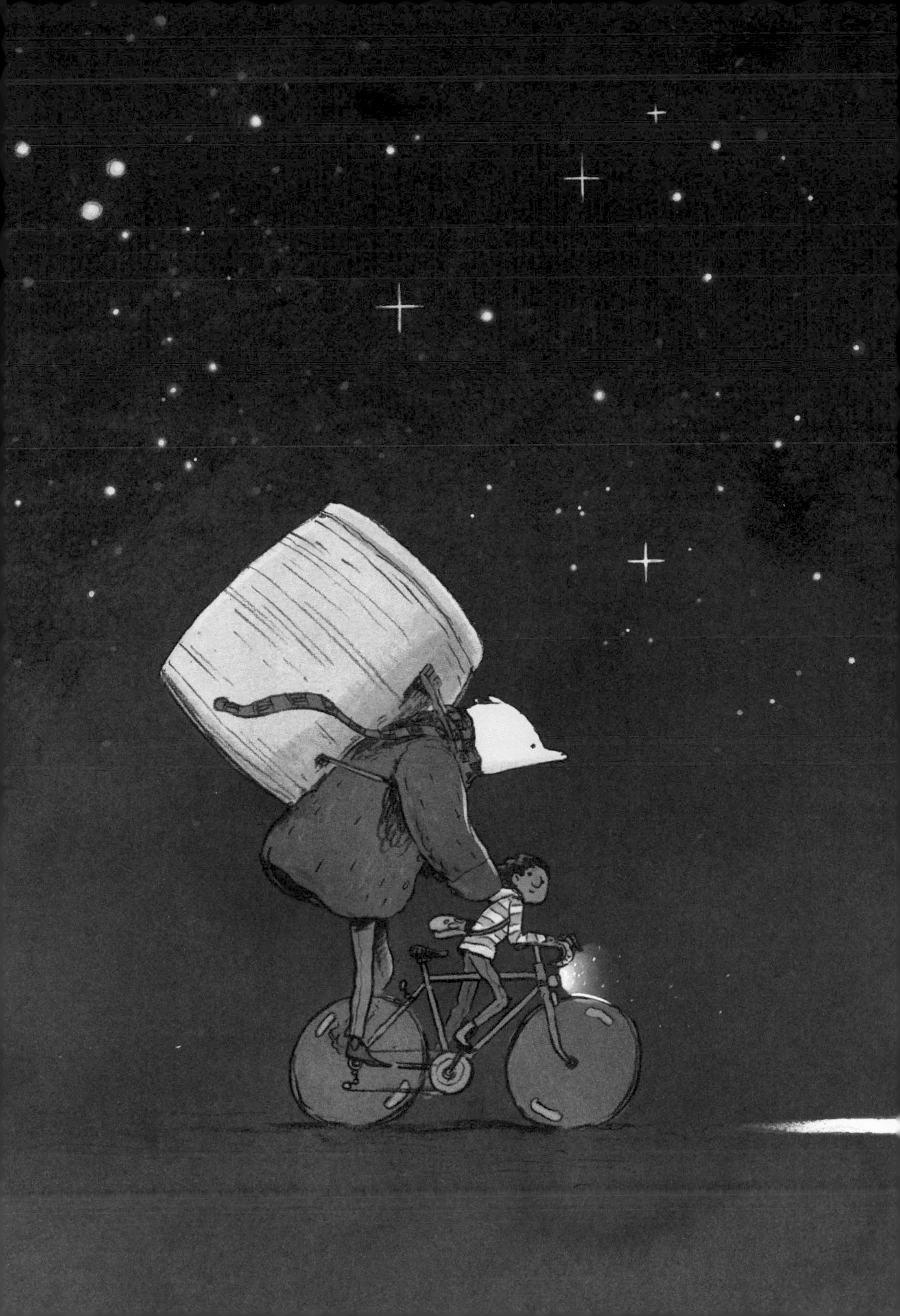

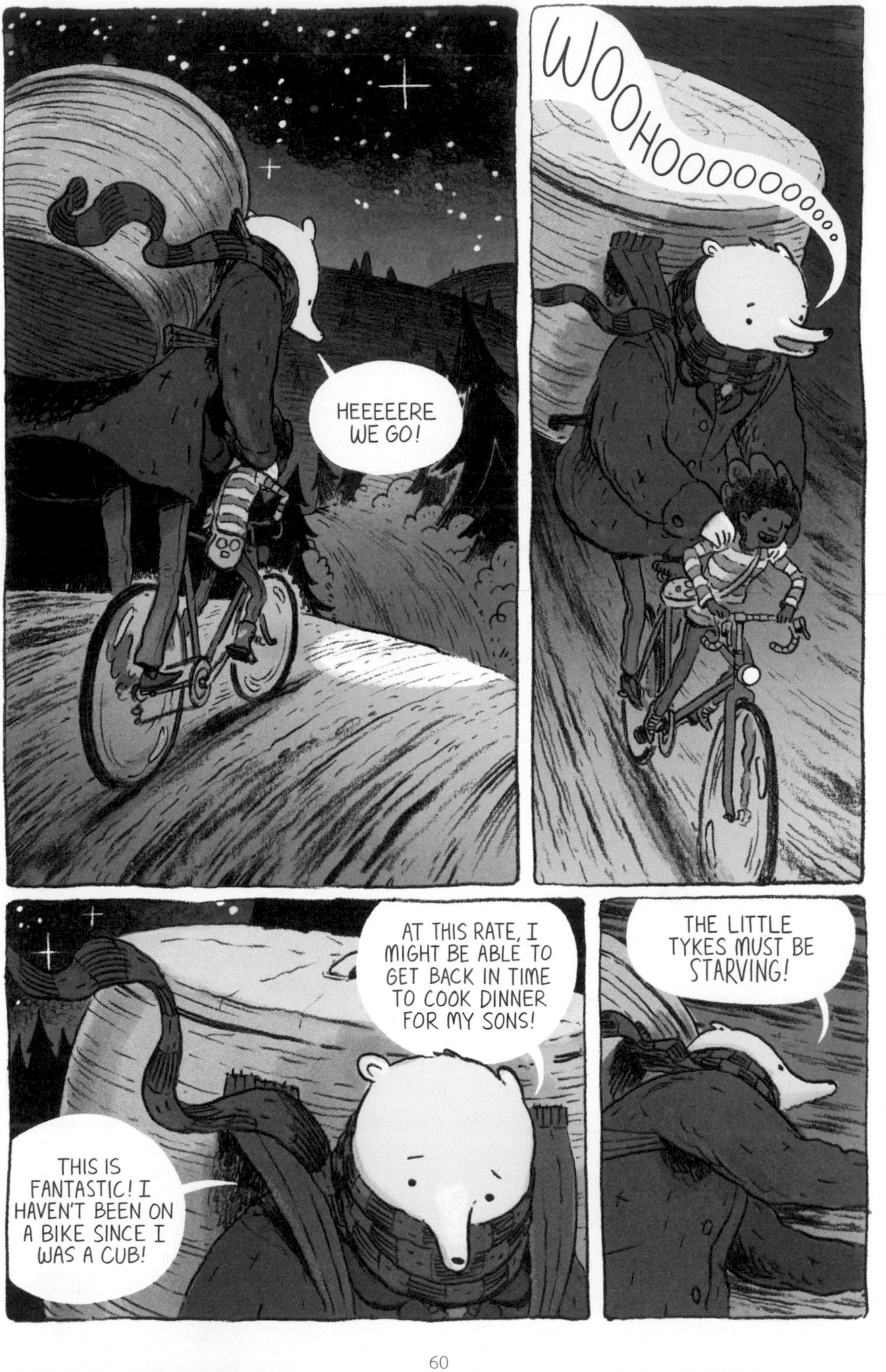
HEEEEERE WE GO!
WOOHOOOOOOOOooo
AT THIS RATE, I MIGHT BE ABLE TO GET BACK IN TIME TO COOK DINNER FOR MY SONS!
THIS IS FANTASTIC! I HAVEN'T BEEN ON A BIKE SINCE I WAS A CUB!
THE LITTLE TYKES MUST BE STARVING!

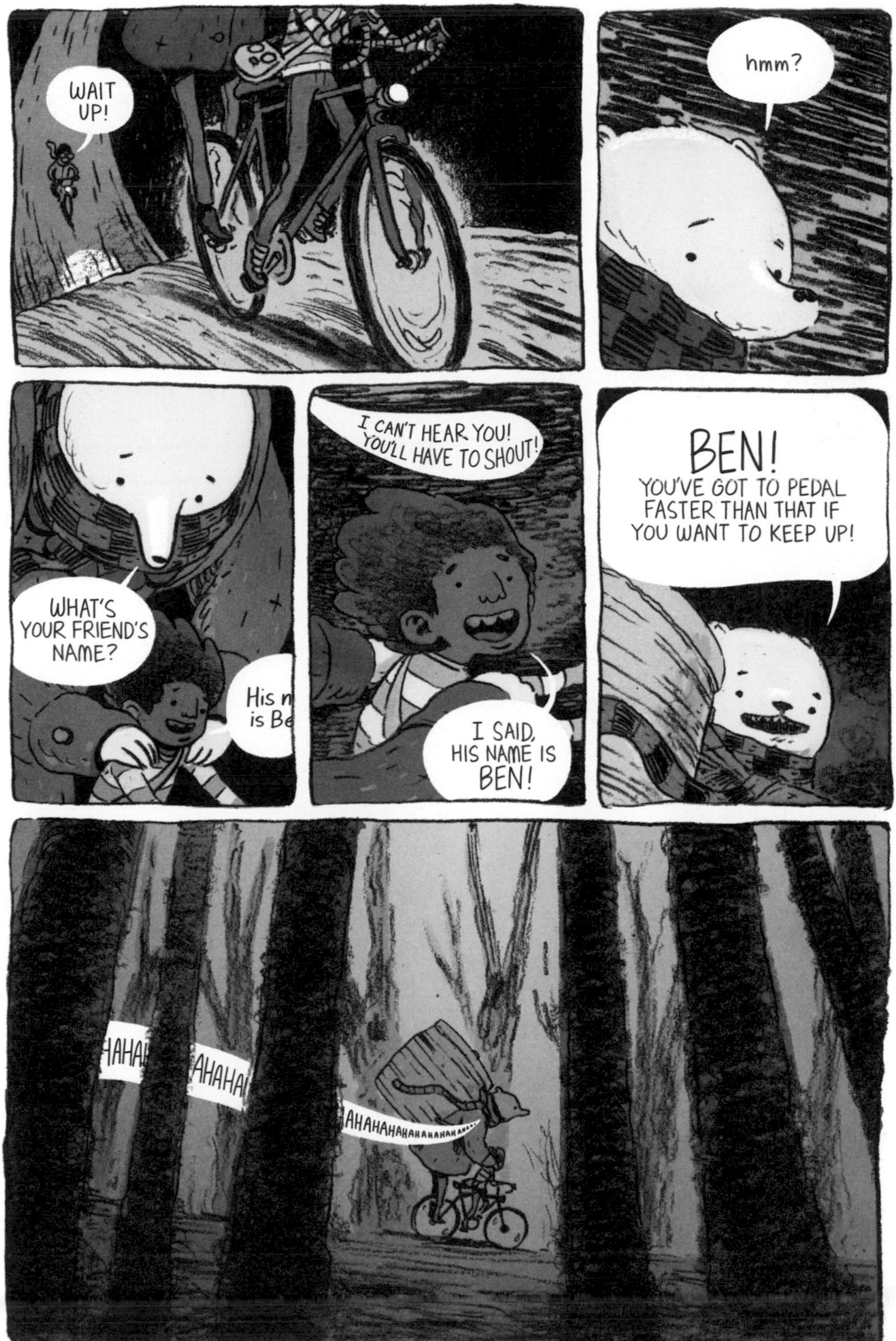
WAIT UP!
hmm?
WHAT'S YOUR FRIEND'S NAME?
His n is Be
I CAN'T HEAR YOU! YOU'LL HAVE TO SHOUT!
I SAID, HIS NAME IS BEN!
BEN! YOU'VE GOT TO PEDAL FASTER THAN THAT IF YOU WANT TO KEEP UP!
HAHAH
AHAHAH
AHAHAHAHAHAHAHAHAHA

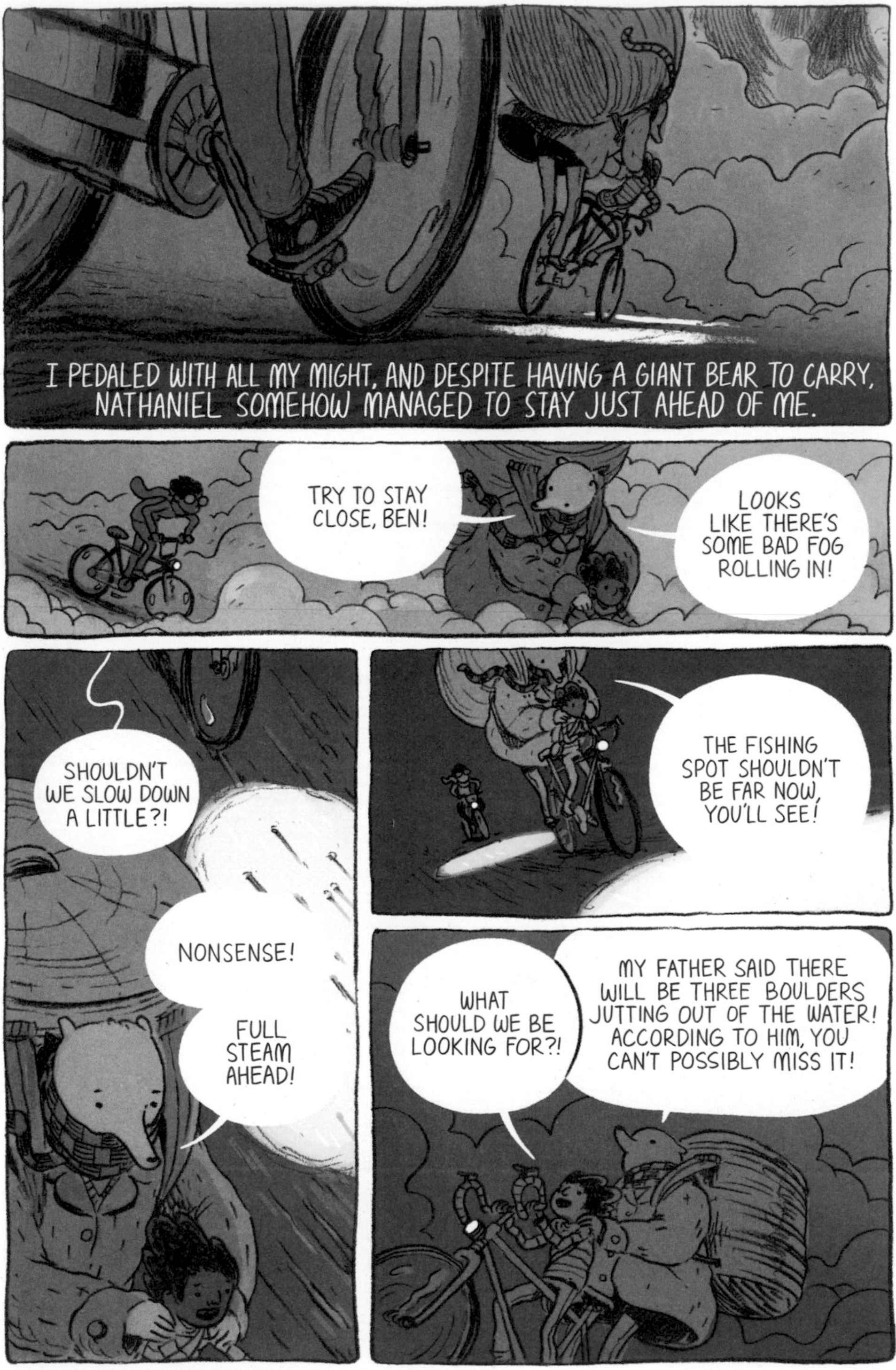
I PEDALED WITH ALL MY MIGHT, AND DESPITE HAVING A GIANT BEAR TO CARRY, NATHANIEL SOMEHOW MANAGED TO STAY JUST AHEAD OF ME.
TRY TO STAY CLOSE, BEN!
LOOKS LIKE THERE'S SOME BAD FOG ROLLING IN!
SHOULDN'T WE SLOW DOWN A LITTLE?!
NONSENSE!
FULL STEAM AHEAD!
THE FISHING SPOT SHOULDN'T BE FAR NOW, YOU'LL SEE!
WHAT SHOULD WE BE LOOKING FOR?!
MY FATHER SAID THERE WILL BE THREE BOULDERS JUTTING OUT OF THE WATER! ACCORDING TO HIM, YOU CAN'T POSSIBLY MISS IT!

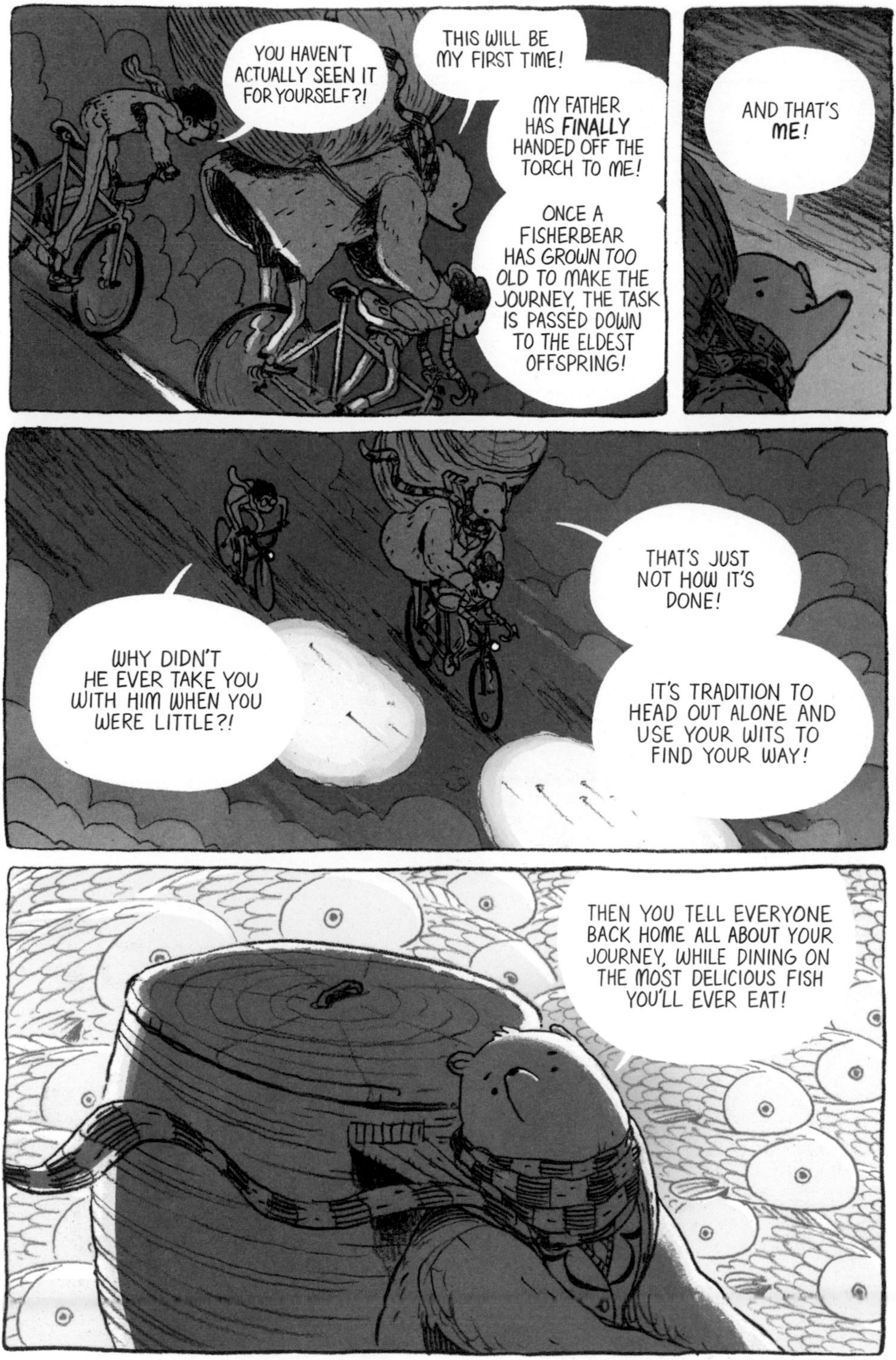
YOU HAVEN'T ACTUALLY SEEN IT FOR YOURSELF?!
THIS WILL BE MY FIRST TIME!
MY FATHER HAS **FINALLY** HANDED OFF THE TORCH TO ME!
ONCE A FISHERBEAR HAS GROWN TOO OLD TO MAKE THE JOURNEY, THE TASK IS PASSED DOWN TO THE ELDEST OFFSPRING!
AND THAT'S **ME**!
WHY DIDN'T HE EVER TAKE YOU WITH HIM WHEN YOU WERE LITTLE?!
THAT'S JUST NOT HOW IT'S DONE!
IT'S TRADITION TO HEAD OUT ALONE AND USE YOUR WITS TO FIND YOUR WAY!
THEN YOU TELL EVERYONE BACK HOME ALL ABOUT YOUR JOURNEY, WHILE DINING ON THE MOST DELICIOUS FISH YOU'LL EVER EAT!

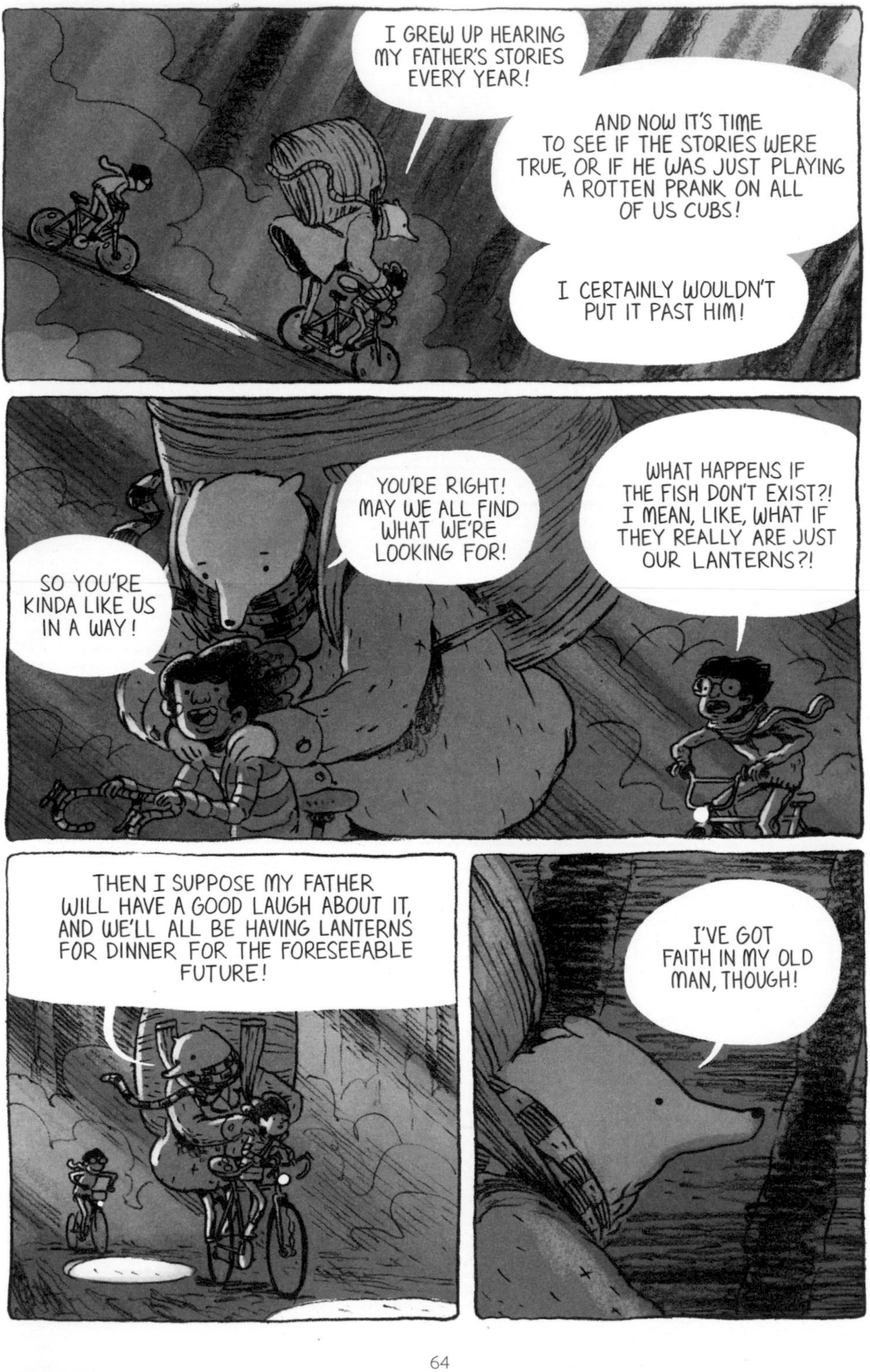

I GREW UP HEARING MY FATHER'S STORIES EVERY YEAR!
AND NOW IT'S TIME TO SEE IF THE STORIES WERE TRUE, OR IF HE WAS JUST PLAYING A ROTTEN PRANK ON ALL OF US CUBS!
I CERTAINLY WOULDN'T PUT IT PAST HIM!
SO YOU'RE KINDA LIKE US IN A WAY!
YOU'RE RIGHT! MAY WE ALL FIND WHAT WE'RE LOOKING FOR!
WHAT HAPPENS IF THE FISH DON'T EXIST?! I MEAN, LIKE, WHAT IF THEY REALLY ARE JUST OUR LANTERNS?!
THEN I SUPPOSE MY FATHER WILL HAVE A GOOD LAUGH ABOUT IT, AND WE'LL ALL BE HAVING LANTERNS FOR DINNER FOR THE FORESEEABLE FUTURE!
I'VE GOT FAITH IN MY OLD MAN, THOUGH!

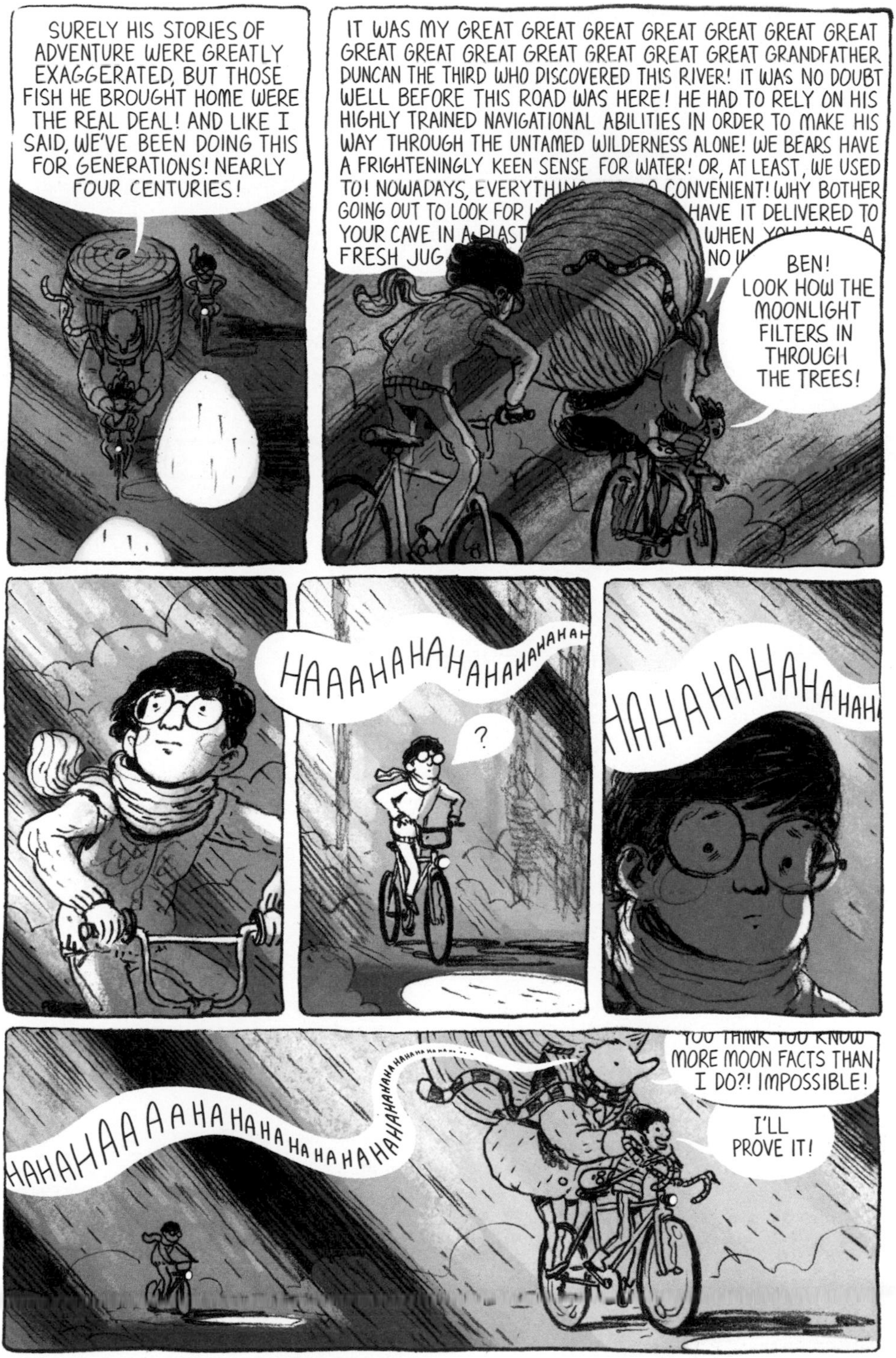
SURELY HIS STORIES OF ADVENTURE WERE GREATLY EXAGGERATED, BUT THOSE FISH HE BROUGHT HOME WERE THE REAL DEAL! AND LIKE I SAID, WE'VE BEEN DOING THIS FOR GENERATIONS! NEARLY FOUR CENTURIES!
IT WAS MY GREAT GREAT GREAT GREAT GREAT GREAT GREAT GREAT GREAT GREAT GREAT GREAT GREAT GRANDFATHER DUNCAN THE THIRD WHO DISCOVERED THIS RIVER! IT WAS NO DOUBT WELL BEFORE THIS ROAD WAS HERE! HE HAD TO RELY ON HIS HIGHLY TRAINED NAVIGATIONAL ABILITIES IN ORDER TO MAKE HIS WAY THROUGH THE UNTAMED WILDERNESS ALONE! WE BEARS HAVE A FRIGHTENINGLY KEEN SENSE FOR WATER! OR, AT LEAST, WE USED TO! NOWADAYS, EVERYTHING
CONVENIENT! WHY BOTHER GOING OUT TO LOOK FOR
HAVE IT DELIVERED TO YOUR CAVE IN A PLAST
WHEN YOU HAVE A FRESH JUG
BEN! LOOK HOW THE MOONLIGHT FILTERS IN THROUGH THE TREES!
HAAAHAHAHAHAHAHAHAH
?
HAHAHAHAHAHAHAH
YOU THINK YOU KNOW MORE MOON FACTS THAN I DO?! IMPOSSIBLE!
I'LL PROVE IT!
HAHAHAAAAHAHAHAHAHAHAHAHAHAHAHAHAHAHA

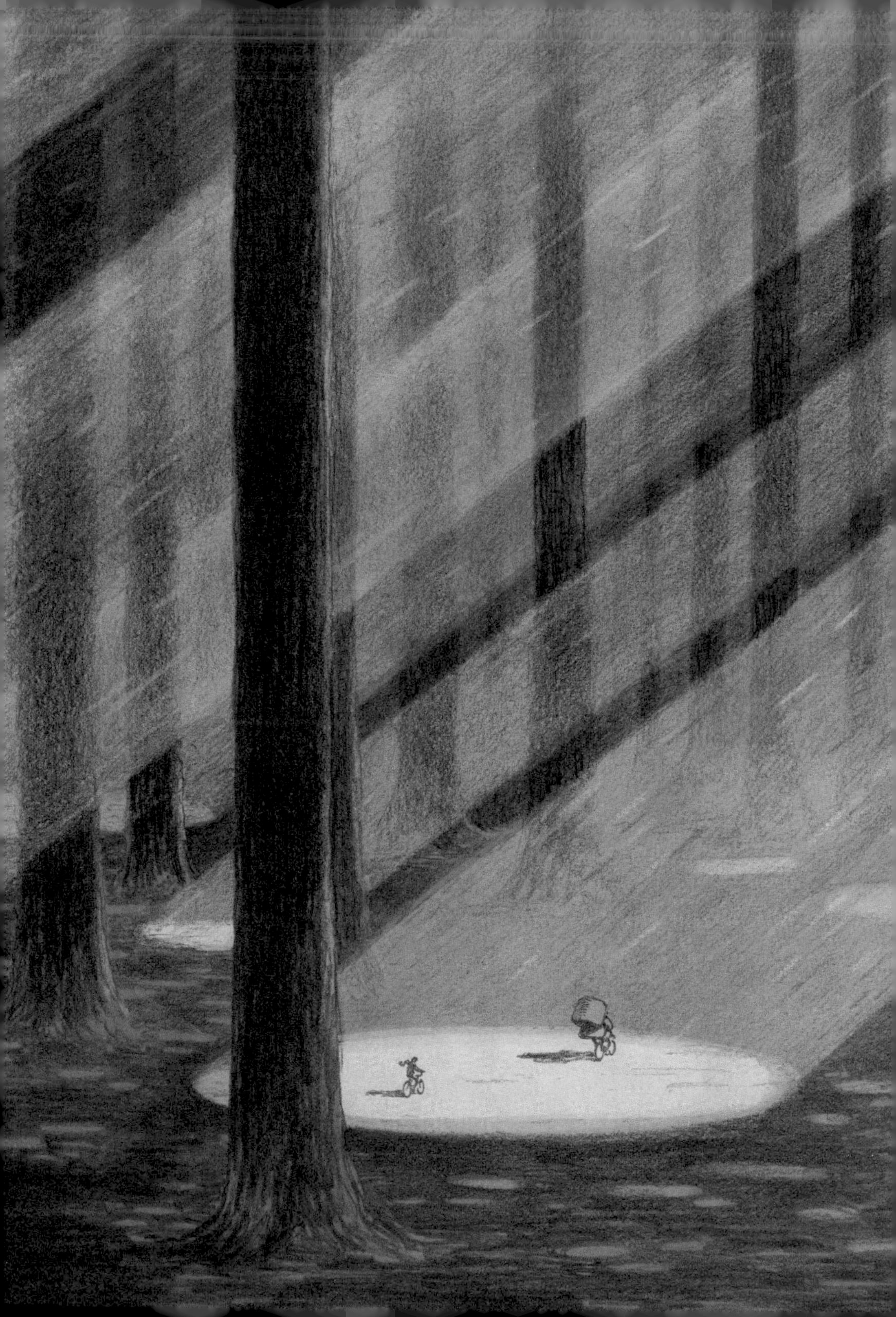

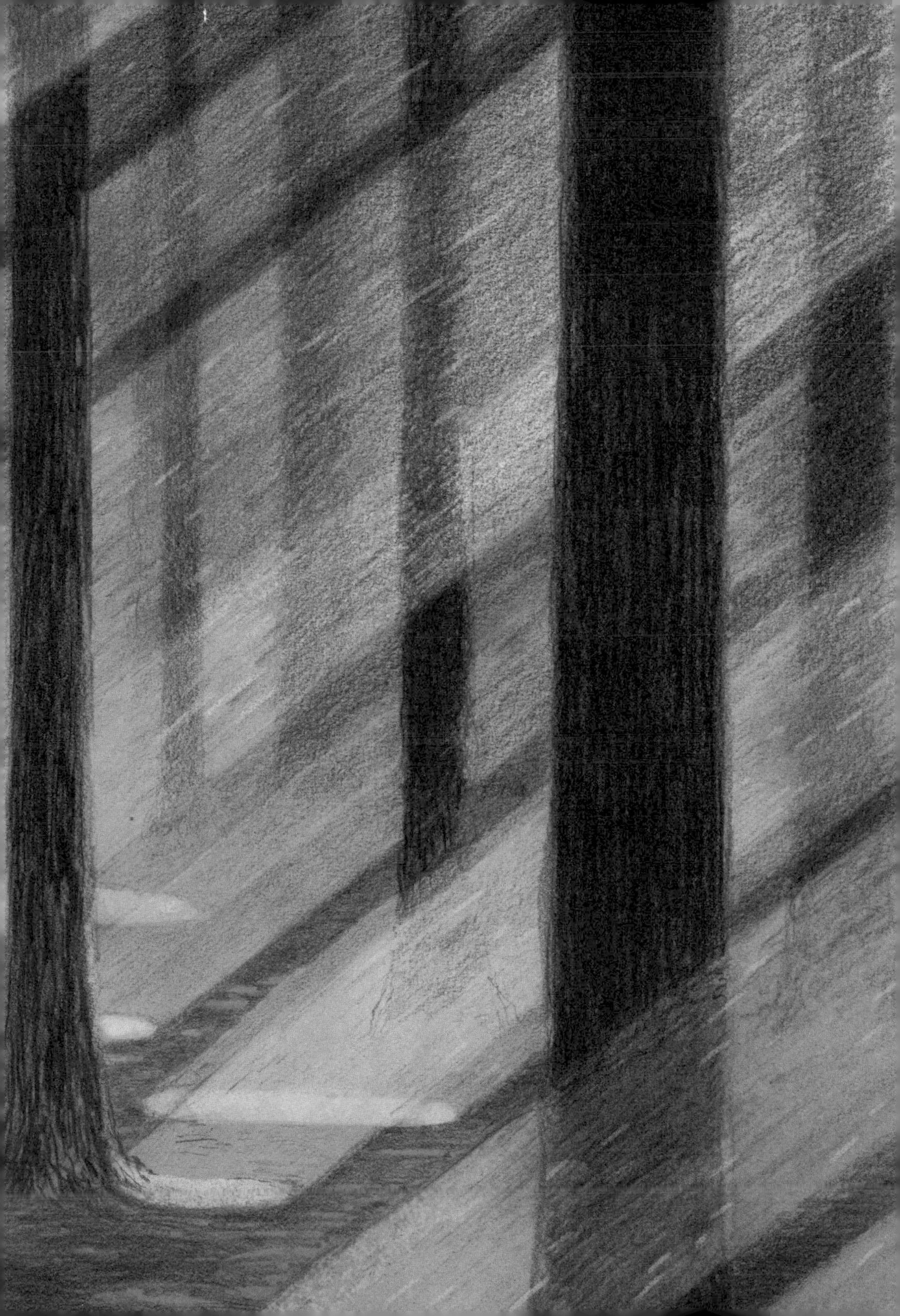

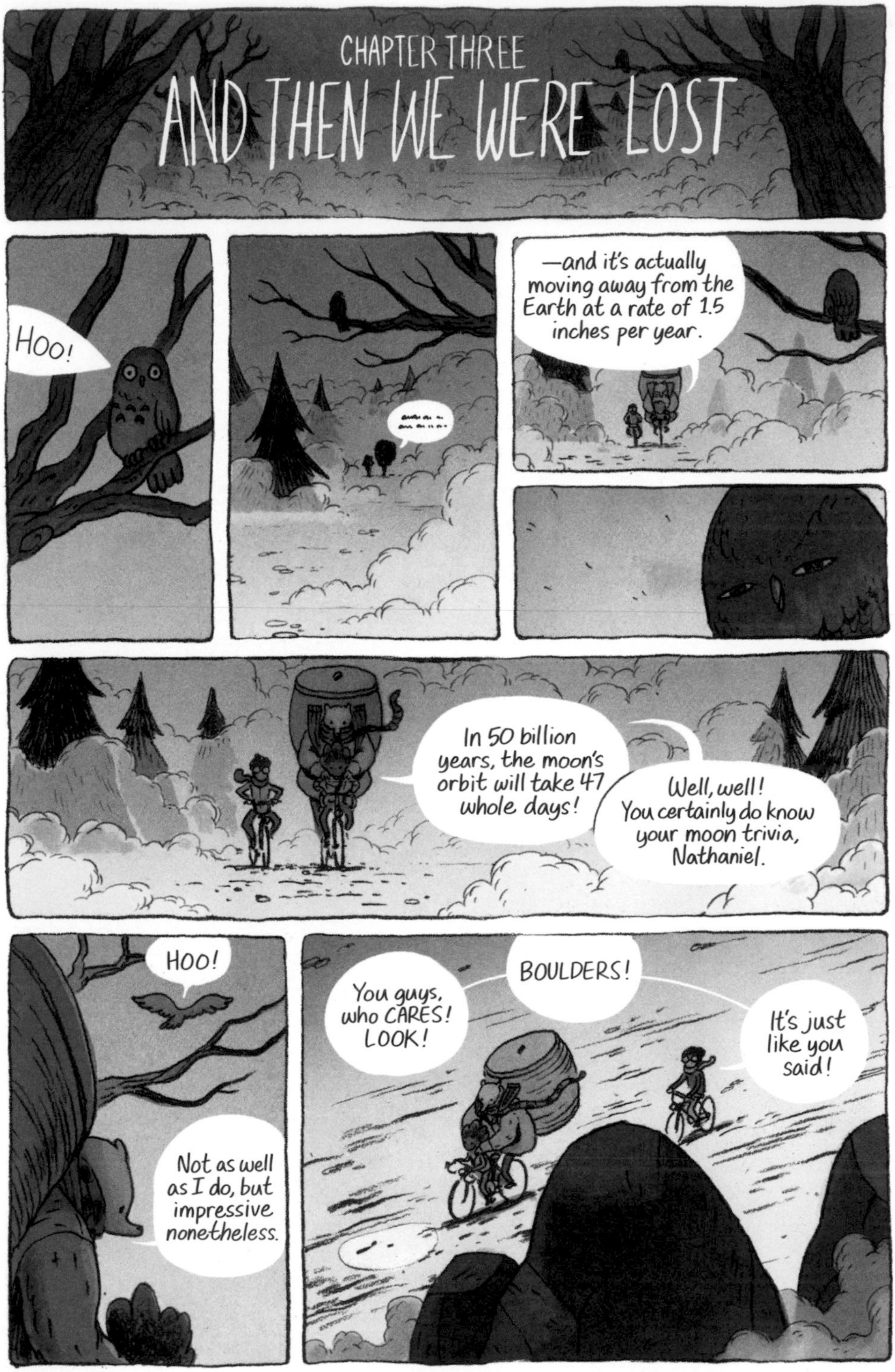
CHAPTER THREE
AND THEN WE WERE LOST
HOO!
—and it's actually moving away from the Earth at a rate of 1.5 inches per year.
In 50 billion years, the moon's orbit will take 47 whole days!
Well, well! You certainly do know your moon trivia, Nathaniel.
HOO!
Not as well as I do, but impressive nonetheless.
You guys, who CARES! LOOK!
BOULDERS!
It's just like you said!

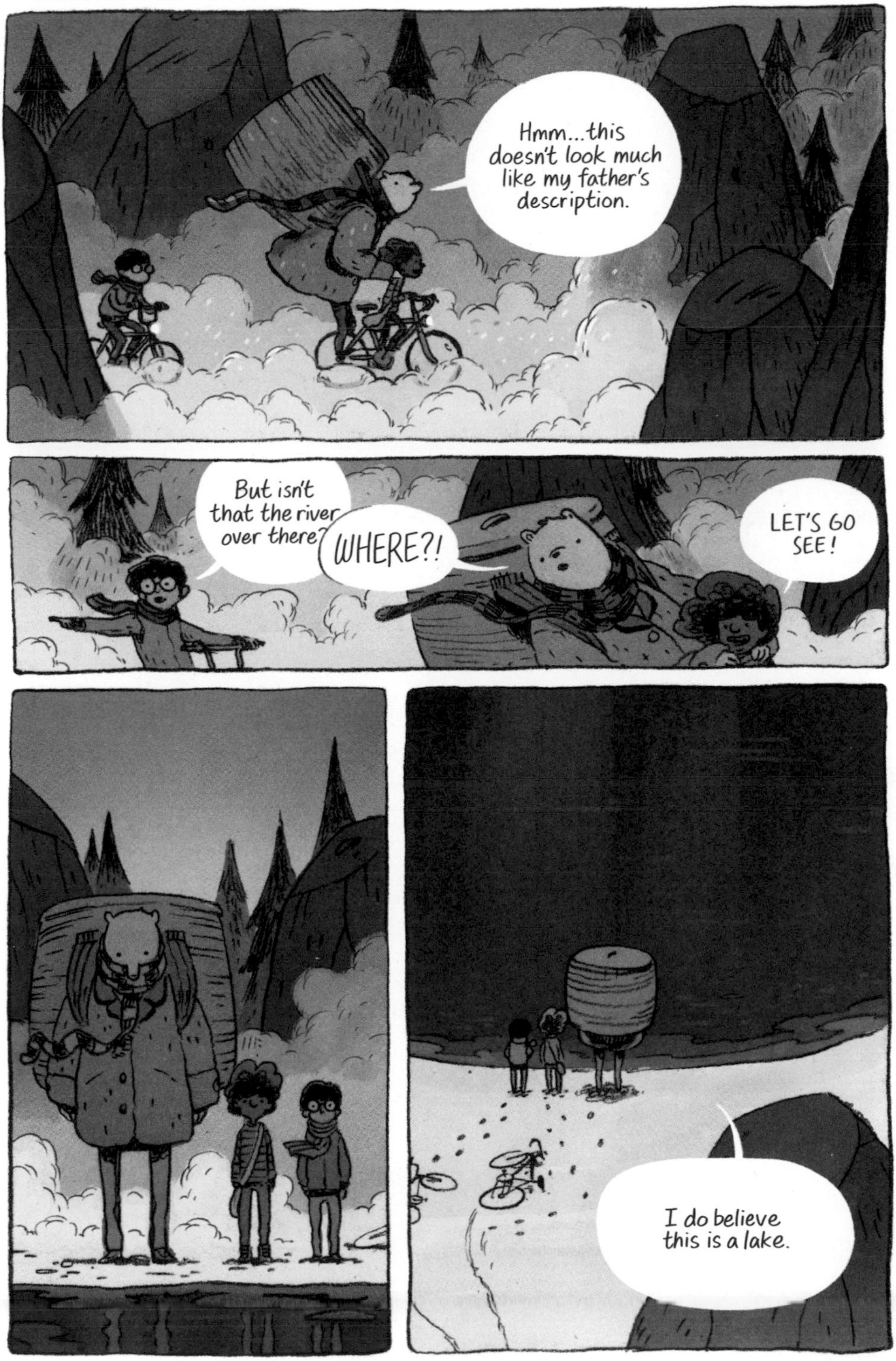
Hmm...this doesn't look much like my father's description.
But isn't that the river over there?
WHERE?!
LET'S GO SEE!
I do believe this is a lake.

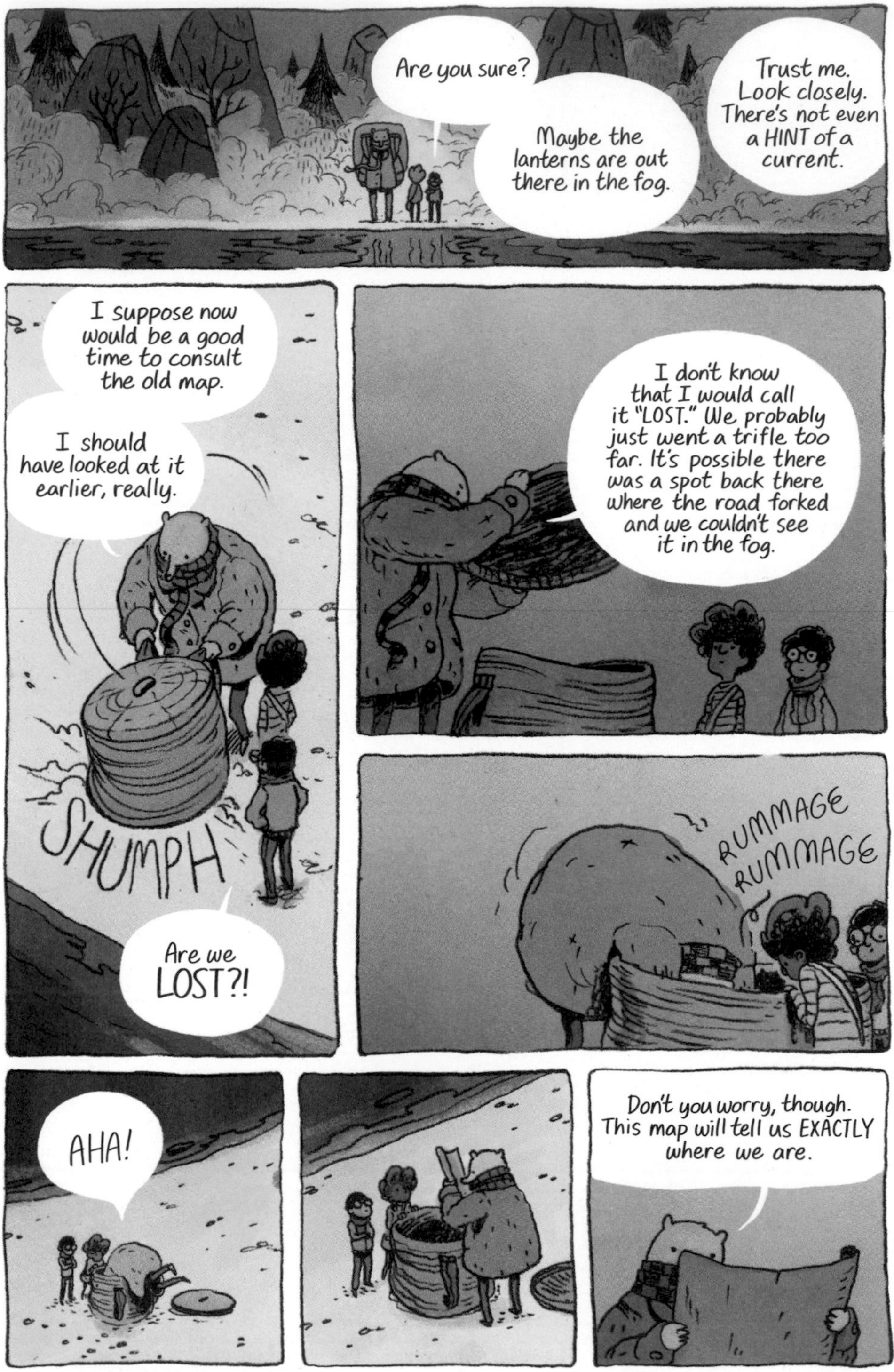
Are you sure?
Maybe the lanterns are out there in the fog.
Trust me. Look closely. There's not even a HINT of a current.
I suppose now would be a good time to consult the old map.
I should have looked at it earlier, really.
SHUMPH
Are we LOST?!
I don't know that I would call it "LOST." We probably just went a trifle too far. It's possible there was a spot back there where the road forked and we couldn't see it in the fog.
RUMMAGE RUMMAGE
AHA!
Don't you worry, though. This map will tell us EXACTLY where we are.

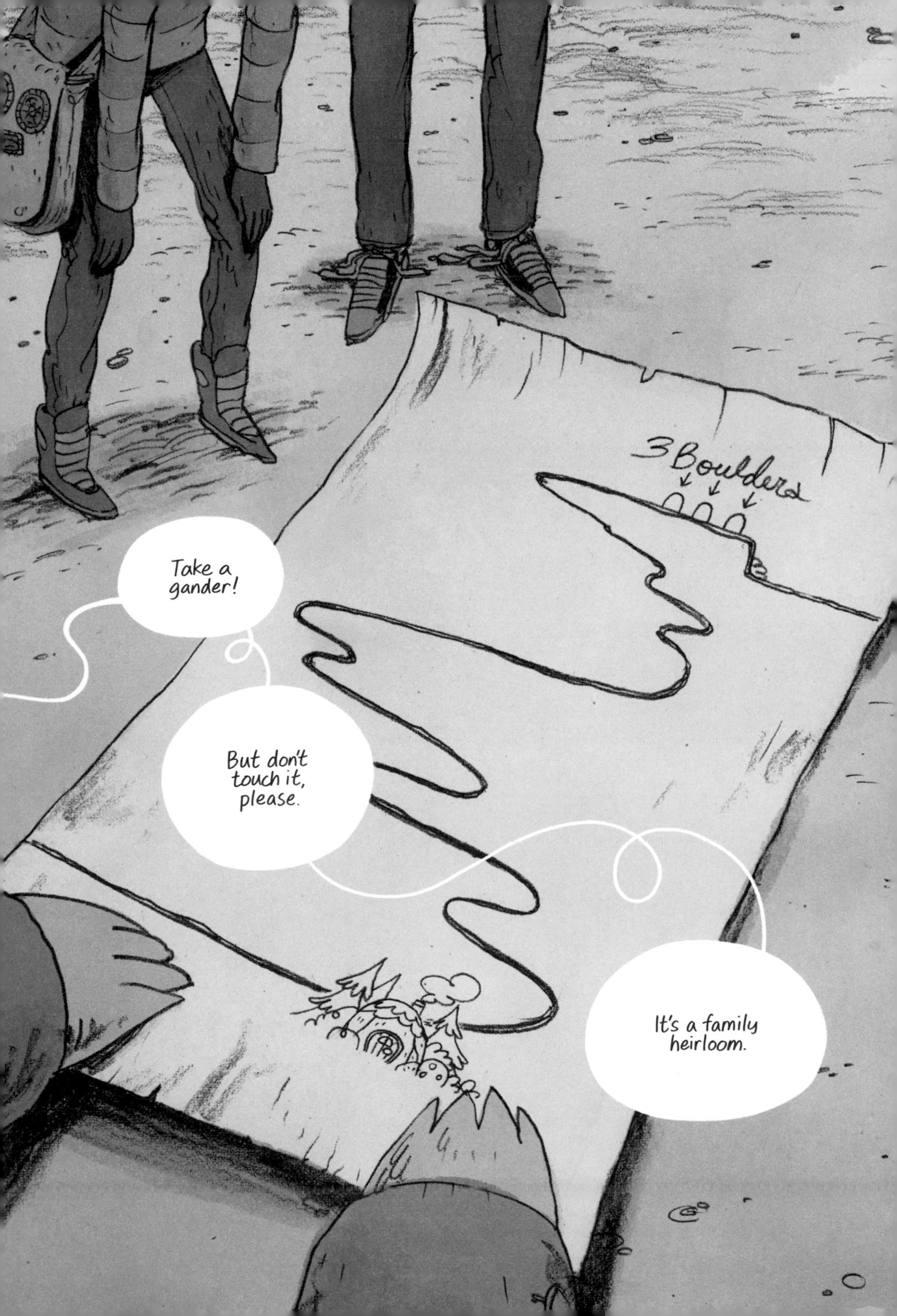
3 Boulders
Take a gander!
But don't touch it, please.
It's a family heirloom.

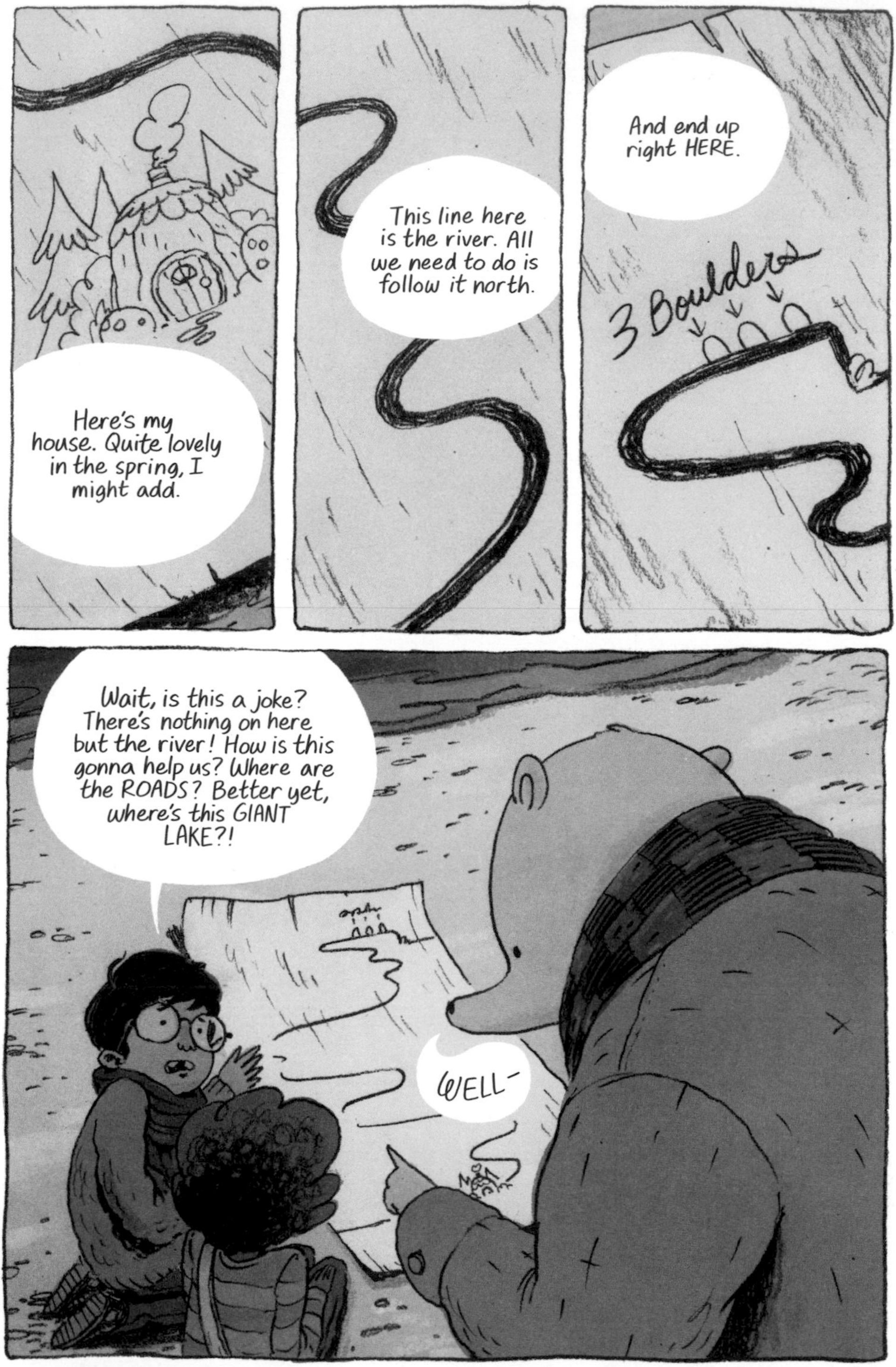
Here's my house. Quite lovely in the spring, I might add.
This line here is the river. All we need to do is follow it north.
And end up right HERE.
3 Boulders
Wait, is this a joke? There's nothing on here but the river! How is this gonna help us? Where are the ROADS? Better yet, where's this GIANT LAKE?!
WELL-

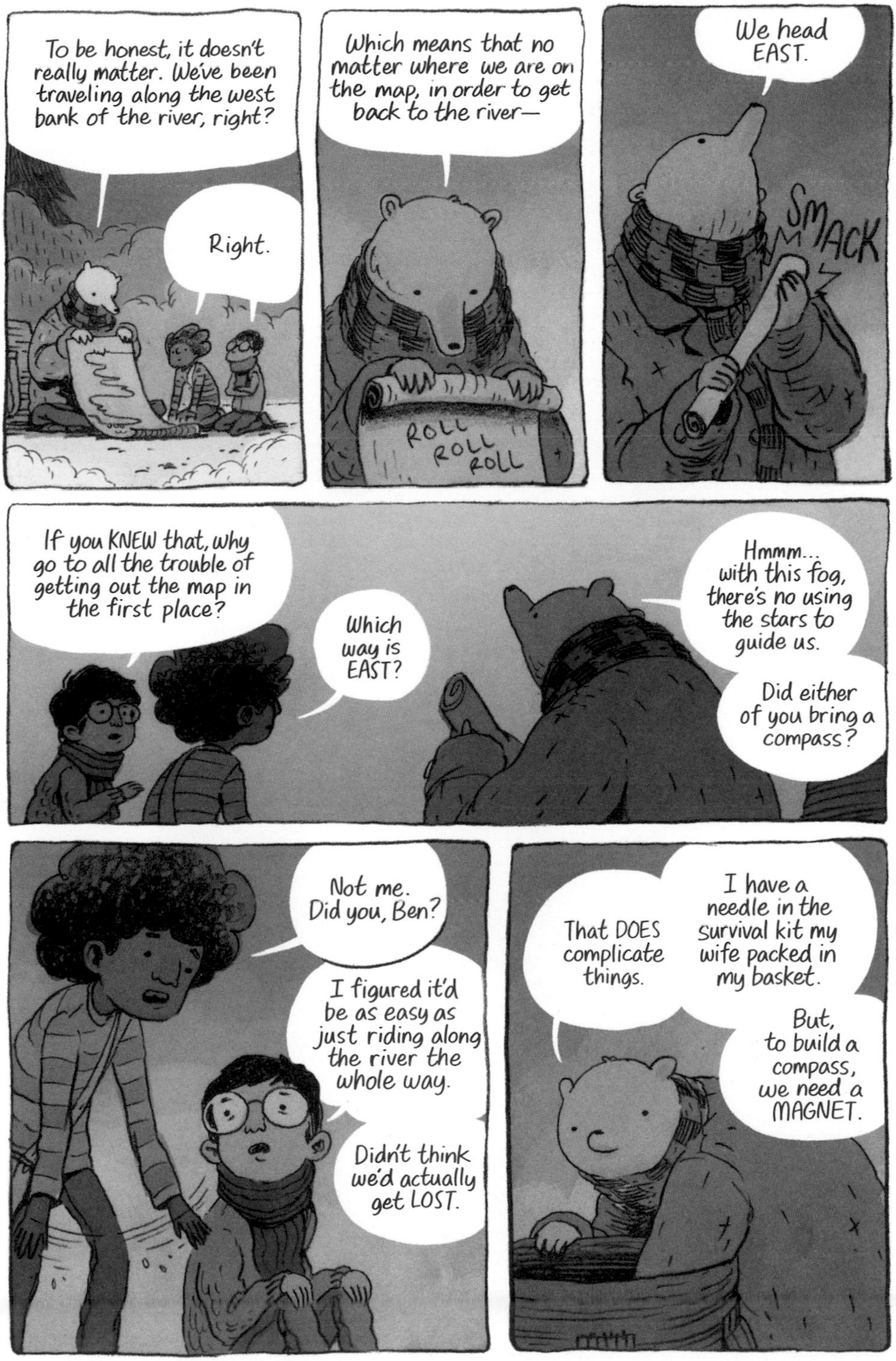

To be honest, it doesn't really matter. We've been traveling along the west bank of the river, right?
Right.
Which means that no matter where we are on the map, in order to get back to the river—
ROLL ROLL ROLL
We head EAST.
SMACK
If you KNEW that, why go to all the trouble of getting out the map in the first place?
Which way is EAST?
Hmmm... with this fog, there's no using the stars to guide us.
Did either of you bring a compass?
Not me. Did you, Ben?
I figured it'd be as easy as just riding along the river the whole way.
Didn't think we'd actually get LOST.
That DOES complicate things.
I have a needle in the survival kit my wife packed in my basket.
But, to build a compass, we need a MAGNET.

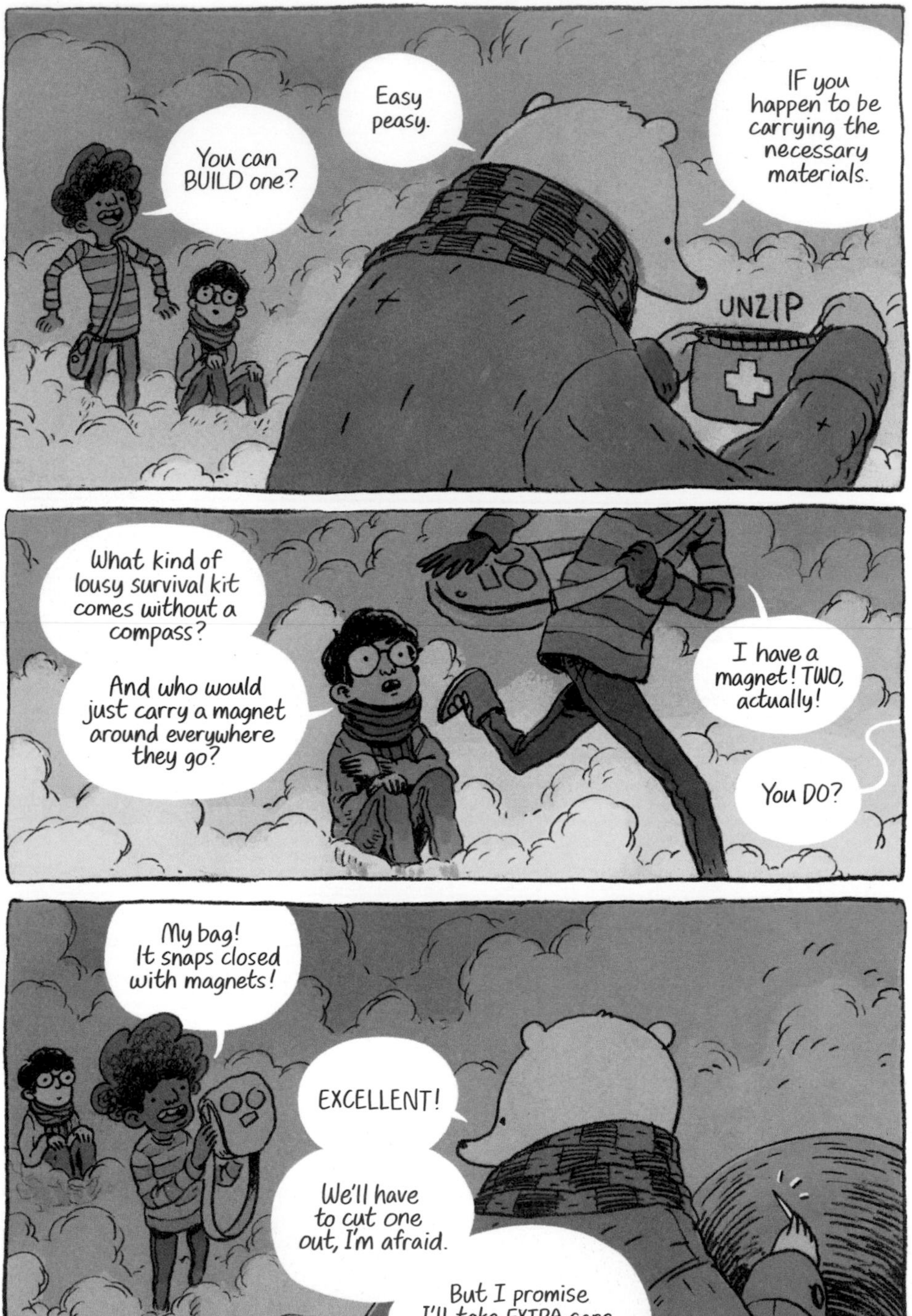
You can BUILD one?
Easy peasy.
IF you happen to be carrying the necessary materials.
UNZIP
What kind of lousy survival kit comes without a compass?
And who would just carry a magnet around everywhere they go?
I have a magnet! TWO, actually!
You DO?
My bag! It snaps closed with magnets!
EXCELLENT!
We'll have to cut one out, I'm afraid.
But I promise I'll take EXTRA care not to ruin your bag.

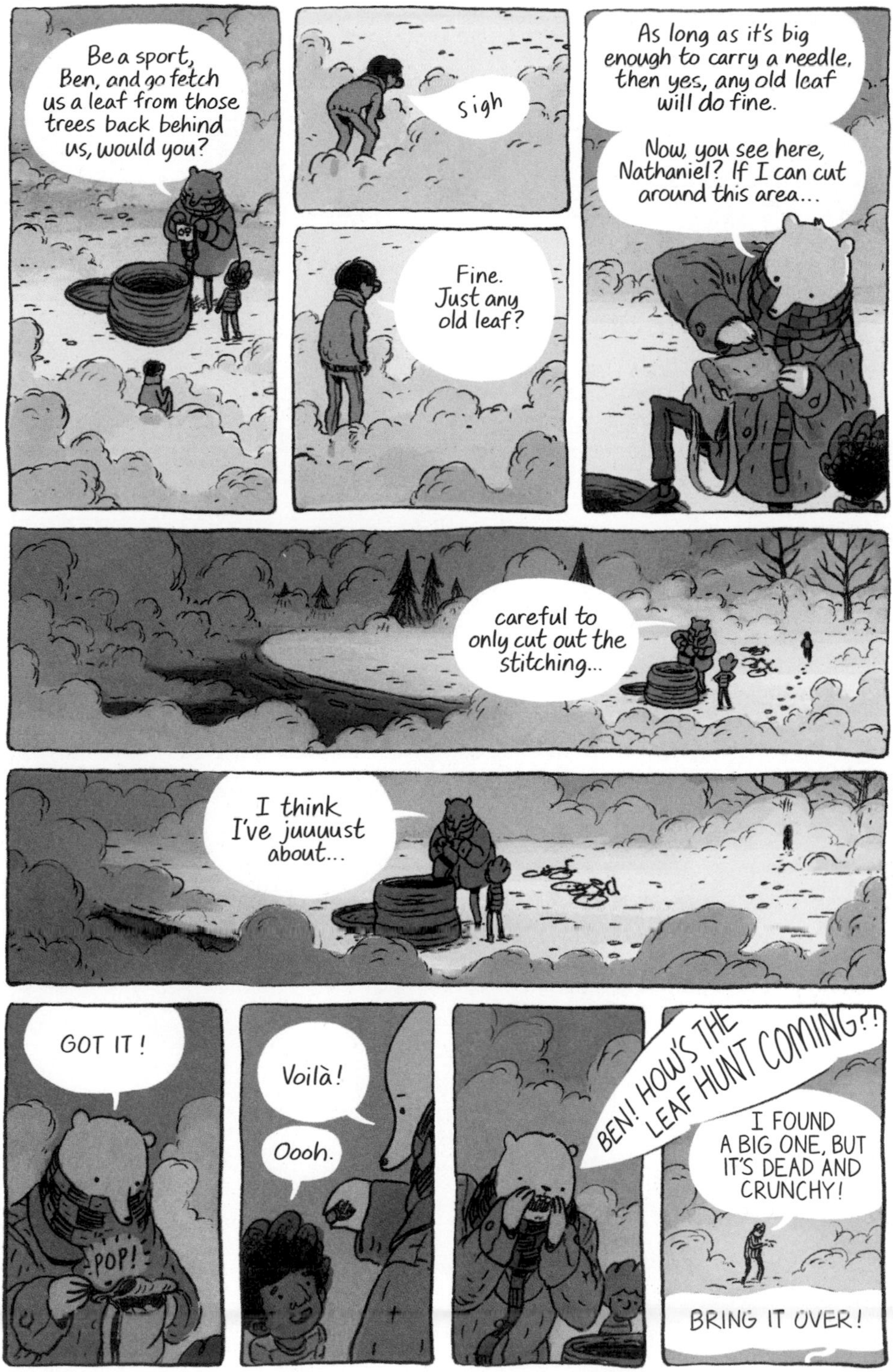
Be a sport, Ben, and go fetch us a leaf from those trees back behind us, would you?
sigh
Fine. Just any old leaf?
As long as it's big enough to carry a needle, then yes, any old leaf will do fine.
Now, you see here, Nathaniel? If I can cut around this area...
careful to only cut out the stitching...
I think I've juuuust about...
GOT IT!
POP!
Voilà!
Oooh.
BEN! HOW'S THE LEAF HUNT COMING?!
I FOUND A BIG ONE, BUT IT'S DEAD AND CRUNCHY!
BRING IT OVER!

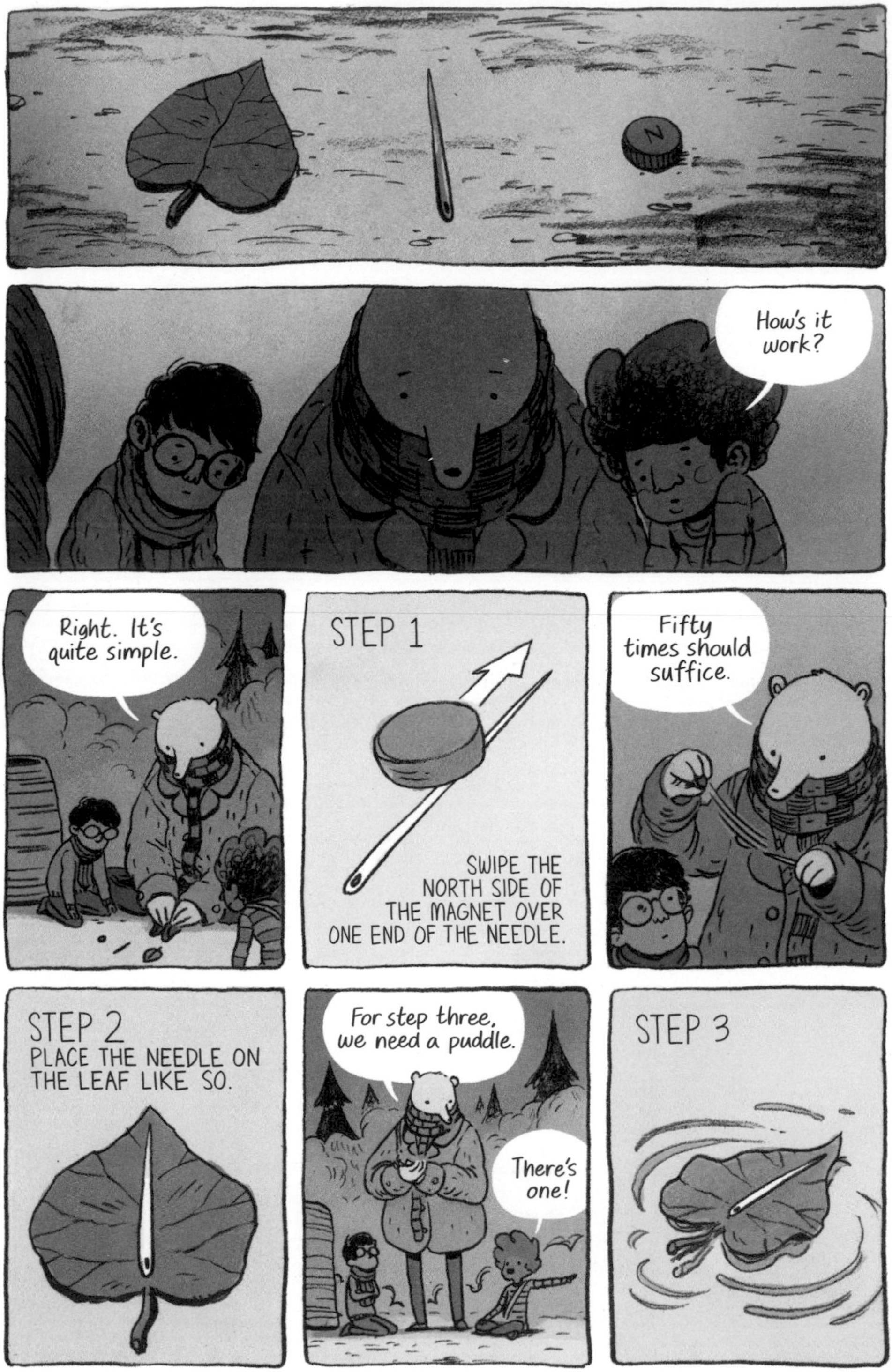
How's it work?
Right. It's quite simple.
STEP 1
SWIPE THE NORTH SIDE OF THE MAGNET OVER ONE END OF THE NEEDLE.
Fifty times should suffice.
STEP 2
PLACE THE NEEDLE ON THE LEAF LIKE SO.
For step three, we need a puddle.
There's one!
STEP 3

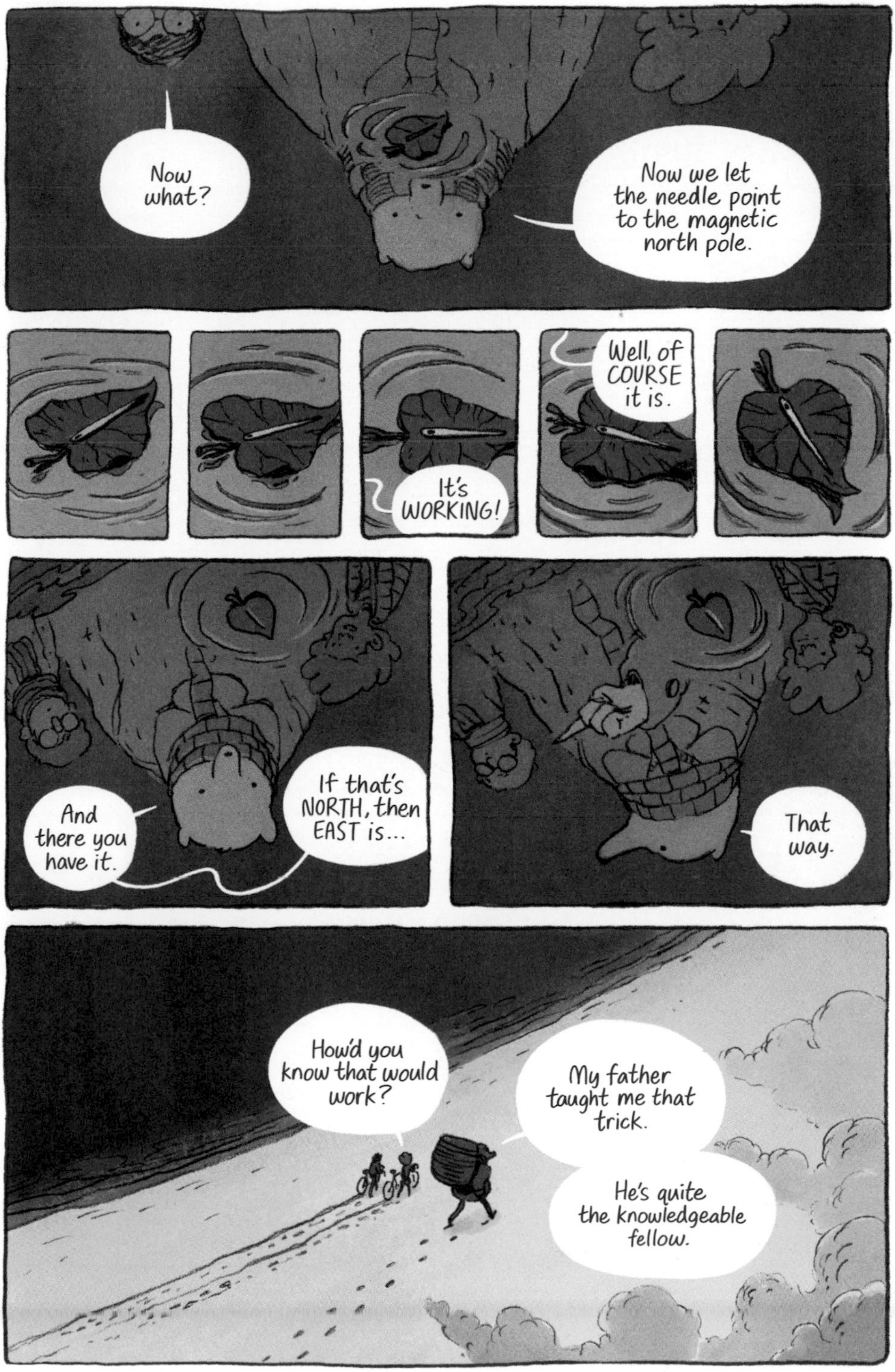
Now what?
Now we let the needle point to the magnetic north pole.
It's WORKING!
Well, of COURSE it is.
And there you have it.
If that's NORTH, then EAST is...
That way.
How'd you know that would work?
My father taught me that trick.
He's quite the knowledgeable fellow.

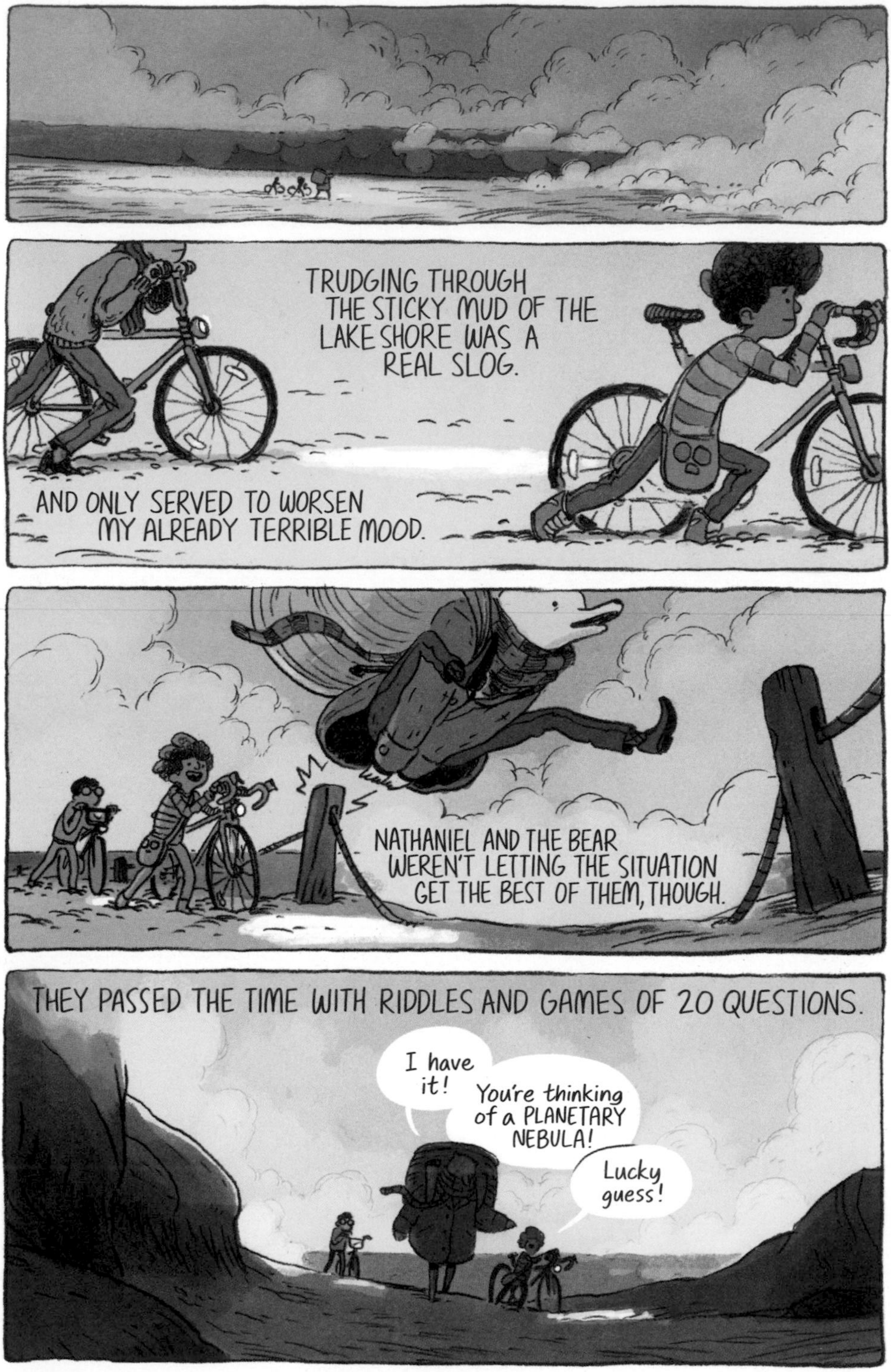
TRUDGING THROUGH THE STICKY MUD OF THE LAKE SHORE WAS A REAL SLOG.
AND ONLY SERVED TO WORSEN MY ALREADY TERRIBLE MOOD.
NATHANIEL AND THE BEAR WEREN'T LETTING THE SITUATION GET THE BEST OF THEM, THOUGH.
THEY PASSED THE TIME WITH RIDDLES AND GAMES OF 20 QUESTIONS.
I have it!
You're thinking of a PLANETARY NEBULA!
Lucky guess!

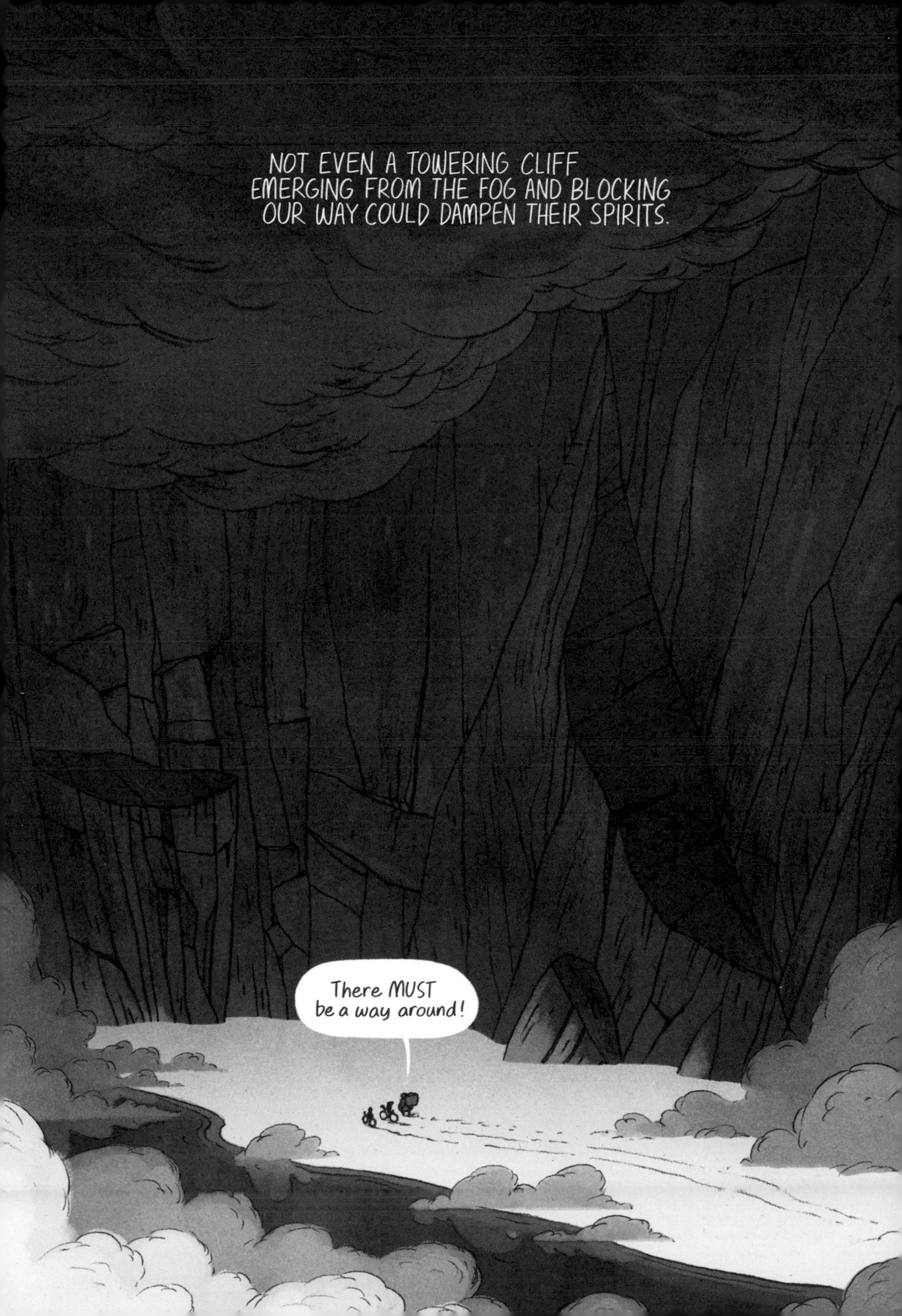
NOT EVEN A TOWERING CLIFF EMERGING FROM THE FOG AND BLOCKING OUR WAY COULD DAMPEN THEIR SPIRITS.
There MUST be a way around!

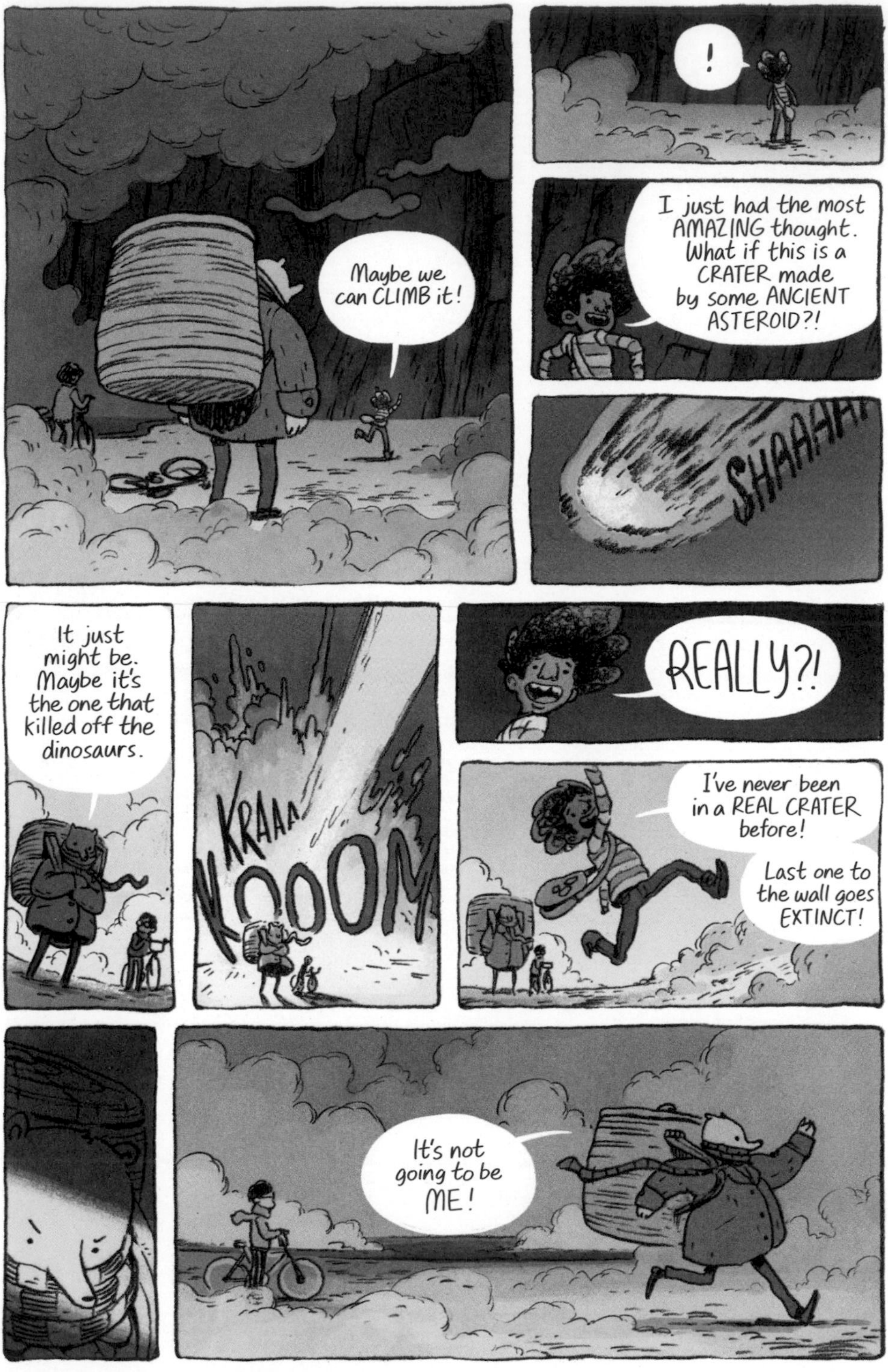
Maybe we can CLIMB it!
!
I just had the most AMAZING thought. What if this is a CRATER made by some ANCIENT ASTEROID?!
SHAAAA
It just might be. Maybe it's the one that killed off the dinosaurs.
KRAAA
KOOOM
REALLY?!
I've never been in a REAL CRATER before!
Last one to the wall goes EXTINCT!
It's not going to be ME!

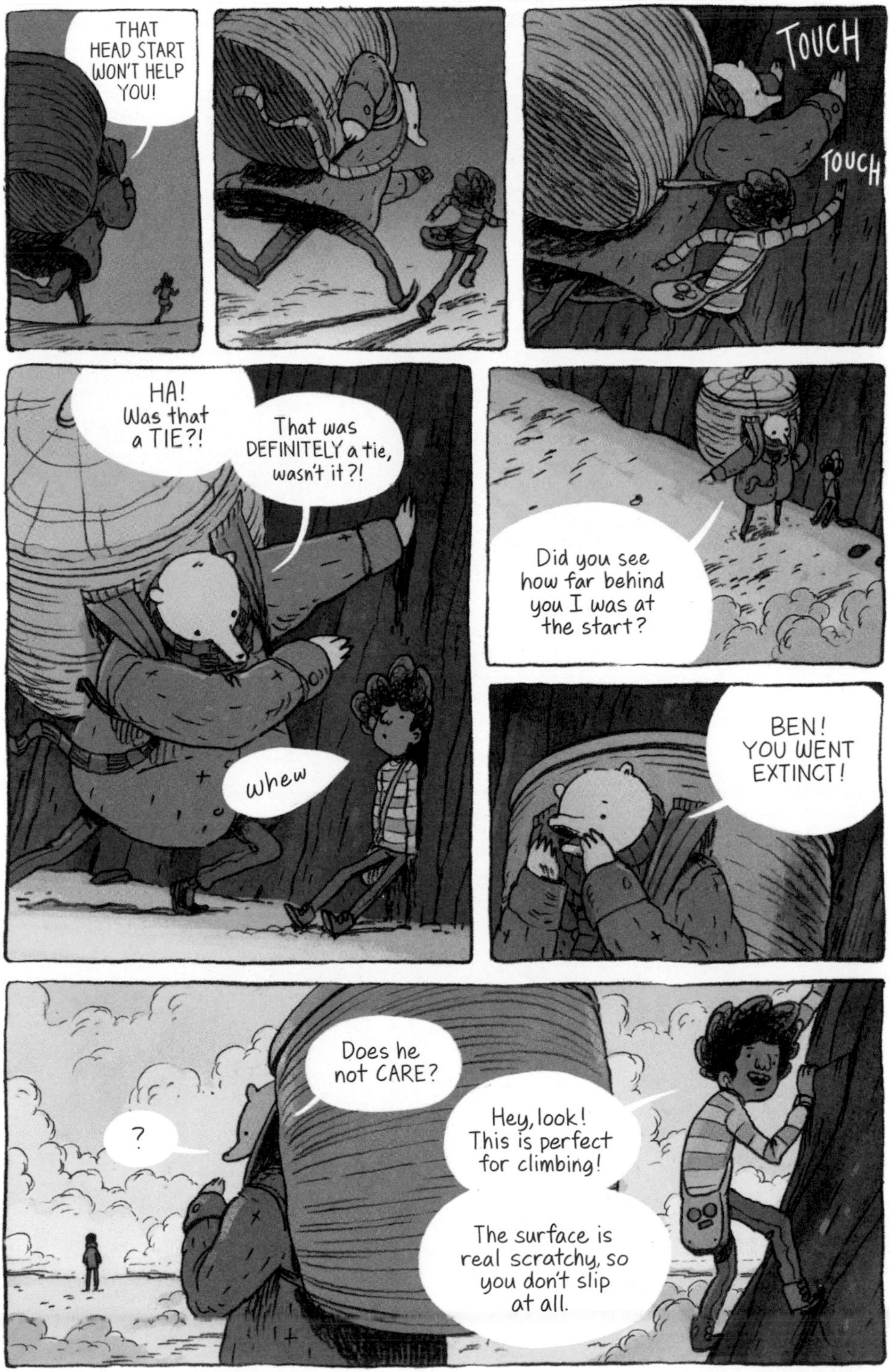
THAT HEAD START WON'T HELP YOU!
TOUCH
TOUCH
HA! Was that a TIE?!
That was DEFINITELY a tie, wasn't it?!
whew
Did you see how far behind you I was at the start?
BEN! YOU WENT EXTINCT!
?
Does he not CARE?
Hey, look! This is perfect for climbing!
The surface is real scratchy, so you don't slip at all.

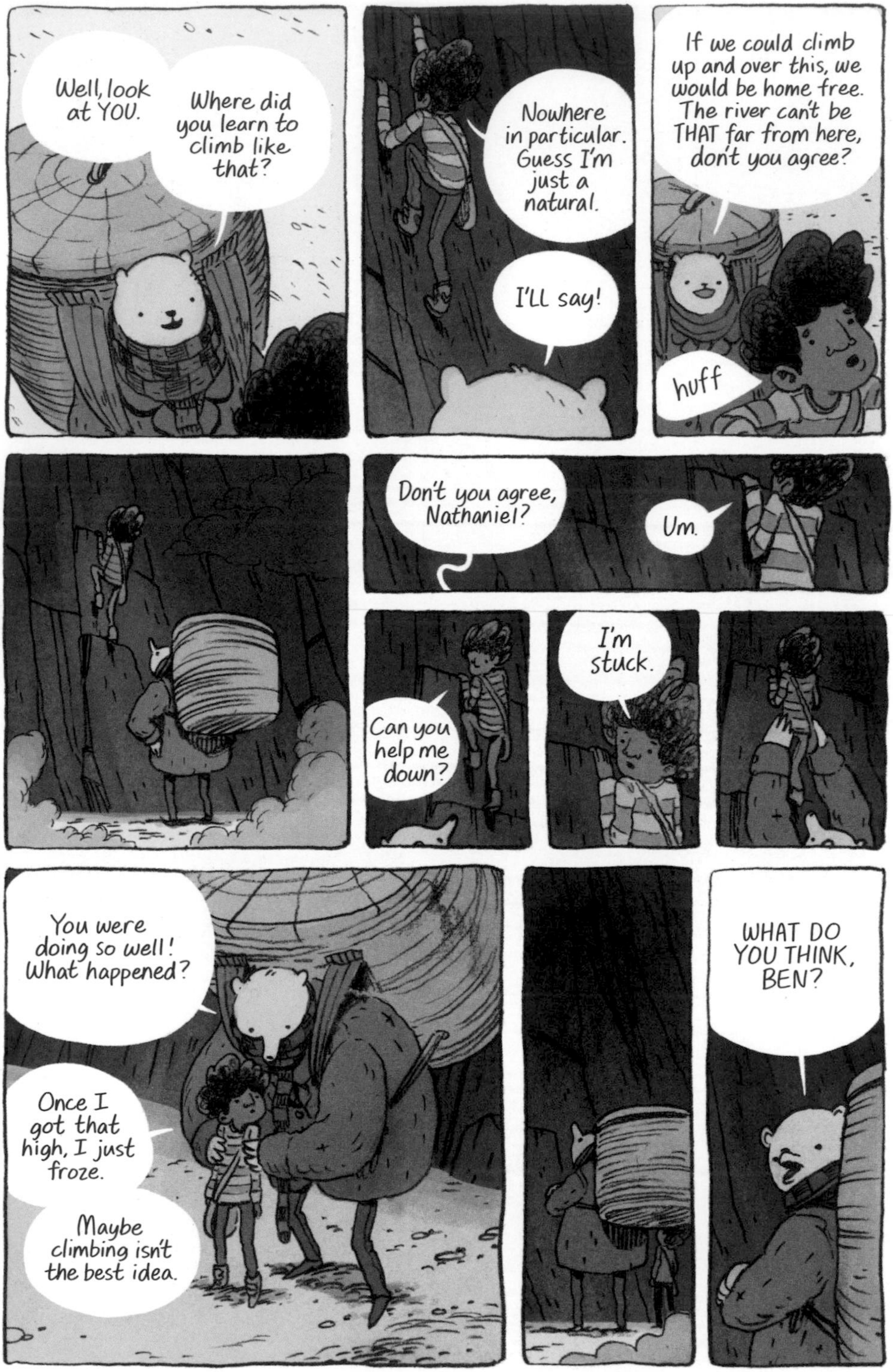
Well, look at YOU.
Where did you learn to climb like that?
Nowhere in particular. Guess I'm just a natural.
I'LL say!
If we could climb up and over this, we would be home free. The river can't be THAT far from here, don't you agree?
huff
Don't you agree, Nathaniel?
Um.
Can you help me down?
I'm stuck.
You were doing so well! What happened?
Once I got that high, I just froze.
Maybe climbing isn't the best idea.
WHAT DO YOU THINK, BEN?

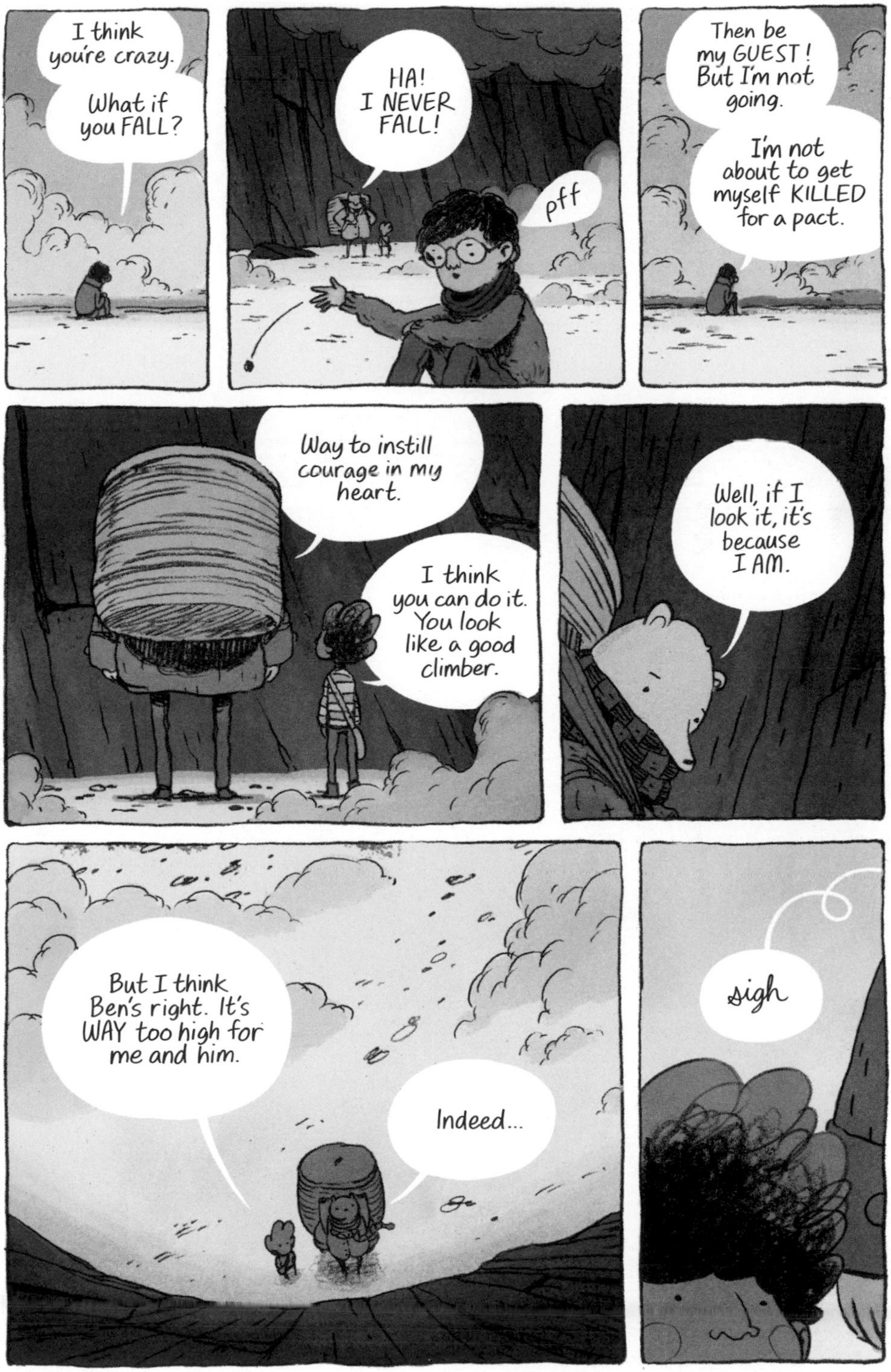

I think you're crazy.
What if you FALL?
HA! I NEVER FALL!
pff
Then be my GUEST! But I'm not going.
I'm not about to get myself KILLED for a pact.
Way to instill courage in my heart.
I think you can do it. You look like a good climber.
Well, if I look it, it's because I AM.
But I think Ben's right. It's WAY too high for me and him.
Indeed...
sigh

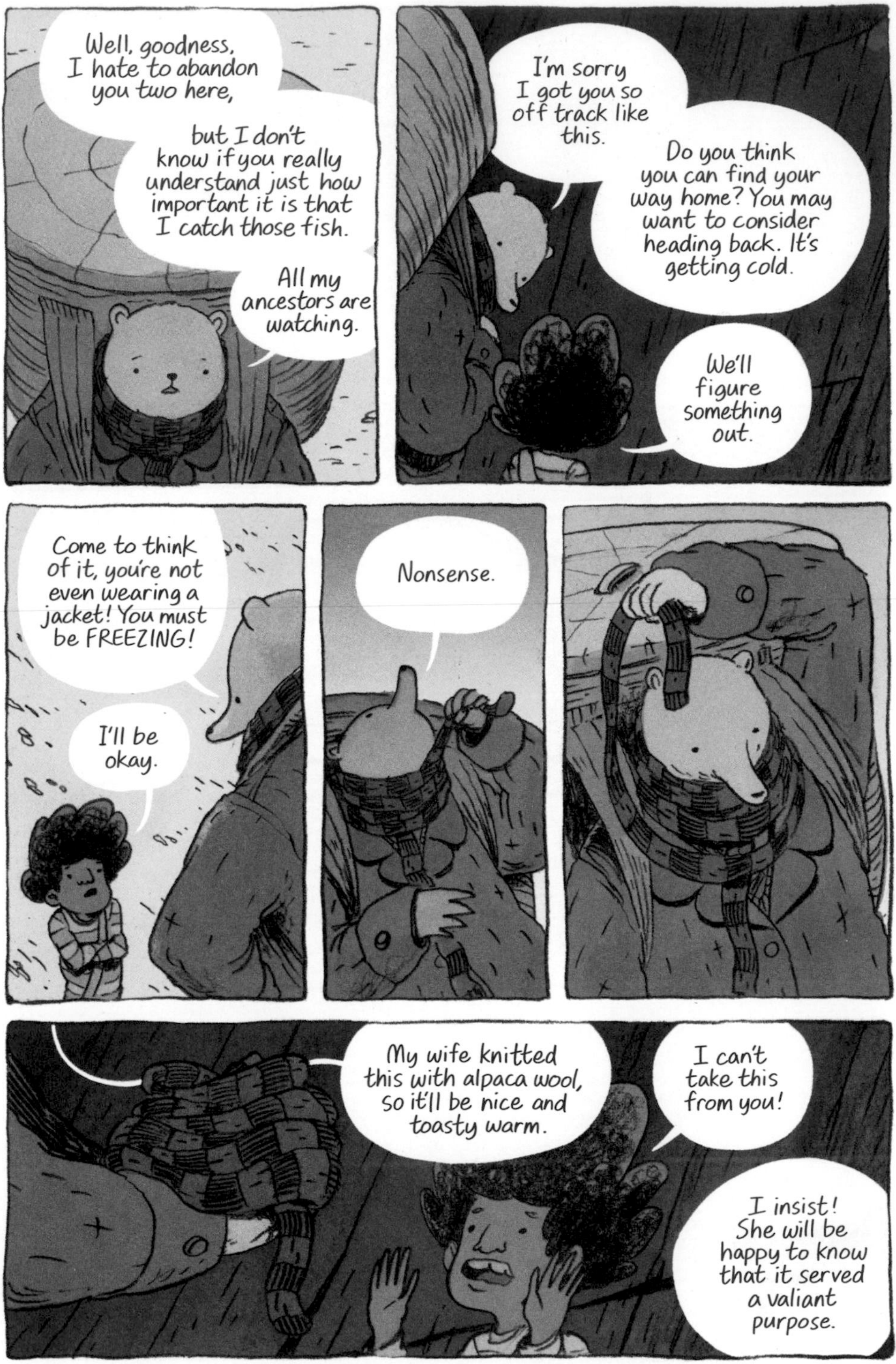
Well, goodness, I hate to abandon you two here,
but I don't know if you really understand just how important it is that I catch those fish.
All my ancestors are watching.
I'm sorry I got you so off track like this.
Do you think you can find your way home? You may want to consider heading back. It's getting cold.
We'll figure something out.
Come to think of it, you're not even wearing a jacket! You must be FREEZING!
I'll be okay.
Nonsense.
My wife knitted this with alpaca wool, so it'll be nice and toasty warm.
I can't take this from you!
I insist! She will be happy to know that it served a valiant purpose.

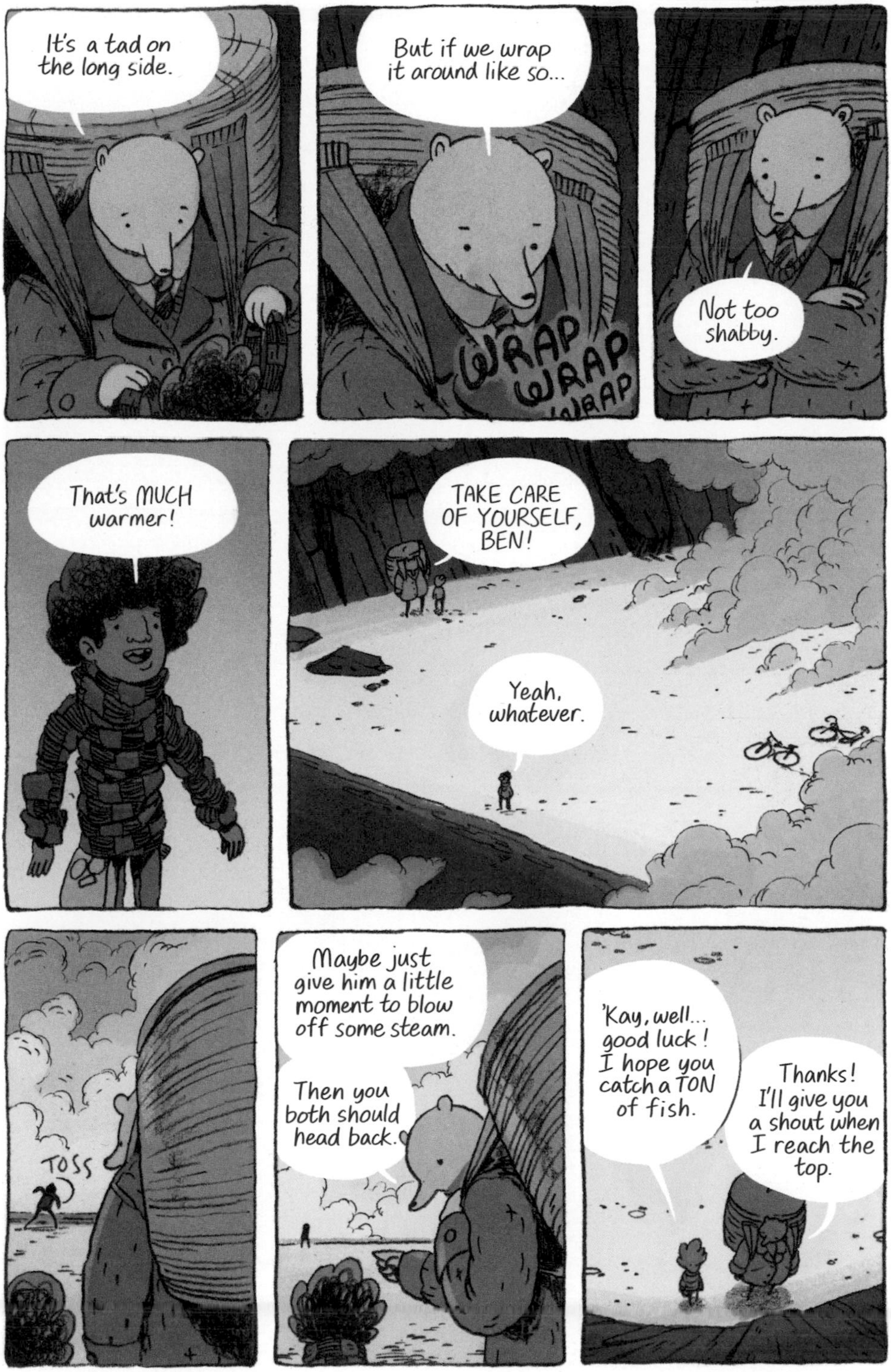
It's a tad on the long side.
But if we wrap it around like so...
WRAP
WRAP
WRAP
Not too shabby.
That's MUCH warmer!
TAKE CARE OF YOURSELF, BEN!
Yeah, whatever.
TOSS
Maybe just give him a little moment to blow off some steam.
Then you both should head back.
'Kay, well... good luck! I hope you catch a TON of fish.
Thanks! I'll give you a shout when I reach the top.

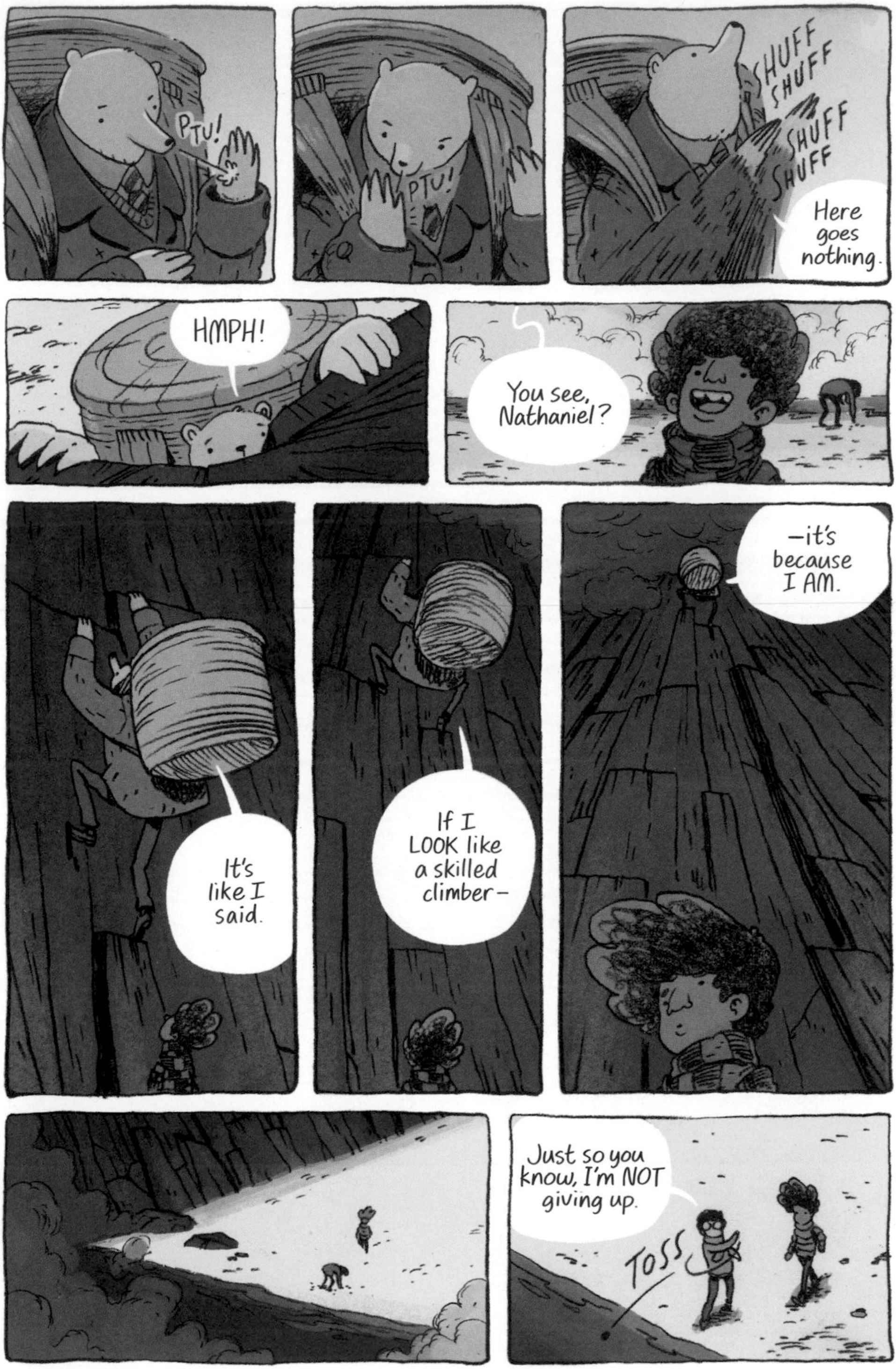
PTU!
PTU!
SHUFF SHUFF
SHUFF SHUFF
Here goes nothing.
HMPH!
You see, Nathaniel?
It's like I said.
If I LOOK like a skilled climber–
–it's because I AM.
Just so you know, I'm NOT giving up.
TOSS

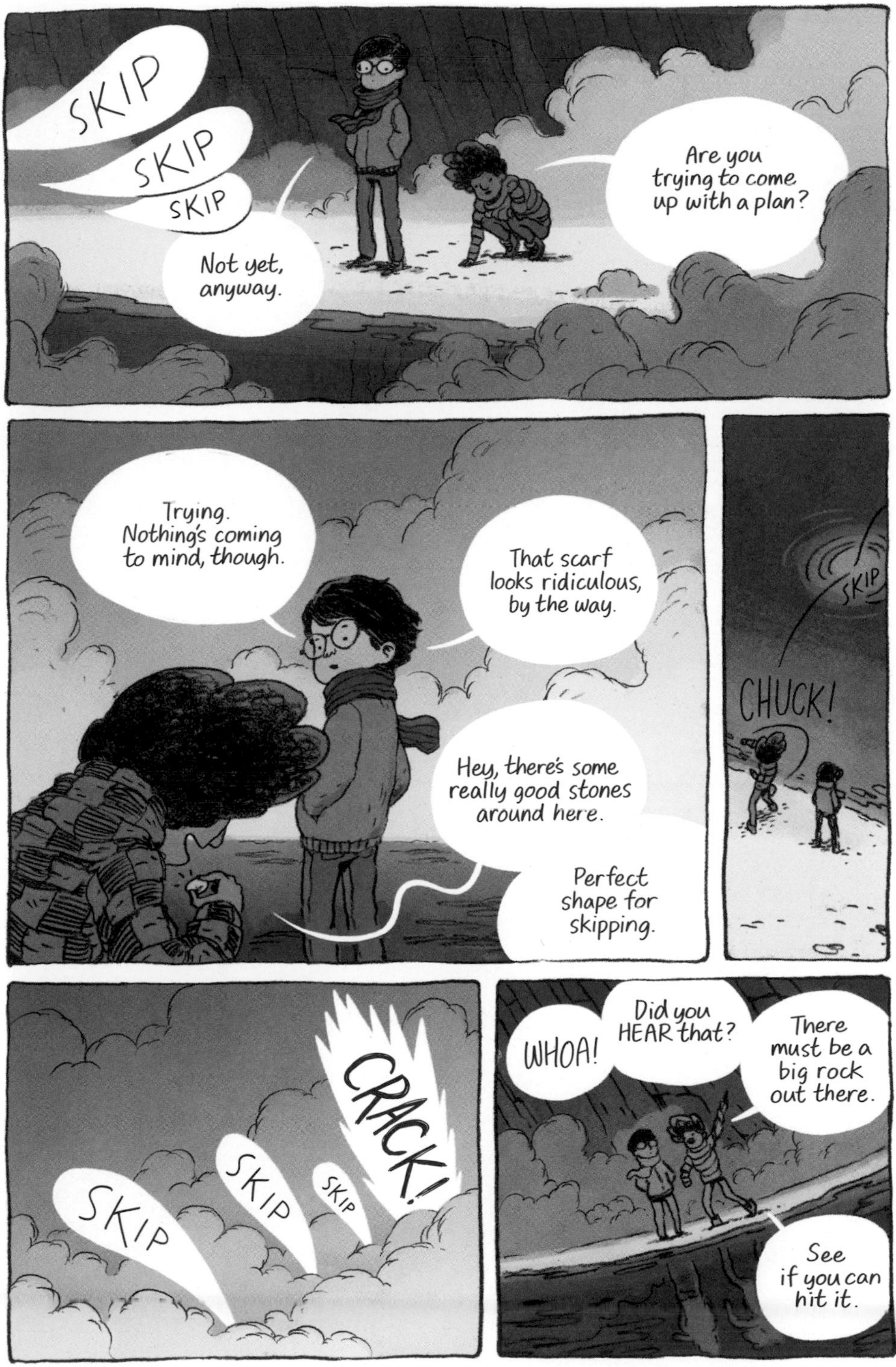
SKIP
SKIP
SKIP
Not yet, anyway.
Are you trying to come up with a plan?
Trying. Nothing's coming to mind, though.
That scarf looks ridiculous, by the way.
Hey, there's some really good stones around here.
Perfect shape for skipping.
CHUCK!
SKIP
SKIP
SKIP
SKIP
CRACK!
WHOA!
Did you HEAR that?
There must be a big rock out there.
See if you can hit it.

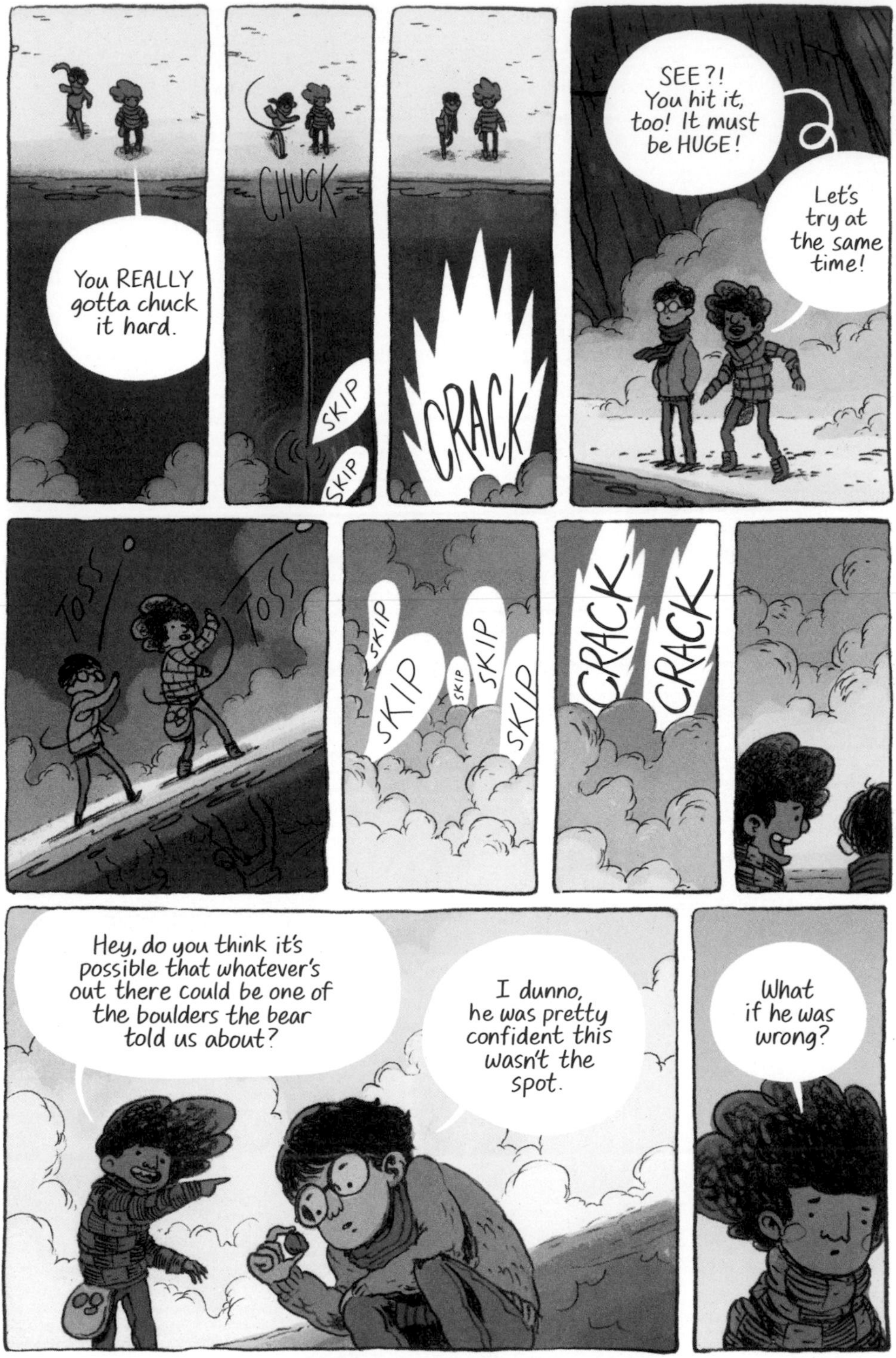
You REALLY gotta chuck it hard.
CHUCK
SKIP
SKIP
CRACK
SEE?! You hit it, too! It must be HUGE!
Let's try at the same time!
TOSS
TOSS
SKIP
SKIP
SKIP
SKIP
SKIP
CRACK
CRACK
Hey, do you think it's possible that whatever's out there could be one of the boulders the bear told us about?
I dunno, he was pretty confident this wasn't the spot.
What if he was wrong?

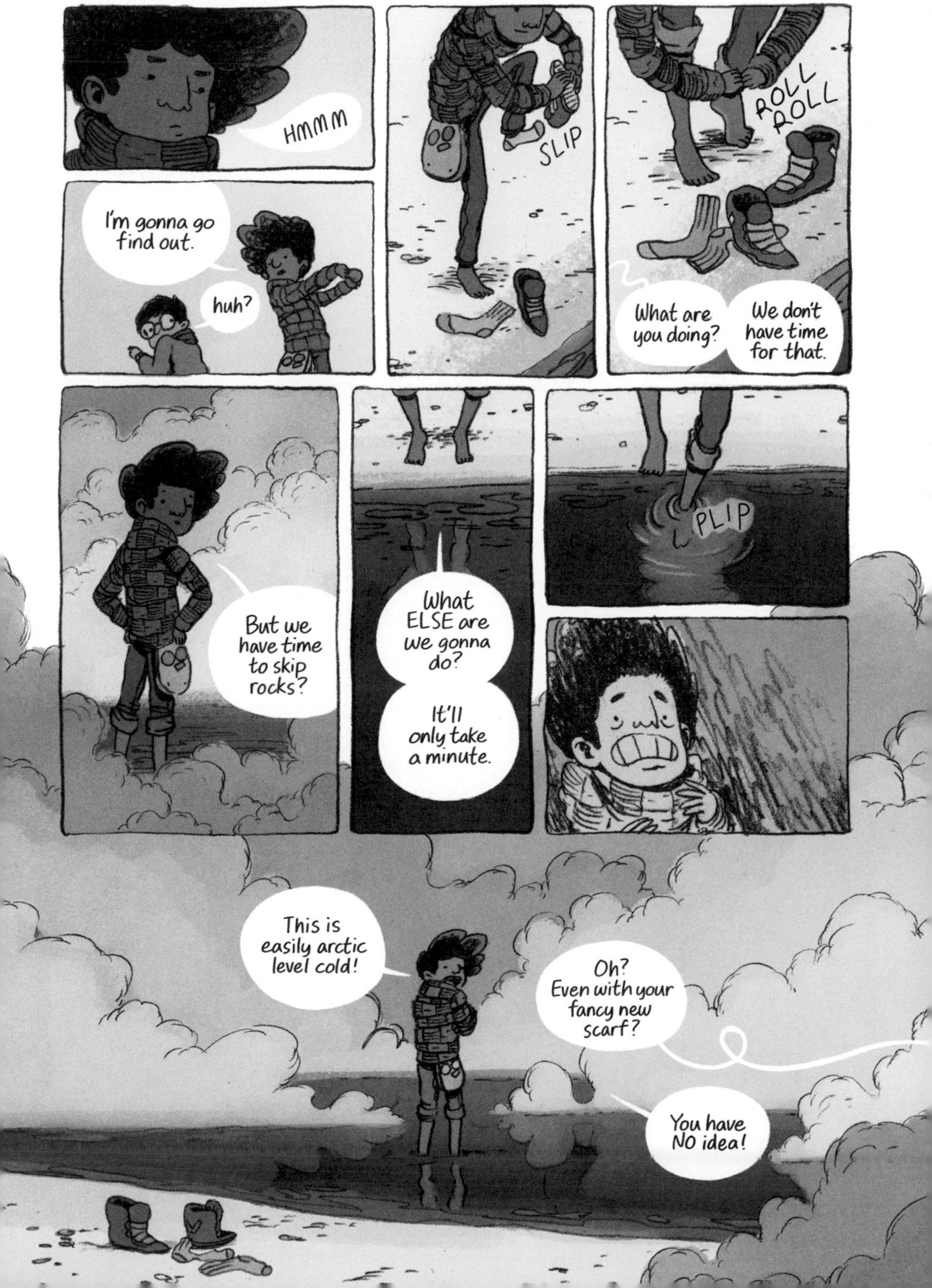
HMMM
SLIP
ROLL ROLL
I'm gonna go find out.
huh?
What are you doing?
We don't have time for that.
But we have time to skip rocks?
What ELSE are we gonna do?
It'll only take a minute.
PLIP
This is easily arctic level cold!
Oh? Even with your fancy new scarf?
You have NO idea!

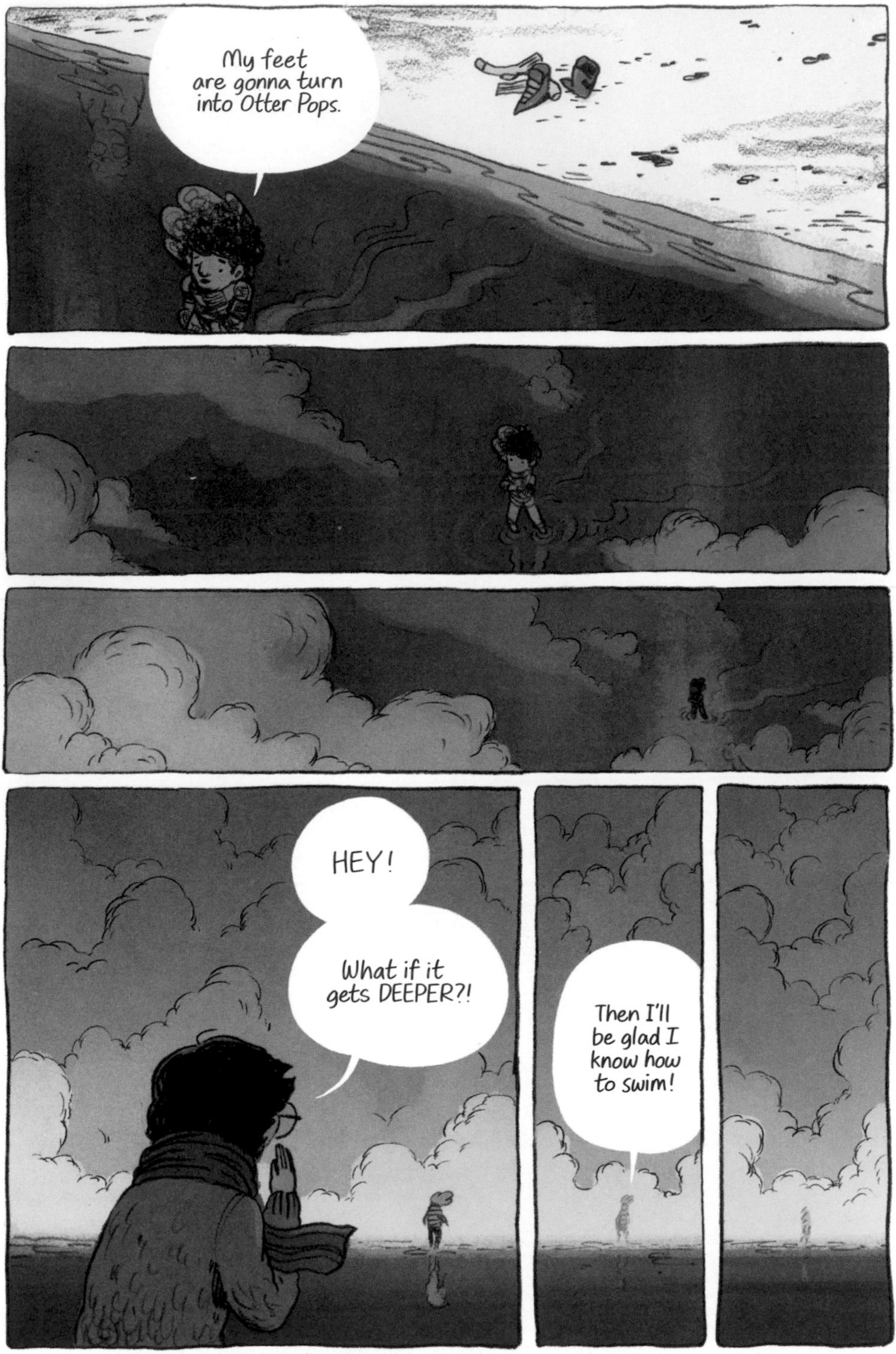
My feet are gonna turn into Otter Pops.
HEY!
What if it gets DEEPER?!
Then I'll be glad I know how to swim!

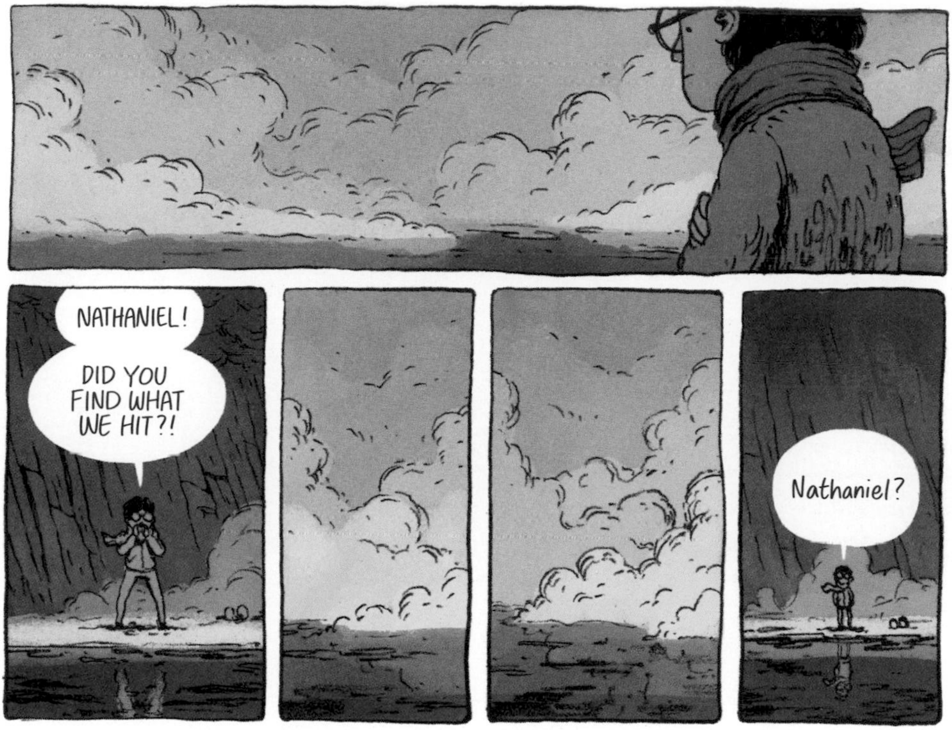
NATHANIEL!
DID YOU FIND WHAT WE HIT?!
Nathaniel?

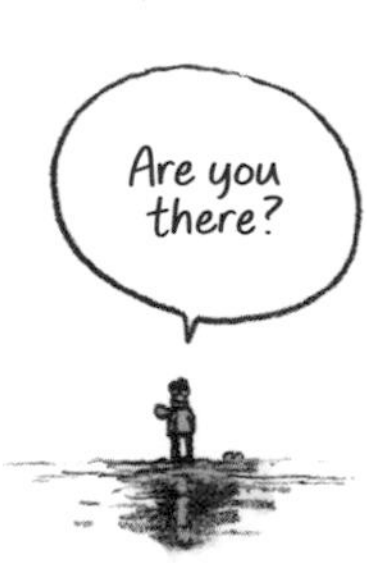
Are you there?

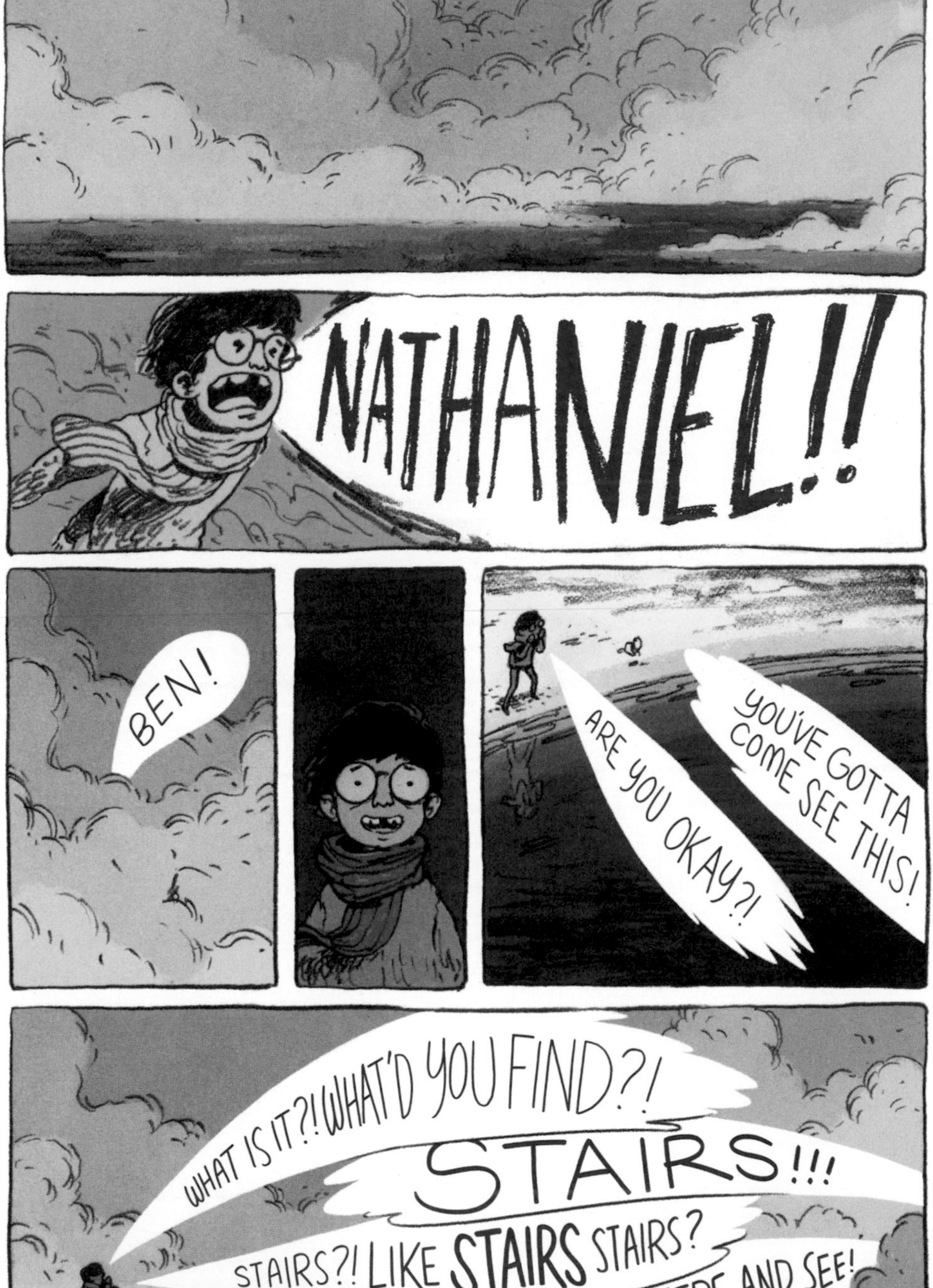
NATHANIEL!!
BEN!
YOU'VE GOTTA COME SEE THIS!
ARE YOU OKAY?!
WHAT IS IT?! WHAT'D YOU FIND?!
STAIRS!!!
STAIRS?! LIKE STAIRS STAIRS?
GET OVER HERE AND SEE!

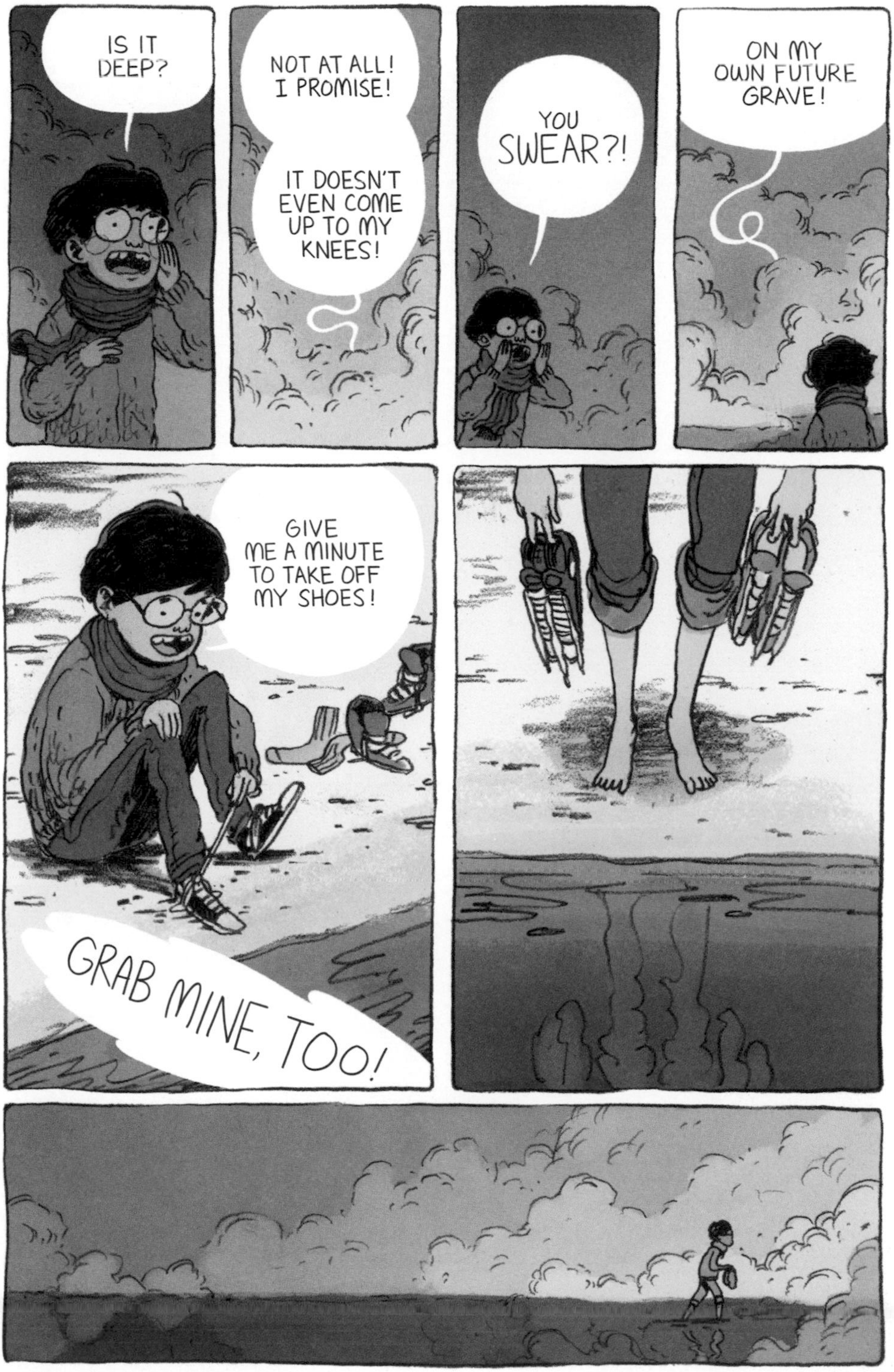
IS IT DEEP?
NOT AT ALL! I PROMISE!
IT DOESN'T EVEN COME UP TO MY KNEES!
YOU SWEAR?!
ON MY OWN FUTURE GRAVE!
GIVE ME A MINUTE TO TAKE OFF MY SHOES!
GRAB MINE, TOO!

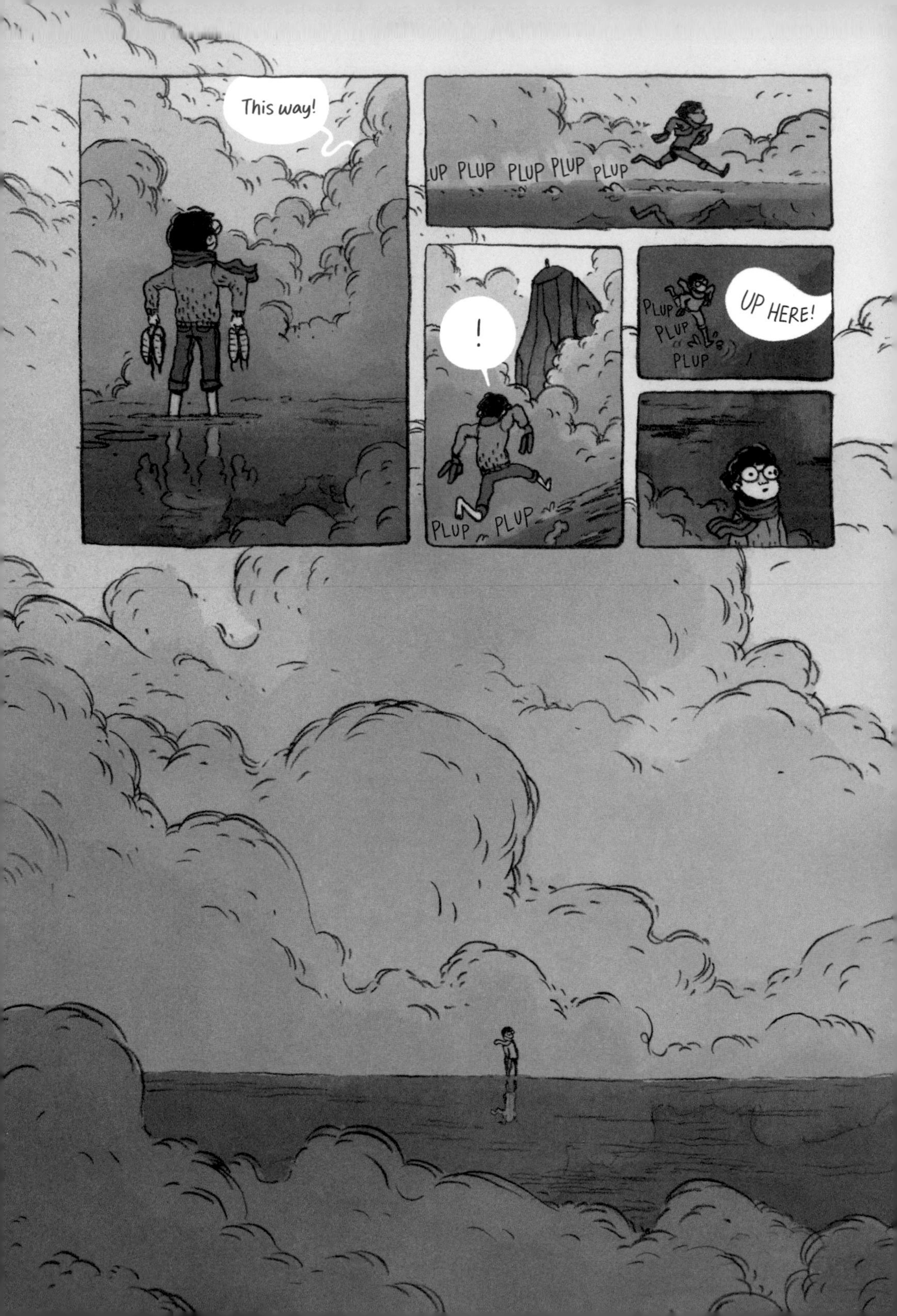
This way!
UP PLUP PLUP PLUP PLUP
!
PLUP PLUP
PLUP PLUP PLUP
UP HERE!

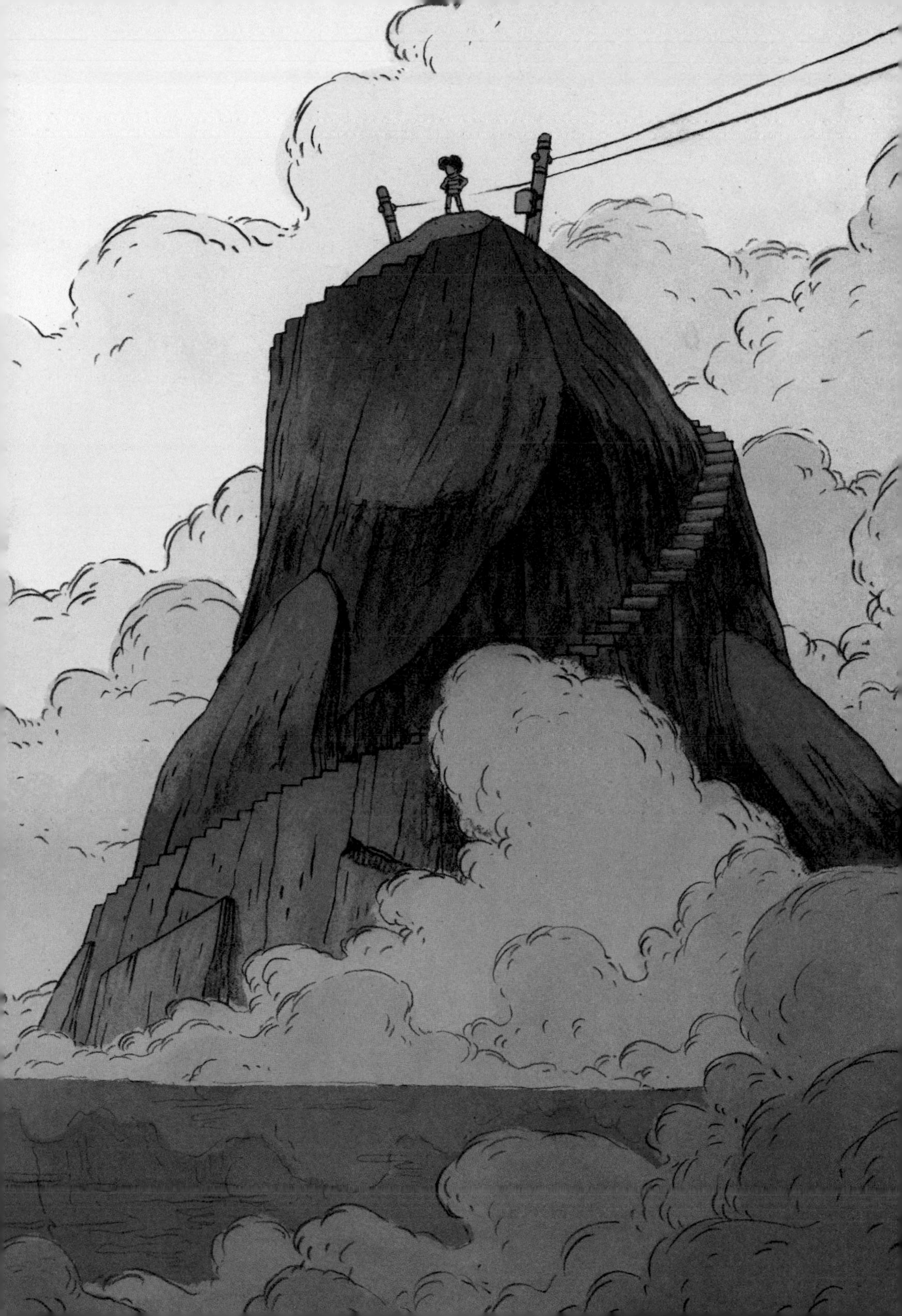

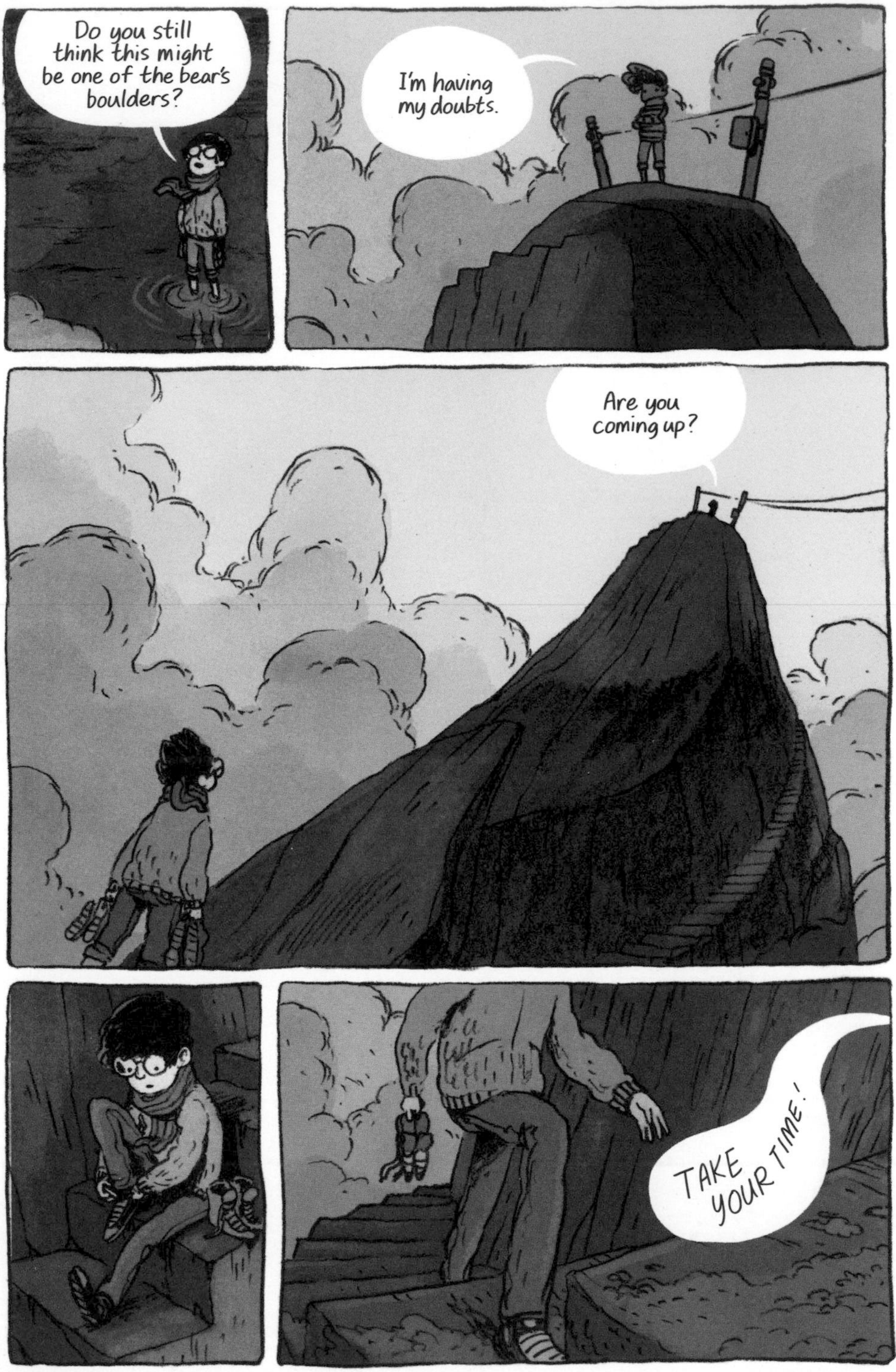
Do you still think this might be one of the bear's boulders?
I'm having my doubts.
Are you coming up?
TAKE YOUR TIME!

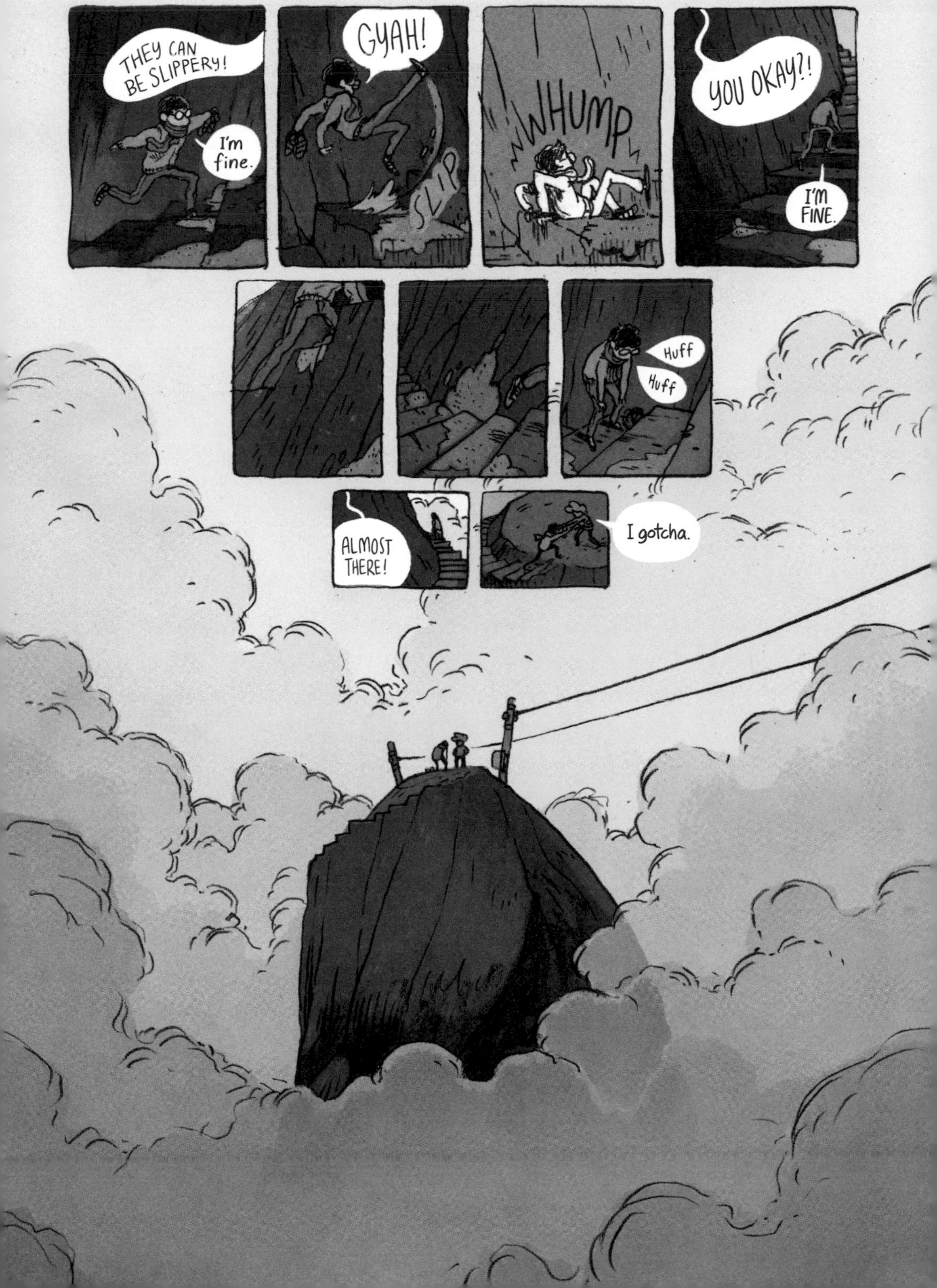
THEY CAN BE SLIPPERY!
I'm fine.
GYAH!
SLIP
WHUMP
YOU OKAY?!
I'M FINE.
Huff
Huff
ALMOST THERE!
I gotcha.

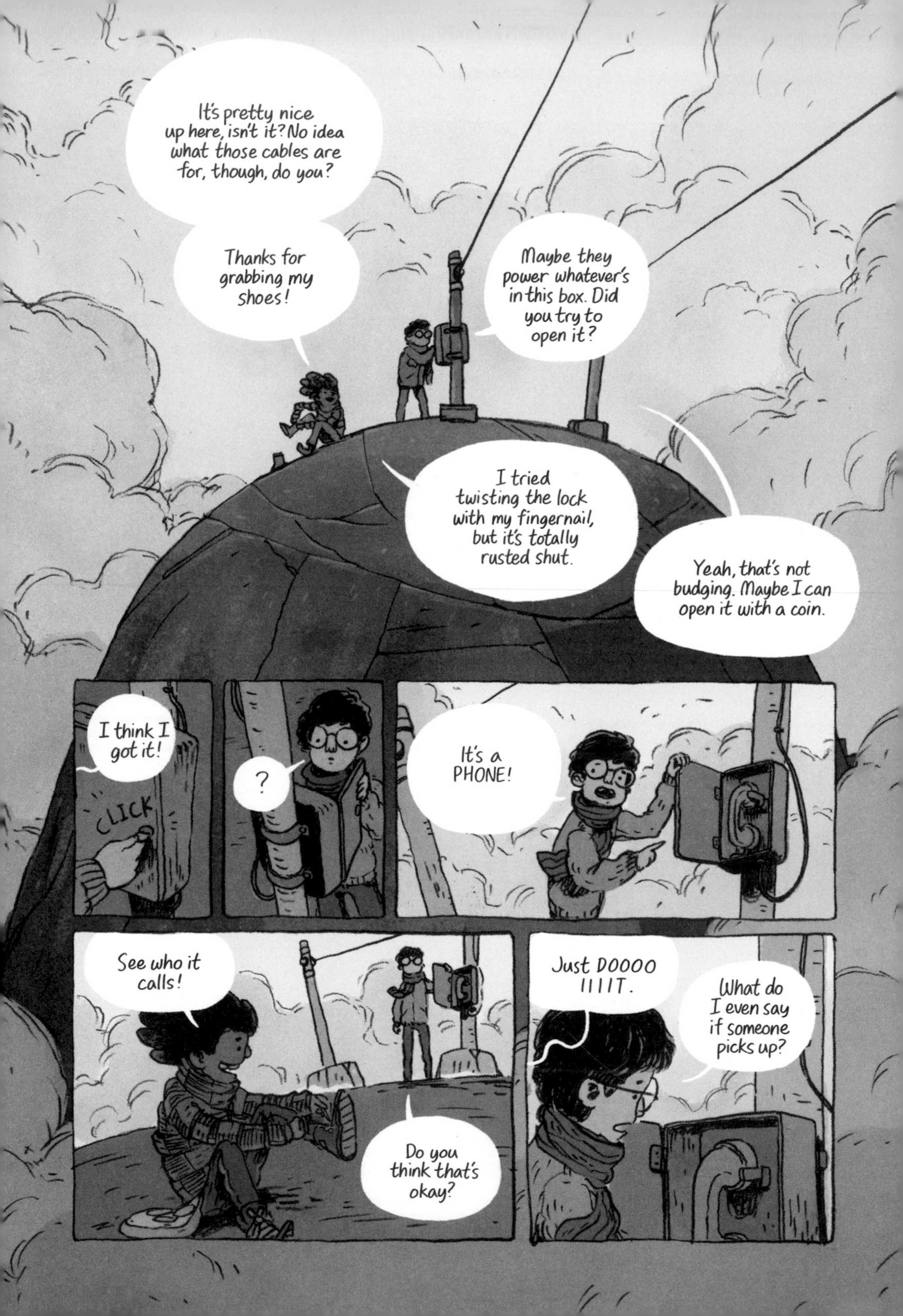
It's pretty nice up here, isn't it? No idea what those cables are for, though, do you?
Thanks for grabbing my shoes!
Maybe they power whatever's in this box. Did you try to open it?
I tried twisting the lock with my fingernail, but it's totally rusted shut.
Yeah, that's not budging. Maybe I can open it with a coin.
I think I got it!
CLICK
?
It's a PHONE!
See who it calls!
Do you think that's okay?
Just DOOOO IIIIT.
What do I even say if someone picks up?

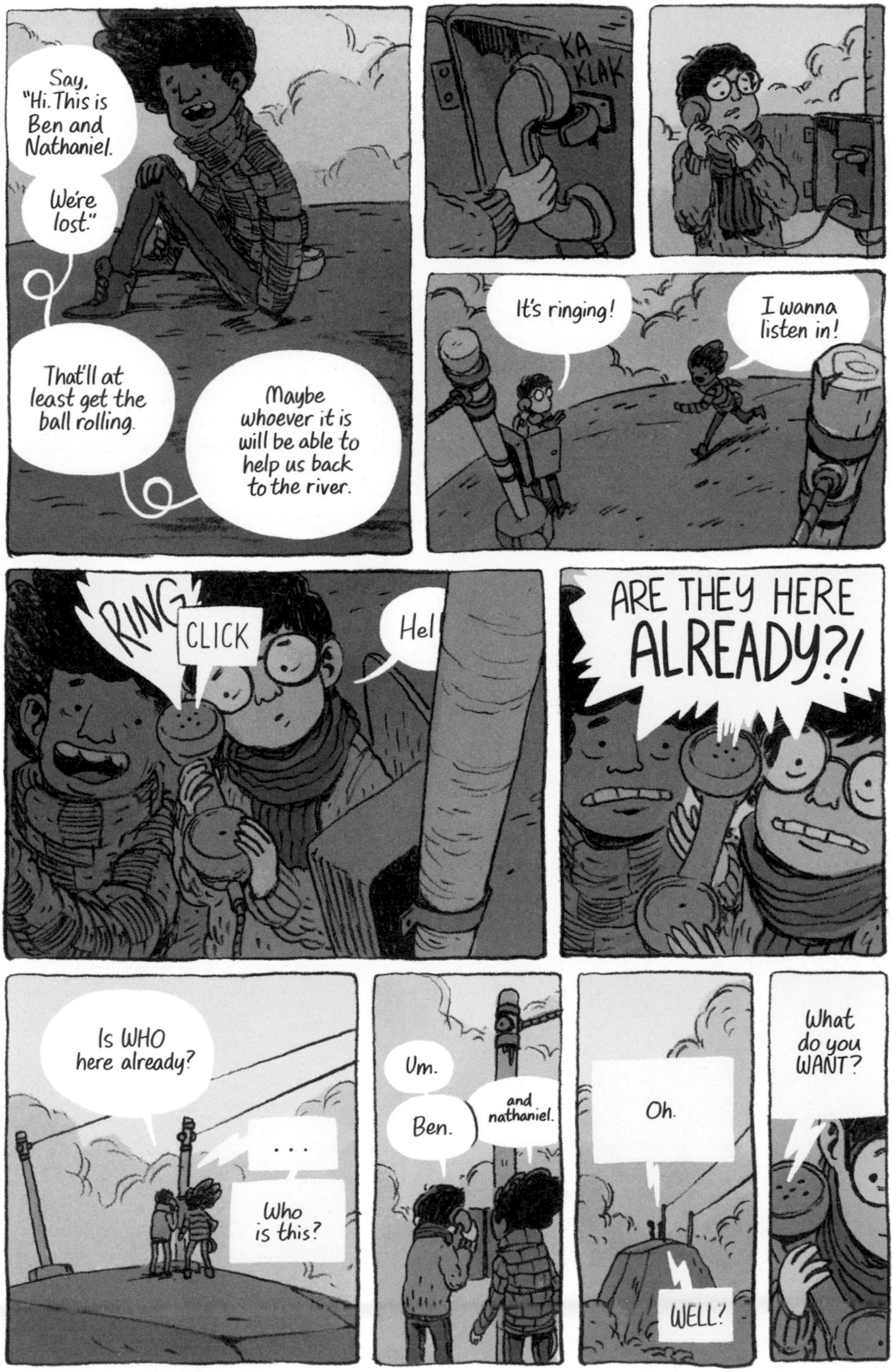
Say, "Hi. This is Ben and Nathaniel.
We're lost."
That'll at least get the ball rolling.
Maybe whoever it is will be able to help us back to the river.
KA KLAK
It's ringing!
I wanna listen in!
RING
CLICK
Hel
ARE THEY HERE ALREADY?!
Is WHO here already?
. . .
Who is this?
Um.
Ben.
and nathaniel.
Oh.
WELL?
What do you WANT?

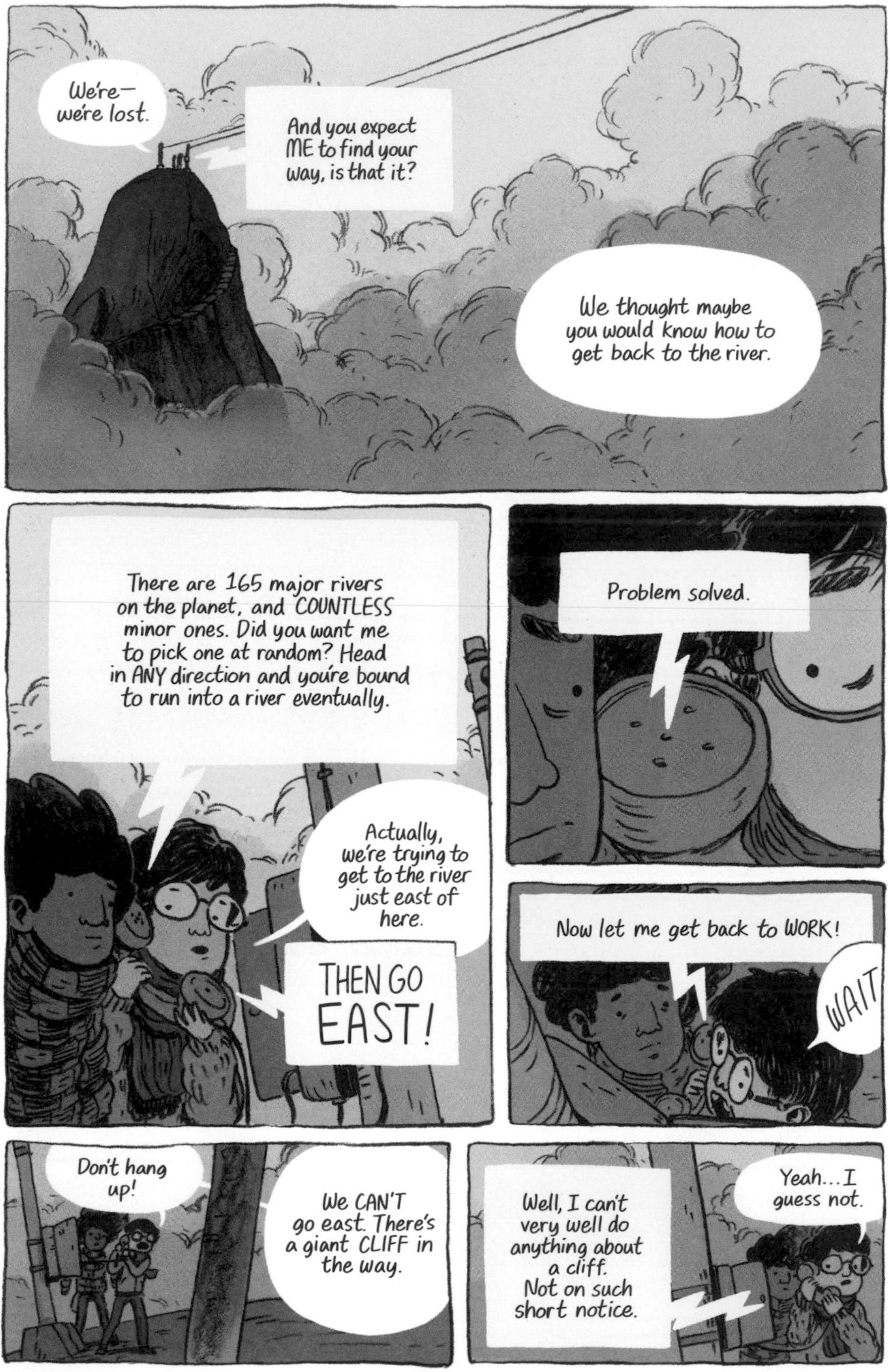

We're—
we're lost.
And you expect ME to find your way, is that it?
We thought maybe you would know how to get back to the river.
There are 165 major rivers on the planet, and COUNTLESS minor ones. Did you want me to pick one at random? Head in ANY direction and you're bound to run into a river eventually.
Actually, we're trying to get to the river just east of here.
THEN GO EAST!
Problem solved.
Now let me get back to WORK!
WAIT
Don't hang up!
We CAN'T go east. There's a giant CLIFF in the way.
Well, I can't very well do anything about a cliff. Not on such short notice.
Yeah... I guess not.

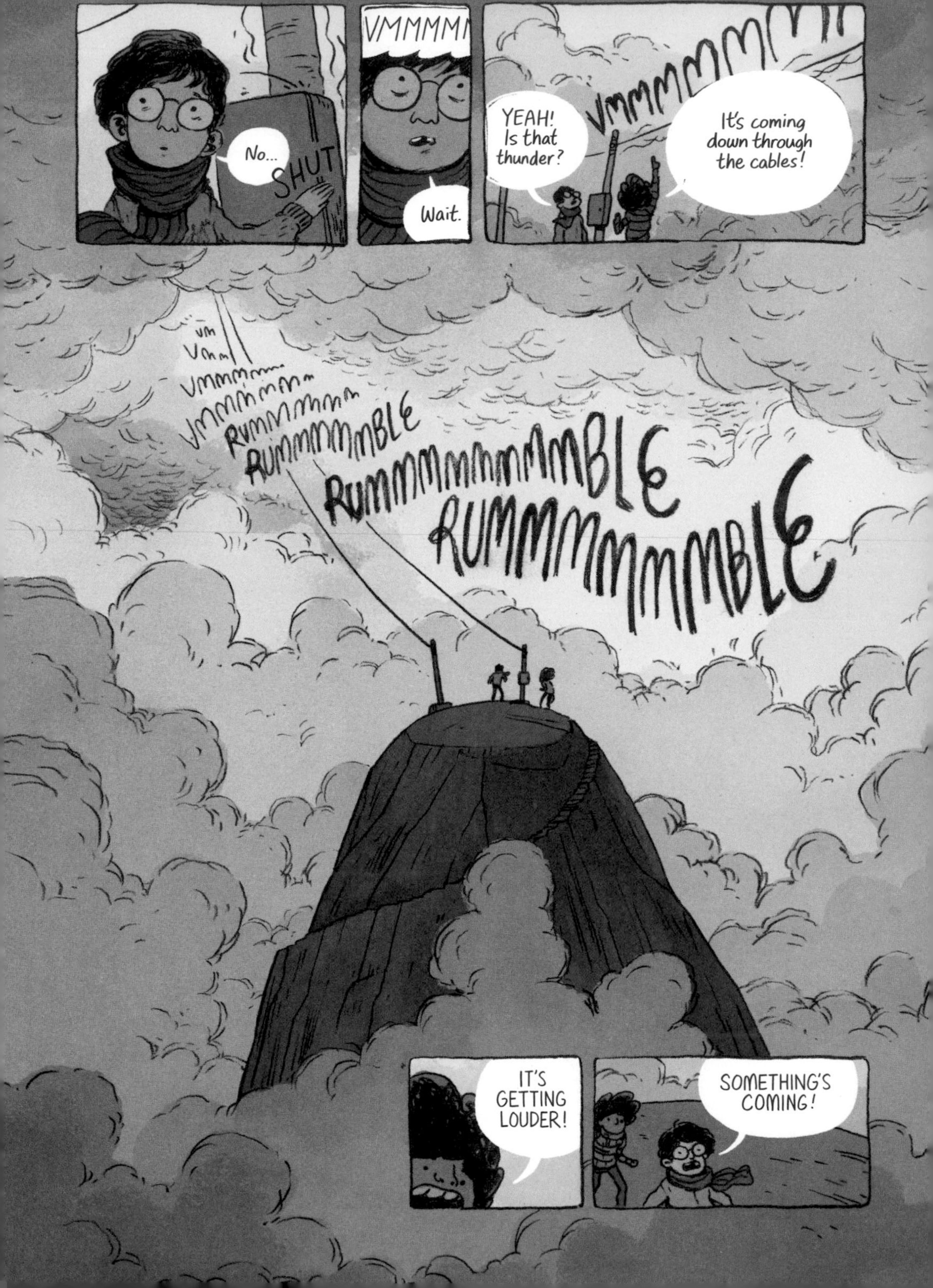
No...
SHUT
VMMMMM
Wait.
YEAH! Is that thunder?
VMMMMMMMM
It's coming down through the cables!
vm
Vmm
VMMMmmm
VMMMMMM
VMMMMMMM
RUMMMMMMM
RUMMMMMMBLE
RUMMMMMMMMMBLE
RUMMMMMMMBLE
IT'S GETTING LOUDER!
SOMETHING'S COMING!

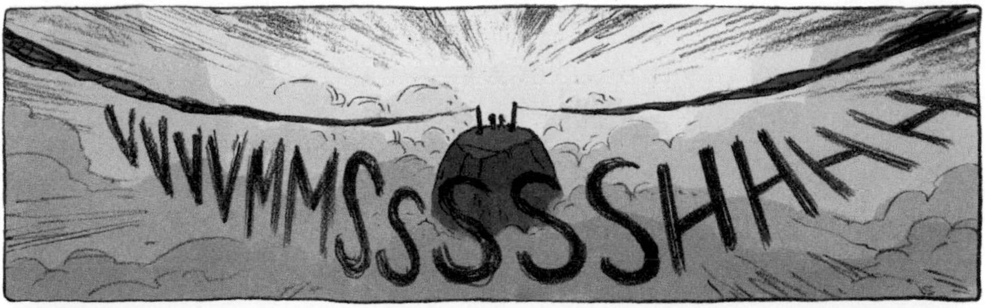
VVVVMMSSSSSHHHHH

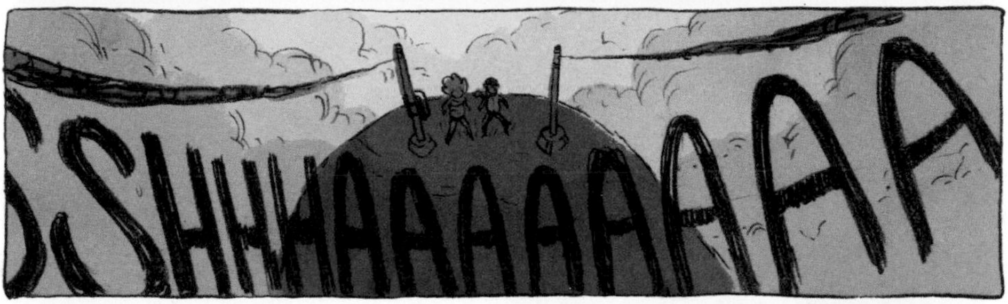
SHHHAAAAAAAAA

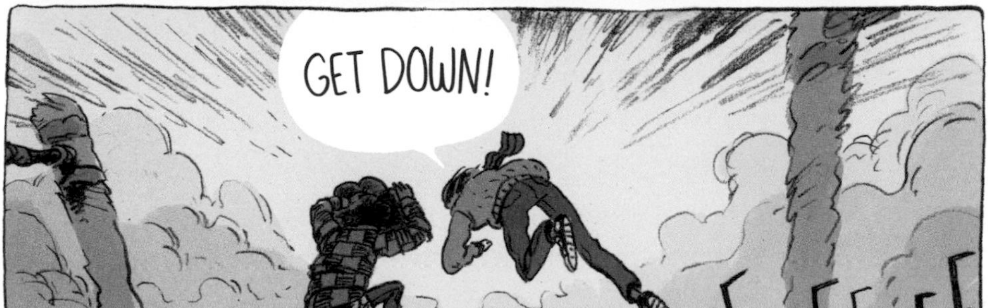
GET DOWN!
SKEEEEEEEEE

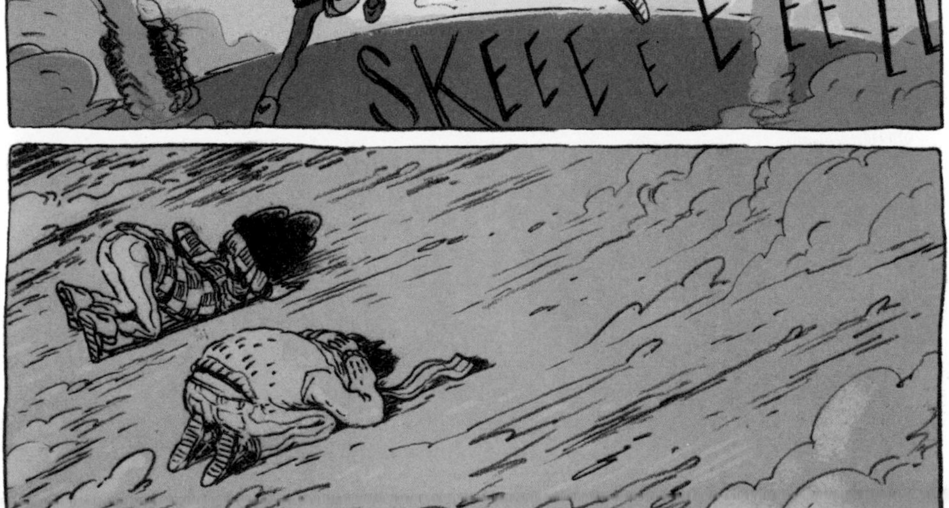

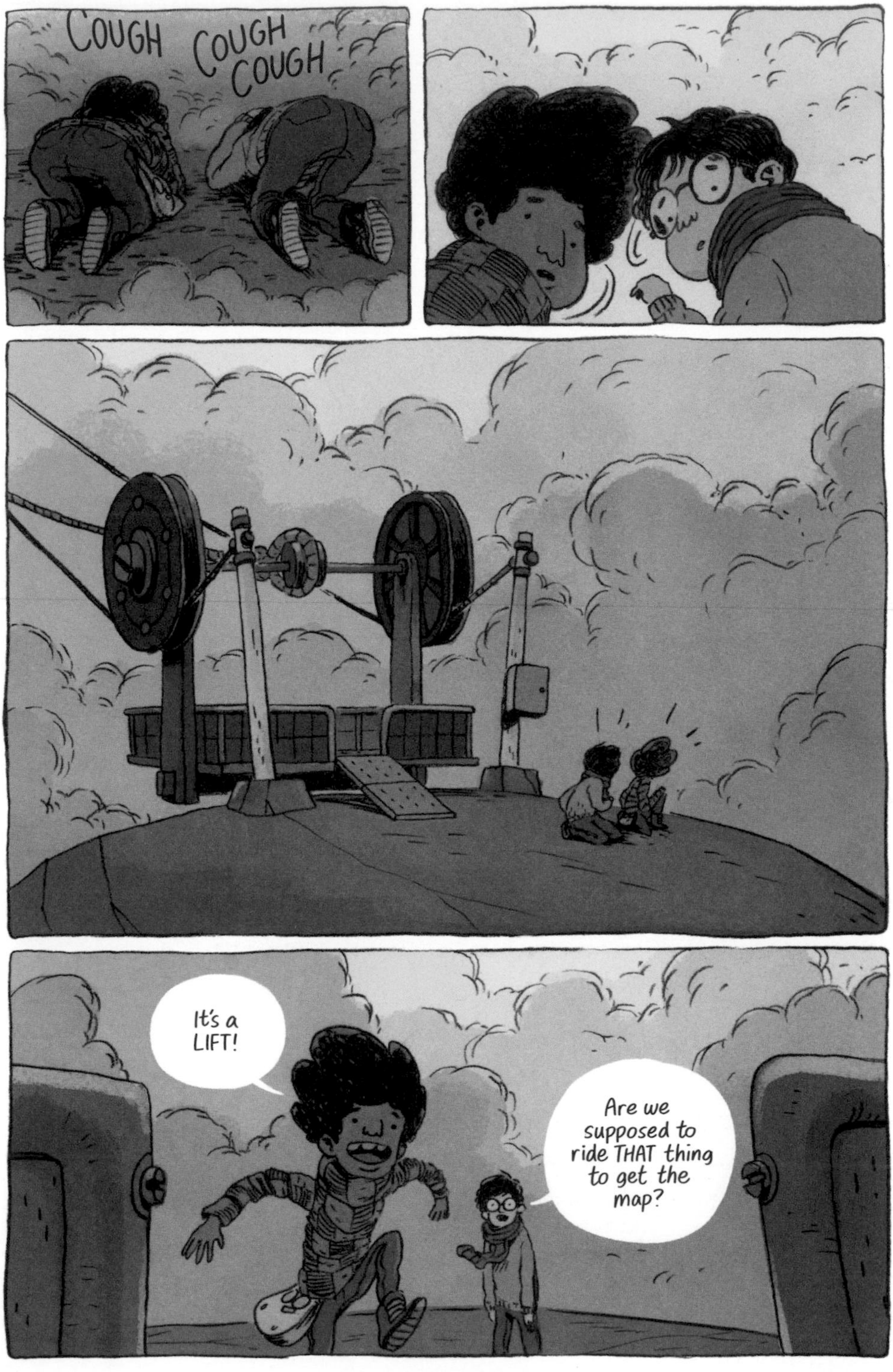
COUGH
COUGH
COUGH
It's a LIFT!
Are we supposed to ride THAT thing to get the map?

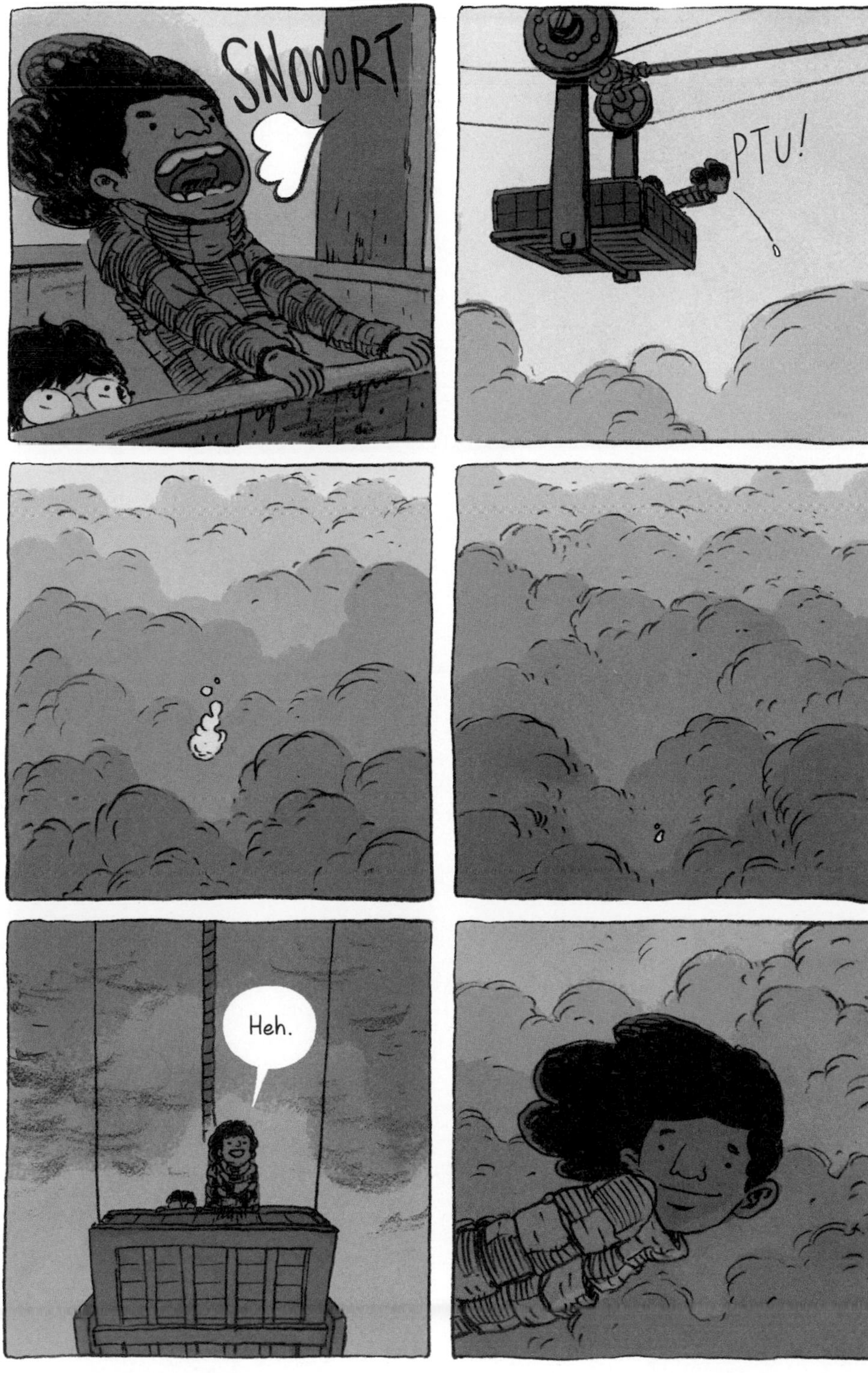
SNOOORT
PTU!
Heh.

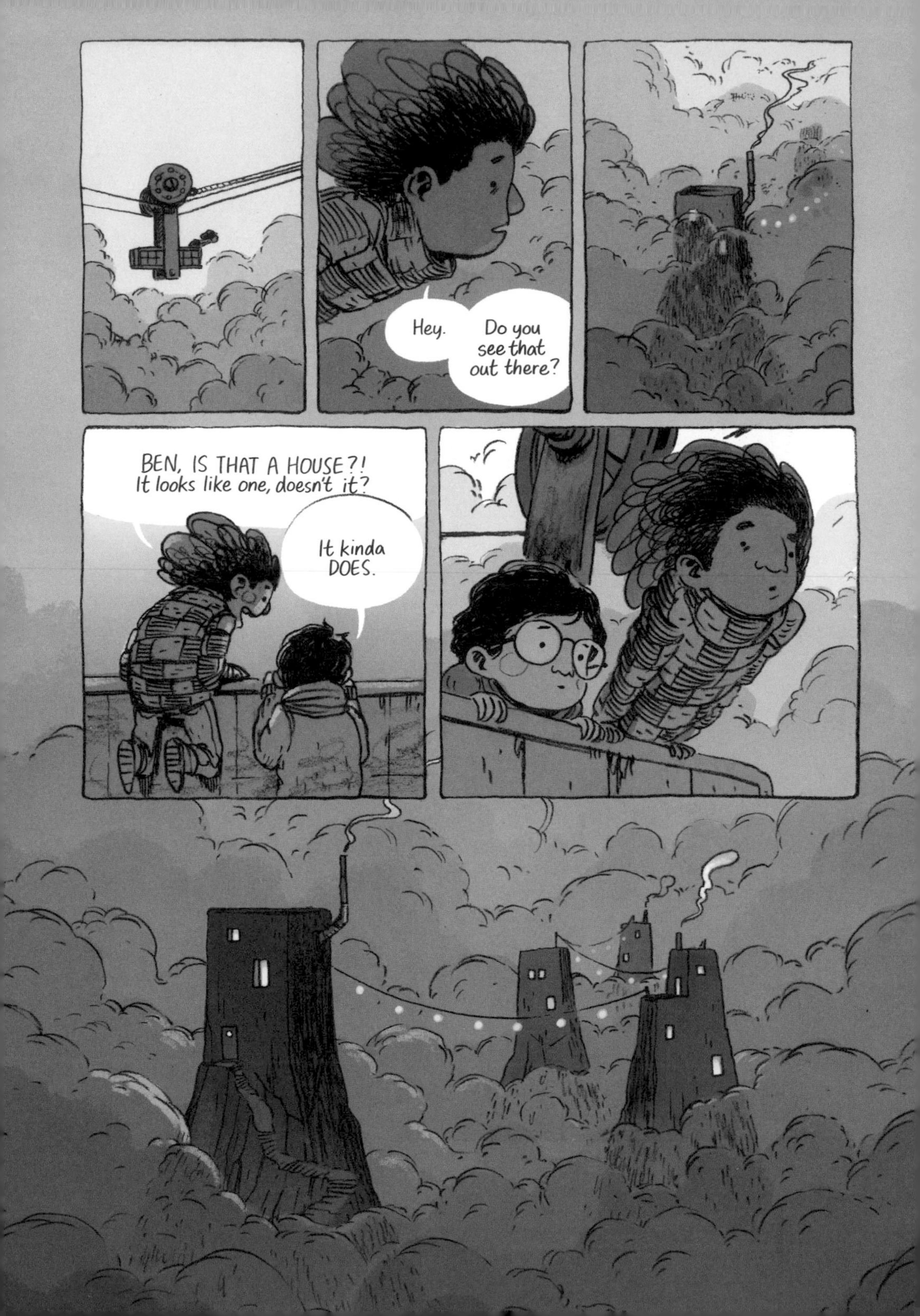
Hey.
Do you see that out there?
BEN, IS THAT A HOUSE?!
It looks like one, doesn't it?
It kinda DOES.

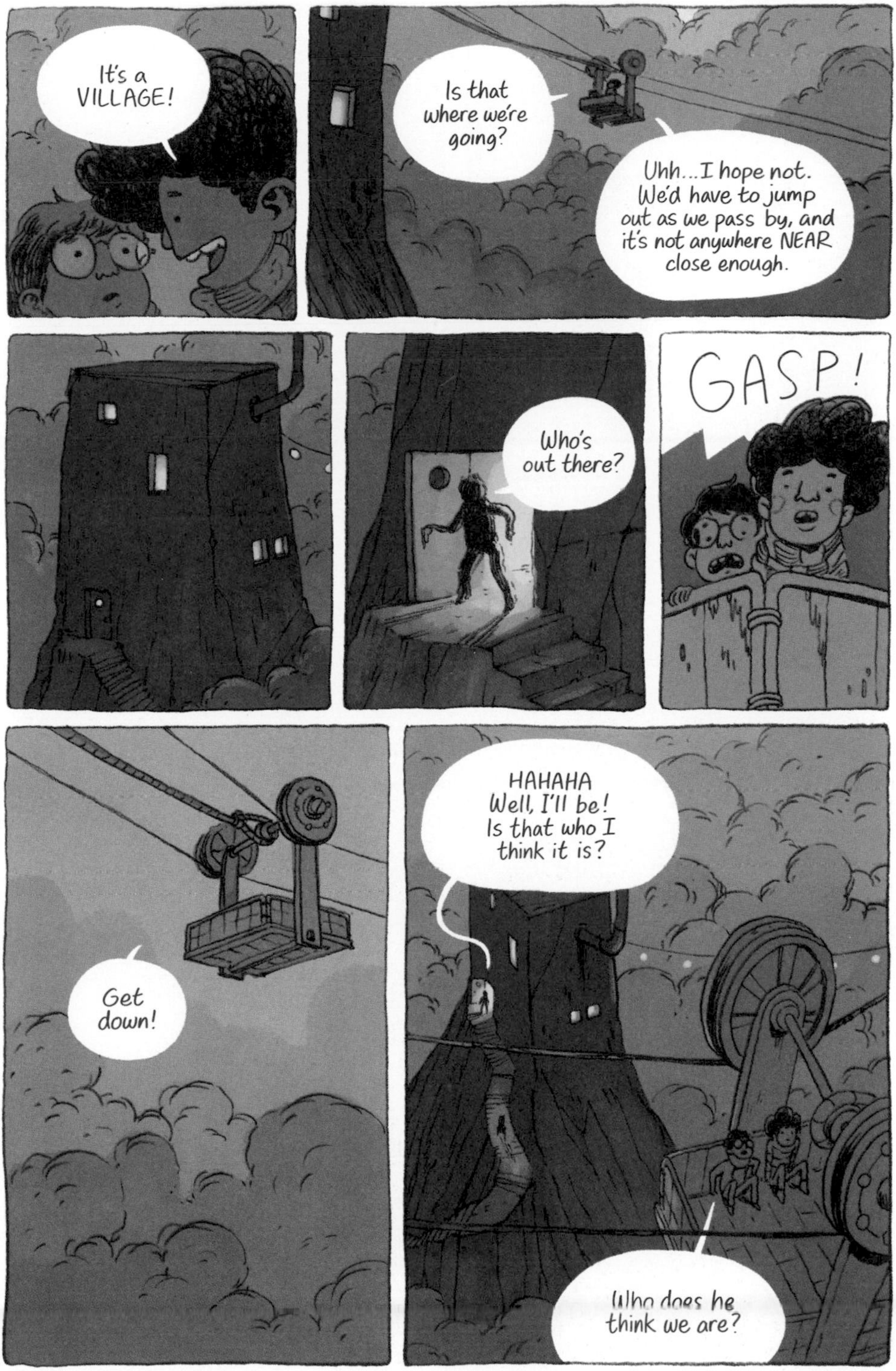
It's a VILLAGE!
Is that where we're going?
Uhh...I hope not. We'd have to jump out as we pass by, and it's not anywhere NEAR close enough.
Who's out there?
GASP!
Get down!
HAHAHA Well, I'll be! Is that who I think it is?
Who does he think we are?

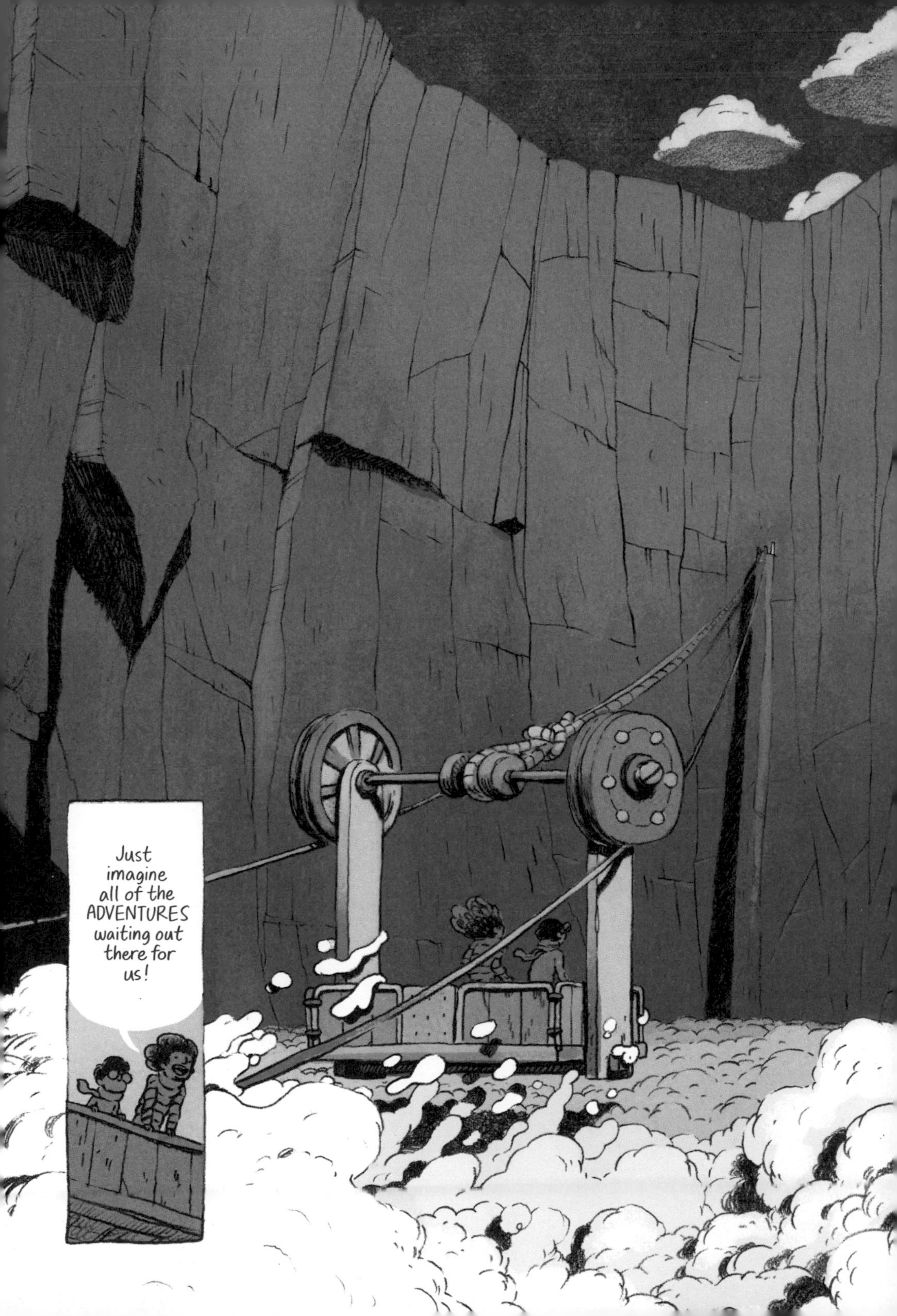
Just imagine all of the ADVENTURES waiting out there for us!

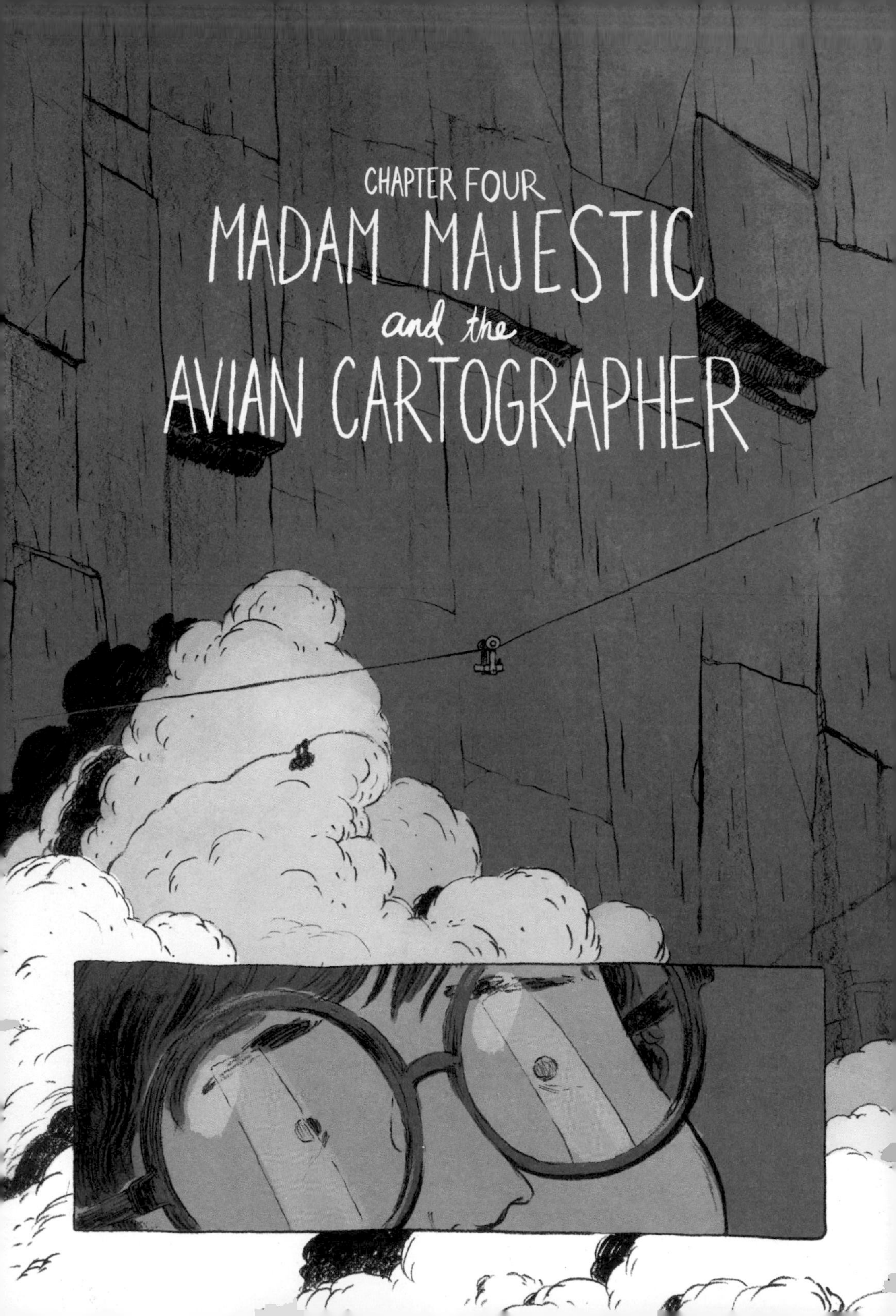

CHAPTER FOUR
MADAM MAJESTIC
and the
AVIAN CARTOGRAPHER

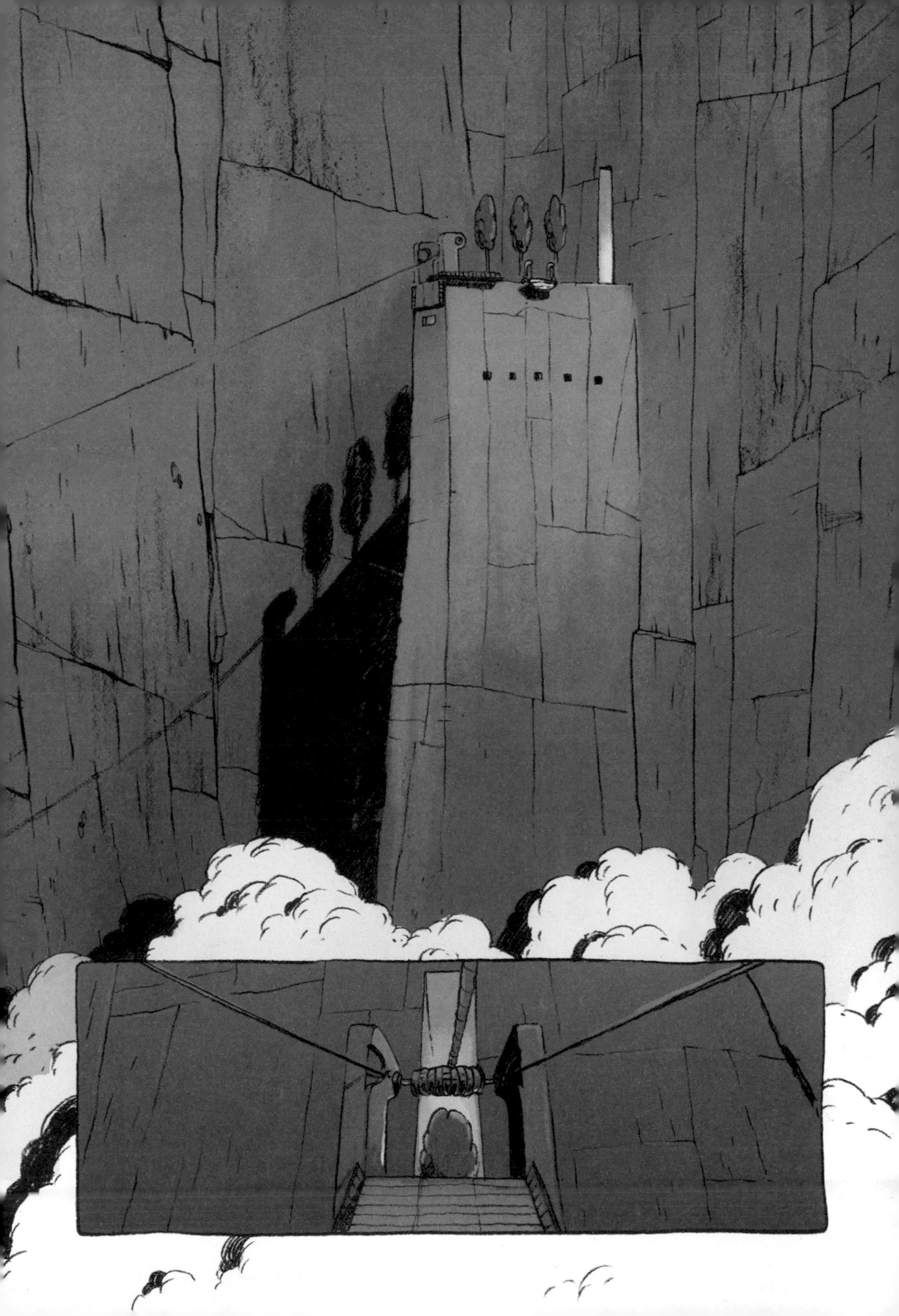

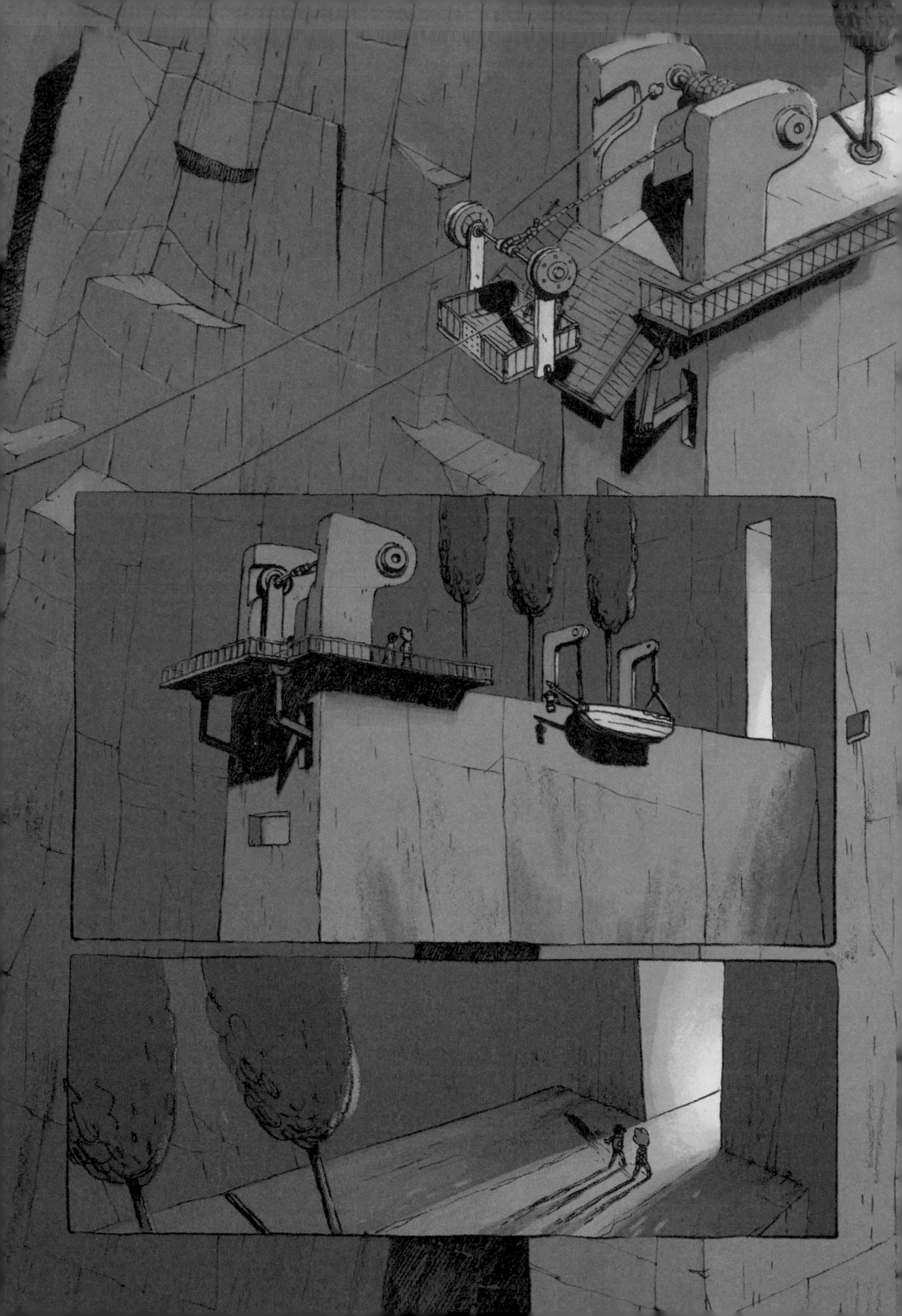

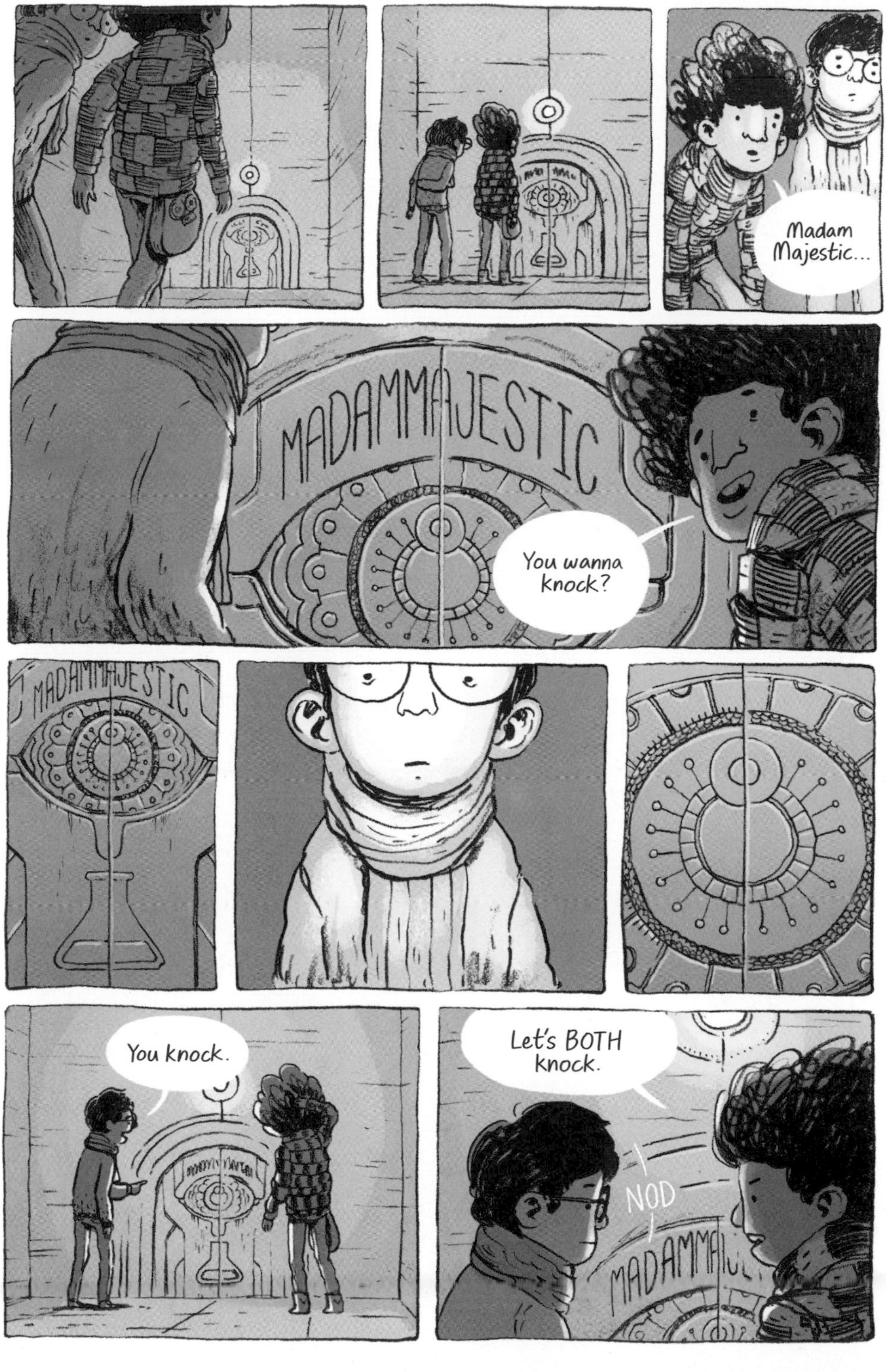
Madam Majestic...
MADAMMAJESTIC
You wanna knock?
MADAMMAJESTIC
You knock.
Let's BOTH knock.
NOD

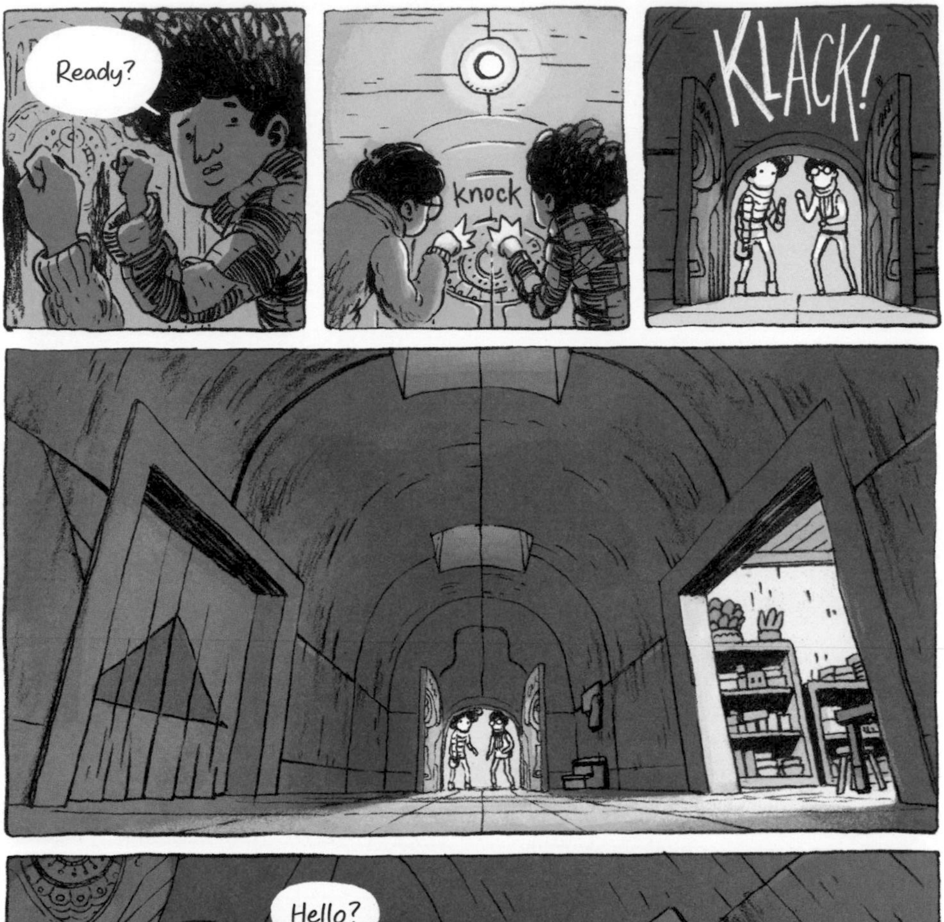
Ready?
knock
KLACK!
Hello?
MAGAMMA
KLAK
Anybody in here?

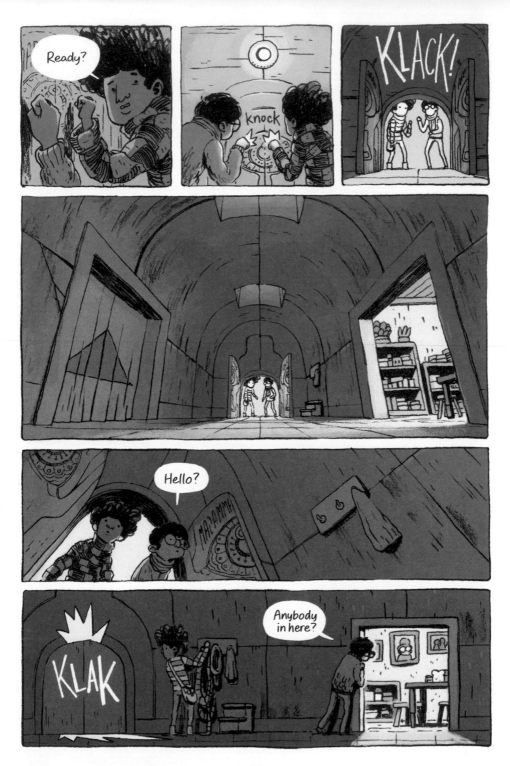

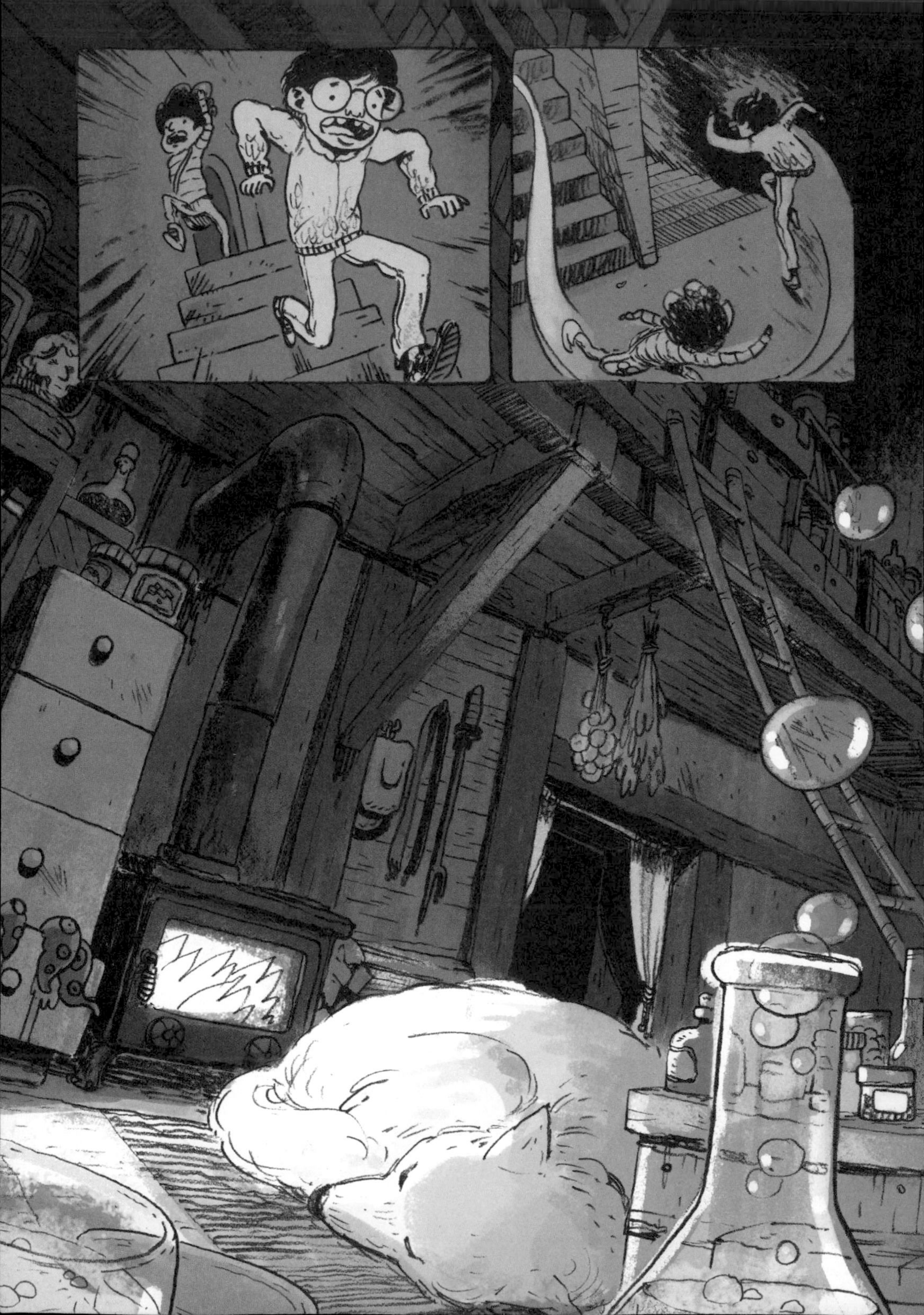

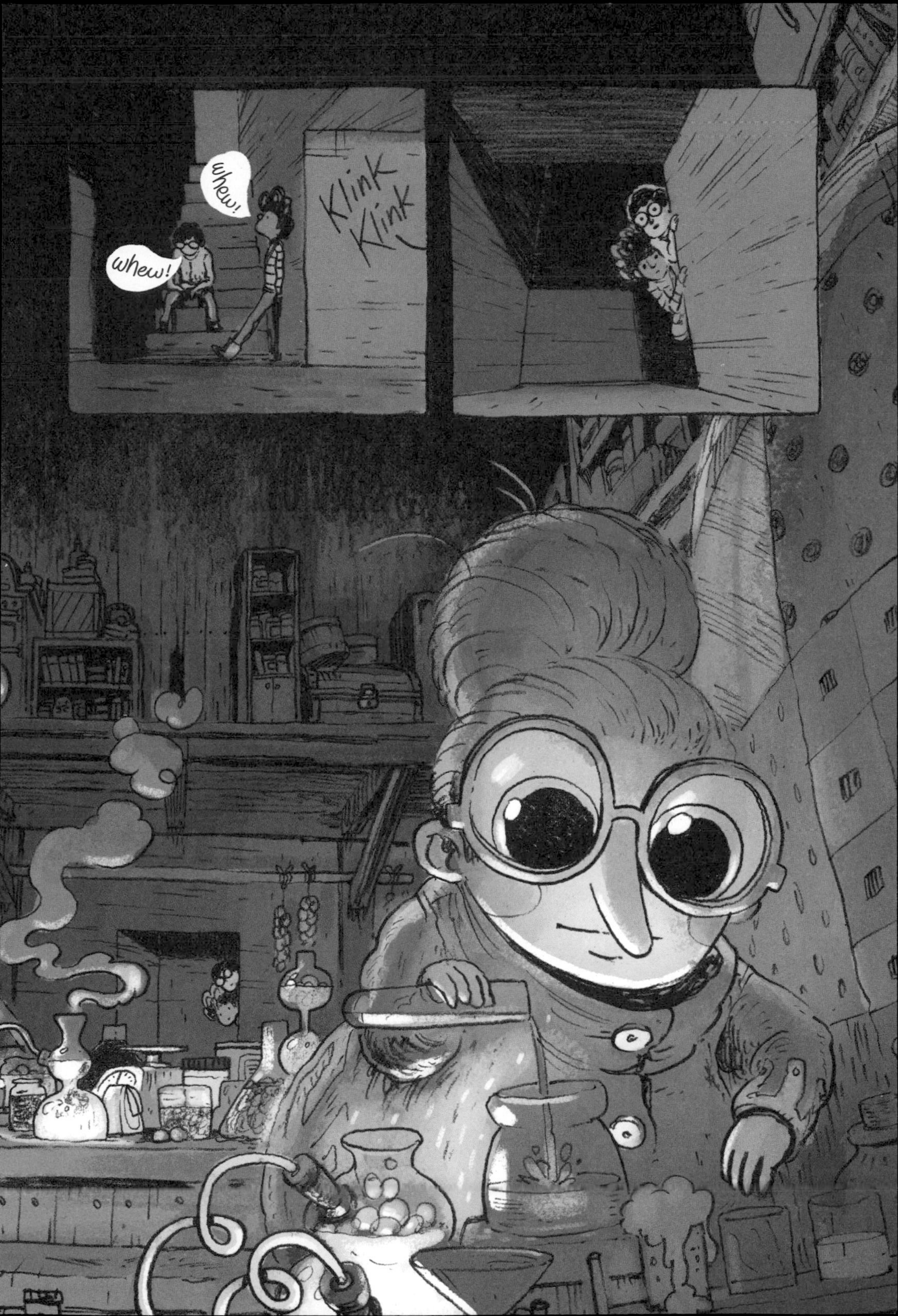
whew!
whew!
Klink
Klink

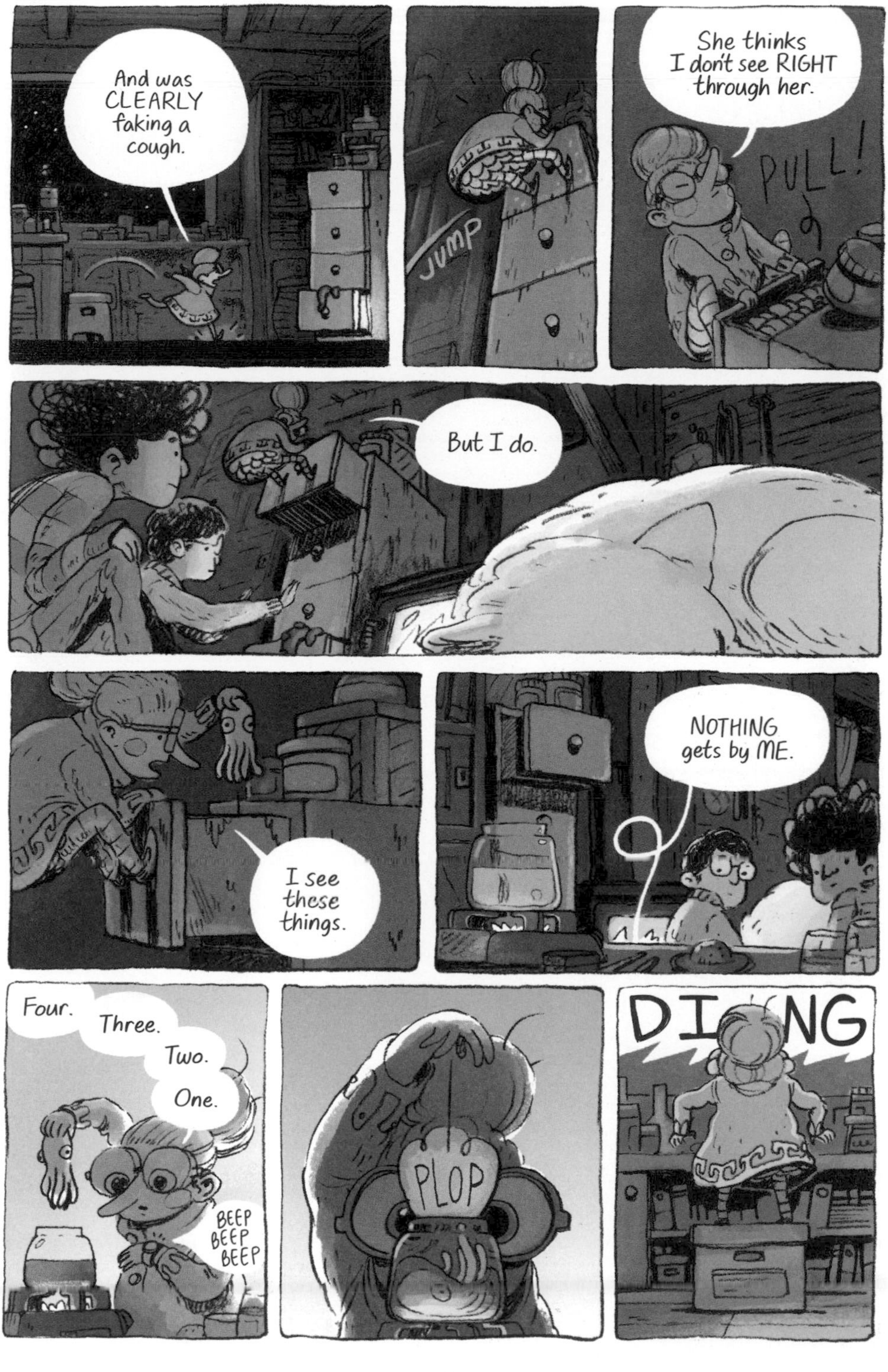
And was CLEARLY faking a cough.
JUMP
She thinks I don't see RIGHT through her.
PULL!
But I do.
I see these things.
NOTHING gets by ME.
Four.
Three.
Two.
One.
BEEP BEEP BEEP
PLOP
DING

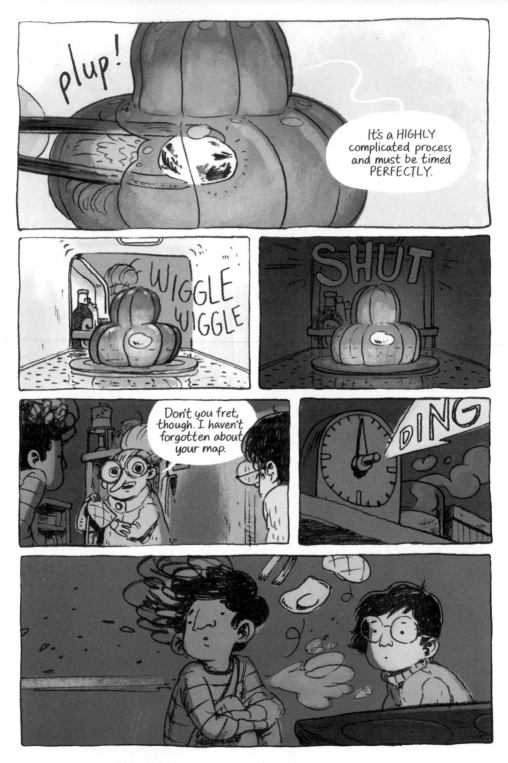

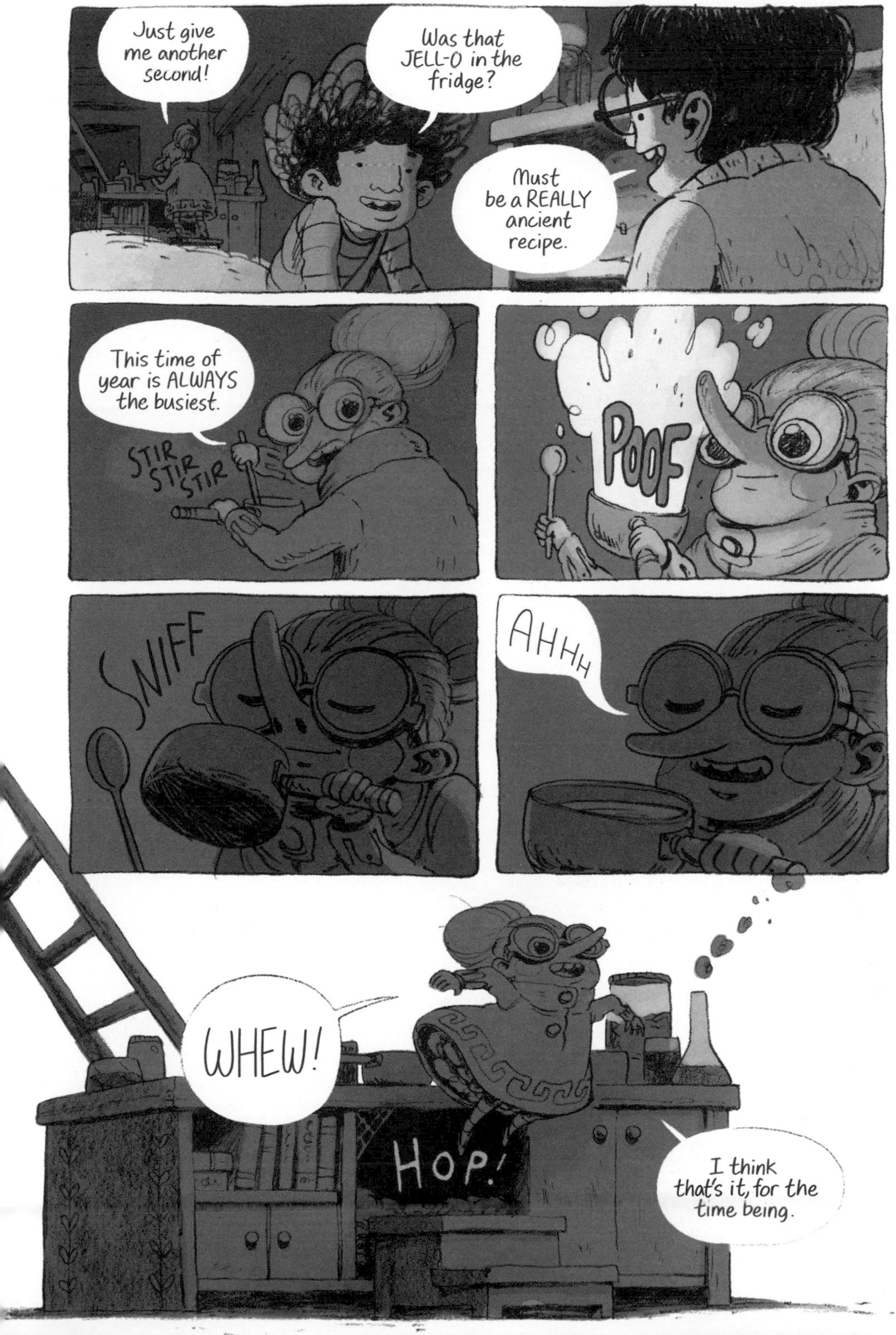
Just give me another second!
Was that JELL-O in the fridge?
Must be a REALLY ancient recipe.
This time of year is ALWAYS the busiest.
STIR STIR STIR
POOF
SNIFF
AHHH
WHEW!
HOP!
I think that's it, for the time being.

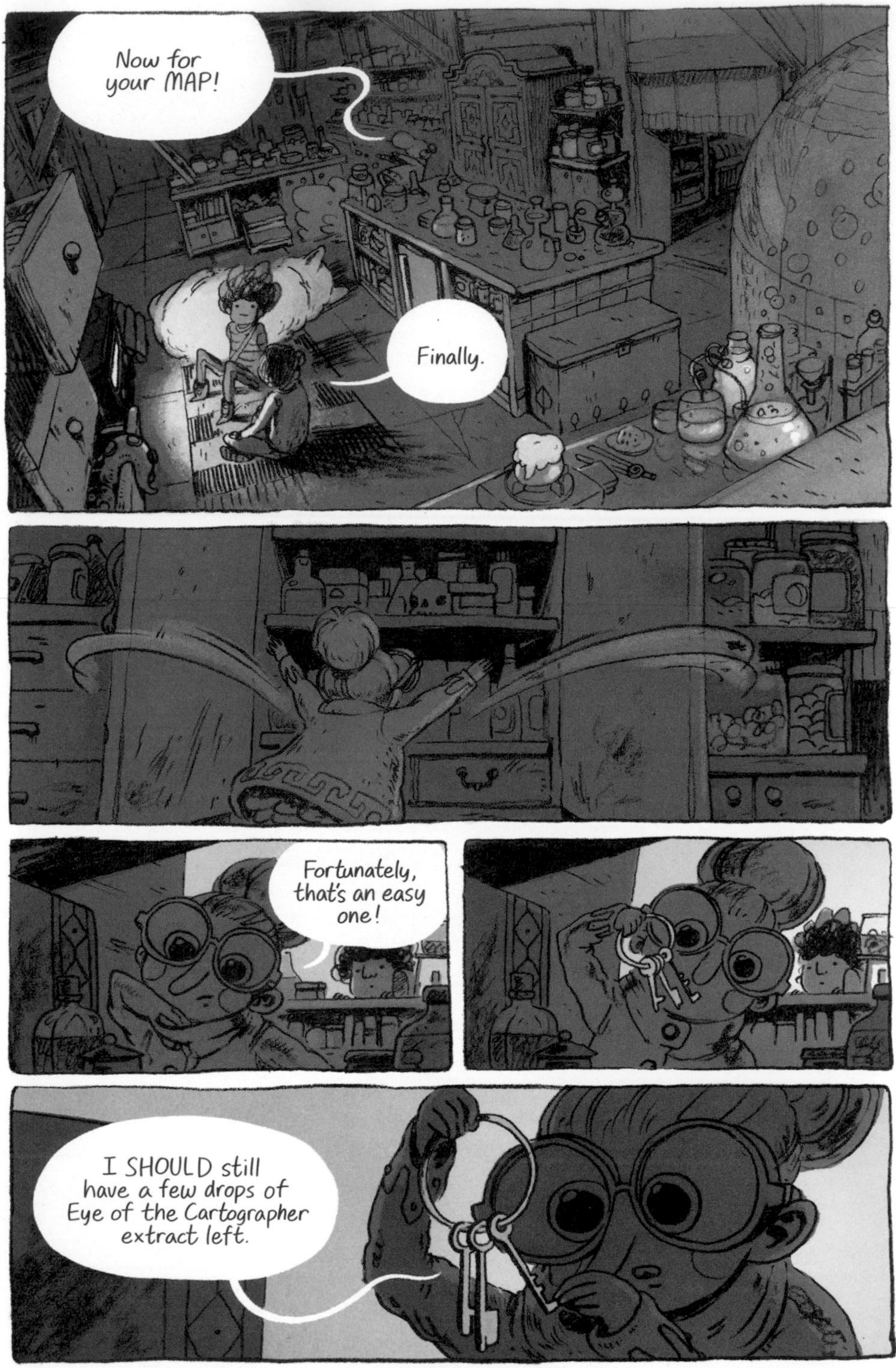
Now for your MAP!
Finally.
Fortunately, that's an easy one!
I SHOULD still have a few drops of Eye of the Cartographer extract left.

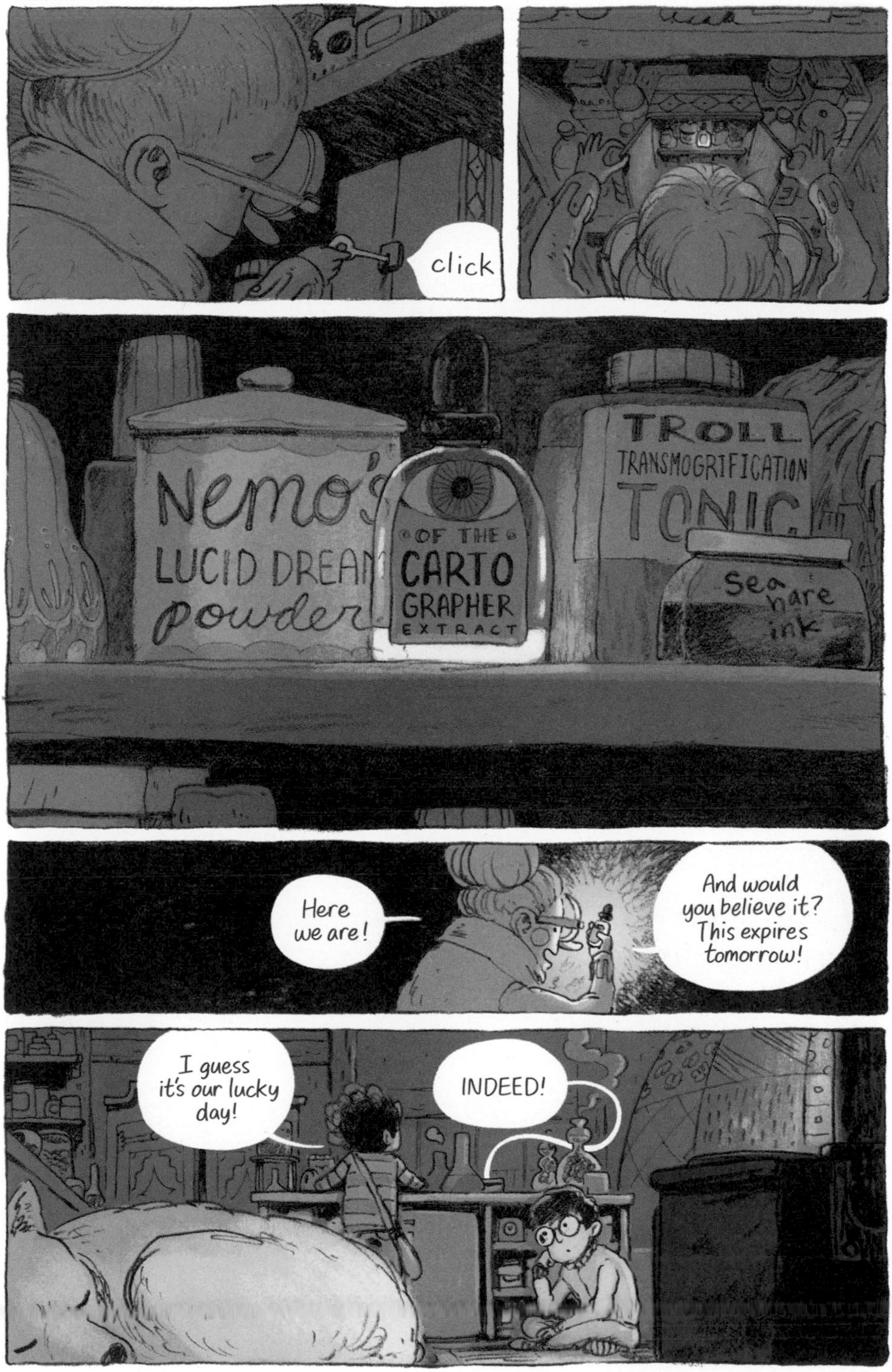
click
Nemo's LUCID DREAM powder
OF THE CARTOGRAPHER EXTRACT
TROLL TRANSMOGRIFICATION TONIC
sea hare ink
Here we are!
And would you believe it? This expires tomorrow!
I guess it's our lucky day!
INDEED!

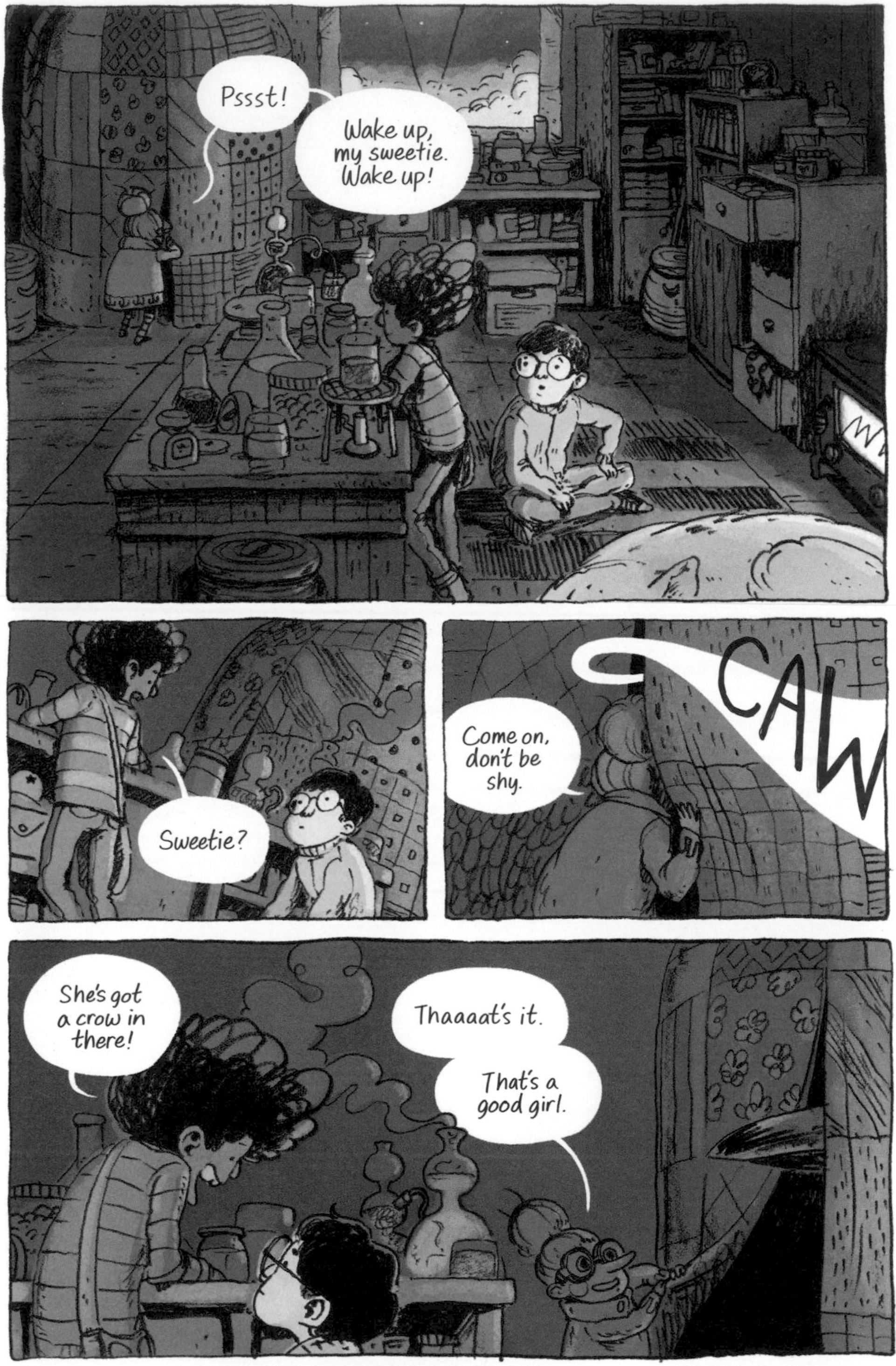
Pssst!
Wake up, my sweetie. Wake up!
Sweetie?
Come on, don't be shy.
CAW
She's got a crow in there!
Thaaaat's it.
That's a good girl.

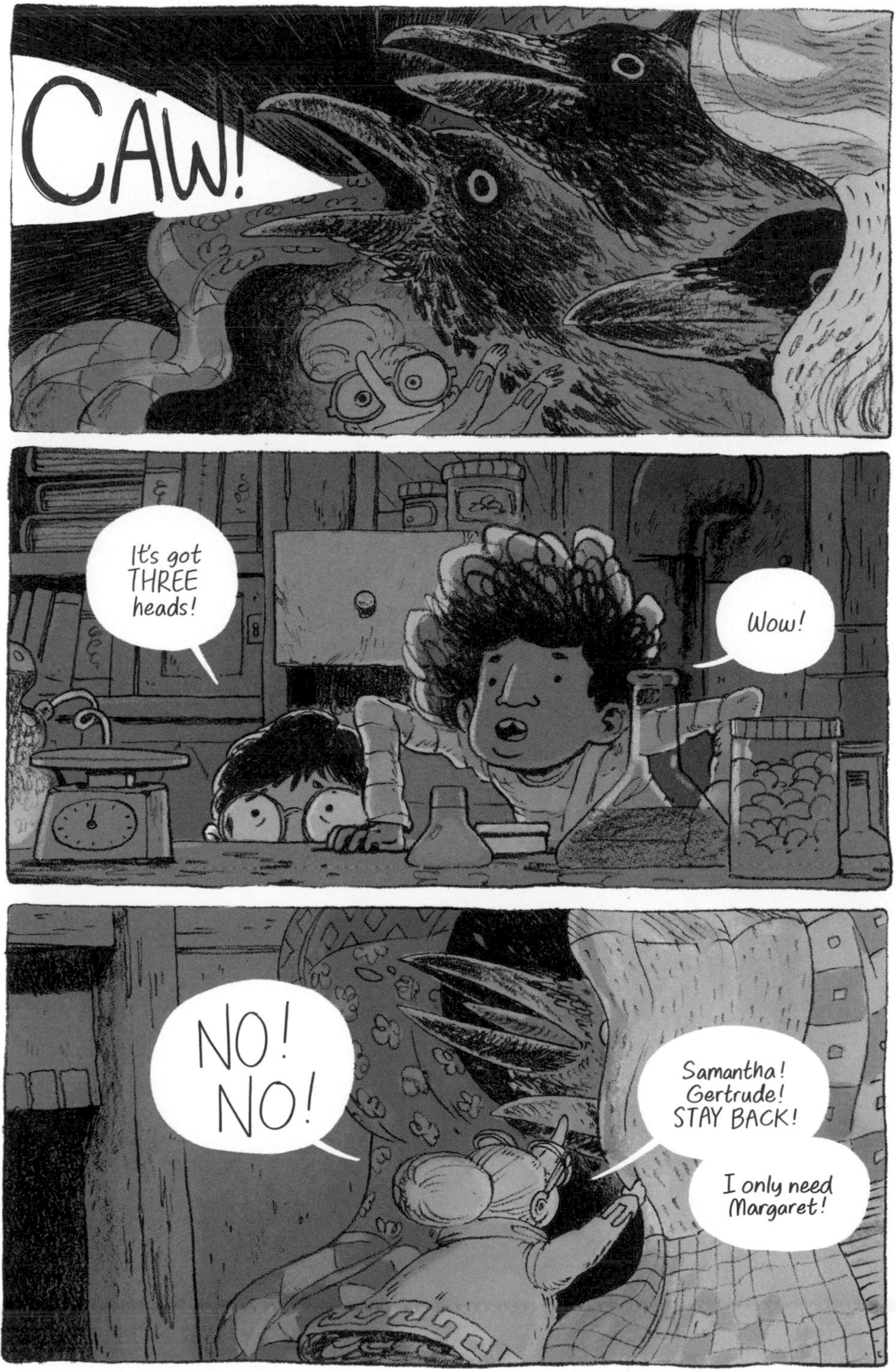
CAW!
It's got THREE heads!
Wow!
NO! NO!
Samantha! Gertrude! STAY BACK!
I only need Margaret!

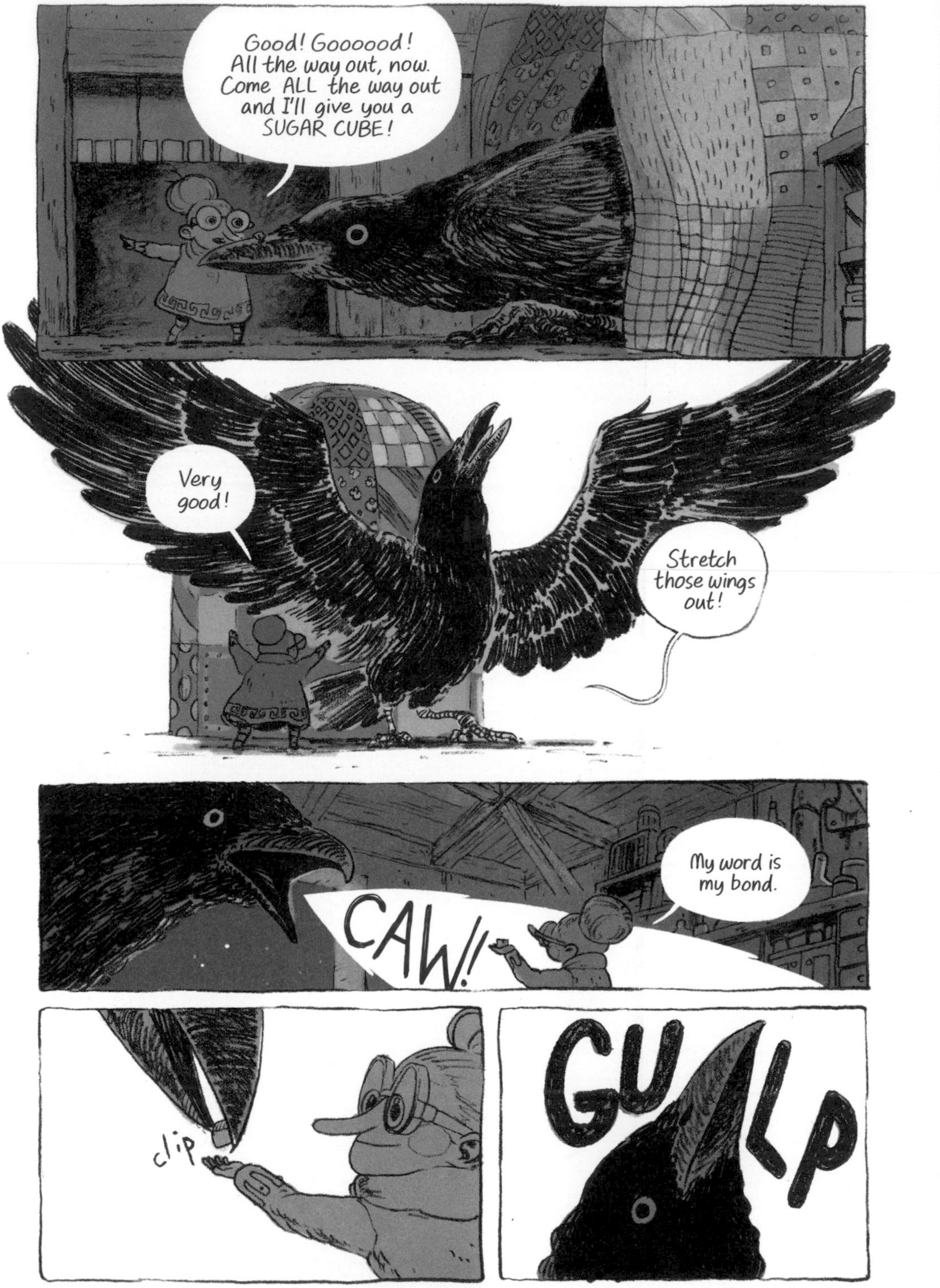
Good! Goooood! All the way out, now. Come ALL the way out and I'll give you a SUGAR CUBE!
Very good!
Stretch those wings out!
CAW!
My word is my bond.
clip
GULP

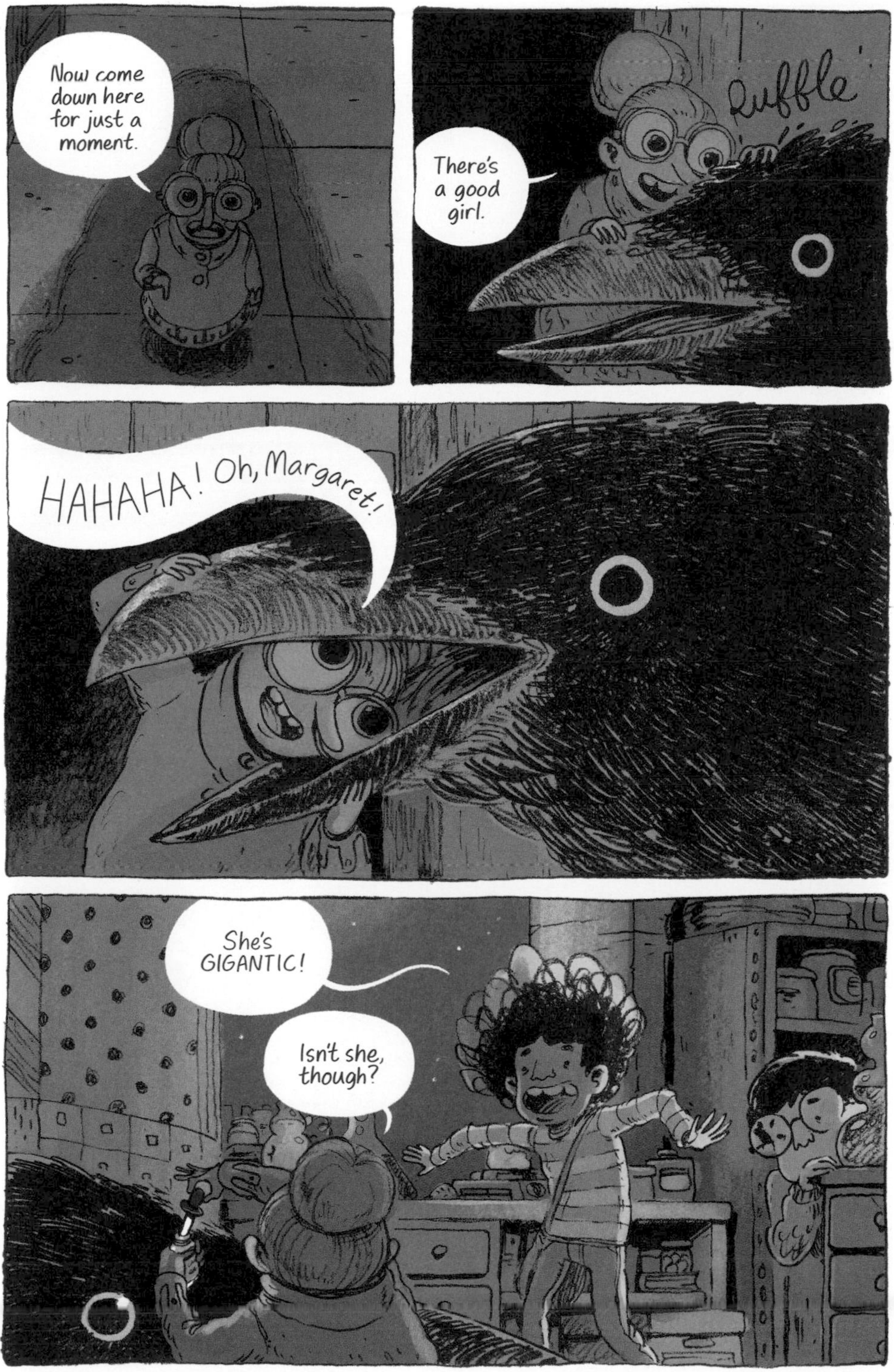
Now come down here for just a moment.
ruffle
There's a good girl.
HAHAHA! Oh, Margaret!
She's GIGANTIC!
Isn't she, though?

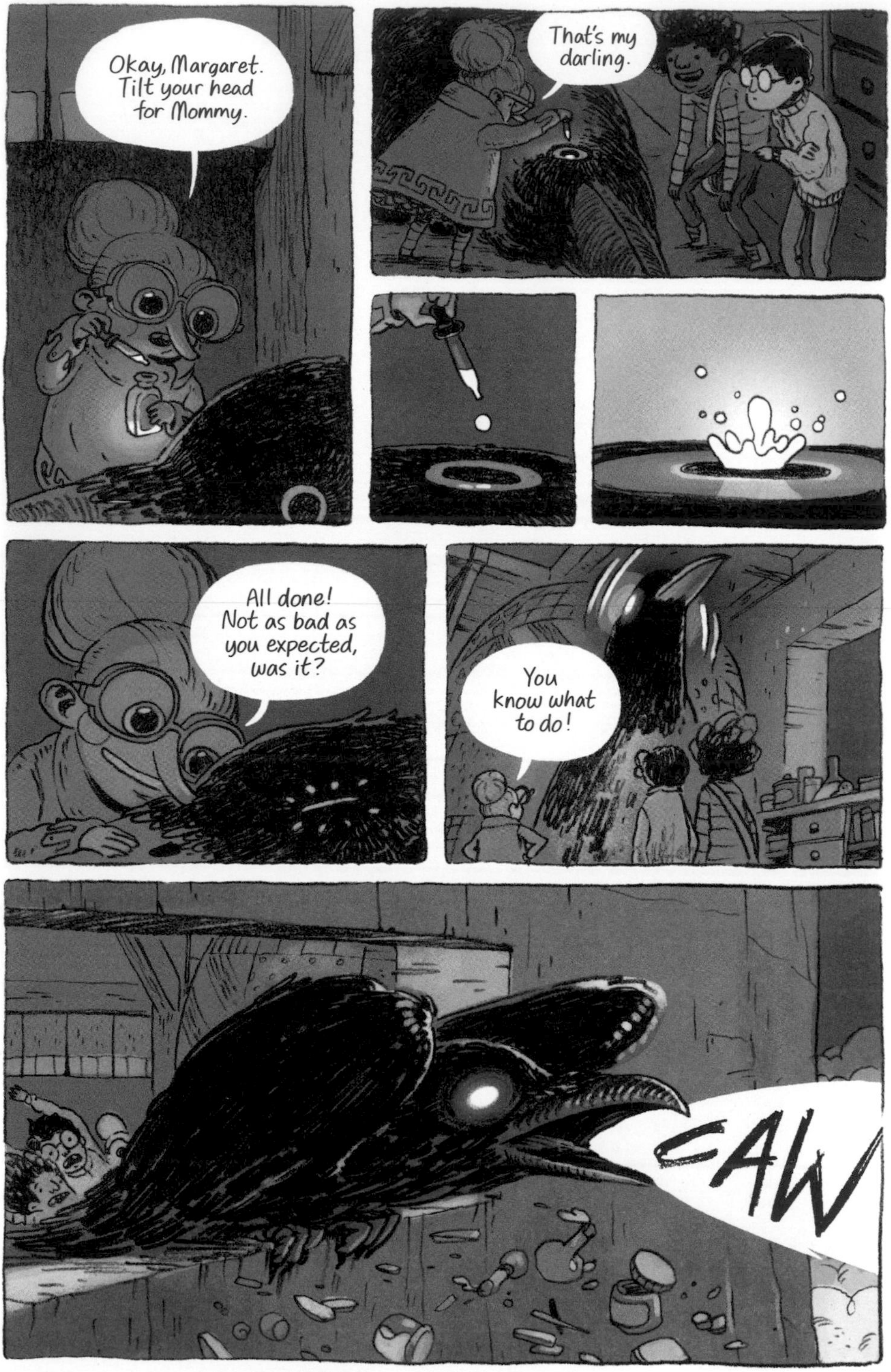
Okay, Margaret. Tilt your head for Mommy.
That's my darling.
All done! Not as bad as you expected, was it?
You know what to do!
CAW

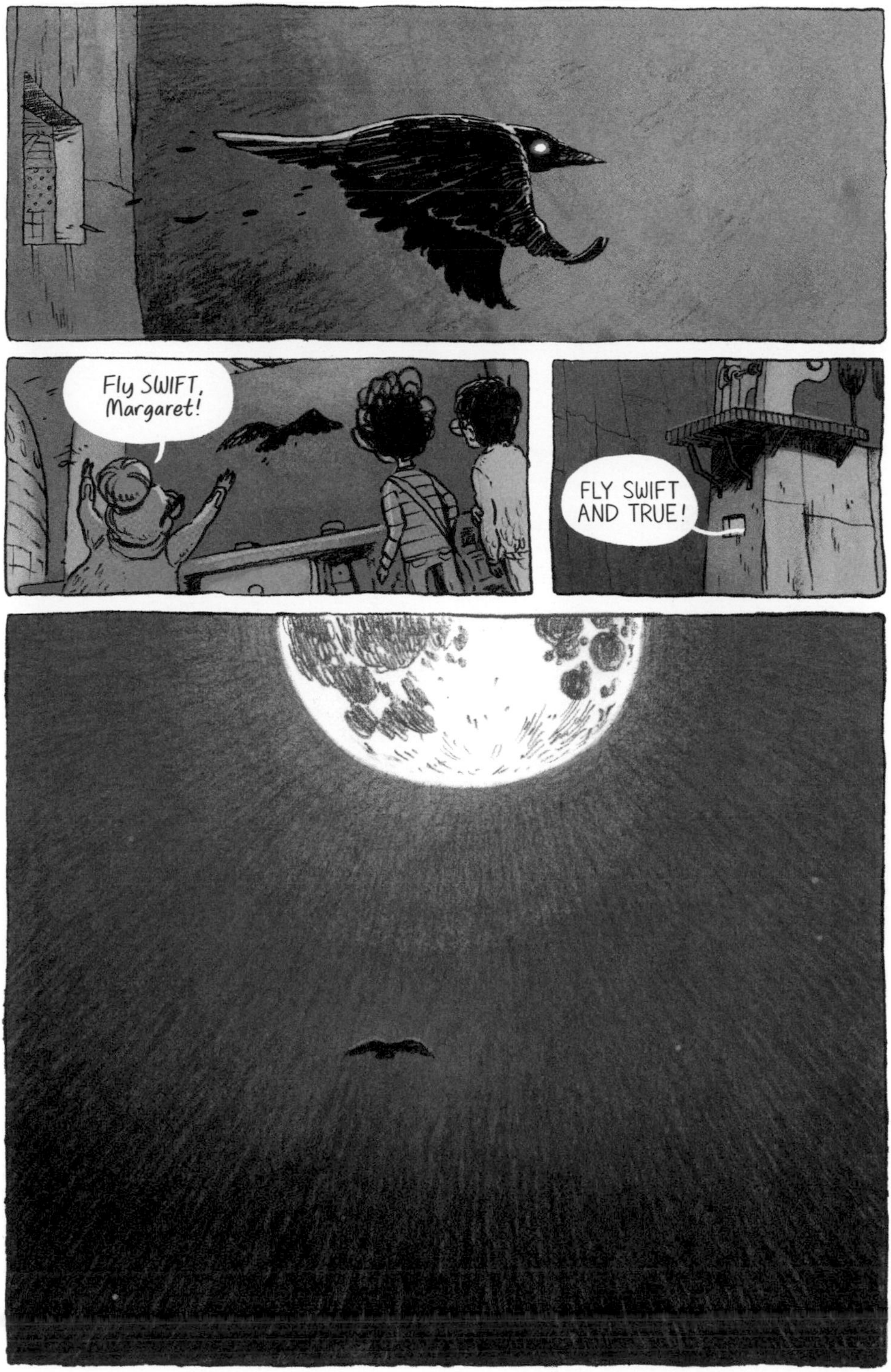
Fly SWIFT, Margaret!
FLY SWIFT AND TRUE!

This happens every few decades. The LAST time a full moon fell directly on the autumn equinox was September 23, 1953.

They don't SOUND very enlightened.

What a disappointing year THAT was.

And so, while NORMALLY I'd be down there with the others, joining in on the day's merrymaking—

nibble

—I've been stuck in HERE, crafting my greatest potion yet!

PTU!

One that will perform the impossible task of blotting out the moon long enough to allow the stars of the Milky Way to FAR outshine it, providing the Enlightened Ones with a foolproof path to our doorstep.

I don't suppose you two would like to stick around and witness their arrival?

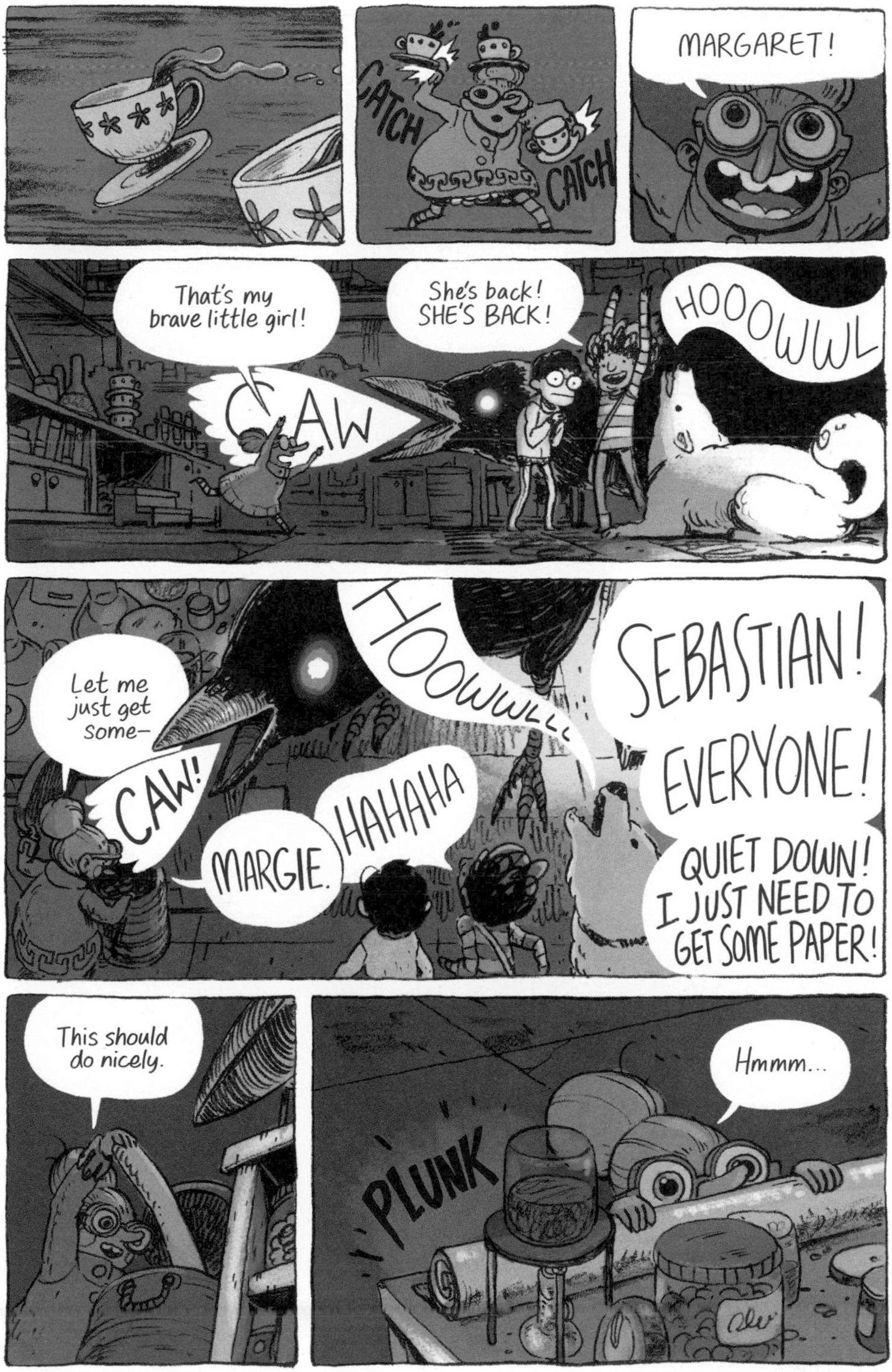
CATCH
CATCH
MARGARET!
That's my brave little girl!
CAW
She's back! SHE'S BACK!
HOOOWWL
Let me just get some–
CAW!
HOOOWWLLL
MARGIE.
HAHAHA
SEBASTIAN!
EVERYONE!
QUIET DOWN! I JUST NEED TO GET SOME PAPER!
This should do nicely.
PLUNK
Hmmm...

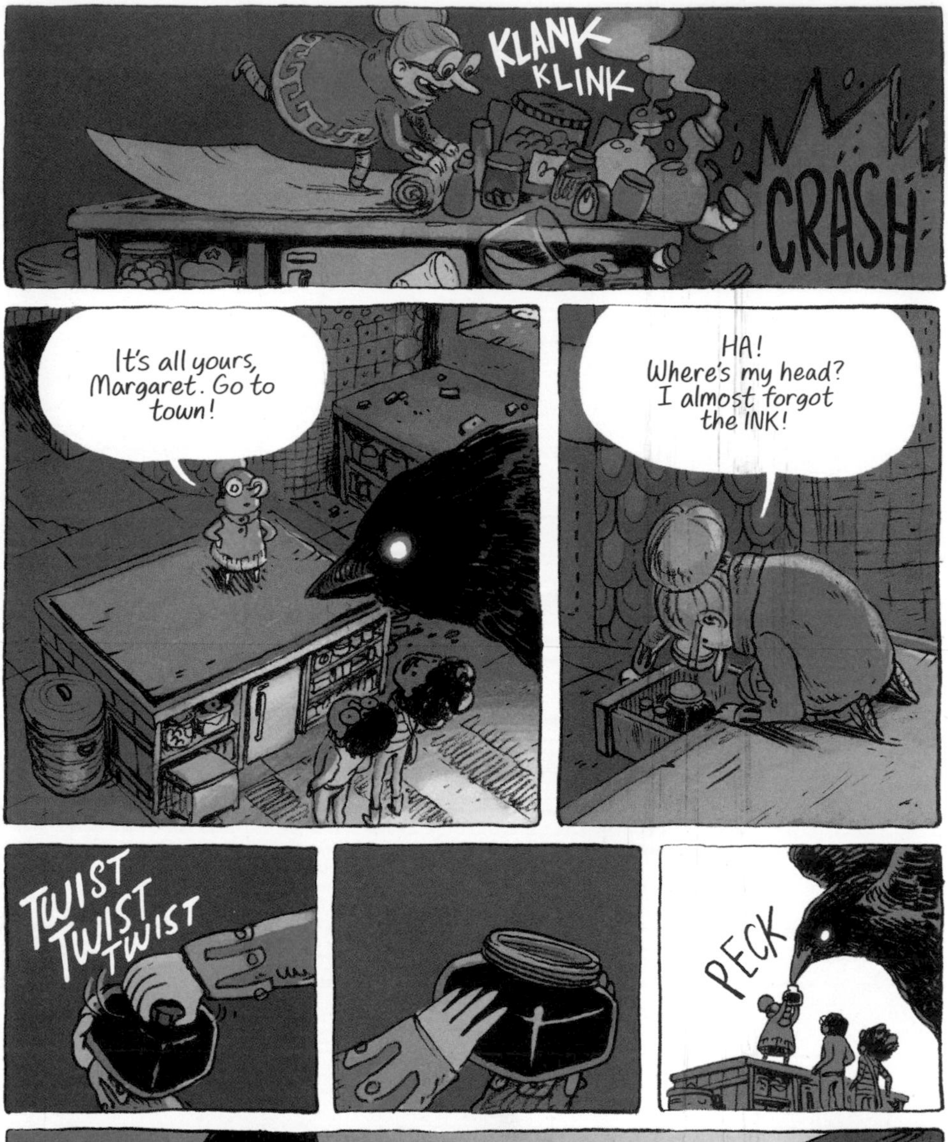
KLANK
KLINK
CRASH
It's all yours, Margaret. Go to town!
HA! Where's my head? I almost forgot the INK!
TWIST TWIST TWIST
PECK
hup!
Wait. Is Margaret going to DRAW our map?

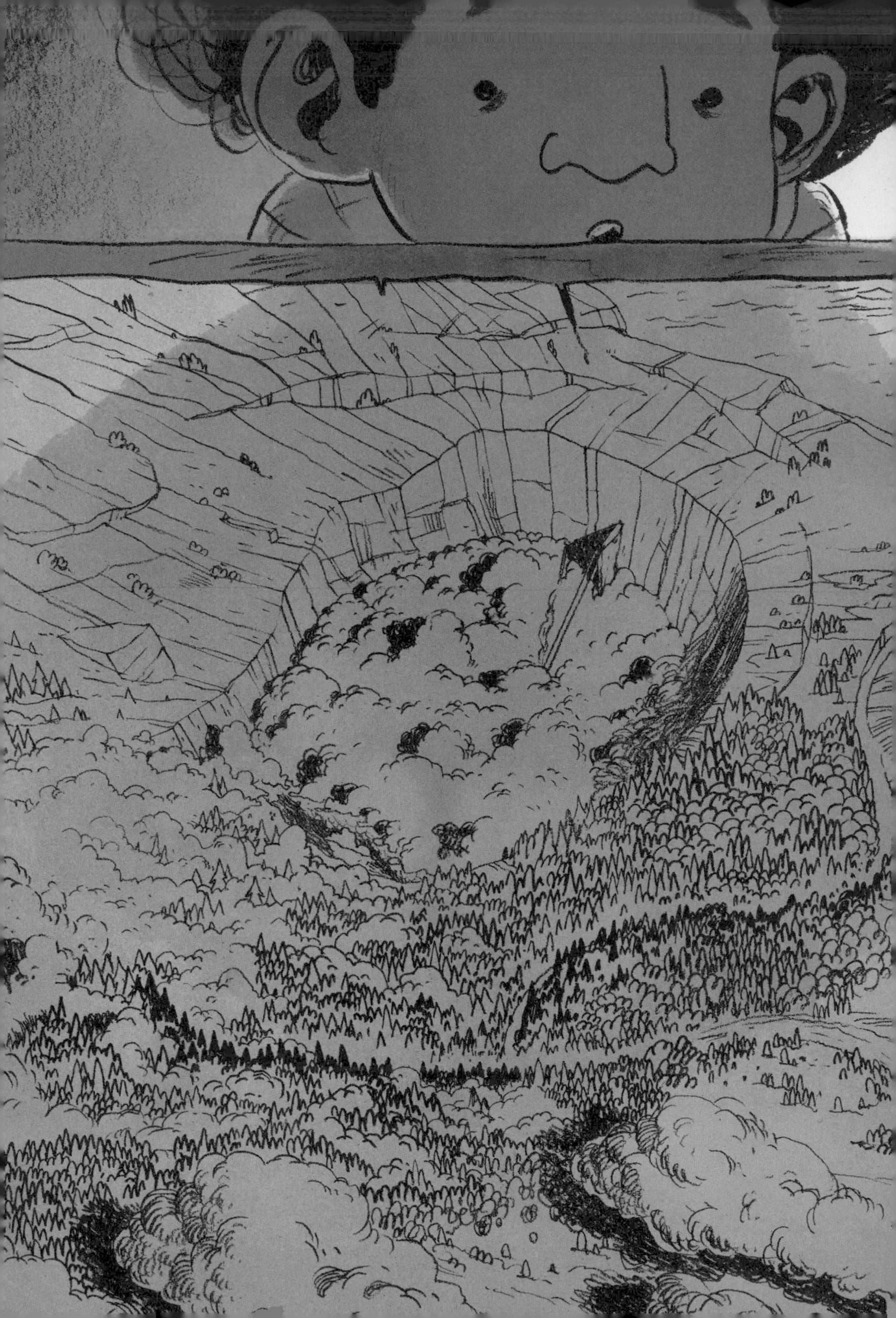

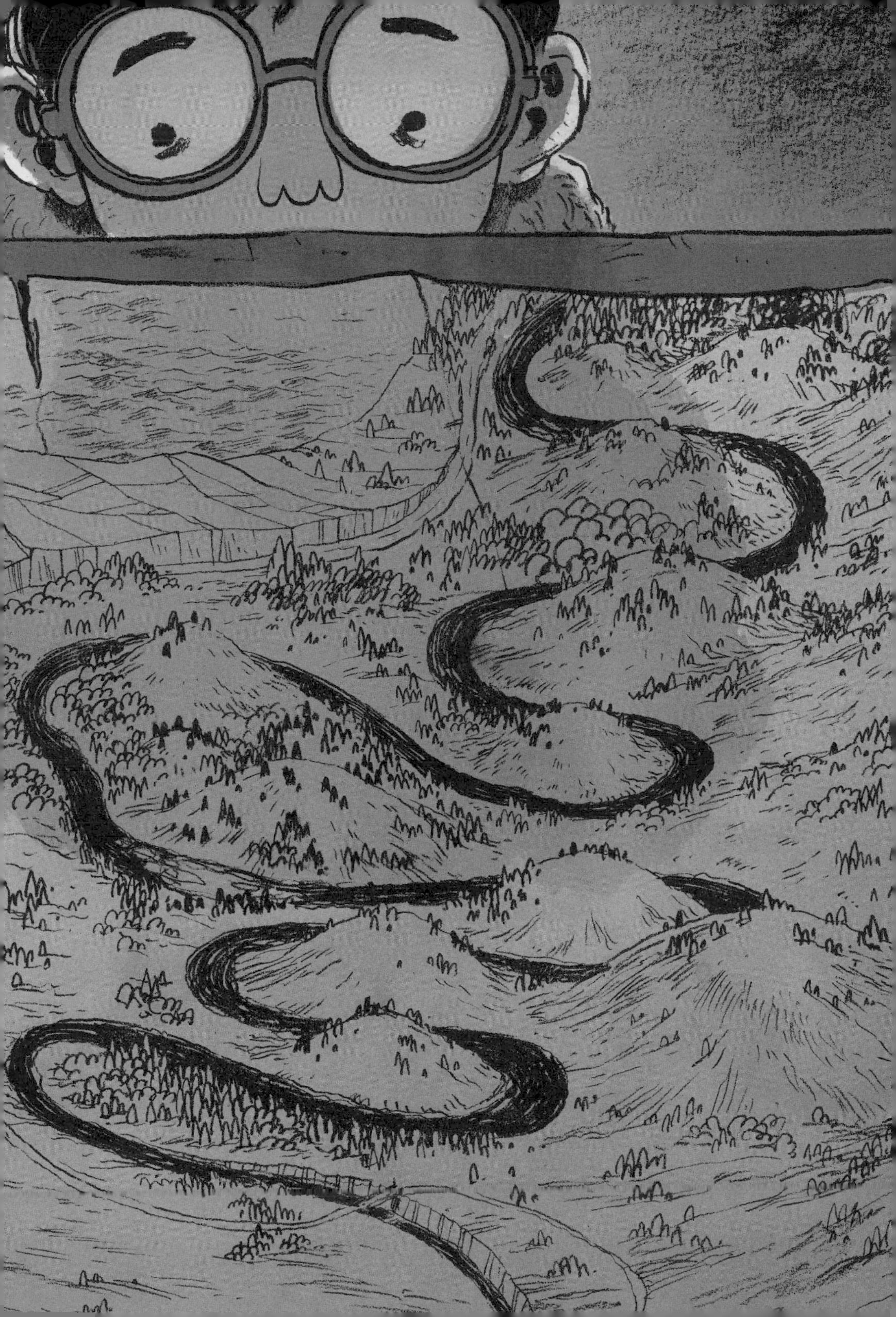

153

154

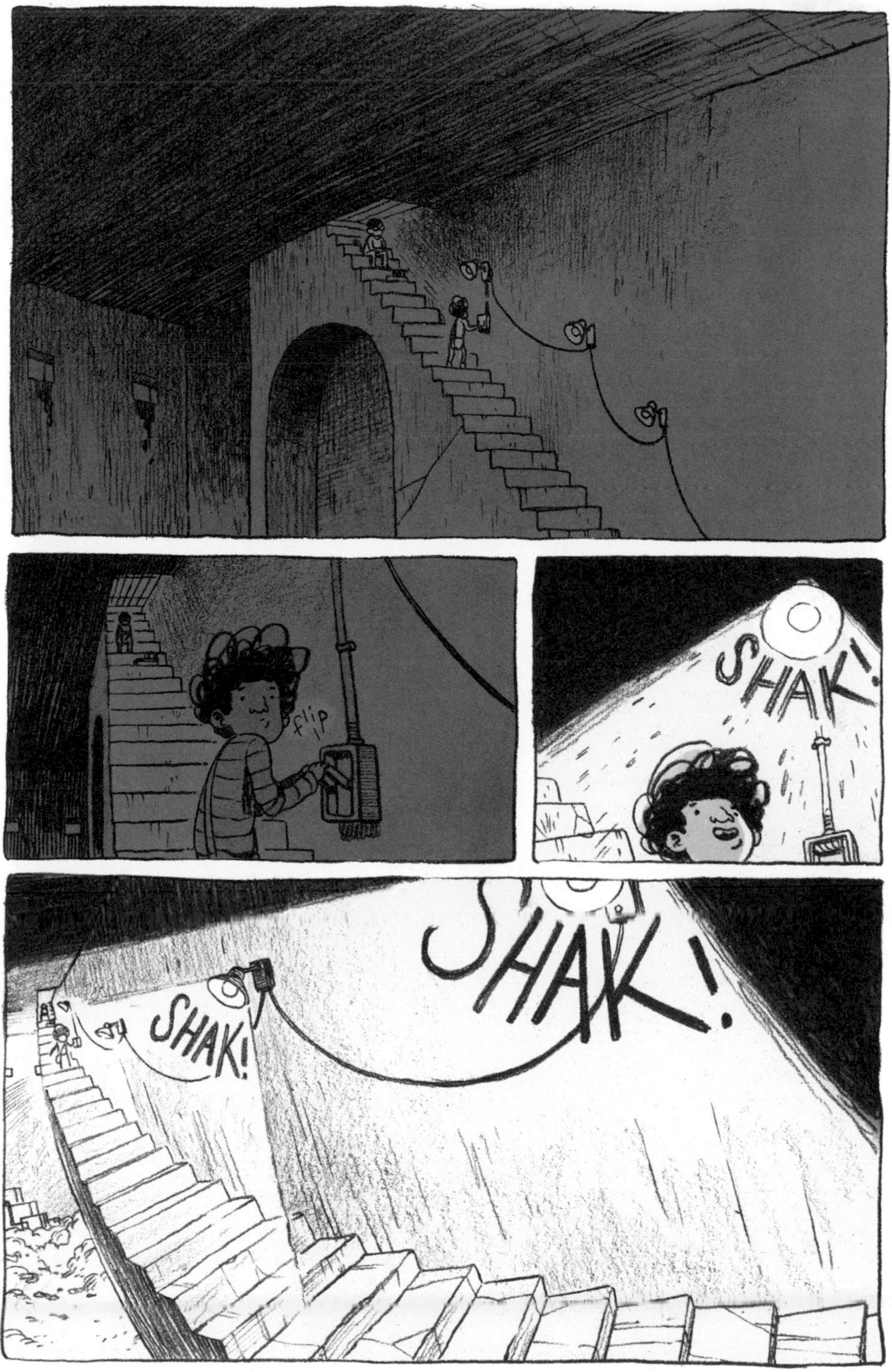
flip
SHAK!
SHAK!
SHAK!

CHAPTER FIVE

THE MUSTY CELLAR

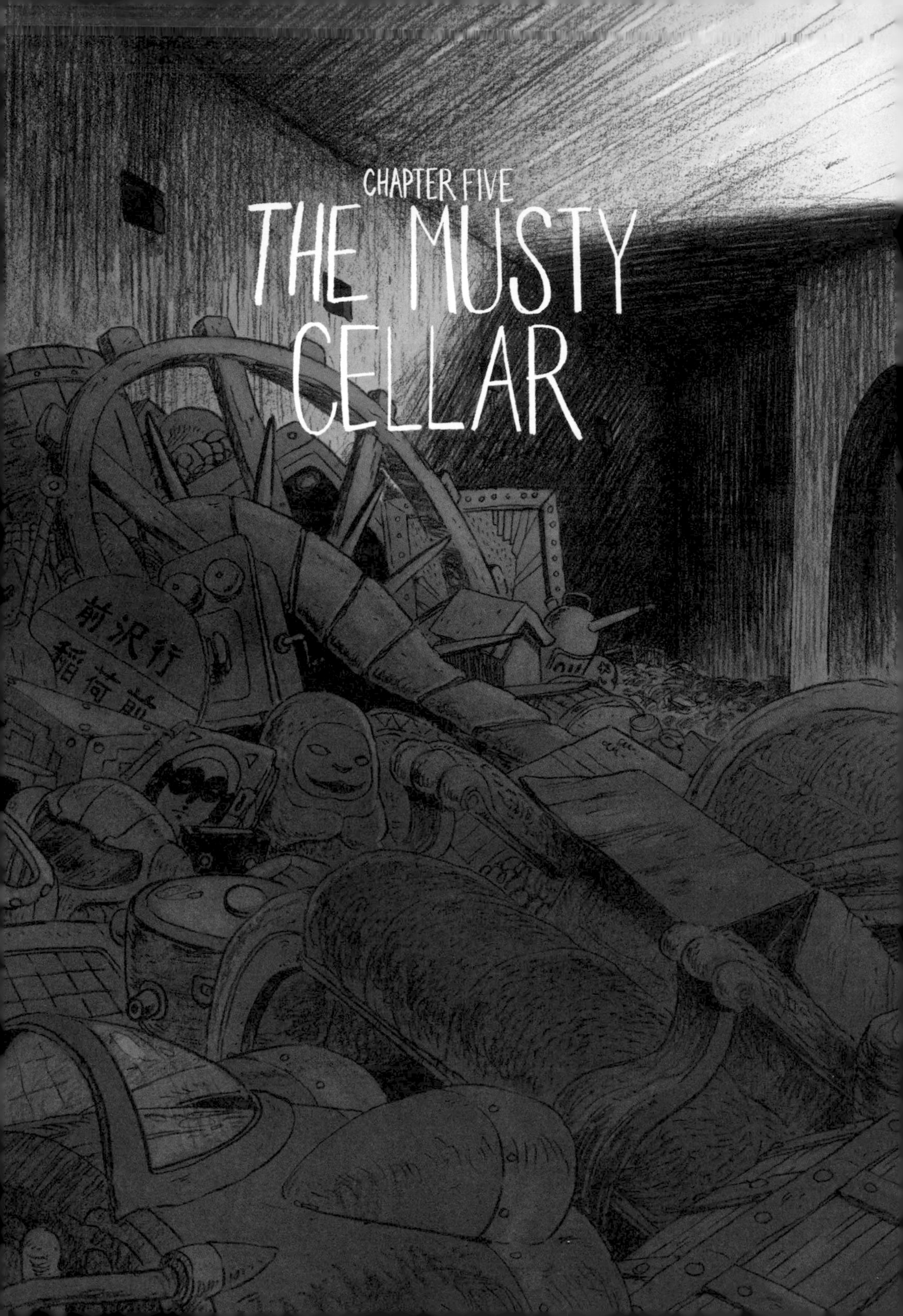
前沢行
稲荷前

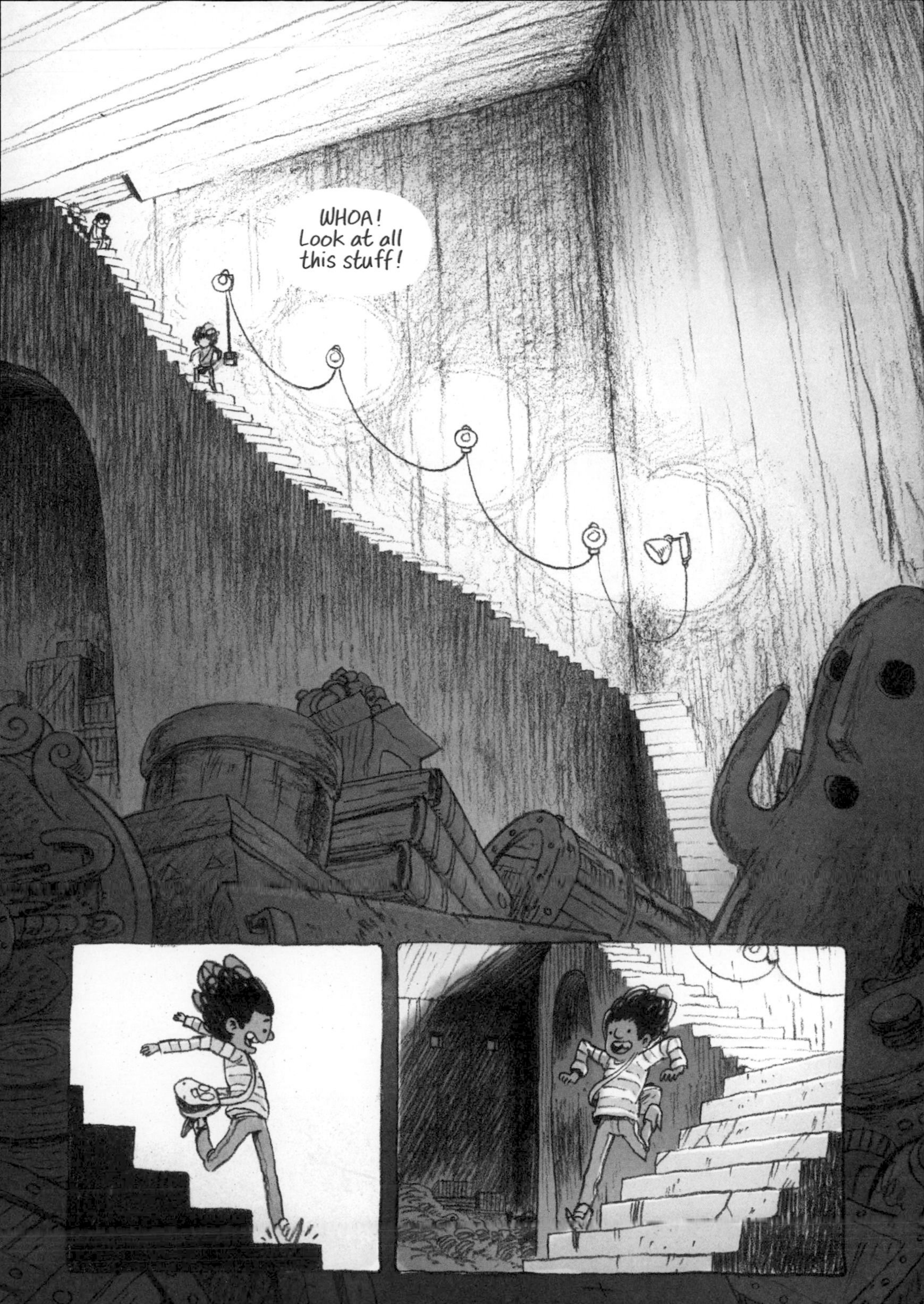
WHOA! Look at all this stuff!

164

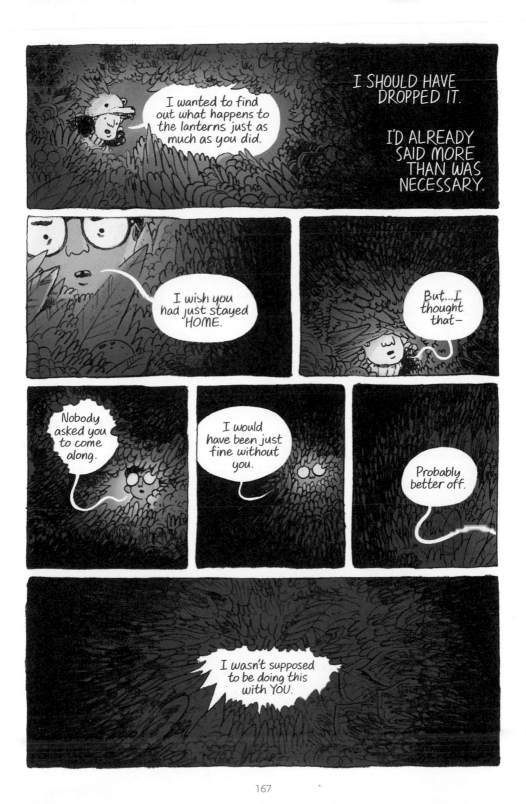

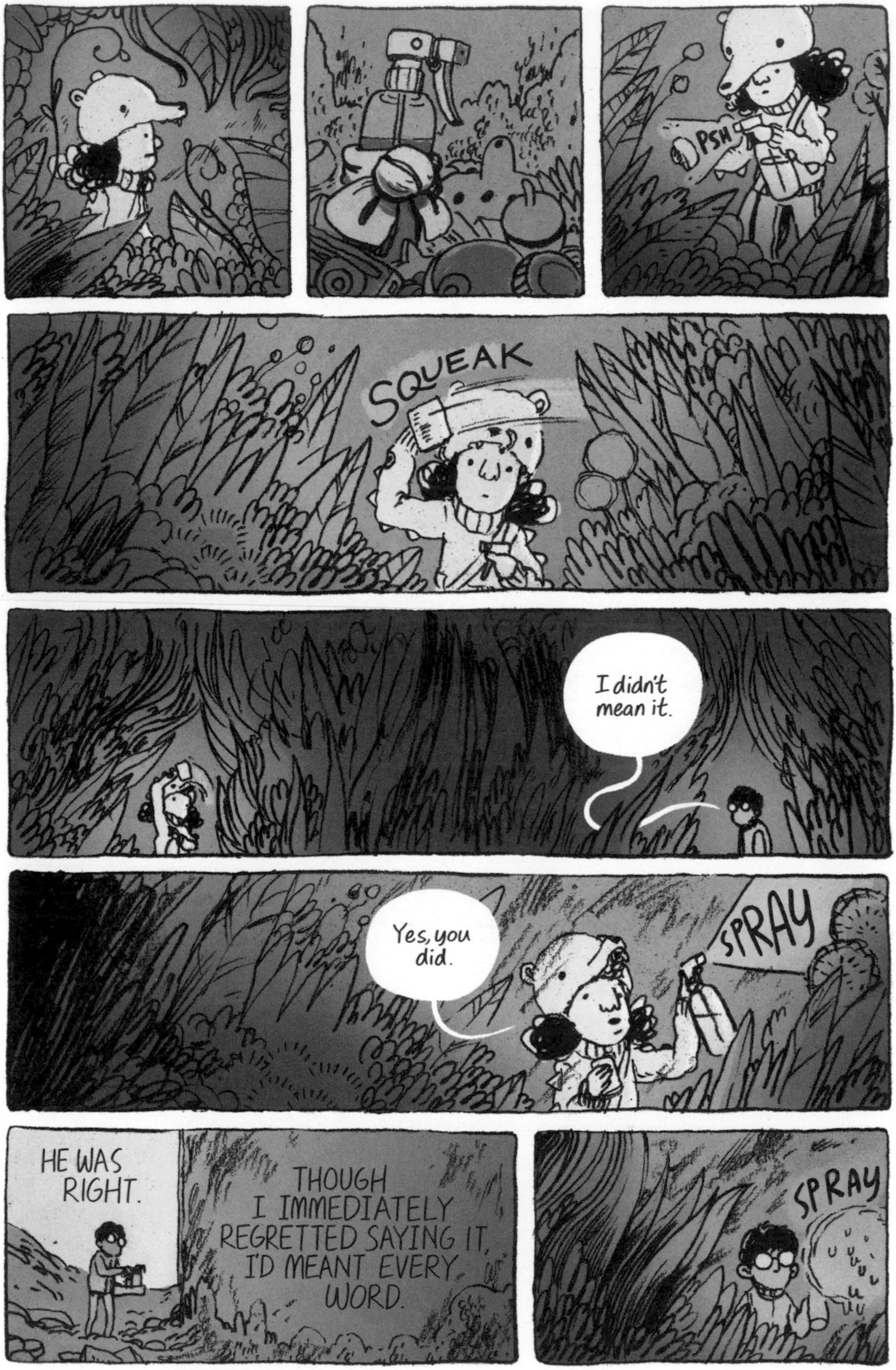
PSH
SQUEAK
I didn't mean it.
Yes, you did.
SPRAY
HE WAS RIGHT.
THOUGH I IMMEDIATELY REGRETTED SAYING IT, I'D MEANT EVERY WORD.
SPRAY

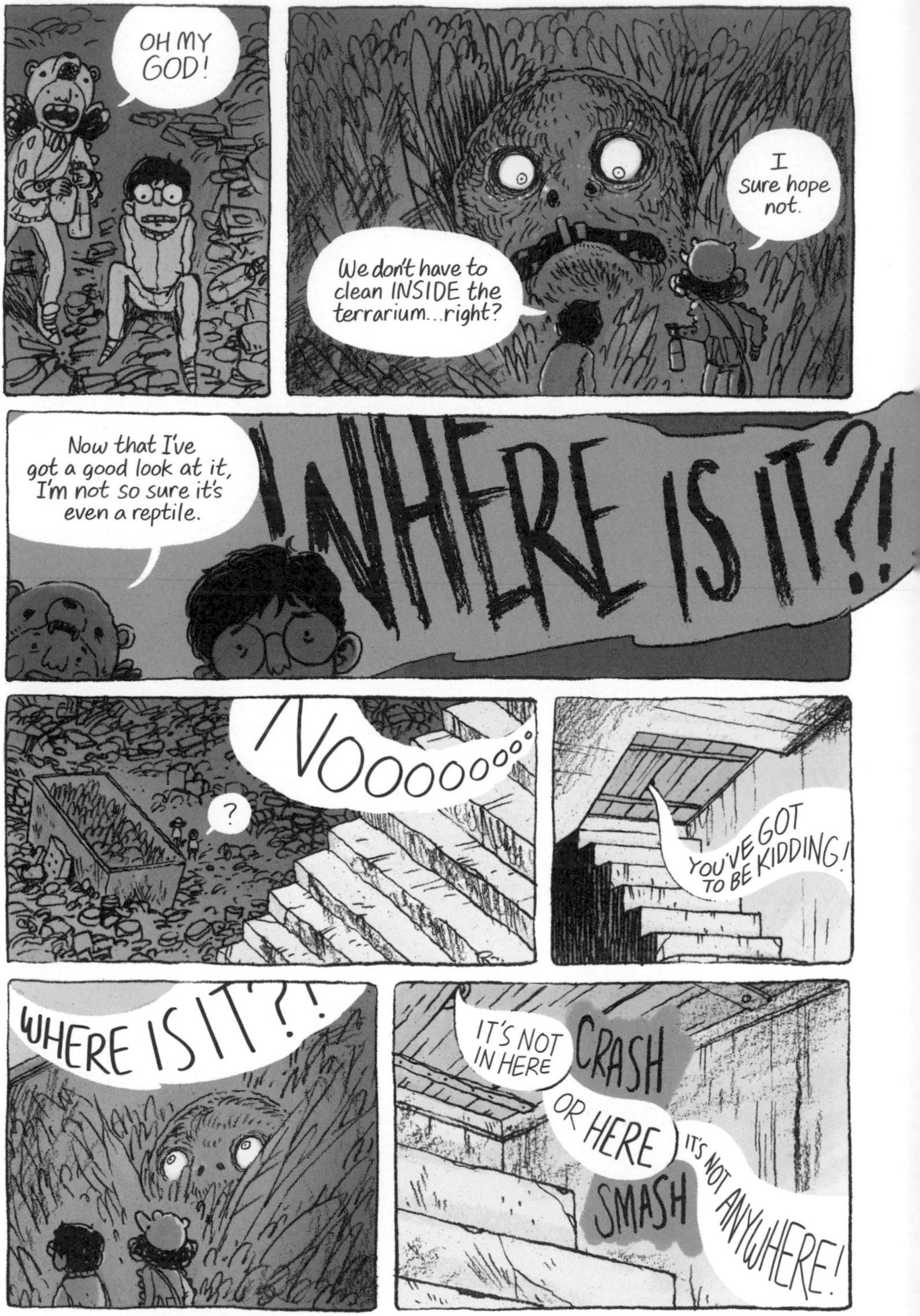
OH MY GOD!
We don't have to clean INSIDE the terrarium...right?
I sure hope not.
Now that I've got a good look at it, I'm not so sure it's even a reptile.
WHERE IS IT?!
NOOOOOOOO
?
YOU'VE GOT TO BE KIDDING!
WHERE IS IT?!
IT'S NOT IN HERE
CRASH
OR HERE
SMASH
IT'S NOT ANYWHERE!

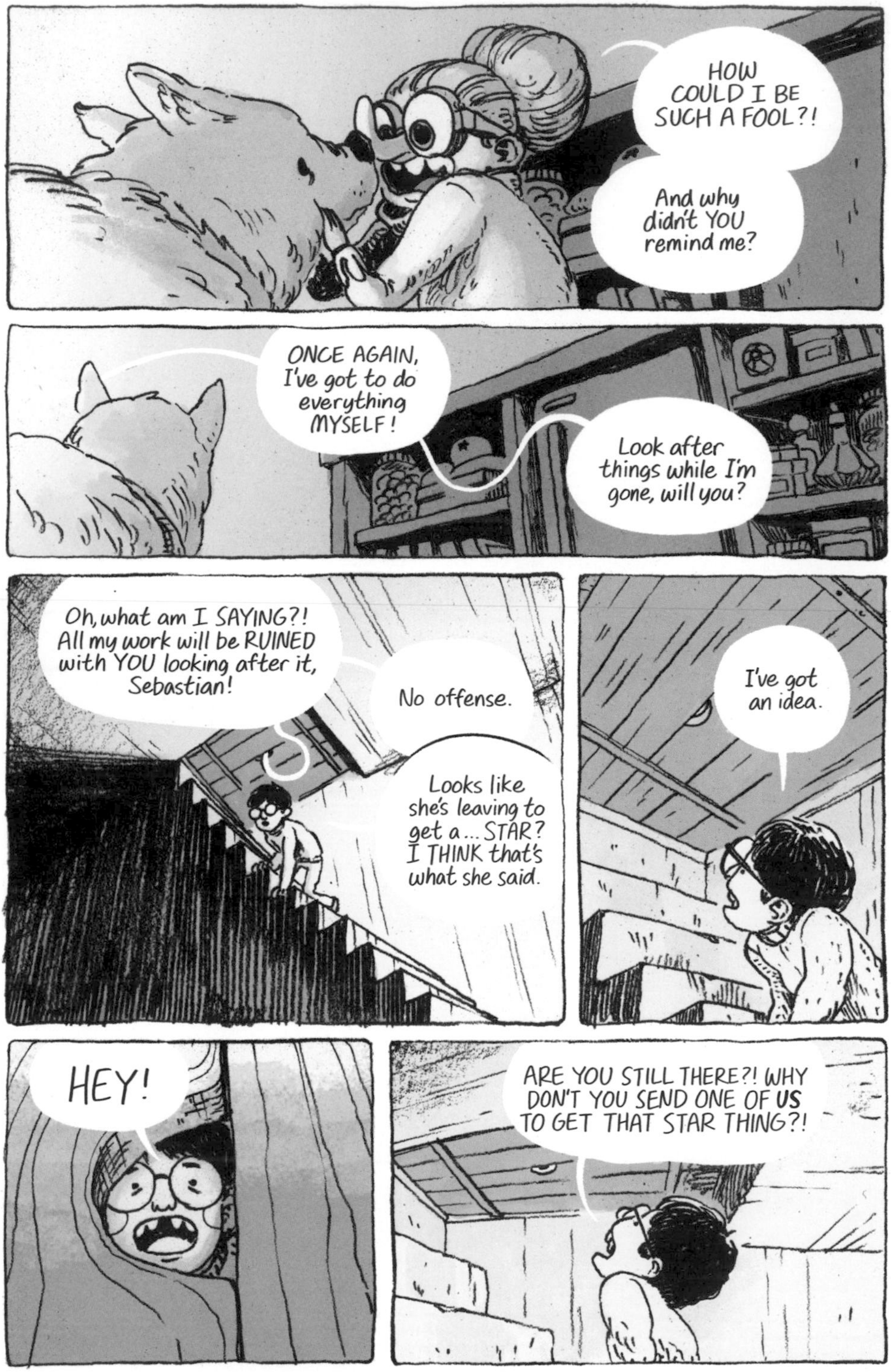
HOW COULD I BE SUCH A FOOL?!
And why didn't YOU remind me?
ONCE AGAIN, I've got to do everything MYSELF!
Look after things while I'm gone, will you?
Oh, what am I SAYING?! All my work will be RUINED with YOU looking after it, Sebastian!
No offense.
Looks like she's leaving to get a... STAR? I THINK that's what she said.
I've got an idea.
HEY!
ARE YOU STILL THERE?! WHY DON'T YOU SEND ONE OF US TO GET THAT STAR THING?!

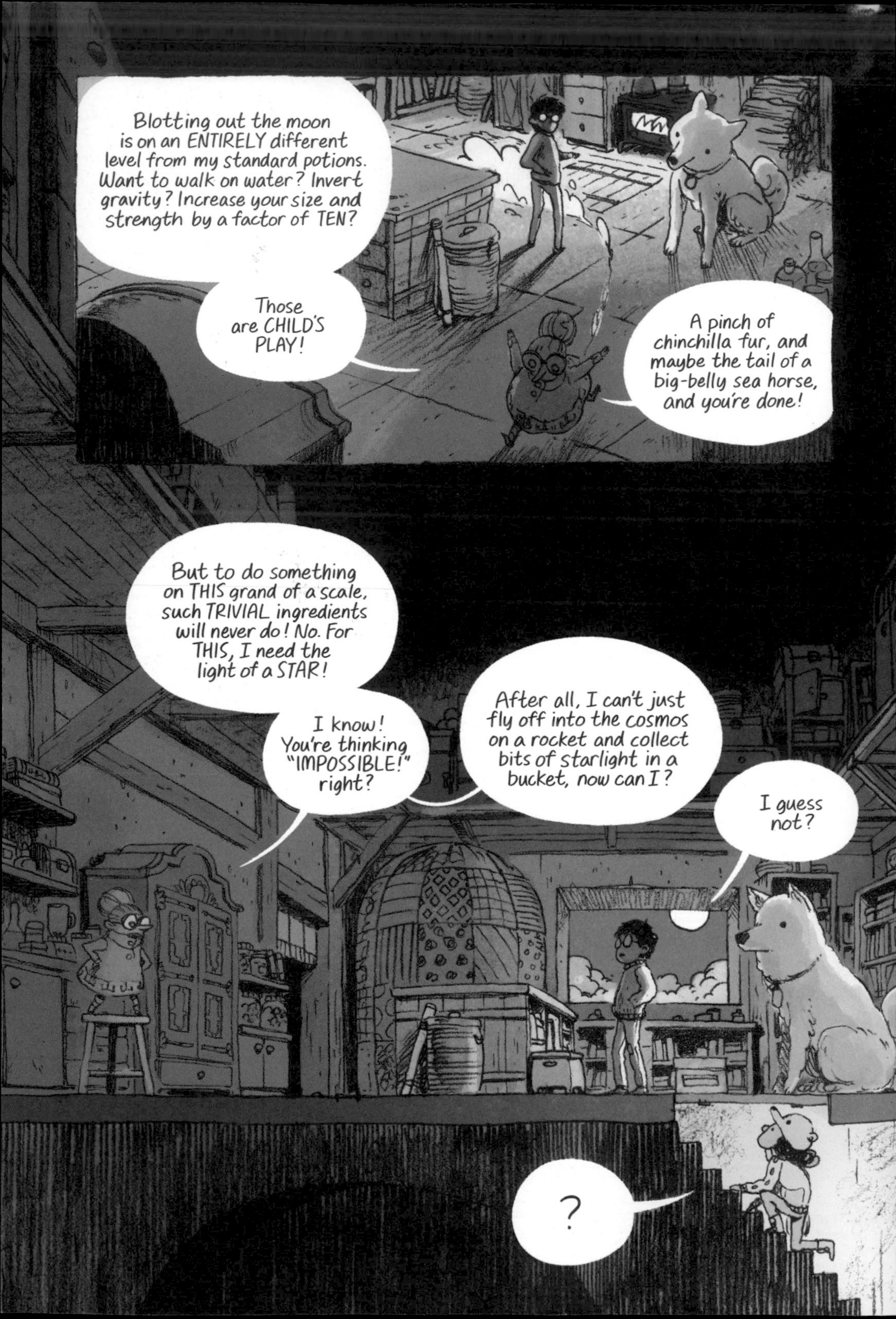
Blotting out the moon is on an ENTIRELY different level from my standard potions. Want to walk on water? Invert gravity? Increase your size and strength by a factor of TEN?
Those are CHILD'S PLAY!
A pinch of chinchilla fur, and maybe the tail of a big-belly sea horse, and you're done!
But to do something on THIS grand of a scale, such TRIVIAL ingredients will never do! No. For THIS, I need the light of a STAR!
I know! You're thinking "IMPOSSIBLE!" right?
After all, I can't just fly off into the cosmos on a rocket and collect bits of starlight in a bucket, now can I?
I guess not?
?

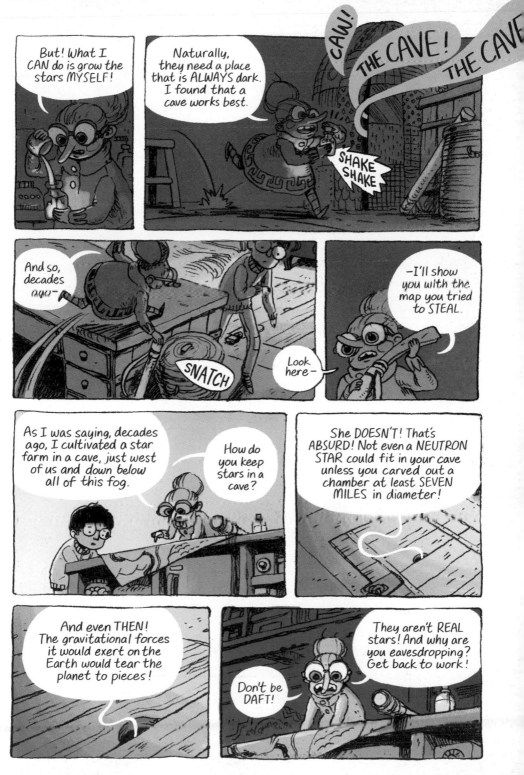

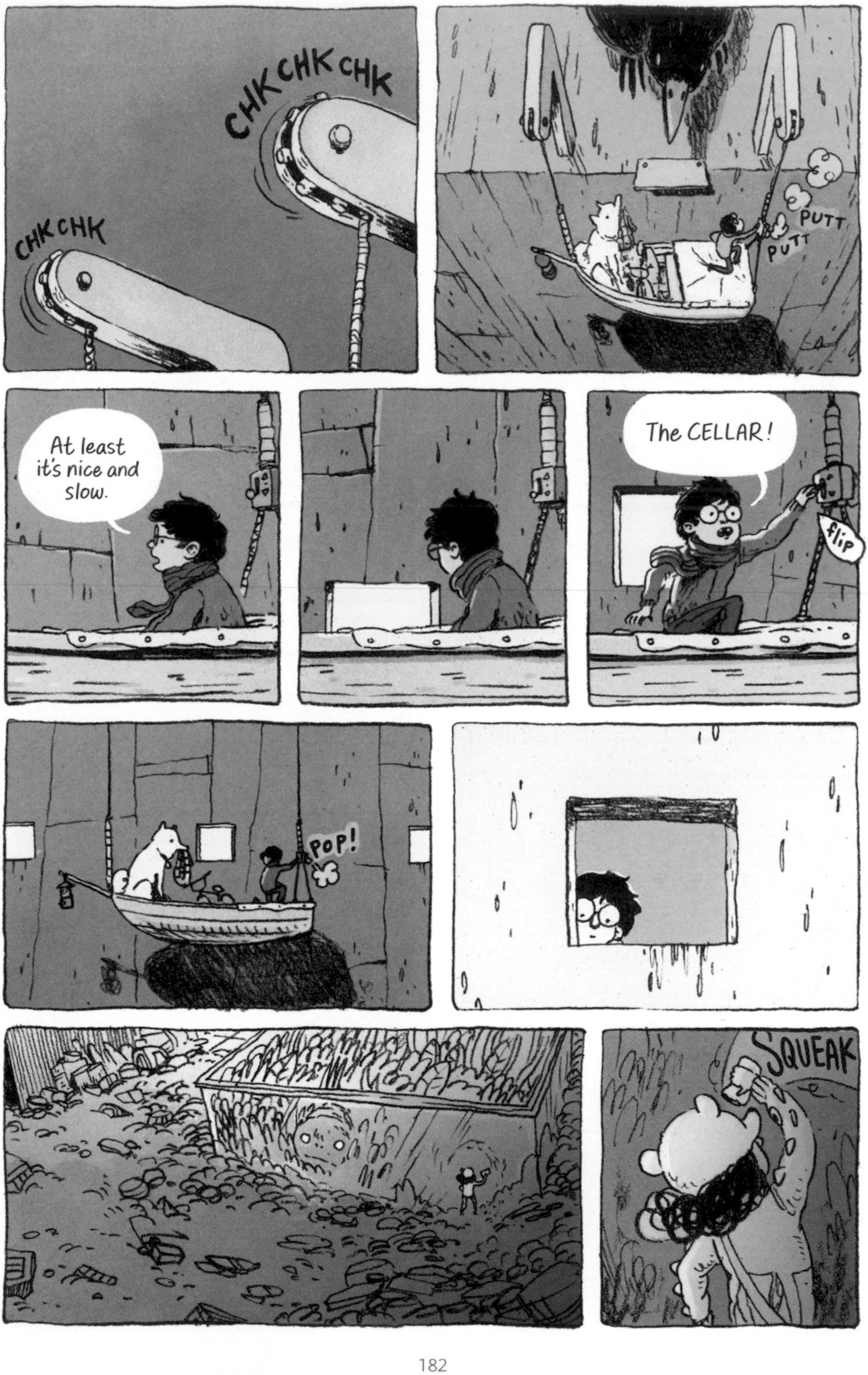
CHK CHK CHK
CHK CHK
PUTT
PUTT
At least it's nice and slow.
The CELLAR!
flip
POP!
SQUEAK

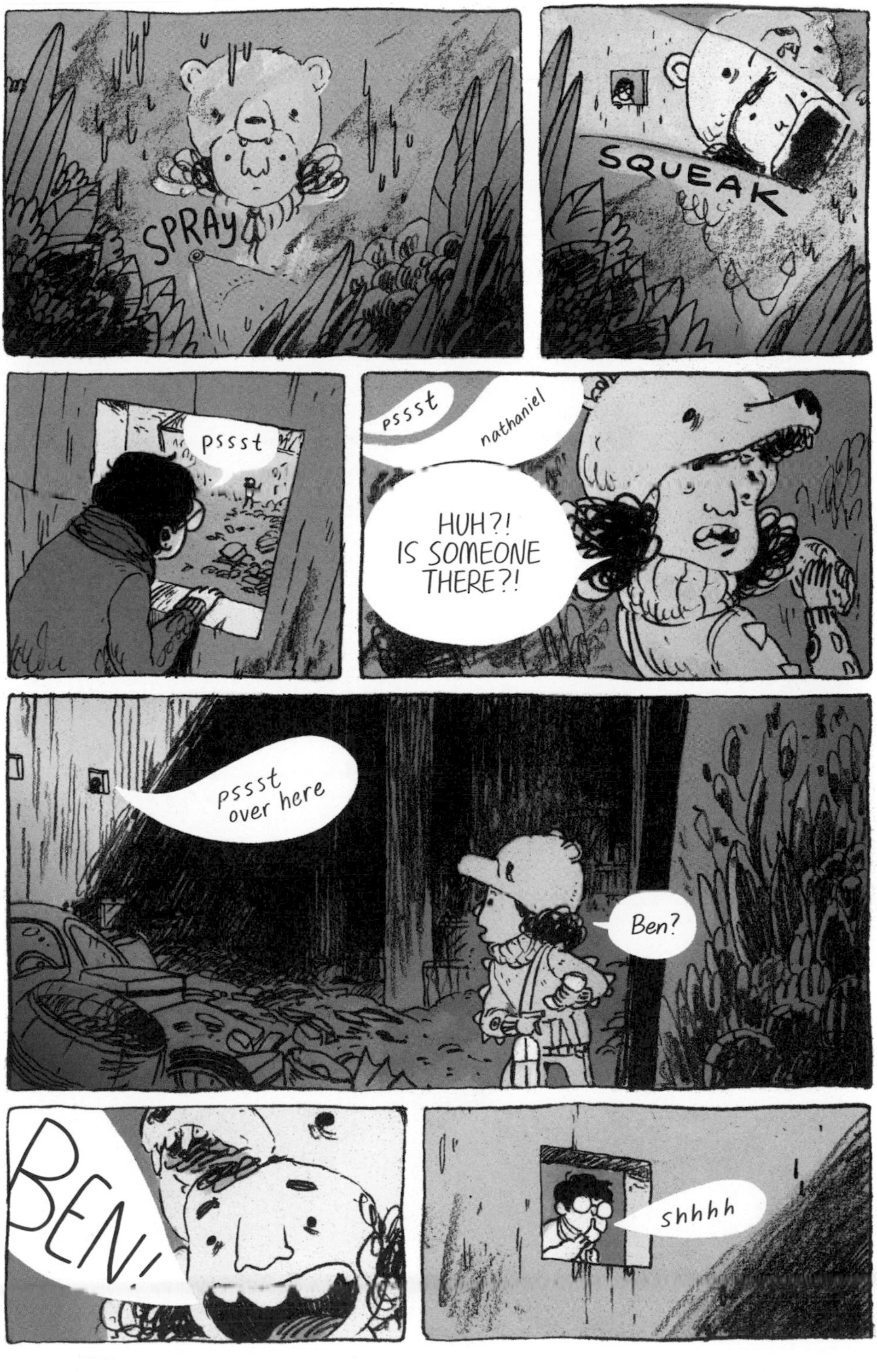
SPRAY
SQUEAK
pssst
pssst
nathaniel
HUH?! IS SOMEONE THERE?!
pssst over here
Ben?
BEN!
shhhh

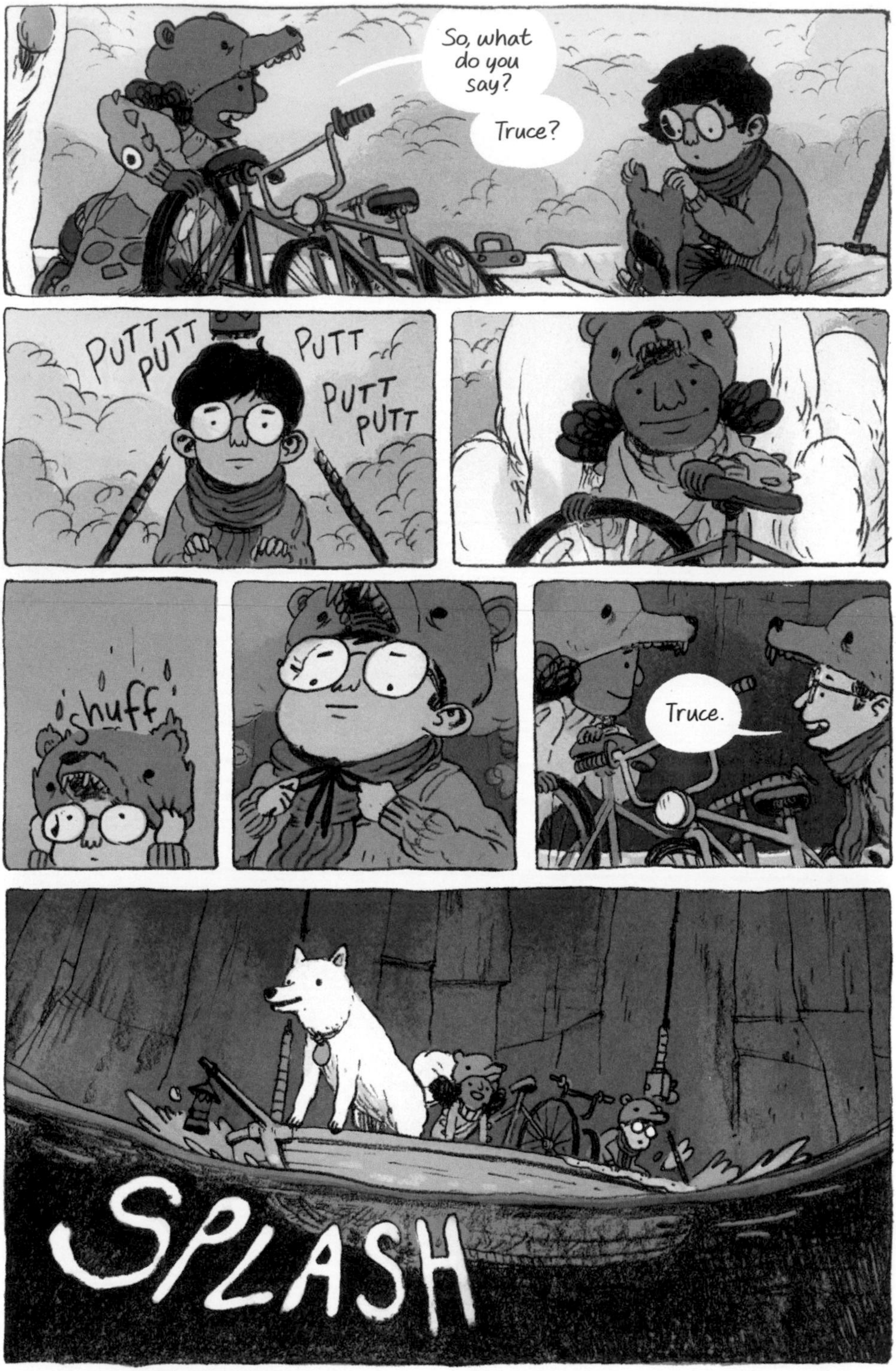
So, what do you say?
Truce?
PUTT PUTT
PUTT
PUTT PUTT
shuff
Truce.
SPLASH

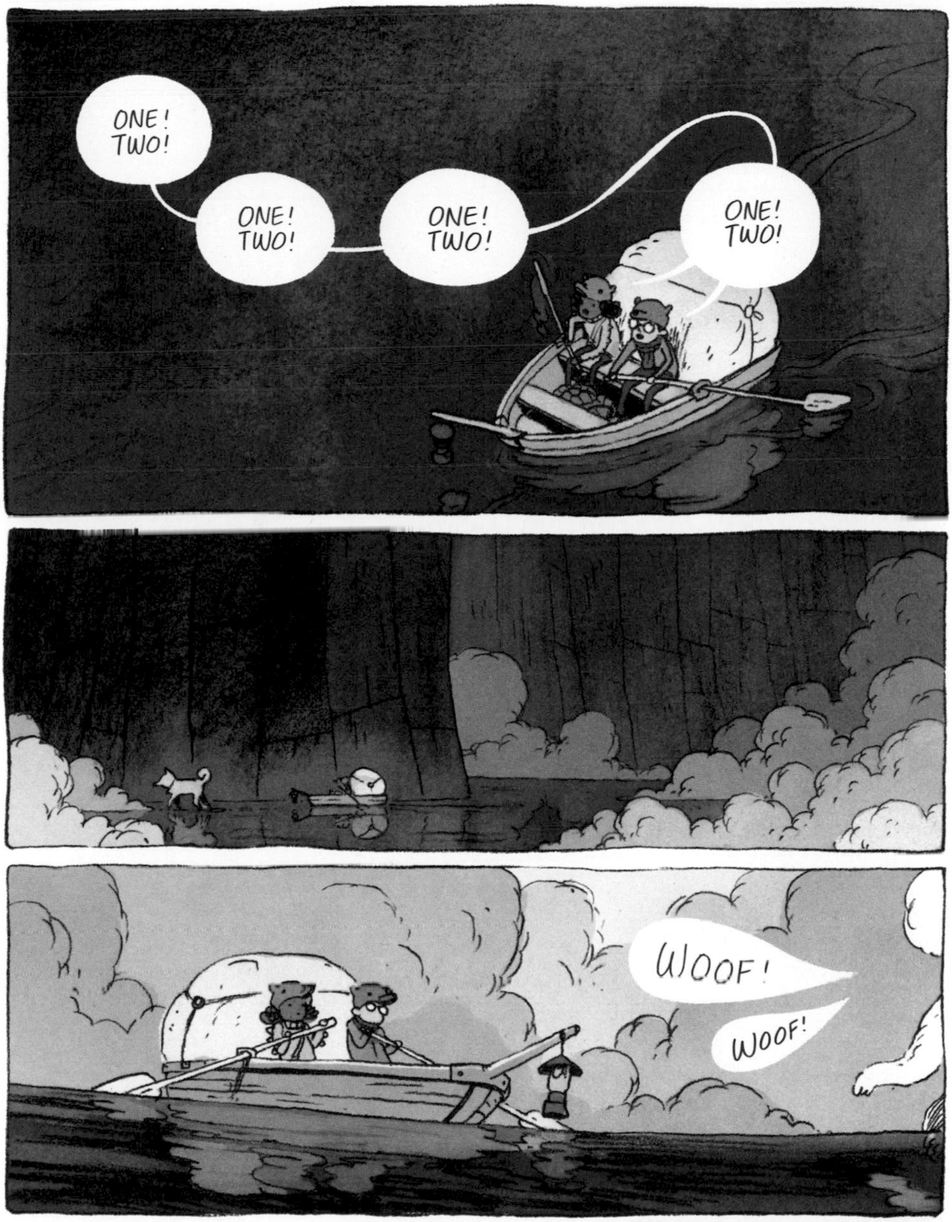
ONE! TWO!
ONE! TWO!
ONE! TWO!
ONE! TWO!
WOOF!
WOOF!

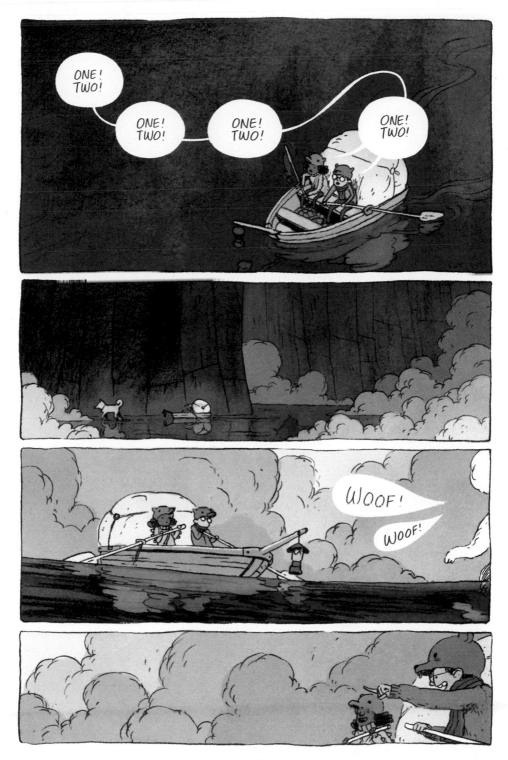

CHAPTER SIX

THE CAVE THAT CARRIED THE COSMOS

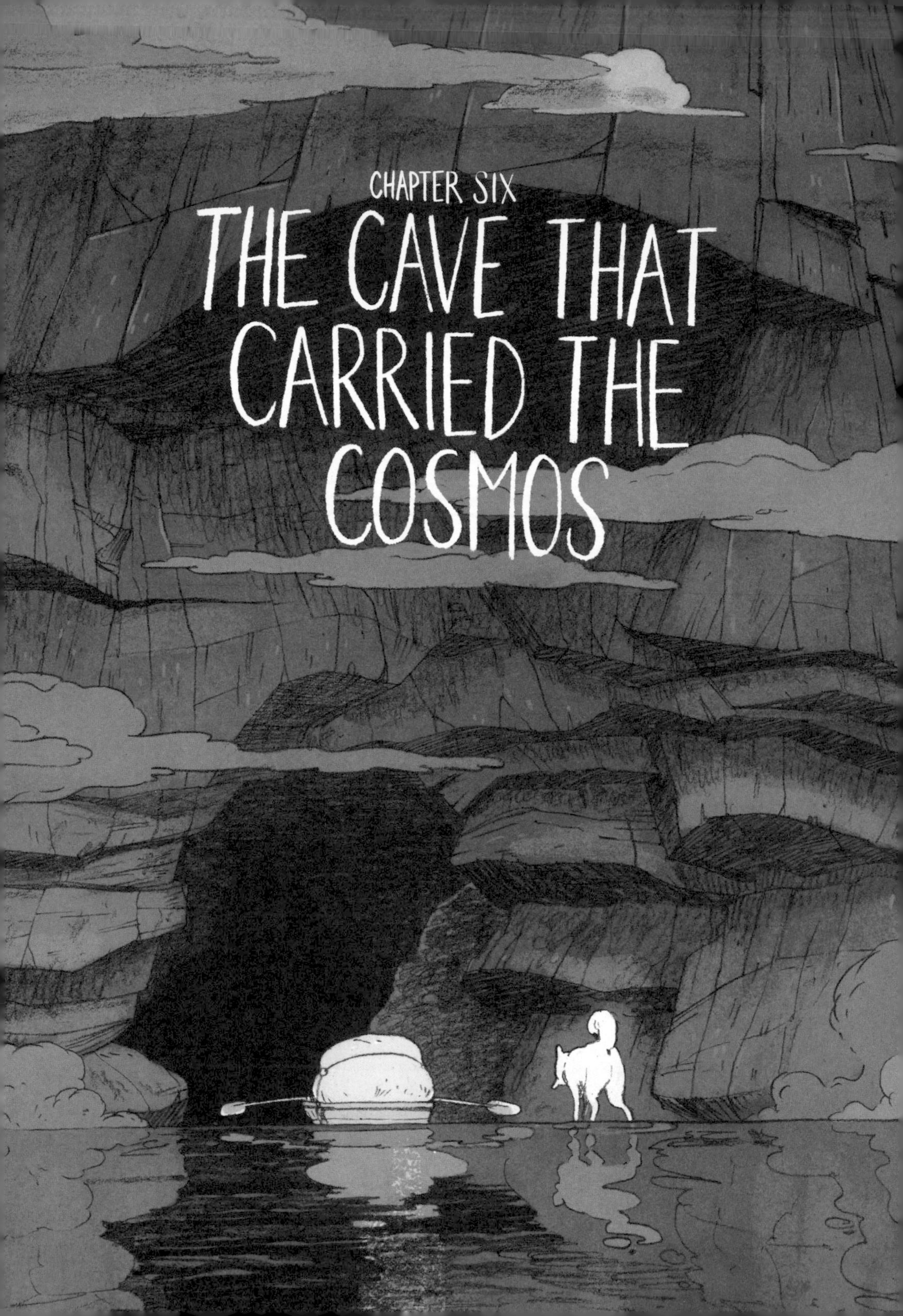

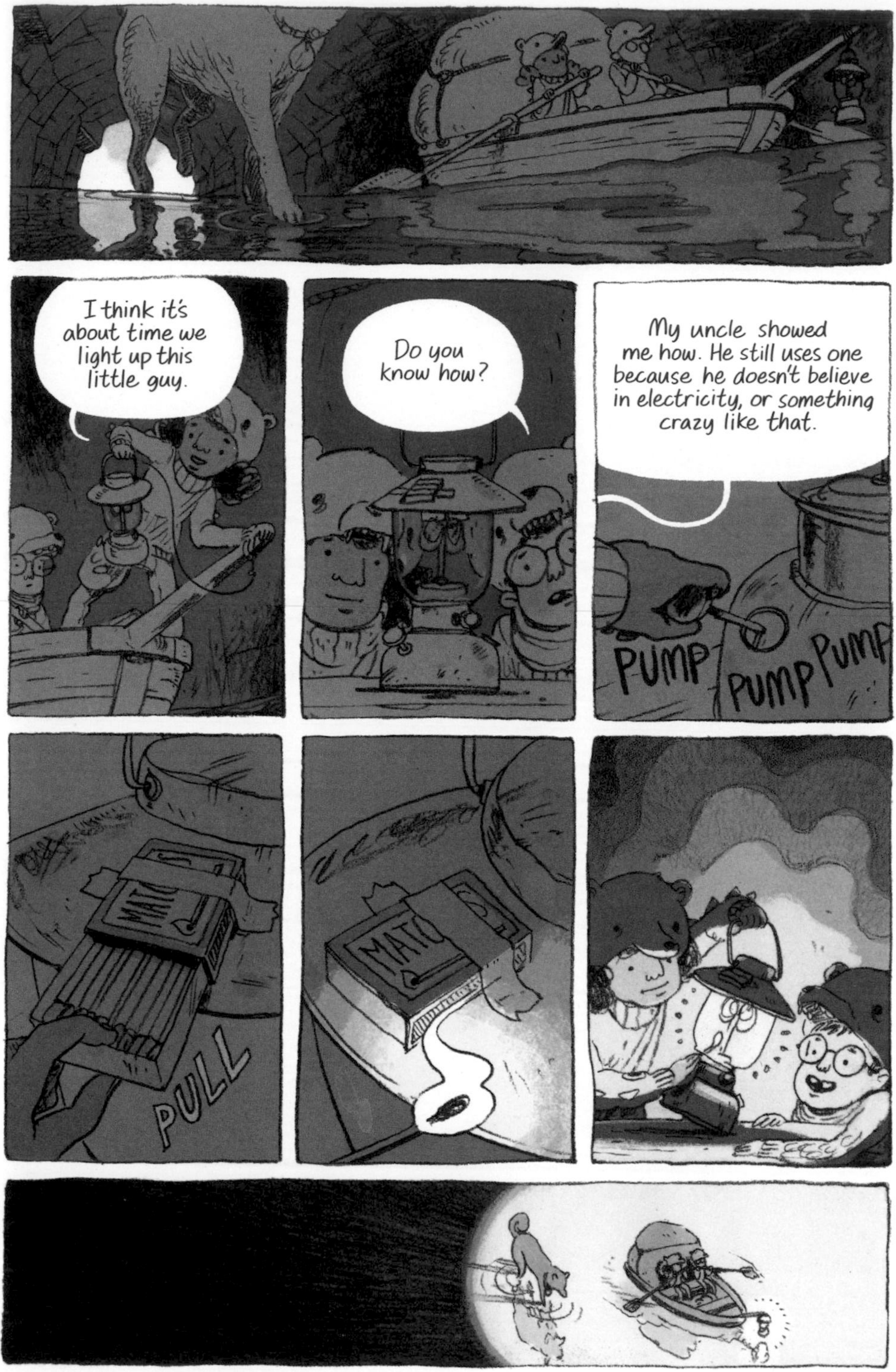

I think it's about time we light up this little guy.
Do you know how?
My uncle showed me how. He still uses one because he doesn't believe in electricity, or something crazy like that.
PUMP
PUMP PUMP
PULL

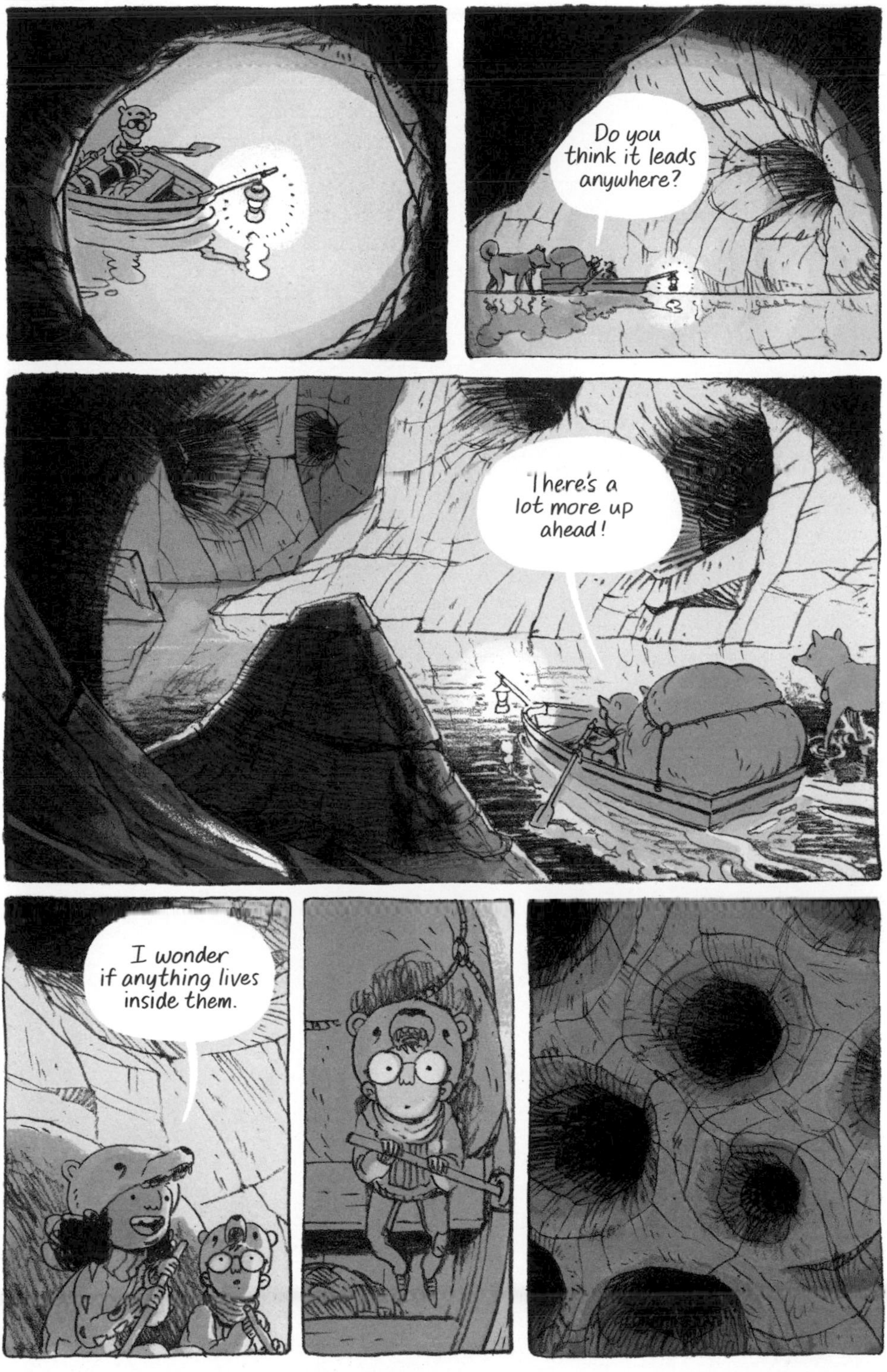
Do you think it leads anywhere?
There's a lot more up ahead!
I wonder if anything lives inside them.

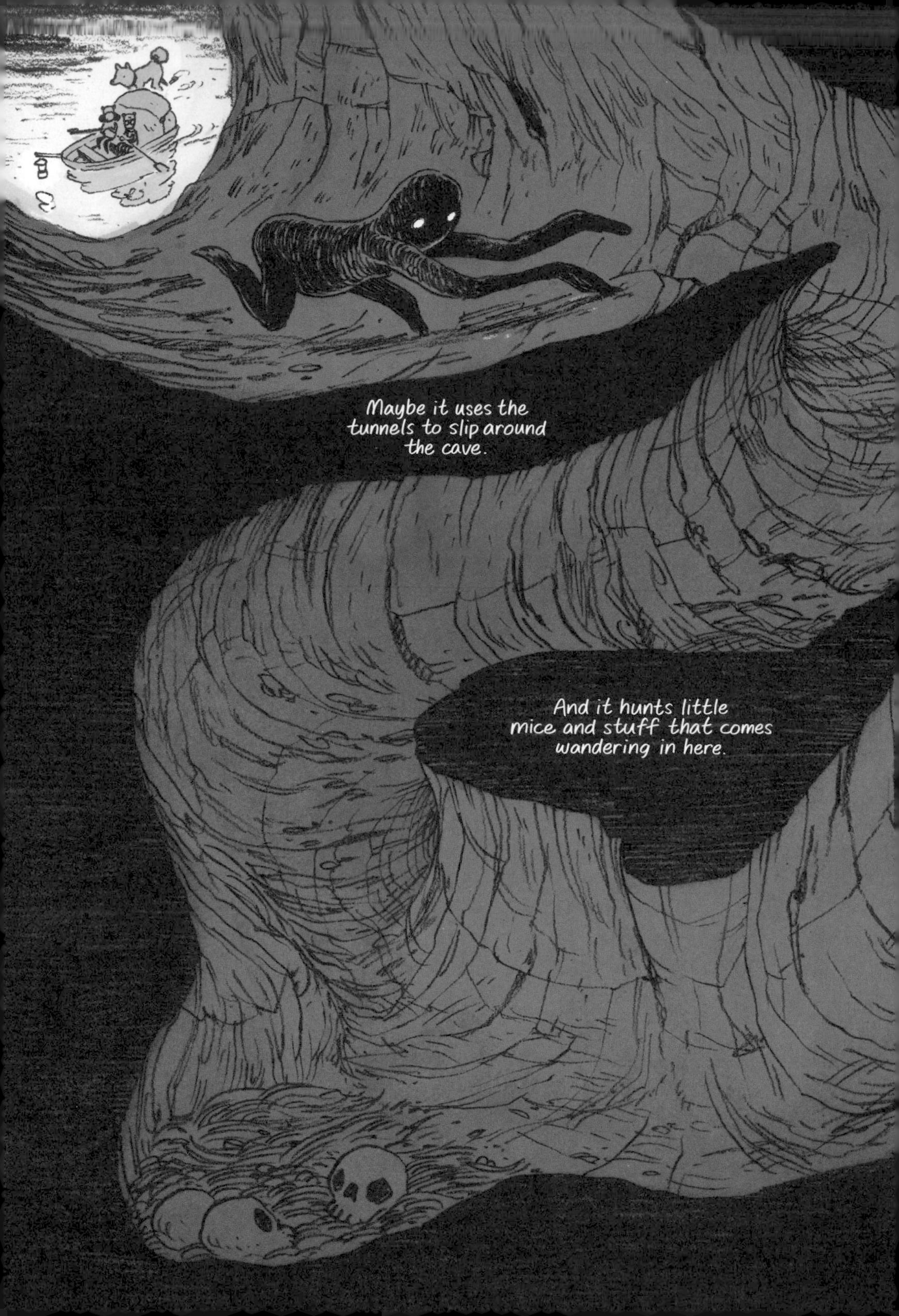
Maybe it uses the tunnels to slip around the cave.
And it hunts little mice and stuff that comes wandering in here.

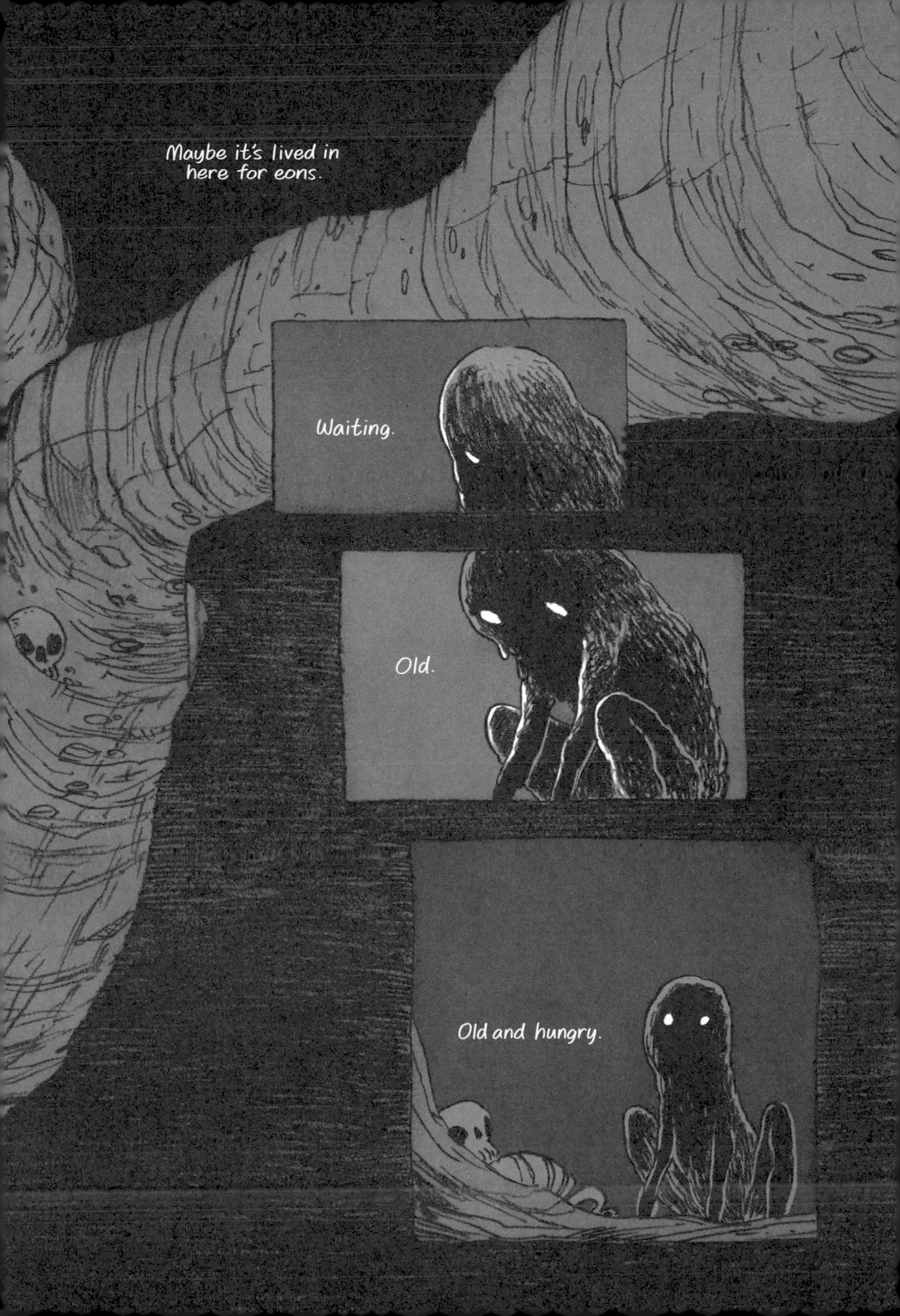
Maybe it's lived in here for eons.
Waiting.
Old.
Old and hungry.

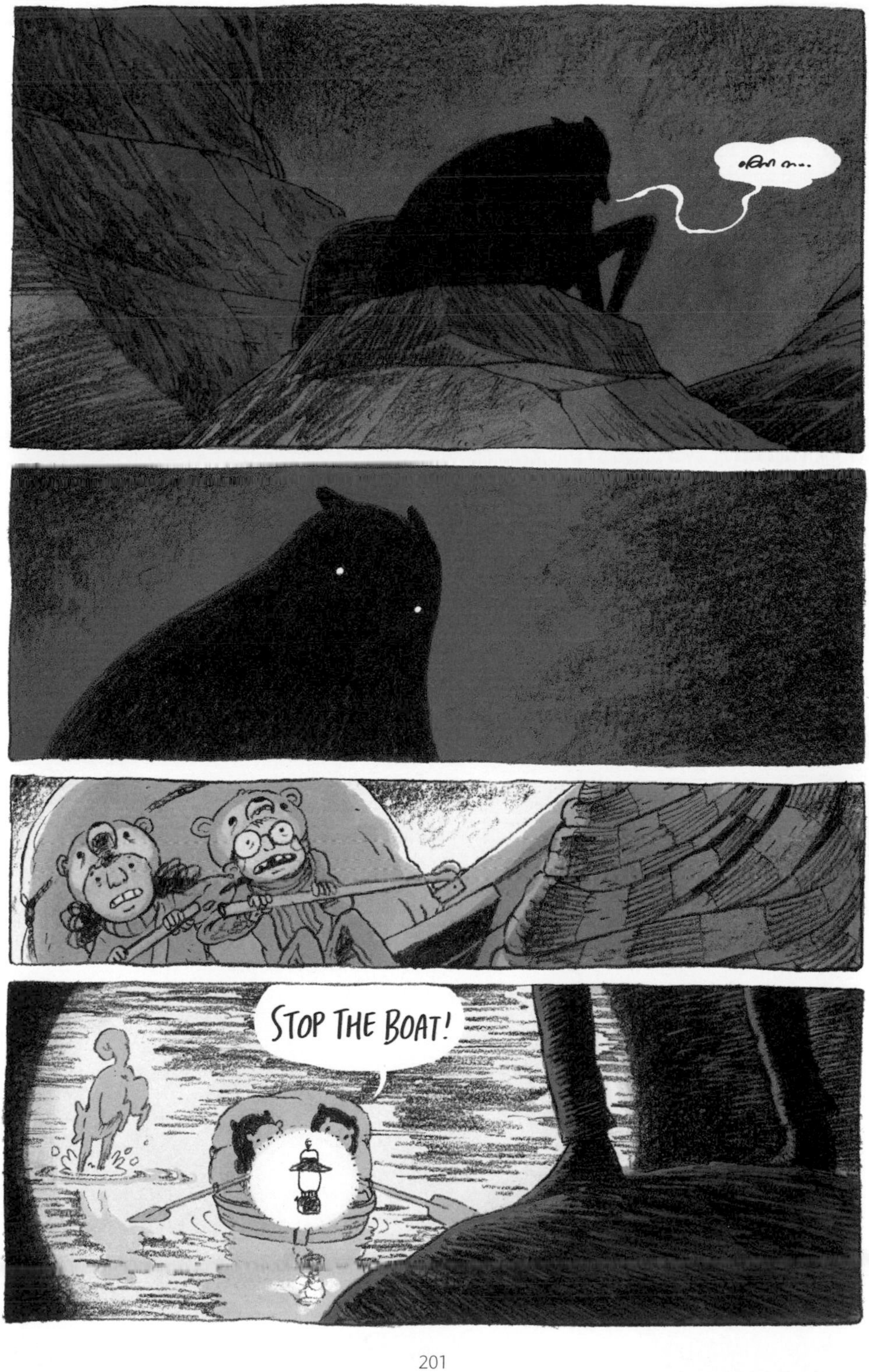
STOP THE BOAT!

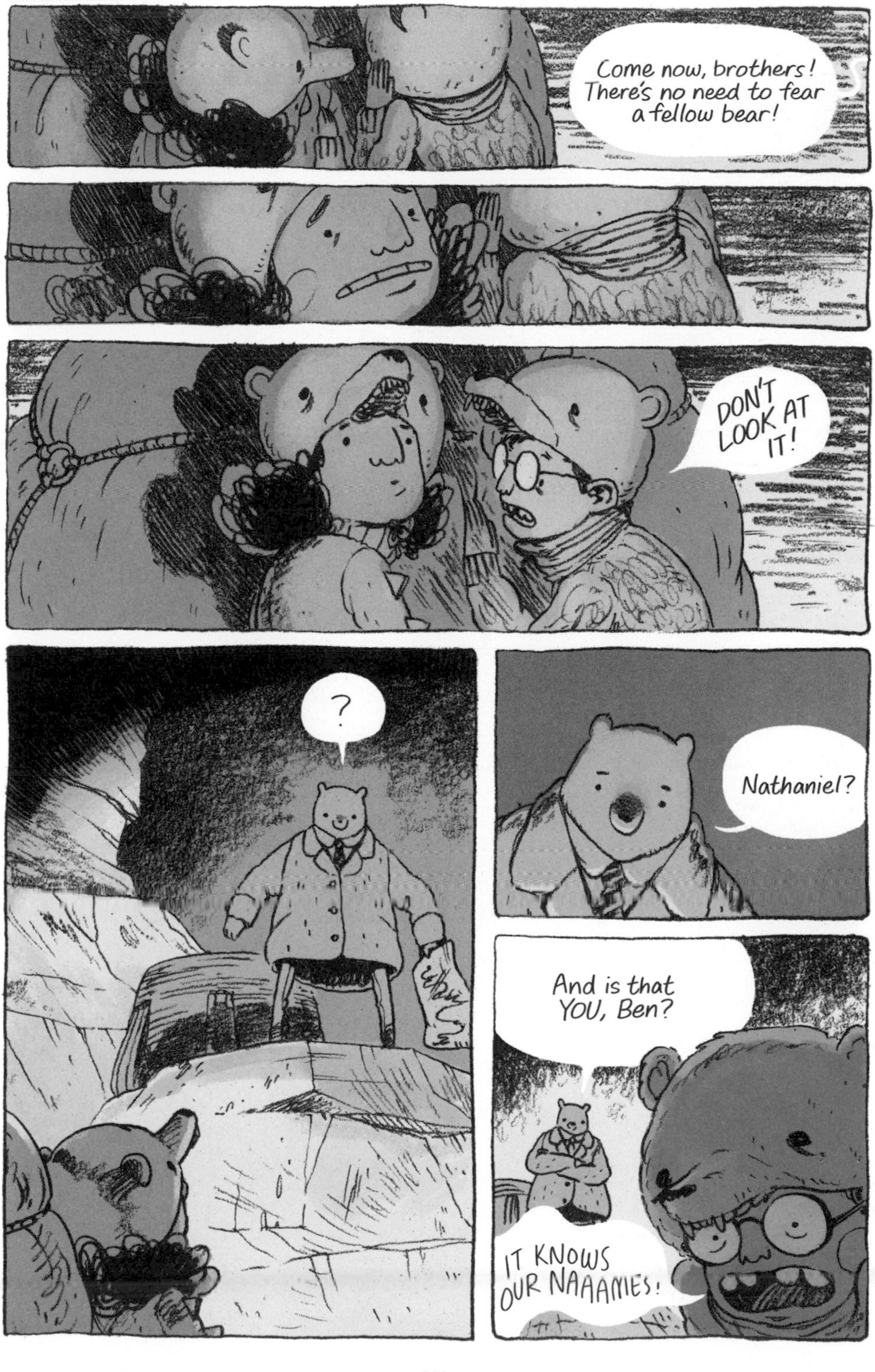
Come now, brothers! There's no need to fear a fellow bear!
DON'T LOOK AT IT!
?
Nathaniel?
And is that YOU, Ben?
IT KNOWS OUR NAAAMES!

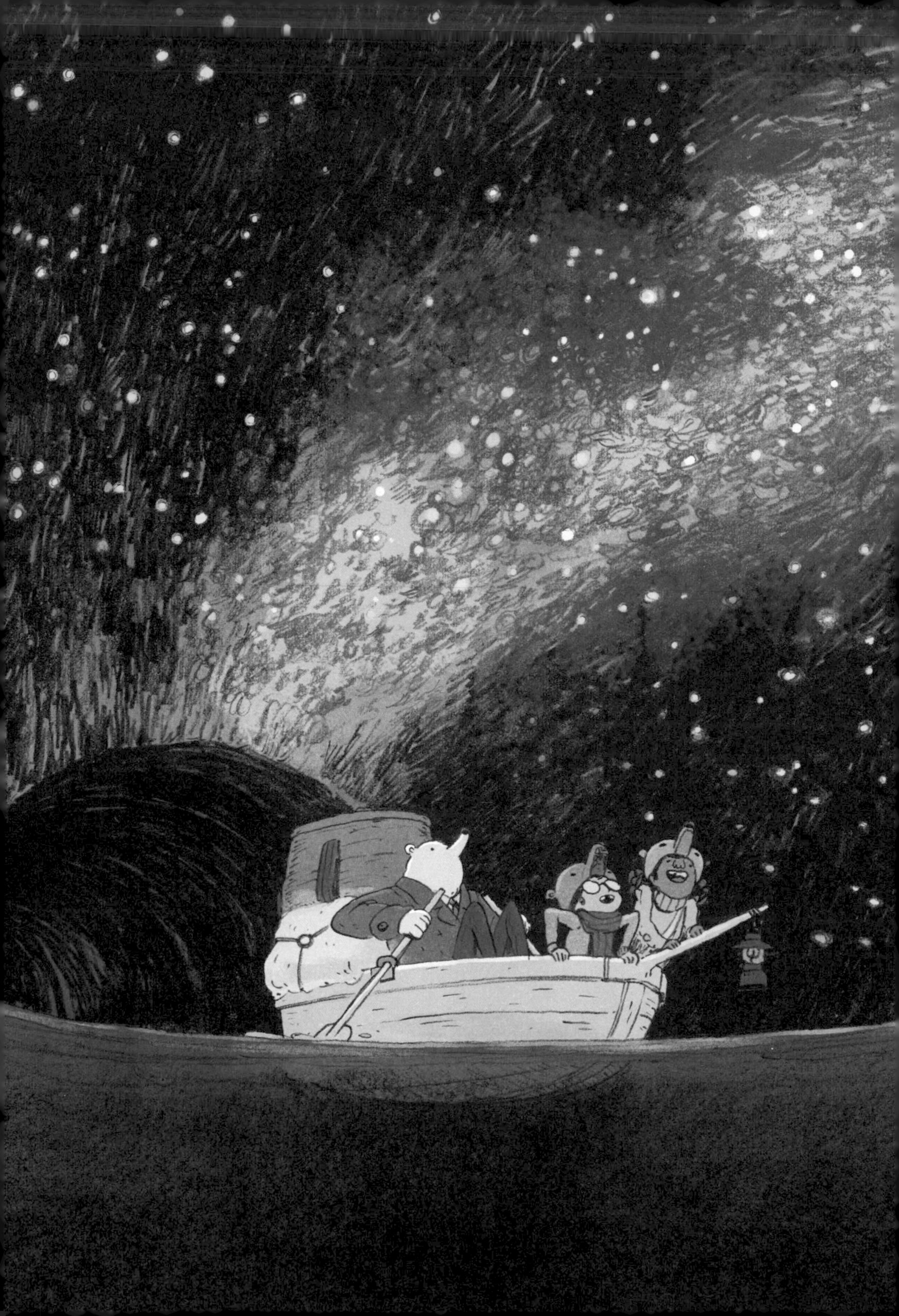

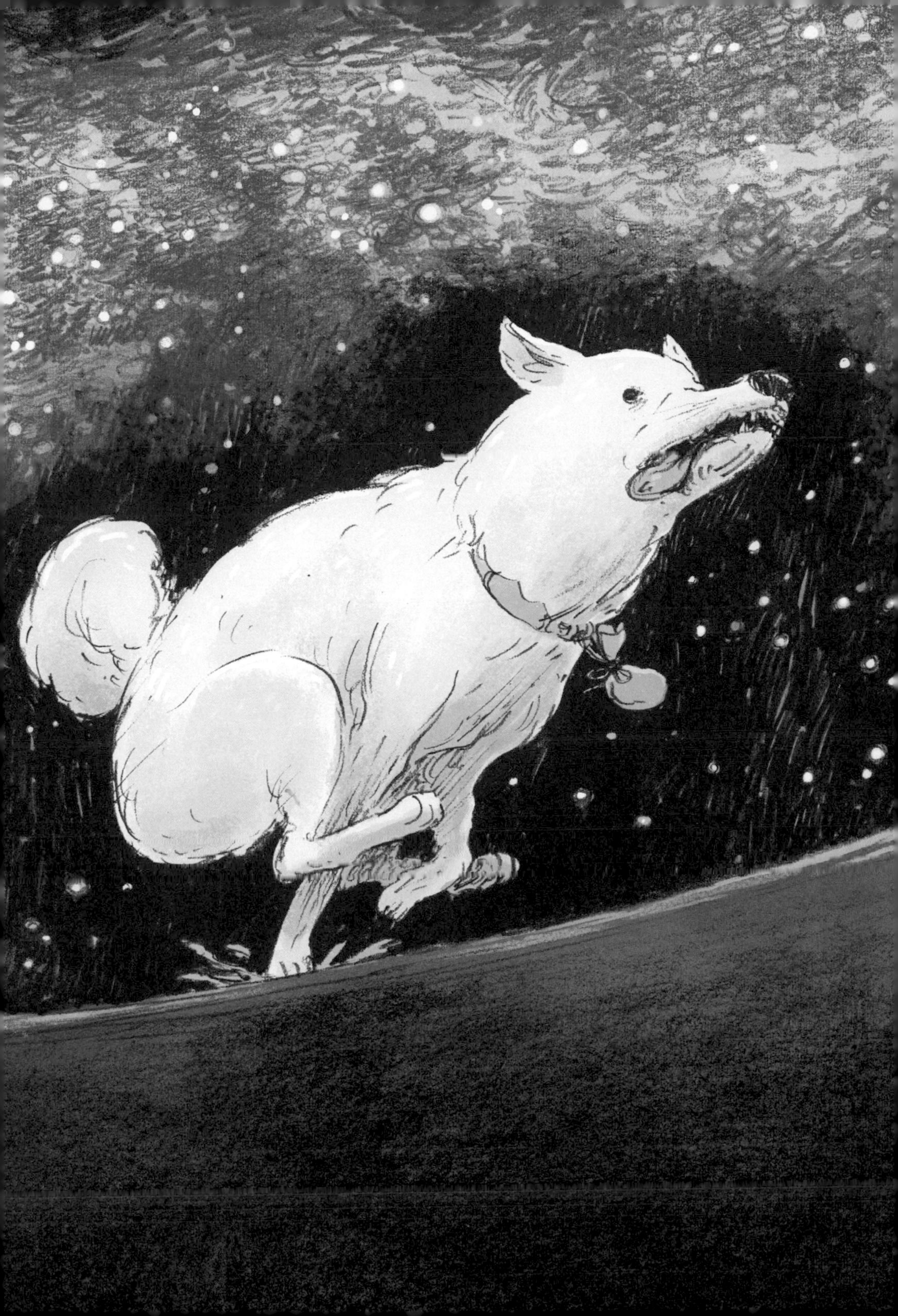

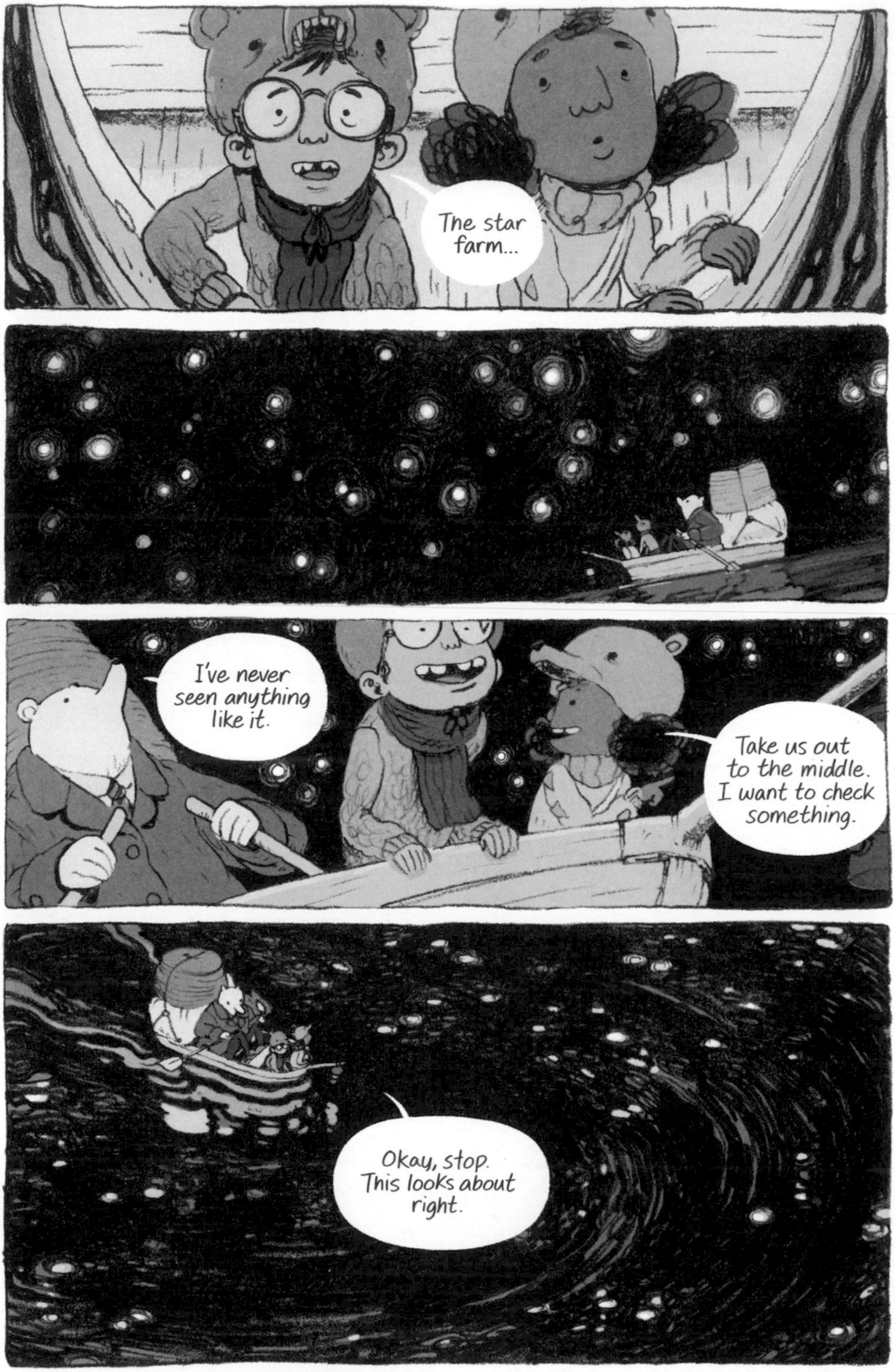
The star farm...
I've never seen anything like it.
Take us out to the middle. I want to check something.
Okay, stop. This looks about right.

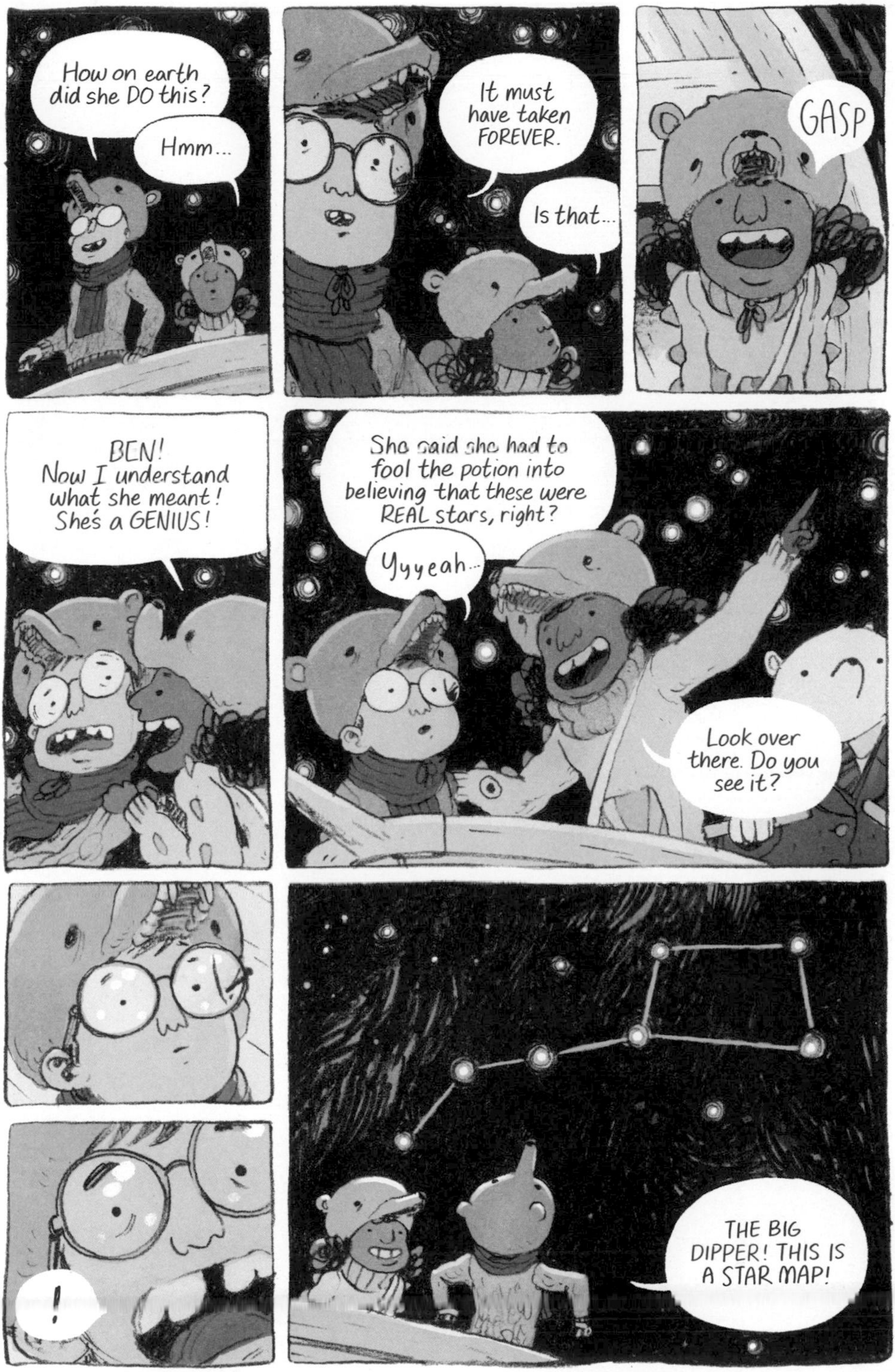
How on earth did she DO this?
Hmm...
It must have taken FOREVER.
Is that...
GASP
BEN! Now I understand what she meant! She's a GENIUS!
She said she had to fool the potion into believing that these were REAL stars, right?
Yyyeah...
Look over there. Do you see it?
!
THE BIG DIPPER! THIS IS A STAR MAP!

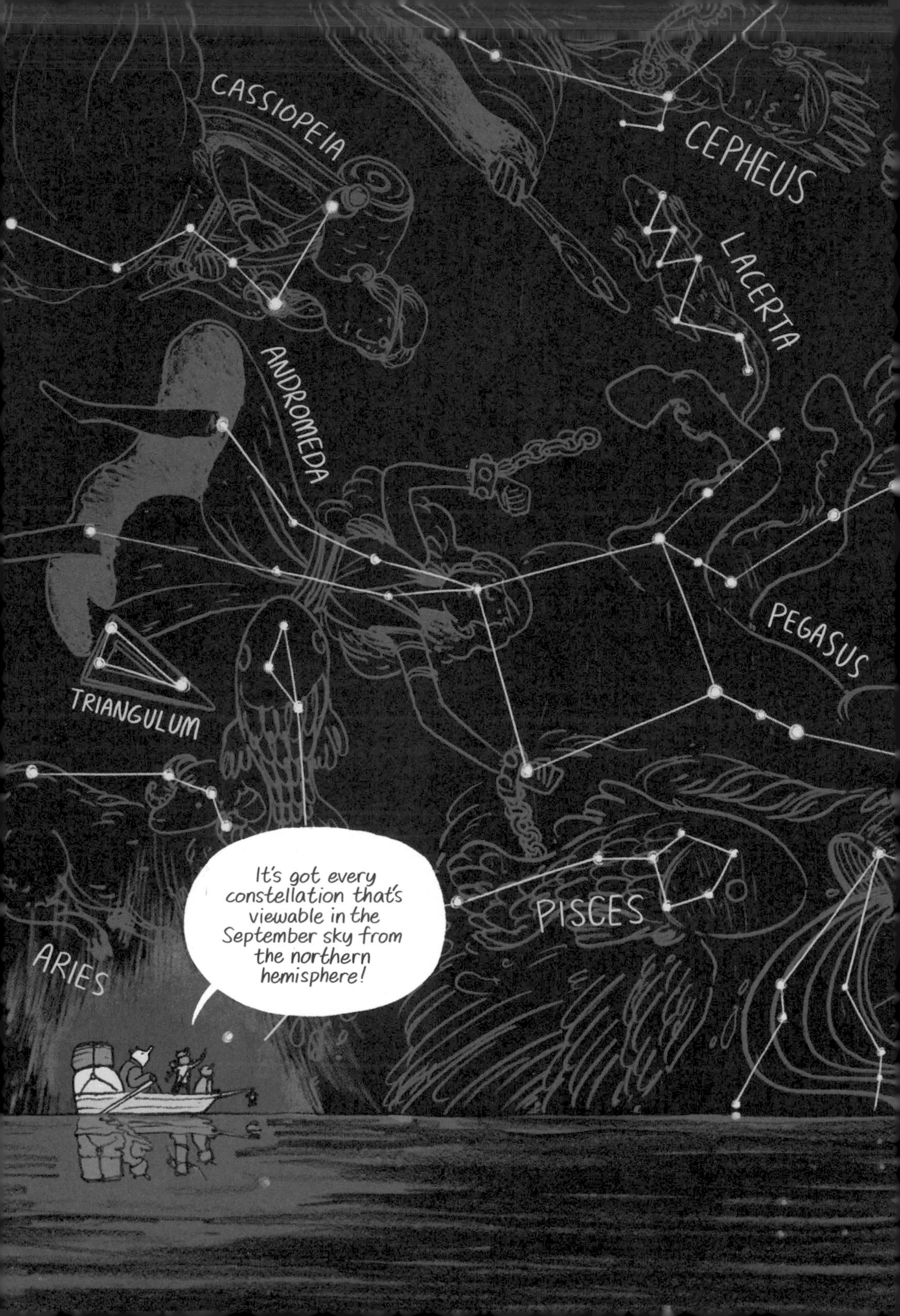
CASSIOPEIA
CEPHEUS
LACERTA
ANDROMEDA
PEGASUS
TRIANGULUM
PISCES
ARIES
It's got every constellation that's viewable in the September sky from the northern hemisphere!

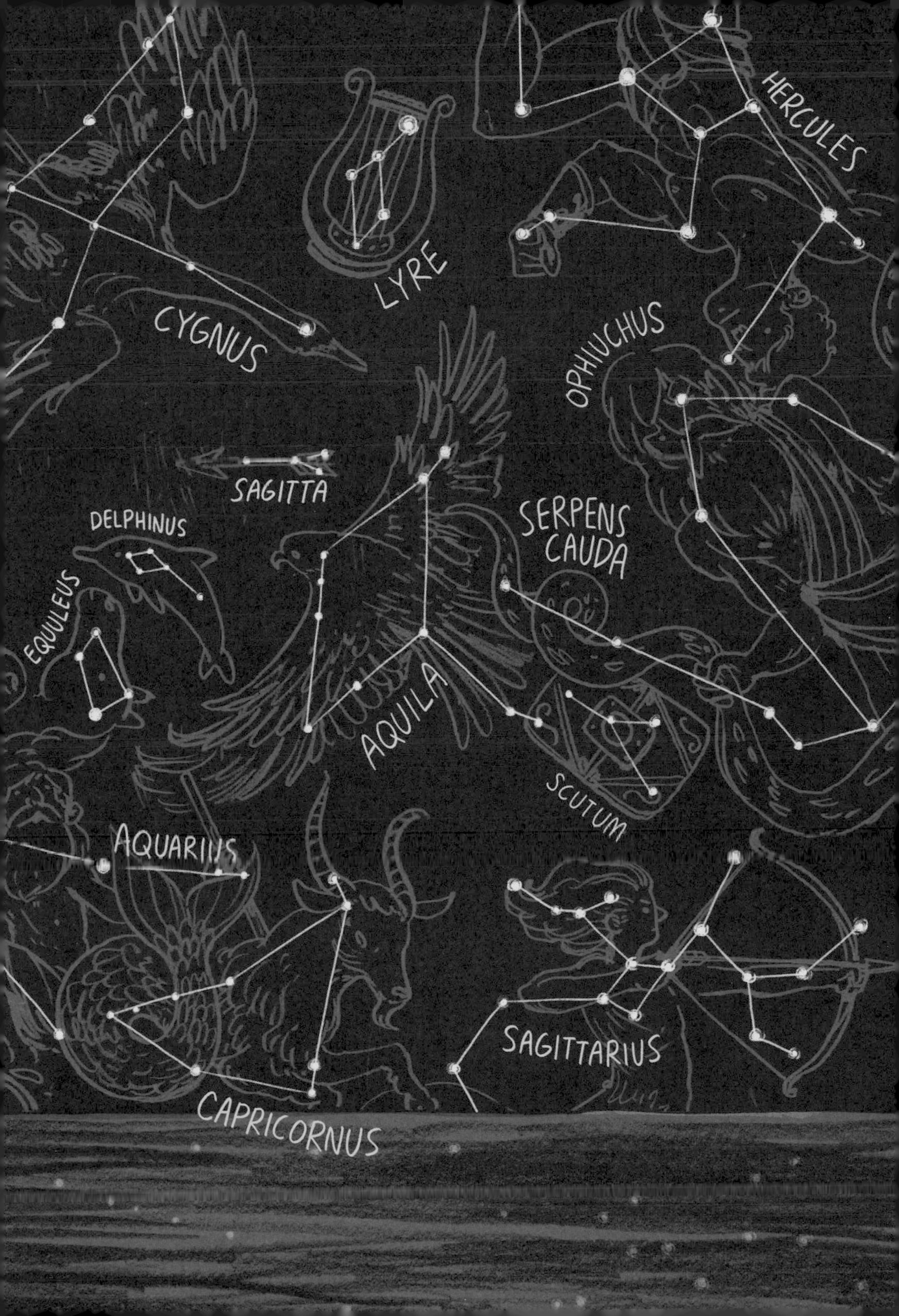

HERCULES
LYRE
CYGNUS
OPHIUCHUS
SAGITTA
DELPHINUS
SERPENS CAUDA
EQUULEUS
AQUILA
SCUTUM
AQUARIUS
SAGITTARIUS
CAPRICORNUS

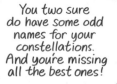

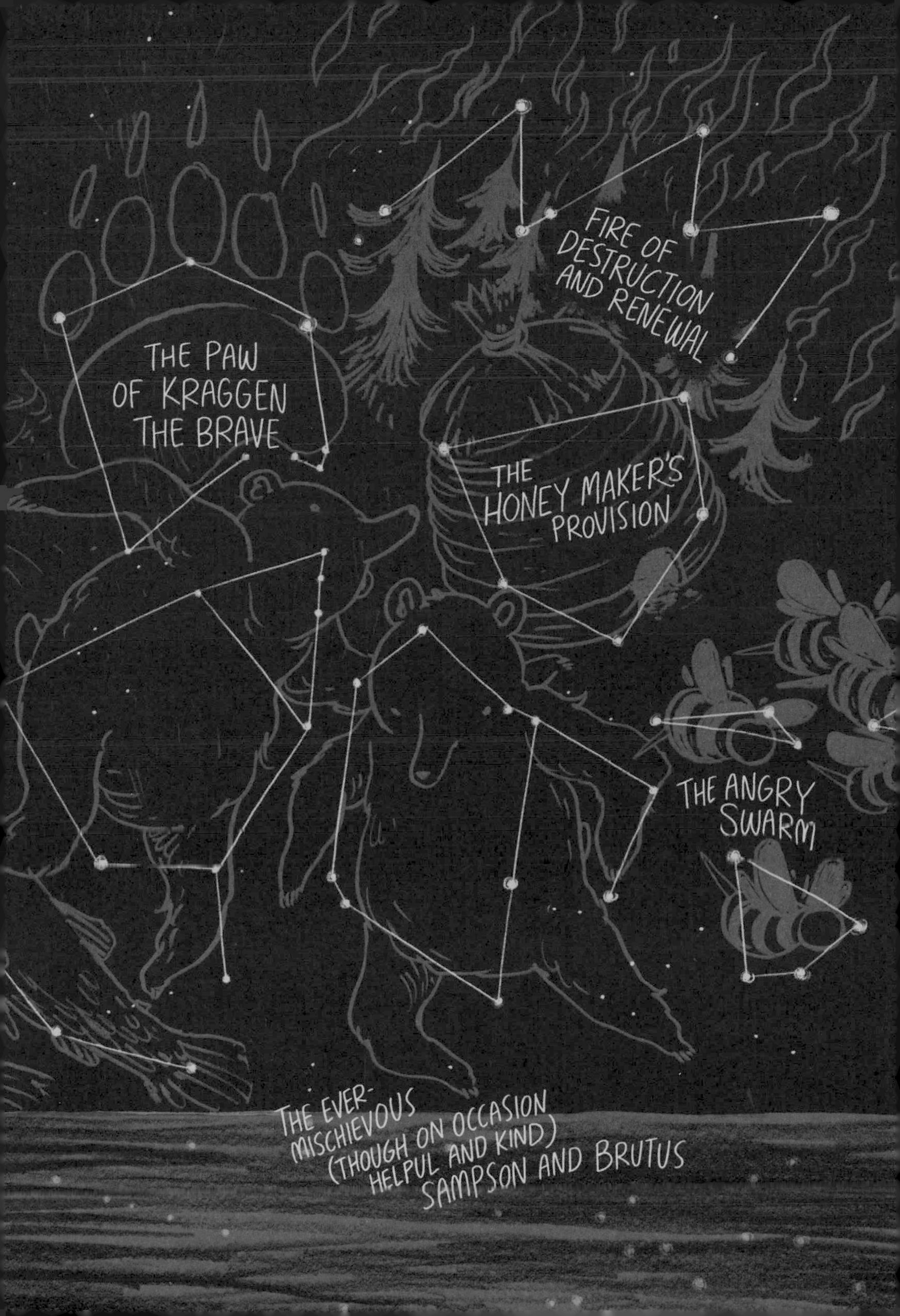
FIRE OF DESTRUCTION AND RENEWAL
THE PAW OF KRAGGEN THE BRAVE
THE HONEY MAKER'S PROVISION
THE ANGRY SWARM
THE EVER-MISCHIEVOUS (THOUGH ON OCCASION HELPUL AND KIND) SAMPSON AND BRUTUS

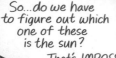

So...do we have to figure out which one of these is the sun?

That's IMPOSSIBLE! There's literally thousands of them!

I must agree. I consider myself quite the stargazer, but even **I** wouldn't know where to begin searching.

It's not impossible. If this map is accurate, then I bet the sun would be somewhere along the ecliptic.

The what?

?

The ECLIPTIC.

It's the path that the sun appears to follow over the course of a year.

Interesting. And is it safe to assume that you know where this path IS, Nathaniel?

Well, sort of.

I know that it runs through all the constellations of the Zodiac.

IUS

SCORPIUS

SAGITTARIUS

CAPRICORNUS

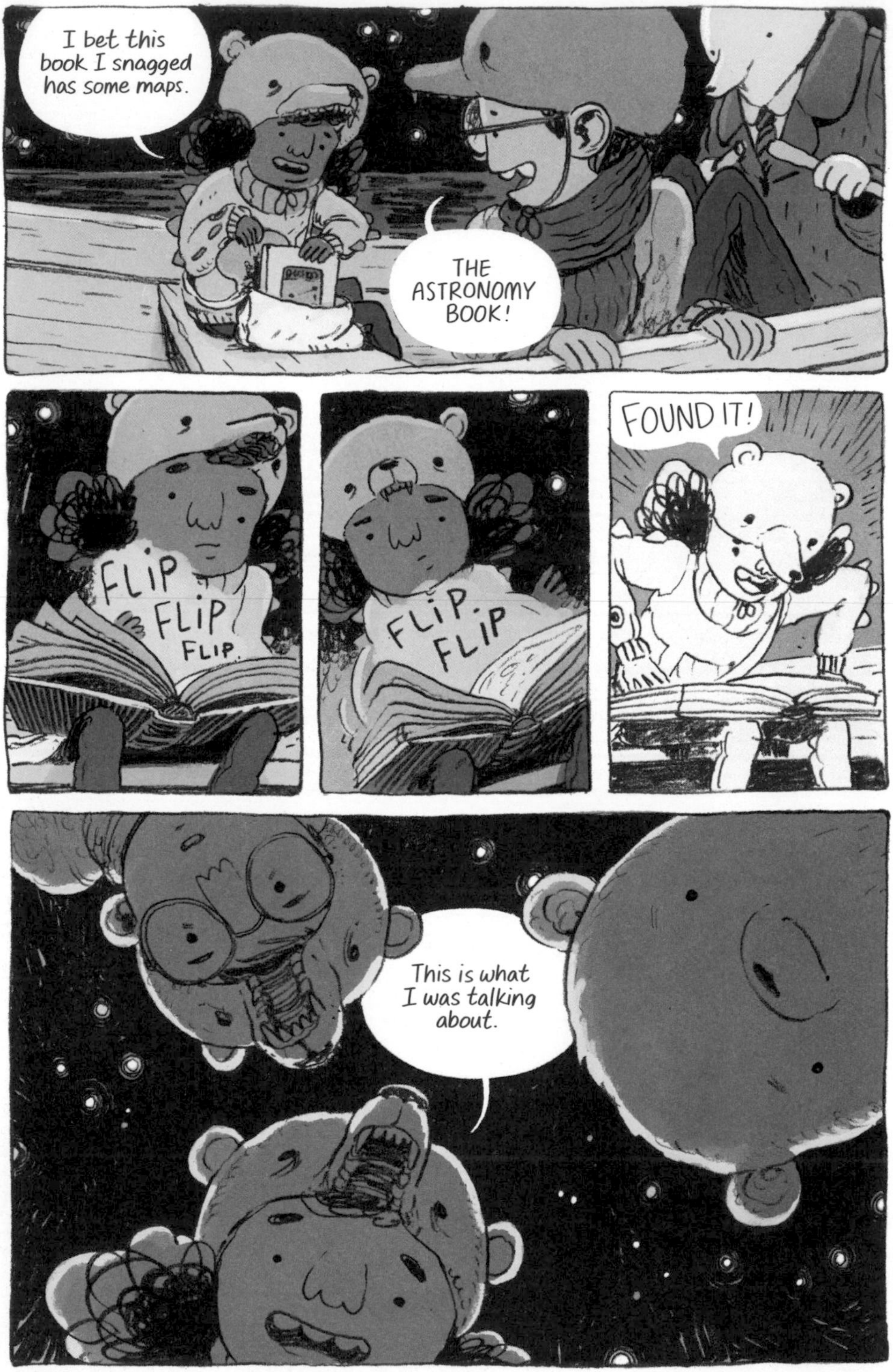
I bet this book I snagged has some maps.
THE ASTRONOMY BOOK!
FLIP FLIP FLIP.
FLIP. FLIP
FOUND IT!
This is what I was talking about.

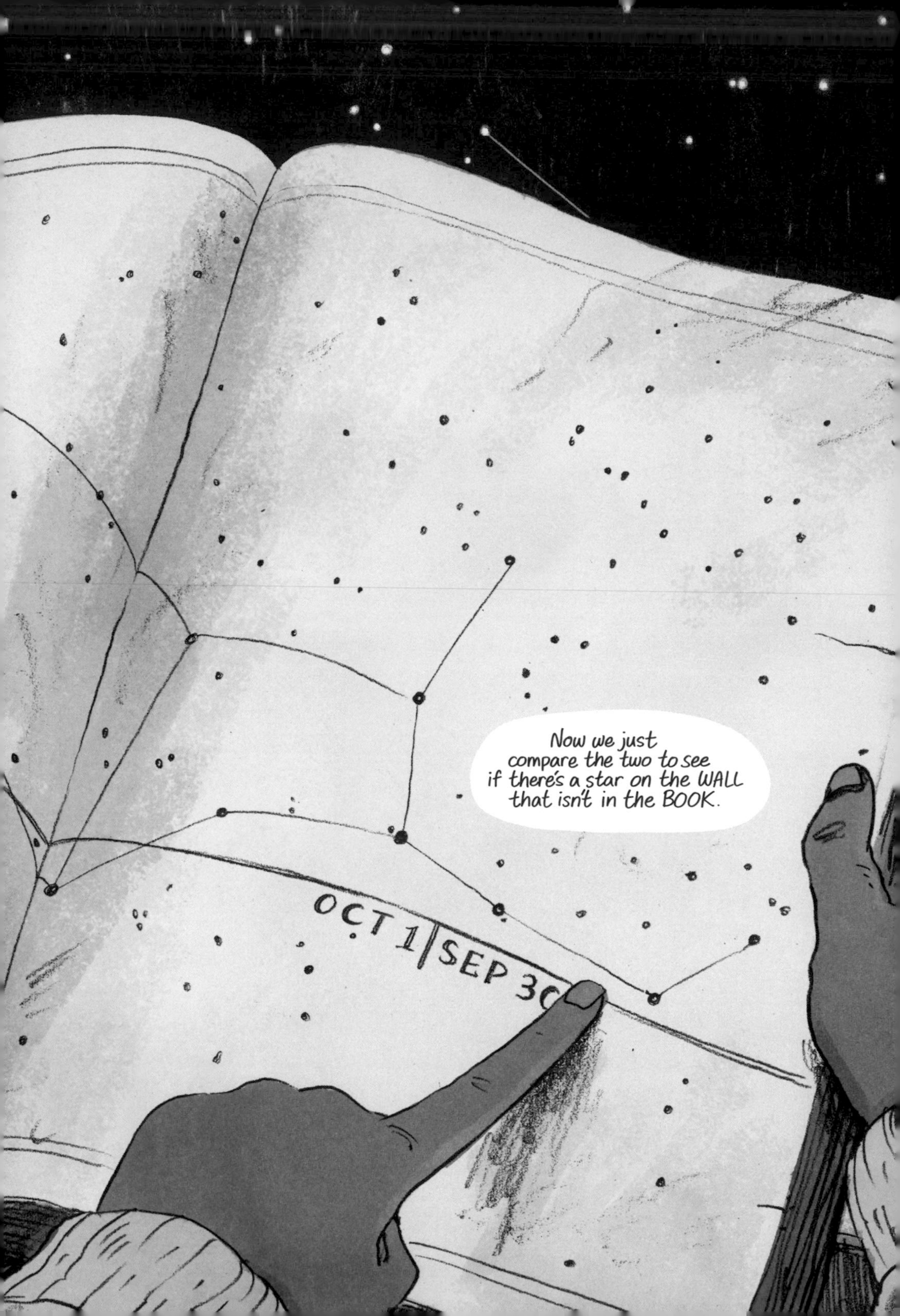
Now we just compare the two to see if there's a star on the WALL that isn't in the BOOK.
OCT 1
SEP 30

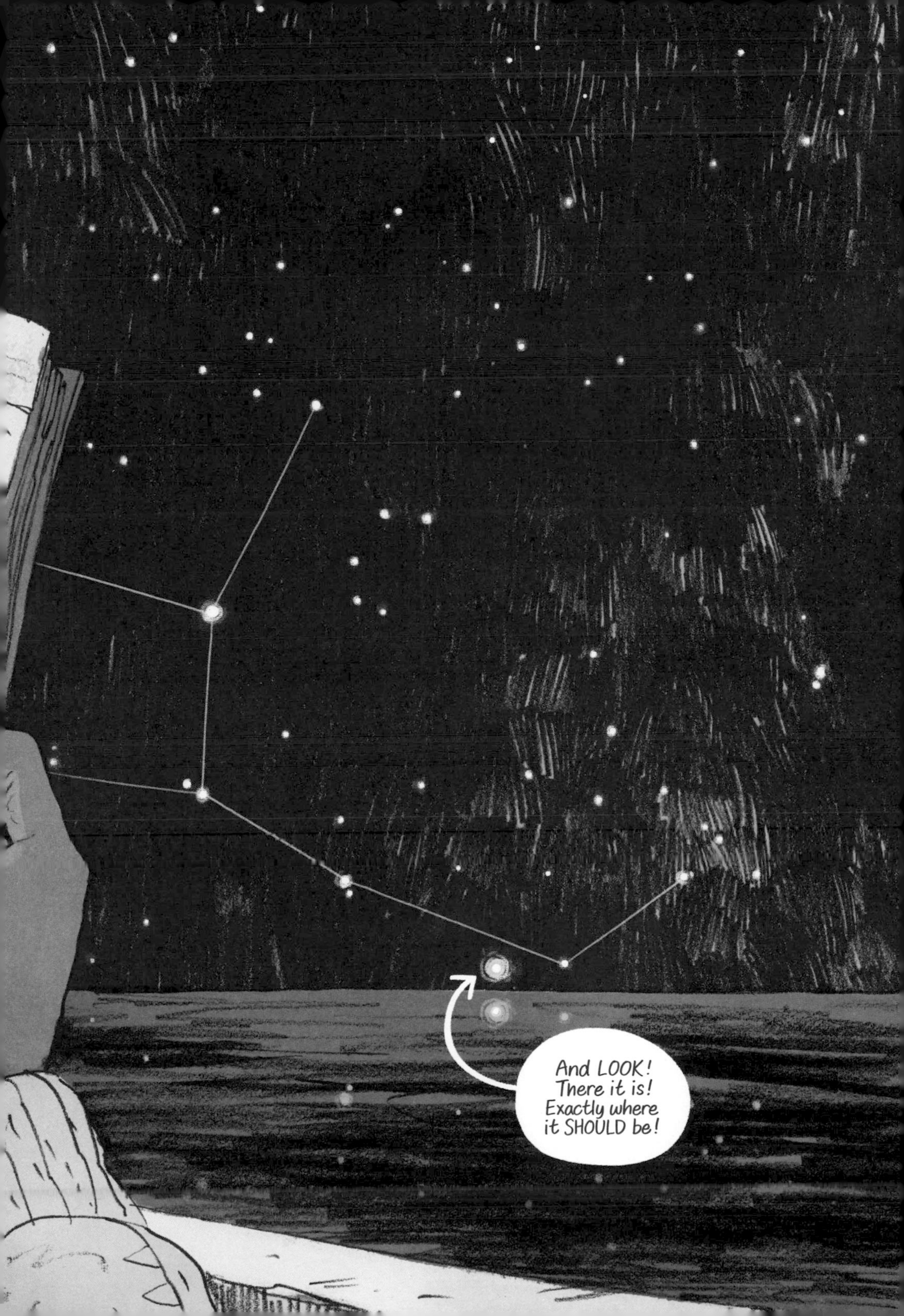
And LOOK! There it is! Exactly where it SHOULD be!

228

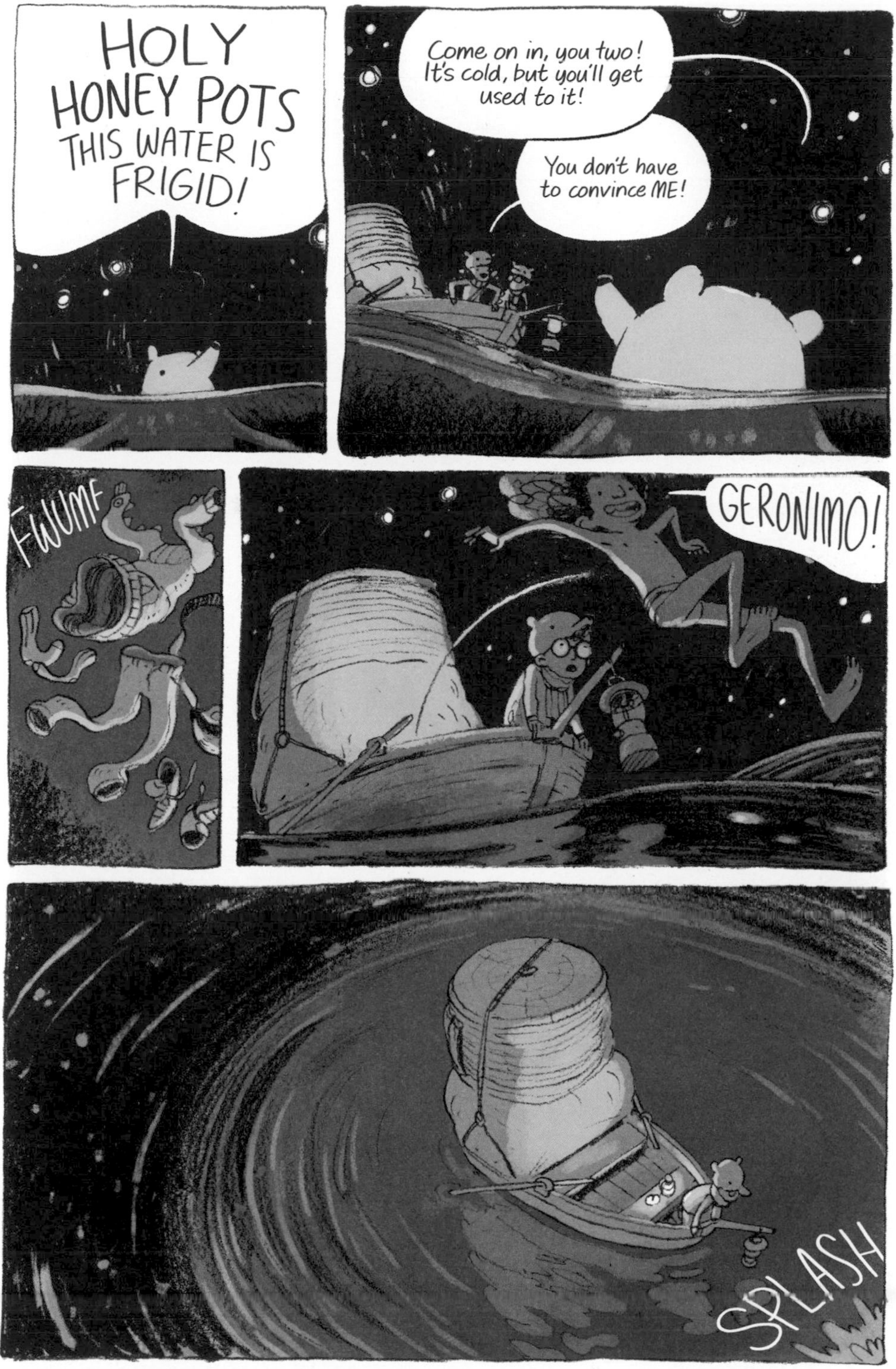
HOLY HONEY POTS THIS WATER IS FRIGID!
Come on in, you two! It's cold, but you'll get used to it!
You don't have to convince ME!
FWUMF
GERONIMO!
SPLASH

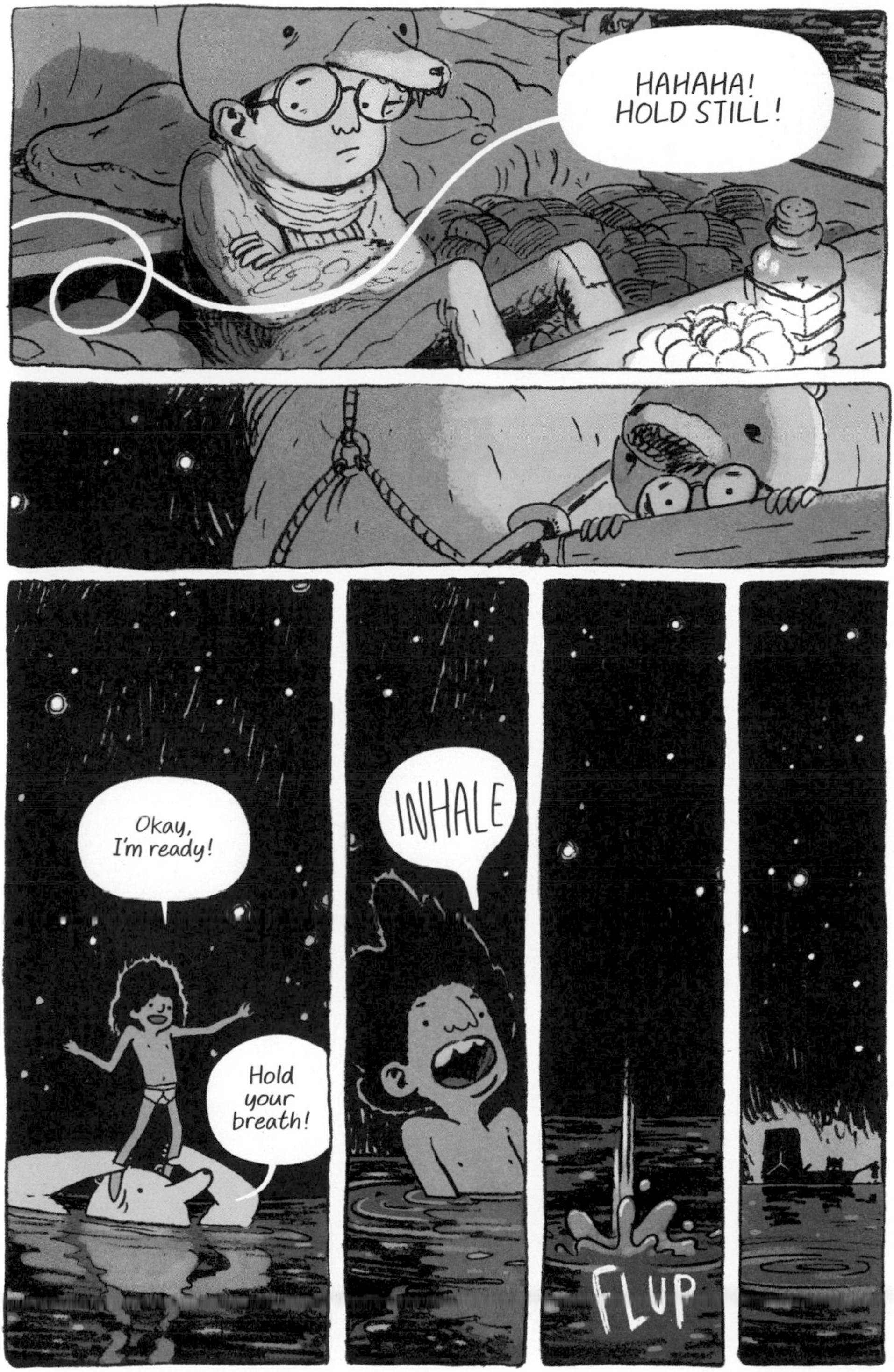
HAHAHA! HOLD STILL!
Okay, I'm ready!
Hold your breath!
INHALE
FLUP

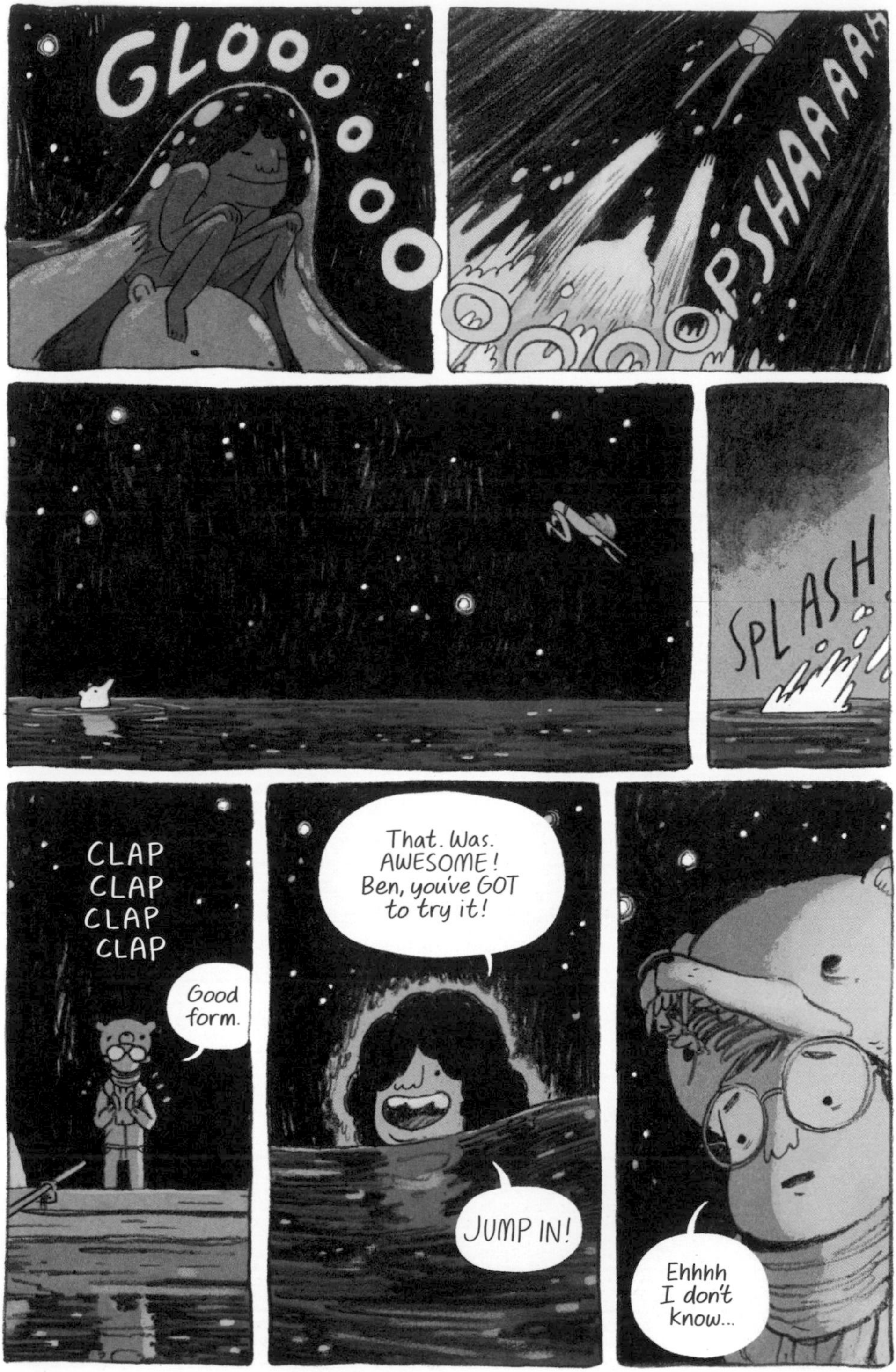
GLOOOOOOOO
PSHAAAA
SPLASH
CLAP
CLAP
CLAP
CLAP
Good form.
That. Was. AWESOME! Ben, you've GOT to try it!
JUMP IN!
Ehhhh I don't know...

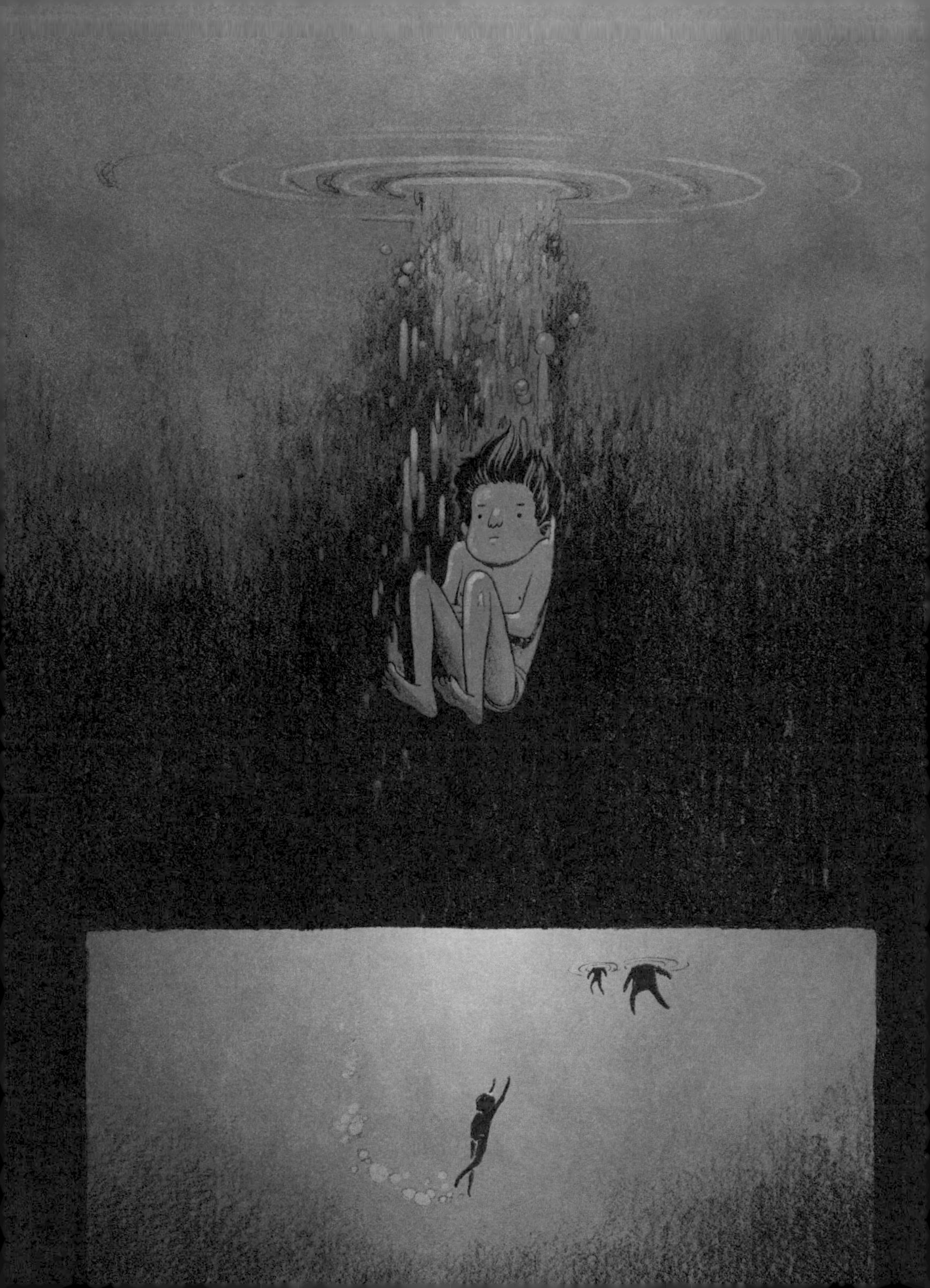

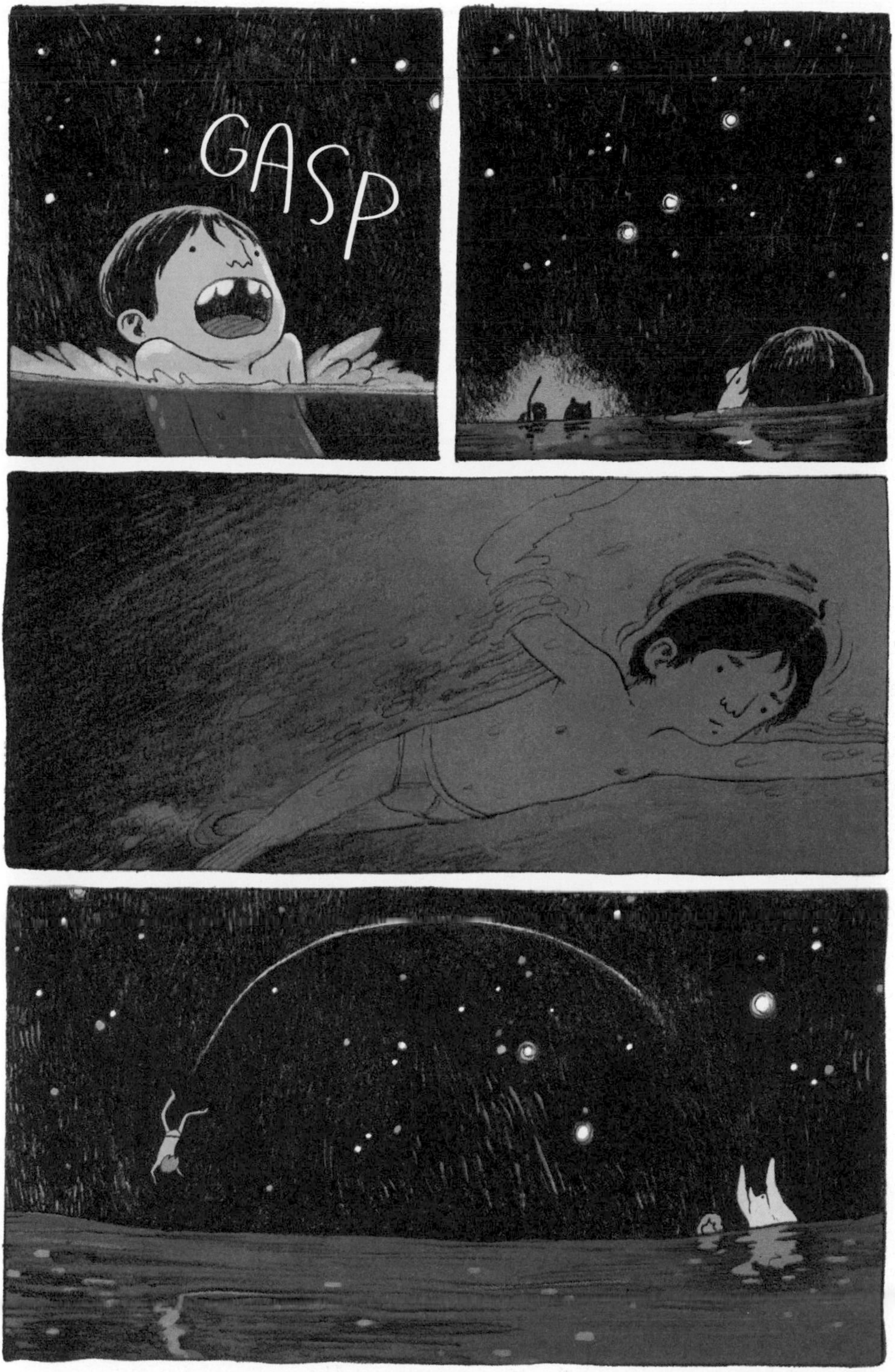
GASP

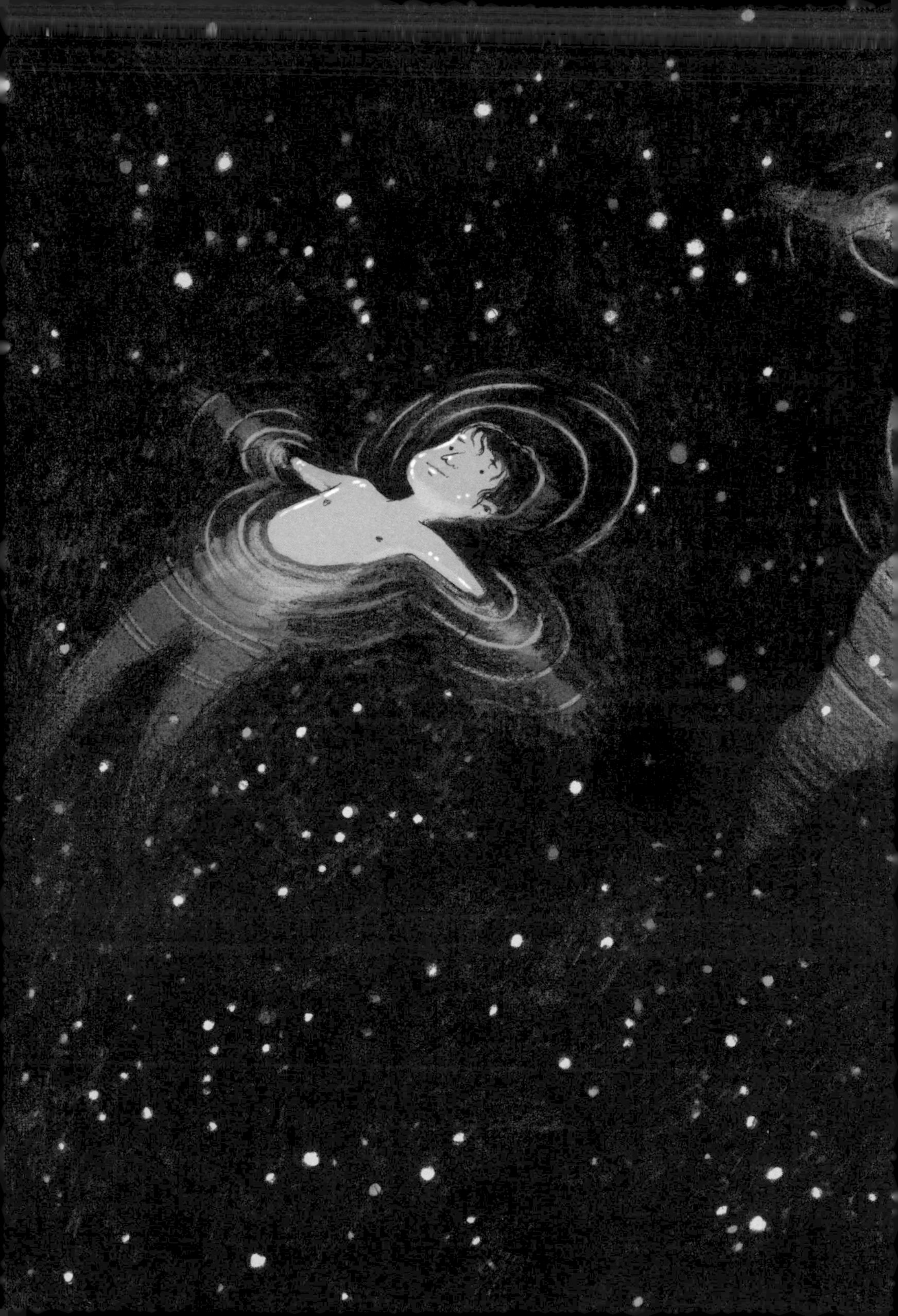

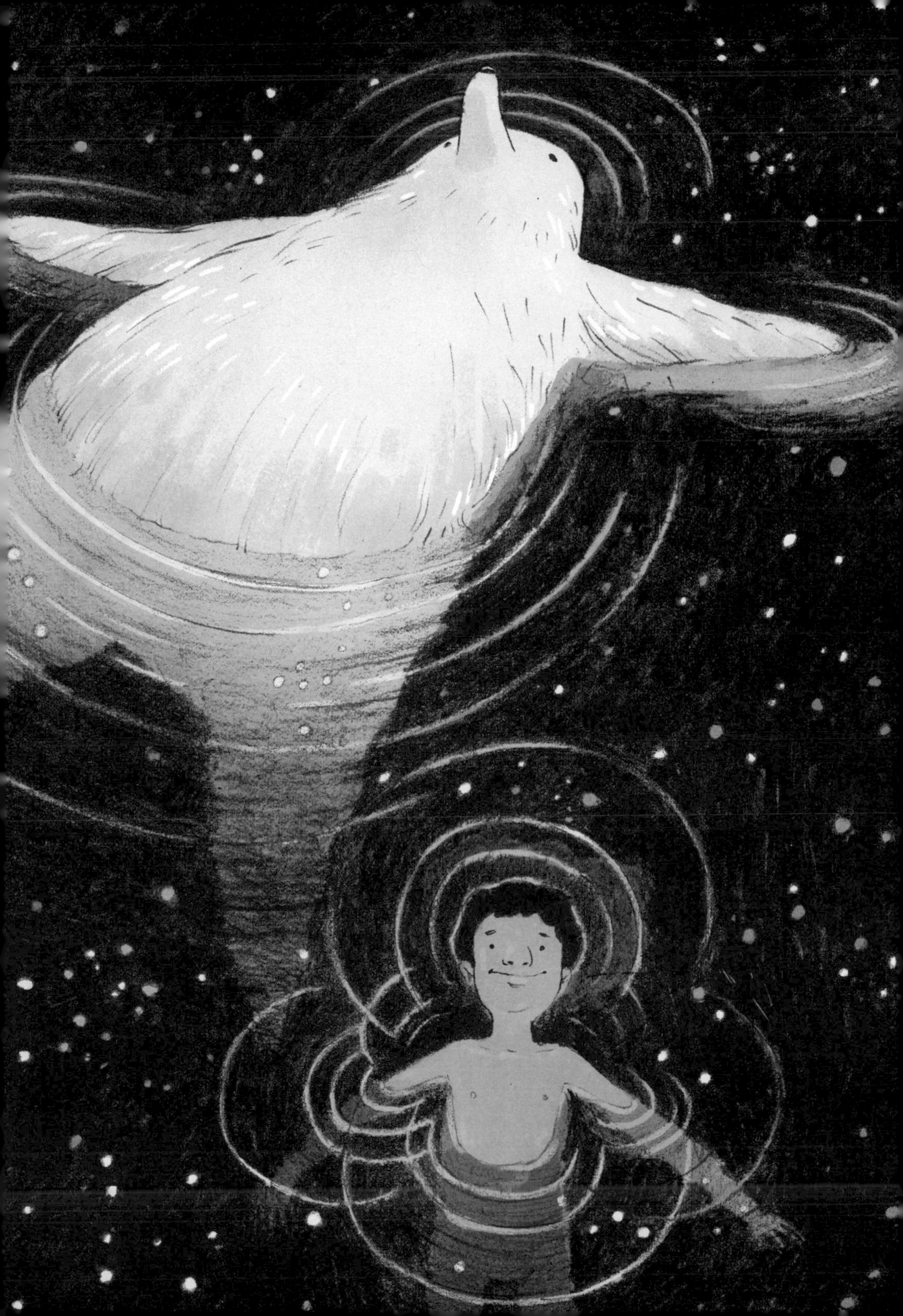

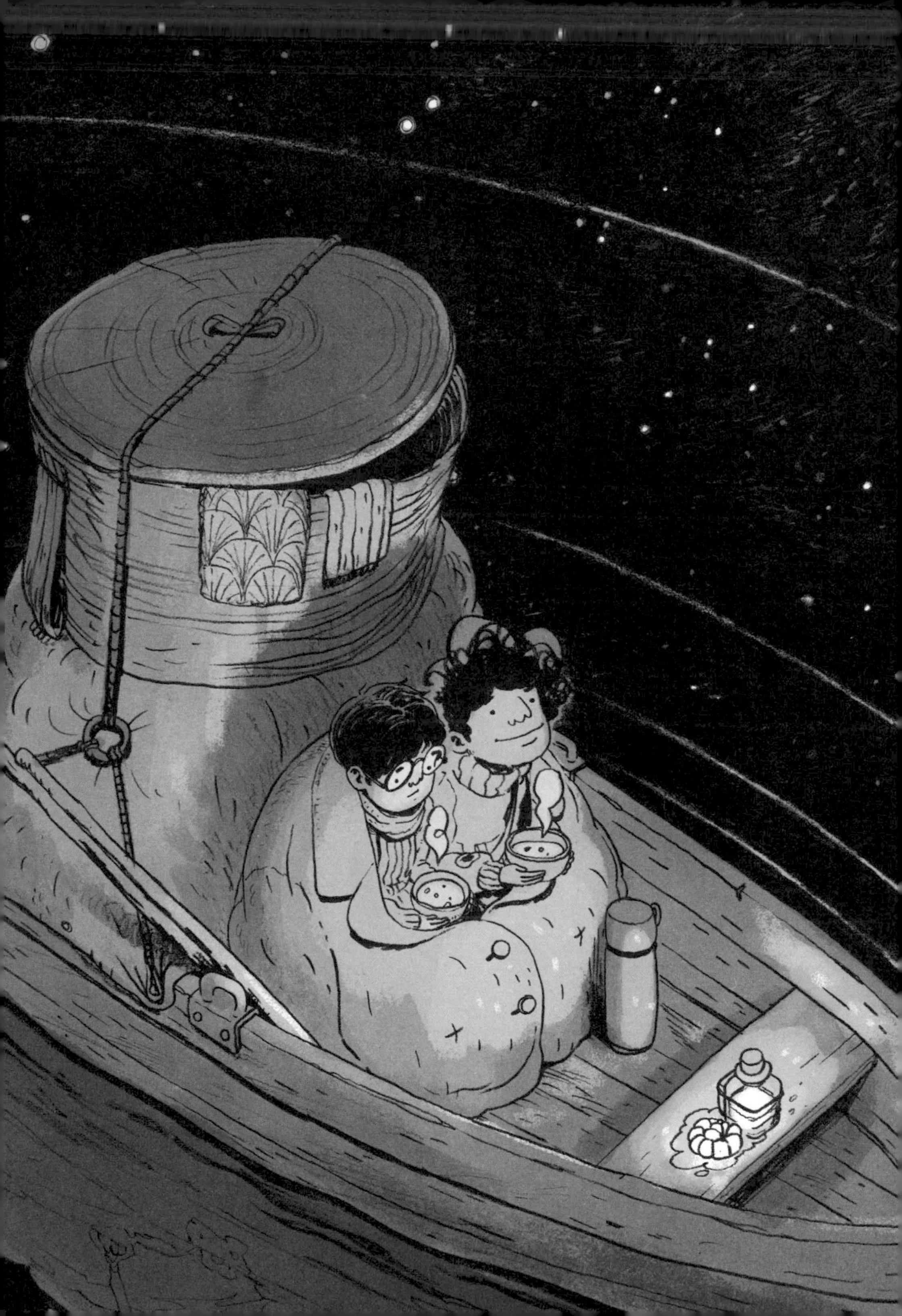

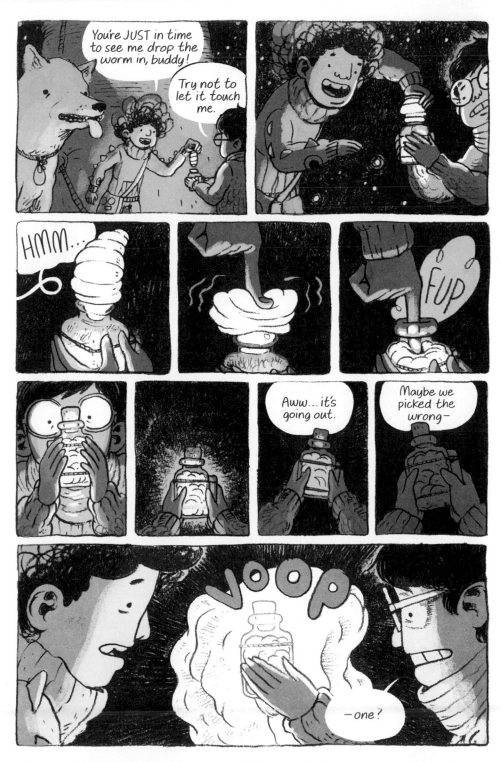

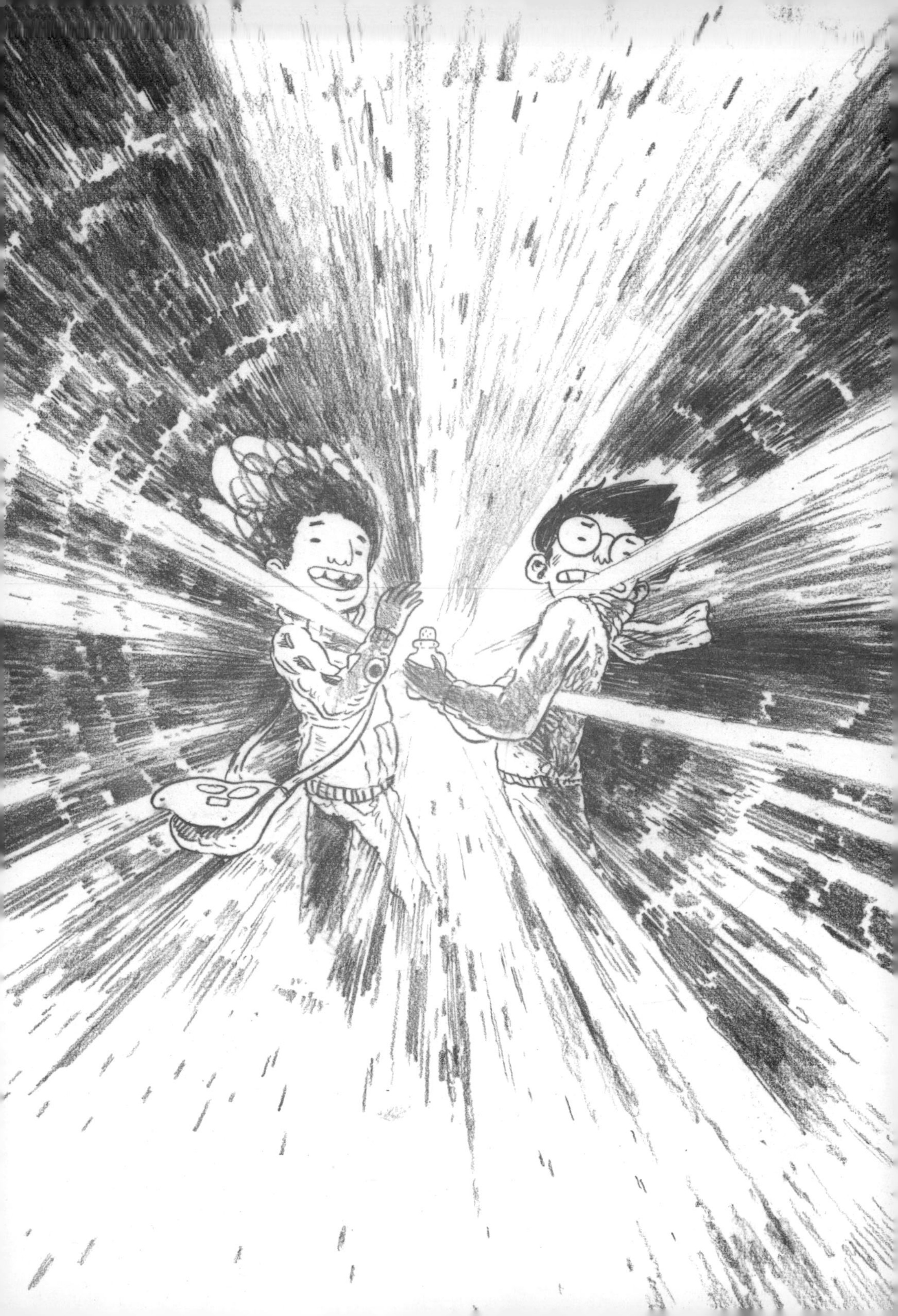

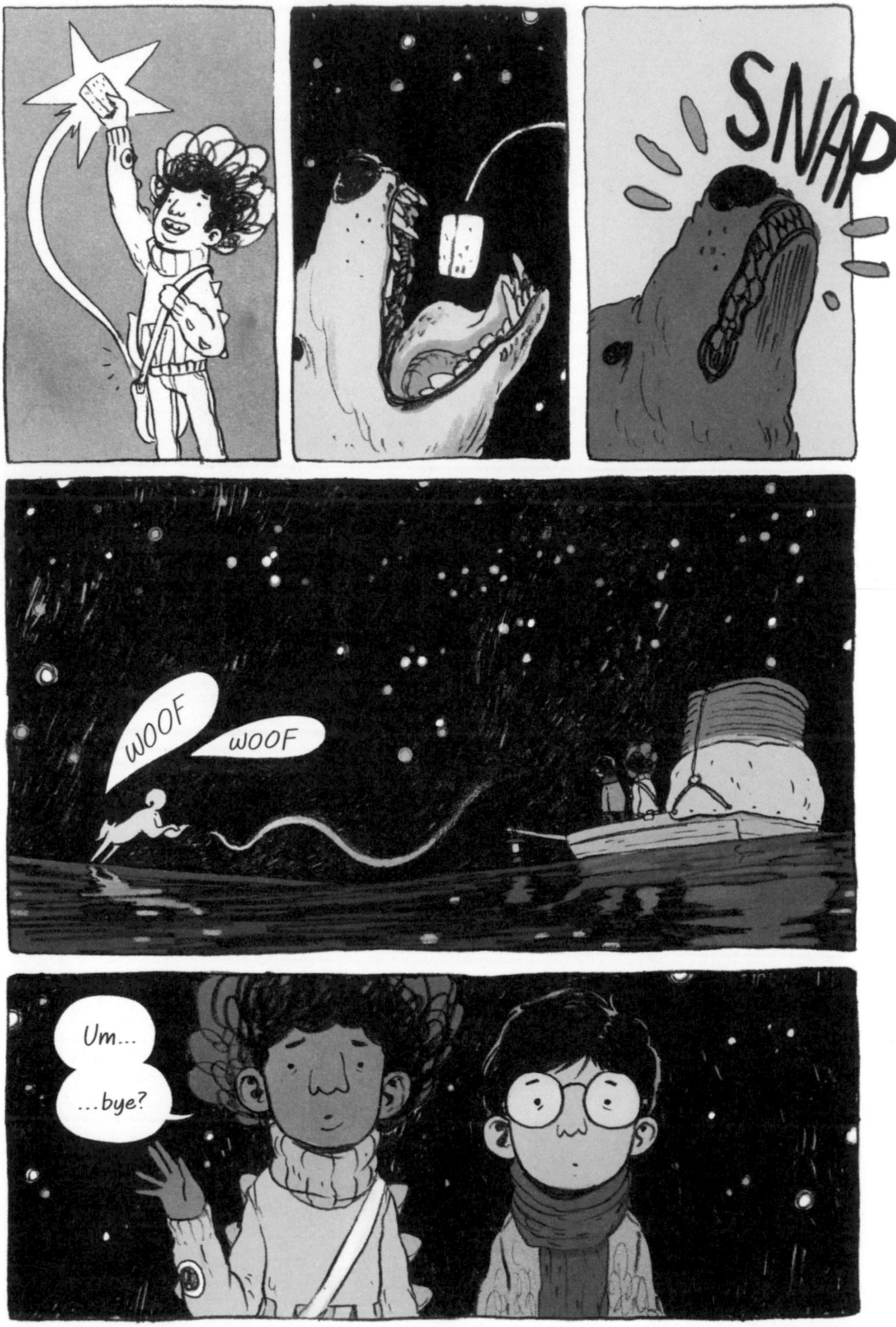
SNAP
WOOF
WOOF
Um...
...bye?

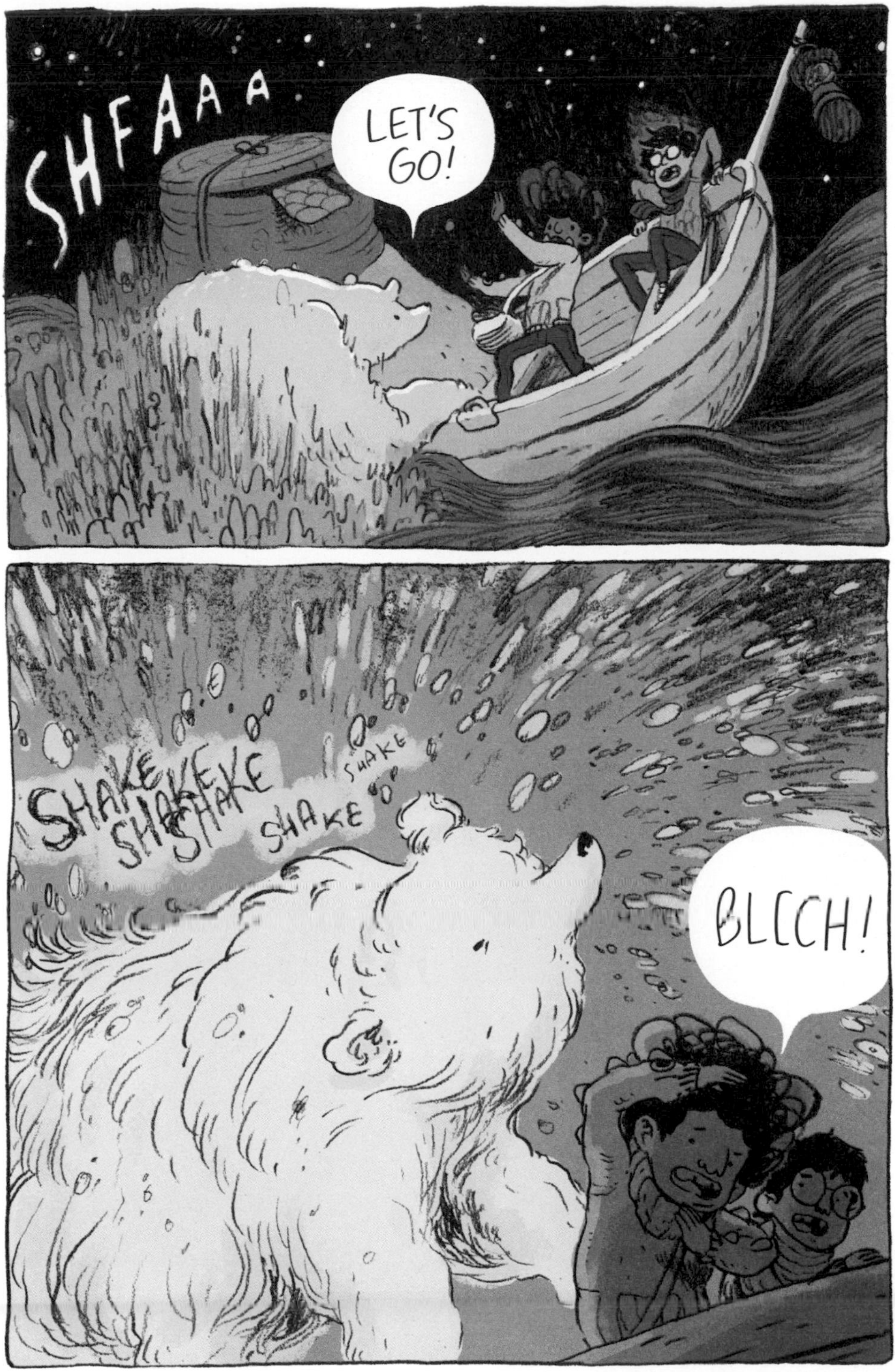
SHFAAA
LET'S GO!
SHAKE
SHAKE
SHAKE
SHAKE
SHAKE
BLCCH!

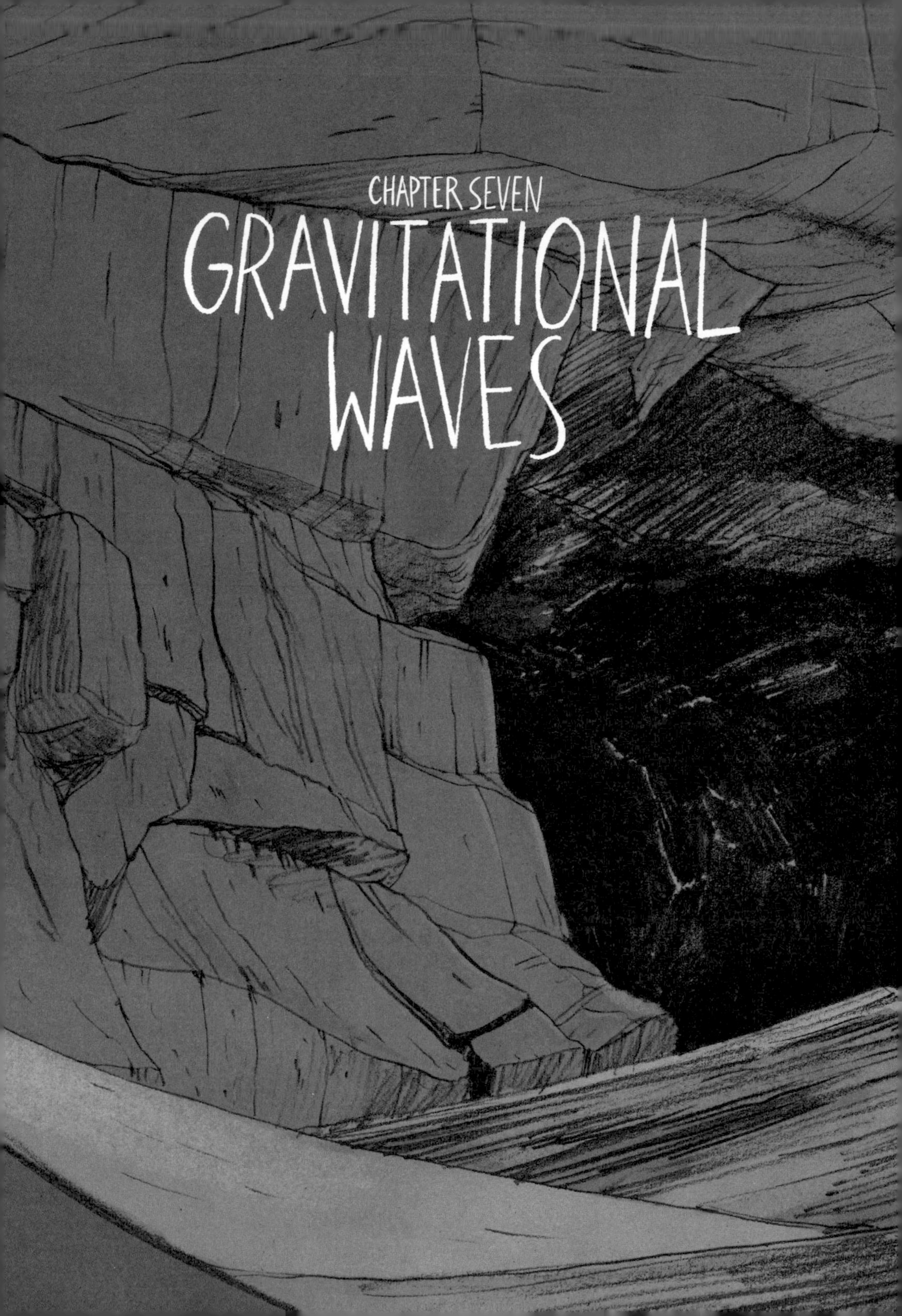
CHAPTER SEVEN
GRAVITATIONAL WAVES

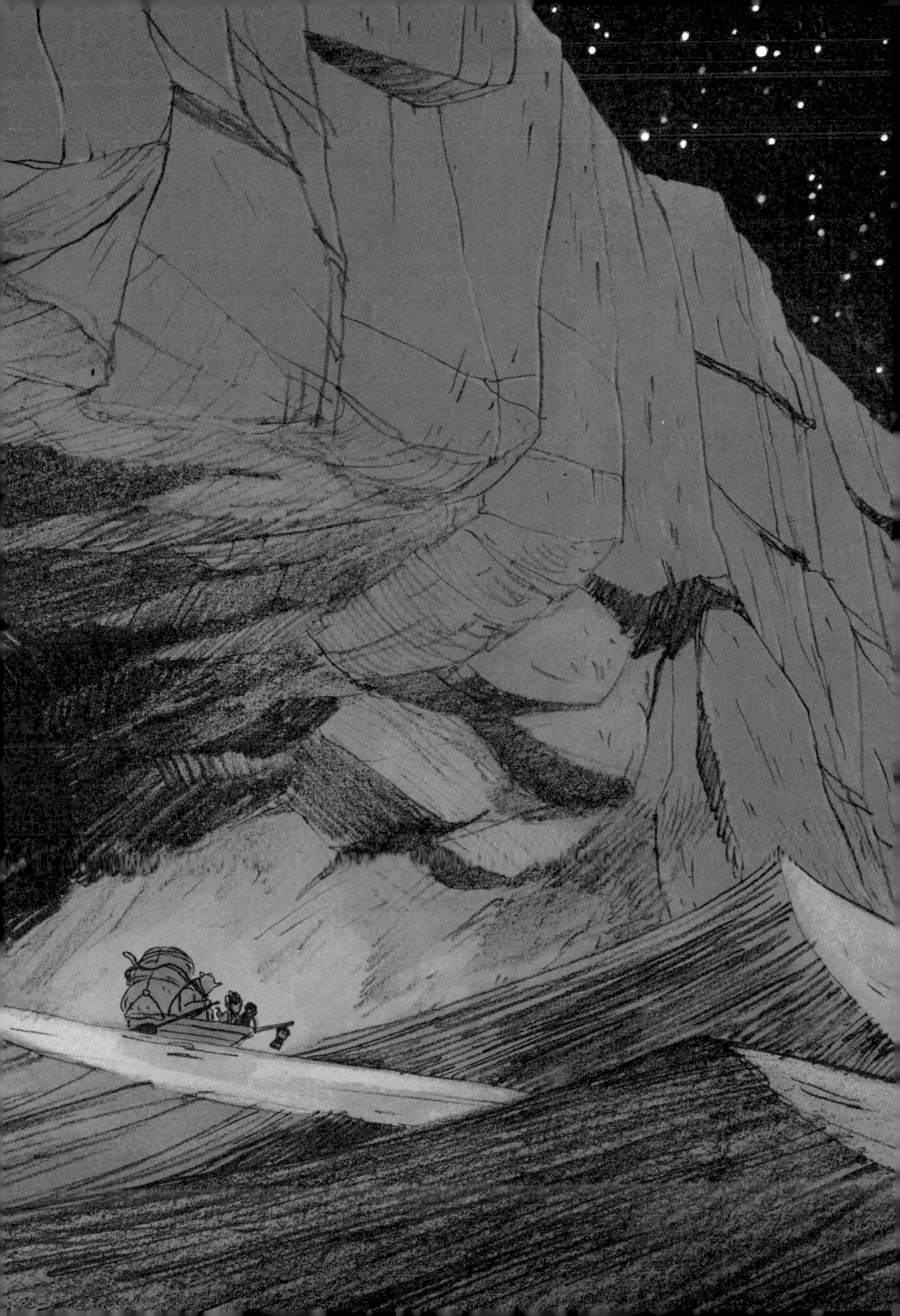

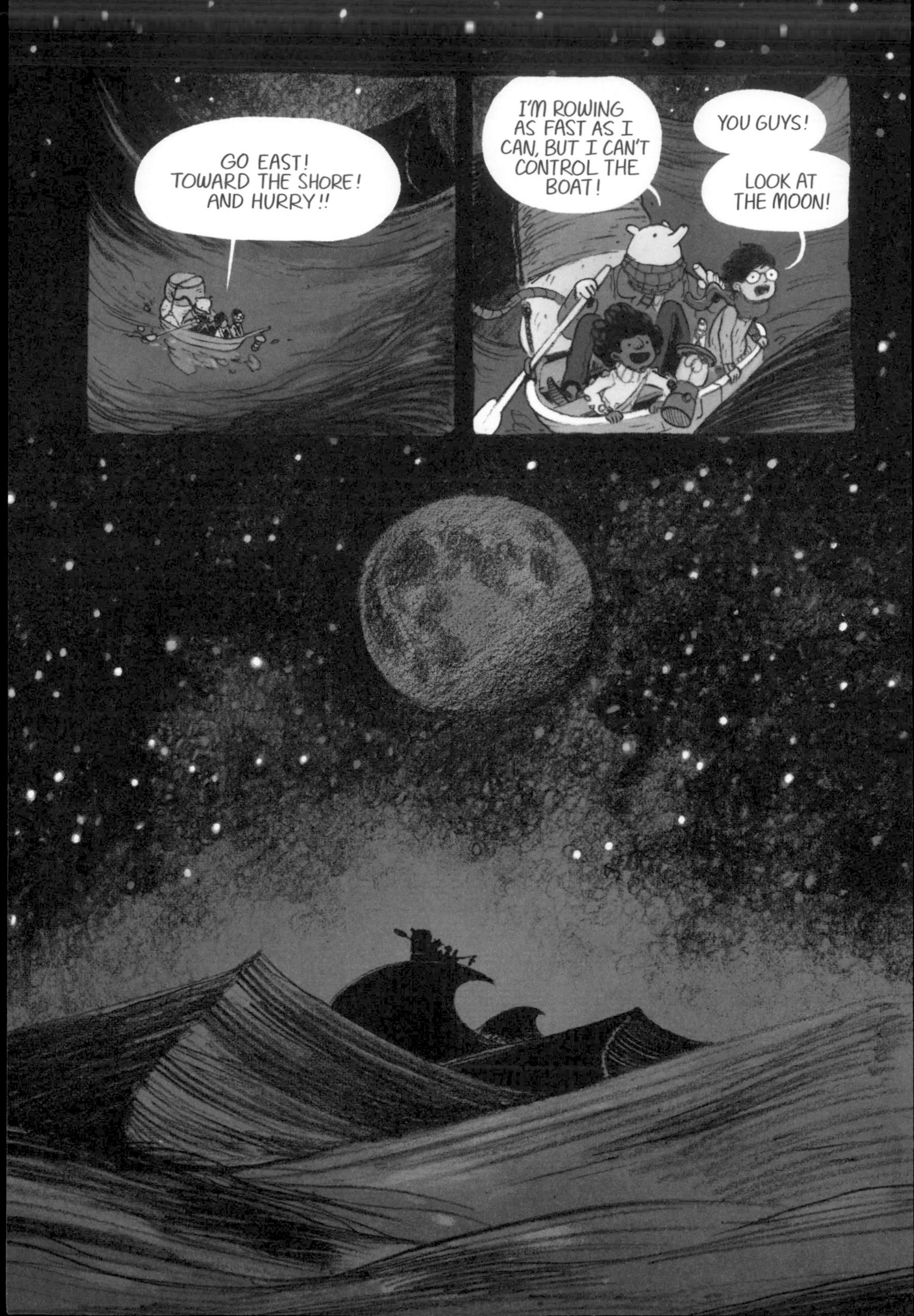
GO EAST! TOWARD THE SHORE! AND HURRY!!
I'M ROWING AS FAST AS I CAN, BUT I CAN'T CONTROL THE BOAT!
YOU GUYS!
LOOK AT THE MOON!

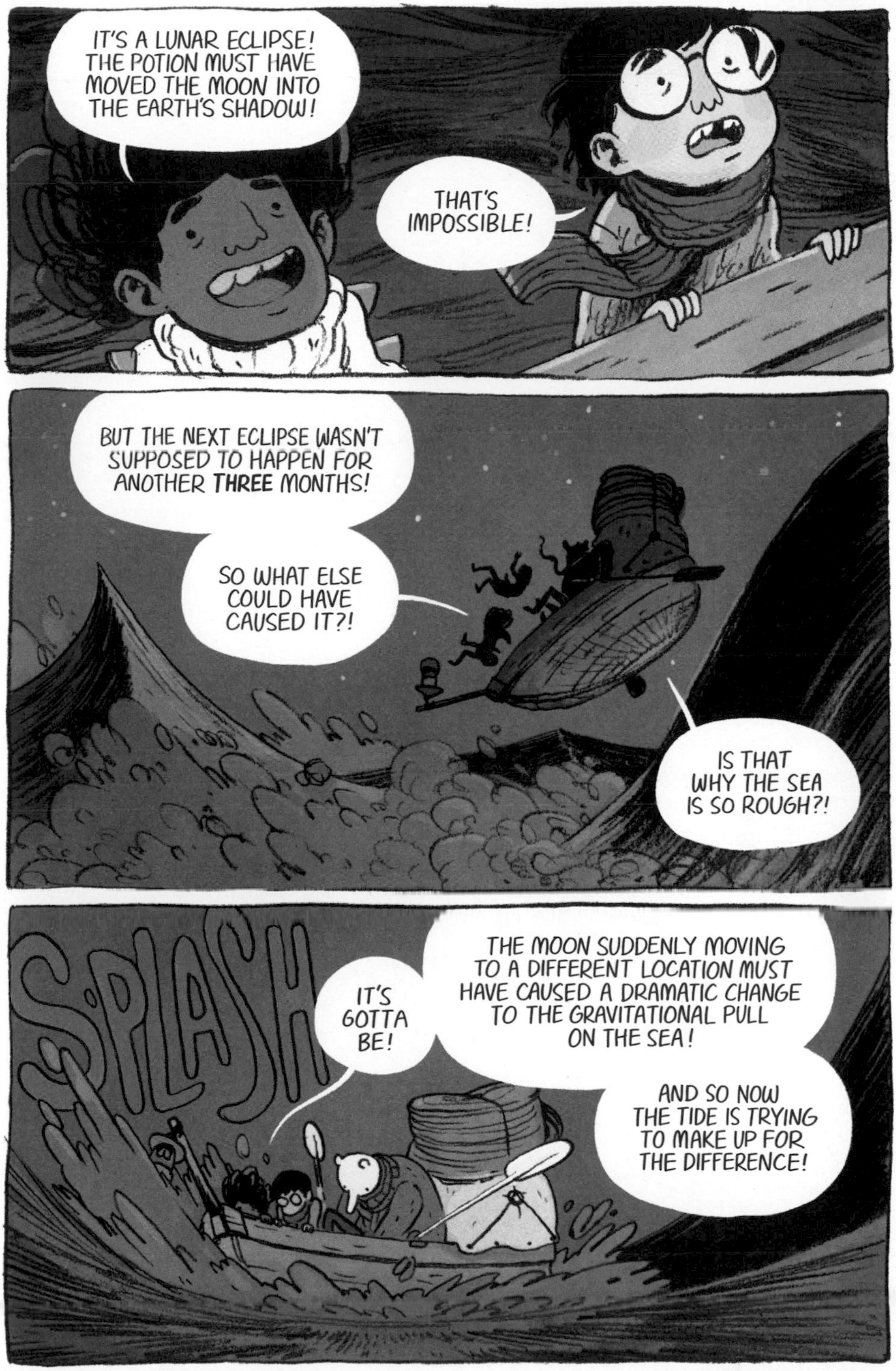

IT'S A LUNAR ECLIPSE! THE POTION MUST HAVE MOVED THE MOON INTO THE EARTH'S SHADOW!
THAT'S IMPOSSIBLE!
BUT THE NEXT ECLIPSE WASN'T SUPPOSED TO HAPPEN FOR ANOTHER **THREE** MONTHS!
SO WHAT ELSE COULD HAVE CAUSED IT?!
IS THAT WHY THE SEA IS SO ROUGH?!
SPLASH
IT'S GOTTA BE!
THE MOON SUDDENLY MOVING TO A DIFFERENT LOCATION MUST HAVE CAUSED A DRAMATIC CHANGE TO THE GRAVITATIONAL PULL ON THE SEA!
AND SO NOW THE TIDE IS TRYING TO MAKE UP FOR THE DIFFERENCE!

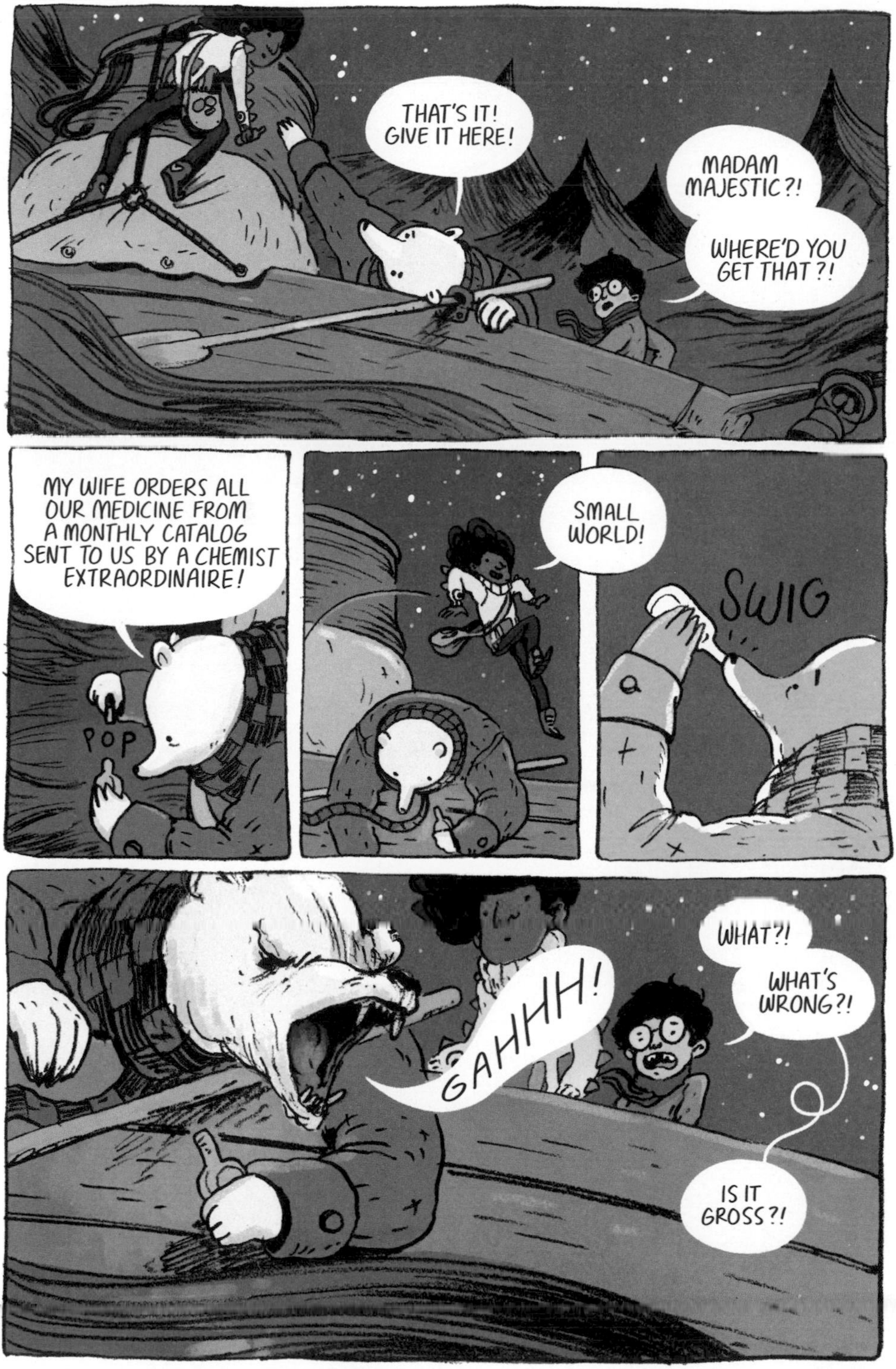
THAT'S IT! GIVE IT HERE!
MADAM MAJESTIC?!
WHERE'D YOU GET THAT?!
MY WIFE ORDERS ALL OUR MEDICINE FROM A MONTHLY CATALOG SENT TO US BY A CHEMIST EXTRAORDINAIRE!
POP
SMALL WORLD!
SWIG
GAHHH!
WHAT?!
WHAT'S WRONG?!
IS IT GROSS?!

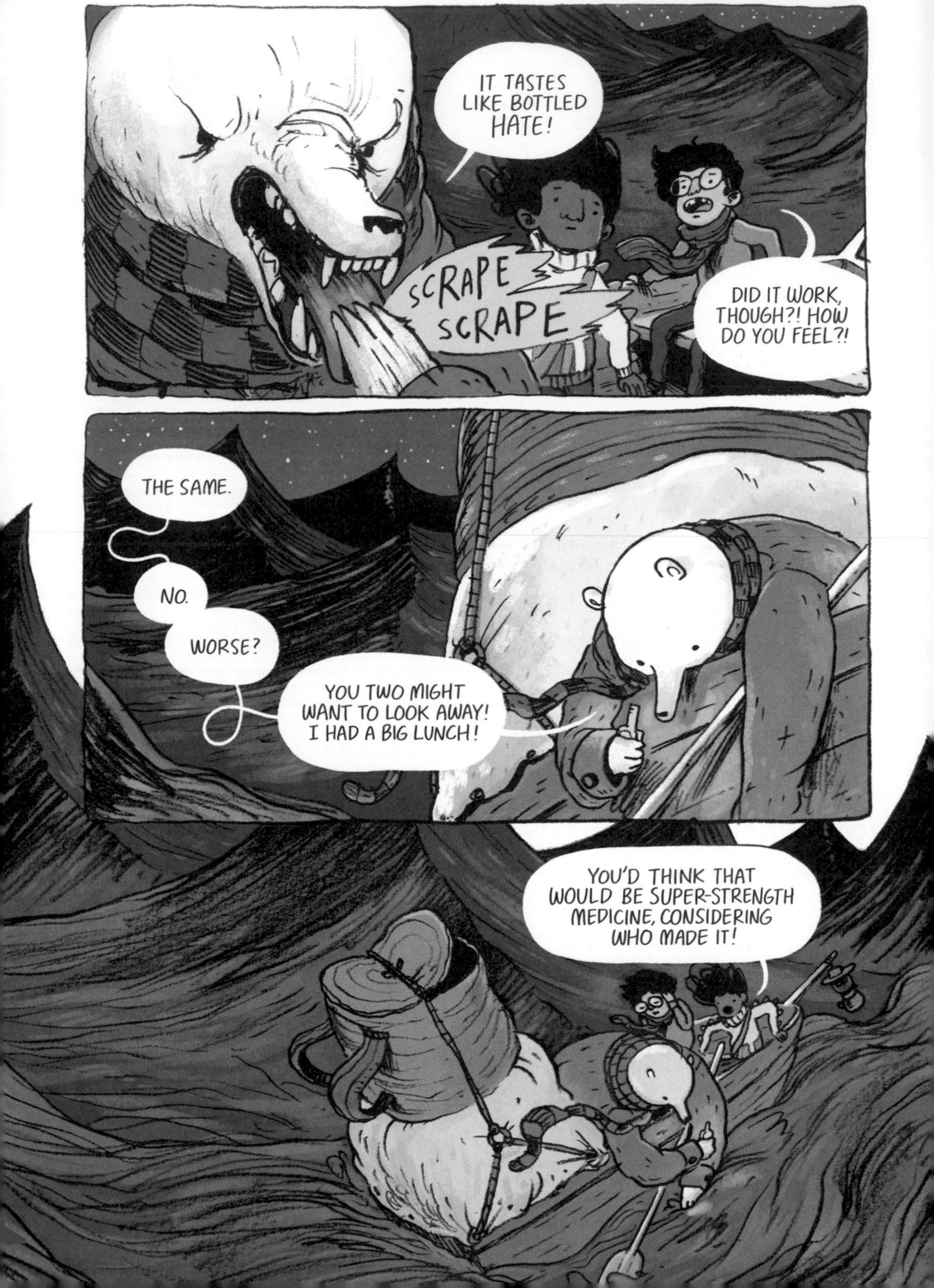
IT TASTES LIKE BOTTLED HATE!
SCRAPE SCRAPE
DID IT WORK, THOUGH?! HOW DO YOU FEEL?!
THE SAME.
NO.
WORSE?
YOU TWO MIGHT WANT TO LOOK AWAY! I HAD A BIG LUNCH!
YOU'D THINK THAT WOULD BE SUPER-STRENGTH MEDICINE, CONSIDERING WHO MADE IT!

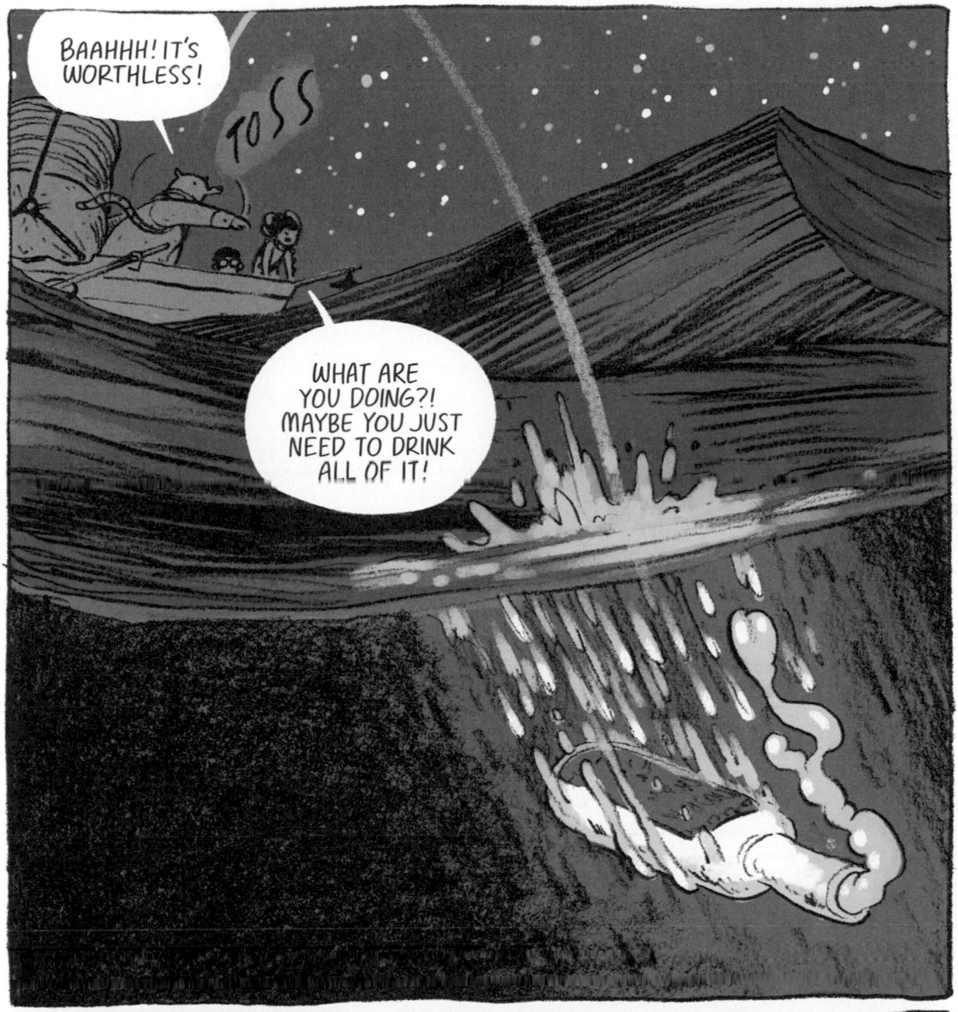
BAAHHH! IT'S WORTHLESS!
TOSS
WHAT ARE YOU DOING?! MAYBE YOU JUST NEED TO DRINK ALL OF IT!

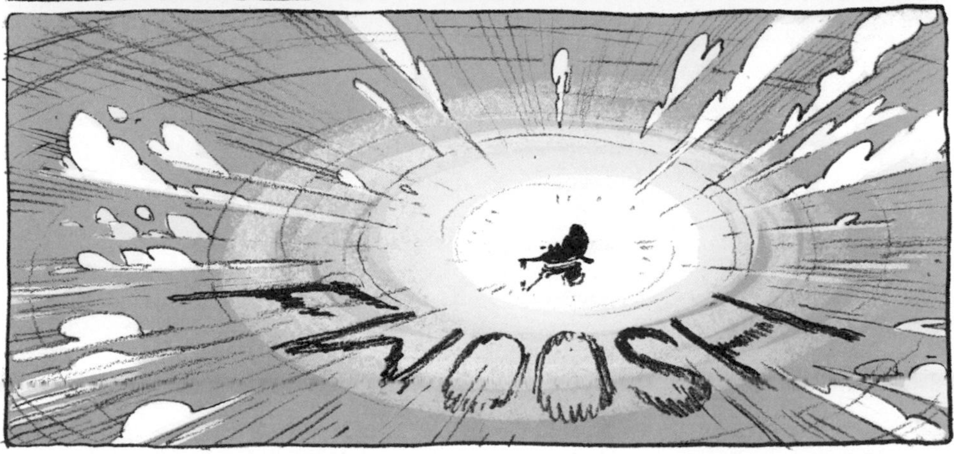
FWOOSH

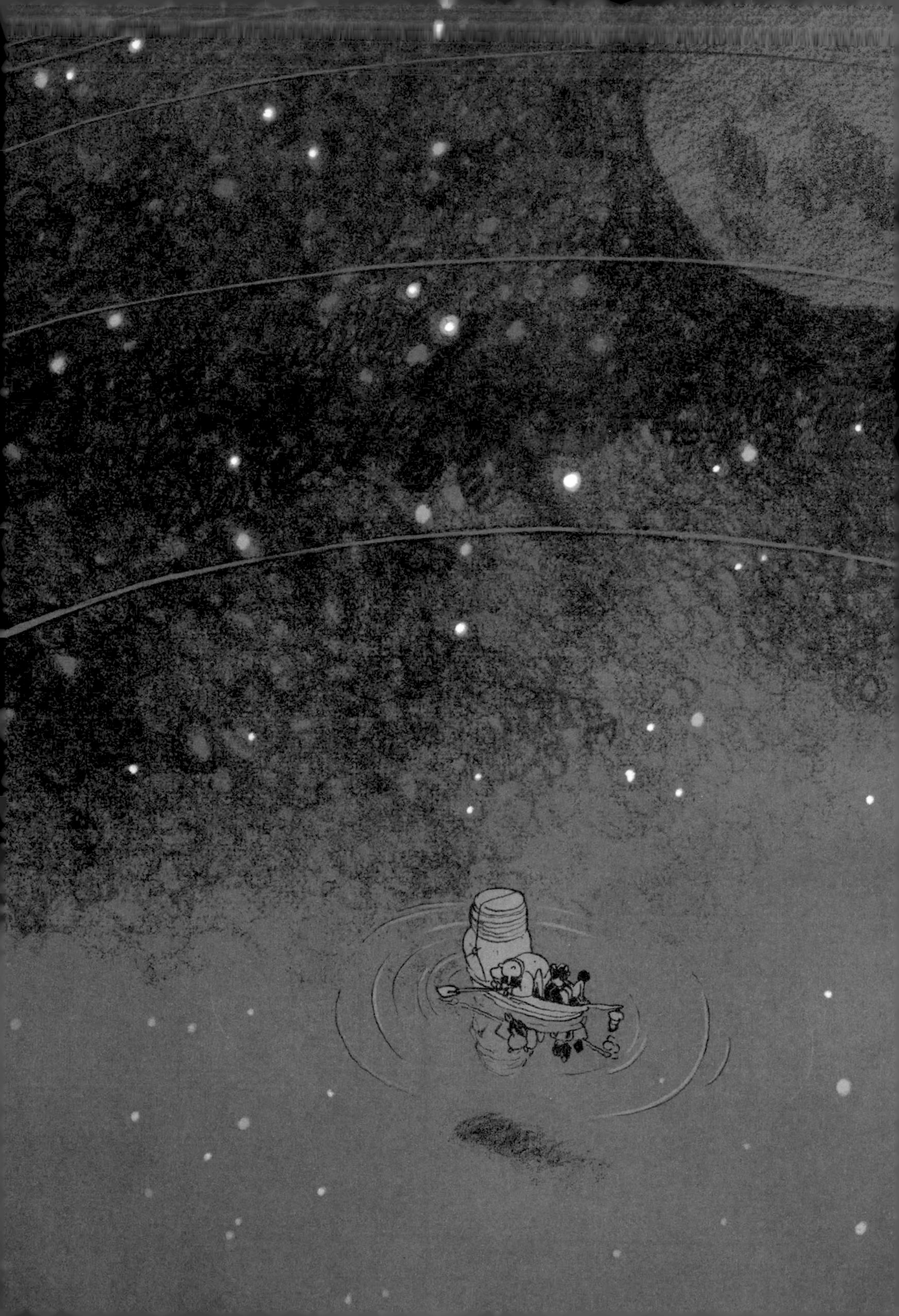

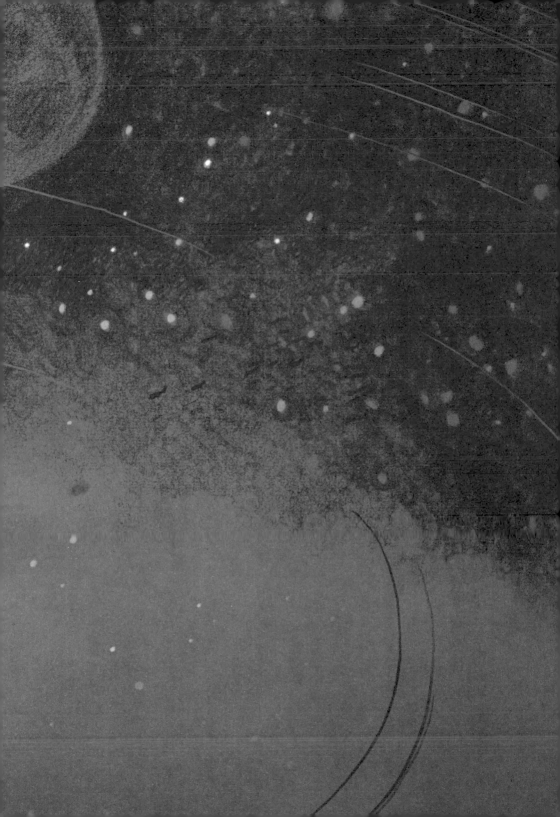

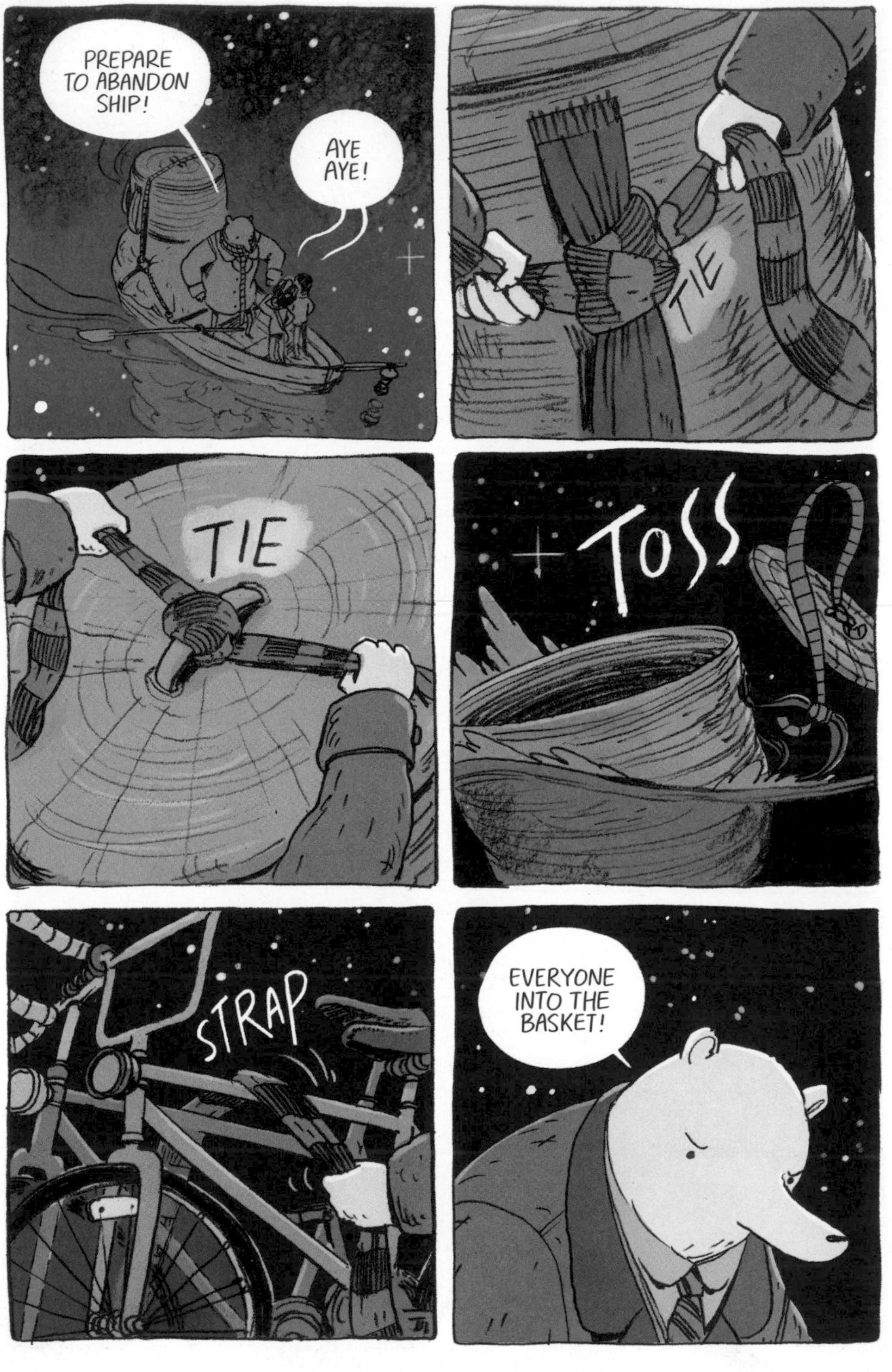
PREPARE TO ABANDON SHIP!
AYE AYE!
TIE
TIE
TOSS
STRAP
EVERYONE INTO THE BASKET!

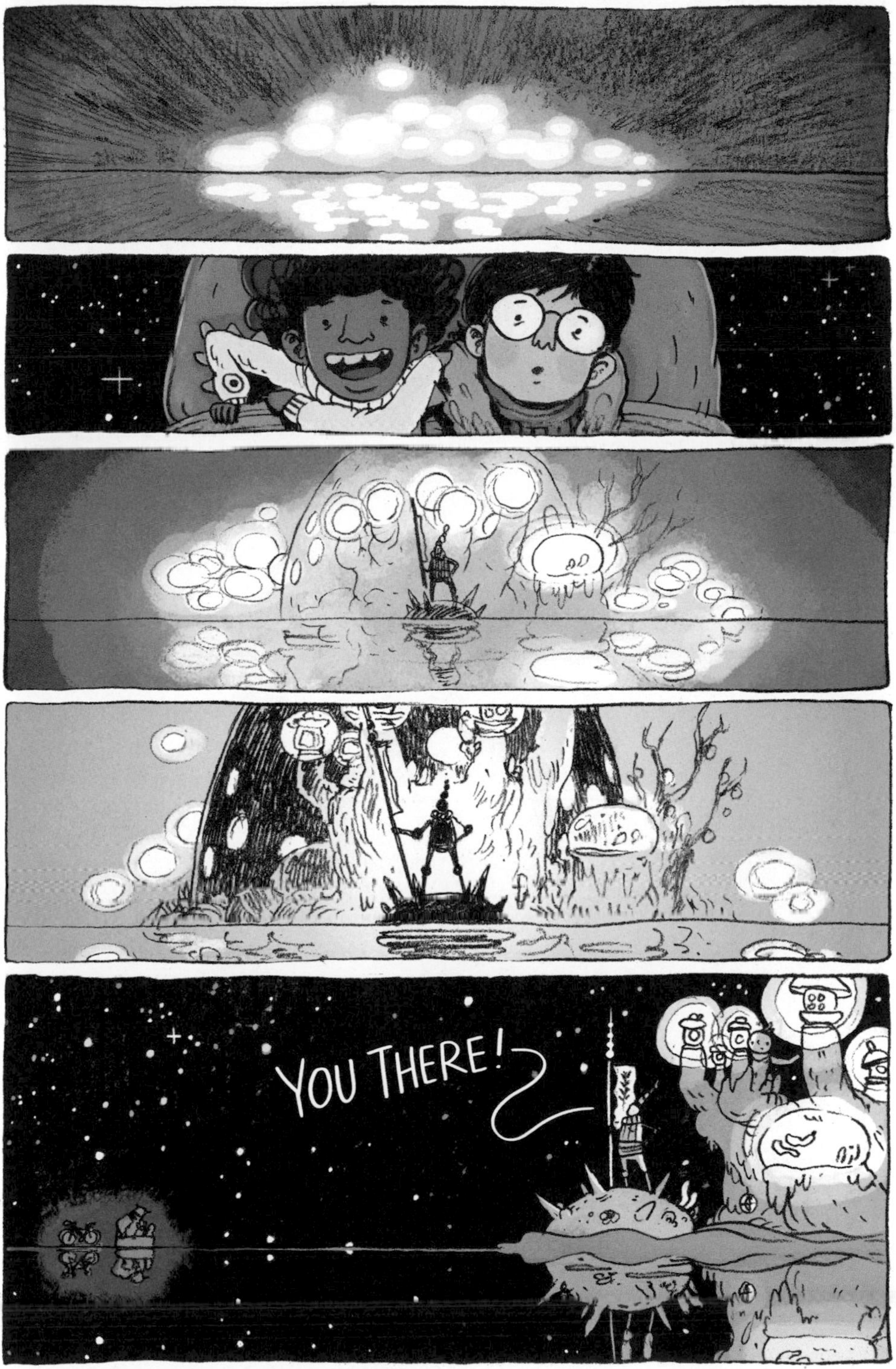
YOU THERE!

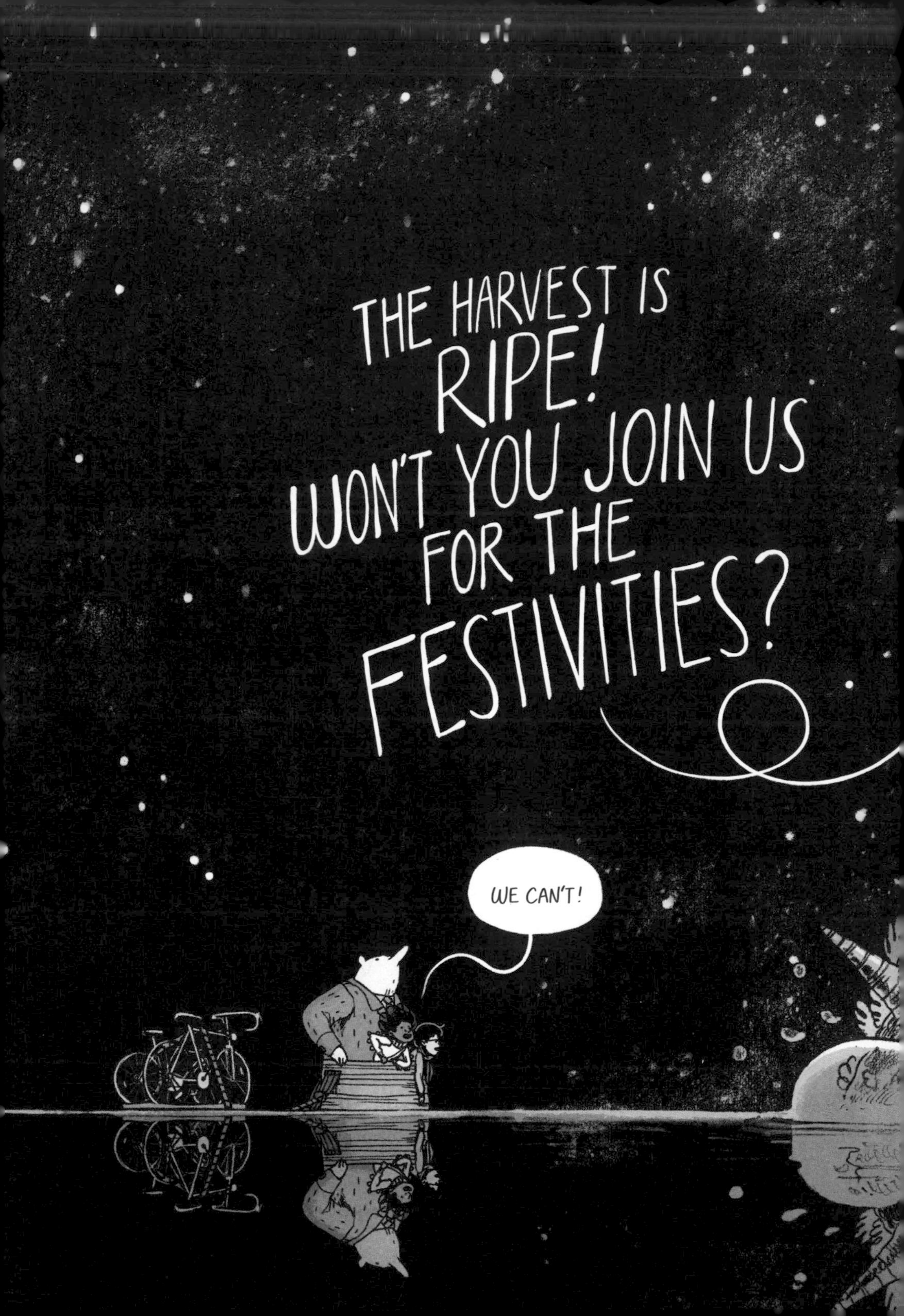
THE HARVEST IS RIPE! WON'T YOU JOIN US FOR THE FESTIVITIES?
WE CAN'T!

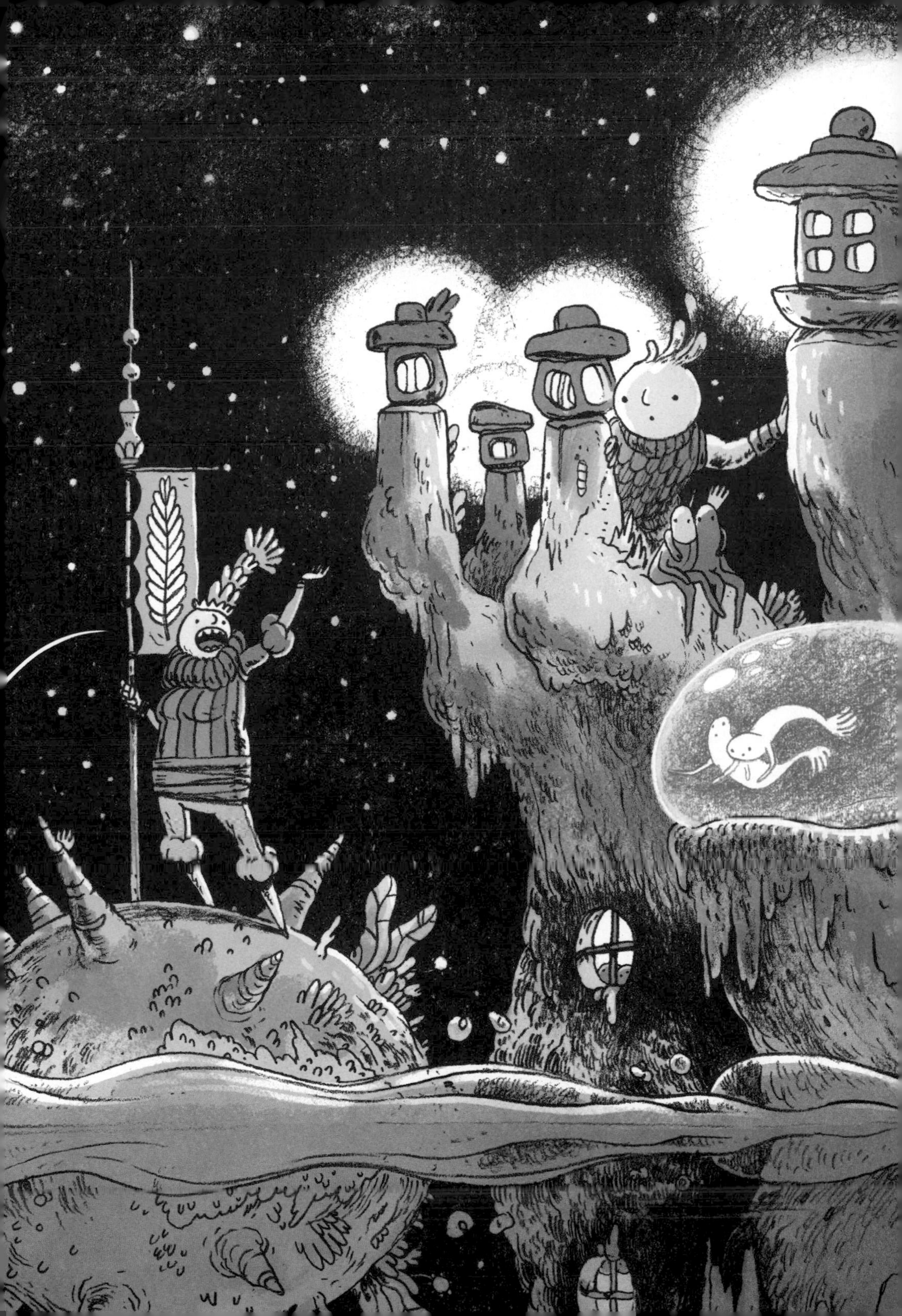

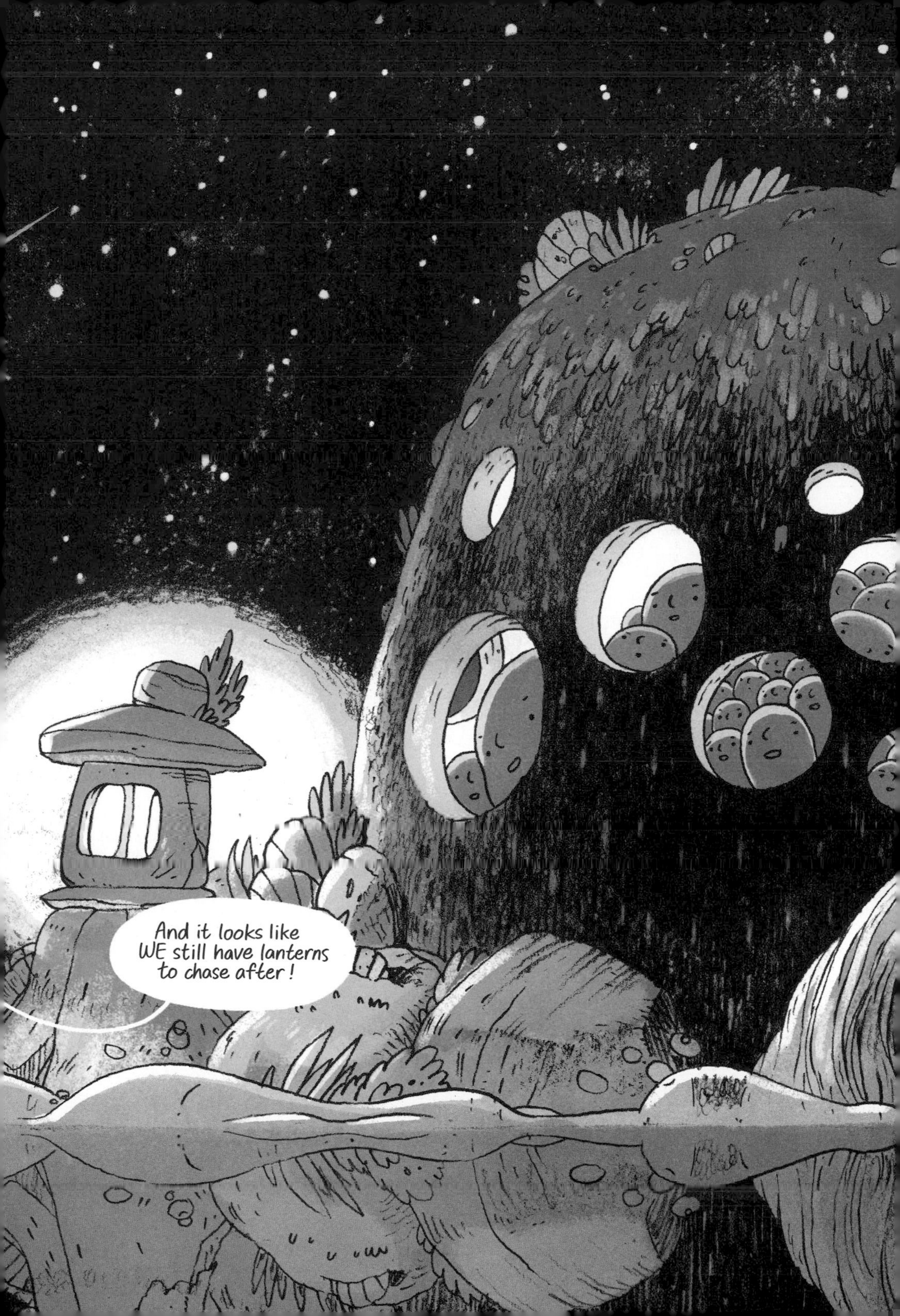
And it looks like WE still have lanterns to chase after!

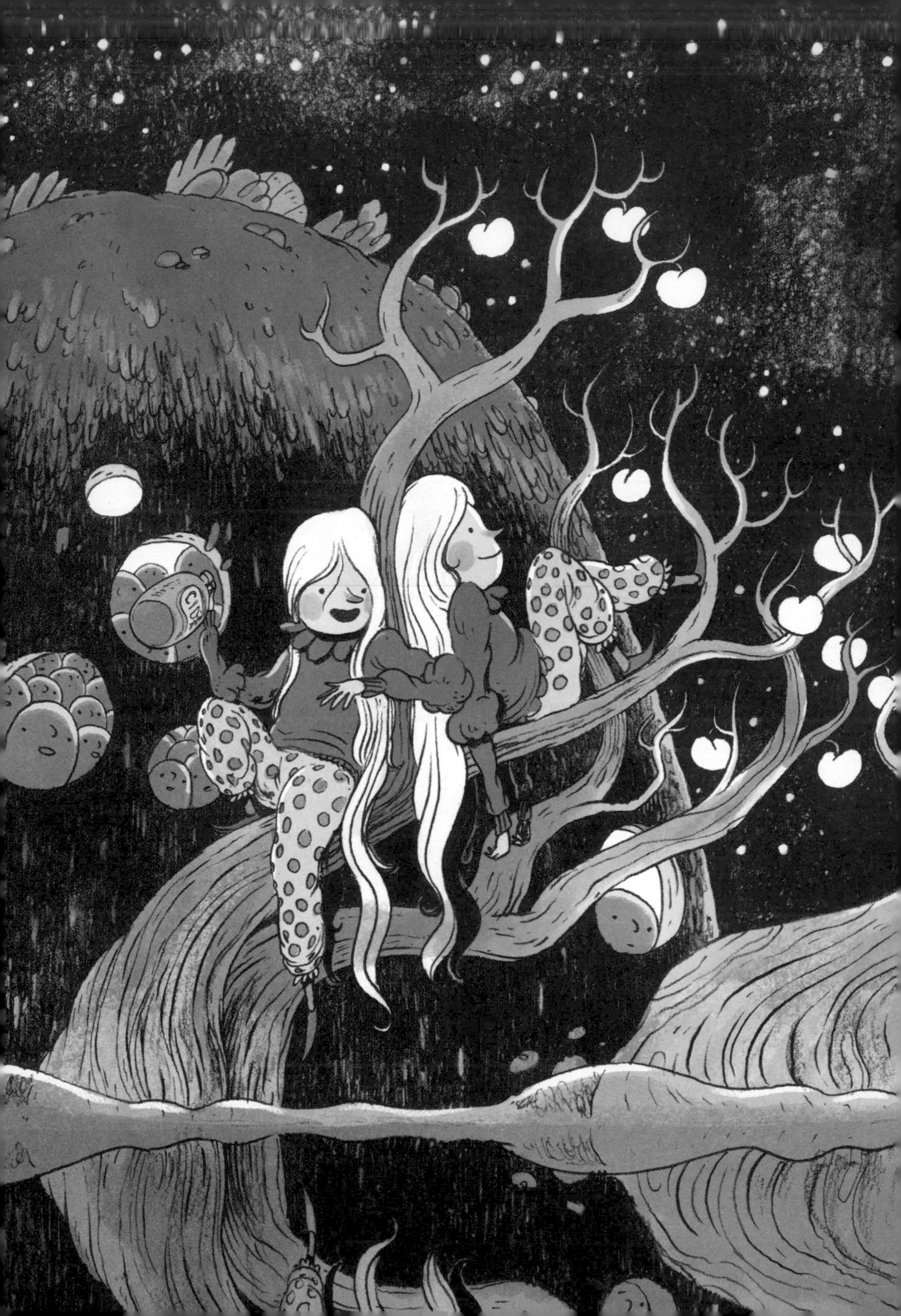

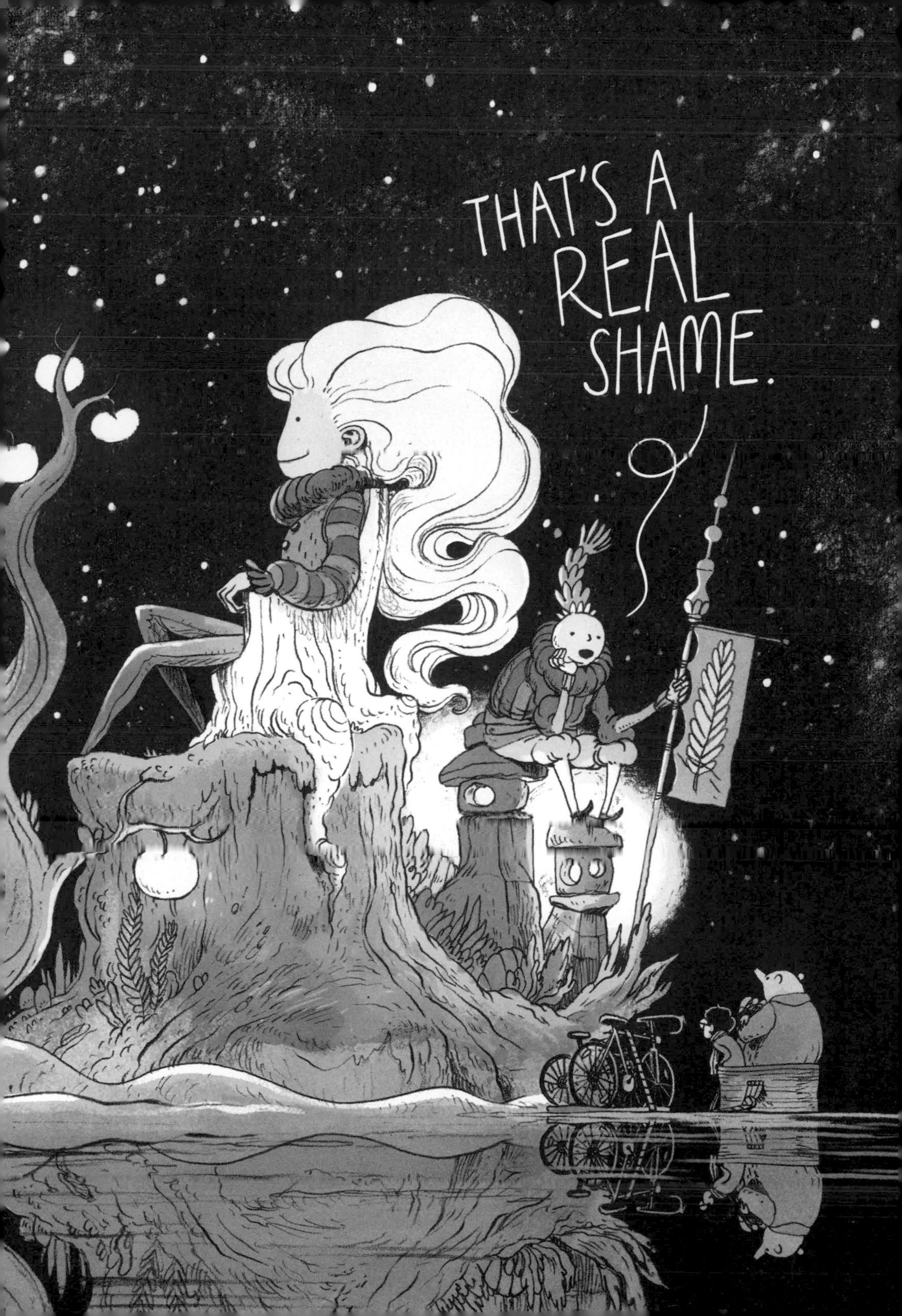
THAT'S A REAL SHAME.

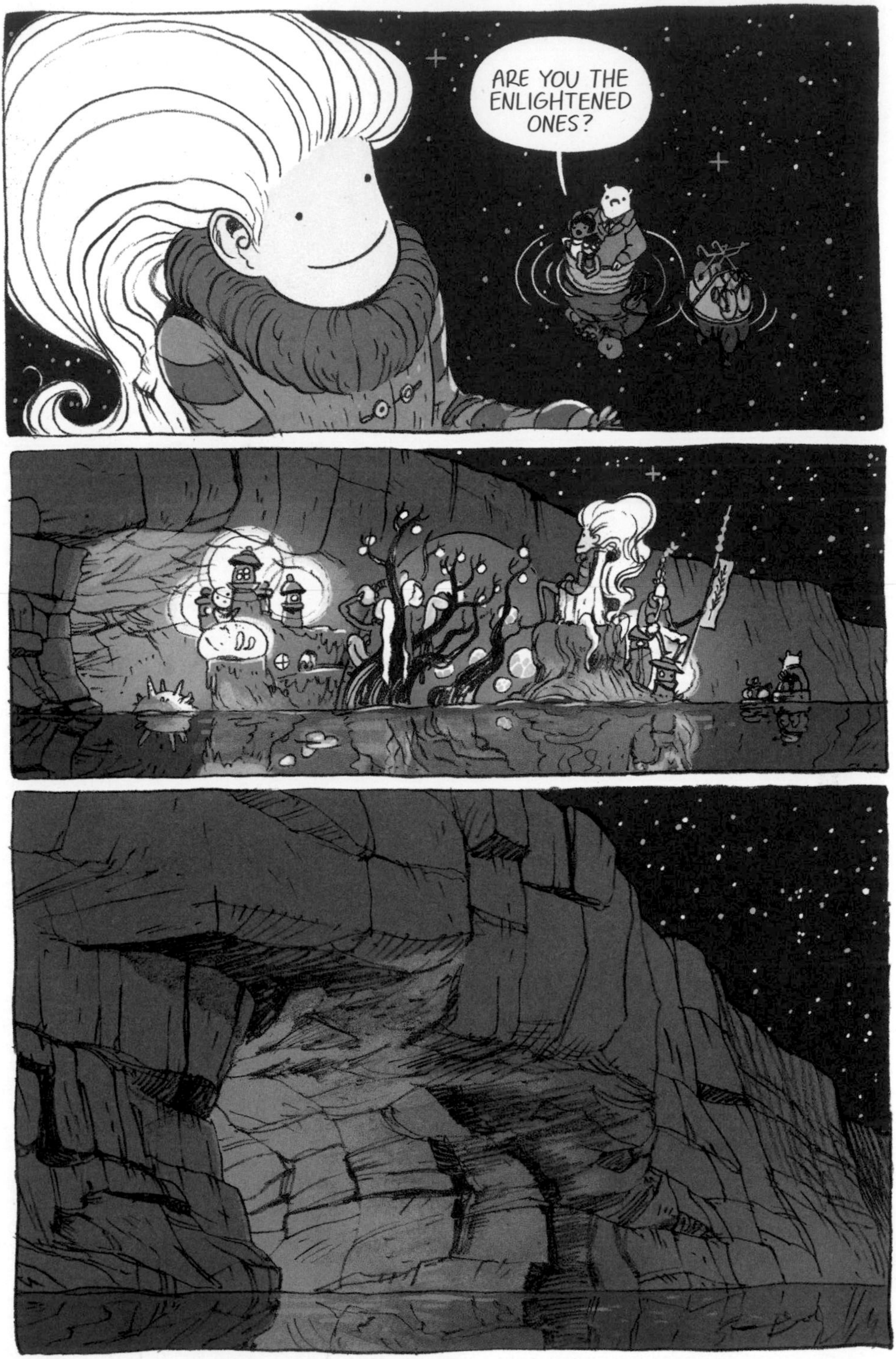
ARE YOU THE ENLIGHTENED ONES?

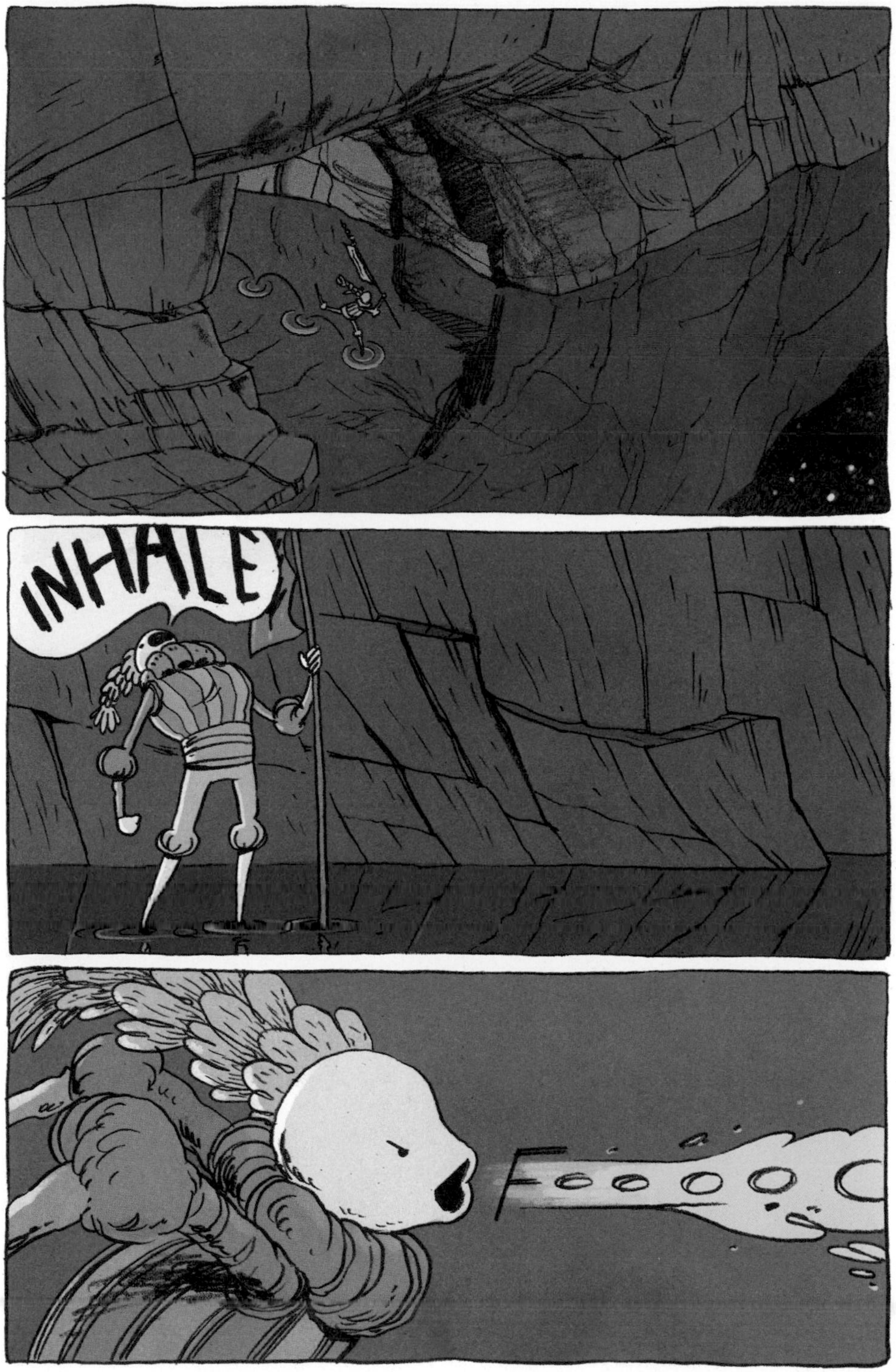
INHALE
FOOOOO

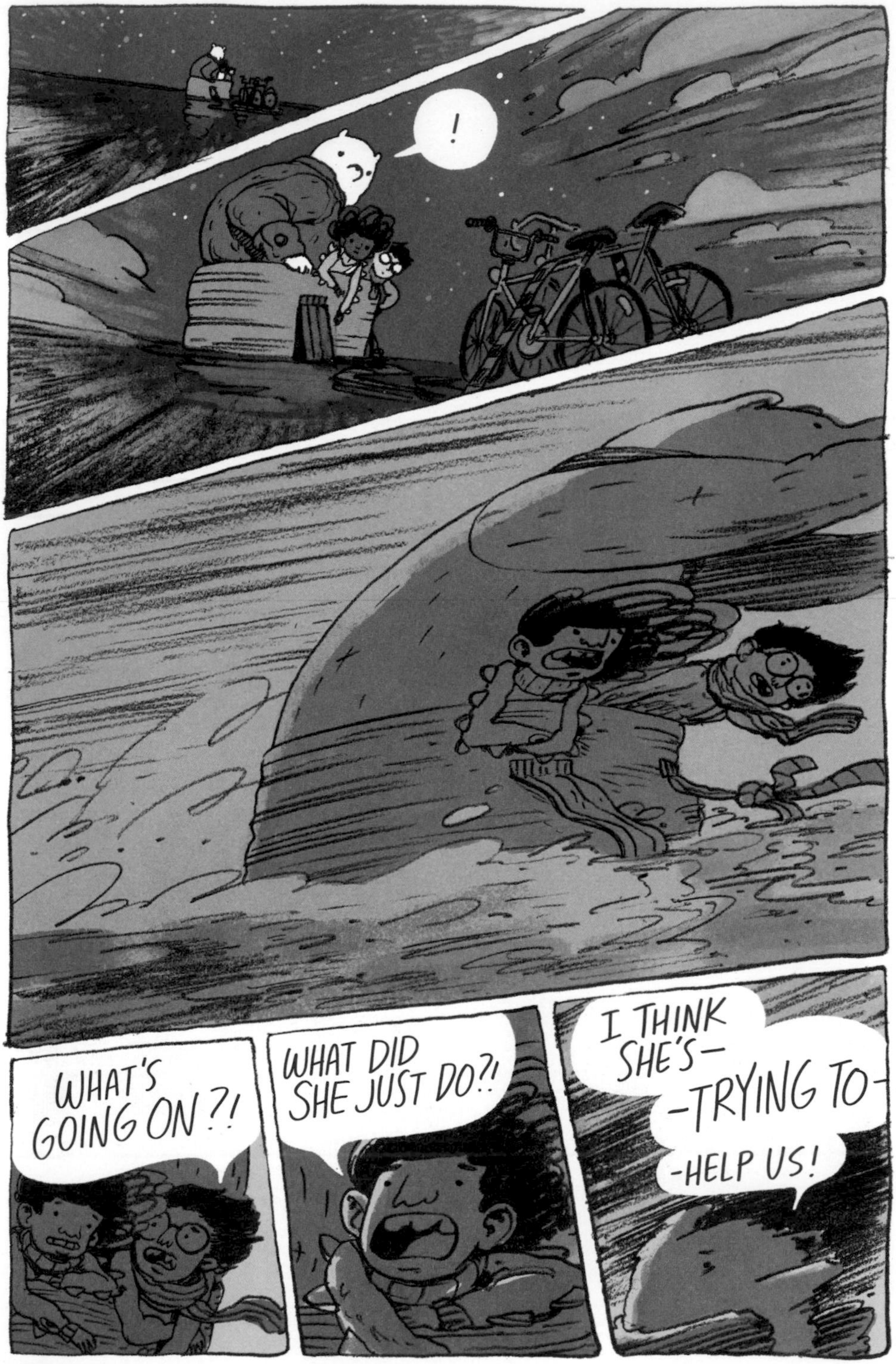
!
WHAT'S GOING ON?!
WHAT DID SHE JUST DO?!
I THINK SHE'S—
—TRYING TO—
—HELP US!

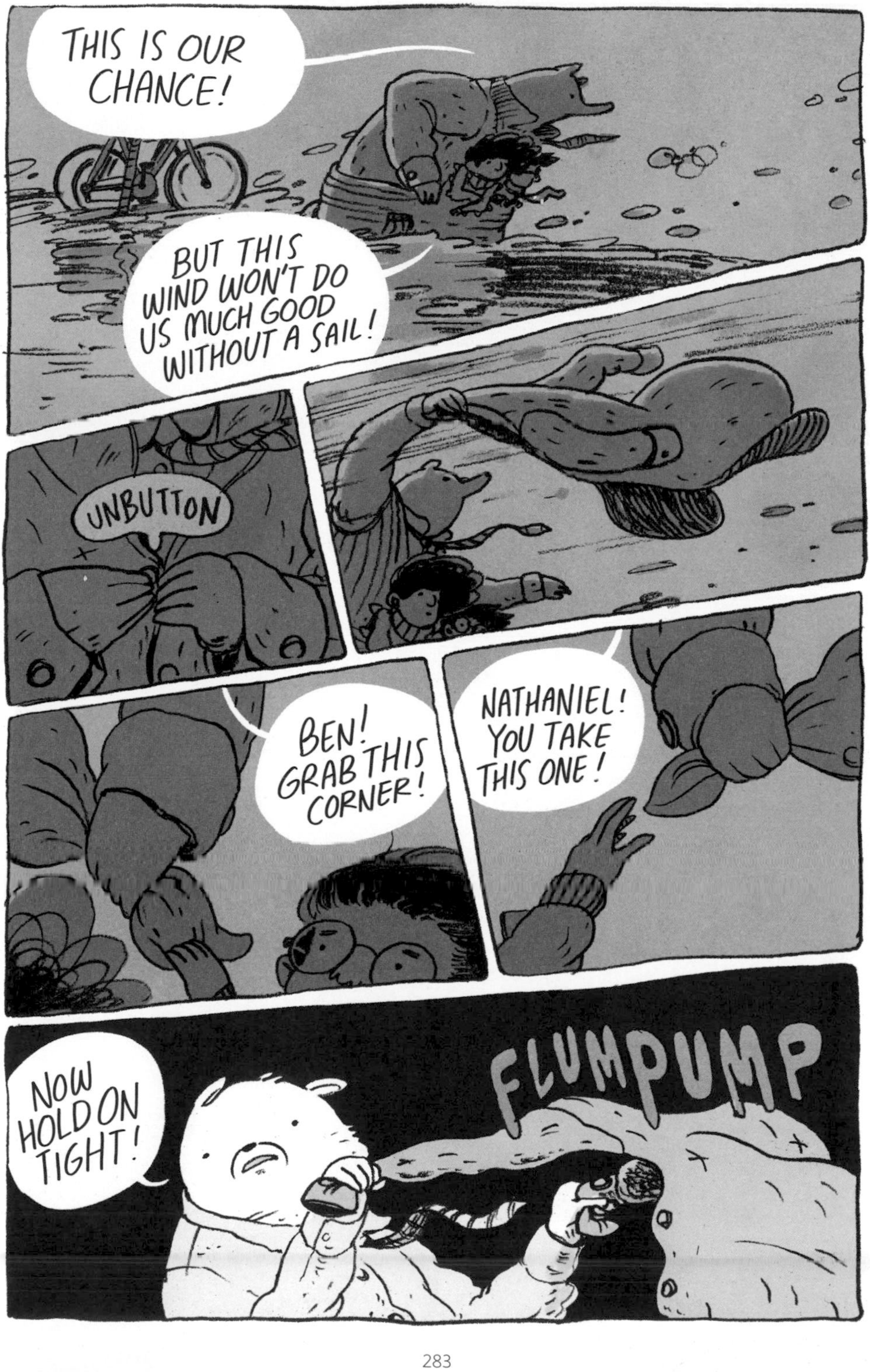

THIS IS OUR CHANCE!
BUT THIS WIND WON'T DO US MUCH GOOD WITHOUT A SAIL!
UNBUTTON
BEN! GRAB THIS CORNER!
NATHANIEL! YOU TAKE THIS ONE!
NOW HOLD ON TIGHT!
FLUMPUMP

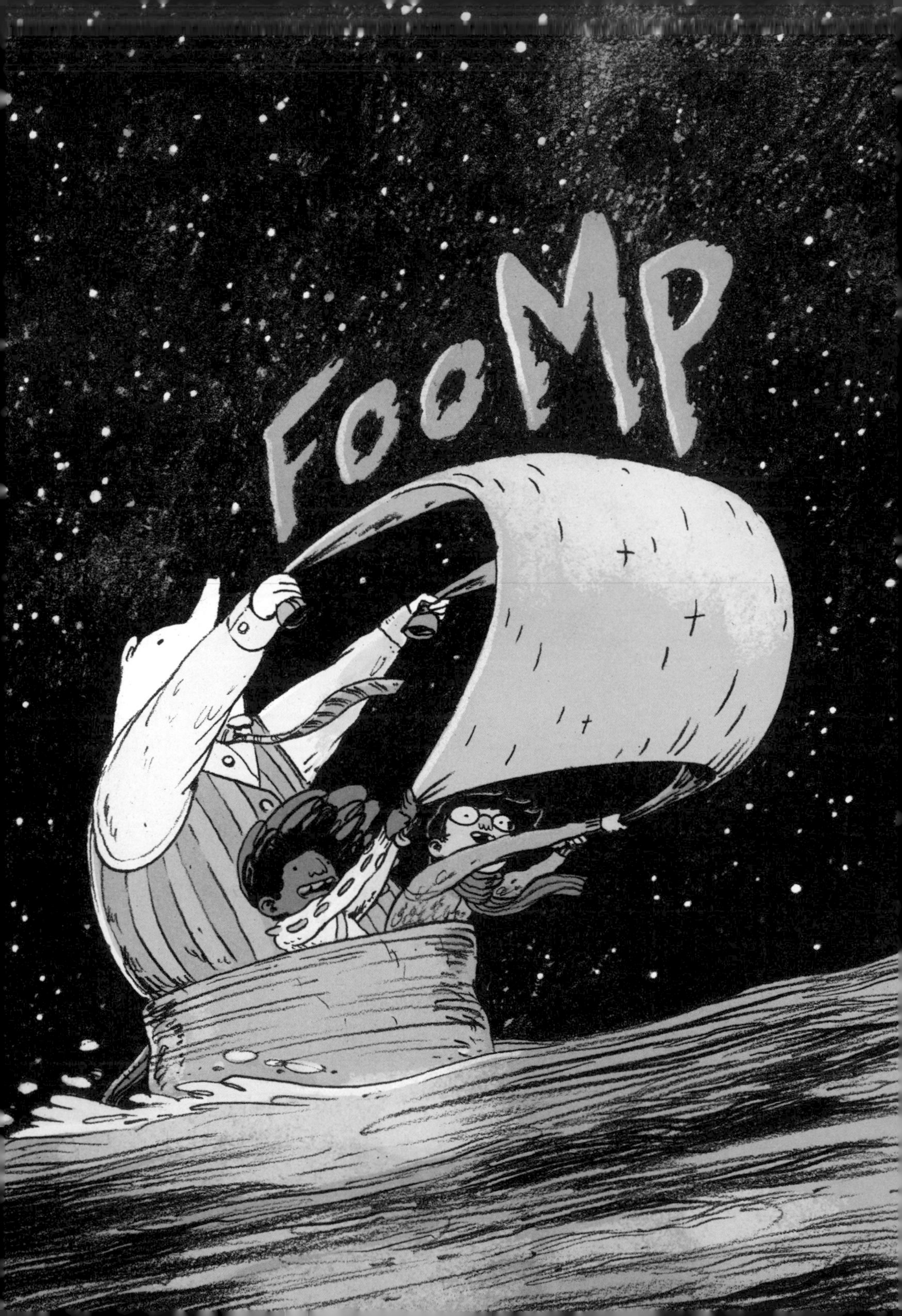
FOOMP

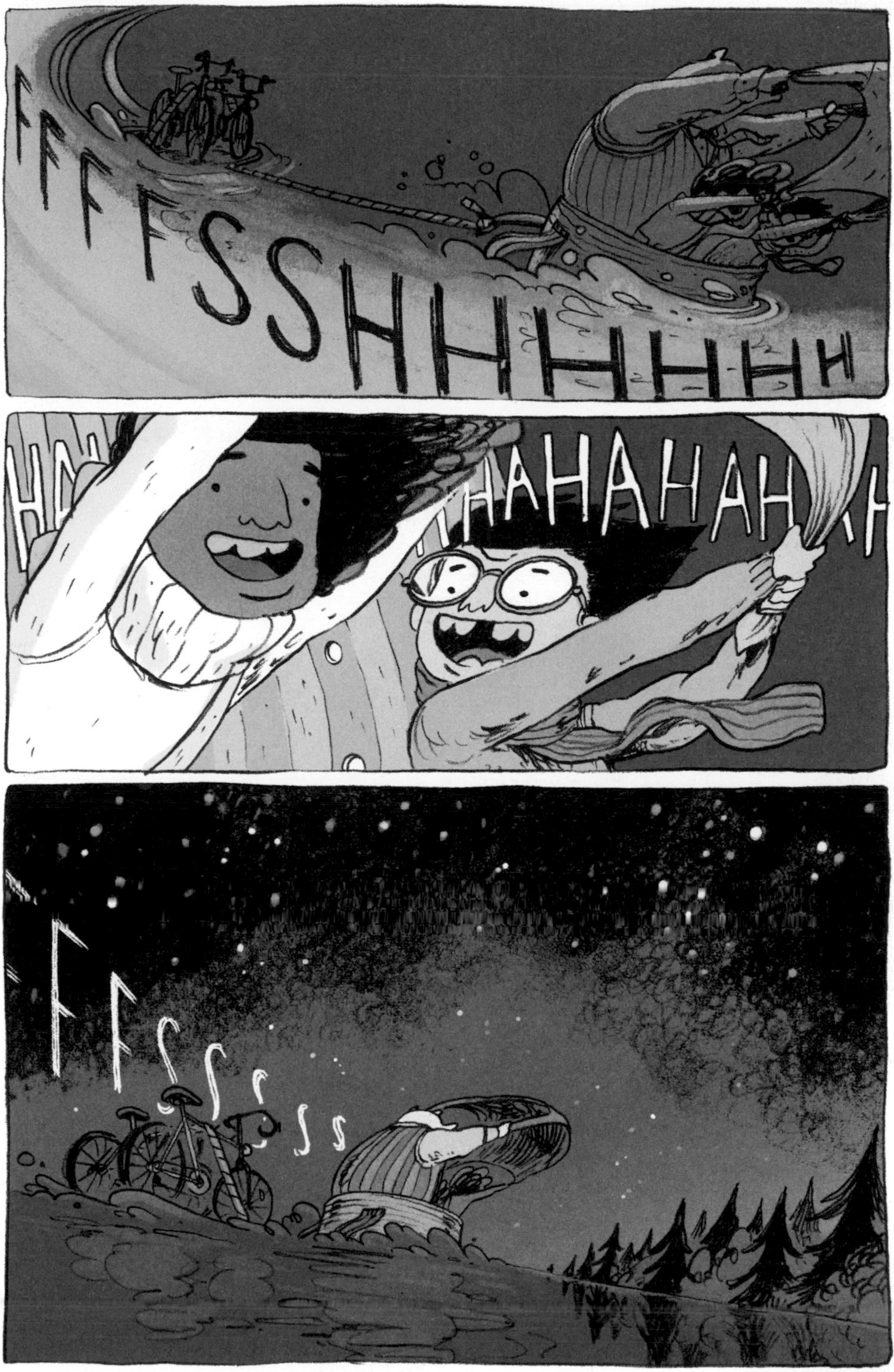
FFFFSSHHHHHHHH
HAHAHAHAHA
FFFSSSSS

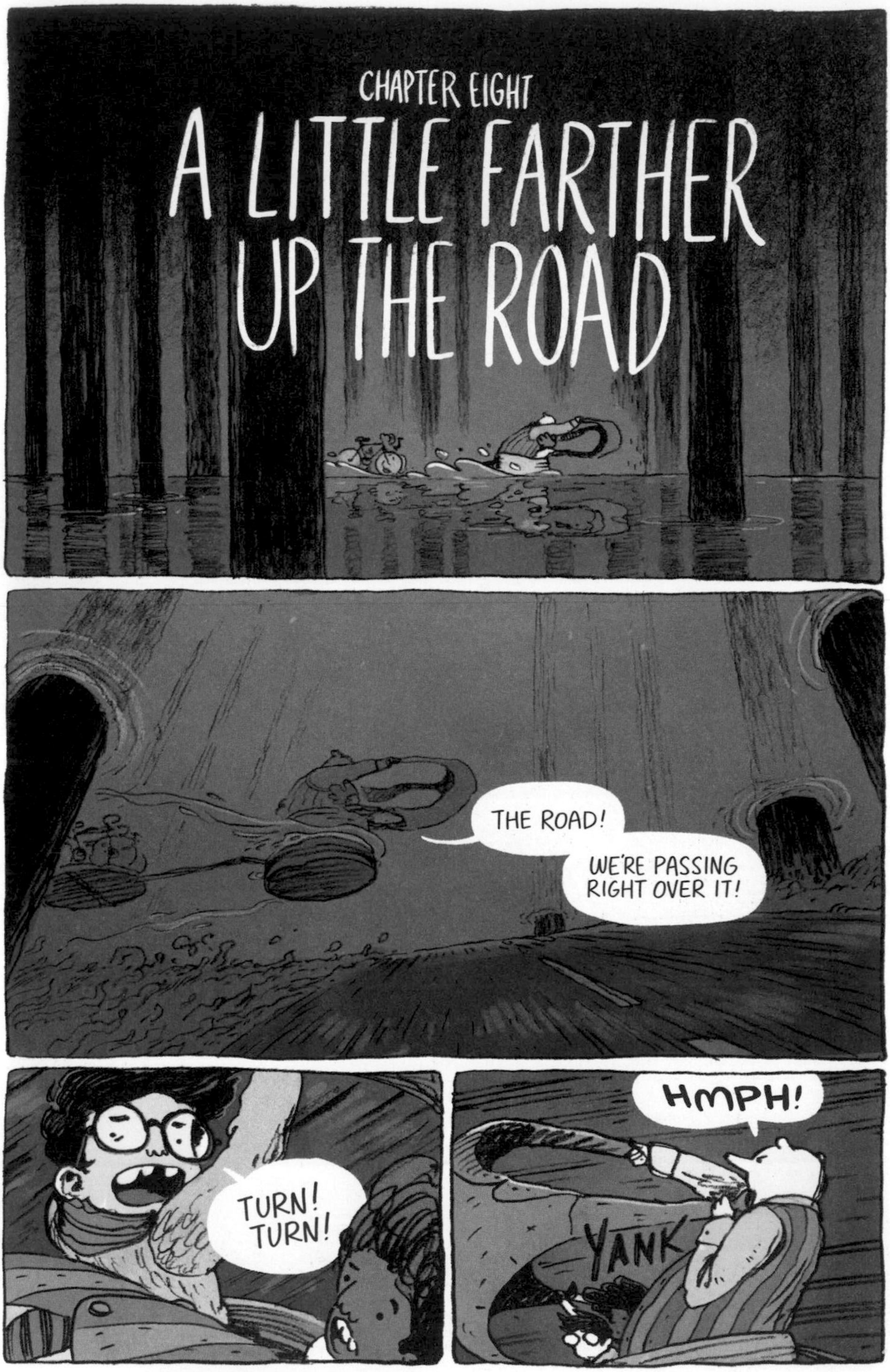
CHAPTER EIGHT
A LITTLE FARTHER UP THE ROAD
THE ROAD!
WE'RE PASSING RIGHT OVER IT!
TURN! TURN!
HMPH!
YANK

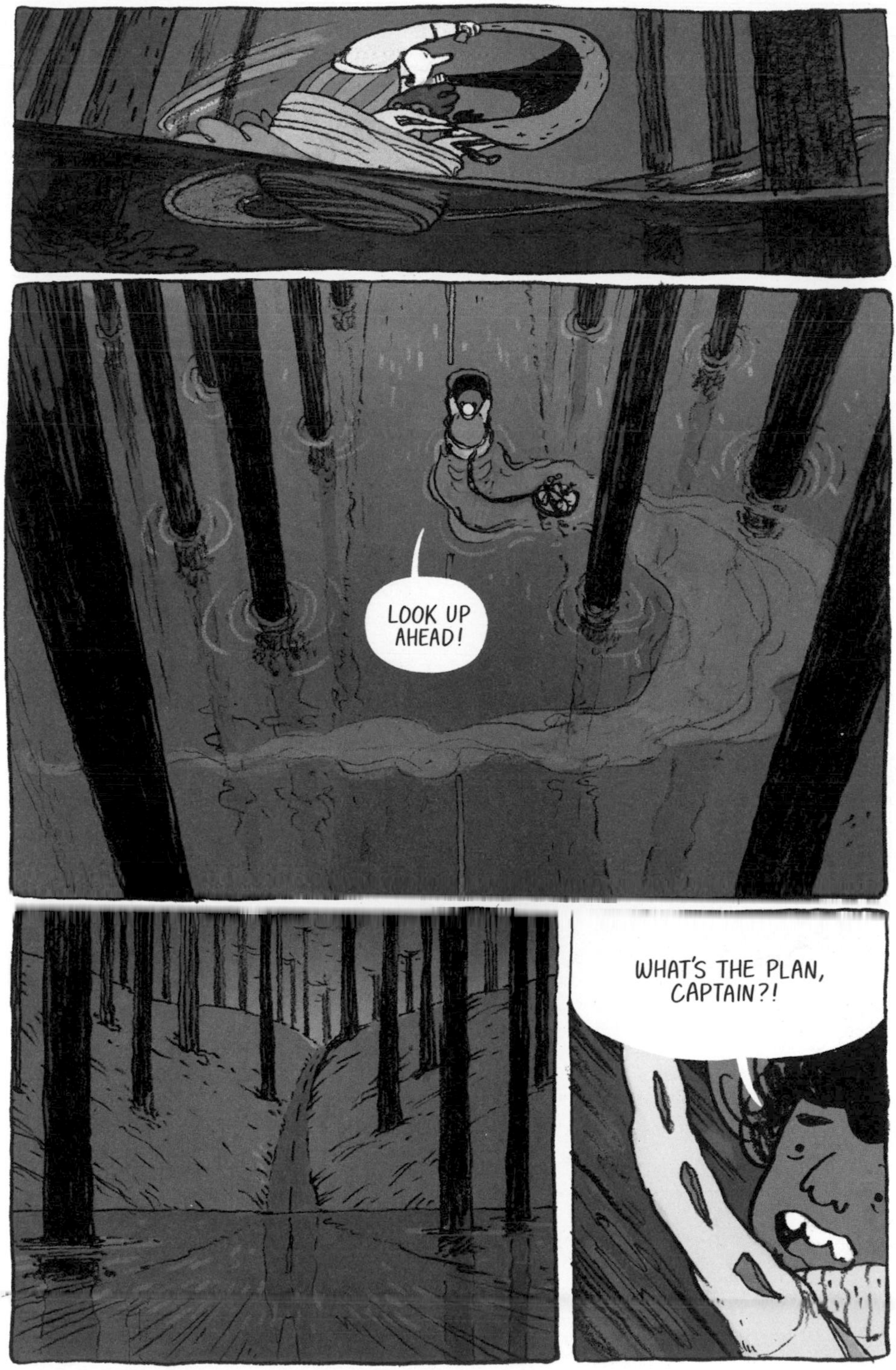

LOOK UP AHEAD!
WHAT'S THE PLAN, CAPTAIN?!

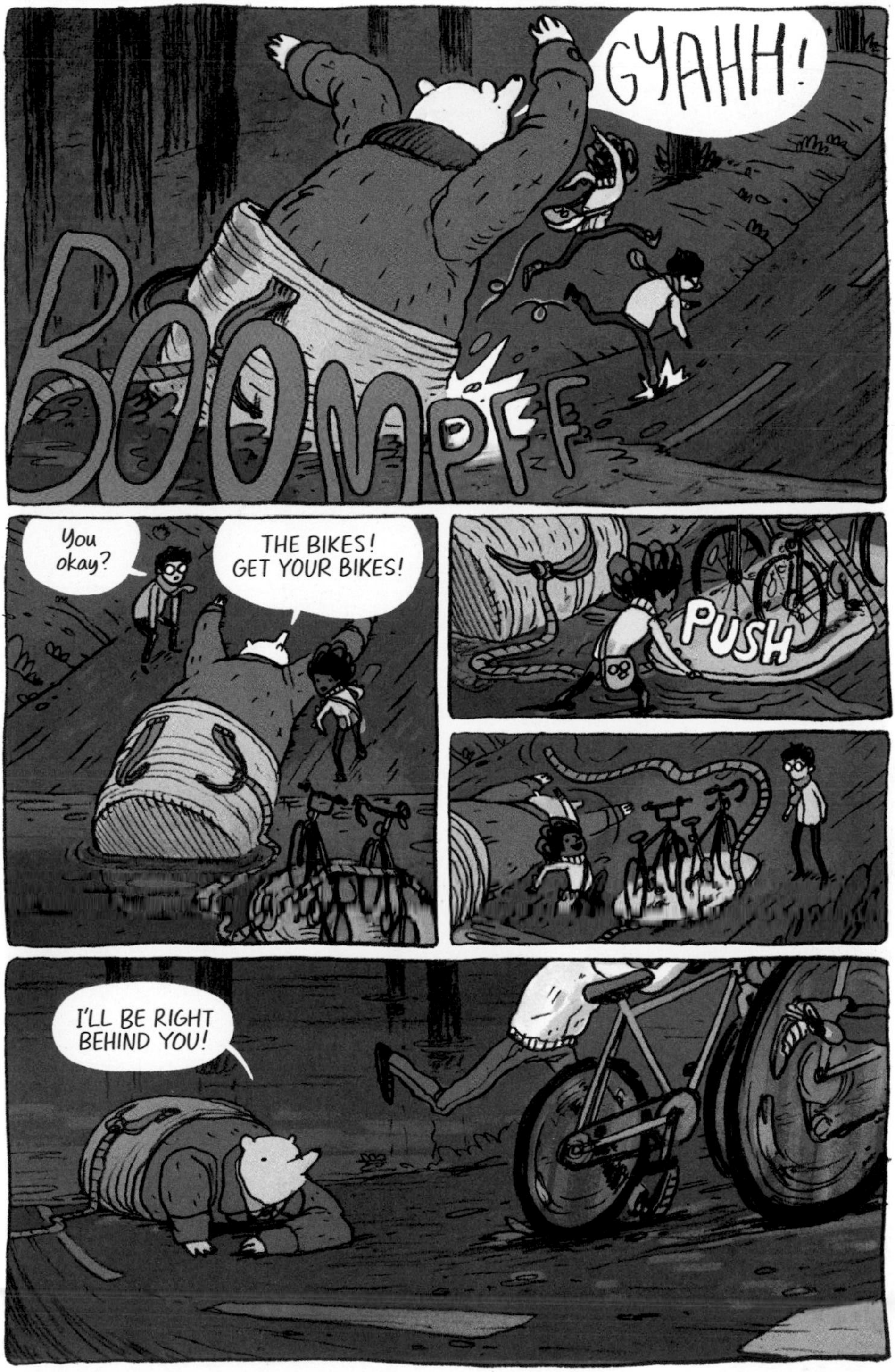
GYAHH!
BOOMPFF
You okay?
THE BIKES! GET YOUR BIKES!
PUSH
I'LL BE RIGHT BEHIND YOU!

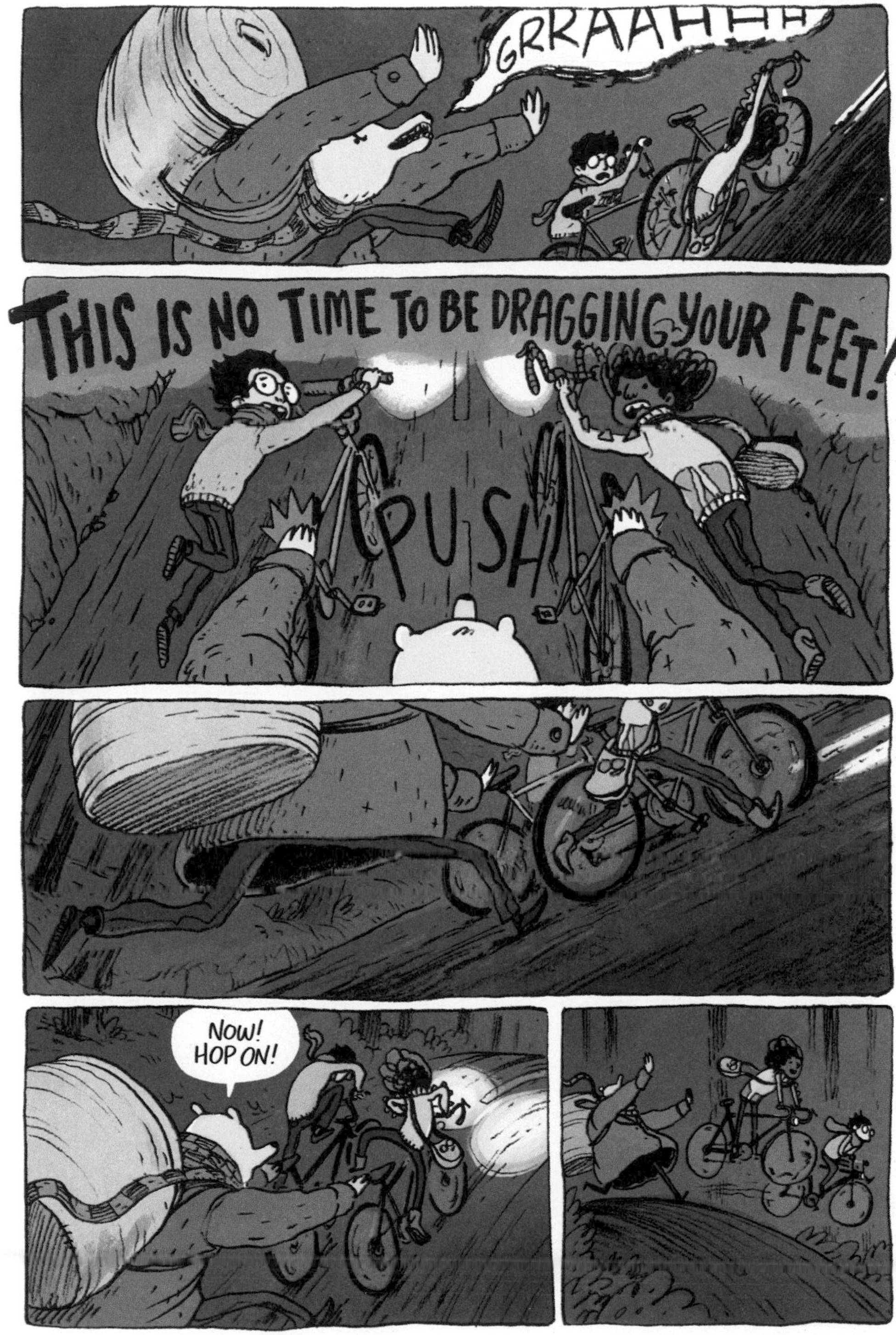
GRRAAHHH
THIS IS NO TIME TO BE DRAGGING YOUR FEET!
PUSH
NOW! HOP ON!

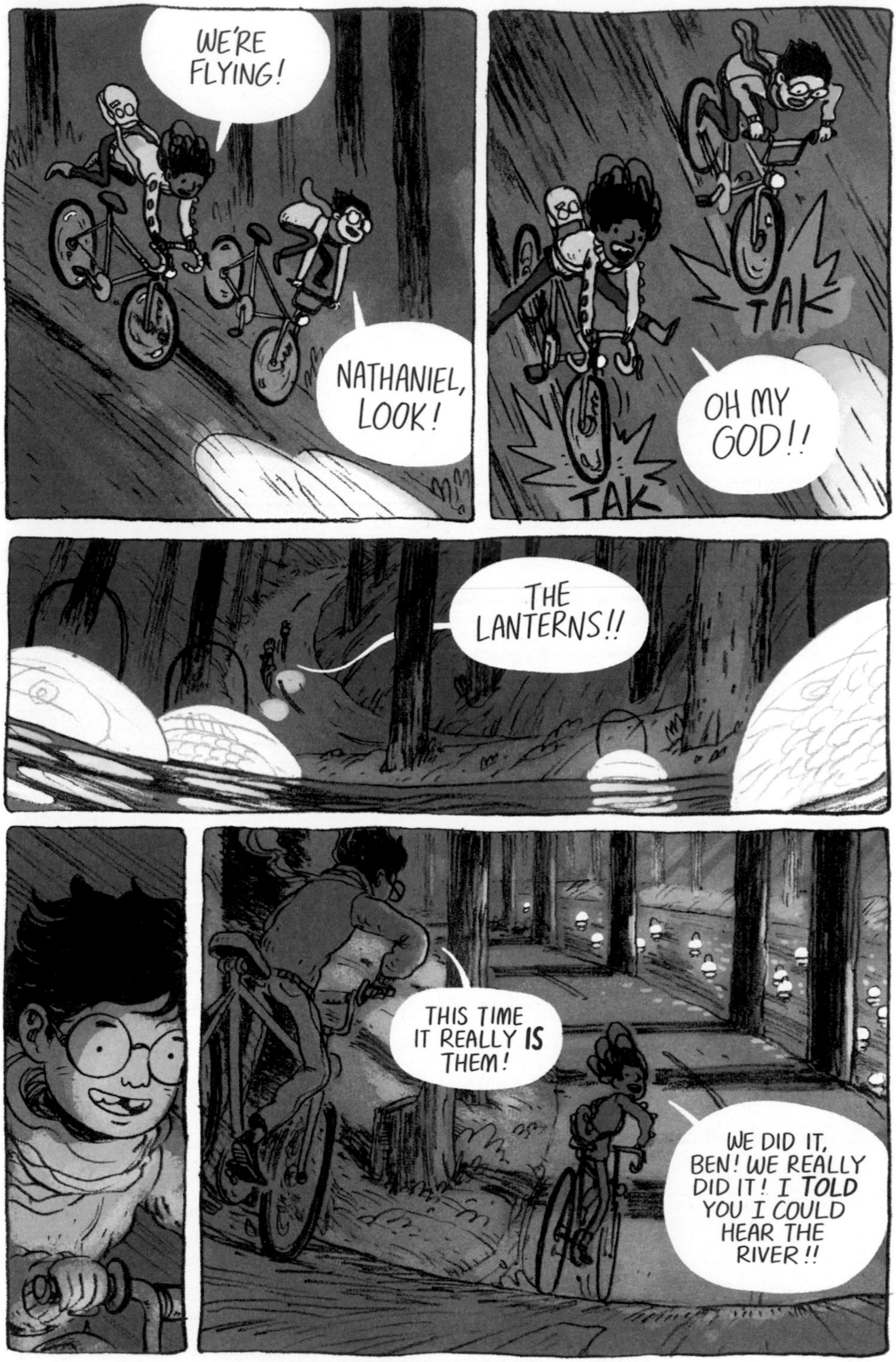
WE'RE FLYING!
NATHANIEL, LOOK!
TAK
OH MY GOD!!
TAK
THE LANTERNS!!
THIS TIME IT REALLY **IS** THEM!
WE DID IT, BEN! WE REALLY DID IT! I **TOLD** YOU I COULD HEAR THE RIVER!!

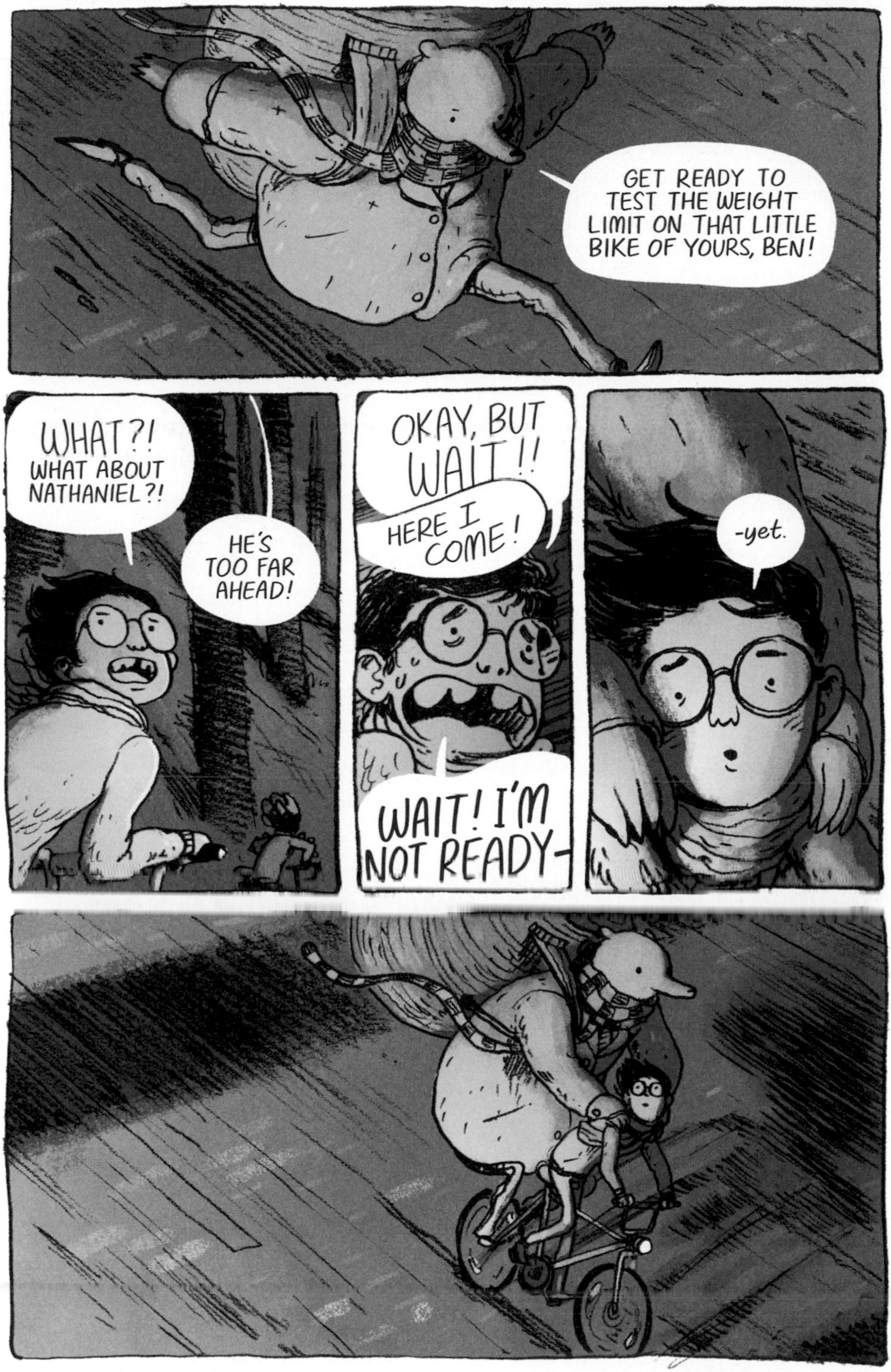
GET READY TO TEST THE WEIGHT LIMIT ON THAT LITTLE BIKE OF YOURS, BEN!
WHAT?! WHAT ABOUT NATHANIEL?!
HE'S TOO FAR AHEAD!
OKAY, BUT WAIT!!
HERE I COME!
WAIT! I'M NOT READY-
-yet.

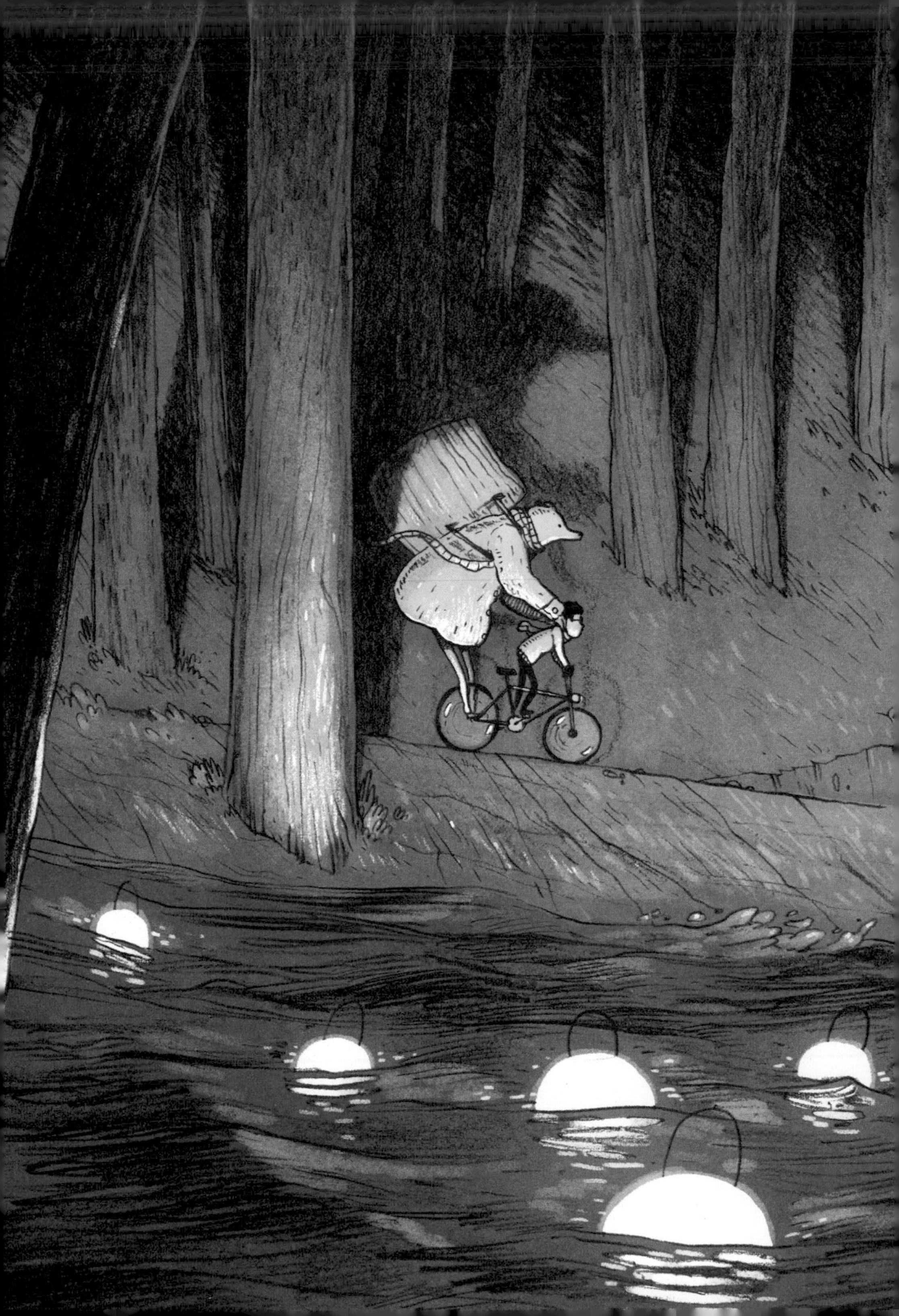

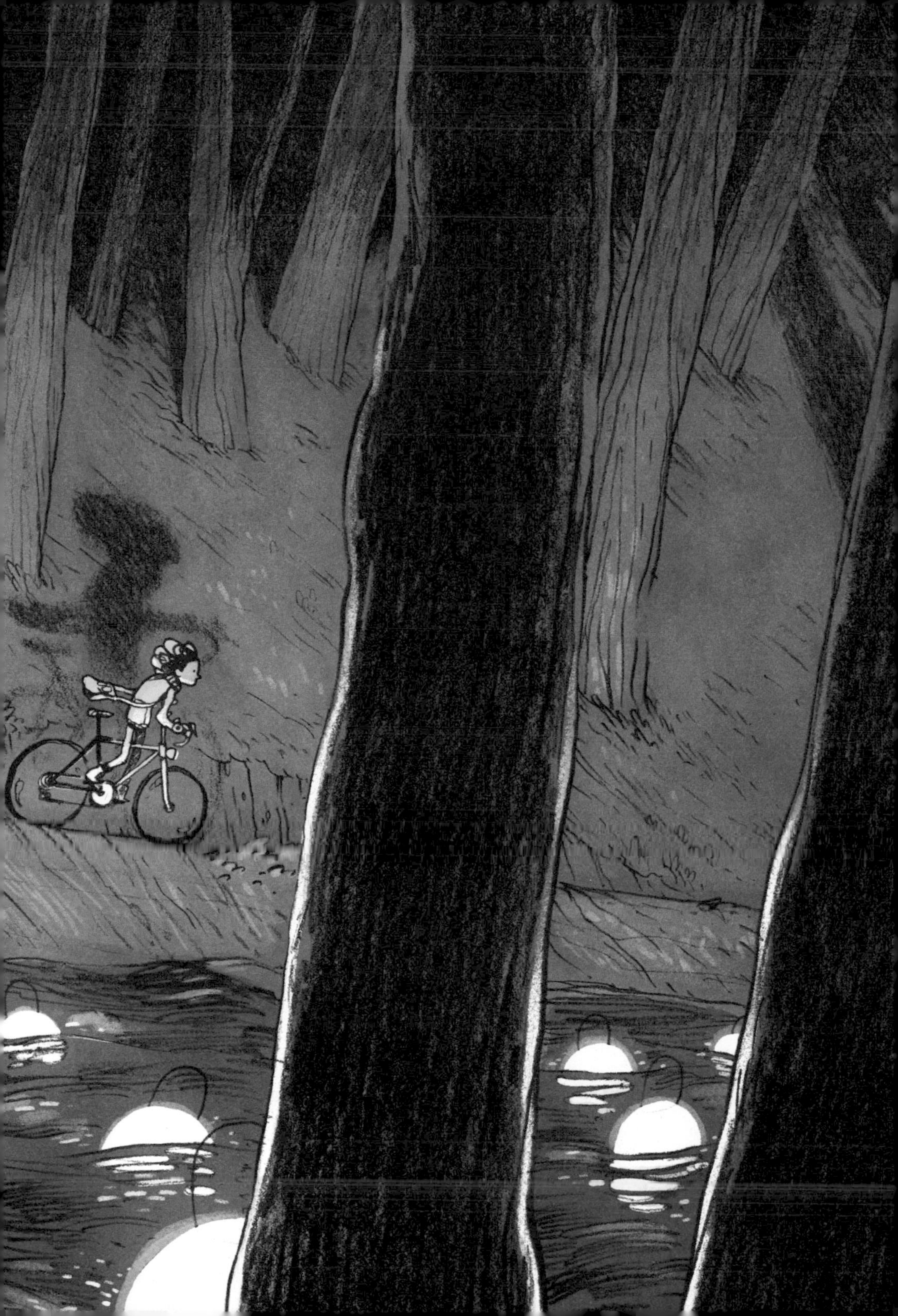

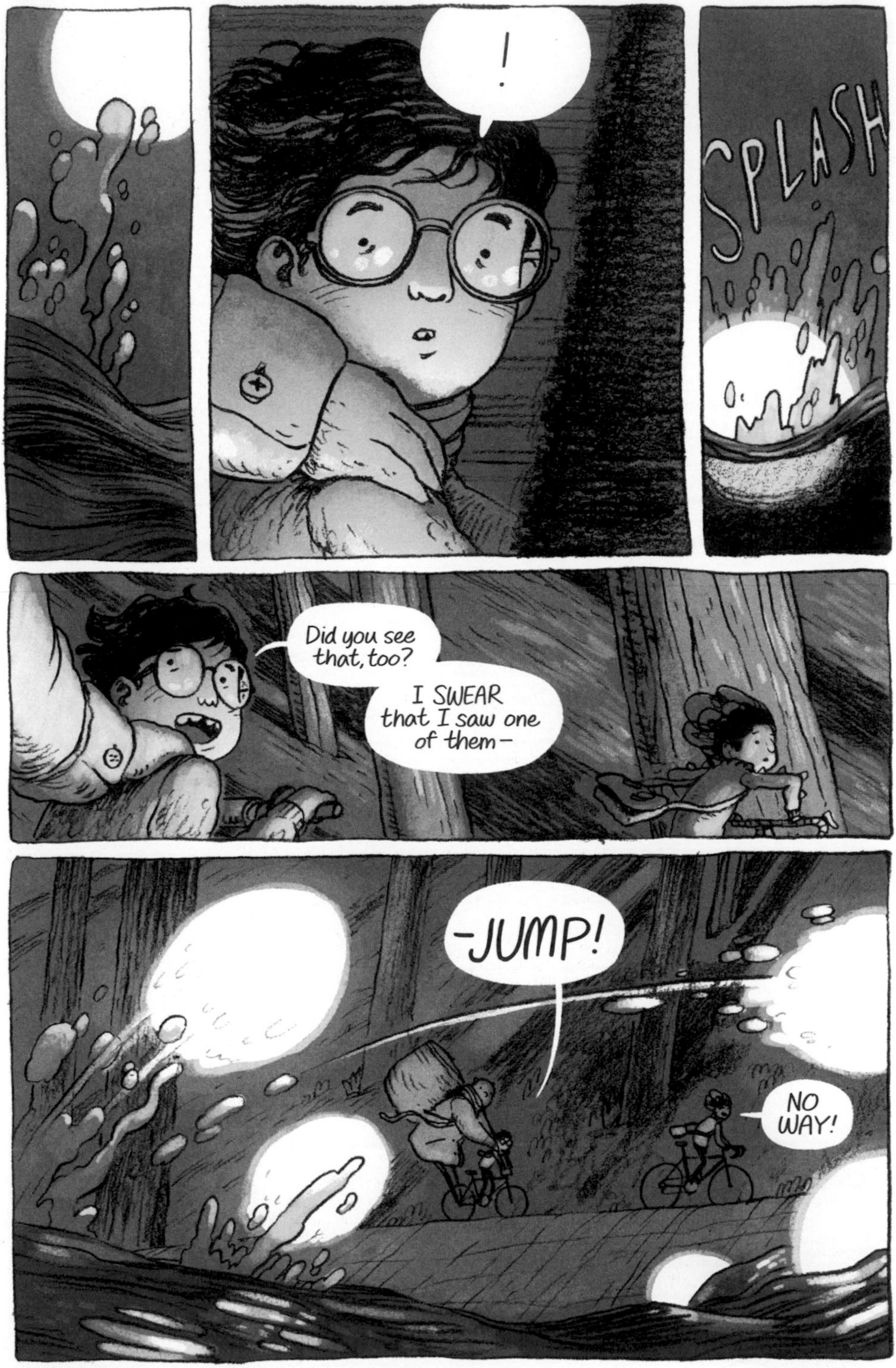
!
SPLASH
Did you see that, too?
I SWEAR that I saw one of them–
–JUMP!
NO WAY!

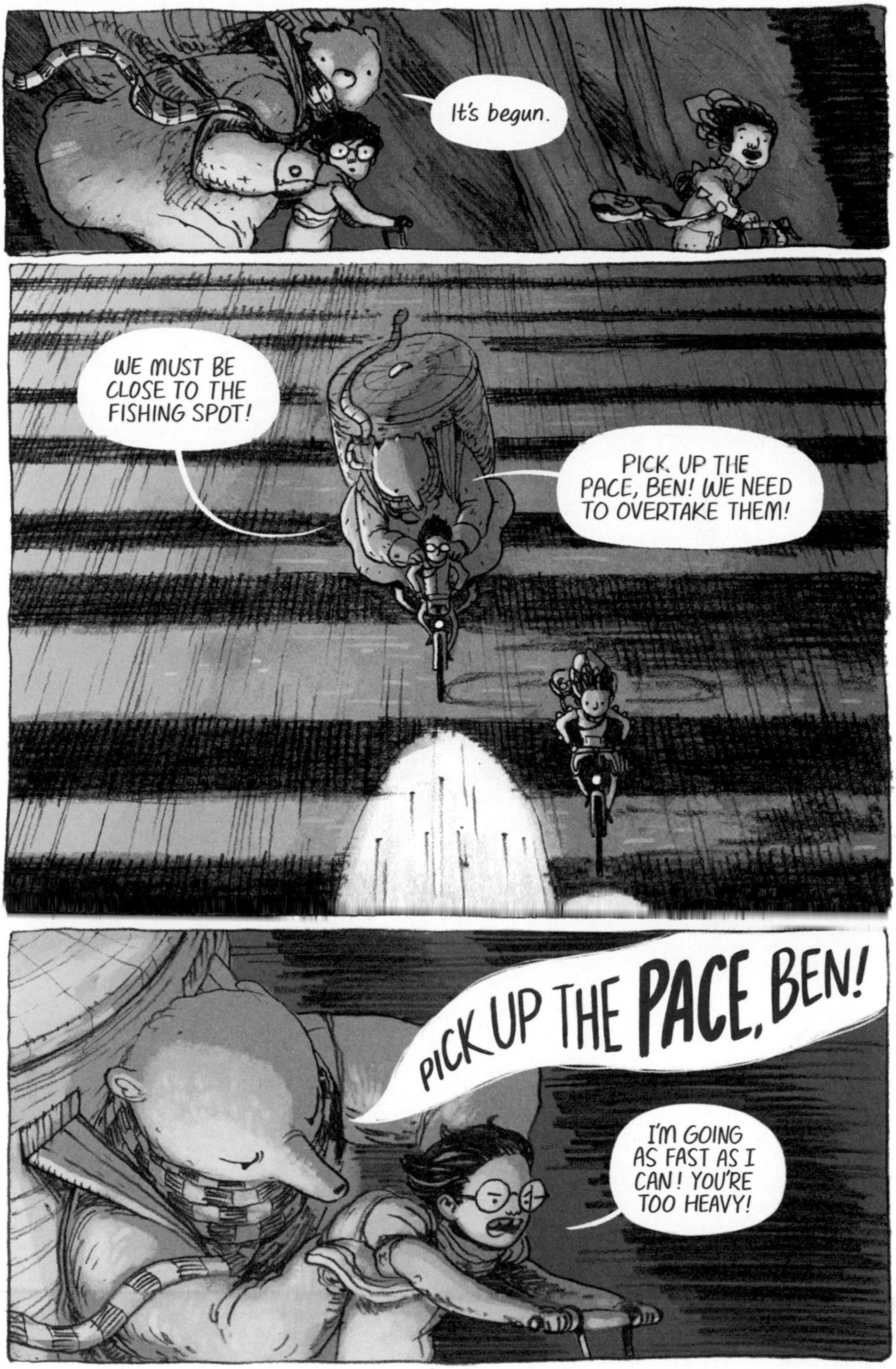
It's begun.
WE MUST BE CLOSE TO THE FISHING SPOT!
PICK UP THE PACE, BEN! WE NEED TO OVERTAKE THEM!
PICK UP THE PACE, BEN!
I'M GOING AS FAST AS I CAN! YOU'RE TOO HEAVY!

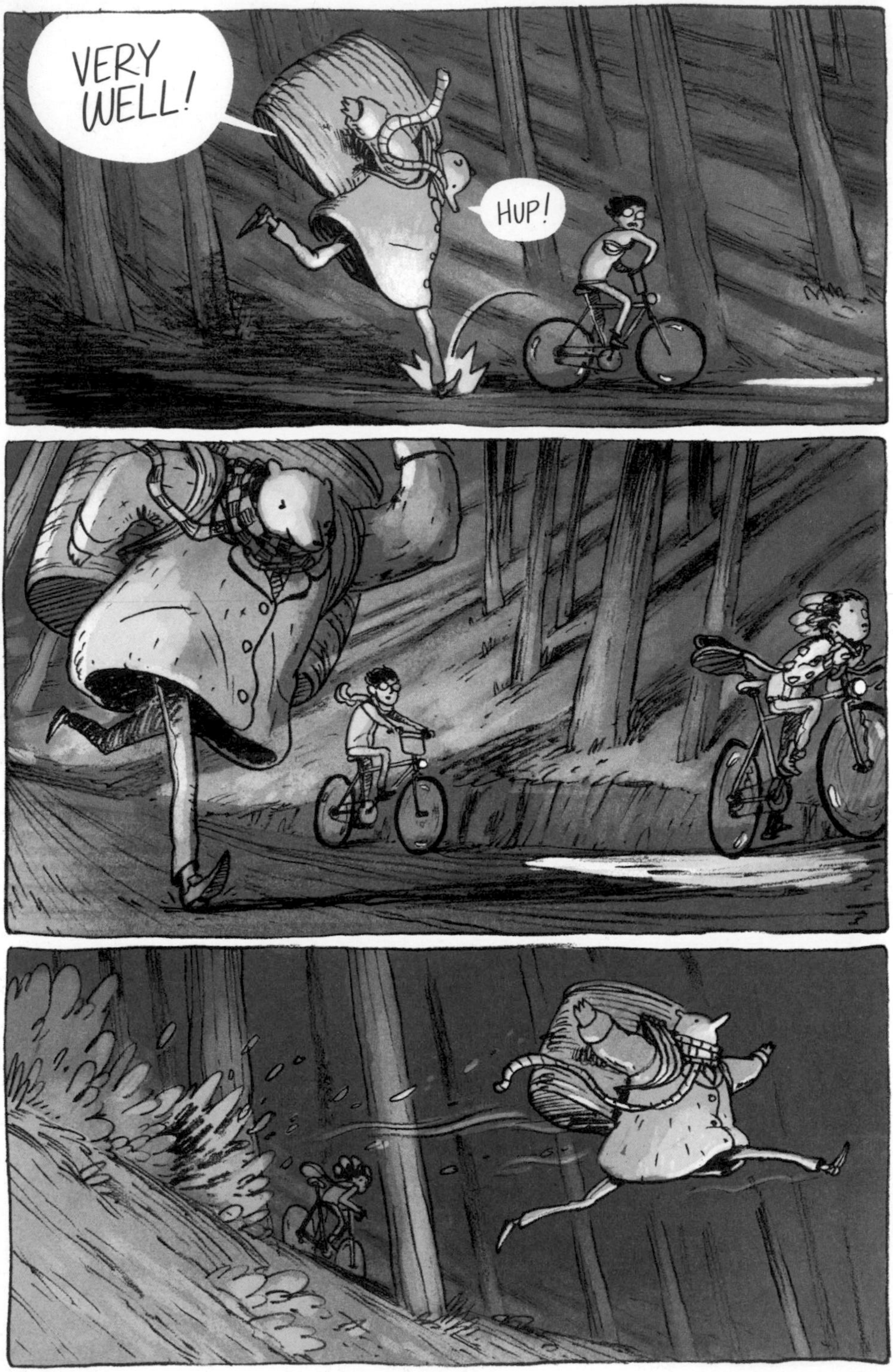
VERY WELL!
HUP!

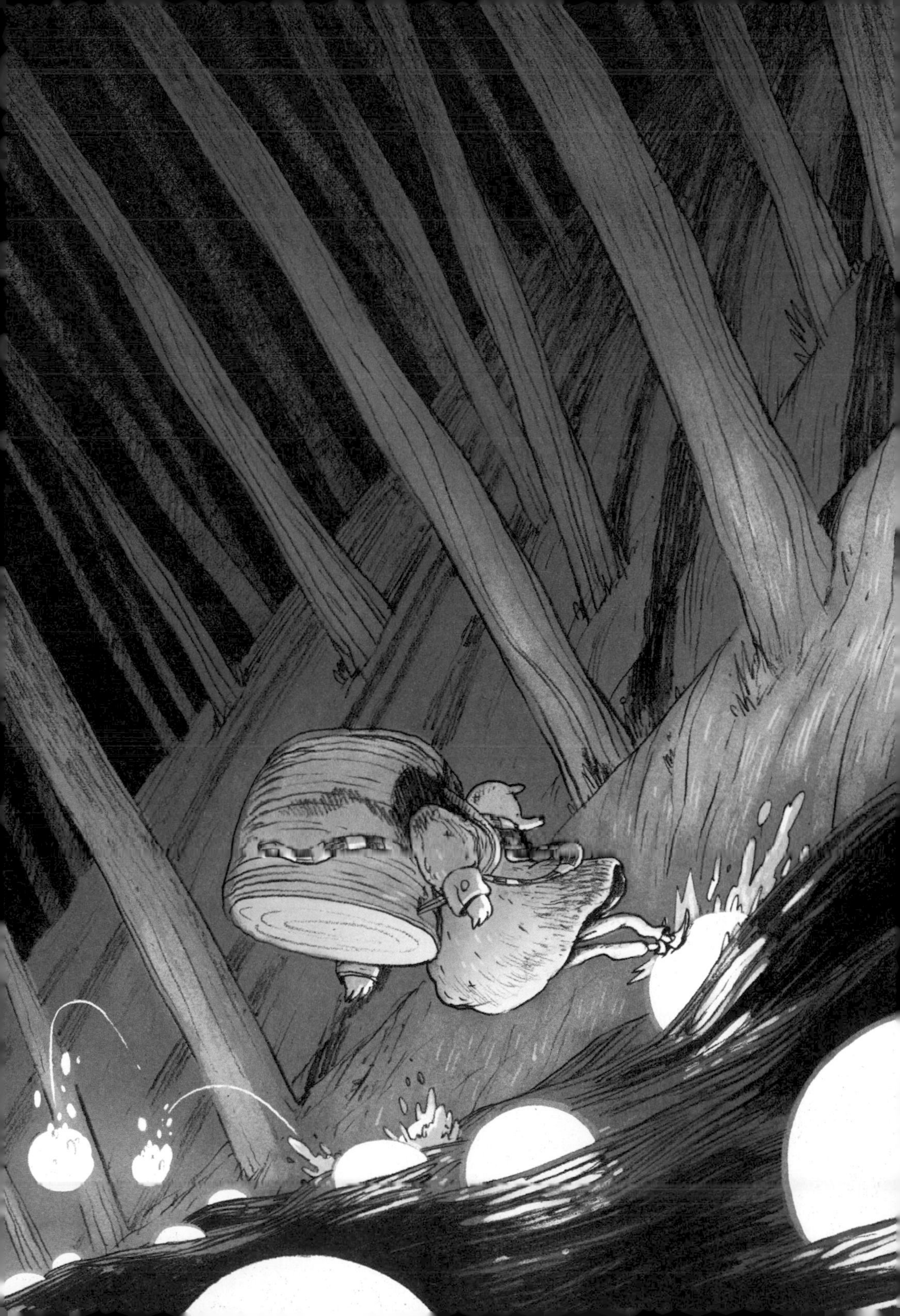

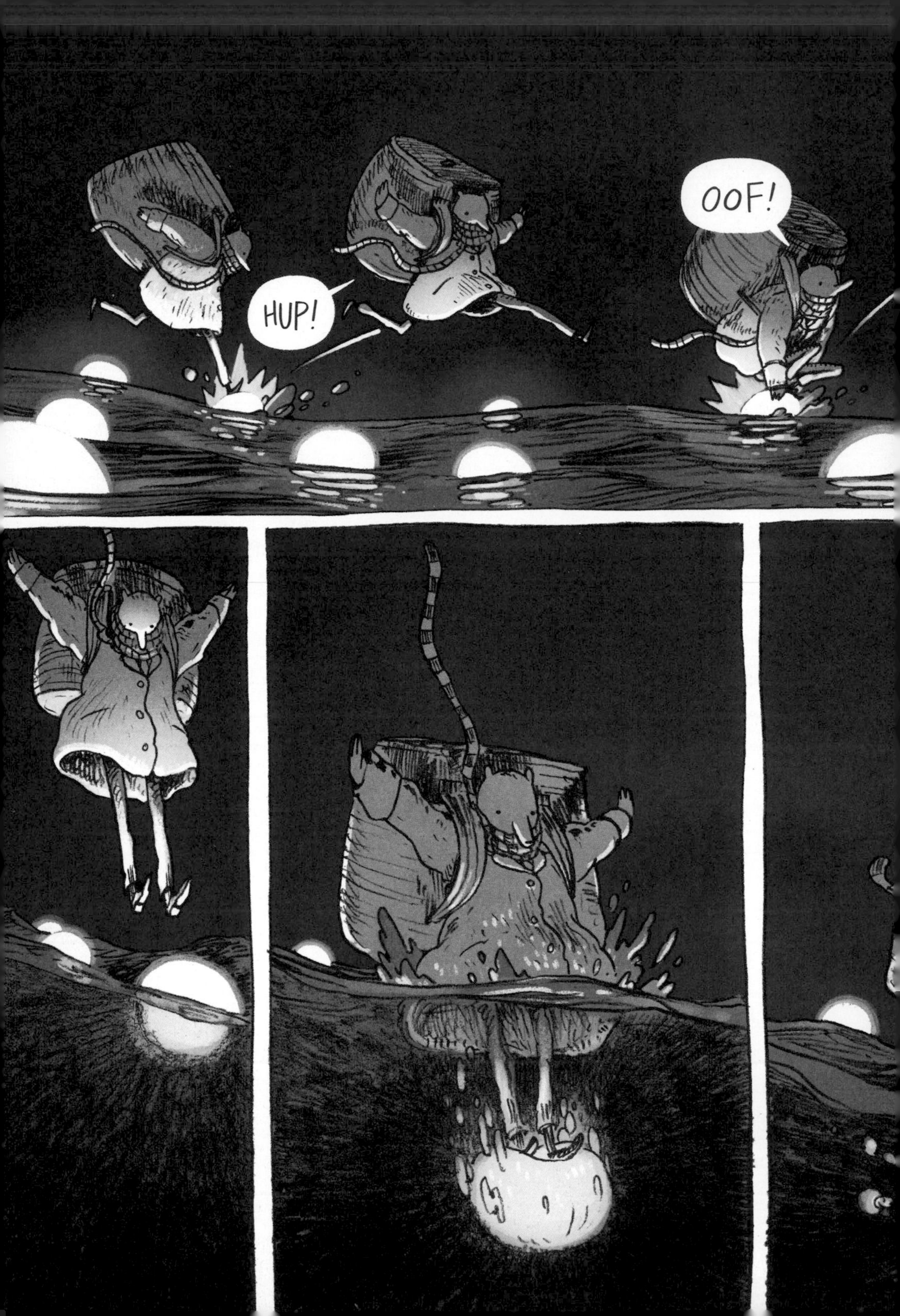
HUP!
OOF!

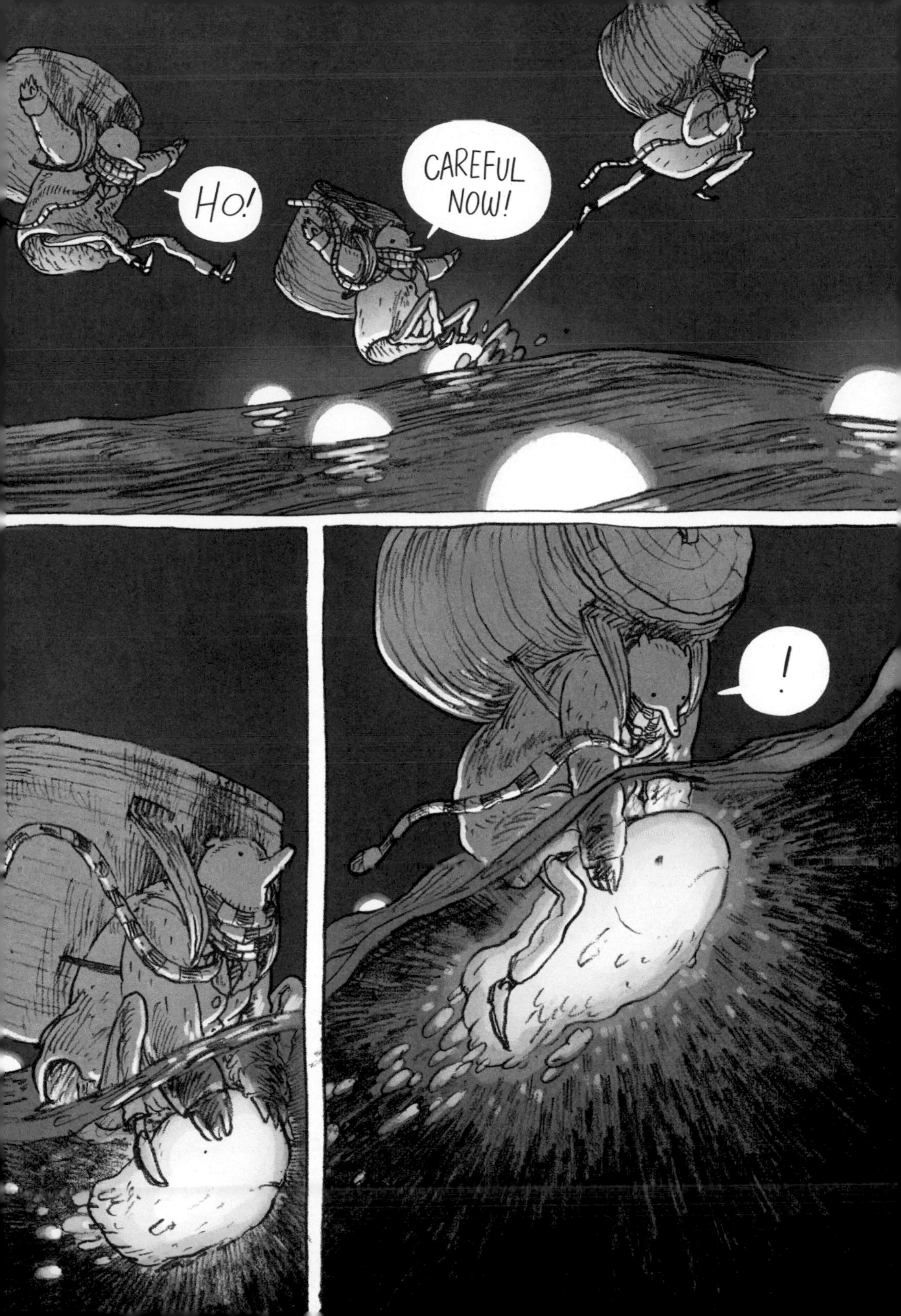
HO!
CAREFUL NOW!
!

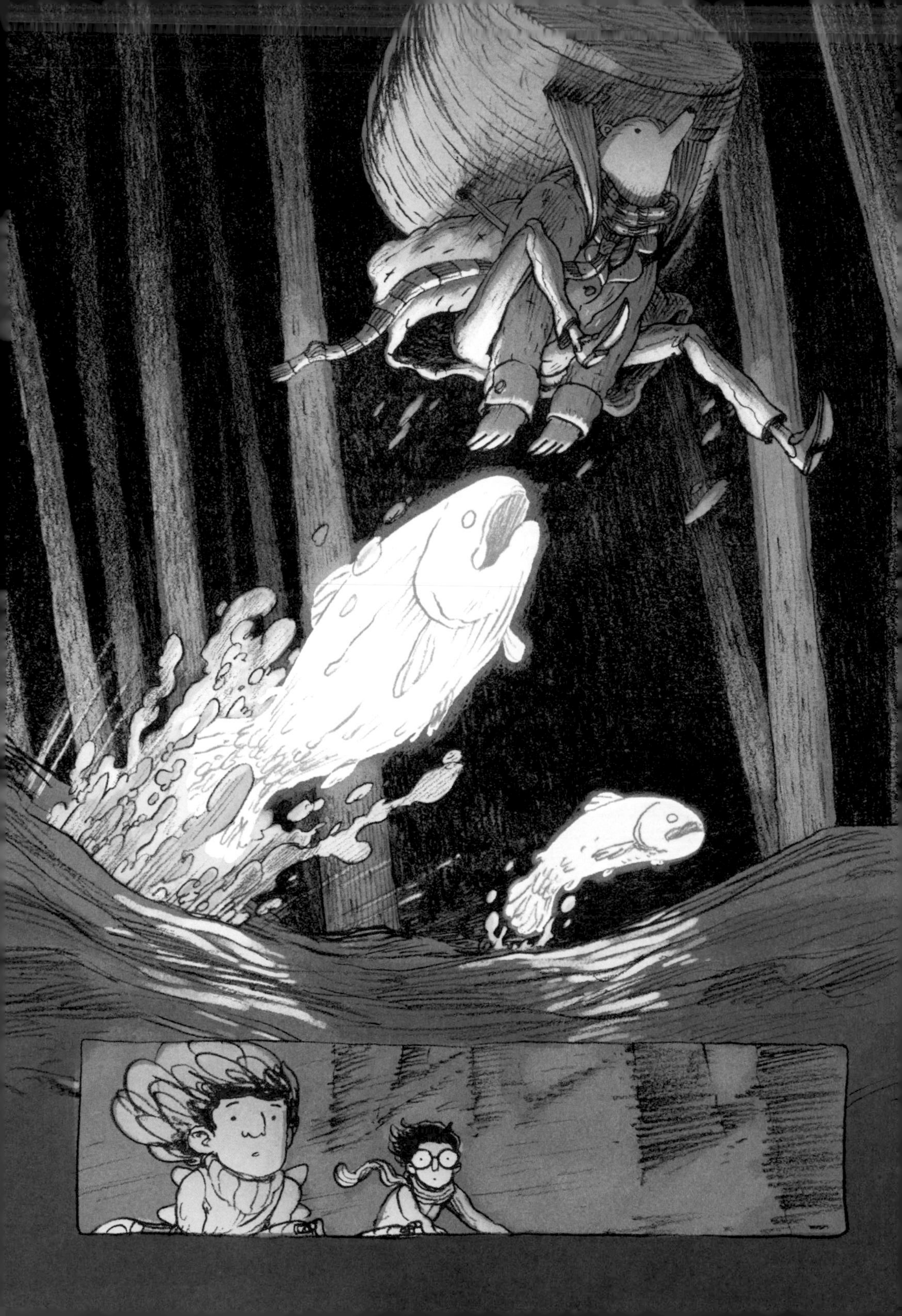

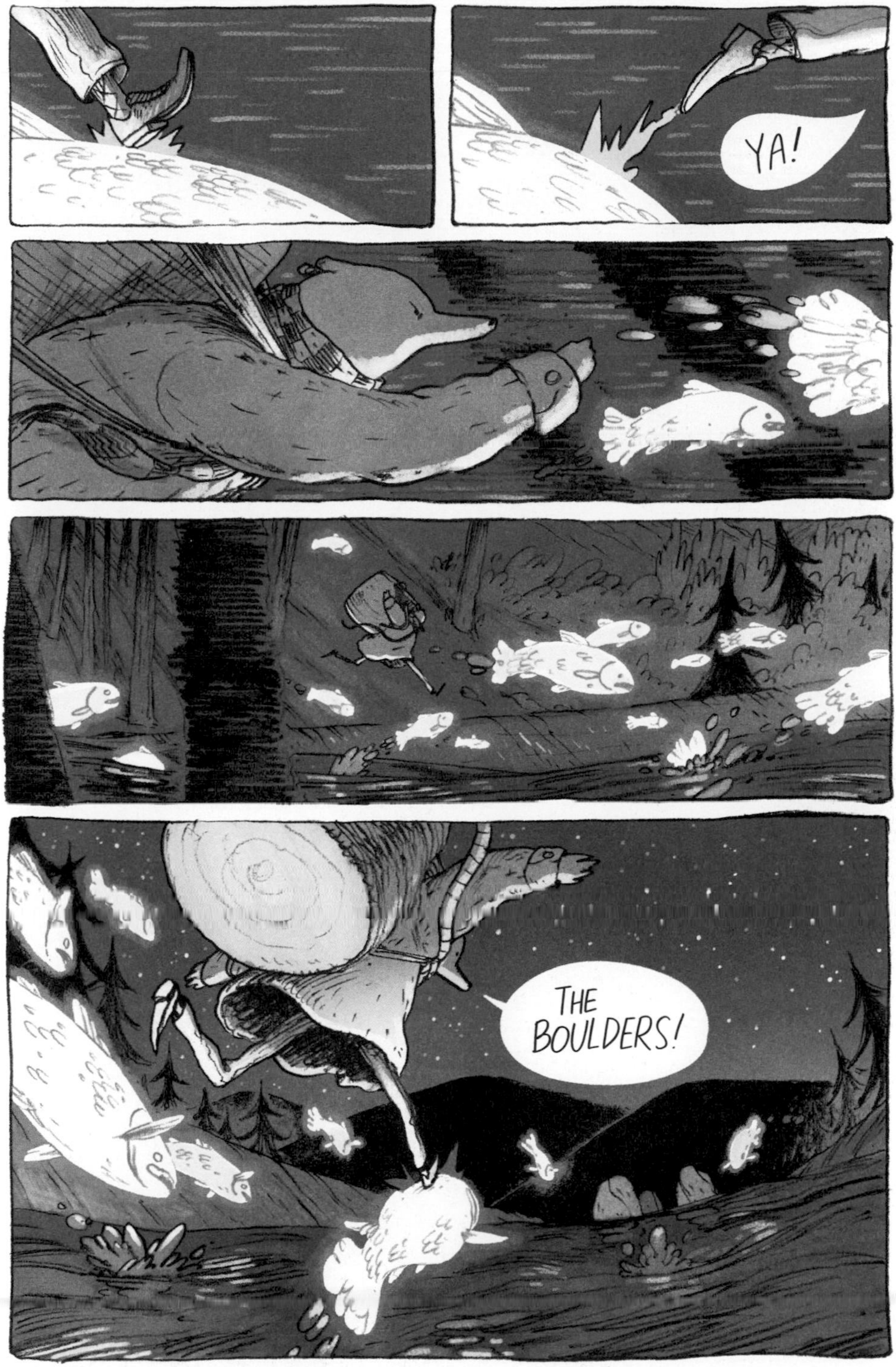
YA!
THE BOULDERS!

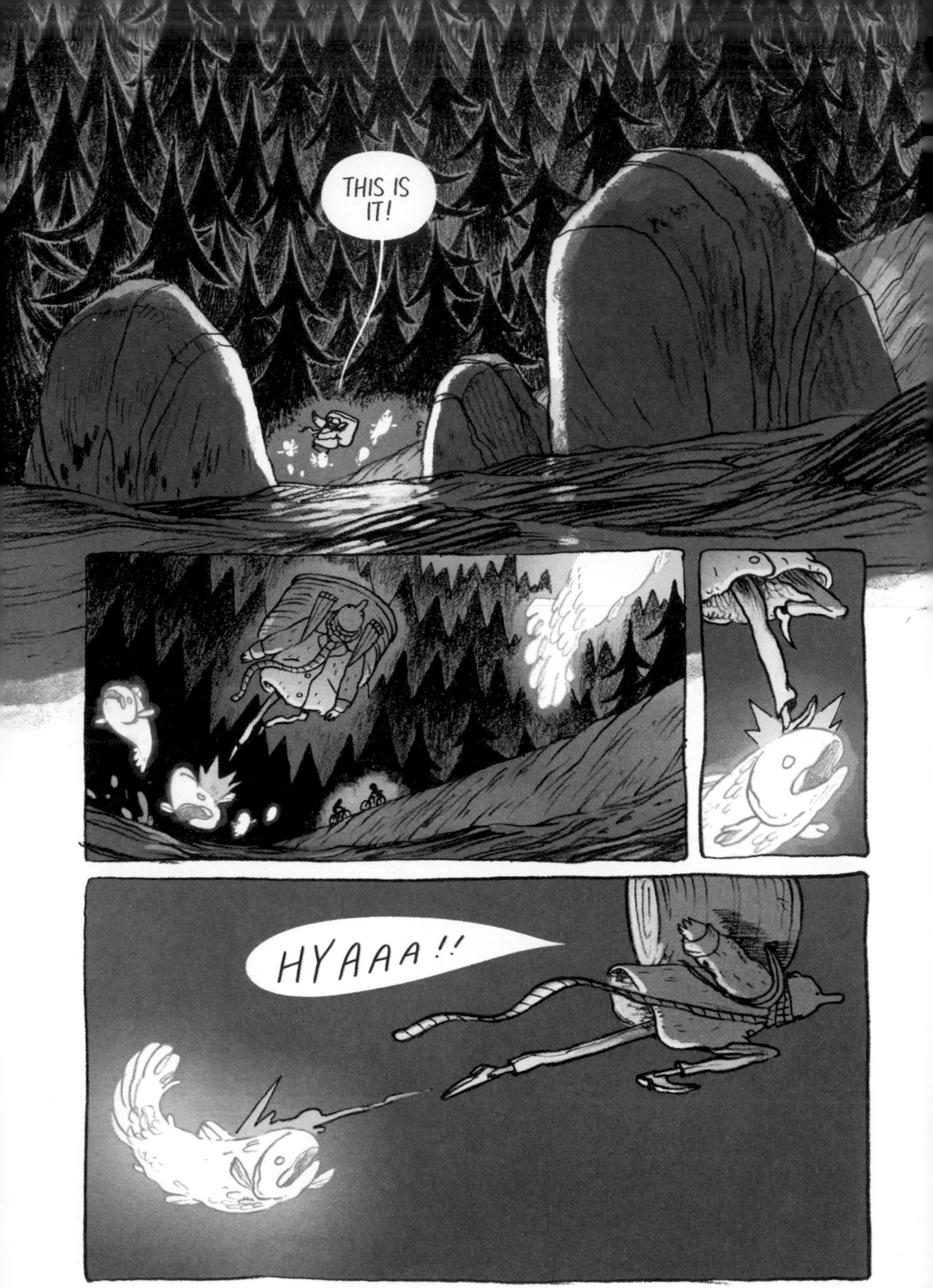
THIS IS IT!
HYAAA!!

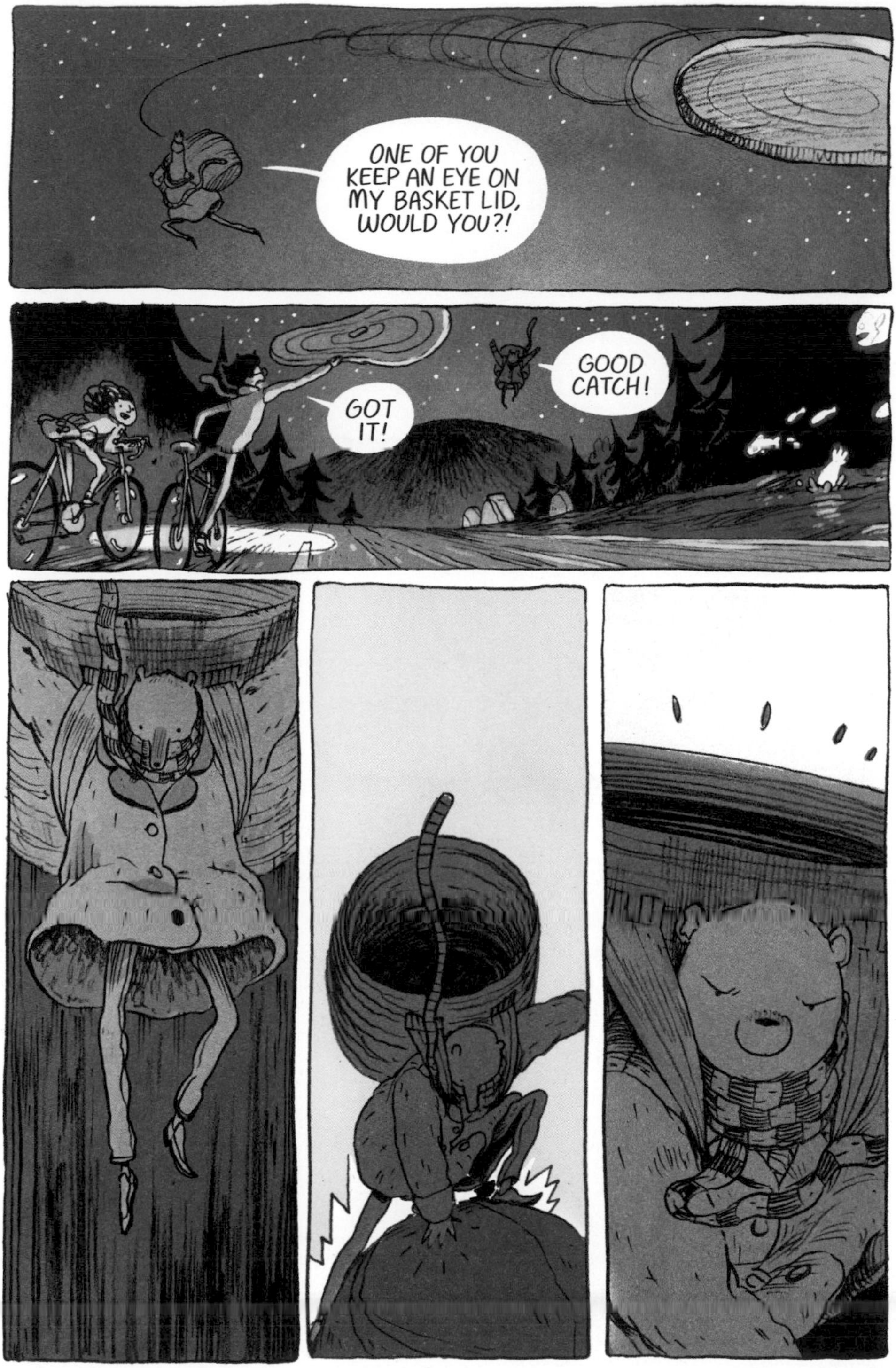
ONE OF YOU KEEP AN EYE ON MY BASKET LID, WOULD YOU?!
GOOD CATCH!
GOT IT!

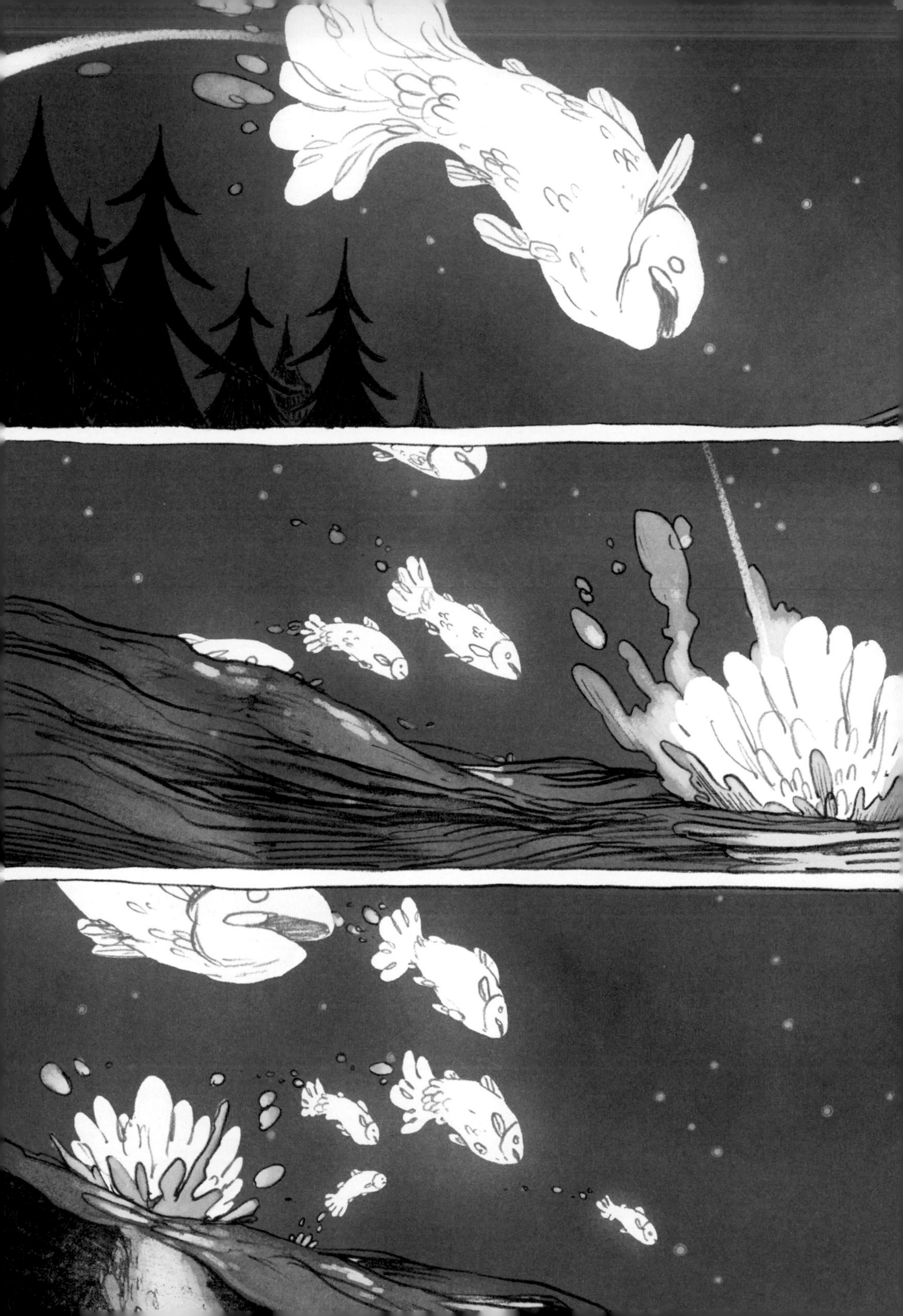

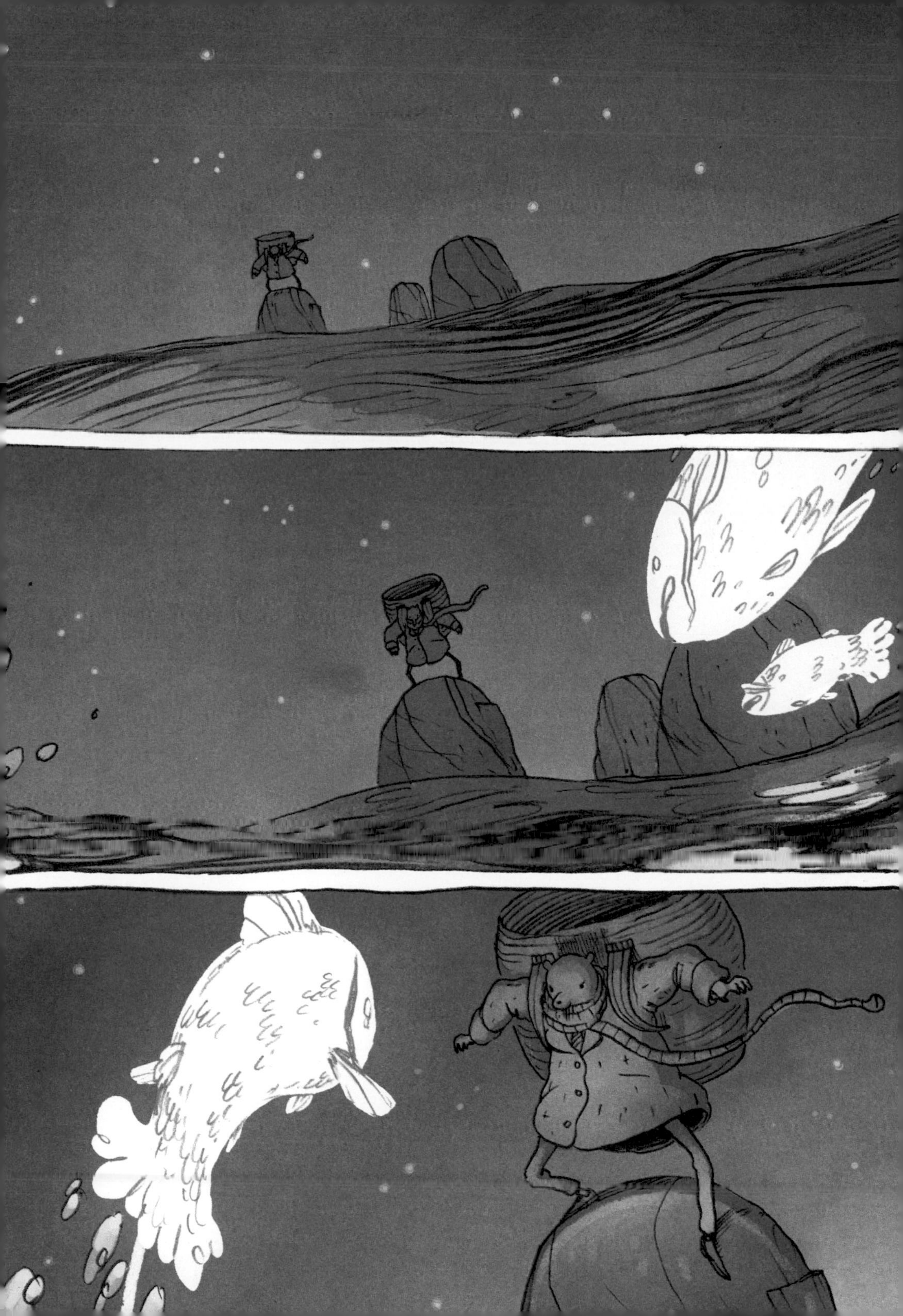

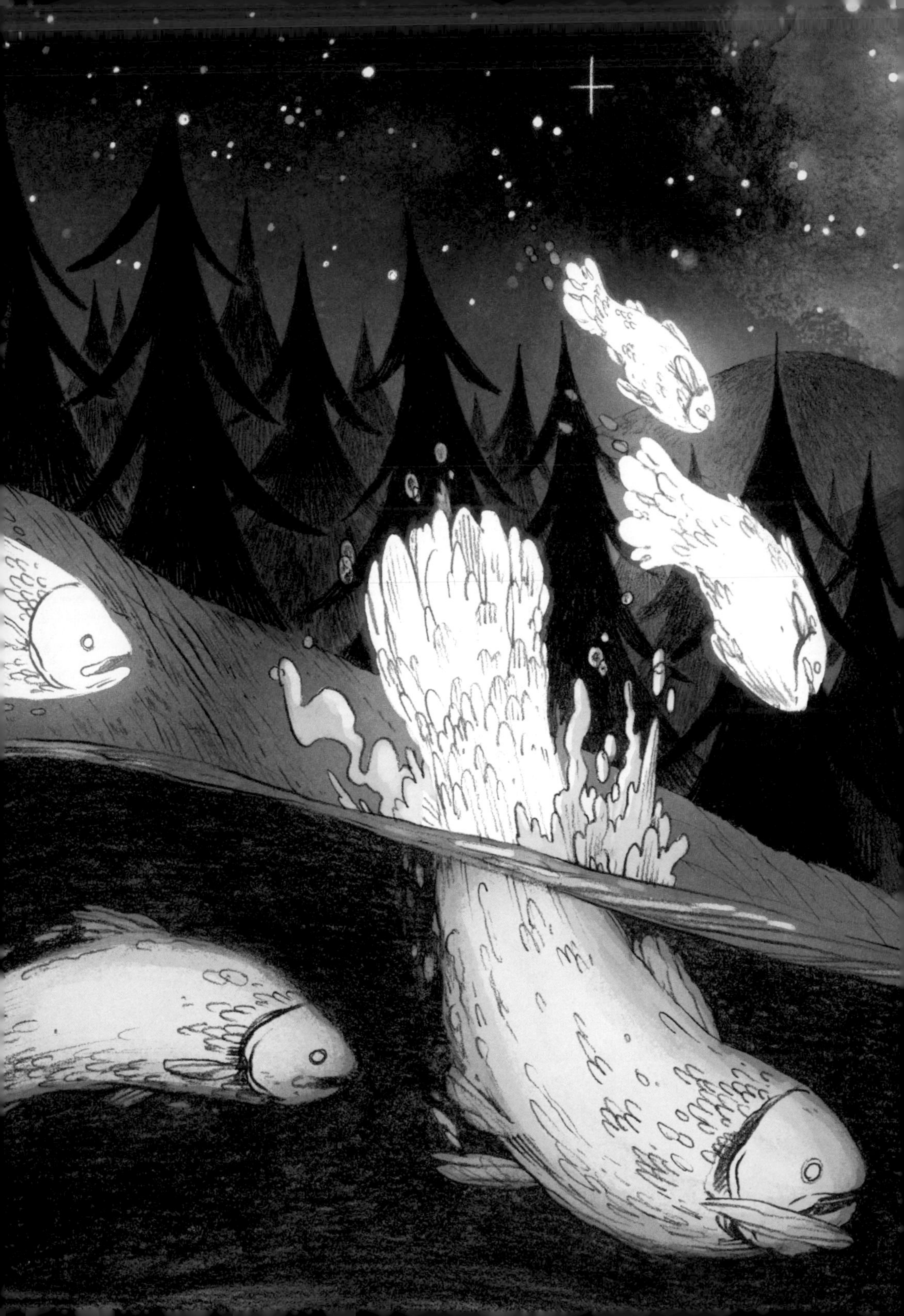

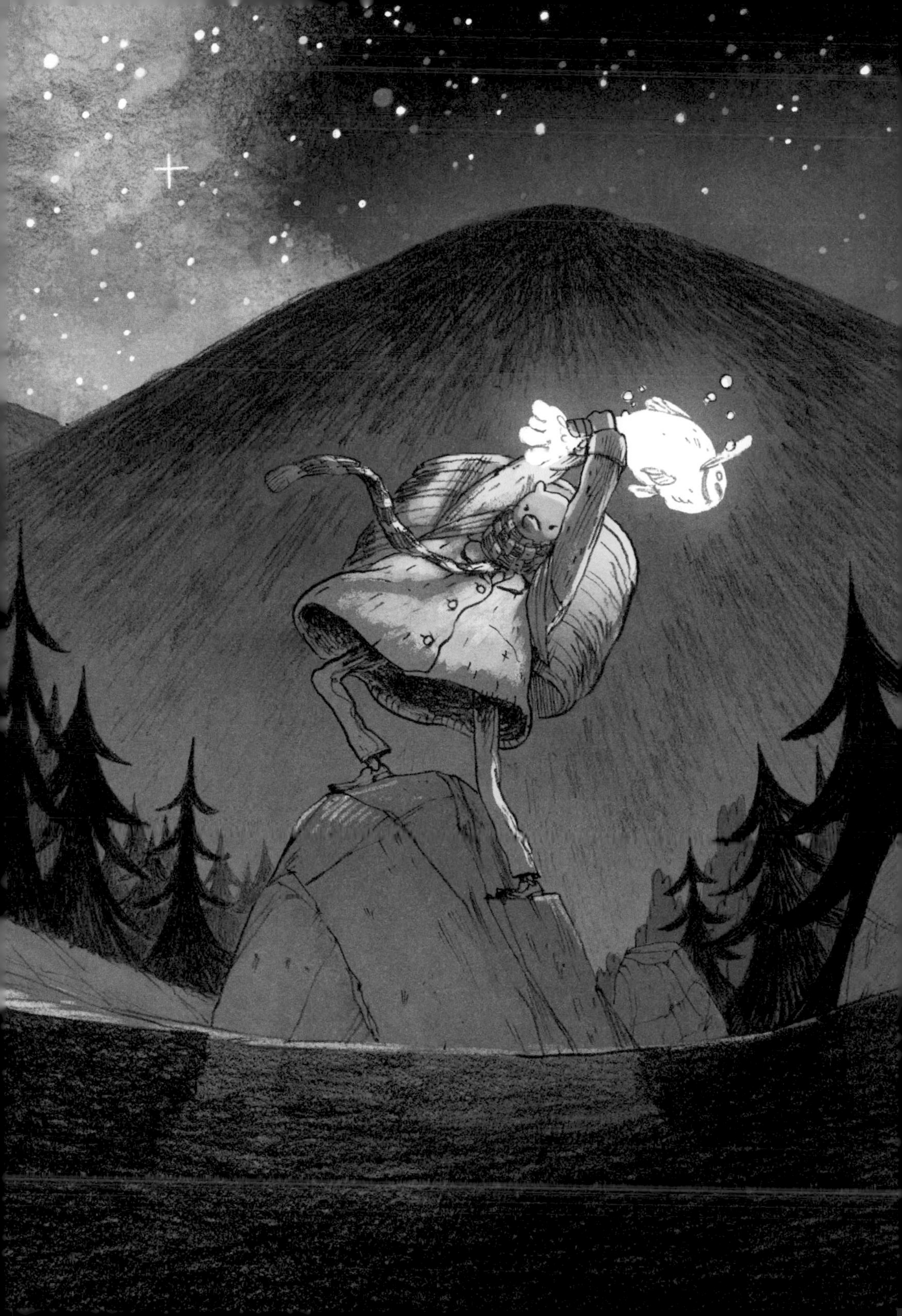

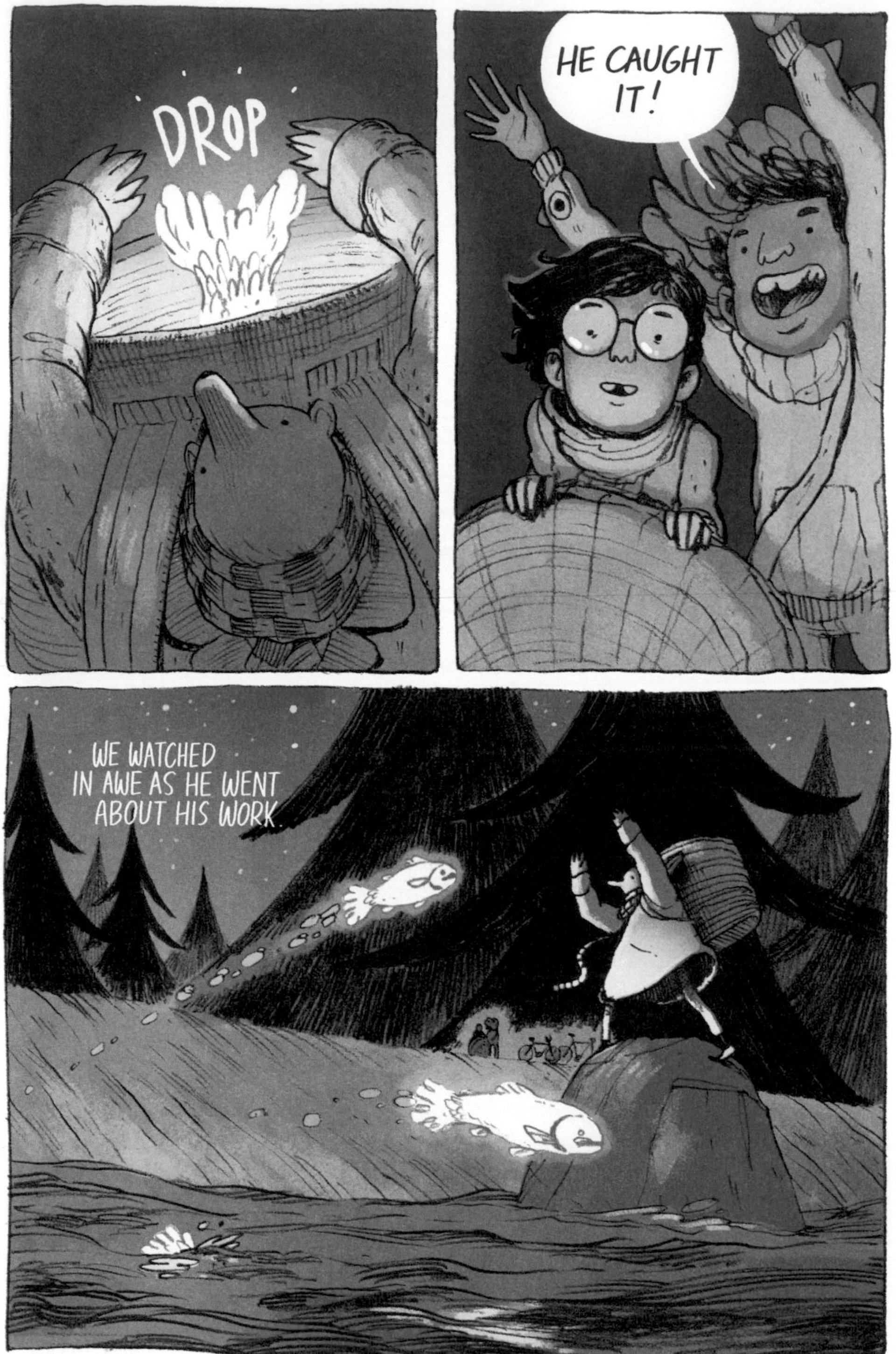
DROP
HE CAUGHT IT!
WE WATCHED IN AWE AS HE WENT ABOUT HIS WORK

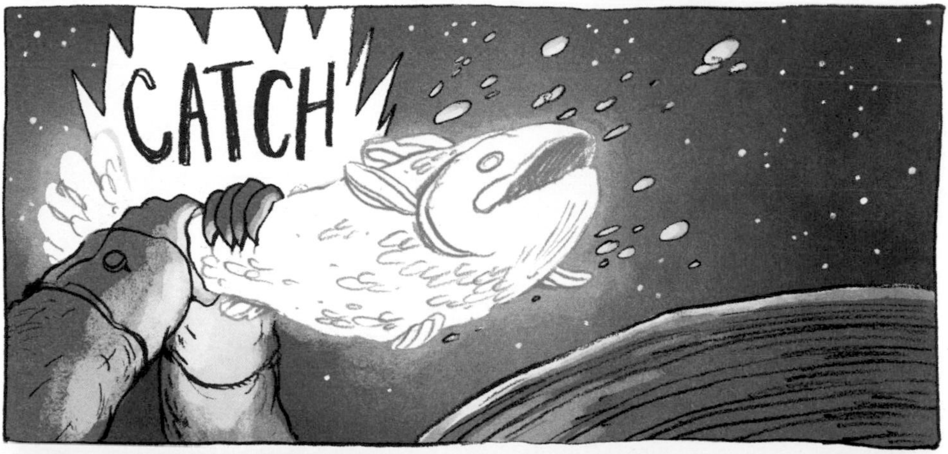
CATCH

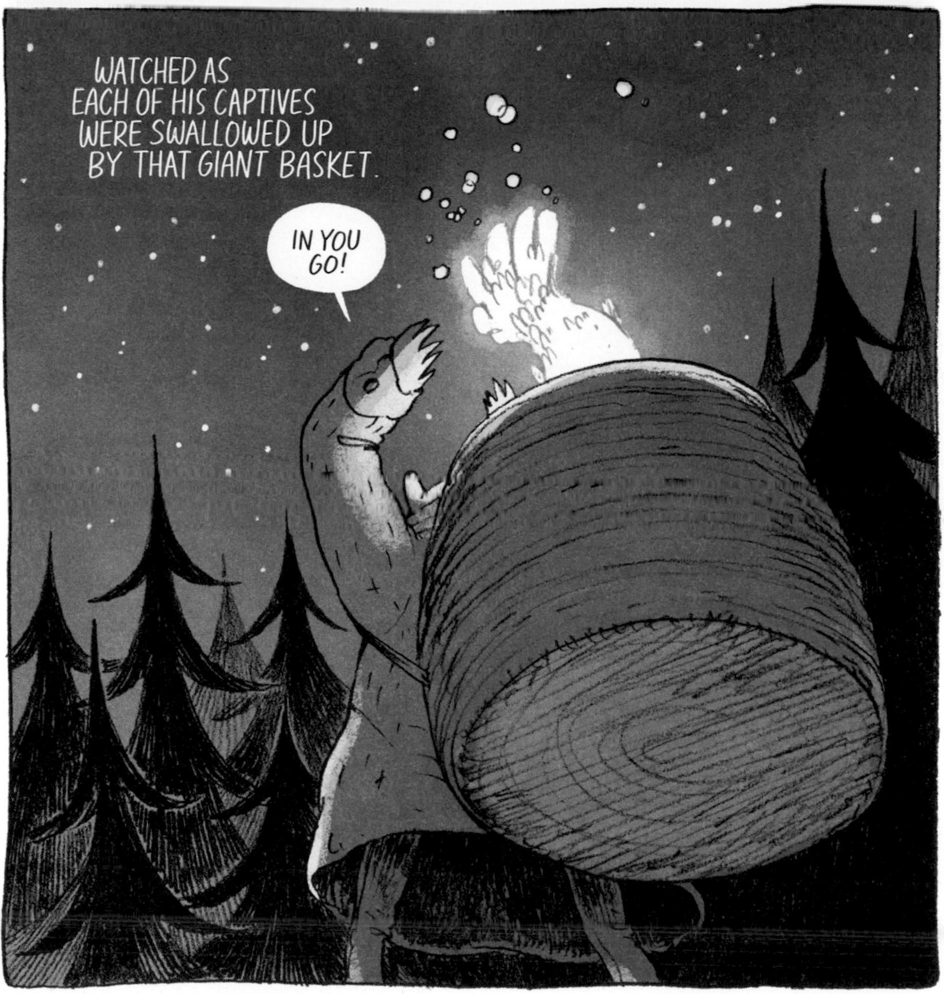
WATCHED AS EACH OF HIS CAPTIVES WERE SWALLOWED UP BY THAT GIANT BASKET.
IN YOU GO!

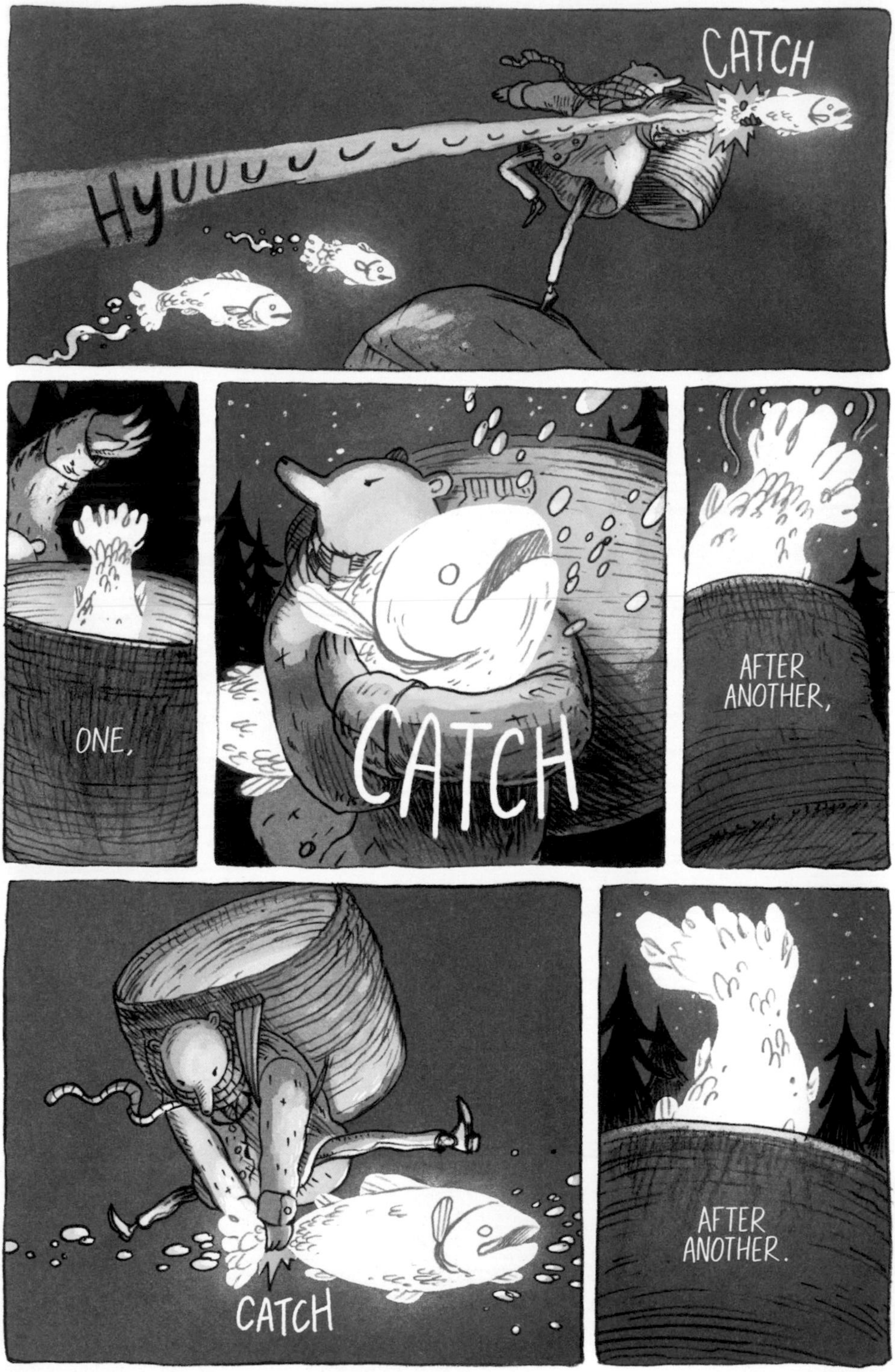
CATCH
Hyuuuuuuuuuuuuu
ONE,
CATCH
AFTER ANOTHER,
CATCH
AFTER ANOTHER.

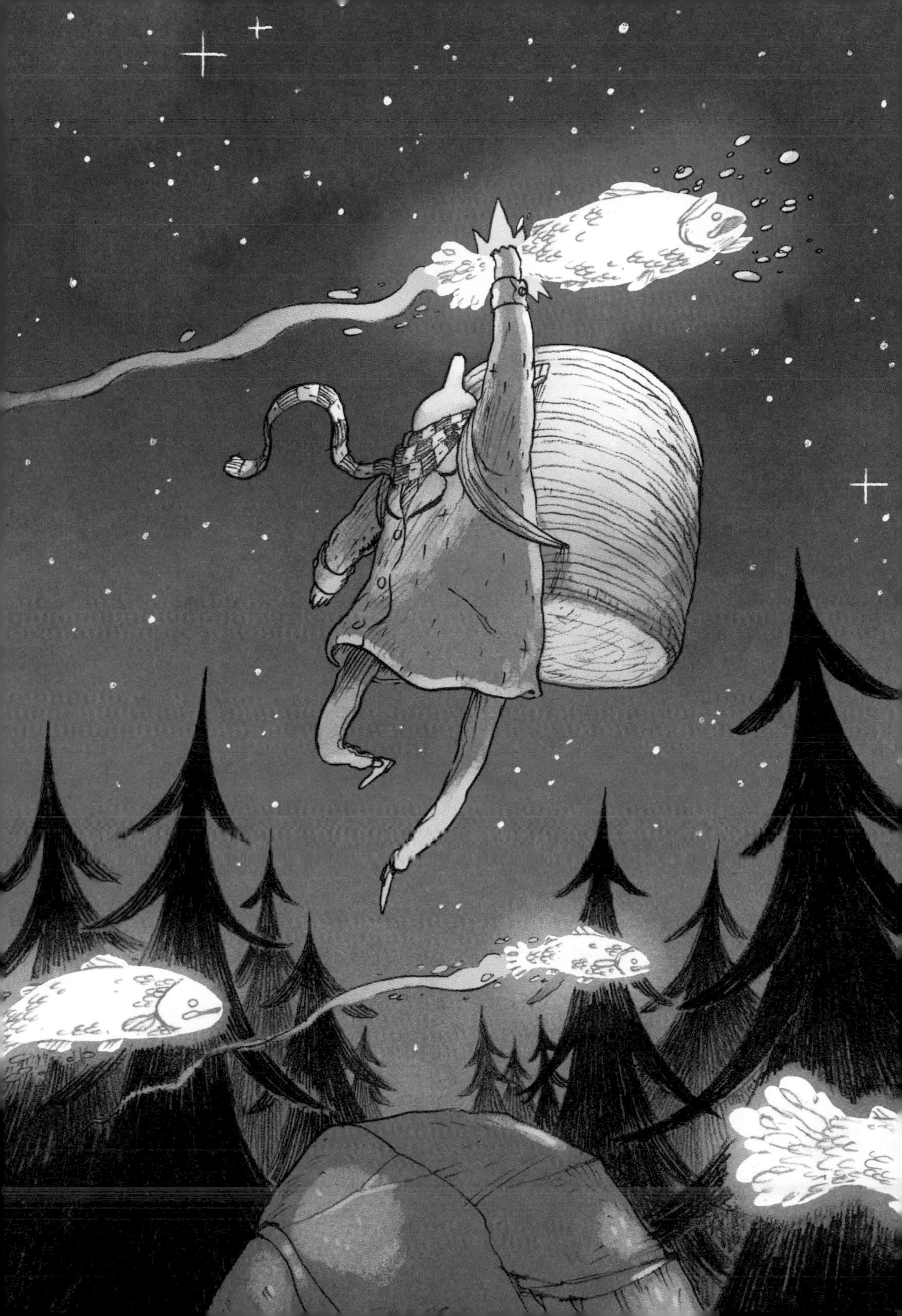

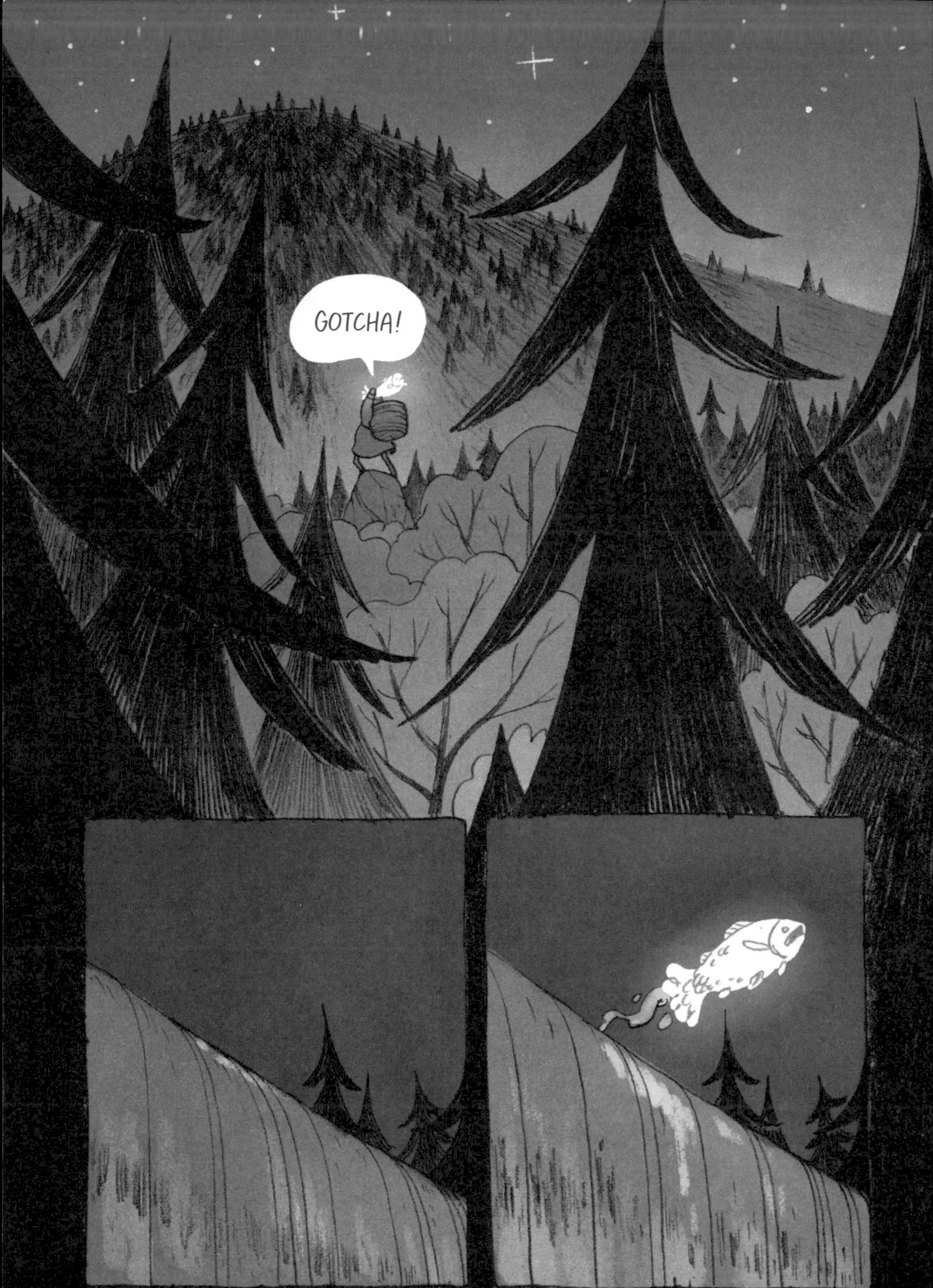
GOTCHA!

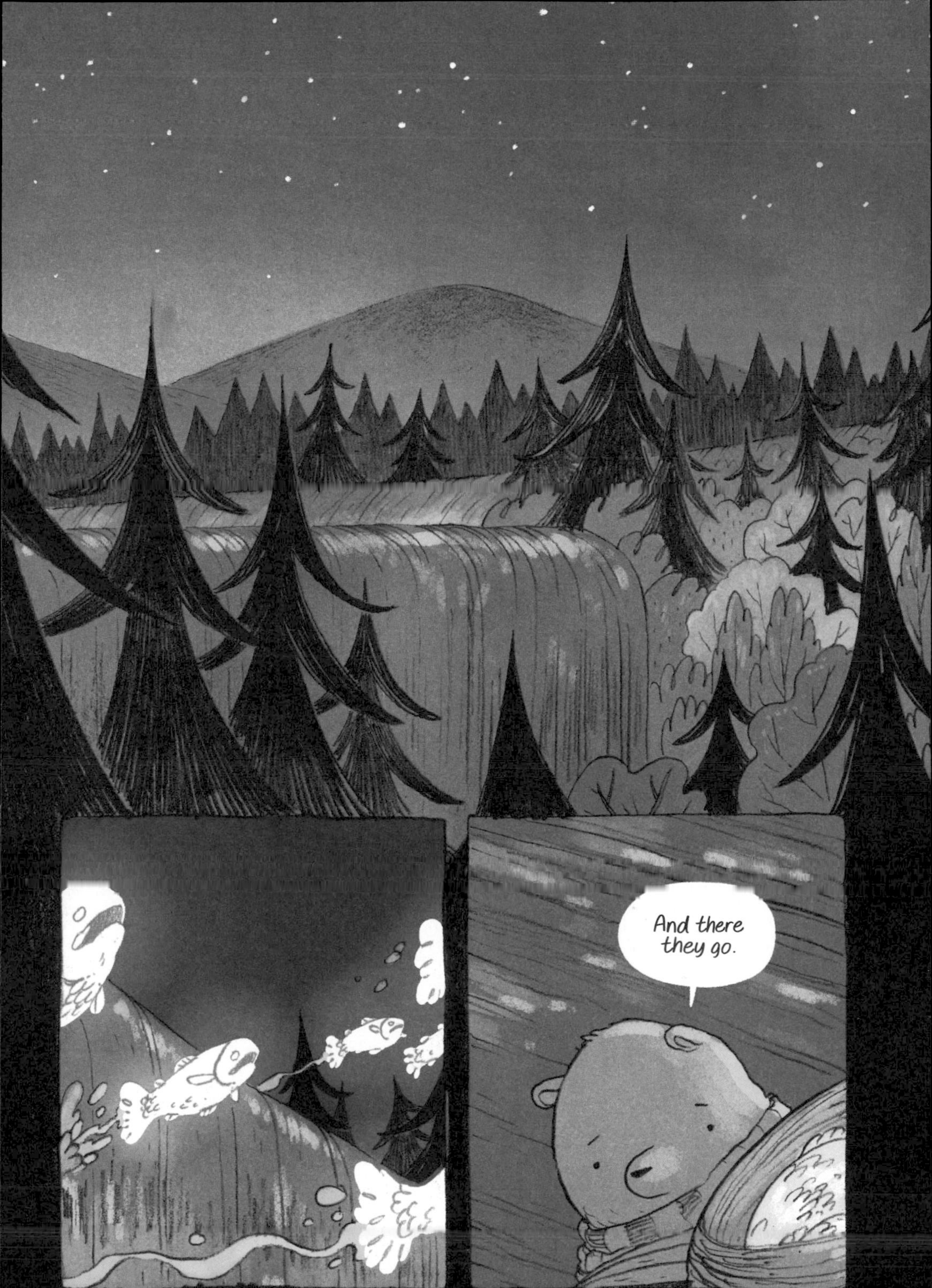
And there they go.

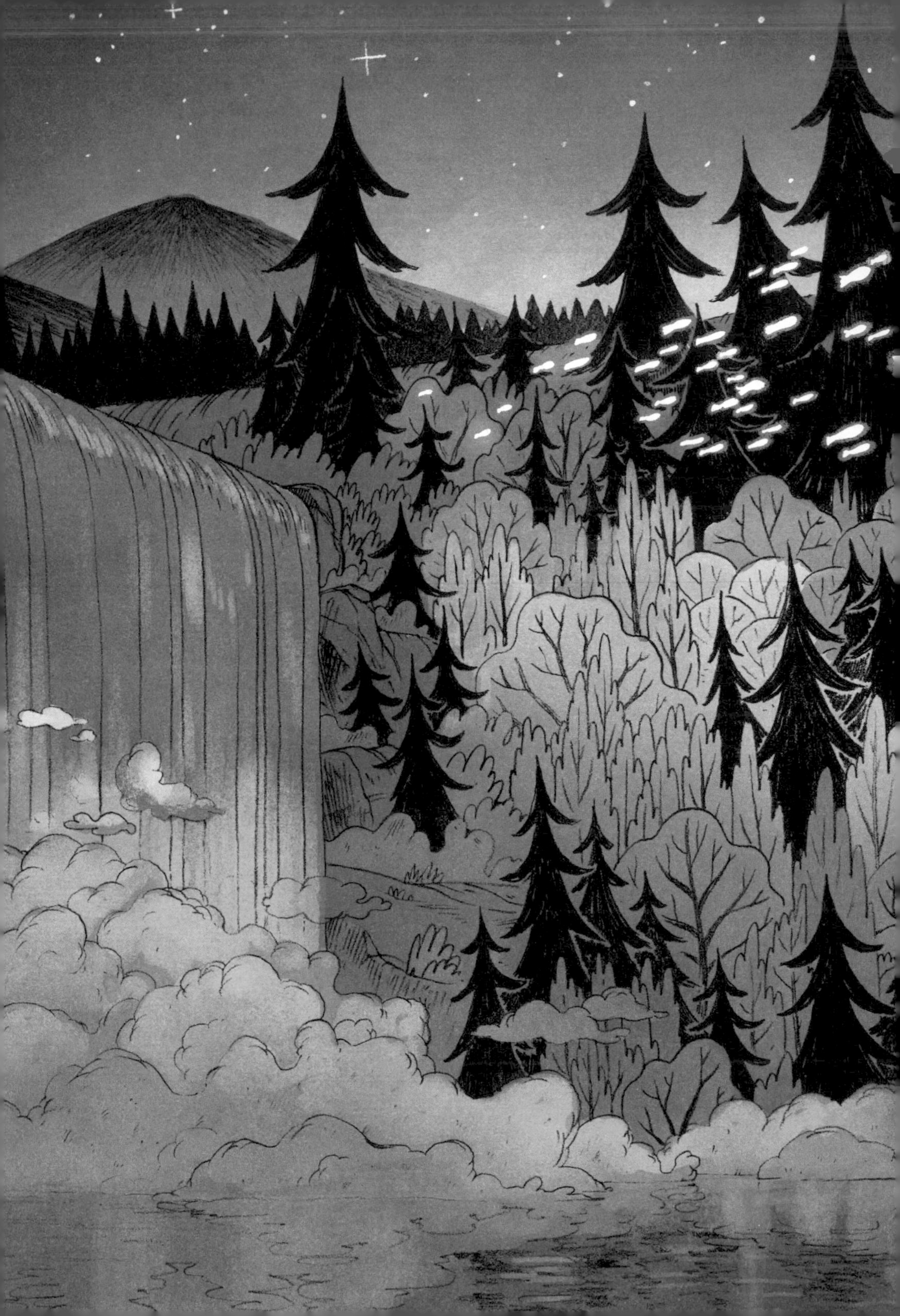

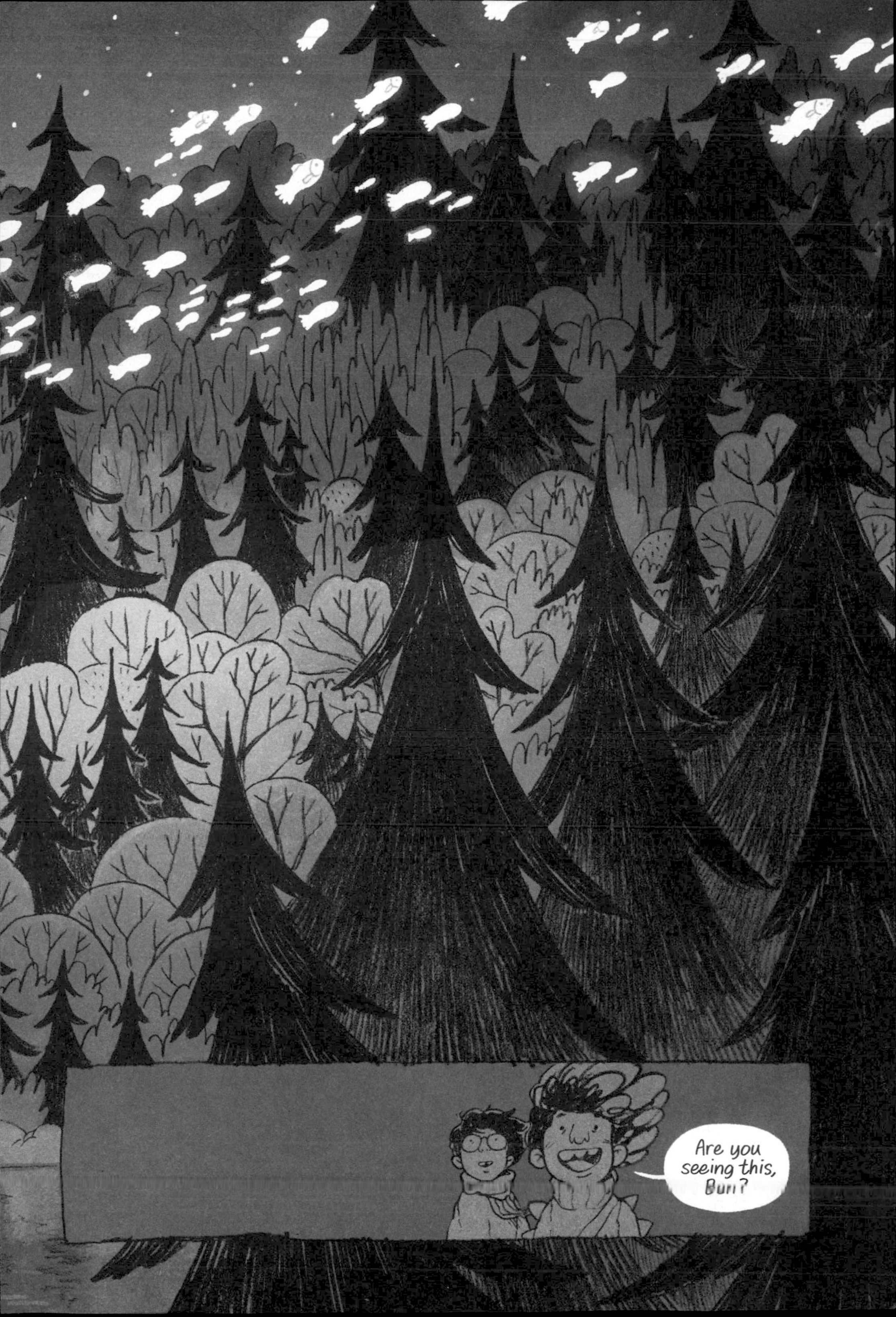
Are you seeing this, Buri?

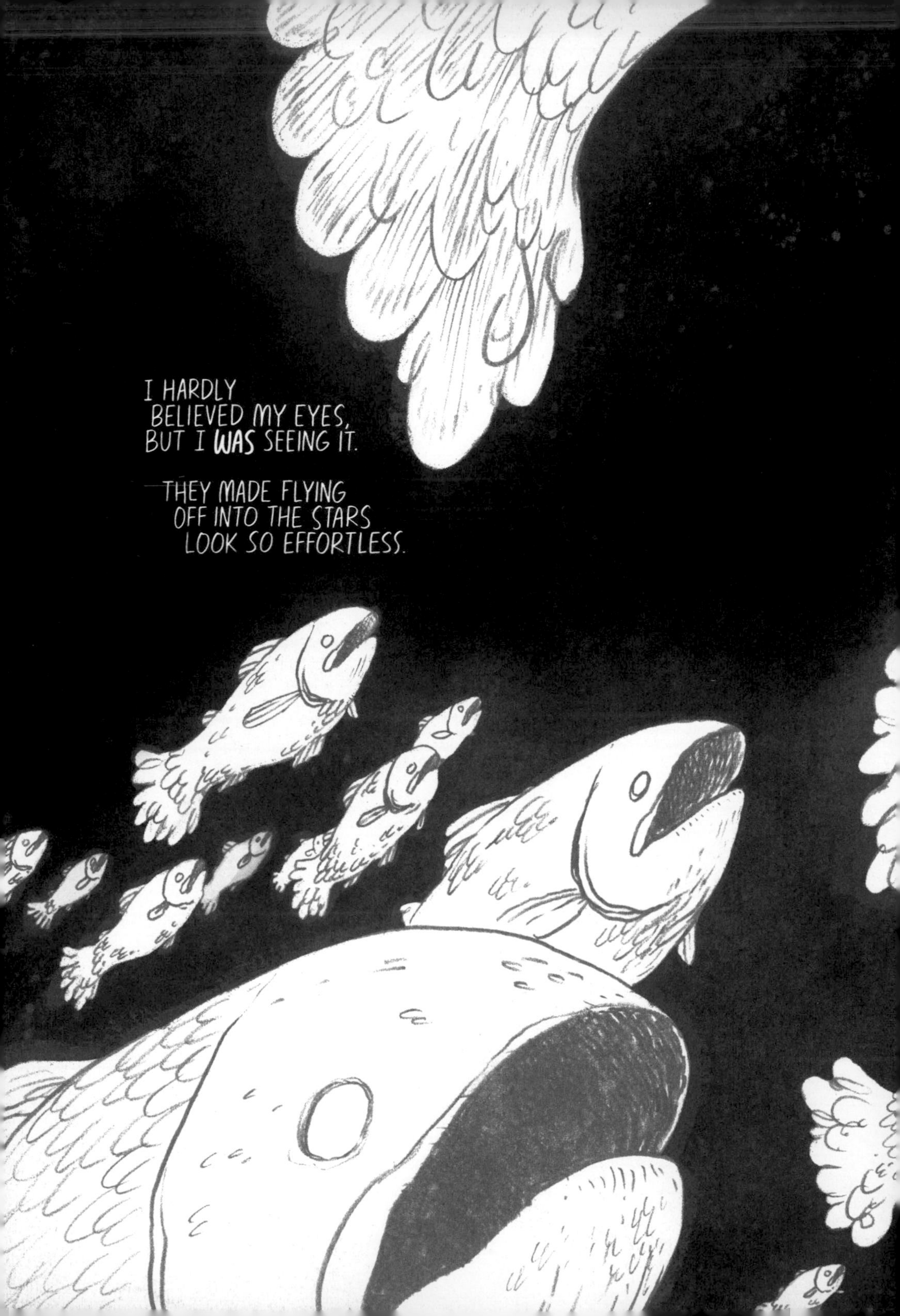
I HARDLY BELIEVED MY EYES, BUT I **WAS** SEEING IT.
THEY MADE FLYING OFF INTO THE STARS LOOK SO EFFORTLESS.

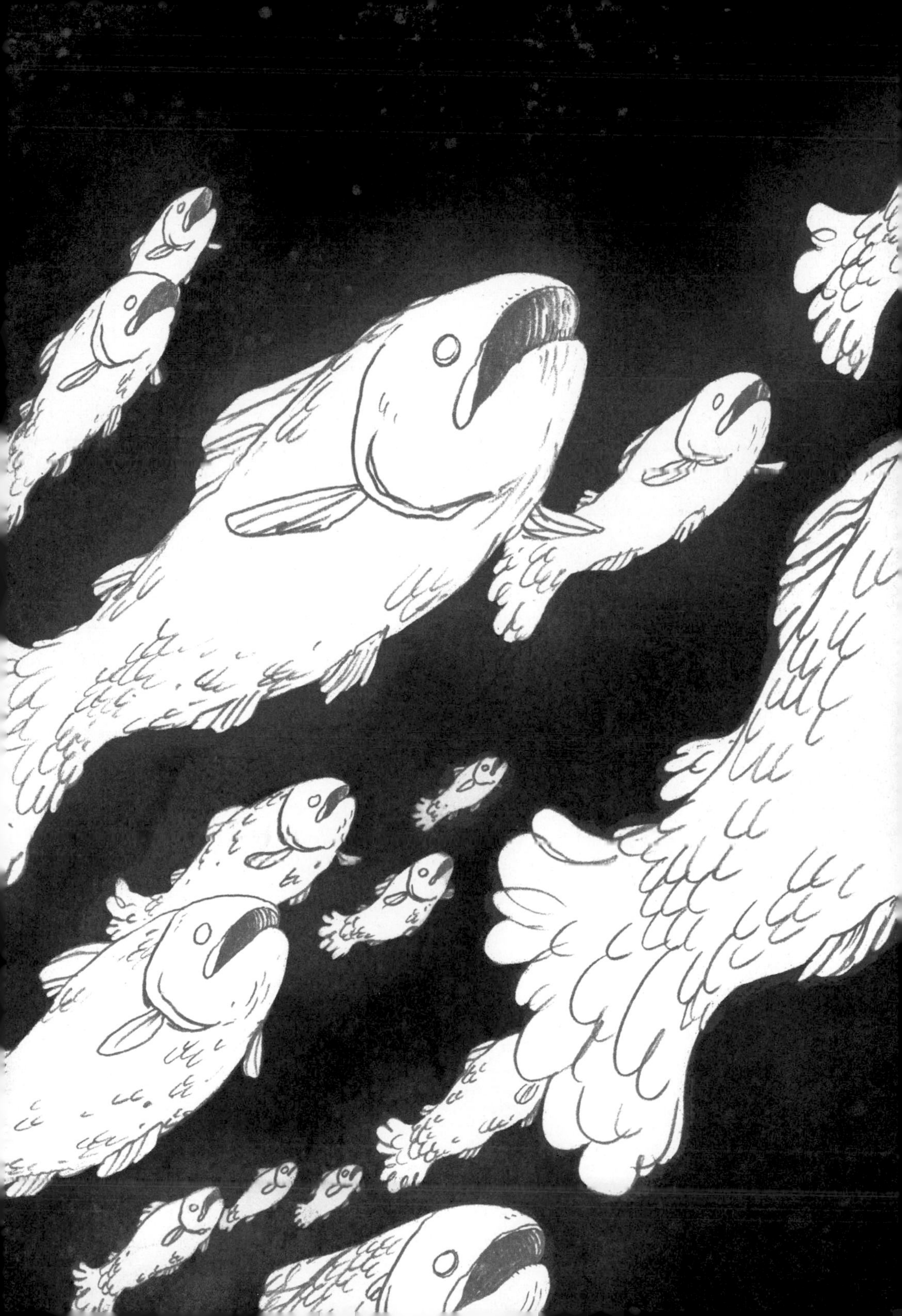

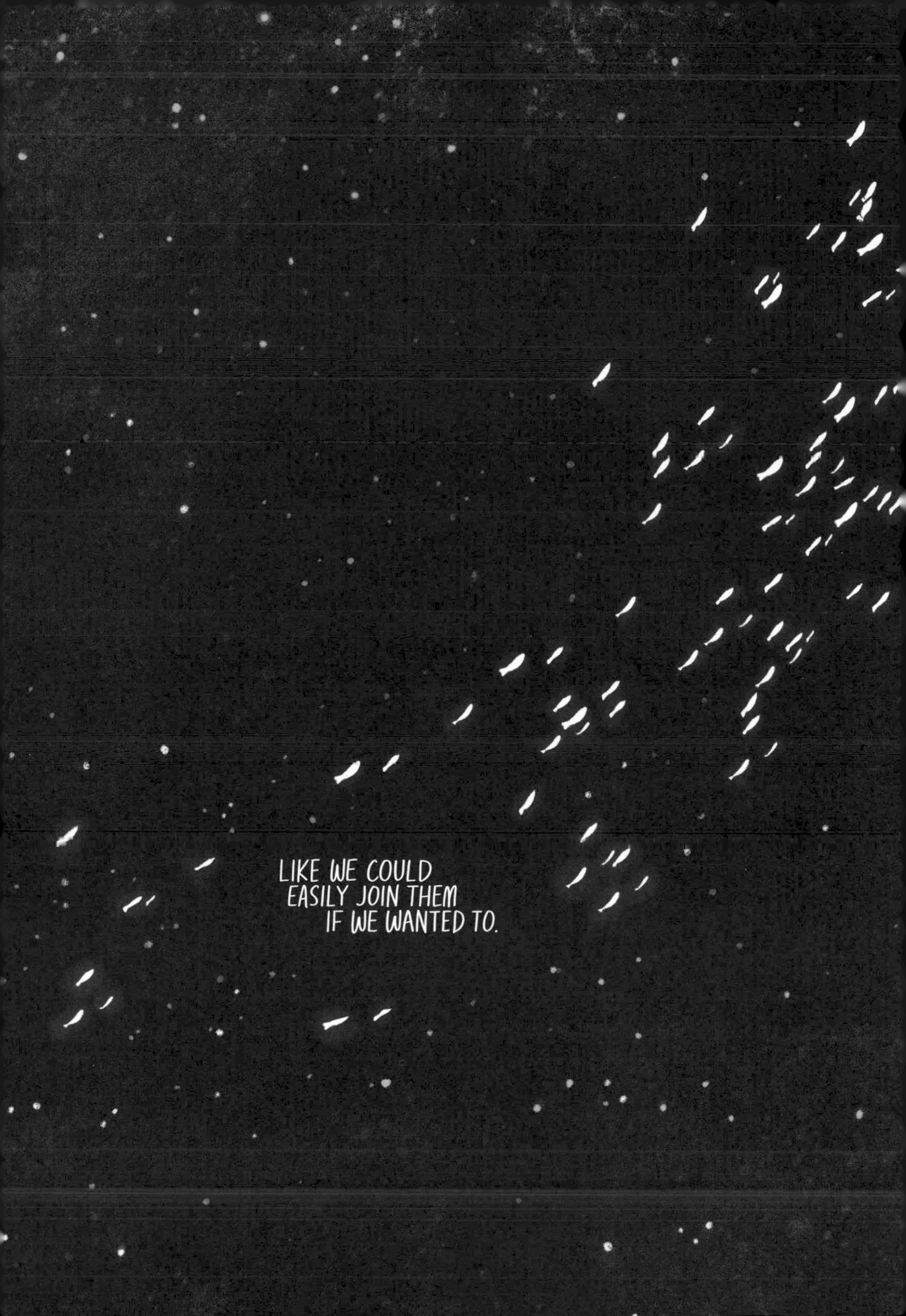
LIKE WE COULD EASILY JOIN THEM IF WE WANTED TO.

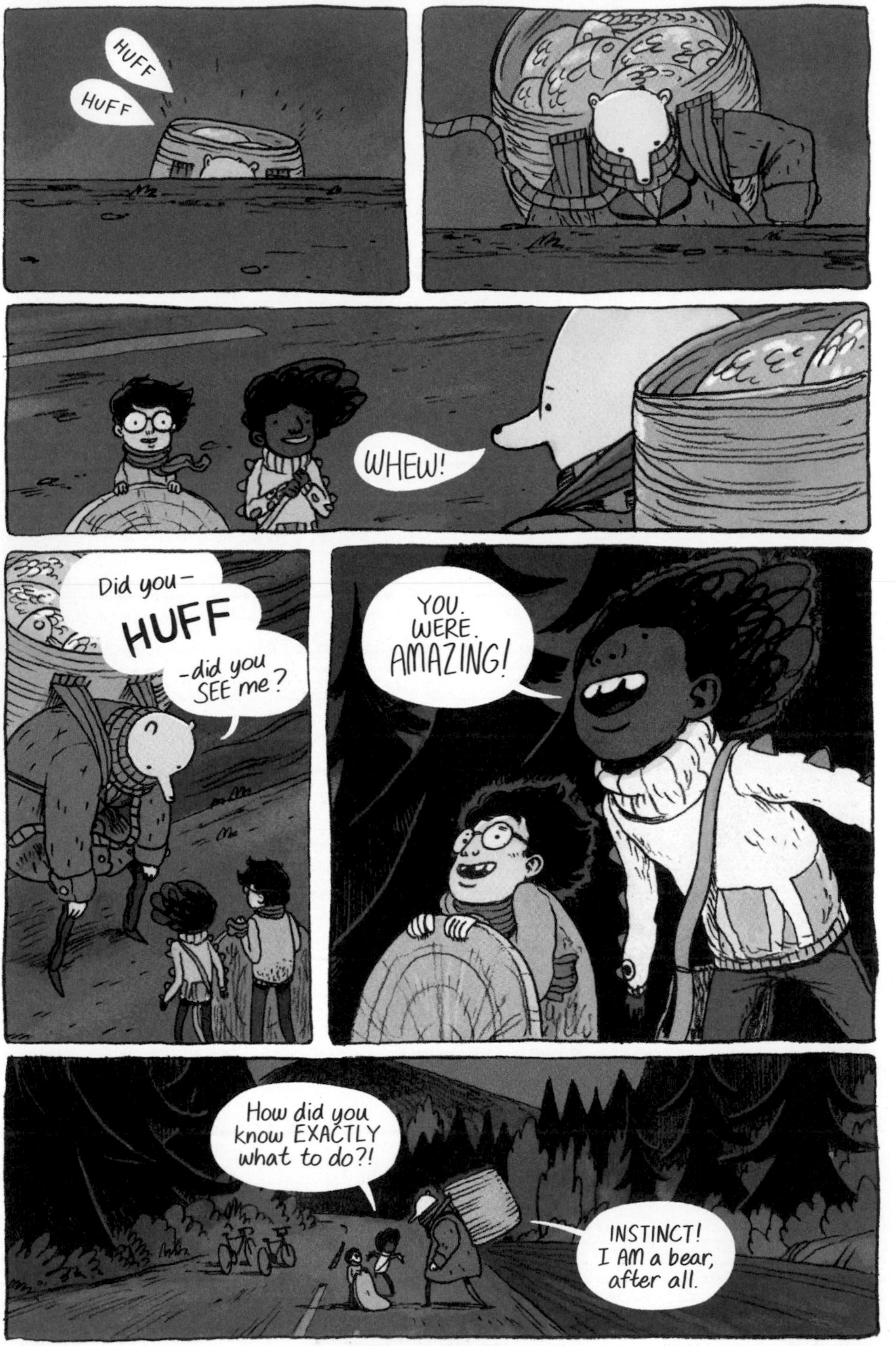
HUFF
HUFF
WHEW!
Did you-
HUFF
-did you SEE me?
YOU. WERE. AMAZING!
How did you know EXACTLY what to do?!
INSTINCT! I AM a bear, after all.

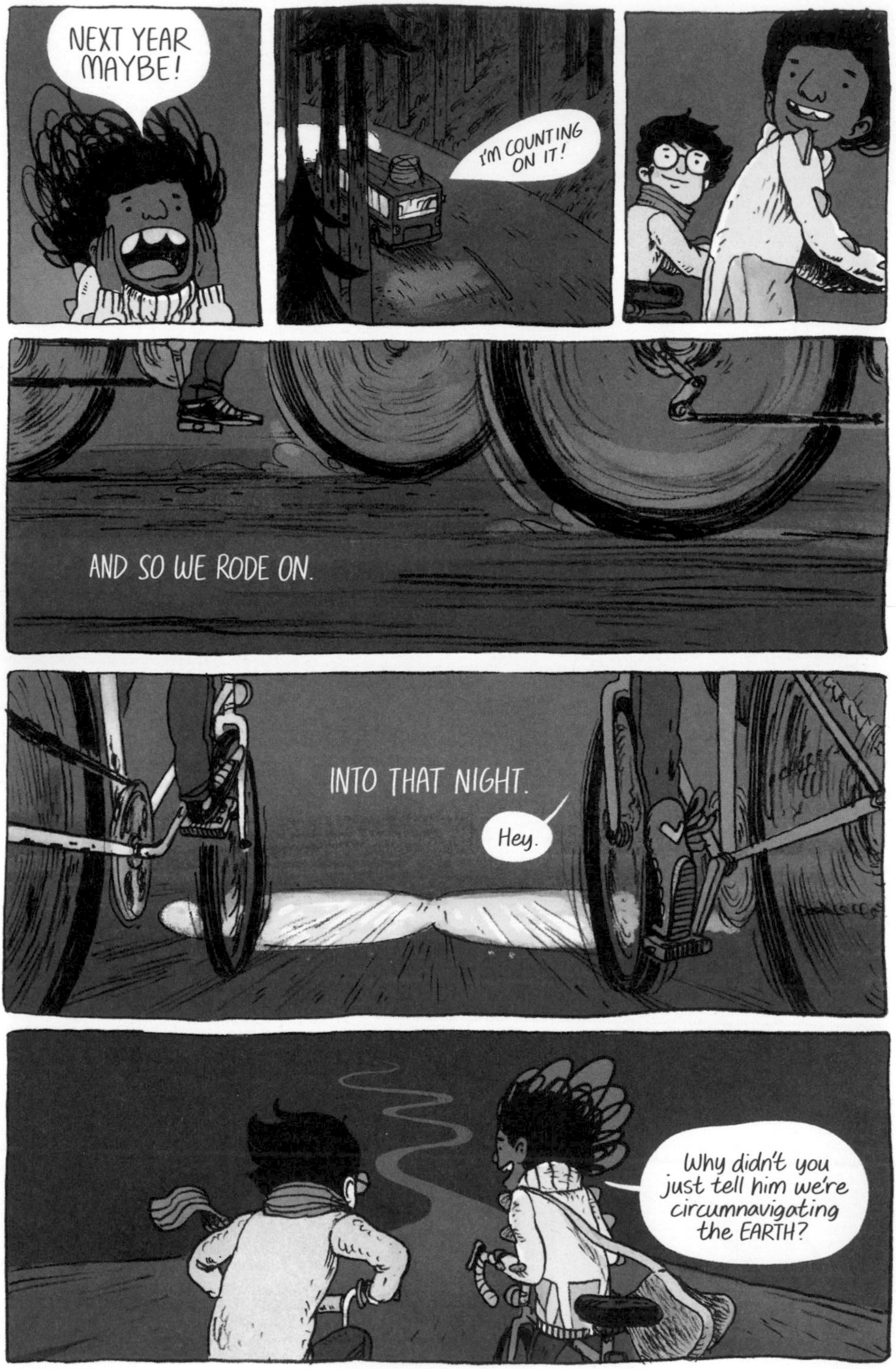
NEXT YEAR MAYBE!
I'M COUNTING ON IT!
AND SO WE RODE ON.
INTO THAT NIGHT.
Hey.
Why didn't you just tell him we're circumnavigating the EARTH?

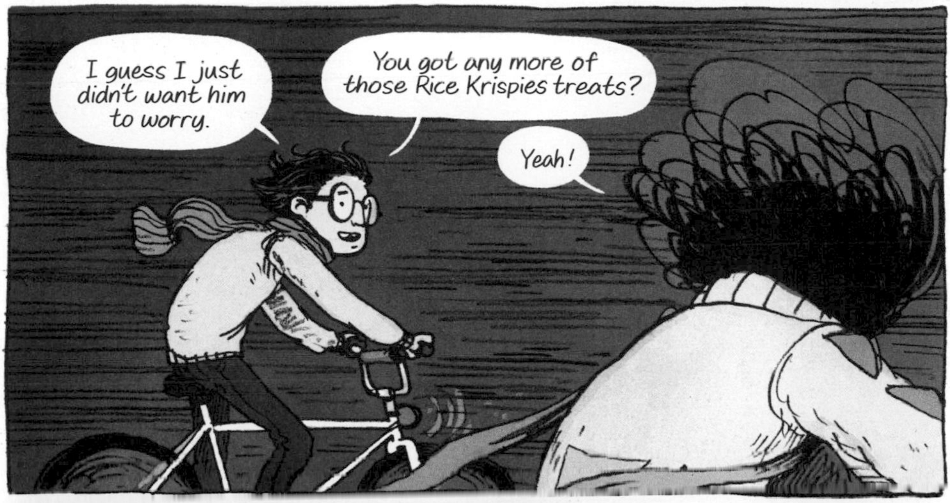
I guess I just didn't want him to worry.
You got any more of those Rice Krispies treats?
Yeah!

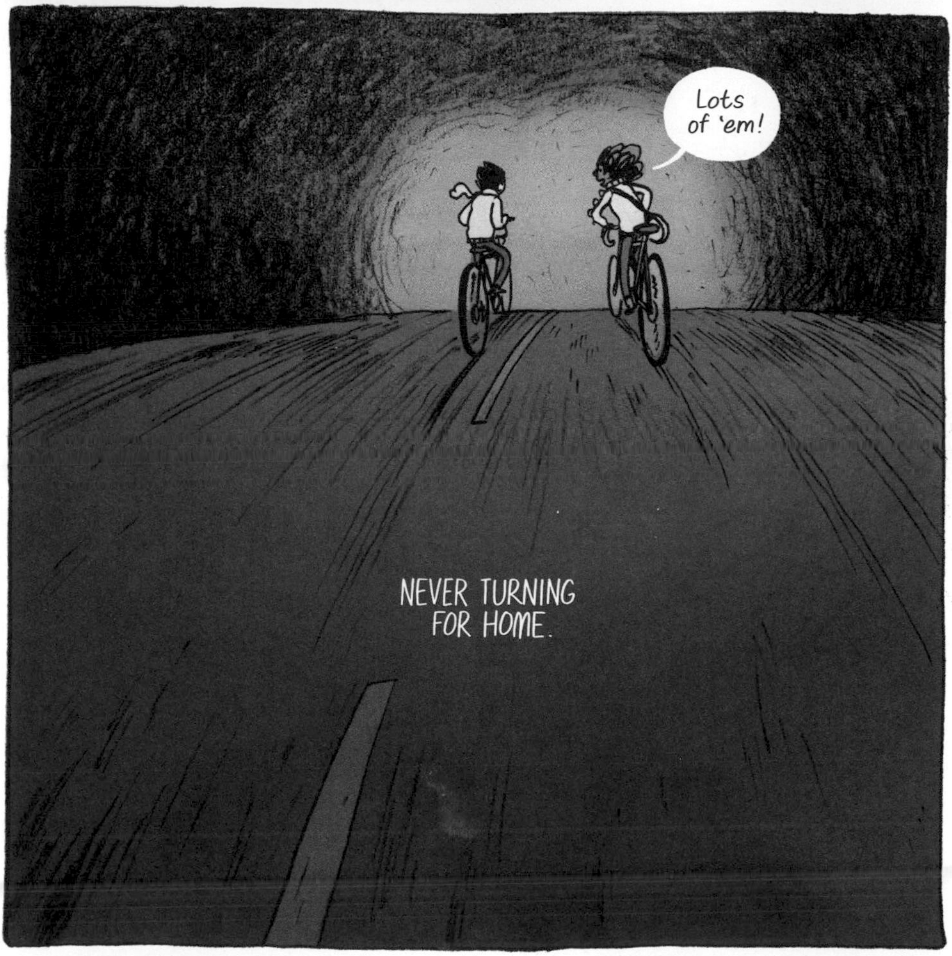
Lots of 'em!
NEVER TURNING FOR HOME.

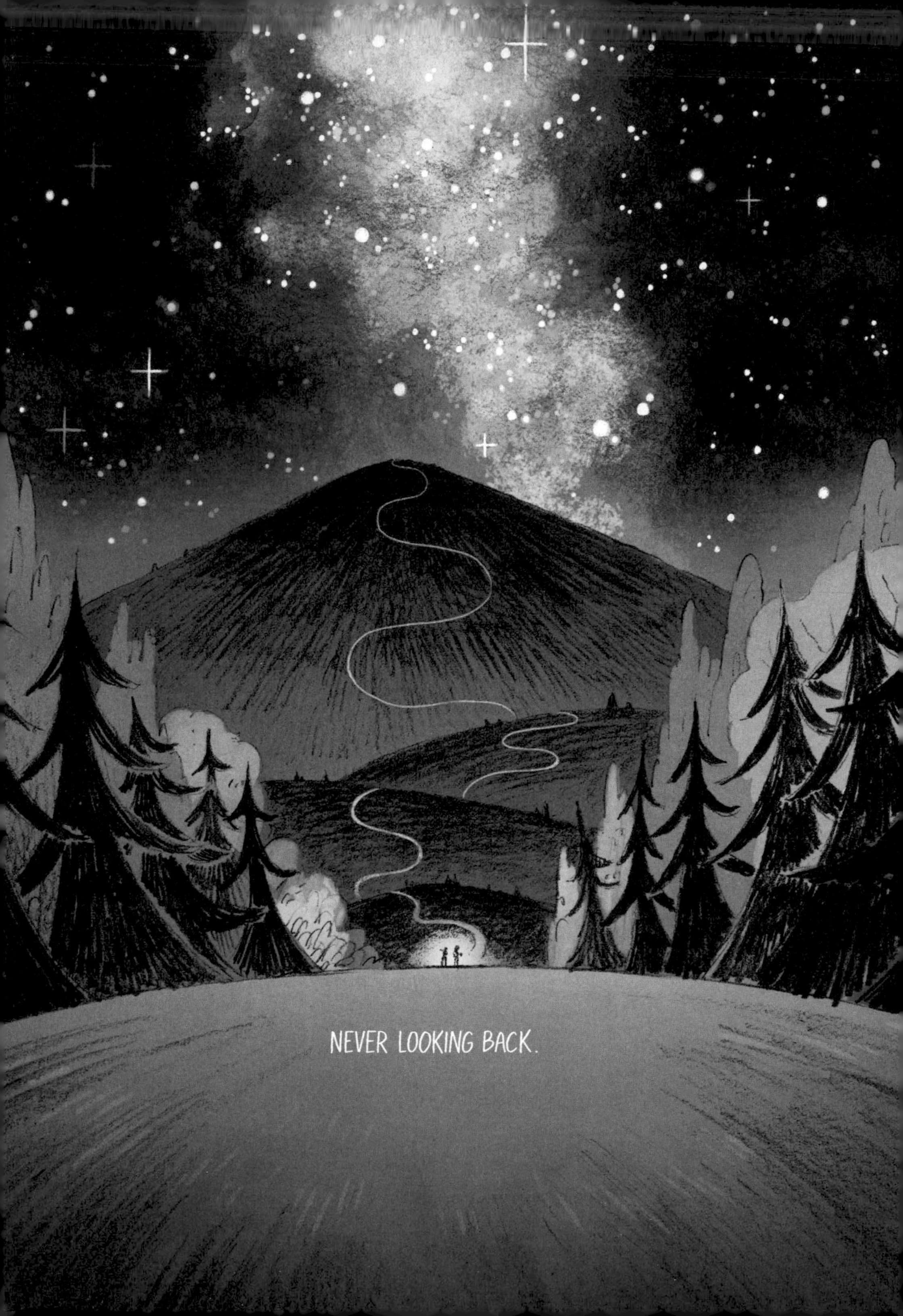
NEVER LOOKING BACK.